PENGUIN BOOKS

THE SECOND RUMPOLE OMNIBUS

John Mortimer is a playwright, novelist and former practising barrister. During the war he worked with the Crown Film Unit and published a number of novels before turning to the theatre with such plays as *The Dock Brief*, *The Wrong Side of the Park* and *A Voyage Round My Father*. He has written many film scripts, radio and television plays, including six plays on the life of Shakespeare, the Rumpole plays, which won him the British Academy Writer of the Year Award, and the adaptation of Evelyn Waugh's *Brideshead Revisited*. His translations of Feydeau have been performed at the National Theatre and are published in Penguin as *Three Boulevard Farces*.

Penguin publish his collections of stories *Rumpole of the Bailey*, *The Trials of Rumpole*, *Rumpole's Return*, *Rumpole for the Defence*, *Rumpole and the Golden Thread*, *Rumpole's Last Case* and *Rumpole and the Age of Miracles*, as well as *The First Rumpole Omnibus*. Penguin have also published two volumes of his plays; his acclaimed autobiography, *Clinging to the Wreckage*, which won the *Yorkshire Post* Book of the Year Award; a series of interviews with some of the most prominent men and women of our time, *In Character* and its follow-up *Character Parts*; and his novels, *Charade*, *Like Men Betrayed*, *The Narrowing Stream*, the bestselling *Paradise Postponed*, which was made into a much-acclaimed television series in 1986, and *Summer's Lease*. His latest novel, *Titmuss Regained*, is a sequel to *Paradise Postponed*. John Mortimer lives with his wife and their two daughters in what was once his father's house in the Chilterns.

John Mortimer

THE SECOND

Rumpole

OMNIBUS

Rumpole for the Defence
Rumpole and the Golden Thread
Rumpole's Last Case

PENGUIN BOOKS

PENGUIN BOOKS

Published by the Penguin Group
27 Wrights Lane, London w8 5tz, England
Viking Penguin Inc., 40 West 23rd Street, New York, New York 10010, USA
Penguin Books Australia Ltd, Ringwood, Victoria, Australia
Penguin Books Canada Ltd, 2801 John Street, Markham, Ontario, Canada l3r 1b4
Penguin Books (NZ) Ltd, 182–190 Wairau Road, Auckland 10, New Zealand

Penguin Books Ltd, Registered Offices: Harmondsworth, Middlesex, England

Rumpole for the Defence first published by Allen Lane,
under the title *Regina* v. *Rumpole* 1981
Published by Penguin Books 1982
Rumpole and the Golden Thread first published by Penguin Books 1983
Rumpole's Last Case first published by Penguin Books 1987
This collection first published by Viking 1987
Published in Penguin Books 1988
7 9 10 8

Copyright © Advanpress Ltd, 1981, 1983, 1987
All rights reserved

Made and printed in Great Britain by
Richard Clay Ltd, Bungay, Suffolk
Typeset in Plantin

Contents

Rumpole
for the Defence

Contents

Rumpole and the Confession of Guilt

This morning a postcard, decorated with an American stamp and a fine view of the Florida freeways, put me in mind of the long-distant day when my son Nick first left these shores, leaving his mother and father staring at each other in wild surmise alone in our 'mansion' flat in Froxbury Court, Gloucester Road. Nick had finished with Oxford and was about to take up the offer of a postgraduate course at the University of Baltimore, which would lead to his teaching sociology and eventually becoming the head of his department in Miami. Today's postcard was yet another invitation from our daughter-in-law, Erica, to hang up the wig, burn the *Archbold on Criminal Law* and retire to join Nick and his wife in the sunshine state, where Senior Citizens loll on beaches and never is heard a discouraging word from the likes of his Honour Judge Bullingham. If the time for such an uprooting were ever to arrive, it had not come yet. I still have enough strength and health to totter to my feet to address the jury. Pommeroy's claret still keeps me astonishingly regular and I am still more or less profitably engaged on the sort of work which I was doing in that far-off day when my son Nick first set off to seek a newer world and found a swimming bath, an outdoor cooking device, a 'car port' for two motors and my daughter-in-law, Erica.

I also remember the day Nick left for America because I was then defending a customer called Mr Gladstone in an attempted murder case which depended, in the main, on his own confession of guilt. Mr Gladstone was black. He lived in Brixton, and he was just sixteen years of age. I was reading his brief at breakfast with my wife Hilda (known to me as 'She Who Must Be Obeyed'), and something in the youth and boyishness of Mr Oswald Gladstone put me irresistably in mind of Wordsworth. Picture me then, dressed for battle in black jacket, winged

collar and striped trousers, champing toast, and quoting the old
sheep of the Lake District.

> ' "There was a boy; ye knew him well ye cliffs
>   And islands of Winander! – Many a time,
>   At evening, when the earliest stars began
>   To move along the edges of the hills,
>   Rising or setting, would he stand alone."

More toast, please, Hilda.

> "Beneath the trees or by the glimmering lake;
>   And there . . .
>   Blew mimic hootings to the silent owls
>   That they might answer him –"

Refill of coffee, please, Hilda!'

'Rumpole, I do wish you'd stop doing your legal work at
breakfast. You're getting butter all over that brief. Now about
Nick, about your son . . .'

'My client today is a boy, younger than Nick and engaged on
rather less harmless pursuits than sociology. A brilliant client! I
mean, he only took out a flick-knife and stabbed a young man in
a bus queue. Outside Lord's Cricket Ground. At four o'clock in
the afternoon! Well, I mean, if you have to do that sort of thing,
at least do it during the hours of darkness and, if possible, not
in St John's Wood Road.'

'Rumpole! I'm trying to have a serious conversation!' She
gave me one of her severest looks.

'Well, I think the fellow who got stabbed took it seriously,' I
told her. 'He was a total stranger, of course. Just someone my
juvenile client felt like stabbing. Absolutely brilliant!'

'When are you going to say goodbye to your son, Rumpole,
before he goes away to the other side of the world?'

There was a sinister charge lurking in Hilda's remark, but I
had enough evidence to rebut her innuendo.

'I'm meeting Nick at twelve,' I told her complacently. 'In
the Army and Navy Stores. I'll buy him a top coat for America,
then we'll have a good lunch, steak and kidney pud, I imagine,
something of that nature. I've got to get back to Chambers for a
four-thirty conference, so you give him tea, and then he's off
to the airport!'

'How can you meet Nick at twelve o'clock? You'll be in the Old Bailey at twelve o'clock.' She launched into her cross-examination. Again I had my answer ready.

'My case'll be over in half an hour. It's just a shortie. The young hopeful will have to plead guilty. Mr Gladstone signed a full confession of guilt to Detective Inspector Arthur, who is a most reliable officer. He grows prize chrysanthemums.' Hilda was momentarily floored by this answer, but She came back fighting.

'I don't know why you have to go down to the Old Bailey at all, on Nick's last day.'

'They say crime doesn't pay, but it's a living, you know. That nice breakfast egg of yours is probably a tiny part of the proceeds of an unlawful carnal knowledge.'

It wasn't an answer that pleased Hilda, and She came back with a sharp one below the belt.

'You're an Old Bailey hack, that's what you are, Rumpole,' She said. 'I heard your Head of Chambers, Guthrie Feather-stone, say that at the garden party. "Dear old Rumpole," he said, "is a bit of an Old Bailey hack!"'

Hilda, I thought, had gone too far. I'm not exactly a hack. I've been at the work for longer than I can remember and, as is generally recognized down at the Old Bailey, there are no flies on Rumpole. After all I cut my teeth on the Penge Bungalow Murders. I could win most of my cases if it weren't for the clients. Clients have no tact, poor old darlings. No bloody sensitivity! They *will* waltz into the witness-box and blurt out things which are far better left unblurted. I suppose, when I was young, I used to suffer with my clients. I used to cringe when I heard their sentences and go down to the cells full of anger. Now I never watch their faces when sentence is passed. I hardly listen to the years pronounced and I never look back at the dock.

These thoughts were occurring to me as I put on the wig and gown, and tied a moderately clean pair of bands round my neck in the robing room. My old friend, George Frobisher, was standing beside me, dressing up for some crime, and we found ourselves chatting about our work for the day.

'My man decided to rob a dance hall on the night of the Police Ball!' George and I appeared to have no luck with our clients.

'We only get the stupid villains, George.' I tried to cheer him up.

'Why's that?'

'The bright ones are all on holiday in Majorca. My little attempted murder's bound to be a plea, of course.'

'Bates isn't too bad on a plea.' George confirmed my own view of my Judge. 'It's when you fight he gets so sarcastic.'

'All over in half an hour! I'm meeting my son Nick, you know. He's off to America.'

'You're proud of him, aren't you, Rumpole?'

'Three years doing politics and sociology. Postgraduate? Of course! Nick's got the brains of the family.'

'You're proud of that boy, Rumpole!'

Of course George was perfectly right. I thanked my lucky stars for Nick, and not for the first time I wondered what on earth I'd do if I'd given birth to one of the Oswald Gladstones of this world, a boy who apparently stabbed cricket fans simply because they were there. He even failed as a murderer and would have no doubt to plead guilty to an attempt only. Try as I might, I couldn't find a satisfactory explanation for Oswald Gladstone. I mean, I believe in Mutual Aid, Universal Tolerance, and the Supreme Individual. At heart, I've long suspected I'm an anarchist. Man is born free and is everywhere in chains. But my darling Count Leo Tolstoy, or jolly Jean-Jacques Rousseau, or even that old sweetheart, Prince Peter Kropotkin, would have drawn the line at shoving a flick-knife into a complete stranger, in broad daylight, waiting outside Lords for a number thirteen bus. For a whim!

I was still troubled by these difficult matters when I met my eager Welsh solicitor, Mr Winter, an ardent reader of *New Society* and a pillar of the Islington Labour Party, who was accompanied by his articled clerk, Jo (who was in turn accompanied, as always, by a well-thumbed copy of *Time Out*). We had arranged to fortify ourselves with cups of coffee (scarcely distinguishable from tea) in the canteen at the Old Bailey.

'What surprises me,' Jo said with deep suspicion, 'is how the other boys got away – including Ginger Robertson.'

'Surprise, surprise! Everyone got away. Except one little black boy.' Winter smiled in a meaningful way. 'Mr Rumpole'll crucify the police on this one.'

'Crucify them? What for exactly, Mr Winter?' I asked.

'Racialism. You'll roast them alive. Like you did in the Penge Bungalow Murders.'

'What was that, Mr Winter?' Young Jo is surprisingly ignorant of the great moments of legal history.

'Before you were born, Jo. Before ever you were born, Mr Rumpole was crucifying the police!' Winter told him proudly.

Poor old Winter! The gullible old sweetheart believes that the customer's always right. He can't tell a dodgy car salesman from the unknown political prisoner. It was a sign of Winter's incorrigible optimism on behalf of his clients that he went on to say, 'You'll have a bit of fun with this one, Mr Rumpole.'

'Fun, Mr Winter? You call standing on your hind legs to plead guilty for a Jamaican teenager who pushes a knife into anyone who crosses his path – fun? What do I say to the Judge? "Do understand, my Lord. He'd just seen the West Indies drop a catch. Can I have a 50p fine, and time to pay?"'

'Did you say, "plead guilty?"' Mr Winter sounded deeply hurt.

'Have you got any other ideas?' I asked him.

'They pick on these boys.' Winter gave me his usual speech. 'That's what we've got to hammer home to the jury. The police victimize them, Mr Rumpole.'

'You mean the dear old British bobby has a blind, unreasoning prejudice against boys who stab people in bus queues?' I asked, purely for information.

'Anyway, can they prove it? No one identified him.' Winter, the optimist, turned his attention to the facts.

'That's true. He was just another boy with a flick-knife. A common sight, apparently, at the St John's Wood roundabout.'

'Fingerprints were all smeared. There were no bloodstains on his clothing,' Winter remembered.

'I really wonder why they dragged us out of bed to come here at all,' I murmured.

'So where's the prosecution case?' My instructing solicitor concluded his well-reasoned address.

'Gone! Vanished into thin air, Mr Winter!' I encouraged him. 'We'd get our costs against the police, a gold watch donated from the poor box, and have every Inspector in court demoted to the rank of P.C. If it wasn't for one tiny triviality.'

'What's that, Mr Rumpole?' Winter frowned.

'Our brilliant client made a full, frank, free confession to the police – signed and witnessed.'

'A confession to the police!' Jo repeated with contempt.

'He confessed to Inspector Arthur of E Division, a gentle, fatherly officer with a green finger for chrysanthemums,' I reminded them both as Mr Winter searched among his papers, and found a much-used photostat.

'Here's an article that might help from the *New Society*, Mr Rumpole. It gives you figures on the arrests of black teenagers in one square mile of London. There's an analysis in depth of racialism in the police. Obviously it's based on strong feelings of sexual jealousy.'

At which point Inspector Arthur, a grey-haired and benevolent-looking man in plain clothes, passed with his side-kick Sergeant Shaw. They were carrying cups of coffee. I wished the Old Bill a cheery goodmorning.

'Nice to see you, Inspector,' I said. 'Chrysanths all right, are they?'

'Managed a First at the Division Flower Show, anyway,' the Inspector said modestly. 'See you in Court, Mr Rumpole.'

'In Court. Yes. What do you want me to do?' I asked Mr Winter as the officers passed by. 'Get Arthur to admit he forged the confession in a blue fit of penis envy? That'd give the old sweetie on the bench a fit of the vapours.' I lit a small cigar and Winter sounded disappointed as he said, 'Well you know best, Mr Rumpole.'

'Yes,' I agreed. Winter was still looking through his file hopefully.

'We've got one character witness,' he said. 'The vicar. A Reverend Eldred Pickersgill. From the Sandringham Road Boys' Club.' Winter seemed proud of his coup and I hated to disillusion him.

'The reckless use of an offensive weapon will be far out-weighed by some clerk in holy orders who says the lad's ping-pong shows promise!' I said unkindly. 'We must face facts, Mr Winter. Oswald Gladstone'll have to plead guilty.'

'I thought it might help us, calling a vicar.'

'You, Mr Winter, a founder member of the Islington Humanist Association?' I looked at him sadly. 'You fall back on a dog-collar?'

'Wouldn't the Judge like it?'

'Nothing inflames a sentence so much as an over-eager cleric. That's my experience. We'd better go down.' I stood up and the soliciting gentlemen followed me with Mr Winter still protesting weakly. 'There's a lot to be said for our client,' he said.

'Always,' I agreed, and then Jo reminded me. 'His mother put him in care when he was four. Can you imagine? Taking a little kid to the Brixton magistrates and handing him over as a menace to society. Can you imagine doing that?' As a matter of fact I couldn't.

It's part of the life of an Old Bailey hack to spend a good deal of his time down the cells. You walk in past the old door of Newgate, kicked and scarred, through which generations of villains were sent to the gallows or the treadmill. There's a perpetual smell of cooking down the Old Bailey cells, and the screws are often to be found snatching odd snacks of six-inch-thick jam butty and gallons of tea. When I asked the officer in charge of the gate if Mr Gladstone was at home, he said, 'I don't think he's gone out to lunch with the Lord Mayor.' He called down the passage, 'Counsel to see the piccaninny!'

You know what life at the Old Bailey blunts? It blunts the sensitivity. When you've been round the place as long as I have the sensitivity comes out like hair on the comb. Mr Gladstone was brought to us in the interview room. He was wearing a sharp suit and had a small trilby hat perched on his head. His smile was wide and he looked determinedly brave. He greeted me with, 'Who are you, dad?'

'This is Mr Rumpole, your counsel; he's defending you,' Mr Winter explained and Oswald Gladstone said proudly, 'I don't need no brief. I'll just tell the Judge, Ginger done it, didn't he?'

'Ginger Robertson,' Winter explained to me, 'is one of the boys that went missing. That's our defence. If you can destroy the police evidence.' I looked at my watch, we hadn't got all the time in the world, if I was to meet Nick in the Army and Navy and keep our appointment for lunch.

'How do you know Ginger did it?' I asked. 'Did you see him with the knife?'

'After. I see him with the cutter after. Ginger throwed it away, didn't he?'

'You tell us, old dear. Did you know he was going to use it?'

'Use it? What you mean?'

'Did you know Ginger might use the cutter?'

'I tell you, dad. I know nothing about that.' Young Oswald Gladstone looked round at us, three men all there because of him, and said proudly, 'Got me in a big Court, haven't they? Number One Court.'

'Oh yes, Mr Gladstone. You're a star,' I assured him. 'Why did Ginger do it?'

'Why?'

'Yes. Why stab a man whom none of you apparently knew?'

'I guess Ginger didn't like them M.C.C. supporters.'

I stared at Oswald then, and Mr Winter supplied his usual explanation. 'There was anti-coloured feeling on the ground. I told you, Mr Rumpole. This case has political undertones.'

'But this old darling at the bus queue. He hadn't even *been* on the ground!' Oswald smiled and blew out smoke from the cigarette Jo had given him. 'Guess Ginger couldn't find any M.C.C. supporters, and this fellow was there like. So Ginger said, "I might as well cut him." '

'Oh, dear me. How would jolly Jean-Jacques Rousseau explain all that?' I heard myself saying it aloud, and Oswald looked at Mr Winter. 'What's he on about,' he asked.

'Mr Rumpole is a very experienced counsel. If we can destroy the police here, sir . . .' Mr Winter turned to me.

' "If", "if". And if the Judge turns out to be a Jamaican teenager with form we might have a chance. Speaking for myself,' – I looked at the diminutive client, and said – 'I don't believe Mr Gladstone meant to kill him.'

'Ginger carried the knife! That's what he says.' Jo was still fighting.

'Ginger formed the intention, quite clearly,' Mr Winter argued.

'See, dad,' Ossie told me. 'Ginger don't take all the trouble to carry no knife unless he use it sometimes.'

'They carry these knives,' Jo gave his favourite explanation, 'to prove their virility.'

'I'll tell the Judge that. In his day it was conkers.' I had to think of a way of saving Mr Gladstone a long stretch and I had Nick's farewell to consider. So I asked, 'Who's prosecuting?' At which Mr Winter went through his papers again and said, 'Mr . . . Piecan.'

'Magnus Piecan? What a bit of luck! I might just get him to swallow A.B.H.?'

'Actual Bodily Harm,' Winter explained to Oswald, and I asked our client, 'You'd plead to that, of course?'

'What they give me for that?' Mr Gladstone sounded interested.

'Nine months – a year. That suit you?'

'You want me to do a year? For something I never done?'

'You'd rather fight, and do four years for what you say you never done? The Judge'll give you full credit for admitting . . .'

'Admitting? What I didn't do.'

'Look at it this way. What's the credit in admitting something you *did* do. Not much credit in that, is there?'

'Are you taking the mick out of me?' Mr Gladstone was right of course. It was a joke in poor taste, and I apologized. 'I'm sorry. It's a bad habit.'

'I tell you truth, dad. I never done this cutting.'

For an answer I dived into my brief (always a rash thing to do) and brought out a single, but most unfortunate, sheet of paper, and started to read from it aloud.

'My name is Oswald Montgomery Gladstone, though in our gang they calls me "Blades",' I read, and then asked Ossie, 'Is that what they call you?'

'Blades,' Mr Gladstone answered proudly. 'That's right. That's my name, with the others like!'

' "I mean," ' I went on reading, sure that Oswald's denials

wouldn't survive in the face of his confession, ' "I know you found the dagger so I better come clean, guv'nor. Anyway if you nabs Ginger he'll grass on me. We was mad at the M.C.C. supporters what annoyed us. So when I left the ground I had my knife ready but the M.C.C. blokes all scarpered. 'Cos I had the weapon I felt a bit of a fool not using it. And there was this bloke standing. So I just let him have it in the Auntie Nellie. I'm very sorry for all the trouble I caused." Signed O. Gladstone and witnessed D.I. Arthur and D.S. Shaw.'

'I told them.' Mr Gladstone shook his head. 'Ginger done all that.'

'Did you read this written confession, when you were in the police station?'

' 'Course I did.' Now Oswald seemed vaguely annoyed at my questions.

'Did you understand it?' I asked.

'I read it through, didn't I?' Oswald was becoming belligerent.

'I wasn't there. You've got to tell me.'

'Yes. I read it through.'

'Why did you sign it. If it wasn't true?'

'I got bored. They was going on so long. You ever had questioning in the nick?'

'Not . . . as far as I remember.'

'It gets boring. You'd do like anything to get it over with.'

'To get back to reading a comic in the cell?' I wondered, and again my question had a curious result. Oswald seemed delighted by it. 'Reading!' Ossie said proudly. 'That's it. I was doing reading. Tell you what. If I signed that, they promised me a smoke.'

'Didn't it strike you as a rather expensive cigarette?'

I looked sadly at Oswald, and decided that my only course was an approach to my learned friend, Mr Magnus Piecan. My worst suspicions about sport had been confirmed, it brings out the very worst in people. Football leads to violence and cricket to murder. God knows what ludo would do to a man.

Magnus Piecan spends his life trying to be a Judge. I believe that he thinks that a Judge is the only person in Court whose hands don't sweat and whose mouth isn't dry with panic, which may not be entirely true. Dear old Magnus is so afraid of doing the wrong thing that he makes notes with ten different coloured pencils, and never gets to his feet without checking his fly buttons.

'You for the black teenager, Rumpole?' he asked me, when we tracked him down, pacing nervously in front of old Bates's Court, waiting for the case in front of us to finish.

'Yes, I am, as it so happens,' and I tried an old gambit calculated to increase his nervous tension. 'As a matter of fact I heard from the Judge's clerk, Bates, J., wants to get away early today.'

'Tickets for Glyndebourne?' Piecan made the assumption.

'Glyndebourne? Probably all-in wrestling at the Wembley public baths. His clerk hopes very much the Judge isn't going to be kept late.'

'Well, this isn't going to take long, is it?' Piecan asked nervously.

'Long?'

'I mean, I can't really see where the defence . . .'

'Give it a couple of weeks,' I interrupted him airily. 'Three possibly. It's not a long point, but I'll have to go into it in a *little* detail. You appreciate the point, of course?'

'The point?' Poor old Piecan looked totally confused.

'The point of law,' I said, mysteriously. 'It's rather a nice one, isn't it? You spotted it, of course.'

'The point of law, Rumpole?'

'I knew you would, you clever old sweetheart, you dear old brain box. I made sure the point would not have eluded you. So we may get a pretty rough ride from the Judge, and you'll have to bear the brunt, of course, opening a two-week case before an impatient chap like Bates. Well, good luck to you.'

'Is it really going to take two weeks?' Piecan's voice was tremulous.

'Up to you, old fellow. Entirely up to you, if you want to shorten it.'

'I mean, I told my clerk it might be a plea.' Piecan sounded hopeful.

'That's what I told my client as well,' I chimed in gleefully. 'This is a case, I told him, where the prosecution will almost certainly make us an offer. Now, old love, what *are* you offering us?'

'I don't quite see what I *can* offer.' Piecan was puzzled and not happy.

'Don't you? Use your imagination, Piecan. Consider the mind of a boy! You see they were only playing games!' I made a few sword passes with my Pentel, to demonstrate. 'Rapier and dagger, that's two of your weapons! Have at you! Cardinal's lackey! Take that! From Rupert of Hentzau! You know how boys play games, don't you?'

'I suppose so,' said the mystified Piecan. Of course he didn't know; he was born aged forty with a thorough knowledge of the law of torts. 'What you're saying is, no criminal intent?' Piecan put it in the legal language he understood.

'They were fooling about,' I told him. 'My boy lunged at an imaginary musketeer, and winged a real live accountant from Muswell Hill.' I put my arm through his and walked him out of my instructing solicitors' hearing.

'As we lawyers say, Magnus, no bloody criminal intent whatsoever. What does that make it? You were at the crammers last.'

'Actual Bodily Harm.'

'I thought you might accept "Possessing an Offensive Weapon".' I tried to look gloomy.

'It'll have to be A.B.H.' Piecan was determined to be tough with me.

'Hard-hearted Magnus! Ah well, you've got your job to do.'

'I'll have to take instructions.'

'Take them, then, quickly.'

'By the way, Rumpole,' Piecan paused with a sudden doubt. 'Why's your chap called "Blades"? Because he's the one that carries the knife?'

'Of course not. The old dear's a snappy dresser. A masher. A dandy. A *blade*! Don't you know the expression?'

Anyway Piecan filtered off to consult his prosecution masters. I was lighting a small cigar as Mr Winter came up to me, and again showed his ignorance of the perilous nature of our position.

'What're they up to, Mr Rumpole? Got cold feet, have they?'

I looked at my watch. It was nearly ten. By eleven, it should all be over. 'I'm meeting my son, you know, Nick,' I told Mr Winter. 'He's off to the United States, to study social sciences, which are a mystery you probably understand. Yes. I think it'll turn out to be a plea.'

'You mean they'll want us to accept Actual Bodily Harm?' Mr Winter looked less than pleased that an agreement was in sight.

'Given a following wind, we might edge them into it.'

'I don't think Gladstone's the type who'll want to play ball, Mr Rumpole.' Mr Winter shook his head gloomily.

'Play ball? He's being offered a remarkably easy way out. He'd be a lunatic not to take it.'

One thing you can never guarantee about clients is that they *won't* behave like lunatics. Piecan came back and offered us a nice quick and easy plea to Actual Bodily Harm. Lunch with Nick now seemed a certainty. But when we put the deal and all its advantages to Mr Oswald Gladstone, he simply said, 'I can't do it.'

'Look, Ossie. Blades. Mind if I call you Oswald?' I started.

'Call me what you like, dad.'

'If only you had someone you trusted. I wish your family were here to advise you. Perhaps your mother?'

'She gave him to the Brixton magistrates,' Mr Winter reminded me.

'That's right. Yes. Well, your father.'

'My baby father?'

'The man his mother was living with at that time,' Winter translated. 'He's back in Jamaica, and his mother is living with Oswald's social worker, a Mr Hammurabi.'

'Well, get Hammurabi here.'

I wanted someone to advise Oswald for his own good, but Mr Winter opened his file again and gave us another jewel. 'Mr Hammurabi wrote us a report. He thinks Oswald should never have been let out of the detention centre.'

'Isn't there *anyone* in your family to advise you?' I asked Oswald, almost desperately.

'You my brief, ain't you? You tell me what to do.'

He was absolutely right of course. I took a deep breath and said. 'All right, Mr Gladstone, I'll advise you, to the best of my poor ability, as your counsel. Plead guilty to Actual Bodily Harm! You're risking four years, maybe five if you fight the attempted murder. It's a hell of a great bloody risk, my dear old thing.'

'You mean I don't have no chance?' Oswald asked the question, and I answered it as well as I could. 'As much chance as I have of leaving these marble halls and spending the evening of my days in a little villa in the South of France, being poured out long pink drinks by expensive secretaries. No chance. No.'

'You got another case you want to do, you want to go work for some of them rich villains?' Oswald looked at me, he seemed very angry. 'What's the matter with my case? Too much like hard work?' I didn't answer him and he sat down, suddenly deflated. 'All right. I'll plead guilty then! If that's what you want, I'll plead bloody guilty! My Mum – she wants me put away. All right. I'll plead guilty to something what I never done!' I lit a small cigar, and then I asked him, quietly. 'Are you still telling me – you didn't stab anyone?'

'Look, dad. I never had the knife!'

'Are you still telling me that?'

'You don't believe me?' Oswald looked deeply hurt.

'What I believe isn't of the slightest importance. Is that what you're still telling me?'

'I'm still telling you that. Yeah.'

The most common question I'm asked by such non-legal characters as cross my path, or get talking to me over a glass in Pommeroy's Wine Bar, is how you can defend a customer when you know he's guilty. Well, the answer is, of course, that you don't. Once the old darling tells you that he did the deed, you've got to advise him to plead guilty, admit all and take the consequences. If he refuses to agree, then you must leave him to his own devices. This is not so much a code of morality as a reflex action, an admission of guilt in conference means the end of the road for Rumpole. But the converse is also true. If a client insists that he's innocent, and maintains this attitude against all odds, you can't finally lead him into Court and force him to plead guilty. I may have been, at this moment, just Mr Oswald Gladstone's humble servant, but if My Master's Voice still insisted that he was innocent there was no possible manner in which I could pretend to the Judge that he was ready to surrender. These were the simple rules I had to obey in the end, even if they put paid to luncheon with my son Nick.

'If you still tell me you didn't stab anyone,' I told Oswald, 'we've got to fight the case, and that's all there is to it.'

It was then, of course, that Mr Winter began to get cold feet. 'Listen, Ossie,' he said, 'perhaps it would be more sensible . . .'

'If he goes on telling us he's innocent we've got to fight,' I repeated. 'Just give me five minutes to ring up the Army and Navy Stores.'

'Oh, is that Coats and Macintoshes? It's about my son Nick. He'll probably walk into your department at approximately midday. Well, I imagine you're pretty empty, aren't you, now we've lost the Empire?'

I was standing in the telephone box outside No. 1 Court, chattering to the Army and Navy. Oswald's instructions had meant a radical change in my plans. As I spoke, I happened to notice a worried-looking person in clerical garb loitering outside the window. However, I carried on my conversation with Coats and Macintoshes.

'Nick? Well, he's about twenty-three. Hair brown. Eyes blue. No visible distinguishing marks, that sort of thing. Please tell him, his father's stuck down at the Old Bailey. Thank you.'

I didn't have enormous hope in my message getting through, but there was nothing else I could do in the time available. As I emerged from the confined space, the cleric called my name.

'Mr Rumpole!'

'Yes.'

'I did so want to meet you. I'm Ossie's father.' I looked at the undoubtedly white padre in some confusion. 'His father in God you understand,' the man of the cloth explained. 'Eldred Pickersgill. I'm priest at St Barnabas Without. There's good in that lad, Mr Rumpole, real good in him, deep down somewhere!'

'Pity he doesn't bring it up and give it an airing occasionally,' I said on my way to the Court door.

'He's a hard worker. He works hard at his classes. No result as yet. Absolutely no result. But Oswald is not discouraged. He is, in my view, a natural optimist.'

'That's why we are fighting this case.'

I was about to go through the swing door and on to the battle-field when the vicar had an afterthought.

'Oh, Mr Rumpole,' he said. 'If you do call me as a witness, I prefer not to swear on the Bible.'

'What's the matter, Vicar,' I said severely. 'Have you no religion?' And I left him to attend to my secular affairs.

When I was a young man, just starting at the bar, the old Judges used to scare the living daylights out of me. Terrible old darlings they were, who went back to their Clubs and ordered double muffins after death sentences. They used to be bright purple with rage, or white as paper with voices like ice cracking as they put the boot in. All the same, you could work on those old Judges. You could divert their rage on to the opposition, or move them to tears about an old lag's army record. 'I agree, he has his faults, my Lord, but he did extremely well on the Somme.' Mr Justice Bates was a newer type of Judge, a civil servant, with not a tear in him. I could never get on terms with Bates. There he was, at the start of R. *v*. Gladstone, giving me a look of vague disgust, as if he were Queen Victoria with a bad period. There was nothing for it, however, but to join battle, and at first R. *v*. Gladstone proceeded uneventfully.

Detective Inspector Arthur had just finished giving evidence at the end of the prosecution case when I rose to cross-examine, and I was aware that the judicial atmosphere was somewhat chilly. Perhaps the old darling on the bench was a member of the M.C.C. All the same, I launched cheerfully into the first ques-tion.

'Mr Arthur. You would agree the only real evidence against my client is this statement he is alleged to have signed at the police station?'

'Isn't that evidence *real* enough for you, Mr Rumpole?' said the learned Judge. You see what I mean by the judicial atmos-phere.

'We shall see, shan't we?' I could see Bates, J., looking displeased as I said that. 'Have you the alleged statement there, Inspector?'

'I have, my Lord.' Mr Arthur addressed the Judge respectfully, and the Judge looked respectfully back. I intruded on this mutual respect with another question.

'Did you read that document through to my client, Mr Gladstone, before he signed it?'

'As I remember, he read it himself.'

'You're sure of that?' I challenged him. A memory of something young Oswald had said in the interview room had given me an idea.

'Yes. Quite sure. As a matter of fact he read it aloud to me.'

'He read it all through out loud?' I thought that was unusual, and decided to pin the Inspector to his story.

'Yes, he did, my Lord.' Mr Arthur again got a glance of approval from the bench.

'And you didn't read it back to him?'

'No. I don't believe so.'

'You swear you did not?' The Judge looked as if he didn't care for my doubting the words of a police officer, but the Inspector gave me his answer.

'I swear I didn't read it to him. Mr Gladstone read it to himself.' I picked up the document in question and looked at it with mild distaste.

'And this is a statement alleged to have been made by a West Indian teenager?'

'It was made by your client.'

'Every word his?'

'Every word.'

'Oh dear me, Inspector, don't you think you officers ought to brush up on your Jamaican?' There was a slight stir of laughter in Court in which the Judge didn't participate. After the usher had called, 'Silence,' the Inspector looked vaguely hurt and said, 'I don't know what you mean sir.'

'Neither do I, Mr Rumpole,' the Judge grumbled. I continued to address the witness. 'Just that you've composed this piece of sparkling prose in the dead language of dear old Edgar Wallace.'

'Mr Rumpole,' the Judge answered for the witness. 'Are you suggesting that your client's statement was *composed* by this officer?' So then I had to explain to the judicial old darling, as to a child, 'I am simply suggesting, my Lord, that the whole shooting match comes out of the old police book of verbals. No self-respecting young criminal talks like that nowadays, does he?'

It was then that my son Nick walked into Court, as he had done in his schooldays to listen to my old murders. Although this was only an 'attempt', I was determined to put on a good show for Nick. I beckoned to him to come and sit beside Mr Winter and Jo in the seat behind me. I whispered my apologies for not turning up in the Army and Navy, and he whispered that he'd telephoned my Chambers and discovered where I was to be found. And then His Lordship asked if he could have a few moments of my valuable time.

'My Lord, by all means.' I gave Mr Justice Bates my full attention.

'You were suggesting to the Detective Inspector that this statement was not couched in the language of "a self-respecting young criminal".'

'Of course it isn't. It's the language of a middle-aged Detective Inspector.'

'Mr Rumpole, the jury may not be as expert as you are on the way "self-respecting" criminals talk.' I ignored the somewhat snide innuendo and said with a smile, 'Then let me demonstrate, my Lord. Let's read it together, Detective Inspector.'

'Very well, sir.' He was always cooperative, the dear old chrysanthemum grower. I started to read from Oswald's statement. ' "I know you found the dagger so I better come clean, guv'nor." You left something out, didn't you? What about "it's a fair cop" and "you've got me bang to rights"?'

There was a louder laugh. The usher called, 'Silence,' again, and the Judge's voice was icy. 'Mr Rumpole, is this cross-examination meant to be taken seriously?'

'Only if this bit of paper is meant to be taken seriously, my Lord,' I said, and went on reading before he had time to interrupt again. ' "If you nab Ginger he'll grass on me." Do you know, Inspector? Had Mr Gladstone been going to evening classes in old-time cockney? Had he written a thesis on the argot of the Artful Dodger?'

'Not that I know of, sir.'

'Mr Rumpole!' It was the Judge again, sounding a warning note which I ignored. I kept on at the Inspector. 'Or did these quaint phrases drift up from your memories of happier times when all confession statements taken by the police started "It's a fair cop" just as a formality?'

'Mr Rumpole!' The Judge took the words out of Mr Arthur's mouth. 'I sincerely hope there'll be some evidence to support this attack on the officer's integrity.'

'At the moment, my Lord, I'm simply attacking his prose style.' Not bad, I hope you'll agree; and I wanted Nick to see me at my best.

'You're suggesting the Inspector is lying?' The Judge seemed slow to follow my drift.

'Oh, my Lord, certainly. No doubt the same suggestion will be made to my client. The compliments are mutual.'

'Mr Rumpole, you have some experience in these Courts.' Now the Judge was trying the effect of being menacingly polite.

'A little, my Lord. Just a little.'

'Over a long period of years?'

'You might say, my Lord, from time immemorial.'

'And you know perfectly well the limits to which defending counsel may go?'

'I've often been reminded of them, my Lord.'

'I imagine you have. If the cross-examination we have just heard is typical of you, Mr Rumpole, I imagine you have had to be reminded often. One does not expect to have to repeat such reminders to counsel of your advanced age and seniority. Now have you any other questions to ask this officer? I mean, *proper* questions.'

'Oh, a great many. I was anxious not to interrupt the flow of Your Lordship's rebuke.' I was delighted Nick was hearing this, and I turned to attack the Inspector with renewed strength.

'Wouldn't you agree, Inspector Arthur? This is really a Golden Oldie of a confession statement?' There was more laughter, another call for 'silence' and a long sigh from the

Judge who said, wearily, 'The jury may have some idea what the question means. I have none.'

Inspector Arthur, I knew, understood the question perfectly well.

'What's the answer, Inspector?'

'As your client knows full well, that is his own confession, Mr Rumpole. His own confession of guilt.'

This clearly appealed to the Judge as a curtain line. He turned apologetically to the jury. 'This case is obviously going to detain us a considerable time. We have yet to learn the nature of the defence. Shall we say, two o'clock, members of the jury?'

The Judge had risen and vanished before I could say certainly not two o'clock, what about half past two, which would give me a decent chance of a farewell lunch with Nick? As it was, Simpsons in the Strand was out of the question, there were no tables to be had in the Newgate Street Wine Bar, and we ended up in a pub round the corner, where the cold beef was off, and all they had left was a cheese sandwich, which was no particular good even as a cheese sandwich, and no pickle! Nick had a half of lager, and I took refuge in a large rum, washed down with a pint of Guinness.

'What time's your plane, Nick?'

'Six o'clock. It's one of those charters.'

'You're having tea with your mother?'

'She wants me to.'

'Then don't try and cut it, eh?' I gave my son a conspiratorial wink. 'Watch out for She Who Must Be Obeyed.'

Nick didn't laugh at that, as he used to in the old days. Perhaps he was hungry and missing the roast at Simpsons. After the disappointments of the morning, I thought a little financial support might be in order, and I pulled out the cheque book accordingly. 'Got all you need in the way of money, Nick?'

'I've got enough. I worked all last August.'

'Oh yes, of course.' He seemed to mean it so I put the cheque book away.

'Dirty sort of work, wasn't it? I take my hat off to you. I could never dig up the Underground!' I saw Nick look at me then, and somehow it wasn't the look of unqualified admiration which I had been used to when he came home from school and dropped in on my murders. 'I don't think I could do your job either,' he said.

'Oh, come on Nick. The Old Bailey's not so bad. You can have quite a lot of good, clean fun down the Bailey.'

'Is that what you were having this morning?' I'd had enough of the cheese sandwich and felt for the box of small cigars.

'I forget. Do you smoke these things?'

'No.'

'No. Of course not.' I prodded one between my lips, lit it and gave a resounding cough. 'Filthy habit.'

'No, but *were* you having fun?' For once I saw my son looking genuinely puzzled.

'Well, now. Yes! Yes, perhaps I was. In my own quiet way.'

'That Judge!' Nick seemed appalled by what he had seen in Court. 'That Judge,' I told Nick, 'was defending bad cases of non-renewed dog licence when I was doing the Penge Bungalow Murders – alone and without a leader!' I was not, as you may have gathered, over-impressed by Mr Justice Bates.

'I don't know how you could go on when that Judge said those things to you, Dad.'

'Bless you, Nick. I'll tell you how you deal with judicial insults. You smile a sweet smile of Chinese inscrutability and say, "If your Lordship pleases". You take the rough with the smooth. In a dozen oysters there's always one that gives you the collywobbles. It's just bad luck that of all the Judges available I had to pick the one who looks as if he's got woman trouble.' I might have added, 'and of all the women available for matrimony I had to pick your mother,' but I looked at Nick and suspected that this thought might not, at that particular lunch-time, get an entirely sympathetic reception.

'I suppose the Judge thought you were wasting his time,' Nick went on.

'*His* time? How long should it take to rob a boy's life of five years?' I looked at my watch, I'd soon have to be back in Court. This is no proper farewell, I thought, to my son Nick. 'I had hoped the case might be a shortie.'

'And the Judge didn't like you pretending.'

'Pretending what, Nick?' For once I wasn't following my son's drift.

'Pretending your mugger's innocent. I mean Judges must get sick and tired of all those phoney defences. Looking at the policeman's notebook and all that sort of nonsense, when surely everyone *knows*.'

'What do they know?'

'Well. That boy actually admitted . . .'

'So they say. No one *knows* anything until it's proved. And even then you may have a nagging doubt.'

Nick was laughing then, imitating one of my stock court-room phrases, ' "Members of the jury, while there remains a particle of doubt." I remember you practising that speech in front of the bathroom mirror, while I put my rubber duck's head under the water, so he wouldn't be embarrassed. Doubt's your stock in trade, isn't it?'

'Better than being a cleric and dealing in improbable beliefs.' I swallowed about a quarter of a pint of Guinness and tried a final apology. 'Nick, I'm sorry I was busy . . .'

'I didn't mind. Not till I saw what you were busy at.'

'Do you find it so disreputable?' I looked at him, in some sorrow, and not much anger.

'If that boy's guilty, which he obviously is . . .'

'They're all guilty of something, my dear old thing. Everyone's guilty of *something*. If anyone gets off it's a plus.'

'A plus for who?'

'For them, of course. It's a strange quality of human nature, Nick.' I signalled for a refill of our glasses. 'People show an almost comic relief at not being locked up. They actually *enjoy* not having to share one chamber-pot through endless nights with vindictive, frightened and sexually frustrated strangers. Do you find that so very odd?' There was silence as the barmaid gave us our drinks. Nick didn't answer my unanswerable question. I raised my glass to him and said, 'My clients relish a good win as much as I do.'

'What about society?' Nick still looked worried. 'I mean, all that getting people off – is it much good to society at large?'

'Society can open a door at night and go to the lavatory.'

'Shouldn't you see it's protected occasionally?'

'Just at the moment I've got my hands full protecting young Ossie Gladstone.'

'By telling lies?'

'By telling his story for him, as well as I can. What do you think I am, Nick? I'm nothing but a ventriloquist's doll, perched on Mr Gladstone's knee.'

'You think that's a very dignified position?'

'Oh, Nick, you can't be born or die in a dignified position. How the hell can you live in one, my old darling?' I drank the Guinness, and remembered something about Mr Gladstone. 'You know about that boy. His mother sent him away, when he was four. Sent him away from home, I mean.'

Curiously enough, Nick didn't seem to be thinking about Oswald Gladstone. He was putting me, for some reason, in the dock.

'But today, when I saw you standing there, saying things you really didn't mean . . .'

'That's *not* what I was doing.'

'I suddenly knew why, well, why you've never said much you meant to me, have you?'

'Nick! I'm sorry we couldn't manage Simpsons. It'd've been so much pleasanter.'

'Yes. We'd've had steak and kidney pud and you'd've been in a good mood and told me a string of funny stories about your favourite murders. But you wouldn't have actually *said* anything. Not something of your own. I suppose it's all that ventriloquist business. You must forget your own voice sometimes.'

That, at last, was an allegation I could rebut. 'Now, my voice. It's a good voice. I do flatter myself.' I tried it out on a snatch of Wordsworth. ' "There was a boy; you knew him well ye cliffs And islands of Winander . . ." '

'I think that's what Mother finds so difficult,' Nick said, and now I was beginning to lose my patience. '*She* finds difficult? And *what* does the Leader of the Opposition find difficult exactly?'

'Knowing exactly who you are,' Nick said, and I felt little sympathy for She's problem. 'Well, we've been married thirty years,' I said. 'If She doesn't know *that* by now . . .'

'It's just that she's not very happy actually. I wanted to talk to you about it before I left,' Nick said.

'It's not easy to talk here.' Indeed the bar was full of noisy jurors and solicitors' clerks, villains and even noisier coppers. I felt helpless and apologized again. 'If only he'd pleaded.'

'No. But I know what she means now. Now, I've seen you in action. Is that what you call it?'

'In action. Yes, I suppose it is.' I drained my glass and Nick went on. 'She says you're always arguing, but she doesn't know if it's an argument or just a game, like the game you were playing in Court this morning. She says you seem to hate her sometimes, but she can't tell if you mean it. In a way, she says, she'd rather you really hated her than pretended to.'

'But I say wonderful things to her. Very often! Wonderful, complimentary things.' I protested at a manifest injustice.

'Of course, she doesn't believe those either.'

'*She's* not very happy. *She's* not. What do you think *I* feel, Nick? What do you think?'

But he could give no answer to my question. 'I don't know. I don't know what you feel, Dad.'

And I don't know what else we might have said to each other if we hadn't been interrupted at that precise moment by my instructing solicitor, Mr Winter, and his side-kick, Jo. The unwelcome Winter announced that he had got a message, through the prison officer, that our client Mr Gladstone required our immediate presence down the cells. He had, it seemed, new instructions to give us. I reminded him that my son Nick was just off to America, but Mr Gladstone, it appeared, would brook no delay.

'My Master's Voice,' I said regretfully. 'Have a good trip then, Nick. I mean, it's not for ever, is it? You'll be back soon, I'm sure. On holidays.'

'I expect so.'

'I'm sorry about the lunch being so scrappy.'

'That's all right.' And Nick smiled.

'Damn it. We haven't had a talk yet even.'

'No. No, we haven't.'

Mr Oswald Gladstone, when we got to the interview room, had plenty of time to talk. He was another young man who seemed not altogether pleased with Rumpole.

'That Judge, dad,' he said in a tone of rebuke. 'He sure don't like you . . .'

'I'm not absolutely crazy about him,' I admitted.

'It's the jury that matters, Oswald.' Mr Winter tried to re-assure him. 'Mr Rumpole's getting through to the jury.'

'From what I seen, that Judge, he's pretty angry with you, dad.' Oswald frowned at me.

'It's part of the wear and tear of legal life.' I was prepared to be philosophical.

'So when I seen that, I decide to plead guilty.'

'But Mr Rumpole explained. If you tell us you didn't do it . . .' Mr Winter protested.

'I tell you now. I don't want this going on.'

'But if you *didn't* do it . . .'

'I made that statement, didn't I?' Oswald shook his head. 'That Judge. He's getting *really* angry.'

'But Oswald. I told you. It's the *jury* that matters, not the Judge.'

'It's gone all against us.' Mr Gladstone had lost his early ebullience. In vain, Winter continued, cheeringly, 'I've seen them all at work, and Mr Rumpole's cross-examination was top hole! I mean, he had D.I. Arthur right on the ropes.'

Oswald gave me a look of pity. 'I'm sorry, dad. I know you tried real hard.'

'Thank you.' Well, it hadn't been a day of kind words for Rumpole.

'Just wasn't working for you, was it? So I'm pleading guilty.'

'If you're quite sure.' I could have wished he'd made his decision in the morning.

'I'm sure.'

'We'd better take written instructions then.' It's always a wise precaution to get a client's signature to a change of plea, so I started to write, just as Inspector Arthur had started to write on a previous occasion.

'Cheer up the old Judge, anyway.' Oswald smiled.

'Well, I think you're doing the wrong thing, Oswald,' my instructing solicitor rambled on. 'I think it's a tragedy. I mean, give Mr Rumpole another half hour with that Inspector and he'll come out as what he is, a nigger hater.'

'He didn't call me no nigger.' Oswald shook his head. 'He never called me that.'

'Well, if you think you know what you're doing.' Winter was still grumbling, but Oswald was looking at me with, I thought, some apprehension.

'What you got there, Mr Rumpole?'

'Written instructions. For you to sign.' I finished writing and handed Mr Gladstone the sheet I had torn out of my notebook. 'You *can* sign that, can't you?'

'Yes. Yes, I can write my name.' Oswald sounded hurt.

'Read it through first. Just read it through. Before you sign it.' I went on playing the Inspector Arthur part. Oswald took the paper, glanced at it, and said confidently, 'O.K. I read it.'

'Are you sure?' I was watching him carefully.

'O.K.' Oswald began to sound irritable.

'Why don't you read it out loud? Come on, old dear. Just so we're sure you've got it perfectly clear. Out loud. Like you did down at the nick.'

There was a long, a very long pause, during which I knew the answer to the case of Mr Oswald Gladstone and his confession of guilt.

'You can't read, can you, Oswald?' I said quietly. 'Why didn't you tell us?'

Ossie was too ashamed of not reading to try to get off a little charge of attempted murder. He looked away from me, and said, 'What do you want me to do?'

'I think,' I told him, 'I want you to fight.'

On my way back to Court I ran into the Rev. Eldred Pickersgill still hanging about and waiting to give evidence. I was able to check a few facts with him before I pushed open the glass swing door and prepared myself to go a few more rounds with Detective Inspector Arthur and Mr Justice Bates.

'Detective Inspector. You remember saying before we adjourned for luncheon that you didn't read out his alleged statement to my client?' I got straight down, you see, to the pith of the argument.

'Yes, sir.' The officer in the witness-box now sounded bored.

'But, you said, the reverse was the case, and he read his statement out to you?'

'That's perfectly true.'

'Would it interest you to know, Inspector, that Oswald Gladstone can neither read nor write?'

'But . . .' The Judge, of course, had picked up the document and was looking at the scribbled signature. I interrupted to explain, and give him further details thanks to the Reverend Eldred Pickersgill.

'Oh, he can scrawl his signature – just, my Lord. But the whole realm of poetry is a closed book to him. Wordsworth is silent. Dickens and Thackeray might not have existed. He can't even look up and tell what street he's in or follow the simplest directions for assembling a model aeroplane!'

'Well, he either can read or he can't. Which is it?' the Judge asked, testily.

'He can't, can he, Inspector?'

For once, Inspector Arthur seemed lost for words. The Judge, bless his little ermine cuffs, repeated the question.

'Do you accept, Inspector, that this young man could not read?'

Another long pause, and then the Inspector made an admission. 'If counsel says so, I must accept that, my Lord.'

'So it follows from that that you never put his reading to the test?' I asked innocently.

'It must do.'

'And your evidence this morning was quite misleading?'

'Yes. But . . .'

'No "buts", Inspector. It was either true of false. Which?' Dear old Arthur spent a long while searching for a word and came up with, 'It was incorrect.'

'And if he couldn't read, my client wouldn't've known if you had written down his words, or *your* words, Inspector?'

'He . . . might not know.' The possibility was enough for me, I breathed a huge sigh of relief.

'He told you, didn't he, about a boy called Ginger Robertson?' I hoped I had prevented the proof of Oswald's guilt. Now I had to do something to suggest he might even be innocent.

'Yes, he did,' the Inspector agreed.

'Who was present at the scene of the crime?'

'Yes.'

'Who is not there in that dock?'

'No.'

'Because the combined power and brilliance of the detective force has not succeeded in catching that young gentleman, Ginger Robertson? Are the police still out looking for him?'

'No.'

'Why not?'

'Because we got Gladstone's confession?'

'And because of that worthless document, you didn't trouble to find the true criminal?'

I thought of how I would describe my triumph to Nick, and settle all his doubts about my profession. I would say, 'You see, Nick, sometimes it goes well. Sometimes it goes beautifully. Sweet and easy as cutting off a hunk of Stilton cheese or knock. ing back a glass of claret. You've got to lay the ground, though. You notice I tied old Arthur down before lunch. Got him committed to his story? Then I didn't really know why I was doing it. But it was the instinct, you see. That's why they use Rumpole, Nick. It's the dear old instinct. See how it's working for us? They're never going to believe his confession now. See how it's working for us, Nick?'

✦ I looked behind me, but the seat beside Mr Winter was empty. My son had gone to start a new sort of life in another country.

At the end of the prosecution evidence, I made a speech to the jury, and didn't call Oswald. They took about an hour to acquit. When I said goodbye to my client he looked discontented, and asked me why I had to show him up for not being able to read.

All the same I was in a moderately satisfied mood as I stood in front of the porcelain of the Gents attached to the Old Bailey robing room and recited a particularly triumphant bit of Wordsworth to myself.

> ' "She was an elfin pinnace; lustily
>   I dipped my oars into the silent lake.
>   And, as I rose upon the stroke, my boat
>   Went heaving through the water like a swan . . ." '

'So you had to fight your case, Rumpole.' George came pottering up beside me.

'Yes, George. It was a pretty good day. Had a bit of fun with the Detective Inspector. He'll probably go home and kick the chrysanthemums.'

'So you never got away to see your son?' George asked.

'Sorry?'

'You had a fight on your hands. You never got away to meet your boy?'

'Well, Nick came up here. He came up to the Bailey. To watch the old man in action.'

'He'll have enjoyed that.'

'Oh yes! Nick's always liked the Bailey. Since he was a schoolboy. He used to come up to my murders and then I'd give him a rattling good tea!'

Back in mufti, I was on my way out of the Bailey when I ran into a gratified Mr Winter and his side-kick Jo.

'You crucified old D.I. Arthur, Mr Rumpole.' Winter beamed. 'You really did.'

At which moment, the Detective Inspector and his Sergeant passed us on their way out to a villainous world. The D.I. looked displeased and didn't answer when I gave him a cheery good night. I felt some sympathy for the officer, and said to Winter, 'Poor old sweetheart. You know, Ossie may have said all that to him. Every word. The only mistake the Inspector made was to ginger it up with a little lie.'

'His *only* mistake? Do you believe that?' Mr Winter gave me a tolerant smile.

'Who knows?' And I told him, 'It's not my job to believe anything.'

After dinner, I sat in the chilly living-room of the 'mansion' flat finishing a bottle of Château Fleet Street, and thumbing through the papers in a rather attractive little murder my clerk had landed for me. My wife, Hilda, was knitting some woollen garment intended as a substitute for a more efficient form of central heating.

'You saw Nick, then,' she said.

'Yes. Yes, I saw him. Well, we had a scrap lunch, but very pleasant. Very pleasant indeed.'

'He said you had a sandwich in the pub!' She Who Must Be Obeyed said accusingly. I looked up from the interesting description of another stab wound and apologized. 'Well, you know how it is in the Bailey. It's difficult to make plans.'

'Nick said he talked about you, about your work. He seemed to think it was a little, well, off-colour somehow.'

'Did he? Did he give you that impression?' I was genuinely surprised when She sounded indignant.

'I must say, I wasn't having that from Nick!' I looked at her questioningly, and Hilda went on. ' "Your father," I told him, "is a member of an Honourable Profession. Besides which, think of all he's done for you. Public school, Oxford, and a lot of help in going to America." '

'All paid for by the proceeds of crime.'

'I certainly did *not* say that! I said, "Nick. You should respect your father." That's what I said.'

'Thank you, Hilda.'

'Well he should.'

I got up and found a small cigar. I was more troubled, perhaps, than I had liked to admit about what Nick had said to me. 'Nick thinks we ask all the wrong questions. Just so we can get the wrong answers. That's what he thinks.'

'He really upset me, talking like that.' Hilda clicked her needles disapprovingly.

'He's perfectly right, of course.'

'Rumpole!'

I applied a torn-off page of the *Criminal Law Review* to the electric fire and lit the small cigar.

'I mean, "Why?" That's what we ought to be asking about Mr Oswald Gladstone. Not "Who did it?" "Who's guilty?" "Can you prove it?" "Yes I can." "No, you can't." "Bags I have the last word and the burden of the proof." But *why*? Why ever did that happen? Outside Lords, for no reason whatsoever. I mean, God knows I believe in freedom. But jolly Jean-Jacques Rousseau, I'd like to ask him a few pertinent questions.' Nothing was heard in the room but the click of Hilda's needles. Then she said, 'I have absolutely no idea what you're talking about. So far as I am concerned, you belong to an Honourable Profession. And you do it very well. I heard that at the garden party.

"Rumpole," Guthrie Featherstone told me, "is stubborn as a mule in cross-examination."' '

'You know what else Nick said?' I asked her.

'So far as I can understand, Nick talked a lot of nonsense.' She went into a spurt of high-speed knitting.

'He said you didn't know exactly who I am.'

'Of course I do. You're Rumpole!' She stopped knitting then and looked at me, only a little puzzled. 'Aren't you?'

Well, yes. I'm Horace Rumpole. What *was* Nick talking about? Everyone down the Bailey knows me. I'm an amiable eccentric who drops ash down his waistcoat and tells the time with a gold hunter and calls Judges old sweethearts. Also I recite Wordsworth in the loo.

That's who I am, isn't it?

Rumpole and the Gentle Art of Blackmail

A certain amount of detachment, the learned Head of my Chambers, Guthrie Featherstone, Q.C., M.P., says, is essential to the life of a barrister. This means that you should be able to see your client sent down for a long stretch, wave him a cheery goodbye and potter off to the Sheridan Club for a touch of cold pheasant with nothing more than a mild 'Oops!' at having backed another loser.

Detachment, I suppose, comes easily to Guthrie. He plays golf with a number of Her Majesty's Judges and when he stands up to defend, he often gets a small smile from His Lordship which seems to indicate, 'Well, we know you've got to go through the motions, old chap. Better luck next time when you'll be appearing for the prosecution.' When I get up on my hind legs, the judicial attitude is to identify me more closely with the criminal classes. Indeed I sometimes think that as I stand in the robes and old horsehair wig I might as well be wearing a cloth cap, mask, striped jersey and carrying a bag marked 'swag', from the glassy-eyed stare of disapproval I get from the old sweetheart on the bench.

Quite frequently, of course, I can rise above it. Sometimes I can even manage a touch of the famous Featherstone detachment. When defending Bertie Timson on yet another charge of carrying housebreaking implements by night, for instance, I know what verdict the old darling expects, and any better result will be accepted with the utmost gratitude.

But when it comes to defending a young man with no previous convictions, about whom you have the horrible suspicion that he may be innocent, then proceedings may become extremely sticky, not to say, hair-raising, and detachment is extremely difficult. Adverse verdicts, in such circumstances, tend to be taken to heart and inflict wounds which can only be soothed by a prolonged dosage of Pommeroy's ordinary claret (Château Fleet Street 1979) and an influx of other briefs. The scars, however, remain.

It is not, happily, very often that you get a client cursed with the possibility of innocence, but it does happen, and such a client was young Vernon, gardener and handyman at St Joseph's College, Oxford, whose case caused me a number of sleepless nights under the dreaming spires. The situation wasn't made any easier by the fact that R. *v.* Vernon was a case concerned with an offence of the kind which draws a swift intake of breath from Her Majesty (who, of course, concerns herself in the prosecution of all potential villains), and usually involves a prolonged stay at one of the Royal Residences in Wandsworth, Pentonville or the Isle of Wight. The crime in question was blackmail, in this case of a 'distinguished public figure', and carried out in a particularly nasty manner.

Blackmail, technically speaking, the demanding of money with menaces, is, as I say, looked on with grave disapproval by the powers that be; but it's an essential part of family life. When it is used, however, it does require a certain amount of basic skill.

> I will do such things ...
> What they are yet I know not – but they shall be
> The terrors of the earth.

That vague menace of King Lear, of course, was absolutely hopeless as a bit of blackmail. The good blackmailer utters a threat which is short, clear and perfectly possible. My wife had that lesson to learn, over the matter of the new loose covers for our drawing-room chairs.

Picture me, that morning, with She Who Must Be Obeyed (or Mrs Hilda Rumpole to give her the name under which she sometimes passes) at breakfast in our matrimonial home at 25B Froxbury Court, Gloucester Road. I was on my way to Oxford, not primarily for the purpose of visiting my old college, but to Her Majesty's Prison, in order to confer with my client, Vernon, and She, having been on a tour of inspection of our 'mansion' flat, looked vaguely discontented and narrowed her eyes in the manner of someone about to put the screws on.

'Rumpole!' she said. 'We need new chair covers.'

There is only one way to deal with such an unnecessary and generally unhelpful remark – pretend you haven't heard it.

'Got to hurry breakfast, I'm afraid,' I muttered. 'I'm catching a train to Oxford.'

Whatever else you may say about my wife Hilda, she gets top marks for persistence. She ignored my convenient deafness and carried on.

'When we went to the Featherstones' sherry party, I was admiring their chintz chair covers. So jolly and spring-like, I told Marigold Featherstone.'

'I'm going there to study a rather jolly and spring-like little case of blackmail.' I was consuming the tea and toast at breakneck speed.

'We can't invite the Featherstones to dinner here until we've got new chair covers, Rumpole.' Hilda reached a verdict: 'Our old chair covers would simply let us down.'

'I don't know. They've held me up for a good many years.' It is a mistake to attempt any sort of pleasantry with She, particularly at breakfast. My wife looked distinctly unamused and trumpeted a warning, 'Really, Rumpole!'

'The charge is blackmail,' I told her, hoping she might take the hint. 'Demanding money with menaces. Within the sacred precincts of St Joseph's, Oxford. My old college, Hilda.'

She was neither deterred by my hint of crime nor interested in my reminiscence. With a carefully sharpened voice she continued:

'Rumpole! Are you going to let me buy new chair covers or not? Marigold Featherstone only paid three hundred pounds to get hers done, and the sofa.'

The mention of this hideously round figure made me choke on my tea.

'Three hundred pounds! Hilda. Do you think I'm made of money? Besides, that represents, at a rough estimate, almost one hundred bottles of Pommeroy's claret-style plonk . . .'

But now the knives were definitely out. In a voice of cold steel Hilda came to the menace: 'Rumpole, I'm giving you fair warning! If you don't give me the money for new chair covers to brighten up our living-room, I'll . . .' But then there was a fatal moment of hesitation. I jumped in fearlessly with, 'What'll you do, Hilda?'

Her bluff was called. She Who Must Be Obeyed visibly faltered. 'I . . . I haven't thought yet. But I'll . . . I'll take a most serious view. I promise you that.'

You see what I mean? She and old King Lear had a lot to learn about the gentle art of blackmail. No doubt they could have profited by lessons from the client I was about to see, languishing in Oxford prison.

However, I wasn't taking any risks and I swallowed the last gulp of tea and bolted for Paddington station and on to a rather grimy diesel, bound in a westerly direction. How long was it since I had taken a train to go up to St Joseph's College, Oxford, for the study of law? Law is a subject which, I may say, never interested me greatly. People in trouble, yes. Bloodstains and handwriting, certainly. The art of cross-examination, of course. Winning over a jury, fascinating. But law! The only honourable way to pass a law exam is to make a few notes on the cuff and take a quick shufti at them during the occasional visit to the bog.

Oxford! They were romantic years I had spent at St Joseph's no doubt. Those were the first nights when I got tipsy on College claret in the company of my boon companion, P. J. Fosdyke. Fozzy Fosdyke was a thinnish and nervous-looking historian who had a devilish method of playing draughts, a cunning way with a limerick, and a tendency to become over-excited at the sniff of a small dry sherry. Fosdyke and Rumpole were as inseparable, in those distant days, as the three musket-eers, with poor old Monty Simpson, whom I had an irresistible desire to call 'Shrimpson' because of his pop eyes and eyebrows like waving antennae, making up the trio. We three used to drink bitter in pubs by the station together, and, on endless Sunday afternoons, go for walks through the countryside.

As the train got into its stride, and we were granted a view of trees, the river and cows champing at sunlit grass, sizeable chunks of *The Oxford Book of English Verse* (Sir Arthur Quiller-Couch edition) came floating into my mind.

> Pale blue convolvulus in tendrils creep
> And air-swept lindens yield
> Their scent, and rustle down their perfumed showers

Of bloom on the bent grass where I am laid,
And bower me from the August sun with shade;
And the eye travels down to Oxford's towers . . .

What a joy it was, I thought, to be getting away from London, far from the terrors of Judge Bullingham and my clerk Henry, and the V.A.T. man and She Who Must Be Obeyed! And then, at last, I got a splendid view of the coal heaps round the canal as the train rattled and gasped its way into Oxford station.

'Rumpole!'

Walking down the platform I was accosted by a stout person whom I didn't recognize. He was accompanied by an elderly grey-haired man whose sprouting eyebrows gave him the appearance of an anxious crustacean.

'It's never Horace Rumpole?' The stout man sounded positive.

'Well, it is sometimes.'

'You remember me, don't you, Rumpole? P. J. Fosdyke. We were up at St Joseph's together.'

'My God, Fozzy Fosdyke!'

'And you recollect old Simpson. Senior Classics Fellow now at St Joseph's.'

'Monty Simpson! Senior Fellow?'

It seemed incredible, until I remembered that standing in front of my two old friends I too must have seemed like some sort of antique or relic from the past. Simpson twitched his eyebrows and said in that high, slightly hysterical voice of his, which always sounded like a scream from the depths of the sea, 'We were all at St Joseph's together!'

'In the year dot,' I said, putting the record straight.

'We climbed in one evening. Over the wall and straight into the Principal's bedroom.' Simpson was becoming nostalgic.

'Which you mistook for the upstairs bog,' Fosdyke reminded me.

'And we were greeted by the sight of the Principal's wife sitting bolt upright in bed in a pink nightie.' Simpson was bubbling with long-remembered mirth.

'And hair curlers.' It was something that stuck in my mind.

'A sight to drive a man to life-long homosexuality,' Simpson thought. And then he asked me, 'What are you doing in Oxford?'

'Oh, a bit of legal business.' Compared to the work of a Senior Classical Fellow it sounded on the sordid side.

'Do you have to hurry back? Come for a drink at the old Coll. this evening. Or something to eat, we dine early.' Fosdyke issued the invitation, and Simpson backed it up by nodding, his eyebrows waving gently in the air.

Fosdyke explained that he was also on the academic staff of my old college, being a Tutor in Modern History. We had no more time for catching up on the news of our various careers as duty called in the shape of a good-looking young girl with nice eyes, clean jeans and a knapsack full of papers.

'Mr Rumpole?' she said. Someone must have described a crumpled sort of legal person in an old hat to her. 'I've come to take you to the prison.'

'Oh Rumpole! What have you done now?' P. J. Fosdyke was laughing like an undergraduate. 'Can it be that landlady's daughter in Longwall Street?'

'Do you want us to come with you and bail you out?' Simpson was signalling joke with his eyebrows. Very wry fellows, these academics.

'This is P. J. Fosdyke and Mr Shrimp ... I beg his pardon, Simpson. Both dons of a sort from St Joseph's, my old college.'

'St Joseph's!' The girl seemed to be looking at all of us with a new wariness, and my old friends with a kind of hostility.

'Yes, and you are . . .'

'Sue Galton. I'm an articled clerk with Newby and Paramore, your instructing solicitor in the Vernon case.'

'Vernon!' This time Fozzy Fosdyke looked slightly uneasy, and the Shrimp gave out one of his piercing underwater laughs.

'Well, Rumpole. Do come and have a drink up at the Coll. For old times' sake.'

'Yes, of course. Of course I will. For the sake of old times.'

'Come on, Mr Rumpole. I've got a taxi outside. We can't keep Peter waiting.'

Peter? Who was Peter? And then I remembered, our client was Peter Vernon.

'Why?' He is not going anywhere, is he?' I said, and because of the hurt look in Sue Galton's eyes I immediately regretted having said it. She must be one of the new sort of instructing solicitor, the sensitive variety.

Peter Vernon, as I'd gathered from a glance through my brief on the way up in the train (always ask your client, at the start of any conference, to tell you his story in *his own words*, that saves a lot of preliminary reading), was a young man in his early twenties. His father was a shop steward in the Cowley works and Peter had a number of A-levels, but just couldn't find work that suited him, rebelling, in a way I found quite understandable, from the tedium of the assembly line. He finally landed a job as a gardener at St Joseph's, a pleasant enough existence, I should have imagined, mowing the croquet lawn and planting out snapdragons. He was all set, it seemed, for a gentle and rustic existence in the heart of Oxford. In fact, his statement had read, 'I was extremely happy at St Joseph's until this business with Sir Michael started.'

Sir Michael Tuffnell, Oxford Professor of Moral Philosophy, Principal of St Joseph's College for the past five years, was a popular guru known to millions. He was a grey-haired and distinguished-looking old party, with a twinkling eye and a considerable sense of humour, always ready to be wheeled on to the telly or 'Any Questions' when anyone wanted a snap answer on such troublesome points as 'What is the meaning of meaning?' Or 'Is God dead?'

Sir Michael was a person, certainly, of the utmost brilliance and respectability, whose grasp of the Nature of the Universe was such that God no doubt relied on him to tell him whether or not He existed, a question that Sir Michael answered with a respectful and tentative negative, meanwhile keeping his options open. Apart from his brilliance as a philosopher, he was known as a patron of the arts, an expert on Italian opera and the holder of progressive and even radical opinions. Perhaps he was rather self-consciously determined not to be thought of as a remote academic or an intellectual snob. He seemed to have gone out of his way to be kind to the new young gardener, to talk to him and to lend him books and records. There was no evidence from the prosecution that the relationship between the Philosopher and the Gardener had ever gone so far as what would be called, in any self-respecting social inquiry report, a deeply caring one-to-one single-sex situation. Indeed, my client, in his statement, denied that anything of the sort had ever occurred.

According to Sir Michael, this represented a change of story by Peter Vernon. The young gardener, he said, had threatened to tell the world, or at least the Senior Common Room, of passionate goings on in the Principal's lodge. For a while Sir Michael gave my client cheques, considerable sums in cash and a handsome gold engraved cigarette case to prevent this baseless accusation being made. Finally, and with considerable courage, the Principal went to the Oxford constabulary and denounced his gardening blackmailer.

It seemed a straightforward, sordid and averagely unpleasant case. But as we sat in the taxi on our way to the prison, Miss Sue Galton, leaned forward, fixed me with her sincere look (blue eyes and brown hair, I noticed, made an attractive combination) and added to my instructions.

'Mr Rumpole. Before we get to the prison, there's something I ought to tell you. You see, Peter's not in the least gay.'

'Well, I'm sure he isn't.' I sympathized entirely. 'Not stuck in Oxford gaol for the past six months awaiting the attentions of one of Her Majesty's Judges on a nasty charge of blackmail.'

'No. You don't understand.' Miss Galton sounded impatient.

'Tell me.'

'Peter's just not queer. He's not homosexual.' There was the smallest hesitation before she added, 'You see, I can guarantee that. Personally.'

'Can you, Miss Galton?'

'Oh yes. You see, Peter's my boyfriend. We're going to get married when you get him off.'

This, I must say, was an added complication. If I lost the case, as, after a brief glance at the papers, seemed highly probable, I should not only have an aggrieved client, but a broken-hearted solicitor on my hands. Moreover, I didn't see how I could question the fiancé without some embarrassment to his legal adviser. I don't think I had ever had a solicitor who'd been to bed with the client before, at least not in such complicated circumstances. I hadn't fully worked out all the implications of

Miss Sue Galton's evidence before our taxi reached the prison and she rang for admittance.

After the gate had opened, after the formalities were complete and the shades of the prison-house began to close upon the growing Rumpole, we were shown into the cupboard they grandly called an interview room, and Peter Vernon was brought to us. As he came in, Miss Sue Galton began to glow in a way which provided little evidence of Vernon's homosexuality. He gave her a smile, and then welcomed me with a mixture of modesty and gratitude.

'Hullo, Mr Rumpole. It's kind of you to come all this way. I know you're busy.'

'I got you some fags, Peter.' Miss Galton dived in her kit bag and came up with a packet of Gauloises.

'Oh, thanks, Sue.' He took one and lit it, the smoke mixed with the usual prison smell of urine and disinfectant to give us a genuine continental atmosphere.

'How are things in the Oxford nick?' I said politely, and he smiled at me.

'Well, it's not the Senior Common Room at St Joseph's. But it's not so bad, I suppose. There's one or two decent screws. Blokes you can talk to.' He was being perfectly fair. Then he looked at my solicitor, concerned. 'You haven't been worrying, have you, Sue?'

'What do you think?' Her smile was rueful.

'Well, you're not to worry,' he reassured her. 'We'll be all right. Now we've got Mr Rumpole. Sue told me, sir, you're marvellous at getting criminals off.'

'Really? She's too kind.' Something about all this politeness was worrying me. But they really were quite the nicest young couple I'd ever been banged up in a nick with.

'Well, you may have a bit more trouble with me.' Peter Vernon blew out smoke thoughtfully, he was still smiling.

'Oh yes? Why?' I asked him.

'Well, I suppose my problem is – I'm not a criminal.'

I looked at Peter Vernon. To say that he was a good-looking boy is an understatement. You can see faces like his on Greek statues and Florentine paintings. And, as I have said, the most disturbing thing, from the point of view of an old hack advocate about to undertake his defence, was that he looked innocent. I started a difficult interview cautiously, still embarrassed by the presence of the clearly devoted young girl, who gazed at our client as he talked, and took copious notes.

'Well now, Peter. How long did you work at St Joseph's?' I decided to begin at the beginning, as far as possible from the unfortunate heart of the matter.

'About ten months.'

'You met Sir Michael soon after you started there?'

'Oh yes. He came up to me in the garden one afternoon. He was very charming.'

'Do you remember what he said?'

'When he first spoke to me?'

'Yes.'

'Well, I do, as a matter of fact. He said . . .' Peter Vernon closed his eyes and repeated the words as though he understood them.

> '"Such was that happy Garden State
> When man first walked without a mate."

And I said:

> "After a place so pure and sweet,
> What other help could yet be meet?"'

There was no reason why anyone should be surprised to hear Andrew Marvell repeated in the nick, but I was. I lit a small cigar and blew out smoke as Peter went on with his story.

'He used to come out and see me – if I was alone in the garden. Sometimes he'd bring me a glass of sherry or a packet of fags. We'd talk . . .'

'What did you talk about?' Uneasily I realized I had asked the stock prosecution question in all homosexual cases. Young men and old men, prosecutors always seemed to assume, with their resolutely filthy minds, have absolutely nothing to talk about except sex. Peter Vernon answered quite calmly, and his answer seemed convincing.

'Oh, we talked about all sorts of things. Music . . .'

'Peter's great on music.' Miss Sue Galton added her pennyworth eagerly.

'And opera,' Peter Vernon went on. 'He told me that opera was another world. I'd never seen one, but he told me I was like Siegfried, Wagner's Siegfried. Then one day he asked me if I'd like to come up to London, to go to Covent Garden with him. We had dinner at his Club.'

'Where?' Would Sir Michael have taken a young gardener he was having an affair with to his London Club? I supposed that might depend on the extent of the philosopher's sublime self-confidence.

'Somewhere in St James's. The food was terrible. You'd do better in a bistro in Oxford. Then we went off to Covent Garden.'

'And Wagner? Pretty hard going I imagine?'

What I know about Wagner's operas could be written on a postcard and still leave room for the stamp. Claude Erskine-Brown is the Wagnerian expert in our Chambers, and he tells me that Tristan and Isolde were in love with death, which seems to me, at my advanced age, a rum sort of thing to fancy. I mean, who wants to hop into bed with a terminal disease?

'I'd have liked to stop listening but I felt I had to. Out of politeness to Sir Michael at first. But then out of ... I don't know why. It upset me. The music upset me terribly.'

Miss Galton looked at her lover with enormous sympathy.

'Did you come back to Oxford that night?'

'Sir Michael drove me back, yes.'

'And then?' I asked, and our instructing solicitor looked at our client; I was reminded of an eager fiancée watching a Wimbledon champion, her breath held, her fingernails stuck into the palms of her hands. What would he do with the question, lob it out of court or smash it into the net? In fact, Peter Vernon made a neat return, and his fan club breathed again.

'I've got a room near the station,' he said. 'He dropped me off there and then ... I suppose he drove back to the College.'

'After that?' Miss Galton looked at me as though, Peter Vernon having won game and set, further play was surely no longer necessary.

'After that we went to dinner in London once or twice. Oh, and I had tea with him in his rooms a few times.'

My client was carefully squashing out his cigarette end in the top of an old tin provided.

'And that's all?'

'Yes, that's all.'

All, at any rate, that I was going to get for the moment. I pulled out my watch, looked at it with incredulous despair and said something about having to telephone my clerk immediately.

'You can do that from the office when we get back.' Miss Galton suggested.

'Henry'll be gone then, I'm afraid. You couldn't ask them if you can make a call at the gate, could you? Just ring my Chambers and say I will be back tonight. But not till much later. I'm having dinner with old friends in Oxford. But I'll be free for the breathalyser case at Chelmsford tomorrow. There's a good girl. Do you want 10p?'

She went reluctantly, almost as though she were leaving her lover alone with a rival.

When she had gone I spent a good deal of time looking at Peter Vernon in silence. Then I said, 'I can't get you off you know, unless you tell the truth.'

His looks betrayed nothing. He was still smiling charmingly, looking a little puzzled, but not in the least offended.

'Because if you don't tell the truth about you and Sir Michael, the jury will never believe you about the blackmail.'

We then went into another bout of silence. Although I had got rid of our solicitor, her presence, like her perfume, was still vaguely about us. I tried the approach direct.

'Look. What do you think? Would Miss Sue Galton rather marry a free man who's had a few strange experiences or wait for four years for a convicted blackmailer? Anyway, there's no defence unless you did it. You went to bed together and he gave you presents for it. Isn't that the story?'

Peter Vernon was no longer smiling. He took another cigarette and lit it carefully.

'How do you know?'

'Because that's always the story, in your sort of case.' There is no experience, I thought, like the experience of an Old Bailey hack.

'So you don't believe it?'

For the first time Peter Vernon looked put out. No one likes to be told that his defence is just Number Two, Standard Size.

'You tell me. And then I'll see if I believe it.'

So then, my client began to tell me the story.

'It happened that first night. After *Siegfried*. I suppose I did it out of politeness. You know. Like the way you're taught to say "thank you" after a children's party.'

'You didn't care for him?' For a moment I almost felt sorry for Sir Michael.

'I don't think it was him I liked, ever. It was his whole world. Oh, the way he talked, and the music he played me and even that freezing old Club with the Regency paintings and the rotten food. I was grateful to him for showing me all that. The rest didn't seem terribly important.'

'He gave you money?' I was anxious to return to the charge on the indictment.

'Yes. Cheques a few times. He must have been mad to do that, mustn't he?' Peter Vernon asked me.

'And you were mad to pay them into your bank account. Why did you keep the money? I mean if you were not a blackmailer?'

'I just kept it . . .' He smiled vaguely.

'And the cigarette case?'

'Yes. That was the last thing he gave me. I kept it all because . . . Well, you know Sue and I are going to get married. We've got a lot to save up for.'

It was, I suppose, an unusual way to furnish a bottom drawer. Oddly enough, he made it sound completely natural. At this point Miss Sue Galton returned to us and said that although she had telephoned my clerk, Henry, he seemed to know nothing about a breathalyser at Chelmsford the next day. I looked suitably puzzled and said I supposed my clerk was always the last to know.

I took my leave of the young engaged couple, having given Peter Vernon a piece of advice which would have been fatal to most of my clients. I counselled, if he wanted to have any prospect of an early marriage, to tell the truth. If there were any lies to be told, they were best left to the Professor of Moral Philosophy, who might even be better at it.

I had expected a quiet drink with Fosdyke and Simpson in one of their rooms, and felt distinctly embarrassed when, having given my name to the porter at St Joseph's (some spotty youth, clearly far too young for the job), I was sent over to the Senior Common Room where a whole flock of dons, looking, with tattered gowns drooping from their shoulders, like bedraggled birds were sniffing the sherry and pecking at the biscuits. I was well into the aperitifs before I realized that I was expected to dine at High Table, in embarrassing proximity to the principal witness for the prosecution in R. *v*. Vernon. It was really, I told Fozzy Fosdyke, not on.

'Of course it is,' Fosdyke filled my glass. 'The food's not bad at all. Ah. You'd like to meet Humphrey Grice, our Senior Law Tutor. This is my old friend, Horace Rumpole. It seems he's known as "Rumpole of the Old Bailey".'

The man to whom I was introduced was the most raven-like of all the dons. He had almost jet-black hair, hardly going grey, which also grew from his ears and on the back of his hands. He had strong yellow teeth.

' "Rumpole of the Old Bailey", eh? How very amusing,' said the law tutor Grice. 'What do you think of academic lawyers down at the Old Bailey?'

'Well to tell you the truth,' I had to admit, 'we hardly think of them at all.'

'But you'll have read my paper on "The Concept of Constructive Intent and Mens Rea in Murder and Manslaughter" in the *Harvard Law Review*?' Humphrey Grice looked puzzled and not a little hurt.

'Oh rather!' I lied to him. 'Your average East End jury finds it absolutely riveting.'

Further badinage along these lines was prevented by Simpson who came up with a distinguished-looking grey-haired man in a black velvet dinner jacket, to whom he introduced me.

'Rumpole, this is our Principal. Sir Michael Tuffnell. My friend, "Rumpole of the Old Bailey".'

'How are you, Rumpole? So glad you could join us.'

Sir Michael had the knack of making you feel that you were just the sort of valued companion he'd been hoping might drop in for dinner. Without switching off the charm for a second he turned to Humphrey Grice: 'Gulls' eggs, tonight, isn't it, Humphrey? We usually have gulls' eggs on the first Thursday in Lent, and we make ourselves stop at three . . .'

I couldn't let this extremely gracious old telly star feed me gulls' eggs on false pretences, so I muttered, 'Sir Michael, could I have a word?'

'Fasting is a state of mind. I do believe that,' the Principal said to the world at large, and then to me, 'Yes, what is it, Rumpole?'

'Fosdyke invited me to dinner, but I should tell you that I'm appearing for young Peter Vernon on the blackmail charge.' I let him into the secret. If the news caused Sir Michael the faintest distress, he didn't show it. In fact he didn't even bother to lower his voice as he said, 'Oh good. Do your best for him, won't you? I feel genuinely sorry for the lad.'

'But it's no doubt embarrassing for you, Sir Michael, having me here . . .' I felt rather awkward myself, carrying on a conversation in a whisper.

'Embarrassing? Why should it be? We shall be drinking some rather seductive Sancerre with the eggs.'

And as Sir Michael took my arm to lead me into dinner, he said: 'And of course, Rumpole, we won't talk "shop".'

So we went into hall, to High Table, where the oak and the old silver glowed in the candle light, and the Principal said grace standing in front of the paintings of former heads of St Joseph's, who had concealed in their gentler academic lives who knows what strange secrets without ever having to give evidence in a criminal Court.

For the first, and I hope the last, time I sat down to gulls' eggs and Sancerre, to be followed by saddle of lamb and Margaux, with a major prosecution witness a week or two before a criminal trial. But Sir Michael was consistently charming to everyone, although he did show, from time to time, an understandable impatience with the academic lawyer, Humphrey Grice. When we returned to the Senior Common Room (coffee, Romeo & Juliettas and vintage Cockburn) the talk was brought round by Grice to what I thought was an uncomfortable subject. He was talking to Fosdyke, but in a voice which carried across the room.

'Interesting piece on Sir Charles Dilke in the *Historical Review*, Fosdyke. Tell me, do you think Dilke might have made a great Liberal prime minister, if he hadn't been caught out by his sexual indiscretions?'

'Dilke was an extraordinary talent.' Fosdyke sniffed his port.

'You know Keir Hardie invited him to lead the Independent Labour Party?'

'Humphrey Grice probably finds that far more shocking than hopping into bed with a couple of ladies at once.' Sir Michael joined fearlessly in the discussion of an ancient scandal.

'If a man is a natural leader, I don't believe his private life makes the smallest difference,' Fosdyke insisted. 'So the answer to your question, Humphrey, is undoubtedly "Yes".'

This didn't seem to please Grice particularly, so he turned to me for support. 'If a man can't run his private life, it's quite obvious that he can't run his country. Wouldn't you agree, Rumpole?'

I looked at the Principal, took a gulp of strengthening port and tried to sound neutral.

'I suppose we've all got things we'd rather not have broadcast to the nation. It's probably just bad luck if you get found out.'

'Quite right. Dilke and Parnell had bad luck. Lloyd George had the luck of the devil.' Simpson's voice came with its muted scream, out of the depths of a chair in the corner of the room.

'It's not luck, in my opinion. It's the use of a little common sense.' Sir Michael was carefully cutting the end off a cigar.

'Yes, Principal. Let's hear your expert opinion.' Grice was stuffing a charred pipe with Old Holborn and giving a yellow smile. Sir Michael settled himself for an elegant oration.

'What is a scandal, if I may ask the rhetorical question? A scandal is a secret that gets found out. It's a subject for lies and cover-ups. If you don't lie, if you don't try and conceal, then there's no scandal. Take Watergate . . .'

'Oh really, Principal. Do we have to?' Simpson shrilled from his corner.

'A tragedy, in my opinion. Those two complacent little scribblers got rid of America's only competent President.' Grice's voice was like a rusty nail on a slate, but Sir Michael came melodiously in to agree with him entirely.

'Exactly! Who'd have given tuppence about Watergate if Nixon had told the truth about it? What was it, a trivial bit of housebreaking, almost a student prank? It became a scandal because of the lies. The moral is, if you want to kill a scandal, tell the truth.'

Sir Michael looked triumphantly round his colleagues. No one spoke, except of course Grice, who said:

'Is that what you intend to do, Principal?'

There was an awkward pause. The dons looked at Grice with varying degrees of antagonism, but Sir Michael said, unperturbed:

'Since you have the bad taste to ask the question, Humphrey, after dinner and in the presence of a guest, the answer is unquestionably "Yes".'

As he said this, the Principal gave me a glowing smile, and an invitation to put up for the night in a College guest room. I telephoned She Who Must Be Obeyed, who didn't seem unduly aggrieved, and walked with Fosdyke and Simpson across the moonlit quadrangle, past the fountain, towards the crumbling golden stone of Founder's Buildings.

'Sir Michael was very charming,' I said. 'I mean I must have been a bit of a spectre at the feast, in all the circumstances.'

'You know we all felt frightfully sorry for him,' Fosdyke told me. 'But he's been so bloody honest about the thing that I don't think it'll do him the slightest harm.'

I thought that on the whole, Sir Michael Tuffnell had handled the scandal which had broken over St Joseph's College with intelligence and skill.

'It'll be so much water off the back of a particularly fly old duck. Is that what you think, Fosdyke?' I asked.

'Much to the fury of Humphrey Grice,' Simpson squawked from the shadows.

'The academic lawyer?'

'He's been after the Principal's job for years.'

At the whiff of college politics, Simpson became audibly excited. 'Grice was the runner-up when Michael was elected. It was Grice who started the scandal really. Went round telling everyone about the Principal's jaunts to London with the gardening boy. All perfectly innocent, of course, but it laid poor Michael wide open to blackmail from two ruthless neurotics.'

'Two . . .?' I didn't follow.

'That's how I'd describe Humphrey Grice.' Simpson was positive. 'And your client too, I'm sorry to say, Rumpole.'

I ignored that. Peter Vernon had more on his plate than Simpson's ill will. Instead I asked, innocently enough, 'So you believe your Principal, when he says nothing happened?'

'The Professor of Moral Philosophy!' Fosdyke sounded shocked. 'Who wouldn't believe him?'

'Yes, I know, Fozzy,' I said, for P. J. Fosdyke had hit on the Achilles' heel of our defence. 'That's exactly what I'm afraid of.'

'And no one's going to believe Vernon, are they?' Monty Simpson turned the knife in the wound. 'No one can stand a blackmailer.'

The next morning I had a leisurely breakfast with Fosdyke and Simpson, and then wandered through the town to land up breathing in the dust and powdered leather of a secondhand bookshop in the Turl. There I propped myself up to read a tattered volume of memoirs by some long dead legal hack, re-calling life on the old south-eastern circuit (when, in his ex-perience, no case seemed to last more than a day, and most ended with the black cap at twilight). I was enjoying myself in a mild sort of way, postponing the evil hour of my return to my clerk, Henry, and She Who Must Be Obeyed when a voice like tearing metal pierced the calm of the bookshop.

'You do actually read books then? Your life isn't entirely practical?' Grice blew a sweet cloud of Old Holborn all over me. It was the academic lawyer, crept out of his lair on a shopping spree. He gave me a cunning and conspiratorial sort of smile as he said, 'I say, a bit of a cheek you turning up to dinner with the Principal. Fosdyke tells me you're defending young Vernon.'

'I'm afraid I got trapped. I apologized. It was most embarras-sing.'

'Not at all. Tuffnell needs reminding,' said Grice. 'The case isn't far off.' At which he grinned in a way I can only describe as ghoulish. He seemed to relish the idea of my playing Banquo's Ghost at Sir Michael's dinner table. 'I don't think he realizes just how serious it is.'

'For my client?'

'Oh no. For the Principal's career. There's no possible doubt, you know, that he's guilty.'

'My client?' I asked again innocently, knowing quite well what the answer would be.

'Oh no, Sir Michael Tuffnell, "Star of Television". The relationship was definitely physical.'

Fortunately, apart from an antique and no doubt deaf cleric reading an illustrated Boccaccio in a corner, the shop was empty. Otherwise, the Senior Law Tutor might have been involved in a quite non-academic action for slander.

'Oh yes.' He piled on the defamation like a starving man filling his plate at a cafeteria. 'Jemms, the porter, distinctly saw the boy Vernon coming out of the Principal's lodge at dawn.'

'Well,' I tried to put the opposing view, 'I came out of Founder's Buildings, which houses P. J. Fosdyke, at dawn, but I hope no one thinks that the relationship is definitely physical.'

'And I have had a long talk with the Principal's cleaning lady . . .' Grice was clearly prepared to call evidence.

'Have you indeed . . .?'

'I just thought,' he ended triumphantly, 'that *someone* should see the truth come out at the trial. What do you think, Rumpole?'

As he stood in front of me, he looked less like a raven and more like an old vulture getting a far-off whiff of recently killed zebra. I said, 'I think, if I may say so, Grice, that your interest in the law doesn't appear to be entirely academic.'

In the weeks that intervened before the trial, my wife Hilda again tried to raise the subject of the loose covers for the drawing-room chairs.

'Rumpole,' she said, 'I wonder you're not ashamed to be sitting on those tattered remnants.'

'I went to Oxford,' I said hastily, 'and I met my two dear old friends, Monty Simpson and Fozzy Fosdyke. We were inseparable you know. We used to set off with a bottle of beer and a slice of cold Christmas pudding, and tramp to Woodstock.'

'If the Featherstones ever came here, they'd think the place was a tip.'

' "Two scholars whom at College, erst he knew" ' –

I did my best to drown her in Matthew Arnold –

    ' "Met him, and of his way of life inquired . . ." '

'They'd think you were down on your luck, Rumpole,' she persisted, but I gave her more of the 'Scholar Gypsy'.

    ' "Whereat he answered that the Gypsy crew,
      His mates had arts to rule as they desired,
      The workings of men's brains . . ." '

'Couldn't you give me a cheque, Rumpole?'

'Not that my mates are a Gypsy crew, you couldn't call Guthrie Featherstone a Gypsy crew, and we can't rule the workings of men's brains, although I might put certain things to a jury, entirely for their consideration of course.'

Under the cover of this nonsense, I had made it to the door, and was almost clear of Froxbury Court when Hilda uttered her final threat.

'If I don't have a cheque for new loose covers, Rumpole, the consequences will be serious.'

'What will the consequences be?'

'I told you. Serious.'

You see my wife had absolutely no understanding of the art of blackmail. For Sir Michael Tuffnell, it was alleged, the consequences of his failure to pay up had been spelled out with the utmost clarity.

I sat in chambers toying with the brief R. *v.* Vernon, and thought about St Joseph's. By my third year I had forsaken the company of Fozzy and Shrimpson. I no longer walked to the Cumnor Hills or Bablock-hithe. I had become engaged to the eldest daughter of Septimus Porter, my tutor in Roman law.

Unhappily my engagement to poor Cissie Porter had to be broken off by reason of her early death. But had she lived, had we married, how would history have been altered? I couldn't believe that Miss Porter, so docile and eager to agree, would have ended up by blackmailing me over a matter of loose covers.

'You were at St Joseph's too weren't you, Rumpole?'

I looked up and saw that Guthrie Featherstone, Q.C., M.P.,

our learned Head of Chambers, had manifested himself beside
my desk.

'What do you mean, *too*?'

'Well, I was at St Joseph's, as you know, from 1952 to 1955.'

'After my time.'

'I know it was. The point is I was up the other night. Giving
a talk to the Law Society on my famous cases.'

'Must have been a pretty short talk.'

'Horace! Of course I don't get the sort of sensational stuff
you do. I don't hit the headlines, or the *News of the World*. I
don't think I'd care to either. What I meant to say is, I had
dinner with the Principal. What a perfectly charming fellow.'

'Oh charming. I agree.'

'The point is, of course he's being enormously brave about
it, but Michael is most frightfully embarrassed about this
case.'

'Not half as embarrassed as my client.'

'It really is an appalling thing to happen, to a man who has
the Order of Merit.'

'Well, if he didn't want it to happen, Sir Michael Tuffnell,
O.M., shouldn't have rushed round to the Old Bill to pour out
his soul.'

'What could he do? He was being blackmailed.'

'Isn't that for the jury to decide?'

'Horace.' Guthrie Featherstone essayed the boyish smile
which he puts on before he's going to attempt something unusually devious. 'How do you feel about defending blackmailers?'

'Much as I feel about defending anyone. Glad of the money.'

'But blackmail's such an extra loathsome crime.'

'Perhaps that's why Peter Vernon needs to be defended extra
carefully. You wouldn't like him convicted out of prejudice?'

'I really think,' Guthrie was choosing his words carefully,
as though he were a Judge at first instance and utterly scared of
the Court of Appeal, 'I really do think that Michael is just a
little *wee* bit upset at the fact that Vernon's being defended by
an old St Joseph's man.'

'I can't think why. Peter Vernon's a St Joseph's man too,
after all. He's a St Joseph's gardener.'

'Oh well, Horace, if that's the attitude.' And Guthrie Feather-stone started to beat a measured retreat.

'Don't come to dinner next week, Guthrie, will you?'

'Have you asked me?'

'No. So please don't come. If you do I'll simply have to spend a fortune on loose covers.' Guthrie then withdrew, feeling per-haps, that his mission on behalf of Sir Michael Tuffnell had not been a total success.

When our Head of Chambers had gone off to govern the country (or at least to sit in moody silence through an all-night sitting), I turned my attention back to the brief, and a thought, as yet no bigger than a very small man's hand, appeared on the horizon. I lifted the telephone and asked Harry to put me through to Miss Sue Galton of the Oxford solicitors. After we had exchanged pleasantries and I had inquired after her fiancé's health ('Bit worried now the trial's next week, actually.' *He* was worried – what on earth did she think I was?), I asked Miss Galton to remind me of the date when Sir Michael first went to the police and complained that he was being blackmailed.

'November the first last year.'

'And what are the dates on the cheques?' I heard the rustling as she consulted her file.

'August, September. One in October.'

'All before the Principal went to the police?'

'Before that, yes.'

'Listen. I want you to find out about the gold cigarette case. Get a photograph of it or something. Go round Oxford jewellers. Find out when Sir Michael bought it.'

'*When*?'

'Yes. The date's important. Find out *when*.'

'Do you think that's going to help us?' Miss Galton asked me.

'I really don't know. Something has to.'

I went back to Oxford the day before the trial for a final con-ference. Miss Sue Galton had, she told me, drawn a blank with the Oxford jewellers. I sent her up to London. I had an idea that Sir Michael might have bought the case when he stayed at his Club in St James, just across the road from Bond Street and the Burlington Arcade. It seemed a forlorn hope, and she hadn't returned the next morning when I sat gloomily in Court, listening to the opening of Her Majesty's case against Peter Vernon.

The Oxford Crown Court was full of students – perhaps they were all learning law and anxious to perfect their knowledge of 'demanding money with menaces'. Perhaps they merely wanted to see a distinguished academic in a spot of bother. The Red Judge in charge of the proceedings was Mr Justice Everglades, known to his few friends as 'Florrie', a highly educated old sweetheart with no affection for the criminal classes, who were mainly the sort of people he never bumped into at Glyndebourne. When Peter Vernon pleaded not guilty to the charge of blackmail, the Judge looked at him with a kind of bored disgust; he had not yet had occasion to acknowledge the presence of Rumpole. He listened to Bernard Crompton, Q.C., opening the case for the Crown, with obvious satisfaction.

'Members of the jury,' old Bernard started, after the usual formal introductions. 'We may be able to forgive some forms of criminal activity. The man who steals because his wife or his children are in need, the man who loses his self-control and commits an assault, may even deserve our sympathy. But blackmail, you may think is a truly unforgivable crime. Blackmail is a slow poison which feeds on its victims' fear and, of course, members of the jury, the higher position a man reaches in his public life, the further he has to fall, and the more he's got to lose. And no one, you may think, is in a more vulnerable position than the distinguished head of a great Oxford college, a man like Sir Michael Tuffnell, whom you probably all know well from your television screens.

'Sir Michael is, of course, Professor of Moral Philosophy and Principal of St Joseph's College in this ancient university.'

Bernard Crompton was my contemporary and a member of the old Oxford circuit. He was a dangerous prosecutor, covering his considerable intelligence with a bluff and common-sense manner, and being able to talk to the jury as though he were one of them, sitting not in counsel's benches, but beside them in their jury-box.

'But the mere fact that blackmail is a crime which we all hate and despise mustn't make you more ready to assume that this young man, Peter Vernon, is guilty. In all criminal trials, the prosecution bring the case and they have to prove it. If you're in any doubt about it, at the end of the day, say "not guilty".'

Bernard was the most dangerous sort of advocate because he was entirely fair. It was a deadly method of prosecuting and the way he got his convictions.

'And remember,' counsel for the Crown reached his peroration, 'these allegations of sexual misconduct are horribly easy to bring and terribly hard to refute. But if you are sure,' he fixed the jury with a frank and serious stare, 'when you've heard all our evidence, that young Vernon threatened to make these dreadful accusations and so extracted money from Sir Michael, and you will have evidence of the cheques actually paid into Vernon's bank account and the valuable gold cigarette case found in his possession, then your only verdict, according to your oath, must be one of guilty.'

The jury looked impressed and deeply conscious of their duty. They tried not to lick their lips as Bernard announced that he was about to call the evidence with the assistance of his learned junior. At which moment, there was a small stir in the bench behind me. Miss Sue Galton, had returned, not a moment too soon, from the jewellers' shops of London. I leant back and she whispered into my ear:

'I found the shop finally. In the Burlington Arcade. I'm going upstairs to get a witness summons.'

'Tell me the date he bought it, just the date.'

She told me while Sir Michael Tuffnell, having stepped modestly into the witness-box, held up the New Testament, and swore by Almighty God that the evidence he was about to give would be the truth, the whole truth and nothing but the truth. Florrie Everglades glared at us for whispering at this solemn moment, and then turned his attention to the distinguished witness. Having seen so many leather-jacketed tearaways, and polo-necked villains in witness-boxes, Florrie was clearly delighted with the appearance of a grey-haired and good-looking holder of the Order of Merit, wearing a double-breasted blue suit and a spotted bow tie, who could speak the Queen's English and didn't think *Rigoletto* was something you eat with tomato sauce. Although a Cambridge man, Mr Justice Everglades clearly had every sympathy with the embarrassing position in which the Principal of St Joseph's found himself. He gave the witness a welcoming smile and said, 'Sir Michael, you understand that in blackmail cases, the victim can remain anonymous, and merely be referred to as Mr X. I will direct the reporters in Court to refer to you in that way.'

'My Lord, I am extremely grateful.' Sir Michael gave the Judge a small but gracious bow. I was sure Everglades, J., was delighted and I saw no chance of poor old Peter Vernon being referred to as 'Mr X'. Bernard Crompton interrupted my reverie by launching into his examination in chief.

'Sir Michael, you are the Principal of St Joseph's College?'

'I am.'

'You are the Oxford Professor of Moral Philosophy, a Fellow of the Royal Society and hold the Order of Merit.'

'Yes, I do.' The admission couldn't have been made more modestly. Bernard went on to trickier matters.

'Sir Michael, when did you get to know the defendant, Vernon?'

'About eighteen months ago, my Lord.' Sir Michael Tuffnell turned respectfully to the Judge as a good witness should. 'When he came to us as an under-gardener and general handyman.'

'Did you have any relationship with him, other than as a college servant?'

There was a slight pause. The witness was clearly choosing his words, but he made an excellent choice. 'I think he became a friend. I hope all the college servants are my friends.'

'Did you offer him any particular form of friendship?'

'My Lord. May I explain?'

Florrie Everglades seemed almost flattered to be spoken to by the witness. The old sweetheart answered with more than usual unction.

'Please, Sir Michael. And do take your time. Would you care to sit down?'

I was only surprised he didn't offer him a glass of port and a nibble of biscuit.

'I got talking to Peter Vernon . . .' There was another slight hesitation, and Bernard helped out.

'In the garden was that?'

'In the garden, yes,' the witness agreed. 'I found that he was a very intelligent young man, with genuine, if unformed, musical tastes. He had done well at school, but his parents had opposed him going on to higher education. And he'd been unable to find a job which suited his very real talents. I thought that he might be feeling jealous of the young men of his age who were enjoying academic life at St Joseph's.'

'So?' Bernard nudged the evidence in gently.

'So I felt I should invite him to take some part, at least, in the intellectual life of our community.'

I looked at him; what a dear old philanthropist the great man was!

'I invited him to my rooms. We talked.'

'About?' Bernard was astute enough to ask my best question, and so anticipate my cross-examination.

'About music. And philosophy. I tried to have the sort of discussion with him I would normally have with an under-graduate.'

The Judge was nodding with approval and writing it all down. Dear old Bernard took another brave step forward.

'Did he ever stay the night in your lodge?'

I looked up, wondering if Sir Michael would be fool enough to deny it. Of course he wasn't.

'Once or twice. When we were talking late. I put him up in my spare bedroom.'

'And did you go to London together?'

'Again, I think it was once or twice. I took him to Covent Garden and dinner at my Club.'

'Did your friendship continue happily?'

Sir Michael, with a look of genuine distress at the Judge, said with deep regret, 'I'm afraid it didn't.'

'What happened?' Bernard nudged again.

'One day, Peter Vernon came to me in the garden and said that if I didn't give him money he would write round to all my colleagues at St Joseph's and tell them we had been sleeping together.'

'And had you?'

Sir Michael looked at the jury then, and became the perfect English gent making the perfectly frank denial.

'Certainly not.'

'How did you react?'

'I'm afraid foolishly. I knew I was innocent of what he was suggesting, my Lord, but I was afraid of the scandal.'

'Naturally.' Florrie looked at the jury and explained the obvious to them – 'A man in your very vulnerable position.' I should have chucked a glass of water at the old darling then, but I refrained.

'And I was afraid that one of my colleagues, at least, might say, "There's no smoke without a fire." ' Sir Michael's explanation sounded perfectly reasonable, and I knew who he was talking about – Grice, the academic lawyer.

'So you gave him the cheques which we have seen?' Bernard was relaxed; his examination was a coast downhill all the way from then on.

'Yes. And sometimes cash.'

'Amounting to some six hundred pounds. And the gold cigarette case which was, how much?'

'I think that was five hundred, my Lord.'

'About five hundred . . .' Florrie was writing it all down.

'And then?' Bernard moved him on gently.

'Then I began to think about it and realized that if I went on paying Vernon, he would blackmail me for ever. I decided that I must face up to the possibility of scandal and go to the police.'

'I'm sure we all realize that required considerable courage, Sir Michael,' said the Judge, and I wondered if he was going to give him his V.C. then or after the trial.

'Yes. Thank you, Sir Michael. Just wait there, will you? In case my learned friend has any questions.'

Bernard Crompton subsided with an air of great satisfaction, and the Judge looked with distaste at counsel for the defence. He sighed and said: 'Have you any questions, Mr Rumpole?'

'A few, my Lord.' I was hoisting myself on to my hind legs, preparatory to going into my act. 'Just a few.'

The Judge looked at the distinguished witness in an apologetic sort of way, and the jury viewed me with the vague interest they always accord to a new character in the drama, as Sir Michael prepared himself with a smile of almost amused cooperation.

'In your book, *Morality and Modern Man*, you said something to this effect. "Modern man will do good, and tell the truth for its own sake, not out of fear or respect for a possibly non-existent deity." '

I had done my homework, but I didn't feel that the jury were immediately grabbed by the question.

'I did, yes.'

'And yet you began your evidence by swearing on the Bible?'

'Yes.'

'Why did you do that? Why didn't you affirm, if you don't believe in God?'

Sir Michael dealt with my ignorance with patience, as though I were a serious but not over-bright pupil at a seminar.

'I said God was possibly non-existent. That means I have to recognize that He possibly exists.'

'And on that outside chance, you took the oath as you did?' I was merely asking for information, but the Judge didn't like it.

'Mr Rumpole,' he asked in a markedly unfriendly manner. 'Are you criticizing Sir Michael for taking the oath in the usual fashion?'

'Oh no, my Lord.' This time *I* was giving the seminar. 'I am criticizing Sir Michael for trying to present himself to this jury as something other than he is.'

I turned to the witness and asked a brutally non-academic question. 'You're lying about yourself, aren't you?'

'Perhaps you could make clear what you mean, Mr Rumpole.'

'The truth is that you and this young man were lovers.'

'No. I have already told you . . .' I knew quite well what he had already told us. I battled on.

'And as a lover, you gave him presents from time to time.'

'Is *that* what they were . . .?' Sir Michael smiled, and the Judge pursed his lips as though he expected nothing better from the defence.

'Certainly that's what they were,' I suggested strongly. 'The sort of expensive presents another man might give his mistress.'

'I have no idea what a man might give his mistress.' Sir Michael smiled at the jury, but I noticed they didn't smile back.

'I expect you haven't! You never married, Sir Michael?'

'No. I have been denied that happiness.' I supposed some of us might say he'd been exceptionally lucky, but I let that pass.

'So you have no one else to give presents to?'

'It's true that I have no immediate family . . .'

'No one but young Peter Vernon?'

'I've already told the Court why I gave him that money.'

My Lord, the learned Judge, who had been listening to the exchange with growing impatience, nodded his agreement.

'Because you were afraid of being accused of something you hadn't done?' I asked with an almost genuine bewilderment.

'Exactly.'

'And you knew that Mr Humphrey Grice, your Senior Tutor in Academic Law, would use any scandal to have you dismissed as Principal, because he coveted your place?'

I followed Sir Michael's eye up to the public gallery, where the law don was leaning eagerly over the rail, waiting for the kill.

'That was something I did have in mind, yes,' the Principal admitted.

'And you were particularly fearful, because you knew the charge was true?'

'Mr Rumpole, this witness has already denied that unpleasant suggestion!' Florrie intervened, and I toyed with the notion of asking the old darling if he'd care to go in to the witness-box and give evidence himself. I rejected the idea and persisted with the material available.

'Sir Michael. We've heard my learned friend, in his opening speech, tell us the date when you went to the police to make this charge of alleged blackmail. It was November the first, was it not? Of last year.'

'I believe so. Yes.' For the first time Sir Michael Tuffnell sounded doubtful.

'You can take the date from me. The police did nothing for well over a month . . .'

'They were making inquiries, my Lord,' Bernard Crompton rose to his hind legs to protect the honour of the force. 'At Vernon's bank, for instance.'

'Yes, of course, Mr Crompton. I'm sure most of us in Court understand that perfectly well.' The Judge looked coldly at Rumpole, who didn't understand. I asked my next question undeterred.

'And it was during that month, but after the first of November, while the police were making their inquiries, that you gave young Peter Vernon this gold cigarette case? Might I just have it, usher. Exhibit twelve.'

The usher obliged, and I stood in Court holding the heavy gold object, weighing it in my hand. The jury paid me the compliment of looking intensely interested. Florrie gave a slight frown and Bernard Crompton lay back in his seat and studied the ceiling. Sir Michael Tuffnell looked as though he'd just stumbled on something which upset his whole theory of the Universe – proof of the existence of God for instance.

'No, I'm sure,' he said, 'I'm sure that can't be right.'

'It can't be right if you're telling the truth, can it? You wouldn't decide to put an end to the blackmailing by complaining to the police, and *then* spend five hundred pounds on a gold cigarette case for Peter Vernon?'

'No. Certainly not!'

Oh, Tuffnell, my dear old sweetheart, I breathed a sigh of relief, you have delivered yourself into my hands.

'But you see, that's exactly what you did, Sir Michael. I will be calling evidence to prove that you bought this case on the fifth of December last year at a jeweller's in Burlington Arcade, near your Club, and gave it to Peter Vernon as a Christmas present!'

'What date was that, Mr Rumpole?'

For the first time in the course of my cross-examination, the learned Judge was preparing to make a note.

'The fifth of *December*, my Lord.'

'Why should I do that, Mr Rumpole?' The witness was asking me the question.

'I'll tell you, Sir Michael. Because you wanted to frame Peter Vernon on a blackmail charge . . .'

'*Frame* him!'

Mr Justice Everglades was showing signs of genuine distress, but I addressed myself entirely to the witness. 'Oh, yes. You wanted to make sure that Peter Vernon wasn't going to be believed if he ever told the truth. You knew that Grice was on to your trail like an old bloodhound, and you also knew Peter was planning to get married to a young lady solicitor. You didn't know him very well, did you? You thought he'd start talking –

about your nights together. And if he was going to talk, you wanted him to talk from the dock, where no one would believe him.'

'But I'd already given him the cheques.' Sir Michael was now driven to try and argue the prosecution case.

'Presents. Presents that could be used to get Peter Vernon arrested and have him convicted as a criminal whom no one could believe. You might have got away with it, Sir Michael, if you hadn't wanted to add one final bit of evidence. The gold cigarette case that you bought him in London *after you'd gone to the police*!'

From then on, in spite of a bumpy ride from the Judge, it was really downhill all the way for Rumpole. We called the jeweller from the Burlington Arcade, who had his books in good order, and there could be no doubt about the date when Sir Michael bought the case that was designed to frame a blackmailer. Peter Vernon went into the witness-box, was greeted with a blast of hostility from the Judge, and left it with the jury looking as if they might all chip in for a set of Tupperware to give the happy couple. When it came to my turn to address the Court I was able to do a bit of a Bernard Crompton for the defence.

'Members of the jury. We may be able to forgive some forms of criminal activity, the man who steals because his wife or his children are in need, the man who loses his self-control and commits an assault. But blackmail, and here I agree with every word that my learned friend, Mr Bernard Crompton, said to you on behalf of the Crown, is really the meanest form of crime! Blackmail, when it means planting false evidence on an innocent young man so that you can have him convicted of an offence he had never committed, so that you can gain the advantage of being safe from scandal, must be the meanest crime of all. Who was the blackmailer in this case, members of the jury? Was it the young man in the dock, or the older man in the witness-box? Who is lying about whom? Ask yourselves that question. And remember that the answer is a gold cigarette case, bought to bolster up a false charge, and bought *after* Sir Michael had complained to the police.'

*

When the case was over, Peter Vernon came out blinking into the sunlight, surprised to be free, and Miss Sue Galton was surprised only that he had never told her everything. They went away, I suppose to flog the cigarette case and buy wallpaper, saucepan scourers, lino tiles, acres of Vim and other domestic articles.

After I had said goodbye to the young couple, I saw Sir Michael getting into a taxi. He smiled his own goodbye at me, I thought very charmingly. He resigned a little while later as Principal of St Joseph's College, a job Humphrey Grice, so Fozzy said in his letter to me, doesn't do as well, and the food at High Table has deteriorated. Sir Michael has just presented a hugely successful telly series on 'Man – the Moral Animal'.

As for me, I caught the train to London immediately after the trial, and like Matthew Arnold's old gypsy

. . . came, as most men deem'd, to little good

But came to Oxford and his friends, no more.

Seated at breakfast in the mansion flat some weeks later I opened an envelope which was lying beside my plate, and regretted having done so when a document fluttered out, marked with a huge sum of money.

'Hilda,' I put the question fearlessly to She Who Must Be Obeyed, 'what on earth's this?'

'It's an estimate, Rumpole. For redecorating the flat.'

'Why should we want the flat redecorated?' I didn't follow.

'To brighten it up, Rumpole.' Hilda then paused dramatically, and said, 'Of course, if you'd agreed to buy new chair covers, that wouldn't be necessary.'

Now that was a decent bit of blackmail, clear and open, and, of course, quite effective. I had absolutely no alternative but to say, 'All right then, Hilda. Chair covers it is.'

Rumpole and the Dear Departed

> Let's talk of graves, of worms, and epitaphs;
> Make dust our paper, and with rainy eyes
> Write sorrow on the bosom of the earth.
> Let's choose executors and talk of wills;
> And yet not so – for what can we bequeath
> Save our deposed bodies to the ground.

The only reason why I, Horace Rumpole, Rumpole of the Old Bailey, dedicated, from my days as a white-wig and my call to the bar, almost exclusively to a life of crime should talk of wills, was because of a nasty recession in felonies and misdemeanours. Criminals are, by and large, of an extraordinary Conservative disposition. They believe passionately in free enterprise and strict monetarist policies. They are against state interference of any kind. And yet they, like the owners of small businesses, seem to have felt the cold winds of the present recession. There just isn't the crime about that there used to be. So when Henry came into my room staggering under the weight of a heavy bundle of papers and said, 'Got something a bit more up-market than your usual, Mr Rumpole; Mowbray and Pontefract want to instruct you in a will case, sir,' I gave him a tentative welcome. Even our learned Head of Chambers, Guthrie Featherstone, Q.C., M.P., could scarce forbear to cheer. 'Hear you've got your foot in the door of the Chancery Division, Horace. That's the place to be, my dear old chap. That's where the money is. Besides it's so much better for the reputation of Chambers for you not to have dangerous criminals hanging about in the waiting-room.'

I said something about dangerous criminals at least being alive. The law of probate, so it seemed to me, is exclusively concerned with the dead.

' "Let's choose executors and talk of wills; and yet not so" –

for, besides having nothing to bequeath, Rumpole knows almost nothing about the law of probate.'

That is what I told Miss Beasley, the Matron of the Sunny-side Nursing Home on the peaceful Sussex coast, when she came to consult me about the testamentary affairs of the late Colonel Ollard. It was nothing less than the truth. I know very little indeed on the subject of wills.

Miss Beasley was a formidable-looking customer: a real heavyweight with iron-grey hair, a powerful chin and a nose similar in shape to that sported by the late Duke of Wellington. She was in mufti when she came to see me (brogues and a tweed suit), but I imagine that in full regimentals, with starched cap and collar, the lace bonnet and medals pinned on the mountainous chest, she must have been enough to put the wind up the bravest invalid.

She gave me the sort of slight tightening of the lips which must have passed, in the wards she presided over, as a smile. 'Never you mind, Mr Rumpole,' she said, 'the late Colonel wanted you to act in this case particularly. He has mentioned your name on several occasions.'

'Oh, really? But Miss Beasley, dear lady, the late Colonel Bollard . . .'

'Colonel Ollard, Mr Rumpole, Colonel Roderick Ollard, M.C., D.S.O., C.B.E., late of the Pines, Balaclava Road, Cheeveling-on-Sea, and the Sunnyside Nursing Home,' she corrected me firmly. 'The dear departed has come through with your name, perfectly clearly more than once.'

'Come through with it, Miss Beasley?' I must say the phrase struck me as a little odd at the time.

'That is what I said, Mr Rumpole.' Miss Beasley pursed her lips.

'We should be alleging fraud against the other side, Mr Rumpole.'

The person who had spoken was Mr Pontefract, of the highly respected firm of Mowbray and Pontefract, an elderly type of solicitor with a dusty black jacket, a high stiff collar and the reverent and deeply sympathetic tone of voice of a reputable undertaker. He was someone, I felt sure, who knew all about wills, not to mention graves and worms and epitaphs. And the word he had used had acted like a trumpet call to battle. I felt myself brighten considerably. I beamed on La Beasley and said with confidence,

'Fraud! Now, there is a subject I do know something about. And whom are we alleging fraud against?'

'Mr Percival Ollard, Mrs Percival Ollard . . .' Mr Pontefract supplied the information.

'That Marcia. She didn't give a toss for the Colonel!' Miss Beasley interrupted with a thrust of the chest and a swift intake of breath. 'And young Peter Ollard, their son, aged thirteen years, represented by his parents as guardians, *ad litem*.' Mr Pontefract completed the catalogue of shame.

'The Colonel thought Peter was a complete sissy, Mr Rumpole!' Miss Beasley hastened to give me the low-down on this shower. 'The boy didn't give a toss for military history, he was more interested in ballet dancing.'

'Young Peter, it appears, had ambitions to enter the West Sussex School of Dance.' Mr Pontefract made this announcement with deep regret.

'You should have heard Colonel Ollard on the subject!' Miss Beasley gave me another tight little smile.

'I can well imagine,' I said. 'Mr Pontefract . . . just remind me of the history of Colonel Ollard's testamentary affairs.'

I needed to be reminded because Pontefract's instructions, as set out in his voluminous brief, were on the dryish side. As a lawyer, Pontefract was no doubt admirable, as an author he lacked the knack, which many criminal solicitors possess, of grabbing the attention. In fact I had slumbered over his papers and a bottle of Pommeroy's plonk in front of the electric fire in Froxbury Court.

'Colonel and Percival Ollard were the only two sons of the late Reverend Hector Ollard, Rector of Cheeveling-on-Sea,' Pontefract started to recap. 'They inherited well and by wise investments both became wealthy men. Percival Ollard started a firm known as Ollard's Kitchen Utensils which prospered exceedingly. During the last six years the brothers never met; and Colonel Roderick Ollard, who was an invalid . . .'

'It was his heart let him down, Mr Rumpole. His poor old ticker.' Miss Beasley supplied the medical evidence.

'Colonel Ollard was nursed devotedly by Miss Beasley at her nursing home, Sunnyside,' Pontefract assured me, and was once again interrupted by Matron.

'He was a real old sport, was the Colonel! Often had my incurable ladies in a roar! Quite a schoolboy at heart, Mr Rumpole. And I'll take my dying oath on this, the Percival Ollards never visited him, not after the first fortnight. They never even wrote to him. Not so much as a little card for a Christmas or birthday.'

I was about to 'tut-tut' sympathetically, as I felt was expected, when Pontefract took up the narrative. 'When the Colonel died all we could find was a will he made in 1970, under which his estate would be inherited by his brother Percival, his sister-in-law Marcia, and his nephew, Peter . . .'

'The ballet dancer!' I remembered.

'Exactly! In equal shares, after a small legacy to an old batman.'

'Of course their will's a forgery.' Miss Beasley clearly had no doubt about it.

'I thought you said it was a fraud.' The allegations seemed to be coming thick and fast.

'A fraud *and* a forgery!'

It was all good, familiar stuff. In some relief I stood up, found and lit a small cigar.

'Concocted by the Percival Ollards,' I said gleefully. 'Yes, I see it all. You know, even though it's only a probate action, I do detect a comforting smell of crime about this case. Tell me, Miss Beasley. Where do you think the Colonel should have left, how much was it, did you say, Mr Pontefract?'

'With the value of The Pines, when we sell it. I would say, something over half a million pounds, Mr Rumpole.'

Half a million nicker! It was a crock of gold that might command a fee which would even tempt Rumpole into the dreaded precincts of the Chancery Division. I sat down and asked Matron the sixty-four-thousand-dollar question.

'Well, of course, he should have left his money to the person who looked after him in his declining years,' Miss Beasley said it in all modesty.

'To your good self?' I was beginning to get the drift of this consultation.

'Exactly!' Miss Beasley had no doubt about it. But Pontefract came in sadly, with a little legal difficulty.

'What I have told Miss Beasley is,' he said, 'that she has no *locus standi*.' I had no doubt he was right but I hoped that the learned Pontefract was about to make his meaning clear to a humble hack. Happily he did so. 'Miss Beasley is in no way related to the late Colonel.'

'In absolutely no way!' Matron was clearly not keen to be associated with the Percival Ollards.

'And she doesn't seem to have been named in any other will.'

'We haven't found any other will. Yet.' Matron looked more than ever like the Duke of Wellington about to meet her Waterloo.

'So she can't contest the February 1970 will in favour of Peter Ollard. If it fails, she stands to gain ... nothing.' Mr Pontefract broke the news gently but clearly to the assembled company.

Little as I know of the law of wills, some vague subconscious stirring, some remote memory of a glance at *Chancery in a Nutshell* before diving into the Bar Finals, made me feel that the sepulchral Pontefract had a point. I summed up the situation judicially by saying,

'Of course in law, Miss Beasley, your very experienced solicitor is perfectly right. I agree with what he has said and I have nothing to add.'

'There is another law, Mr Rumpole.' Miss Beasley spoke quietly, but very firmly. 'The higher law of God's justice.'

'I'm afraid you won't find they'll pay much attention to that in the Chancery Division.' I hated to disillusion her.

'Miss Beasley insisted we saw you, Mr Rumpole. But you have only confirmed my own views. Legally, we haven't got a leg to stand on.' Mr Pontefract was gathering up his papers, ready for the 'off'.

'Well, we'll jolly well have to find one, won't we?' Matron sounded unexpectedly cheerful, 'Mr Rumpole. I won't keep you any longer. I'll be in touch as soon as we find that leg you're looking for.'

And now Miss Beasley stood up in a business-like way. I felt as though I'd been ordered a couple of tranquillizers and a blanket bath and not to fuss because she'd be round with Doctor in the morning. Before she went, however, I had one question to ask:

'Just one thing, Miss Beasley. You say the late Colonel recommended me, as a sound legal adviser?'

'He did indeed! He was mentioning your name only last week,' Miss Beasley answered cheerfully.

'Last week? But, Miss Beasley, I understand that Colonel Ollard departed this life almost six months ago.'

'Oh yes, Mr Rumpole.' She explained, as though to a child, 'that's when he died. Not when he was speaking to me.'

At which point I sneezed, and Matron said, 'You want to watch that cold, Mr Rumpole. It could turn into something nasty.'

Miss Beasley, of course, was right. The reason I hadn't been able to concentrate with my usual merciless clarity on the law governing testamentary matters was that I had the dry throat and misty eyes of an old legal hack with a nasty cold coming on. A rare burst of duty took me down to the Old Bailey for a small matter of warehouse breaking, and four nights later saw me drinking, for medicinal reasons, a large brandy, sucking a clinical thermometer and shivering in front of my electric fire at Froxbury Court, dressed in pyjamas and a dressing-gown. She Who Must Be Obeyed looked at me without any particular sympathy. There has never been much of the Florence Nightingale about my wife Hilda.

'Rumpole! That's the third time you've taken your temperature this evening. What is it?'

'It's sunk down to normal, Hilda. I must be fading away.'

'Really! It's only a touch of flu. Doctor MacClintock says there's a lot of it about.'

'It's a touch of death, if you want my opinion. There's a lot of that about too.'

'Well, I hope you'll stay in the warm tomorrow.'

'I can't do that! Got to get down to the Bailey. The jury are coming back in my murder in the morning.' I sneezed and continued bravely, 'I'd better be in at the death.'

'That's what you will be in at. If you *must* go traipsing down to the Old Bailey, don't expect me to feel sorry for you.'

I was about to say, of course I never expected Hilda to feel sorry for me, when the telephone rang. She rushed to answer it (unlike me, she takes an unnatural delight in answering telephones), and announced that a Miss Rosemary Beasley was on the line and wished to communicate with her counsel as a matter of urgency. Cursing the fact that Miss Beasley, unlike my other clients, wasn't tucked up in the remand wing of the nick, safe from the telephone, I took the instrument and breathed into it a rheumy, 'Good evening.'

Matron came back, loud and clear, 'Mr Rumpole. I am sitting here at my planchette.'

'At your *what*?' Miss Beasley had me mystified.

'Sometimes I use the board, or the wine glass or the cards. Sometimes I have Direct Communication.'

'That must be nice for you. Miss Beasley, what *are* you talking about?'

'Tonight I am at the planchette. I have just had such a nice chat with Colonel Ollard.'

'With the *late* Colonel Ollard?'

I was, I had to confess, somewhat taken aback. When Matron answered, she sounded a little touchy. 'He wasn't late at all. He came through bang on time! It was just nine o'clock when we started chatting. He says the weather over there's absolutely beautiful! It's just not fair, I told him, when we're going through this dreary cold spell.'

'Miss Beasley.' I asked for clarification. 'Did Colonel Ollard come over from the dead, simply to chatter to you about the weather?'

'Oh no, Mr Rumpole. I shouldn't be telephoning you if that were all. He said something *far* more important.'

'Oh did he? And can you let me into the secret?' My temperature was clearly rising during this conversation. I longed for bed with both my feet on a hot water bottle.

'The Colonel said that Mr Pontefract had never looked in the tin box where he kept his dress uniform, in the loft at The Pines.'

'Well. Suppose Mr Pontefract never has . . .'

'If he looked there, the Colonel told me, Mr Pontefract would find, wrapped in tissue paper, between the sword and the . . . trousers, a later will, signed by himself in the proper manner.'

I could see the way things were drifting and quite honestly I didn't like it at all. The day might not be far distant when Miss Beasley might in fact find herself tucked safely up in the nick.

'Is that what the Colonel said?' I asked, warily.

'His very words.'

'You're quite *sure* that's what he said . . .'

'How could I possibly be mistaken?'

'Well, I suppose you'd better ring Pontefract and get him to take a look. I just hope . . .'

'You hope *what*, Mr Rumpole?'

'I hope you're not considering anything *dangerous*, Miss Beasley.'

After all, what could all this planchette nonsense be but a rather obvious prelude to forgery?

'Of course not! I'm perfectly safe, Mr Rumpole. I've just been sitting here chatting.' Matron sounded her usual brisk self. I tried to remember if there'd ever been a woman forger, with a nursing qualification.

'Yes. Well, if you ring Mr Pontefract,' I suggested, but apparently all that had been taken care of.

'I've done that, Mr Rumpole. I just thought I'd ring you too, to tell you the joyful tidings. Oh, and Mr Rumpole. The Colonel sent you his best wishes, and he hopes he's been a help to you, giving you a leg to stand on. Cheerio for now! Oh, and he hopes your cold's better.'

As I put down the receiver, I felt, as I have said, a good deal worse.

'Who on earth's Miss Rosemary Beasley?' Hilda asked when I had finished sneezing.

'Oh her. She's just someone who seems to be on particularly good terms with the dead.'

The next day, still feeling in much the same condition as the late Colonel Ollard, but without the blue skies to cheer me up, I staggered off to the Old Bailey and heard my warehouse breaker get three years. When the formalities and the official good-byes were over I walked back to Chambers and there, awaiting me in my room, was the lugubrious Pontefract. He came straight out with the news.

'It was just as she told us, Mr Rumpole. There was a tin box under a pile of old blankets in the loft at The Pines, which we had overlooked. In it was the full dress uniform of a colonel of the Royal Dorsets.'

'And between the sword and trousers?'

'I found a will, apparently dated the first of March 1974. Over four years after the other will in favour of the Percival Ollards. It revokes all previous wills and leaves his entire estate to . . .'

'Miss Rosemary Beasley?' I hazarded a guess.

'You've hit it, Mr Rumpole!'

'It didn't need great powers of divination.'

I couldn't help looking round nervously to see that we weren't in the presence of the mysterious matron.

'Mr Pontefract, as our client isn't with us today . . .'

'I'm quite thankful for it, Mr Rumpole.'

'You are? So am I. You know that the late Colonel apparently spoke from the other side of the grave, to tip our client off about this will?'

'So I understand, Mr Rumpole.'

'Mr Pontefract. I know you are accustomed to polite civil law and my mind turns as naturally to crime as a vicar's daughter does to sex, but . . .'

I didn't know how to make the suggestion which might wound the old gentleman; but he was out with the word before me.

'You suspect *this* will may be a forgery?'

'That thought had crossed your mind?'

'Of course, Mr Rumpole. There is no field of endeavour in which human nature sinks to a lower depth than in the matter of wills. Your average Old Bailey case, Mr Rumpole, must seem like a day out with the Church Brigade compared to the skul-duggery which surrounds the simplest last will and testament.'

As he spoke I began to warm to this man, Pontefract. He was expressing my own opinions fairly eloquently, and I listened with an increased respect as he went on.

'Naturally my first thought was that our client, Miss Beasley, had invented this supernatural conversation in order to direct our attention to a will which she had, shall we say, manufactured?'

'A neutral term, Mr Pontefract.' But well put, I thought. 'That was my first thought, also.'

'So I took the precaution of having this new-found will examined by a well-known handwriting expert.'

'Alfred Geary?'

There is only one handwriting expert Her Majesty's judges pay any attention to. Geary is now an old man peering at blown-up letters through thick pebble glasses, but he is still an irrefutable witness.

'I went, in this instance, and regardless of expense, to Mr Geary. You approve, sir?'

'You couldn't do better. The Courts listen in awe to this fellow's comparison between the Ms and the tails on the Ps. What did Geary find?'

'That the signature on the will we discovered . . .'

'Between the dress sword and the trousers?'

'Is undoubtedly the genuine signature of the late Colonel.

It was the one piece of evidence I hadn't expected. If the will was not a forgery, if it were a genuine document, could it possibly follow that the message which led us to its hiding-place was also genuine? The mind, as they say, boggled. I was scarcely listening as Mr Pontefract told me that the Percival Ollards would be attacking our new will on the grounds of the deceased's insanity. It was my own sanity I began to fear for, as I wondered if the deceased Colonel would be giving us any more instructions from beyond the grave.

When I got home I was feeling distinctly worse. I mentioned the matter to She Who Must Be Obeyed and she swiftly called my bluff by summoning in the local quack who was round, as he always is, like a shot, in the hope of a fee and a swig of my diminishing stock of sherry (a form of rot-gut I seem to keep entirely for the benefit of the medical profession).

'He's not looking in a particularly lively condition is he?' Doctor MacClintock remarked to Hilda on arrival. 'Well, we've got to remember, Rumpole's no chicken.'

I was unable to argue with the doctor's diagnosis, as it was undoubtedly true, and what's more, I had a clinical thermometer stuck between my jaws. I could only grunt a protest when Hilda, with quite unnecessary hospitality, said, 'You will take a glass of sherry, won't you, Doctor? So good of you to come.'

I mean to say, when I do my job of work, the Judge doesn't start proceedings with, 'So nice of you to drop in Rumpole, do help yourself to my personal store of St Émilion.' I was going to say something along these lines when the gloomy Scots medico removed the thermometer, but he interrupted me with, 'His temperature's up. I'm afraid it's a day or two in bed for the old warrior.'

'A day or two in bed? You'll have to tell him, Doctor, he's got to be sensible.'

'Oh I doubt very much if he'll feel like being anything else.'

I began to wish they'd stop talking as if I'd already passed on, and so I intruded into the conversation.

'Bed? I can't possibly stay in bed . . .'

'You're no chicken, Rumpole. Doctor MacClintock warned you.'

I noticed that the thirsty quack had downed one glass of Pommeroy's pale Spanish-style and was getting a generous refill from the family.

'You warned me? What did you warn me about?'

'You're not getting any younger, Rumpole.'

'Well, it hardly needs five years' ruthless training in the Edinburgh medical school and thirty years in general practice to diagnose that!'

'He's becoming crotchety.' Hilda said, with satisfaction. 'He's always crotchety when he's feeling ill.'

'Yes, but what are you warning me about? Pneumonia, botulism, Parkinson's disease?'

'There is an even more serious condition, Rumpole,' the doctor said. 'I mean there's no reason why you shouldn't go on for a good few years, provided you take proper precautions.'

'You're trying to warn me about death!'

'Well, death is rather a strong way of putting it.'

The representative of the medical profession looked distressed, as though he realized that if Rumpole dropped off the twig there might be no more free sherry.

'Odd thing about the dead, Doctor.' I decided to let him into a secret. 'You may not know this. They may not have lectured you on this at your teaching hospital, but I can tell you on the best possible authority, the dead are tremendously keen on litigation. Give me a drink, Hilda. No, not that jaundiced and medicated fluid. Give me a beaker full of the warm south, full of the true, the blushful Château Pommeroy's ordinary claret! Dr MacClintock, you can't scare me with death. I've got a far more gloomy experience ahead of me.'

'I doubt that, Rumpole,' said the Scot, sipping industriously. 'But what exactly do you mean?'

'I mean,' I said, 'I've got to appear in the Chancery Division.'

The Chancery Division is not to be found, as I must make clear to those who have no particular legal experience, in any of my ordinary stamping grounds like the Old Bailey or Snaresbrook. It is light years away from the Uxbridge Magistrates' Court. The Chancery Division is considered by many, my learned Head of Chambers in particular, to be an extremely up-market Court. There cases are pleaded by lawyers who spring from old county families in a leisurely and courteous manner. It is a tribunal, in fact, which bears the same sort of relation to Inner London Sessions as the restaurant at Claridges does to your average transport café.

The Chancery Division is in the Law Courts, and the Law Courts, which prefer to be known as the Royal Courts of Justice, occupy a stately position in the Strand, not a wig's throw from my Chambers at Equity Court in the Temple. The Victorian building looks like the monstrous and overgrown result of a misalliance between a French château and a Gothic cathedral. The vast central hall is floored with a mosaic which is constantly under repair. There are many church-shaped windows and the ancient urinals have a distinctly ecclesiastical appearance. I passed into this muted splendour and found myself temporary accommodation in a robing room where there was, such is the luxurious nature of five-star litigation, an attendant in uniform to help me on with the fancy dress. Once suitably attired, I asked the way to the Chancery Division.

I knew that Chancery was a rum sort of Division, full of dusty old men breaking trusts and elegant young men winding up companies. They speak a different language entirely from us Criminals, and their will cases are full of 'dependent relative revocation' and 'testamentary capacity', and the nice construction of the word 'money'. As I rose to my hind legs in the Court of Chancery, I felt like some rustic reveller who has blundered into a convocation of bishops engaged in silent prayer. Nevertheless, I had a duty to perform which was to open the case of 'In the Estate of Colonel Roderick Ollard, deceased. Beasley *v.* Ollard and ors'. The judge, I noticed, was a sort of pale and learned youth, probably twenty years my junior, who had looked middle-aged ever since he got his double first at Balliol, and who kept his lips tightly pursed when he wasn't uttering some thinly veiled criticism of the Rumpole case. This chilly character was known, as I discovered from the usher, as Mr Justice Venables.

'May it please you, my Lord,' I fished up a voice from the murky depths of my influenza and put it on display, 'in this case, I appear for the plaintiff, Miss Rosemary Beasley, who is putting forward the true last will of a fine old soldier, Colonel Roderick Ollard. The defendants, Mr and Mrs Percival Ollard and Master Peter Ollard, are represented by my learned friends, Mr Guthrie Featherstone, Q.C. . . .'

It was true. The smooth-talking and diplomatic Head of our Chambers had collared the brief against Rumpole. Never at home in the rough and tumble of a nice murder, the Chancery Division, as I have said, was just the place for Guthrie Featherstone.

'. . . and Mr . . .' I made a whispered inquiry and said, 'Mr Loxley-Parish.'

Guthrie had got himself, as a Chancery Junior, an ancient who'd no doubt proved more wills than I'd had bottles of Pommeroy's plonk. I turned, as usual, to the jury-box and got in the meat of my oration.

'My client, Miss Beasley, is the matron and presiding angel of a small nursing home known as Sunnyside, on the Sussex coast. There she devotedly nursed this retired warrior, Colonel Ollard, and was the comfort and cheer of his declining years.'

Mr Justice Venables was giving a chill stare over the top of his half glasses, and clearing his throat in an unpleasant manner.

Here was a judge who appeared to be distinctly unmoved by the Rumpole oratory. I carried on, of course, regardless.

'Declining years, during which his only brother, Percival, and Percival's wife, Marcia, never troubled to cross the door of Sunnyside to give five minutes of cheer to the old gentleman, and Master Peter Ollard was far too busy cashing the postal orders the Colonel sent him to send a Christmas card to his elderly uncle.'

It was time I thought that the Chancery Court heard a little Shakespeare.

> 'Blow, blow thou winter wind
> Thou art not so unkind . . .
> As man's ingratitude.'

At which point the judicial throat-clearing took on the sound of words.

'Mr Rumpole,' the Judge said. 'I think perhaps you need reminding. That jury-box is empty.'

I looked at it. His Lordship was perfectly right. The twelve puzzled and honest citizens, picked off the street at random, were conspicuous by their absence. Juries are not welcome in the Chancery Division. This was one of the occasions, strange to Rumpole, of a trial by Judge alone . . .

'It is therefore, Mr Rumpole, not an occasion for emotional appeals.' The Judge continued his lesson. 'Perhaps it would be more useful if you gave me some relevant dates and a comparison of the two wills.'

'Certainly, my Lord,' I said, always anxious to oblige. 'By his true last will of the first of March 1974 the late Colonel recognized the care of a devoted Matron . . .'

'Just the facts, Mr Rumpole. Just give me the plain facts,' snapped the old spoil-sport.

'And the plain fact is, under the previous will of the fifteenth of February 1970 the Percival Ollards had managed to scoop the pool.'

'Scoop the pool' was, it seemed, not a phrase or saying in current use in the Chancery Division.

'You mean, I suppose,' the Judge corrected me, 'that Mr Percival Ollard, together with his wife and son were the sole beneficiaries of the deceased's residuary estate.'

Somehow I managed to finish giving the Judge the brief facts of the case without open warfare breaking out. But the atmosphere was about as convivial as a gathering of teetotal undertakers.

I then called Matron to give evidence. She filled the witness-box with authority, she was dressed in respectable and respectful black, she gave her answers in ringing and resonant tones, and yet I could tell that the Judge didn't like her. As she gave her touching description of her devoted care of the late Colonel, and her harrowing account of the Percival Ollards' neglect of their relative, Mr Justice Venables looked upon Matron as though she was a person who had come to his Court for one reason only, money. Well, it was a charge which might, with equal justice, be levelled against me, and Guthrie Featherstone and even, let it be said, the learned Judge.

'Finally, Matron,' I asked the last question with a solemnity which would have deeply moved the jury, if there had been a jury. 'What did you think of the deceased?'

'He had his little ways, of course, but he was always a perfect gentleman.' She looked at the Judge; he averted his eye.

'What did you call each other?' I asked.

'It was always "Matron" and "Colonel Ollard".'

'But you were friends?'

'It was always on a proper basis, Mr Rumpole. I don't know what you're suggesting.' Miss Beasley gave me an 'old-fashioned' look, whereat Featherstone, seeing a rift in our ranks, levered himself to his hind legs and addressed a sympathetic Judge.

'I hope my learned friend isn't suggesting anything, by way of a leading question . . .?'

'Certainly not, my Lord!' And I went on before His Lordship had time to answer. 'Miss Beasley, during the years that Colonel Ollard was with you, did Mr Percival Ollard visit him at all?'

'I think he came over once or twice in the first couple of weeks. Once he took the Colonel for a run on the Downs, I think, and a tea out.'

Featherstone had the grace to subside, and my questioning continued.

'But after that?'

'No. He never came at all.'

'And his family, his wife Marcia, and the young Nijinsky?'

'The *what*, Mr Rumpole?' Mr Justice Venables was not amused.

'Master Peter Ollard, my Lord. A lad with terpsichorean tastes.'

'Oh no. I never saw them at all.'

'Yes. Thank you. Just wait there a moment, will you, Miss Beasley?' I subsided and Guthrie Featherstone rose. I had no particular worries. The middle-of-the-road M.P. was merely a middle-of-the-road cross-examiner.

'Miss Beasley. You say that Colonel Ollard had his little ways,' Guthrie began in a voice like hair oil poured on velvet.

'He did, yes.' Matron faced the old darling with confidence.

'Is Miss Mary Waterhouse one of your nurses?'

'She *was* one of my nurses. Yes.' The name brought a small sign of disapproval from the generalissimo of Sunnyside.

'Did the Colonel take boiled eggs for breakfast?' Featherstone asked what I thought at the time was not much of a question.

'On some days. Otherwise he had bacon and sausage.'

'And did the Colonel once fling his boiled eggs at Nurse Waterhouse and instruct her, and I quote, "To sit on the bloody things and hatch them out"?'

I let out a small guffaw, in which the Judge didn't join. I even began to warm to the memory of Colonel Ollard.

'He . . . may have done,' Matron conceded.

'The Colonel disliked hard-boiled eggs.' Featherstone, bless his timid old heart, seemed to be making a fair deduction.

'He disliked a lot of things, Mr Featherstone. Including young boys who indulged in ballet lessons.' Matron tried to snick a crafty one through the slips, and, of course, fell foul of the Judge immediately.

'Just answer the questions, Miss Beasley. Try not to score points off the other side,' Venables, J., warned her. Again, I got the strong impression that his Lordship hadn't exactly *warmed* to Matey.

'Did he also dislike slices of toast which were more than exactly four inches long?'

'The Colonel liked things just so, yes,' Miss Beasley admitted.

'And did he measure his toast with a slide-rule each morning to make sure it was the correct length?'

'Seems a perfectly reasonable thing to do,' I said to Mr Pontefract, in what I hoped was an audible mutter.

'Did you say something, Mr Rumpole?' The Judge inquired coldly. I heaved myself to my feet.

'I just wondered, my Lord, does the fact that a man measures his toast mean that he's not entitled to dispose of his property exactly as he likes?'

At this, the old sweetheart on the bench decided to do his best to polish up my manners.

'Mr Rumpole,' he said. 'Your turn will come later. Mr Guthrie Featherstone is cross-examining. In the Chancery Division we consider it improper to interrupt a cross-examination, unless there's a good reason to do so.'

Of course I bowed low, and said, '*If* your Lordship pleases. As a rank outsider I am, of course, delighted to get your Lordship's instructions on the mysteries of the Chancery Division.' I supposed old Venables thought that down the Old Bailey we interrupted opponents by winking at the jury and singing sea shanties. It was then my turn to subside and let Featherstone continue.

'Let me ask you something else, Matron. Colonel Ollard had fought, had he not, at the battle of Anzio?'

'That was where he won his Military Cross,' said Miss Beasley, with some understandable pride in the distinction of her late patient.

'Yes, of course. Very commendable.'

That was a tribute, of course, coming from Featherstone. I seemed to remember that he did his military service in the Soldiers' Divorce Division.

Then Featherstone asked another question. 'Matron,' he purred with his usual charm, 'did Colonel Ollard tell you that he had frequently discussed the battle of Anzio with the Prime Minister, the late Sir Winston Churchill?'

'I know that Sir Winston was always interested in Colonel Ollard's view of the war, yes.' Miss Beasley sounded proud, and even the Judge looked impressed.

'And that he had also discussed it with Field-Marshal Lord Montgomery of Alamein?'

'Colonel Ollard called him "Bernard".'

'And with the then Soviet leader, Mr Stalin. Did Colonel Ollard call him "Josef"?' Oh dear, I sighed to myself, things were becoming grim when Featherstone tried to make a funny.

'No. He always called him "Mr Stalin".' Miss Beasley answered primly.

'Very respectful. If I may say so.' Featherstone gave the Judge a chummy little smile and then turned back straight-faced to the witness.

'You know he told Nurse Waterhouse, one morning last October, that he had been talking to Sir Winston, Lord Montgomery and Mr Stalin the evening before. Does that surprise you?' I had the awful feeling that Featherstone had struck gold. There was a sudden silence in Court as Pontefract and I held our breath, waiting for Matron's answer.

When it came, it was a simple, 'No.'

'You say it *doesn't* surprise you, Miss Beasley?' Venables J. leant forward, frowning unpleasantly.

'Not in the least, my Lord.' The answer was positively serene. I wanted to tell the Judge not to interrupt the cross-examination, after all, we didn't do that sort of thing in the Chancery Division. But Featherstone, as he went on, was doing quite well, even without a little help from the Judge.

'Nurse Waterhouse will also say that Colonel Ollard told her that he had been chatting to Alexander the Great, the Emperor Napoleon and the late Duke of Marlborough,' my opponent suggested.

'Well, of course he would, you know.' Miss Beasley smiled back at him.

'He would say that because he was suffering from mental instability?'

'Of course not!' The witness was outraged. 'The Colonel had as much mental stability as you or I, Mr Featherstone.'

'Speak for yourself, Miss Beasley.' Oh, very funny, Featherstone, I thought. What a talent! He ought to go on the Halls.

'Why did you say that the Colonel *would* speak to those gentlemen?' Featherstone asked for clarification.

'Because they were all keenly interested in his subject,' Miss Beasley explained, as though to a rather backward two-year-old.

'Which was?'

'Military matters.'

'Oh, military matters. Yes. Of course.' Featherstone paused, and then asked politely, 'But all the names I have mentioned, Churchill and Montgomery, Marlborough and Napoleon, Stalin and Alexander the Great. They're all *dead*, aren't they, Matron?'

'Yes, indeed. But that wouldn't have worried the Colonel.' She gave the Opposition Leader a patient smile. 'Colonel Ollard was most sympathetic to people who were ill. Being dead wouldn't have put him off at all.'

'But did the Colonel think he *could* talk to those deceased gentlemen?'

'Oh yes. Of course he could.' As Pontefract and I began to see the last will of Colonel Ollard going up in smoke, the Judge said, 'You really believe that, Miss Beasley?'

I must say the answer that Matron gave was not particularly helpful. She merely looked at the Judge with some pity and said, '*You* could talk to the Emperor Napoleon, my Lord. If *you* were a believer.'

'A believer, Miss Beasley?' No doubt a churchwarden and Chairman of the Parish Council, the Judge looked more than a little irked by her reply.

'A believer in communication with the other side.' At least she had the grace to explain.

'And both you and Colonel Ollard were believers?' Featherstone led her gently on, down the primrose path to disaster.

'Oh yes. We had that much in common.'

'Can you communicate with the late Josef Stalin, Miss Beasley?' It was a shot in the dark by Featherstone, but it scored a bull's eye.

'Of course I could,' Miss Beasley said modestly. 'But let's just say I wouldn't care to.'

'Perhaps not. But can you communicate, for instance, with the late Colonel Ollard?'

'Yes indeed.' She had no doubt about that.

'When did you last do so, Miss Beasley?' said the Judge, following his leader, Featherstone, like a bloodhound.

'Yesterday evening, my Lord.'

'Oh dear! Oh, my ears and whiskers!' I groaned to myself as

the psychic Matron blundered on, addressing her remarks to the learned Judge.

'And I may say that the Colonel is very distressed about this case, my Lord. Very distressed indeed. In fact, he thinks it's a disgraceful thing to argue about it when he'd made his will perfectly clear and left it in his uniform box. I wouldn't like to tell you, my Lord, the things that the Colonel had to say about his brother Percy.'

'I think you had better not, Miss Beasley.' Featherstone brought her smoothly to a halt. 'That would be hearsay evidence. We shall have to wait and see whether my learned friend Mr Rumpole calls the deceased gentleman as a witness.'

Oh hilarious, I told myself bitterly. Guthrie Featherstone is being most hilarious. My God, he's working well today!

We, that is, Matron, Mr Pontefract and self, had luncheon in the crypt under the Law Courts, a sepulchral hall, where, it seemed, very old plaice and chips come to die. Miss Beasley's legal team were not in an optimistic mood.

'The Judge doesn't like you all that much I'm afraid, Miss Beasley.' I thought it best to break the news to her gently.

'Never mind, Mr Rumpole. The feeling is entirely mutual.' She looked, all things considered, ridiculously cheerful.

'If you take my advice, Miss Beasley, you should go for a settlement.' Pontefract was trying to talk some sense into her. 'Save what you can from the wreckage. You see, once you had to admit that the late Colonel used to talk to the Emperor Napoleon . . .'

'What's wrong with talking to the Emperor Napoleon?' Miss Beasley frowned. 'He can be quite charming when he puts his mind to it.'

'I don't think the Judge is likely to accept that,' I warned her.

'You'd talk to the Emperor Napoleon, I'm sure, if he came across to you.' Miss Beasley didn't seem to be getting the drift of my argument. I put it more bluntly.

'Mr Pontefract is right. The time has come to chuck in the towel. On the best terms we can manage.'

'You mean, surrender?' She looked at us both, displeased.

'Well, on terms, Miss Beasley.' Mr Pontefract tried to soften the blow, but her answer came like the bugle call which set off the Charge of the Light Brigade.

'Colonel Ollard will never surrender!' she trumpeted. 'Anyway, you haven't cross-examined that wretched Percy Ollard yet. The Colonel says Mr Rumpole's a great cross-examiner!'

'That's very kind of him.' I tried to sound modest.

'He says he'll never forget reading your cross-examination about the bloodstains in the Penge Bungalow Murders. He read every word of it, in the Sunday paper.'

'My dear lady. That was thirty-five years ago. Anyway, I had a jury to play on in that case. I'm at my best with a jury. This is a cold-blooded trial in the Chancery Division, by Judge alone, and that Judge is distinctly unfriendly.'

'The Colonel says, "Mr Rumpole will hit my brother Percy for six." ' She repeated the words as if they were Holy Writ.

'Tell the Colonel,' I asked her, 'that Mr Rumpole isn't at his best, without a jury.'

A trial without a jury is like an operation without anaesthetic, or a luncheon without a glass of wine. 'Shall we drown this old fish, Pontefract, my old darling,' I suggested, 'in a sea of cooking claret?'

What I can't accept about spiritualism is the idea of millions of dead people (there must be standing room only in the Other Side) kept hanging about just waiting to be sent for by some old girl with a Ouija board in a Brighton boarding house, or a couple of table-tappers in Tring, for the sake of some inane conversation about the Blueness of the Infinite. I mean at least when you're dead you'll surely be spared such tedious social occasions. Nevertheless, there was Colonel Ollard apparently at Matey's beck and call, ready and willing to cross the Great Divide and drop in on her at the turn of a card or the shiver of a wine glass. I was expressing some of these thoughts to Hilda in a feverish sort of way that evening as I hugged my dressing-gown round me and downed medicinal claret by the electric fire in Froxbury Court.

'Really, Rumpole,' said She, 'don't be so morbid.'

'I can smell corruption.' I sneezed loudly. 'The angel of death is brushing me with his wings.'

'Rumpole, Dr MacClintock has told you it's only a cold.'

'Dr MacClintock gave me a warning, on the subject of death.'
At which there was a ring at the door, and Hilda said, 'Oh good
heavens. That's never the front door bell!'

With a good deal of clucking and tutting, Hilda went out to
the hall and eventually ushered Miss Rosemary Beasley, who
appeared to be carrying some kind of plastic holdall, into the
presence of the sick. When she asked me how I was, I told her I
was dying.

'Well, don't die yet, Mr Rumpole. You've got our case to
win.'

'Don't you think I could conduct it perfectly well from beyond
the grave?' I asked Matron.

'Now you're teasing me! Your husband is the most terrible
tease,' she told a puzzled Hilda. 'Listen to this, Mr Rumpole.
The Colonel says that he has an urgent message for you. He'll
deliver it here tonight. So I've brought the board.'

'The what?'

'The planchette, of course.'

To my dismay, Matron then produced, from her black
plastic holdall, a small heart-shaped board on castors, which
she plonked on to our dining table. There was paper fixed on the
board, and Miss Beasley held a pencil poised over it and the
board then moved in a curious fashion, causing writing to appear
on the paper. It looked illegible to me, but Miss Beasley de-
ciphered some rather cheeky communications from a late and no
doubt unlamented Red Indian Chief who finally agreed to fetch
Colonel Ollard to the planchette. Tearing himself away from the
Emperor Napoleon, the Colonel issued his orders for the day,
emerging in Miss Beasley's already somewhat masculine voice as
she read the scribbles on the board. 'The Colonel says, "Hullo
there, Rumpole," ' Miss Beasley informed us.

'Well, answer him, Rumpole. Be polite!' Hilda appeared
enchanted with the whole ludicrous performance.

'Oh, hullo there, Colonel.' I felt an idiot as I said it.

'It's very blue here, Rumpole. And I am very happy,' Miss
Beasley came through as the late holder of the Military Cross.

'Oh good.' What else could I say?

'Tomorrow you will cross-examine my brother Percival.'

'Well, I hope to. I'm not feeling . . .' here I sneezed again, 'quite up to snuff.'

'Brace up, Rumpole! No malingering. Tomorrow you will cross-examine my brother in Court.' Miss Beasley relayed Colonel Ollard's instructions.

'Yes, Colonel. Aye, aye, sir.'

'Ask him what we said to each other when he visited me in the nursing home, and he drove me up to the Downs. Ask him what the conversation was when we had cream tea together at the Bide-A-Wee tea-rooms. Go on, Rumpole. Ask Percy that!' Colonel Ollard may have been a very gallant officer and an inspired leader of men. I doubted if he was a real expert in the art of cross-examination.

'Is it a good question?' I asked the deceased, doubtfully.

'Percy won't like it. Just as Jerry didn't like cold steel. Percy will run a mile from that question,' Miss Beasley croaked.

'Colonel, I make it a rule to decide on my own cross-examination.' I wanted to make the position clear, but the answer came back almost in a parade-ground bellow.

'Ask that question, Rumpole. It's an order!'

'I'll . . . I'll consider it.' I suppose it doesn't do to hurt the feelings of the dead.

'Do so! Oh, and see you over here some time.' At which, it seemed, the consultation was over and Colonel Ollard returned to some celestial bowling-green to while away eternity. It was perfectly ridiculous, of course. I knew quite well that the deceased Colonel wasn't manipulating the planchette. But, as for asking his question, I could tell by the Judge's attitude next morning that we had absolutely nothing to lose.

Percival Ollard was not, I thought, a particularly attractive-looking customer. The successful manufacturer of kitchen utensils had run to fat, he had a bristling little ginger moustache and small flickering eyes that seemed to be looking round the Court for ways of escape. Featherstone led him smoothly through his evidence in chief and then I rose to cross-examine. The learned Judge put a damper on my first question.

'I'm really wondering,' he said, 'how much longer this estate is going to be put to the expense of this apparently hopeless litigation.'

'Not long, my Lord,' I said with a confidence I didn't feel, 'after I have cross-examined this witness.' And I turned to the witness-box.

'Mr Percival Ollard. Were you on good terms with your brother, before he went into the nursing home?'

'Extremely good terms. We saw each other regularly, and he always sent my boy, Peter, a postal order for Christmas and birthdays.'

'That was before the Colonel started talking to the dead?' the Judge asked in a way unfriendly to Rumpole.

'Yes, my Lord.' Percy looked gratefully at my Lord.

'Before he became, shall we say, eccentric in the extreme?' the Judge went on.

'Yes, my Lord.'

'Very well.' Venables, J., now seemed to have worn himself out. 'Carry on, if you must, Mr Rumpole.'

'Two weeks after he went into the nursing home, you took him for a drive on the Downs?' Rumpole carried on.

'I did, yes.' Percy's nervousness seemed to have returned, although I couldn't imagine why the memory of tea on the Downs posed any sort of threat to him.

'You were then on good terms?'

'Yes.'

'You shared tea, scones and clotted cream at the Bide-A-Wee café?' It was strange the effect on the witness of this innocent question. He took out a silk handkerchief, wiped his forehead and had to force himself to answer, 'Yes, we did.'

'And talked?'

'We talked, yes.' Percy answered so quietly that the Judge was constrained to tell him to speak up.

'And after that conversation you and your brother never met or spoke to each other again?'

There was a long pause. Had I stumbled, guided by a Dead Hand, on some vital piece of evidence? I couldn't believe it.

'No. We never did.'

'And he made a will cutting out your family, and leaving all his considerable property to my client, Miss Beasley?'

'He made an *alleged* will, Mr Rumpole,' the Judge was at pains to remind me.

I bowed respectfully, and said, 'If that's what you call it in the Chancery Division, yes, my Lord. What I want to ask *you*, Mr Percival Ollard, is simply this – what did you and your brother say to each other at the Bide-A-Wee café?'

Now the pause seemed endless. Percy looked at Featherstone and got no help. He looked at his wife and his ballet-dancing son. He looked vainly at the doors and the windows, and finally his desperate gaze fell on the learned Judge.

'My Lord. Must I answer that question?' he said.

'Mr Rumpole, do you press the question?' His Lordship asked me with distaste.

'My Lord, I do.' For some reason, I was on to a good thing, and I wasn't letting it go.

'Then it is relevant and you must answer it, Mr Ollard.' At least the Judge knew his business.

'My L-L-Lord,' Percival Ollard stammered. He was clearly extremely distressed. So distressed that the Judge had time to look at the clock and relieve the witness's agony for an hour. 'I see the time,' he said. 'You may give us your answer after luncheon, Mr Percival Ollard. Shall we say, two o'clock . . .?'

We all rose obediently to our hind legs, with Rumpole muttering, 'Bloody Chancery Judge. He's let old Percy off the hook.'

Miss Beasley vanished somewhere at lunchtime, and when I had returned from a rather unhappy encounter with the plaice in the crypt, I found Guthrie Featherstone waiting for me outside the Court. He offered me a cigarette, which I refused, and he lit my small cigar with a gold lighter.

'Horace,' he said, 'we've always got on pretty well at the Bar.'

'Have we, Guthrie?'

'My client has come to a rather agonizing decision.'

'You mean he's going to answer my question?'

'It's not that exactly. You see, Horace, we're chucking in the sponge. Our hands are up. We surrender! Matron can have her precious will. We offer no further evidence.'

You could have knocked me down with a Chancery brief, but

I tried to sound nonchalant. 'Oh really, Featherstone,' I said, 'that's very satisfactory.' It was also somewhat incredible. But Guthrie, it became clear, had other matters on his mind.

'I say, Rumpole. A fellow must be certain of his fee. You'll let me have my costs out of the estate, won't you?'

'I suppose so.' I warned him, 'I'd better just check.'

'With your client?'

'Not *only* with her,' I said, 'with the deceased. I mean it's his money, isn't it?' And I left him thinking, no doubt, that old Horace Rumpole had completely lost his marbles.

When Matron came into view I put the proposition to her; I told her that the Percival Ollards would give her all the boodle, only provided that Guthrie, and their other lawyers, got their costs out of the estate. She and the dear departed must have had a convivial lunch together, agreement was reached, and the deal was on. With about as much joy and enthusiasm as King John might have shown when signing Magna Carta, Mr Justice Venables pronounced, in the absence of further argument, for the will of the first of March 1974 benefiting Miss Beasley, and against the earlier will which favoured the Percival Ollards. All parties were allowed their costs out of the estate.

When we came out of Court, Matron seized my hand in her muscular grasp.

'Thanks most awfully, Mr Rumpole,' she said. 'The Colonel knew you'd pull it off and hit them for six.'

'Miss Beasley. May I call you "Matey"?'

'Please.'

'What's the truth of it? What did the brothers say to each other over the scones and Darjeeling?'

There was a pause, and then Miss Beasley said with a small, secret smile, 'How would I know, Mr Rumpole? Only the Colonel and his brother know that.'

However, I was not to be left in total ignorance of the truth of 'In the Estate of Colonel Ollard, deceased'. After we had taken off our robes, Guthrie Featherstone did me the honour of inviting me to crack a bottle of claret at the Sheridan Club, and, as he had given me my first (and my last) Chancery will, I did him the honour of accepting. As we sat in a quiet room, under the portraits of old actors and even older judges, Featherstone said, 'No reason why you shouldn't know, Rumpole. Your client had been Percy's mistress for years.'

'Miss Beasley, Matey, the old dragon of the nursing home, his *mistress*!' I was astonished, and I let my amazement show. 'His *what*?'

'Girlfriend.' Featherstone made it sound even more inappropriate.

'It seems odd, somehow, calling a stout, elderly woman a "girlfriend". Are you trying to tell me, Guthrie, intimacy actually took place?'

'Regularly, apparently. On a Wednesday. Matron's afternoon off. But when Colonel Roderick Ollard went into Sunnyside she dived into bed with *him*, and deserted Percy. The meeting at the tea-room was when the Colonel told his brother all about it and said he meant to leave his money to Rosemary Beasley.'

I was silent. I drank claret. I began to wonder where the planchette came in.

'But why couldn't your client have *told* us that?' I asked my ex-opponent.

'His wife, Rumpole! His wife Marcia! She's a battle-axe and she was kept completely in the dark about Matey. It seems there would have been hell to pay if she'd found out. So we had to settle.'

'Well, well, Featherstone. Matron, the *femme fatale*. I'd never have believed it.'

What did I believe? That the Colonel spoke from the grave? Or that Matron invented all the séances to tell us a truth which would have caused her deep embarrassment to communicate in any other way? As it was, she had told me nothing.

All I knew was that I didn't fancy the idea of the 'other side'. I knew I shouldn't care for long chats with Colonel Ollard and the Emperor Napoleon even if Josef Stalin were to be of the party. Dying, as far as I was concerned, had been postponed indefinitely.

Rumpole and the Rotten Apple

Nothing shocks your Old Bailey Judge more than a bent copper. There the Judge is, his simple world proceeding nicely, with the villains committing enough crimes to keep his Honour in business, and the public-spirited Old Bill out catching them and lobbing them neatly into the dock, and then, horror of horrors, a copper gets on to the wrong side! The Old Bailey universe comes grinding to a halt, and the Judge tends to look on the twisted bobby with the amount of smiling tolerance that Savonarola would have had for a pregnant nun; his only answer would be to kick her out of the convent and into the nick before she starts infecting other members of the Serious Crimes Squad. Of course, the truth is never quite so simple as it appears to an Old Bailey Judge. Coppers and villains spend so much time in each other's company that they often begin to look alike (as dog owners grow to look like their pets). They have the same short-back-and-sides haircut and wear the same navy blue blazers and cavalry twill trousers. King Lear put it in a neat phrase, 'Handy dandy, which is the Justice, which is the thief?'

This was the point at issue in the case of dear old Inspector Dobbs of the Detective Force. I remember leaving Casa Rumpole, our flat in Froxbury Court, Gloucester Road, for a conference with the Inspector one soggy February morning, when I was submitted to a brief interrogation from She Who Must Be Obeyed.

Now it is not, it is certainly not, that I am going deaf. It is just that everyone seems to talk more quietly nowadays, particularly my wife Hilda. I have no doubt that She said something to me on the stairs and the subsequent evidence went to show that her general drift was, 'Will you come straight back this evening, Rumpole?'

Now this may, indeed, be what she said. What I *thought* she said was rather different. From the blurred mumble that reached me over the roar of the traffic and the babble of other people's radios, I thought she said, 'Will you come late back this evening, Rumpole?' To which I replied, with the utmost courtesy, 'I bloody well hope not.' You can imagine my dismay, therefore, when Hilda received my soft answer with a swift intake of breath and retreated back into our matrimonial home as though I had announced a previous engagement with a couple of ladies of the town in an opium den. In a shifting world I felt only one rule was certain, there was no accounting for She.

When I got to my chambers in Equity Court, the clerk's room presented the usual scene of frenzied activity. Henry, my clerk, was making telephone calls. Henry is the devoted servant who is the true master of our Chambers; if he says go, we go, even to the Uxbridge Magistrates' Court. Dianne, his helper, was training as usual for the slow typers' competition, and Uncle Tom, our oldest and most briefless barrister, was practising mashie shots into the waste paper basket. Miss Trant, the Portia of our Chambers and our only lady barrister (now known to some, but not to me, as Phillida Erskine-Brown, having married one of our barristers, Claude Erskine-Brown) was eagerly undoing the tape on her brief in a lengthy 'gang bang' with scarlet finger-nails. Her husband, who now spends a good deal of his time at home drafting affidavits and looking after their baby, was thoughtfully stirring his coffee and Guthrie Featherstone, Q.C., M.P., our Head of Chambers, was picking over his letters in the hope of finding an invitation to play golf with the Lord Chief Justice.

'Inspector Dobbs is in your room, Mr Rumpole, along with Mr Morse from the instructing solicitors.' Henry put down the telephone momentarily to announce my engagements.

'Rumpole! Are you under arrest? Have they caught up with you at last?' Ever since Featherstone was asked to sit as a Commissioner of Assize, or type of part-time Judge, he has shown a regrettable tendency to attempt jokes. All the same I thought I detected, beneath the levity, a certain wishful thinking.

'Not yet, Guthrie, my old darling,' I told him. 'The Inspector comes to me as a client. Like most of the rest of mankind, he's got himself into some sort of trouble with the law.'

'Your letters, Mr Rumpole.' Dianne came up and pressed a number of unwelcome communications into my hand. I took a look at them and threw them into the waste paper basket.

'Little brown envelopes,' I said with horror. 'Communications from Her Majesty's Commissioners of Revenue!'

'All the same, there's no need to throw them away.' Claude Erskine-Brown spoke with disapproval.

'There certainly is, Erskine-Brown. Reading communications from the Revenue only produces palpitations of the heart and quite unnecessary anxiety.'

'You don't deal with the Revenue properly, Rumpole. Philly'll tell you. I've just won a long battle with them on the subject of pin-striped trousers, which I say are absolutely necessary for our work at the Bar. Haven't I, Philly?'

His wife Phillida, appealed to, went on reading her brief. She looked as if she couldn't care less about her husband's pin-striped trousers. Erskine-Brown was our expert on revenue law, good on figures and absolutely hopeless on bloodstains.

'I'm now deducting two pairs of pin-striped trousers a year. It's a perfectly legitimate claim, which has been recognized as such by the Inland Revenue,' the proud father and tax lawyer told me.

'Would you like a cup of coffee up in your room, Mr Rumpole?' Dianne was being remarkably attentive that morning. However, I declined her offer as I knew that Dianne's idea of coffee was a tepid brew tasting faintly of meat extract.

'You might as well have it, Mr Rumpole. You're paying regularly into the coffee money,' Dianne pointed out.

'No time for luxurious living, Dianne. Inspector Dobbs awaits my attention.'

When I went into my room I found dear old Dobbs, a grey-haired, slow-speaking officer sitting stolidly in my client's chair. I had known the Inspector about the Courts for years and we had crossed swords on a number of occasions. I respected him as hard-working and, within his limits, an honest officer. The other man present was Mr Morse, an old solicitor's clerk who had brought me criminal work for longer than I care to remember. He was re-lighting his pipe and my room was filled with the familiar reek of his quite revolting tobacco.

'I never expected to see you in a defending barrister's Chambers, Inspector,' I greeted him. 'Good of Mr Morse to trundle you along.'

'Inspector Dobbs has long been aware, Mr Rumpole, of your talent for getting persons acquitted,' Morse grinned through the smoke-screen.

'I've found your talents frustrating,' Dobbs grumbled. 'Especially when you and I both know the lads are damn well guilty.'

'Really, Inspector! Is it my talent for getting the guilty off you'd like me to exercise in your case?' I couldn't resist it.

'I didn't say that, Mr Rumpole.' Dobbs looked gloomy and I did my best to cheer him up with some gentle reminiscences.

'We met last year, didn't we, after Charlie Pointer's latest warehouse-breaking charge?'

'You had a ridiculous win there, Mr Rumpole.'

'Because you went into the witness-box and swore that he'd said, "It's a fair cop, Mr Dobbs," when you first got him into the nick. Charlie may break into warehouses but he never admits it to the police. He was so incensed at the insult to his intelligence that he was determined to fight.' I'd always wanted to tell old Dobbsy why he lost R. *v.* Pointer.

'And you won!' The Inspector sounded unexpectedly bitter.

'If you hadn't put that little bit of gilt on the gingerbread, it might've been a guilty verdict.'

'Well, I can see we're never going to agree, Mr Rumpole. I told Mr Morse it was going to be hopeless. I'll not waste any more of your time!' He seemed about to struggle up from my easy chair, so I said, as soothingly as possible,

'Agree? Of course we're going to agree.'

'We've never been on the same side in Court.'

'We're on the same side now,' I reminded him.

'Why? What's changed?' The Inspector still seemed to doubt it.

'What's changed, Inspector Dobbs,' I told him, 'is that now *you're* the one in trouble. You've caught a nasty disease and just look at me as the doctor who's here to cure you.'

'What disease is that?'

I found my papers and opened them. Dobbs waited patiently and then I said, 'A little charge of bribery and corruption ... five hundred pounds. Don't worry, though. The most that can happen to you is a spell in an open prison, that's where they send the bent coppers. Cheer up, Dobbs, my old darling. You can exercise your natural talent for hedge clipping and spreading manure.'

My natural high spirits had got the better of me, and I had gone too far at last. Dobbs got up then and grabbed his mac.

'Come along, Mr Morse. I'm not going to sit here and have Mr Rumpole crow over me! He's the chosen representative of the criminal fraternity.' Dobbs made for the door and was out of it, leaving Mr Morse to make his apologies.

'I'm sorry about this, Mr Rumpole.'

'That's quite all right, Mr Morse. 'I told him. 'Charlie, Pointer's just the same. He's always extremely difficult when we start working together. He's been trained to be a model client by the time I get him into the witness-box.'

I was sitting brooding on the departure of the Inspector in trouble, when I received a visit from my learned friend Claude Erskine-Brown. He had the grave face and suppressed excitement of a man who has just unearthed a serious scandal.

'Rumpole, in this not undistinguished set of Chambers ...' He started as if opening a ten-week case to the jury.

'You mean this stable of moderate legal hacks?'

'... what do we stand for above all else?' Erskine-Brown ignored the interruption.

'What do we stand for? I would say we provide a place of refuge, for villains in distress.'

'I would say we stand for justice and for honesty! Surely it's up to us, Rumpole, to set an example.'

An example? I wasn't sure I agreed with him. God save us from a state where everyone goes around imitating lawyers.

'That's why it is so particularly distressing when lawlessness is to be found, even in these very Chambers!' Something of grave importance seemed to be distressing poor old Claude. I set about to probe into the mystery.

'What've you done, Erskine-Brown? Unburden yourself to me, Claude. You've been taking home the law reports for solitary reading, or did you indecently assault Mrs Justice Appleby after a long and sultry divorce case?'

'Rumpole. I implore you to be serious for a moment.' His voice sank to a conspiratorial whisper. 'It's Henry.'

'What?' I was handicapped by the habit people have, nowadays, of speaking beyond the level of human audibility, like dog whistles.

'Our clerk, Henry.' Erskine-Brown raised his voice slightly.

'Henry made an improper suggestion to Mrs Justice Appleby?' I was puzzled. We were obviously entering deep waters, but Erskine-Brown brushed the suggestion aside and said, 'Rumpole! Have you any idea what you pay for coffee money? Of course you haven't. Because Henry deducts the coffee money with the rest of our Chambers' expenses and gives us no particulars. But I happened to be in the clerk's room and saw the petty cash book lying on Henry's desk . . .'

'You want to confess an indecent assault upon Henry's petty cash book?' I was still failing to follow the fellow's drift.

'He is charging us two pounds a week each for coffee money!'

'You astonish me, Claude!'

'I have made careful inquiries at my local supermarket. And a large tin of instant coffee . . .'

'That is not instant coffee we drink, Erskine-Brown. Don't flatter the stuff. It's dishwater lightly flavoured with meat extract.'

'Well, a large tin of whatever it is costs no more than £6.50 at the *most*. There are twenty members of Chambers. Henry is getting £40 a week coffee money and making a profit of £33.50. On our coffee!'

'Unbelievable!' I did my best to sound aghast. 'There's only one thing that disturbs me.'

'What's that, Rumpole?'

'Will they have room for a waxwork of our clerk Henry, between Dr Crippen and Herr Hitler in the Chamber of Horrors at Madame Tussaud's?'

I could see that, once again, I had said the wrong thing and given offence. Erskine-Brown got up and prepared to leave in some dudgeon. I seemed to be doing nothing but drive my visitors away that morning.

'Oh really, Rumpole! It's no use talking to you. I should have gone straight to the Head of Chambers.'

As he reached the door, a thought occurred to me. I thought it just might be worth trying to stop Claude creating endless trouble in the clerk's room. 'Just before you go. That's a very elegant new pair of pin-striped bags you're wearing, Erskine-Brown.'

'Nonsense, Rumpole!' My learned friend looked puzzled. 'I haven't had a new pair of pin-striped trousers for years.'

'Haven't you really?' I smiled at him in the friendliest fashion. 'That's what I rather thought!'

I had to turn my thoughts from the vital matter of Erskine-Brown's trousers when Inspector Dobbs, true to the form of Charlie Pointer, the celebrated warehouse breaker, returned in a more docile mood the next day. He was back in the depths of my clients' chair, sitting where some of the most notable villains on his East London patch had sat before him, and I was studying the officer's pained and honest expression through the smoke of Mr Morse's pipe and my own small cigar.

'I'm back here, Mr Rumpole, on the advice of my senior officer.' Left to himself, it was clear, the Inspector would never have darkened the doors of my Chambers in Equity Court again.

'That's remarkably civil of your senior officer, Inspector. Who is he, by the way?'

'Superintendent Glazier. He called at my home special.'

'Inspector Dobbs has been suspended from duty. For over a year,' Mr Morse explained.

'Of course. You've been out of touch with police matters.' I tried to put it as tactfully as I could.

'The Super came to tell me that you were an outstanding brief, Mr Rumpole.'

A 'brief' is just what Charlie Pointer calls me. Once again, I remembered that villains and the Old Bill speak the same language.

'Superintendent Glazier agrees you are outstanding at getting customers off. That being your job of course.'

I must say I was a little surprised. I knew Glazier as a remarkably efficient officer, proud of his conviction rate, and a cautious and unshakeable witness. I would never have guessed that he cherished a warm admiration for the Rumpole talents. However, I felt proper gratitude to the Super for his friendly action and for encouraging Inspector Dobbs to confide his troubles in me, as he was now doing in the measured monotone which he always used when giving evidence.

'I was as surprised as anyone when Charlie Pointer asked to come and see me. He telephoned me at the station. Suggested we had a Chinese together.'

'A Chinese what exactly?' I asked, purely for clarification.

'Meal, of course,' Dobbs explained tolerantly.

'What did you think about that?' It seemed, on the face of it, a strange invitation from a con to a copper. Dobbs gave me a small, reassuring laugh and said, 'I thought he was trying to Doggett a Chinese dinner.'

'Did you say "Doggett", Inspector?' Mr Morse was puzzled. This time I was able to translate.

'Of course he did, Morse. "Doggett's coat and badge". Means "cadge". Thieves' rhyming slang. The language used by Charlie Pointer and Detective Inspector Dobbs. In any event, you agreed to meet Charlie?'

'At the Swinging Bamboo. In the High Street.'

'*Why* did you meet him?'

'I was curious. It was my night off and I was on the lonely side, not being a married man.' I looked at Dobbs; of course, it was a solitary life being a copper, a man with few friends except among the criminals he pursues.

'So the idea of picking over a chop suey with Charlie Pointer appealed to you. You went on your own?'

'I did, yes. Soon it became, well, a regular date we had together.'

'You weren't suspicious?'

'No. Charlie's the old-fashioned type. Sticks to simple warehouse breaking. No violence, an honest sort of tea leaf, in his way.'

'Just as you're an honest sort of copper, in your way. Even though you invented a couple of verbals at Charlie's trial.' I couldn't help myself and this time the Inspector looked only slightly pained. 'Mr Rumpole,' he said, 'do we have to go into that again?'

'I'm sorry. You're quite right. Don't let's dig up old verbals. Go on.'

'As I say, you could've knocked me down with a feather when Charlie offered to be a grass.'

It amazed me too. Charlie Pointer was an old-fashioned type of villain, born before the age of the super-grass, with old-fashioned ideas of honour among thieves. I asked Dobbs if Charlie would have been any use as an informer. 'He's in touch with three or four big firms of shop and warehouse breakers. I thought he might be useful, yes.'

'So what did you do?'

'I consulted my superior officer.'

'Superintendent Glazier?'

'That's right. He told me to carry on at my discretion.'

'Did Charlie give you anything useful?' I wondered.

'Little bits and pieces. Nothing enormous. But when we checked it over, we found it was reliable.'

'And you were prepared to pay him for it?'

'Yes. We owed him five hundred nicker at the time.'

'At the time of the alleged bribery? So *that's* what you were talking about!' I began, with a feeling of elation, to sniff the faint odour of a defence. I rose from my seat and found and lit another small cigar.

'Of course, Mr Rumpole.' Dobbs sounded vaguely rebuking, as though it should have been obvious to a child.

'That's the defence! You didn't want Charlie to pay you five hundred. You were going to pay *him*.'

'Certainly I was. I'll swear on the book on that. He's a liar who says different.'

Inspector Dobbs looked so solid and convincing when he protested his innocence that I rashly began to assume that we were on a winner. However, one witness was found to contradict the words of the inspector, and to do so, awkwardly enough, in his own words and even with his slow and reassuring voice.

In the good old days when I did the Penge Bungalow Murders, and scored a remarkable success, although I say it myself, alone and without a leader, witnesses were, by and large, human beings. And as human beings, they could be cross-examined, suggestions could be made to them and they were subject to merciful confusion and welcome failures of recollection. Things, I regret to have to say it, have not improved since those distant days, and many of the faults must be laid at the door of automation. Not only have witnesses changed. String quartets, which were once the pride of the tea room, have now been replaced by an abominable form of mechanical music. The toasting fork has given way to an alarming machine that fires singed bread at you like a minute gun. The comforting waitress in black bombazine has become a device that contrives to shoot a warmish and unidentifiable fluid into a plastic cup and over your trousers at the drop of a considerable sum of money. None of these engines is an improvement on the human factor, neither are trials made any easier by the replacement of the living witness with the electronic device. It is hard to cross-examine a machine or to try and shake its recollection.

'Have you seen the additional evidence, Mr Rumpole, in the case of R. *v.* Dobson?'

I confessed I hadn't. Mr Morse and I had had a busy and unpleasant week with an unlawful handling before Judge Bullingham. I staggered away after a day of being chased round the Court by the demented Bull, barely able to raise the glass of Pommeroy's plonk to my parched lips, or read anything more demanding than the *Times* crossword puzzle.

'They've served us with the inspector's little chat with Charlie Pointer in the Chinese restaurant. They've got it word for word.'

'You mean . . .' we were in my favourite wine bar at the time, and I paused to absorb the first glass of the evening, '. . . poor old Dobbsy was bugged?'

'I'm afraid so, Mr Rumpole. Not a lot we can do about it.'

'We can listen to the beastly machine. I mean, don't let's take the word of any sort of transcript.'

Listening to the machine meant a visit to New Scotland Yard where the mechanical witness was in the safe custody of Superintendent Glazier, the officer in charge of the case.

Superintendent Glazier was a tall, rather pale officer with dark hair brushed straight back, wearing a blue suit and a police Rugby Club tie. He greeted Mr Morse and me politely and I took the opportunity of thanking him for recommending my services to the reluctant Inspector.

'I know you're good, Mr Rumpole,' he said, 'and I want Dobbs to have the best. I want him given every chance to put his defence, if he has one. But, if he's crooked, I want him out of my manor and I want him in the nick. I can find a good word to say for all sorts of villains, Mr Rumpole, it's my Christian duty to do so, but I can't stand a bent copper.'

There was a small badge on the officer's lapel, the insignia of the Police Witness to God Society. 'Clean living and high thinking' was the style of Superintendent Glazier.

'This little matter of the additional evidence?'

'Sorry about that, Mr Rumpole. Must have come as a nasty shock to Dobbs that we had that.'

'Tell me, why didn't you put it in at the Magistrates' Court? Was it a little threat you were saving up till the last moment?'

'Let's say, we wanted to spare your feelings, sir.' The Superintendent gave a wintry smile. 'We didn't want to destroy your faith in your client.'

'Oh, I think I can bear to hear the truth about dear old Inspector Dobbsy.'

'A rotten apple, Mr Rumpole! One that could poison the whole barrel if he's not thrown out.' Glazier spoke and I could hear the voice of an officer in Cromwell's army, determined to stamp on corruption and backsliding.

'A rotten apple? He seems to me much more like a swede.'

'A *what*, Mr Rumpole?' The Superintendent frowned.

'Isn't that what you sophisticated officers call the poor old turnip-heads, the simple-minded ploddies who'd look far happier in cycle clips?'

'Simple-minded?' He gave another flicker of a smile. 'I don't think you'd call Dobbs simple-minded, Mr Rumpole. Not when you've heard this tape.'

So the performance we had come to attend began as Superintendent Glazier switched on the little machine. Act One, Scene One. The set, I take it, was the Swinging Bamboo restaurant, the dramatis personae were Detective Inspector

Dobbs and new super-grass Charlie Pointer. The background noises were the crunch of prawn crackers and the gentle simmering of sweet-and-sour pork on the table heaters. On this the curtain rose, or rather, the tape was turned on. Mr Morse and I listened, with growing depression, as Charlie Pointer spoke first.

'You want another payment, Inspector?'

There was a pause, and then the Inspector came through loud and clear. The dialogue went as follows:

DOBBS: No one works for nothing, Charlie.

CHARLIE: What's going to happen if I can't pay?

DOBBS: I've got the whole Squad behind me. And I want to get my fingers on what you promised me. When are you coming through, Charlie?

CHARLIE: How much do you want off me, Mr Dobbs?

DOBBS: Five hundred nicker, Charlie.

CHARLIE: Can I have a few more days to collect the money? I'll sell my old banger.

DOBBS: Next Thursday, Charlie. I want it by then. Next Thursday's pay day.

CHARLIE: Same time and place then, Mr Dobbs.

Glazier clicked off the tape. The performance was over, but we had heard quite enough.

'Still got a lot of faith in your client, have you, Mr Rumpole?'

'Interesting recording that.' I was thinking it over. 'You can hear the clatter of plates and the crackle of crispy noodles throughout. It must have been made in the Chinese restaurant.'

'Of course it was, Mr Rumpole.' Glazier was clearly proud of his evidence. 'Got the transcript of all that, have you?'

I looked at the document Morse produced from the filing system of his overcoat pocket.

'Yes. Dobbs's answers were . . .' I read them out. ' "No one works for nothing, Charlie." "I've got the whole squad behind me. And I want to get my fingers on what you promised me. When are you coming through, Charlie?" "Five hundred nicker, Charlie." And, "Next Thursday, Charlie. Next Thursday's pay day." '

'Those are only Dobbs's answers! You forgot Charlie's

questions.' Superintendent Glazier looked at me as though he were starting to lose his faith in my legal abilities.

'Forgot dear old Charlie the grass's questions, did I?' I did my best to look innocent. 'How particularly stupid of me! Oh well. Come on, Mr Morse. Perhaps it doesn't matter after all.'

When I came home worn out from another day with the Bull, topped up by that somewhat chilling visit to Scotland Yard, I was in a mood to unburden my soul to some sympathetic companion. Imagine my bewilderment when I discovered that She Who Must Be Obeyed had apparently taken a vow of silence and entered a Trappist order. All my attempts to keep up a jolly bubble of conversation fell on very stony ground indeed.

'Had a nice day, have you, Hilda?' was my opening gambit. It got no sort of response.

'Did you buy plenty of Vim to go with the saucepan scourers? Did you treat yourself to a coffee and a couple of ginger nuts upstairs at Pontings and then take a long slow, luxurious turn round the hat department? What did you do this afternoon, Hilda? Put your feet up with the ladies' pages of the *Daily Telegraph*?' All this was greeted by a solemn silence. Perhaps I hadn't made myself heard. I raised the voice a little.

'I said, have a nice day, did you, Hilda?'

'It's all right, Rumpole. You needn't shout. I'm not deaf.' My wife spoke at last. 'Yet.'

'Good. That's marvellous news! I thought I was sending out words like troops to some hopeless battle on the Somme. Knowing they'd never return.'

The vast silence fell again.

'Well, Hilda. Aren't you going to ask me what sort of day *I* had?' She clearly wasn't, so I carried on with the monologue.

'Aren't you going to say, "Had a good day, Rumpole?" Yes, thank you, dear. A very good day. Dear old Inspector Dobbs! Apart from a marked tendency to invent verbal admissions by the villains he felt sure were guilty anyway, I always thought he was rather an honest old copper. Just the sort to send bicycling round the village to clip little boys on the ear-hole when he detected a bad case of scrumping apples. But he's been charged with all sorts of nasty practices. Accepting bribes. Corruption. Perverting the course of justice! And the interesting thing about it is, they've got it all on tape. They've recorded his very incriminating words. Question and Answer. What did you say, dear?'

There was a seemingly endless pause, but at last She gave tongue. 'If you have had such a fascinating day, Rumpole, I really don't know why you bothered to come home at all!'

All things happen if you wait for them long enough, and in due course Inspector Dobbs was called to give an account of himself in Number One Court at the Old Bailey. He stood to attention before Mr Justice Vosper, a cold-hearted Judge who was never particularly fond of rotten apples. Her Majesty, regardless of expense, had secured the service of Mr Martin Colefax, Q.C., to prosecute, and I sat containing myself as best I could whilst that aristocratic voice opened the case to the jury as though, if Dobbs were not convicted, there would be a total breakdown of law and order, rioting in the streets and human sacrifices in the crypt of St Paul's Cathedral.

'Members of the jury,' Colefax spoke with deep disapproval, 'it is fashionable nowadays to "knock" the police. Left-wingers, "do-gooders", protectors of so-called civil liberties . . .'

'Defending barristers such as my learned friend, old Rumpole of the Bailey,' I thought Colefax wanted to add that to his list of villains.

'. . . even some defending barristers.' Martin Colefax said it at last. 'All these people take every opportunity to suggest dishonesty in the police. But you may think, I'm sure you *do* think, members of the jury, that our police are quite the best in the world, and *they* are the sure protectors of our liberties.' Here, I thought the old darling was overdoing it a bit; there might be some hostile reaction. The man with the handlebar moustache top left of the jury-box looked as though he'd just been done for speeding. 'But when one policeman goes wrong. When one copper, as we say, "goes bent" . . .' I wondered if Martin Colefax really did use that sort of language, when chattering to his pals round the Sheridan Club on a Saturday night '. . . that one single bent copper can bring the entire police force into ill-deserved disrepute. That one rotten apple, members of the jury, can infect the whole barrel. He must be weeded out.'

Colefax clearly wasn't a gardener, you don't 'weed out' rotten apples. 'Weeded out,' he repeated. 'And crushed! Detective Inspector Dobbs is a rotten apple, the tape-recordings I have to play you in this case will leave no doubt about that. He was taking bribes from a habitual criminal, a man of the worst possible character, who may yet redeem himself by giving evidence for the Crown in this case . . .' I could hear the sound of distant violins as Colefax concluded, '. . . a man called Charles, or "Charlie" Pointer, whom the Crown will call, after, of course, you have heard the tape-recorded evidence.'

As Colefax concluded his opening speech, I dragged myself to my feet. 'My Lord, while the evidence is being given, I should like Mr Glazier to be outside Court.'

'But he's the officer in charge of the case!' Colefax protested.

'Precisely. I would like him out of Court *because* he's the officer in charge of the case.'

'Oh, very well. Will you leave us, officer?' Mr Justice Vosper conceded with an ill grace. Mr Glazier left the Court, giving me a brief smile to show he didn't blame me for going through the motions, but we all knew the trial could only have one result.

Later, I was cross-examining Charles, or Charlie, Pointer – a cheerful little sparrow of a man who had the decency to look somewhat ashamed as he gave evidence in support of the Old Bill.

'Charlie Pointer. Are you giving evidence for the prosecution?' I asked him, more in sorrow than in anger.

'I'm here to tell the truth, Mr Rumpole,' Charlie said modestly.

'Are you really? Did you tell the truth when you pleaded not guilty to warehouse breaking in 1974?'

'Yes.'

'And yet the jury didn't believe you, and you got convicted?'

'Maybe that's because you were defending me at the time.' There was general laughter in which the Judge was delighted to join. When he had recovered, His Lordship said, 'You asked for that, didn't you, Mr Rumpole?'

I ignored this rudeness and continued to address my questions to Charlie. 'Inspector Dobbs gave evidence against you then, didn't he?'

'So he did last year, when I got off. You did better for me that time, Mr Rumpole!' Charlie carried on with snappy back-chat and was rewarded by another flurry of laughter.

'You don't like Inspector Dobbs, do you, Charlie?' I asked him.

'I've nothing against the man. Not personally, like.'

'Nothing against him personally?'

'No.'

'In fact you became quite friendly with Inspector Dobbs, didn't you – you rang him and asked him to a Chinese dinner?'

There was a pause. Charlie looked incredulously round the Court and gave an exaggerated gasp of amazement.

'*I* asked him? *I* invited out the Old Bill? You're joking!'

'No, Charlie,' I said seriously. 'Inspector Dobbs's entire career is at stake, and his pension. I'm not joking.'

'Look, Mr Rumpole.' Charlie, it seemed, had decided to take me into his confidence. 'He came to see *me*. He said they'd charge me with the job at Fresh Foods, which I never done.'

'Oh, of course.'

'And he said they had my dabs on the frozen-food store.'

'Did you believe him – about the dabs?'

'About the *what*, Mr Rumpole?' One of Mr Justice Vosper's weaknesses is that he needs simultaneous translation in criminal cases.

'The fingerprints, my Lord,' I explained to the old darling.

'No, I didn't really. But I didn't want to face no trial about it. He said he wouldn't do me if I paid him . . .' Charlie looked accusingly at the grey-haired figure in the dock.

'Paid him five hundred nicker?' I suggested and got an explosion from the learned Judge. 'Mr Rumpole! This is intolerable! There may be members of the jury who are not as familiar as you with criminal argot. Would you kindly translate again.'

'Certainly.' I gave him the retort courteous. 'Five hundred pounds, my Lord.'

'I couldn't pay him straight away,' Charlie suggested. 'So I suggested we meet for a Chinese and talk it over like.'

'You went, wired for sound?' In the pause that followed, the jury started to look interested.

'Yes,' Charlie admitted.

'Who suggested that?'

Charlie looked around the Court as if for help. He saw no officer in charge of the case and finally his eye rested on the Judge. 'My Lord. Do I have to say?'

'Mr Rumpole has asked the question. He may not like the answer,' Mr Justice Vosper told him, so Charlie answered, 'Superintendent Glazier.'

'You see, Mr Rumpole. I did warn you that you might not like the answer.' The Judge looked down on me, pleased with himself.

'On the contrary, my Lord. I like it very much indeed!' I was delighted to disappoint him. Then I turned to Charlie. 'You reported this alleged conversation?'

'This alleged request for a bribe, Mr Rumpole,' the Judge corrected me.

'If your Lordship pleases.' I gave him a brief bow, and then went back to work on Charlie. 'You reported this alleged request for a bribe to my client's superior officer?'

'Yes.'

'So you *are* a grass, aren't you, Charlie Pointer?'

At last I had irritated Mr Justice Vosper beyond endurance. 'Mr Rumpole!' he thundered. 'Are you going to conduct this entire case in what the jury may well find to be a foreign language?'

'You *are* a police informer, aren't you, Charlie?' I asked to make my meaning clear. Charlie cast down his eyes, ashamed.

'On that occasion, I have to admit it, yes.'

'And when you went to Inspector Dobbs, and promised to tell him the name of the firm – I beg your pardon, my Lord, the gang – who did the Fresh Foods job . . .'

'I never!' Charlie sounded genuinely outraged. But I pressed on, 'Oh yes you did, Charlie. And Inspector Dobbs was going to pay you for your information. He promised you five hundred nicker, or, for the benefit of His Lordship, pounds. So that's how the sum of money got to be mentioned in the Chinese restaurant.'

'He was offering to pay *me*?' Charlie pointed to himself, grinning incredulously.

'Exactly!'

'Mr Rumpole.' The Judge appeared to think that it was time he took a hand in the proceedings. 'May I remind you that that suggestion is quite contrary to the evidence of tape-recording the jury have heard.'

'It's inconsistent with this witness's questions, my Lord. It's not in the least inconsistent with my client's answers.' I gave a reply which I hoped was enigmatic and was rewarded by seeing the Judge look totally confused.

'I'm afraid, Mr Rumpole,' he said, 'I no longer follow you.'

'Then perhaps, my Lord, we can have a little demonstration. I would just like to remind the Court of the words of the tape again. May it be played?'

A mechanically minded officer switched on the device. We heard the familiar clatter of the Chinese restaurant, and then the voices.

CHARLIE: You want another payment, Inspector?

DOBBS: No one works for nothing, Charlie.

CHARLIE: What's going to happen if I can't pay?

DOBBS: I've got the whole Squad behind me. And I want to get my fingers on what you promised. When are you coming through, Charlie?

CHARLIE: How much do you want off me, Mr Dobbs?

DOBBS: Five hundred nicker, Charlie.

CHARLIE: Can I have a few more days to collect the money? I'll sell my old banger.

DOBBS: Next Thursday, Charlie. I want it by then. Next Thursday's pay day.

I was painfully aware that the recording was having a depressing effect on the jury: there could not, they must have thought, possibly be stronger evidence of Dobbs's guilt. All the same, I was determined to press on with my little experiment.

'Charlie. We're going to play that tape again with your questions left out. Instead of them, I want you to read the list of questions the usher will hand to you. Will you do that for us?'

I gave the usher a sheet of paper which he took round to the witness-box. Charlie looked at it, gave a small, sporting shrug and said, 'I don't mind.'

'I'm sure you don't. With your new interest in assisting the course of justice. Yes. Shall we begin?' Mr Morse gave the officer the copy of the tape we had prepared with silent gaps instead of Charlie's questions. In these pauses, he read from the list I had handed him. It came out like this:

CHARLIE (*reading*): I'm going to get paid, aren't I, Inspector Dobbs?

DOBBS: No one works for nothing, Charlie.

CHARLIE (*reading*): What's going to happen if the old firm find out I'm a grass?'

DOBBS: I've got the whole Squad behind me. And I want to get my fingers on what you promised. When are you coming through, Charlie?

CHARLIE (*reading*): How much are you paying me for the info, Mr Dobbs?

DOBBS: Five hundred nicker, Charlie.

CHARLIE (*reading*): Can I have a few more days to get the gen on the Fresh Foods job? Then I'll come through with the names.

DOBBS: Next Thursday, Charlie. I want it by then. Next Thursday's pay day.'

The officer switched off the tape. The Court was silent. The jury looked at me, as though I had just lifted my wig and released a pigeon. Even the Judge had the decency to appear thoughtful.

'Very clever, Mr Rumpole,' Charlie conceded.

'Thank you, Charlie.'

'It's just not true. That's all,' Charlie began to bluster. 'That's not how it happened. I'll take my oath.'

'Mr Rumpole.' The Judge saw the consequences of my experiment. 'If what you are suggesting is correct, then someone has been guilty of falsifying this tape.'

'That is so, my Lord.' I was glad of the chance of agreeing with the old darling. 'A falsification to which this witness was clearly a party.'

'And the other party?' His Lordship asked.

'That is something, my Lord, which I hope we may be able to find out, before this trial is over.'

'I'll call Mr Glazier.'

Martin Colefax said this, quite casually, at the end of the prosecution case. The name was called outside and presently the senior officer, still in his blue suit and Rugby Club tie, marched modestly to the witness-box. Glazier lifted the New Testament in an experienced manner, and swore to tell the truth, the whole truth and nothing but the truth. As he did so, I wondered why Colefax had called him 'Mister Glazier'. I mean just '*Mister*' Glazier. Wasn't my learned friend for the prosecution rather underdoing it? Why not give the Super his full title? Why not say proudly: 'I call *Superintendent* Glazier, a most senior and experienced officer, of the Serious Crimes Squad. Step forward, *Superintendent*.' That's what I'd do. So why plain '*Mister*'?

'Mister Glazier, on the fourth of March, when this conversation in the Chinese restaurant took place, were you Inspector Dobbs's senior officer?' Colefax began his examination in chief.

'I was.'

'And as such, would you supervise Dobbs's contacts with police informers?'

'I would expect to do so, yes.'

'And would you have to authorize any proposed payment of five hundred pounds to a police informer?'

'If it was a sum of that size, yes,' Glazier agreed.

'Did Inspector Dobbs ever tell you he meant to use the man Pointer as a police informer?' There was a moment's pause, and Colefax asked again. 'Did he, Mr Glazier?'

'No, my Lord.' The officer turned respectfully to the Judge. 'He never did.'

'Or ever ask your permission to pay Pointer five hundred pounds?'

'No, my Lord.' Now Glazier answered without hesitation.

'Or any sum of money whatsoever?'

'No.'

'But Mr Rumpole, our client says he told the Super all about it.' An agitated Mr Morse was whispering into my ear in an excited manner, but I silenced him.

'Sit quiet, Morse, old darling,' I whispered back, 'and let's listen to the damning evidence of *Mr* Glazier.'

'Mr Glazier.' Colefax had done it again. 'At the end of April, did the man Pointer come to you with a complaint against Inspector Dobbs?'

'Yes, he did.'

'What was the nature of that complaint?'

'Just a moment. Do you object to that question, Mr Rumpole?' The Judge looked at me as though he was expecting an attempt to stifle the witness.

'Oh no, my Lord,' I told him cheerfully. 'I'd like to hear the full extent of the case that can be fabricated against my client.'

'Mr Rumpole.' Vosper, J., was not pleased. 'Whether or not it is fabricated is entirely a matter for the jury!'

'Exactly, my Lord!' I looked at the twelve old darlings in the jury-box with the deepest respect, and said as meaningfully as I could, 'and for no one else in this Court.'

'What was Pointer's complaint?' Colefax went back to work with the witness.

'He said that Inspector Dobbs had demanded money from him and threatened to charge him with participating in the Fresh Foods robbery if he didn't pay up.'

'So what course did you take?'

'I provided Pointer with a pocket tape-recorder and asked him to keep an appointment with Dobbs in a Chinese restaurant, my Lord.' At this Vosper, J., nodded his understanding, and made a note.

'And, as a result of that instruction, was this conversation recorded?' Colefax asked.

'*Part* of this conversation was recorded.'

'Thank you, Mr Glazier.' Colefax sat down and the Judge looked in my direction.

'Mr Rumpole. I imagine you have questions for this officer?'

'Just a few, my Lord.'

'Then I've no doubt the jury will be better equipped to understand your case after a little *rest*. Ten thirty tomorrow morning then, members of the jury.'

His Lordship rose, we stood and bowed him out with more or less respect, and then I gave my orders to the faithful Morse.

'Mr Morse. I'll have to tear you away from your tomato plants. I want you to call on my friend Fred Timson, head of the Clan Timson, biggest family of south London villains, valued clients of mine. Oh, and send someone up to see the waiters in the Swinging Bamboo, we might unearth something. Your man needn't speak Chinese, but he should be prepared to invest in a mound of sweet-and-sour lobster.'

'What do I ask Fred Timson?'

'Ask him to tell us all he knows about Charlie Pointer, and everything he's heard about *Mr* Glazier. Now Dobbs, my old darling.' The Inspector had been released from the dock and set at liberty for the night. 'Why does your Super dislike you so?' The Inspector scratched his head and mused a little.

'I can only think,' he said at last. 'Well, I did once make a complaint. It's ironic really, what I complained about . . .' This was exactly what I'd wanted to hear. I interrupted him in some excitement. 'Why didn't you say so to me before? Never mind, Dobbsy. It's not too late to tell me all about it . . .'

That evening, in front of the electric fire in Casa Rumpole, I did my best to engage my better half in conversation. 'Not a bad day, Hilda.' Silence. 'Quite an effective little trick with a tape-recorder. I think the ladies and gentlemen of the jury enjoyed it.' More silence. 'You know what we always say in Court? Listen to the questions. The questions are so much more important than the answers.' Still more silence. 'My questions, Hilda. Are more important than your answers!' Still more silence. 'Just as well, seeing that you haven't got any answers to provide.' A prolonged pause, after which I said. 'What's the matter? Are you about to enter a nunnery? Have you taken a vow to ever hold your peace? Oh please, don't even bother to tell me.'

I found it hard to sleep and was up early the next morning. By seven thirty I was having breakfast with old Morse in Rex's café opposite the Old Bailey. As he puffed his smouldering pipe tobacco over my bacon and fried slice, he gave me news which caused me to rise to cross-examine my client's superior officer with a good deal of interest and some anticipation of pleasure to come.

'*Mister* Glazier.'

'Yes, *Mister* Rumpole?' The witness looked at me, unperturbed.

'When did you first know that Charlie Pointer was a grass?'

'When he came to me and told me that your client had asked for a bribe, Mr Rumpole.' Glazier was a cool customer and I would have to be careful.

'Did that surprise you?'

'Surprise me that your client was a rotten apple? I *was* surprised, sir. And extremely upset.' The jury looked at Dobbs; it was a look of great suspicion.

'Oh, I'm so sorry. No, I meant did it surprise you that Charlie should be prepared to act as a police informer, for the first time in an honourable career as a warehouse breaker?'

'Did you say "honourable", Mr Rumpole?' Mr Justice Vosper asked in a carefully calculated tone of surprise.

'Yes, my Lord. Charlie Pointer was breaking his own code of honour when he decided to grass. That's why I suggested he didn't do so voluntarily.' I did my best to explain my meaning to His Lordship, who merely sighed and said, 'I should be interested to know just what you *are* suggesting.'

'Certainly, my Lord.' I called Glazier to provide an explanation and asked him, 'You thought Charlie was involved in the Fresh Foods job, didn't you?'

'Shall we say he was under suspicion.'

'Did you tell him his fingerprints were on the store-room door at Fresh Foods?'

'I think I may have done.' Glazier admitted that a little less readily.

'So you interviewed him, did you? Long before he told you that Inspector Dobbs was asking for a bribe?'

There was a long pause; then Glazier saw that the Judge was looking at him, waiting for an answer. He gave one at last.

'I may have done.'

'Yes, you may have done. And told him he might be involved in a serious charge?'

'Is that what Pointer has said?' Glazier looked a little confused and I blessed the day we had the officer in charge out of
Court.

'Don't you worry about what Pointer has said. You just try
to tell us the truth, Superintendent. Oh, I'm sorry . . .'

'Why are you apologizing, Mr Rumpole?' the Judge asked, and
I smiled at Mister Glazier with some sympathy. 'It's no longer
Superintendent, is it? You've been demoted.' Martin Colefax
had the grace to look slightly guilty then, and the jury were
clearly interested.

'I have been . . . re-ranked. Yes.'

'After a disciplinary hearing?'

'My Lord, has that got anything to do with this case? . . .'
Glazier tried appealing to the Judge, but I interrupted him.

'I suggest it has everything to do with this case. There was a
complaint, wasn't there, that you had failed to investigate? Was
it a little matter of an officer receiving bribes? Your superiors
took the view that you had been culpably negligent.'

'There was a complaint.' The witness agreed cautiously.

'And the prosecution have tried to conceal your demotion by
referring to you in Court as plain "Mister", and not disclosing
your new rank?'

'My Lord, I really must protest.' The elegant Colefax shim-
mered to his feet, but I motioned him to subside.

'Oh, don't bother,' I said. 'The jury know the truth about
that now. Just as they will soon learn the *whole* truth about this
case!'

'Mr Rumpole.' The Judge felt, perhaps, that he was losing
his grasp of the proceedings. 'If he was once negligent in investigating bribery, this officer has surely made up for it by
the thoroughness with which he has had your client investigated.'

'Or was my client investigated so thoroughly, *Mister* Glazier,'
I ignored the Judge and asked the witness, 'because he *wasn't*
taking bribes?'

'I don't know what you mean, Mr Rumpole.' Glazier played
for safety.

'Do you not? Let me make it clear to you. My client, Inspector
Dobbs, was a "swede", wasn't he?'

'You are saying your client's not English?' Poor old Vosper. He had the greatest difficulty in keeping up with the dialogue.

'I'm sorry. I'll interpret again, for the benefit of your Lordship. A "swede" is an old-fashioned policeman, a "turnip-head", a "vegetable", one who is honest according to his lights, and never takes bribes. Have you heard that description used by less scrupulous officers?' I asked Glazier.

'I have heard it. Yes.'

'But the "swede" was getting suspicious. Old Dobbsy was starting to smell a rat. Was it Inspector Dobbs who made the first complaint against you? Don't bother to lie, Mr Glazier, I can call for the record . . .'

'I'm not at all sure if this is relevant.' Colefax was stirring again, but I interrupted him by almost shouting at the witness, '*Will* you answer?'

'I think it was. Yes.' The words came out of Glazier like pulled teeth.

'You *think* it was! So Dobbsy had to be shut up. You put pressure on Charlie Pointer! You threatened to do him for the Fresh Foods job, which was one of those he *hadn't* done. You lied and told him you had his fingerprints on the frozen-food store, and got him to help you frame Inspector Dobbs. Oh, by the way, does the word "frame" require translation for your Lordship?'

'No thank you, Mr Rumpole. I understand it perfectly well.' At last the Judge appeared to be cooperating. I helped him to understand the rest of the case.

'Pointer offered Inspector Dobbs information and took him to the Chinese restaurant where he led him into some answers you could slot into the other tape you made later. It was careful of you to make that second tape in the same restaurant, so you could get the right background noises.'

'It's not true! I never went to that restaurant with Charlie – with Pointer. I swear that on my oath!'

It was when he talked about his oath that I knew the witness was lying, and I told him so. 'You *are* rather a careless officer, aren't you, Mr Glazier? You see, I shall be calling a Mr Wah Li Po, who remembers Charlie eating in the Swinging Bamboo with certain solid gentlemen in plain clothes, among them your good self, on a number of occasions. Perhaps Mr Wah would just step into Court, so that we can make quite sure he identifies you later.'

The next day I returned from the Old Bailey in good spirits. After a quick and refreshing glass at Pommeroy's Wine Bar I wandered into Chambers and joined our Head, Guthrie Featherstone, Mr and Mrs Claude Erskine-Brown, Uncle Tom and various barristers for one of those meetings in which we decide high and important matters of Chambers policy. As I entered the room, Guthrie noticed my cheerful appearance and asked if I'd had another triumph at the Bailey.

'A *bit* of a triumph, I suppose, Featherstone.' Well, there was no point in being modest about it. 'You see, they were looking for a rotten apple. They found the right one in the end. Ex-Superintendent Glazier'll end up in an open prison, spreading muck and slipping out to the pub on Saturdays.'

'It's the question of a rotten apple which I have to raise at this Chambers meeting,' Erskine-Brown weighed in. 'It's also a question of morality in Chambers.'

'Claude Erskine-Brown has a problem about the coffee made in the clerk's room,' Featherstone explained.

'And I have a problem about trousers,' I told the meeting.

'What on earth do you mean, Rumpole?' Our Head of Chambers wanted to be put in the picture.

'Pin-striped trousers, barristers, for the use of. What would you say if I, if anyone, charged the Commissioners of Inland Revenue for the purchase of two brand new pairs of pin-striped trousers a year, and went on sporting the same faded old bags that had been run up for us on our call to the Bar.'

'I'd say that would clearly amount to deception, and making a false return.' Featherstone pronounced judgement severely.

'I suppose we all have to live with a certain amount of deception,' I said thoughtfully. 'Gingering up the verbals or the coffee money. It can go too far though, like false tape-recordings, or profiting from non-existent trousers.'

'Horace. I'm not sure I follow.' Featherstone looked left behind.

'Never mind. Let's go on with the Chambers meeting.

Claude did you want to raise the question of coffee money?'
There was a long pause before Claude Erskine-Brown had the
decency and good sense to answer:

'No. I don't think so. On second thoughts . . . I don't think
so.'

I took a bottle of claret home to share with Hilda. I even
bought her a handful of ruinously expensive chrysanths at the
Tube station, but She still wasn't communicative, even when
I told her about my excellent win in the case of R. *v.* Dobson.

'The worst part of it all was, Hilda, that Glazier recommended
me as a barrister to poor old Dobbsy. He must've thought that I'd
got such a dislike for the police, having attacked them so often,
that I wouldn't defend a copper properly. Doesn't he know my
religious faith? A client is a client, no matter how disreputable
and unattractive his profession. You understand that, Hilda,
don't you?' Silence. 'Hilda. Would you mind telling me. *What's
eating you?*'

'Oh, very well.' She Who Must Be Obeyed spoke out at last.
'It was your answer to my question.'

'When?'

'A month ago. You were off to a conference with that policeman.'

'Inspector Dobbs?'

'Yes. You were leaving to see him. And I asked you, "Will
you come straight back this evening, Rumpole?" And you
said . . .'

'What did I say?'

'You said, "I bloody well hope not." '

I began to see a light at the end of the tunnel. Normal relations might at last be resumed with She.

'Nonsense. I said that when you asked me if I'd be late back.'

'But . . .'

'I didn't hear any other question.'

'Rumpole. Are you sure?'

'Sure? Of course I'm sure. It's the questions that are important, you see Hilda. Never the answers.'

Rumpole and the Expert Witness

> Canst thou not minister to a mind diseased,
> Pluck from the memory a rooted sorrow,
> Raze out the written troubles of the brain,
> And with some sweet oblivious antidote
> Cleanse the stuffed bosom of that perilous stuff
> Which weighs upon the heart . . .

Certainly not young Dr Ned Dacre, the popular G.P. of Hunter's Hill, that delightful little dormitory town in Surrey, where nothing is heard but the whirr of the kitchen mixers running up Provençal specialities from the Sunday supplements and the purr of the Hi Fis playing baroque music to go with the Buck's Fizz.

Ned Dacre lived in a world removed from my usual clients, the Old Bailey villains whose most common disease is a criminal conviction. He had a beautiful wife, two cars, two fair-haired children called Simon and Sara at rather nice schools, an au pair girl, an Old English sheepdog, a swimming pool, a car port and a machine for recording television programmes so that he didn't have to keep watching television. His father, Dr Henry Dacre, had settled in Hunter's Hill just after the war and had built up an excellent practice. When his son grew up and qualified he was taken into the partnership and father and son were the two most popular doctors for many miles around, the inhabitants being almost equally divided as to whether, in times of sickness, they preferred the attentions of 'Dr Harry' or 'Dr Ned'. With all these advantages it seemed that Ned Dacre had all that the heart of man could desire, except that he had an unhappy wife. One night, after they had enjoyed a quiet supper together at home, Dr Ned's wife Sally became extremely ill. As she appeared to lose consciousness, he heard her say,

'I loved you Ned . . . I really did.'

These were her last words, for although her husband rang the casualty department of the local hospital, and an ambulance was quickly dispatched, the beautiful Mrs Sally Dacre never spoke again, and died before she was taken out of the house.

I learned, as did the world, about the death of Sally Dacre and its unfortunate consequences from *The Times*. I was seated at breakfast in the matrimonial home at Froxbury Court in the Gloucester Road, looking forward without a great deal of excitement to a fairly ordinary day practising the law, ingesting Darjeeling tea, toast and Oxford marmalade, when the news item caught my eye and I gave a discreet whistle of surprise. My wife, Hilda, who was reading her correspondence (one letter on mauve paper from an old schoolfriend) wanted her share of the news.

'What's the news in *The Times*, Rumpole? Has war started?'

'A Dr Dacre has been arrested in Hunter's Hill, Surrey. He's charged with murdering his wife.'

Hilda didn't seem to find the intelligence immediately gripping. In fact she waved her correspondence at me.

'There's a letter from Dodo. You know, my friend Dodo, Rumpole?'

'The one who keeps the tea-shop in Devon?' I had a vague recollection of an unfriendly female in tweed who seemed to imagine that I tyrannized somewhat over She Who Must Be Obeyed.

'She's always asking me to pop down and stay.'

'Why don't you?' I muttered hopefully, and then returned to the Home News. ' "Dr Dacre . . .? Dacre!" The name's distinctly familiar.'

'Dodo never cared for you, Rumpole,' Hilda said firmly.

'The feeling's mutual. Isn't she the one who wears amber beads and smells of scones?' I repeated the name, hoping to stir some hidden memory, 'Harry Dacre.'

'Dodo's been suffering from depression,' Hilda rambled on. 'Of course, she never married.'

'Then I can't think what she's got to be depressed about!' I couldn't resist saying it, perhaps not quite audibly from behind the cover of *The Times*. 'Dr Harry Dacre!' I suddenly remembered. 'He gave evidence in my greatest triumph, the Penge Bungalow Murders! He'd seen my client's bruises. Don't you remember?'

'Dodo writes that she's taking a new sort of pill for her depression. They're helping her, but she mustn't eat cheese.'

'Poor old Dodo,' I said, 'deprived of cheese.' I read the story in the paper again. 'It couldn't be him. This is Dr "Ned" Dacre. Oh well, it's just another nice little murder that's never going to come my way. "Cause of death, cerebral haemorrhage", that's the evidence in the Magistrates' Court, "sustained in an alleged attack . . ." '

As I read, Hilda was casting a critical eye over my appearance. 'You're never going to Chambers like that, are you, Rumpole?'

'Like what, Hilda?' I was wondering what sort of a savage attack by a local doctor could explain his wife's cerebral haemorrhage.

'Well, your stud's showing and you've got marmalade on your waistcoat, and do you *have* to have that old silk handkerchief half falling out of your top pocket?'

'That was the silk handkerchief I used to blow my nose on three times, tearfully, in my final speech in the double murder in the Deptford Old People's Home. It has a certain sentimental value. Will you leave me alone, Hilda?' She was dabbing at my waistcoat with a corner of a table napkin she had soaked in the hot water jug.

'I just want you to look your best, Rumpole.'

'You mean, in case I get run over?'

'And I'll put that old hanky in the wash.' She snatched the venerable bandana out of my breast pocket. 'You'd be much better off with a few nice, clean tissues.'

'You know what that fellow Dacre's been accused of, Hilda?' I thought I might as well remind her. 'Murdering his wife.'

As I had no pressing engagement until two thirty, when I was due for a rather dull touch of defrauding the Customs and Excise at the Uxbridge Magistrates' Court, I loitered on my way to the Tube station, walked up through the Temple gardens smoking a small cigar, and went into the clerk's room to complain to Henry of the run-of-the-mill nature of my legal diet.

'No nice murders on the menu, are there?' When I asked him this, Henry smiled in a secretive sort of way and said,

'I'm not sure, sir.'

'You're not *sure*?'

'There's a Dr Henry Dacre phoned to come and see you urgently, sir. It seems his son's in a bit of trouble. He's come with Mr Cossett, solicitor of Hunter's Hill. I've put them in your room, Mr Rumpole.'

Old Dr Dacre in my room! I began to sniff the memory of ancient battles and a never-to-be-forgotten victory. When I opened my door, I was greeted by a healthy-looking country solicitor, and a greying version of a witness whose evidence marked a turning point in the Penge Bungalow affair. Dr Harry Dacre held out his hand and said,

'Mr Rumpole. It's been a long time, sir.'

How long, was it, perhaps a legal lifetime, since I did R. *v.* Samuel Poulteny, better known as the Penge Bungalow Murders, which altered the course of legal history by proving that Horace Rumpole could win a capital case, alone and without a leader? Young Dr Harry Dacre, then a G.P. at Penge, gave valuable evidence for the defence, and young Rumpole made the most of it. I motioned the good doctor to my client's chair and invited Mr Cossett, the instructing solicitor, to take a seat.

'Well now, Doctor,' I said, 'what can I do for you?'

'You may have read about my son's little trouble?' The old doctor spoke of the charge of wife murder as though it were a touch of the flu which might be cured by a couple of aspirin and a day in bed.

'Yes. Was it a stormy sort of marriage?' I asked him.

The doctor shook his head.

'Sally was an extraordinarily pretty girl. Terribly spoilt, of course. Ned gave her everything she wanted.'

I wondered if that included a cerebral haemorrhage, and then told myself to keep my mouth shut and listen quietly.

'She had her problems, of course,' Dr Dacre went on. 'Nervous trouble. Well. Half the women in Hunter's Hill have got a touch of the nervy. All these labour-saving devices in the kitchen, gives them too much time to think.'

Not a pioneer of women's lib., I thought, old Dr Harry. And I asked him, 'Was she taking anything for her nerves?'

'Sally was scared of pills,' the doctor shook his head. 'Afraid she might get hooked, although she didn't mind taking the odd drink too many.'

'Do you think she needed medical treatment?'

'Ned and I discussed it. He thought of a course of treatment but Sally wouldn't cooperate. So he, well, I suppose he just put up with her.' Dr Harry seemed to think that no one would have found his daughter-in-law particularly easy to live with.

'And on, as the prosecutors say, the night in question?' I decided it was time to get down to the facts.

'Mr Rumpole! That's why we need you,' Dr Harry said flatteringly enough. 'I know from past experience. You're the man who can destroy the pathologist's evidence! I'll never forget the Penge Bungalow case, and the way you pulverized that expert witness for the Crown.'

I wouldn't have minded a lengthy reminiscence of that memorable cross-examination, but I felt we should get on with the work in hand.

'Just remind me of the medical evidence. We don't disagree with the Crown about the cause of death?'

'Cerebral haemorrhage? No doubt about that. But it's the other findings that are the difficulty.'

'Which are?'

'Multiple bruising on the body, particularly the legs, back and buttocks, and the wound on the head where the deceased girl fell and knocked the edge of the coffee table.'

'Which caused the haemorrhage to the brain?' I frowned. The evidence of bruising was hardly encouraging.

'No doubt about it,' Dr Harry assured me. 'The trouble is the pathologist says the bruising was inflicted *before* death; the implication being that my son beat his wife up.'

'Is that likely?' It sounded rather unlike the home life of a young professional couple in Hunter's Hill.

'I told you Sally was a spoilt and highly strung girl, Mr Rumpole.' Dr Harry shrugged. 'Her father was old Peter Gaveston of Gaveston Electronics. She always had everything she wanted. Of course she and Ned quarrelled. Don't all married couples?'

Not all married couples, of course, include She Who Must Be Obeyed, but I had reason to believe that the good doctor was right in his diagnosis.

'But Ned would never beat his wife up like that,' Ned's father assured me. 'Not beat her up to kill her.'

It sounded as if I would have to do battle with another pathologist, and I was anxious to find out who my opponent would be.

'Tell me, who's the Miracle of the Morgues, the Prosecution Prince of the Post Mortems? Who's the great brain on the other side?'

'It's a local pathologist. Does all the work in this part of the country.'

'Would I have heard of him?' I asked casually.

'It's not a "him". It's a Dr Pamela Gorle. And the irony is, Ned knows her extremely well. They were at Barts together, before he met Sally, of course. He brought her home for the weekend once or twice, and I almost thought they might make a go of it.'

'You mean, get married?'

'Yes.' Dr Harry seemed to think that the lady with the formaldehyde might have been a better bet than Sally.

By this time I was beginning to feel some sympathy for Dr Ned. It's enough to be put on trial for murder without having your ex-girlfriend examine your deceased wife's body, and provide what turns out to be the only real evidence for the prosecution.

'I just don't understand! I simply don't understand it.'

Friendly young Dr Ned sat in the unfriendly surroundings of the prison interview room. He looked concerned but curiously detached, as though he had just hit on a mysterious tropical disease which had no known cure.

'Doctor,' I said, 'did you and your wife Sally get on moderately well together?'

'We had our quarrels, of course. Like all married couples.'

It was the second time I had heard that. But, I thought, all married couples don't end up with one dead and the other one in the nick awaiting trial on a charge of wilful murder.

I looked at Dr Ned. He was better-looking than his father had been at his age; but Dr Harry, as I remembered his appearance in the Penge Bungalow Murders trial, had seemed the stronger character and more determined. As I looked at the charming, but rather weak younger doctor (after all, he hadn't had to struggle to build up a practice, but had picked up his father's well-warmed stethoscope and married an extremely wealthy young woman) I found it hard to imagine him brutally beating his wife and so killing her. Of course I might have been mistaken; the most savage murder I was ever mixed up in was the axeing of a huge Regimental Sergeant-Major by a five-foot-nothing Sunday school teacher from East Finchley.

'Your father told me that Mrs Sally Dacre was depressed from time to time. Was she depressed about anything in particular?'

'No. In fact I always thought Sally had everything she wanted.'

'But did she suffer from depression?'

'I think so. Yes.'

'And took nothing for it?'

'She didn't approve of pills. She'd heard too many stories about people getting hooked. Doctors and their wives.'

'So she took nothing?' I wanted to get the facts established.

'My father was her doctor. I thought that was more professional. I'm not sure if he prescribed her anything, but I don't think he did. There was nothing found in the stomach.'

He said it casually and seemed only politely concerned. I don't know why I felt a sudden chill at discussing the contents of his dead wife's stomach with the doctor.

'No pills,' I agreed with him. 'The medical evidence tells us that.'

'Dr Pamela Gorle's report,' Dr Ned went on, still quite dispassionately. I fished out the document in question.

'Yes. It talks of the remains of a meal, and a good deal of alcohol in the blood.'

'We had a bottle of Chianti. And a soufflé. We were alone that night. We ate our supper in front of the television.'

'Your wife cooked?' I asked, not that there was any question of the food being anything but harmless.

'Oh no.' Dr Ned smiled at me. 'I may not be an absolutely brilliant doctor, but my soufflés are nothing short of miraculous.'

'Did you quarrel that evening?' I asked him. 'I mean, like all married couples?'

'Not at all. We had a discussion about where we'd go for our holiday, and settled on Crete. Sally had never been there, and I had only once. Before we met, actually.'

Had that been, I wondered, a romantic packaged fortnight with the pathologist for the Crown? Mine not to reason who with, so I kept him at the job of telling me the story of that last night with his wife.

'And then?'

'Then Sally complained of a headache. I thought it was perhaps due to watching the television for too long, so I switched it off. She was standing up to get herself a brandy.'

'And?'

'She stumbled and fell forwards.'

'Face *forwards*? Are you sure of that?'

'Yes, I'm certain. It was then that her forehead hit the corner of the coffee table.'

'And caused the cerebral haemorrhage?'

Dr Ned paused, frowning slightly. He seemed to be giving the matter his detached and entirely professional opinion. At last, he said cautiously,

'I can only think so.'

'Doctor, your friend, the pathologist . . .'

'Hardly my *friend* any longer.' Dr Ned smiled again, ruefully this time, as though he appreciated the irony of having an old colleague and fiancée giving evidence against him on a charge of wilful murder.

'No,' I agreed with him. 'She isn't your friend, is she? She says she found extensive bruising on your wife's back, her buttocks and the back of her legs.'

'That's what I can't understand.' My client looked genuinely puzzled.

'You're quite sure she didn't fall backwards?' I asked after a careful silence. Dr Ned and his wife were quite alone. Who would quarrel with the description of her falling backwards and bruising herself? I had given him his chance. A professional villain, any member of the Timson family for instance, would have taken that hint and agreed with me. But not Dr Ned.

'No, I told you. She fell forwards.' He was either being totally honest or wilfully obtuse.

'And you can't account for the alleged bruises on her back?'

'No.' That was all he had to say about it. But then he frowned, in some embarrassment, and said,

'There is one thing perhaps I ought to tell you.'

'About your wife?'

'No. About Dr Pamela Gorle.' Again, he hesitated. 'We were at Barts together, you know.'

'And went to Crete together once, on a packaged holiday.'

'How did you know that?' He looked at me, puzzled. It was an inspired guess, so I didn't answer his question. As I am a perpetual optimist, I asked, 'Do you think the Crown's expert witness might be a little helpful to us in the witness-box?'

'Not at all. In fact, I'm afraid she'll do everything she can to get me convicted.'

As I have said, I am an incorrigible optimist, and for the first time in my conference with Dr Ned I began to sniff the faint, far-away odour of a defence.

'Pamela was an extraordinarily possessive girl,' the doctor told me. 'She was always unreasonably and abnormally jealous.'

'When you married Sally?'

'When I met Sally. I suppose, well, after that holiday in Crete Pam thought we might get married. Then I didn't ring her and I began to get the most awful letters and phone calls from her. She was threatening . . .'

'Threatening what?'

'It was all very vague. To tell my father, or my patients, or the G.M.C., that she was pregnant.'

'Would any of those august bodies have cared?'

'Not in the least. It wasn't true anyway. Then she seemed to calm down for a while, but I still got letters – on my wedding anniversary and on some date which Pamela seemed to think was important.'

'Perhaps the day your affair started, or ended?'

'Probably. I really can't remember. She'd got her job with the Home Office, retained as a pathologist for this part of the county. I hoped she might settle down and get married, and forget.'

'She never did? Get married, I mean?'

'Or forget. I had a dreadful letter from her about a month ago. She said I'd ruined her life by marrying a hopeless drunk, and that she'd tell Sally we were still meeting unless . . .'

'Yes?' I prompted him, he seemed reluctant to go on.

'Well. Unless we still met. And continued our affair.'

'Did your wife see the letter?'

'No. I always get up early and opened the post.'

'You've kept the letter, of course?'

'No. I tore it up at once.'

If only people had the sense to realize that they might be facing a murder trial at any moment, they might keep important documents.

'And what did the letter say?'

'That she'd find some way of ruining my life, however long it took her.'

Hell, I supposed, hath no fury like a lady pathologist scorned. But Dr Pamela Gorle's personal interest in the Dacre murder seemed to provide the only faint hope of a cure for Dr Ned's somewhat desperate situation. I didn't know if a murder case had ever been won by attacking the medical evidence on the grounds of a romantic bias, but I supposed there had to be a first time for everything.

Everything about the Dacre murder trial was thoroughly pleasant. The old, red brick, local Georgian courtroom, an object of beauty among the supermarkets and boutiques and the wine bar and television and radio stores of the little Surrey town, was so damned pleasant that you expected nice girls with Roedean accents to pass round the Court serving coffee and rock cakes whenever there was a lull in the proceedings. The jury looked as though they had dropped in for a rather gentle session of 'Gardeners' Question Time', and Owen Munroe, Q.C., was a pleasant prosecutor who seemed thoroughly distressed at having to press such a nasty charge as wilful murder against the nice young doctor who sat in the dock wearing his well-pressed suit and old Barts tie.

Worst of all, Nick McManus was a tremendously pleasant judge. He was out to be thoroughly fair and show every courtesy to the defence, ploys which frequently lead to a conviction. It is amazing how many villains owe their freedom to the fact that some old sweetheart on the Bench seemed to be determined to get the jury to pot them.

We went quickly, and without argument, through the formal evidence of photographs, fingerprints and the finding of the body, and then my learned friend announced that he intended to call the pathologist.

'Will that be convenient to you, Mr Rumpole?' The Judge, as I have said, was a perfect gent.

'Certainly, my Lord. That will be quite convenient.' I made myself perfectly pleasant in return.

'I wish to make quite sure, Mr Rumpole, that you have every opportunity to prepare yourself to cross-examine the expert witness.'

You see what I mean? Old McManus was making sure I would have no alibi if I didn't succeed in cracking Dr Pamela. I'd've been far better off with someone like the mad Judge Bullingham, charging head-on at the defence. In this very pleasant trial, Rumpole would have no excuses. However, there was no help for it, so I bowed and said,

'I'm quite prepared, my Lord. Thank you.'

'Very well. Mr Munroe, as you are about to call the pathologist . . .'

'Yes, my Lord.' My opponent was on his feet.

'I suppose the jury will *have* to look at the photographs of the dead lady?'

'Yes, my Lord. It is Bundle No. 4.'

Pictures of a good-looking young woman, naked, bruised, battered and laid on a mortuary slab, are always harrowing and never helpful to the defence. McManus, J., introduced them to the jury quietly, but effectively.

'Members of the jury,' said the Judge. 'I'm afraid you will find these photographs extremely distressing. It is necessary for you to see them so you may understand the medical evidence fully, but I'm sure counsel will take the matter as shortly as possible. These things are never pleasant.'

Death isn't pleasant, nor is murder. In the nicest possible way, the Judge was pointing out the horrific nature of the crime of which Dr Ned was charged. It was something you just didn't do in that part of Surrey.

'I swear by Almighty God that the evidence I shall give shall be the truth, the whole truth and nothing but the truth.'

I was aroused from my thoughts by the sound of the pathologist taking her Bible oath. Owen Munroe hitched up his gown, sorted out his papers and started his examination in chief.

'Dr Pamela Gorle?' he asked.

'Yes.'

'Did you examine the body of the late Sally Dacre, the deceased in this case?'

'I did. Yes.'

'Just tell us what you found.'

'I found a well-nourished, healthy woman of thirty-five years of age who had died from a cerebral haemorrhage. There was evidence of a recent meal.' The demure pathologist had a voice ever gentle and low, an excellent thing in a woman, but a bit of a drawback in the witness-box. I had to strain my ears to follow her drift. And unlike the well-nourished and healthy deceased, Dr Pamela was pale and even uninteresting to look at. Her hair was thin and mousy, she wore a black suit and National Health spectacles behind which her eyes glowed with some obsession. I couldn't be sure whether it was love of her gloomy work or hatred of Dr Ned.

'You say that you found widespread bruising on the deceased's back and buttocks. What was that consistent with?'

'I thought it was consistent with a violent attack from behind. I thought Mrs Dacre had probably been struck and kicked by . . . well, it appeared that she was alone that evening with her husband.'

'I object!' I had risen to protest, but the perfect gent on the Bench was ahead of me.

'Yes, Mr Rumpole. And you are perfectly right to do so. Dr Gorle, it is not for you to say *who* beat this lady and kicked her. That is entirely a matter for the jury. That is why Mr Rumpole has quite rightly objected.'

I wished his Lordship would stop being so lethally pleasant. 'But I understand,' the Judge continued, 'that your evidence is that she was kicked and beaten – by *someone*.' McManus, J., made it clear that Sally Dacre had been attacked brutally, and the jury could have the undoubted pleasure of saying who did it.

'Yes, my Lord.'

'Kicked and beaten!' His Lordship repeated the words for good measure, and after he'd written them down and underlined them with his red pencil, Munroe wound up his examination in chief.

'The immediate cause of death was?'

'A cerebral haemorrhage, as I said!'

'Could you form any opinion as to how that came about?' Munroe asked.

'Just a moment.' McManus, J., gave me one of his charming smiles from the Bench. 'Have you any objection to her opinion, Mr Rumpole?'

'My Lord, I wouldn't seek to prevent this witness saying anything she wishes in her effort to implicate my client in his wife's tragic death.'

McManus, J., looked slightly puzzled at that, and seemed to wonder if it was an entirely gentlemanly remark. However, he only said, 'Very well. Do please answer the question, Dr Gorle.'

'My opinion, my Lord, is that the deceased had received a blow to the head in the course of the attack.'

'The attack you have already described?'

'That is so, my Lord.'

'Thank you, Dr Gorle,' said Owen Munroe, and sat down with a quietly satisfied air and left the witness to me.

I stood up, horribly conscious that the next quarter of an hour would decide the future of my client. Would Dr Ned Dacre go back to his pleasant house and practice, or was he fated to vanish into some distant prison only to emerge, pale and unemployable, after ten or more long years? If I couldn't break down the medical evidence our case was hopeless. I stood in the silent Court, shuffling the photographs and the doctor's notes, wondering whether to lead up to my charge of bias gently laying what traps I could on the way, or go in with all my guns blazing. I seemed to stand for a long time undecided, with moist hands

and a curious feeling of dread at the responsibility I had undertaken in the pit of my stomach, and then I made a decision. I
would start with my best point.

'Dr Gorle. Just help me. You knew Dr Ned Dacre well,
didn't you?'

The first question had been asked. We'd very soon find out if
it were the right one.

'We were at Barts together.' Dr Gorle showed no sign of
having been hit amidships.

'And went out together, as the saying is?' I said sweetly.

'Occasionally, yes.'

' "Going out" as so often nowadays meaning "staying in"
together?' I used a slightly louder voice, and was gratified to see
that the witness looked distinctly narked.

'What do you mean?'

'Yes. I think you should make that a little clearer, Mr Rumpole,' the Judge intervened, in the pleasantest possible way.

'You and Dr Ned Dacre went on holiday to Crete together,
didn't you? Before he was married.'

There was a distinct pause, and the doctor looked down at the
rail of the witness-box as she admitted it.

'Yes. We did.'

The dear old 'Gardeners' Question Time' fans on the jury
looked suddenly interested, as if I had revealed a new and deadly
form of potato blight. I pressed on.

'Did you become, what expression would you like me to use,
his girlfriend, paramour, mistress?'

'We shared a bed together, yes.' Now the pathologist looked
up at me, defiant.

'Presumably not for the purpose of revising your anatomy
notes together?' I got a small chuckle from the jury which increased the witness's irritation.

'He was my lover. If that's how you want to put it.'

'Thank you, Dr Gorle. I'm sure the members of the jury
understand. And I would also like the jury to understand that
you became extremely angry when Dr Ned Dacre got married.'
There was another long pause, but the answer she came up
with was moderately helpful.

'I was disappointed, yes.'

'Angry and jealous of the lady whose dead body you examined?' I suggested.

'I suppose I was naturally upset that Ned Dacre had married someone else.'

'So upset that you wrote him a letter, only a week or so before this tragedy, in which you told him you wanted to hurt him as much as you possibly could?' Now the jury were entirely hooked. I saw Munroe staring at me, no doubt wondering if I could produce the letter. The witness may have decided that I could, anyway she didn't risk an outright denial.

'I may have done.'

'You may have done!' I tried the effect of a passage of fortissimo incredulity. 'But by then Dr Ned Dacre had been married for eight years and his wife had borne him two children. And yet you were still harbouring this terrible grudge?'

She answered quickly this time, and with a great intensity.

'There are some things you don't forget, Mr Rumpole.'

'And some things you don't forgive, Dr Gorle? Has your feeling of jealousy and hatred for my client in any way coloured your evidence against him?'

Of course I expected her to deny this. During the course of cross-examination you may angle for useful admissions, hints and half-truths which can come with the cunning cast of a seemingly innocent question. But the time always comes when you must confront the witness with a clear suggestion, a final formality of assertion and denial, when the subtleties are over. I was surprised, therefore, when the lady from the morgues found it difficult to answer the question in its simplest form. There was a prolonged silence.

'Has it, Dr Gorle?' I pressed her gently for an answer.

Only Dr Gorle knew if she was biased. If she'd denied the suggestion hotly no one could have contradicted her. Instead of doing so, she finally came out with,

'I don't *think* so.' And she said it so unconvincingly that I saw the jury's disapproval. It was the first game to Rumpole, and the witness seemed to have lost her confidence when I moved on to deal with the medical evidence. Fortunately a long career as an Old Bailey hack has given me a working knowledge of the habits of dead bodies.

'Dr Gorle. After death a body becomes subject to a condition called "hypostasis"?'

'That is so. Yes.'

'The blood drains to the lowest area when circulation ceases?'

'Yes.'

'So that if the body has been lying on its back, the blood would naturally drain to the buttocks and the backs of the legs?'

'That's perfectly right,' she answered, now without hesitation.

'Did you say, Mr Rumpole's right about that?' The Judge was making a note of the cross-examination.

'Yes, my Lord.'

'Yes. Thank you, Doctor.' I paused to frame the next question carefully. 'And the draining of the blood causes discoloration of the skin of a dead body which can *look like bruising*?' I began to get an eerie feeling that it was all going too well, when the pale lady doctor admitted, again most helpfully,

'It can look exactly like bruising, yes.'

'Therefore it is difficult to tell simply by the colour of the skin if a patch is caused by "hypostasis" or bruising? It can be very misleading?'

'Yes. It can be.'

'So you must insert a knife under the skin to see what has caused the discoloration, must you not?'

'That is the standard test, yes.'

'If some blood flows, it is "hypostasis", but if the blood under the skin has coagulated and does *not* flow, it is probably a bruise?'

'What do you have to say about that, Dr Gorle?' the Judge asked the witness, and she came back with a glowing tribute to the amateur pathologist in the wig.

'I would say, my Lord, that Mr Rumpole would be well equipped to lecture on forensic medicine.'

'That test was carried out in a case called the Penge Bungalow Murders, Dr Gorle.' I disclosed the source of almost all my information, and added a flattering, 'No doubt before you were born.' I had never got on so well with a hostile witness.

'I'm afraid it was.'

'So what happened when you inserted a knife into the

coloured portions?' I had asked the question in a manner which was almost sickeningly polite, but Dr Pamela looked greatly shaken. Finally, in a voice of contrition she admitted,

'I didn't.'

'What?'

'I didn't carry out that particular test.'

'You didn't?' I tried to sound encouragingly neutral to hide my incredulity.

'No.'

'Can you tell us *why* not?' The Judge now sounded more like an advocate than the calm, detached Mr Justice Rumpole.

'I'm afraid that I must have jumped to the conclusion that they were bruises and I didn't trouble to carry out any further test, my Lord.'

'You *jumped* to the conclusion?' There was no doubt about it. The courteous McManus was deeply shocked.

'Yes.' Dr Pamela looked paler, and her voice was trembling on the edge of inaudibility.

'You know, Dr Gorle, the jury aren't going to be asked to convict Dr Dacre by "jumping to conclusions".' I blessed the old darling on the Bench when he said that, and began to see a distinct hope of returning my client to piles and prescriptions in the not-too-distant future.

'My Lord is, of course, perfectly right,' I told the witness. 'The case against Dr Ned Dacre has to be proved beyond reasonable doubt, so that the jury are *sure*. Can I take it that you're not sure there were any bruises at all?'

There was a pause and then out came the most beautiful answer.

'Not as you put it now. No. I'm not sure.'

Again I had the strange feeling that it was too easy. I felt like a toreador poised for a life-and-death struggle, seeing instead the ring doors open to admit a rather gentle and obedient cow.

'I'm not *sure* there were any bruises,' His Lordship repeated to himself as he wrote it down in his note.

'And so you're not sure Mrs Dacre was attacked by anyone?' It was a question I would normally have avoided. With this witness, it seemed, I could dare anything.

'I can't be sure. No.'

And again, the Judge wrote it down.

'So she may simply have stumbled, hit her head against the coffee table, and died of a cerebral haemorrhage?'

'It might have happened in that way. Yes.' Dr Gorle was giving it to me with jam on it.

'Stumbled because she had had too much to drink?'

The cooperative witness turned to the Judge.

'Her blood alcohol level was considerably above the breathalyser limit, yes, my Lord.'

'And you knew this family?'

'I knew about them. Yes.'

'And was it not one of your complaints that, in marrying Sally, Dr Ned had married a drunk?'

'I did say that in my letter.'

'The sort of girl who might drink too much wine, stumble against a chromium coffee table, hit her head and receive a cerebral haemorrhage, *by accident*?' It was the full frontal question, but I felt no embarrassment now in asking it. The Judge was also keen on getting an answer and he said,

'Well, Dr Gorle?'

'I must admit it might've happened that way. Yes.'

It was all over then, bar the odd bit of shouting. I said, 'Thank you very much, Dr Pamela Gorle.' And meant it. It was game, set and match to Rumpole. We had a bit of legal argument between counsel and then I was intoxicated by the delightful sensation of winning. The pleasant Judge told the jury that, in view of the concessions made by the expert witness, there really was no evidence on which they could possible convict the good doctor, and directed them to stop the case and pronounce those two words which are always music to Rumpole's ears, 'Not guilty'. We all went outin to the corridor and loyal patients came to shake Ned's hand and congratulate him as politely as if he'd just won first prize for growing the longest leek.

'Mr Rumpole. I knew you'd come up trumps, sir. I shall never forget this, never!' Old Dr Harry was pumping my hand, slapping my shoulder, and I thought I saw tears in his eyes. But then I looked across the crowd, at a door through which the expert witness, the Crown's pathologist, Dr Pamela Gorle had

just appeared. She was smiling at Dr Ned and, unless I was very
much mistaken, he was smiling back. Was it only a smile, or did
I detect the tremble of a wink? I left his father and went up to
the young doctor. He smiled his undying gratitude.

'Mr Rumpole. Dad was right. You're the best!' Dr Ned was
kind enough to say.

'Nonsense. It was easy.' I looked at him and said, 'Too easy.'

'Why do you say that?' Dr Ned looked genuinely puzzled.

I didn't answer him. Instead, I asked a question.

'I was meaning to ask you this before, Doctor. I don't suppose it matters now, but I'd like to know the answer, for my own
satisfaction. What sort of soufflé was it you cooked for your
wife that evening?' He might have lied, but I don't suppose he
thought there was any point in it. Instead he answered as if he
enjoyed telling the truth.

'Cheese.'

I was at breakfast with She Who Must Be Obeyed a few days
later, after I had managed to spring the charming young doctor,
and my wife was brandishing another mauve letter from her
friend Dorothy or 'Dodo', the nervous tea-shop owner from the
West Country.

'Another letter from Dodo! She's really feeling much better.
So much more calm!'

'She's been taking these new pills, didn't you say?'

'Yes, I think that's what it must be.'

I remembered about a drug Dr Ned was discussing with his
father for possible use on his nervous wife. Was it the same
drug that was keeping Dodo off cheese?

'Then Dodo will be feeling better. So long as she doesn't eat
cheese. If she eats cheese when she's on some sort of tranquillizer
she's likely to go the way of the doctor's beautiful wife, and end
up with a haemorrhage of the brain.'

I had a letter too. An invitation to a cocktail party in Hunter's
Hill. Dr Ned Dacre, it seemed, felt that he had something to
celebrate.

'Mr Rumpole! I'm so glad you could come.' Dr Ned greeted
me enthusiastically.

I looked round the pleasant room, at the pleasant faces of grateful patients and the two thoroughly nice children handing round canapés. I noticed the Queen of the Morgues, Dr Pamela Gorle, dressed up to the nines, and then I looked at the nice young doctor who was now pouring me out a generous Buck's Fizz made, regardless of the expense, with the best Krug. I spoke to him quietly.

'You got off, of course. They can't try you again for the same murder. That was the arrangement, wasn't it?'

'What "arrangement"?' The young doctor was still smiling in a welcoming sort of way.

'Oh, the arrangement between you and the Crown pathologist, of course. The plan that she'd make some rather silly suggestions about bruises and admit she was wrong. Of course, she lied about the contents of the stomach. You're a very careful young man, Dr Ned. Now they can never try you for what you really did.'

'You're joking!' But I saw that he had stopped smiling.

'I was never more serious in my life.'

'What did I really do?' We seemed to be alone. A little whispering oasis of doubt and suspicion in the middle of the happy, chattering cocktail party. I told him what he'd done.

'You opened a few of those new tranquillizer capsules and poured them into your wife's Chianti. The cheese in the soufflé reacted in just the way you'd planned. All you had to do was make sure she hit her head on the table.'

We stood in silence. The children came up and we refused canapés. Then Dr Ned opened an alabaster box and lit a cigarette with a gold lighter.

'What're you going to do about it?' I could see that he was smiling again.

'Nothing I can do now. You know that,' I told him. 'Except to tell you that I know. I'm not quite the idiot you and Dr Pamela took me for. As least you know that, Dr Ned.'

He was a murderer. Divorce would have given him freedom but not his rich wife's money; so he became a simple, old-fashioned murderer. And what was almost worse, he had used me as part of his crime. Worst of all, he had done his best to spoil the golden memory of the Penge Bungalow Murders for me.

'Quiet everyone! I think Ned's got something to say!' Old Dr Harry Dacre was banging on a table with his glass. In due course quiet settled on the party and young Dr Ned made his announcement.

'I just wanted to say. Now all our friends are here. Under one roof. That of course no one can ever replace Sally. For me and the children. But with Simon and Sara's approval . . .' He smiled at his charming children. 'There's going to be another doctor in the Dacre family. Pamela's agreed to become my wife.'

In the ensuing clapping, kisses, congratulations and mixing of more Buck's Fizz, Rumpole left the party.

I hear it was a thoroughly nice wedding. I looked hard at the photograph in the paper and tried to detect, in that open and smiling young doctor's face, a sign of guilt.

> '. . . that perilous stuff
> Which weighs upon the heart.'

I saw none.

Rumpole and the Spirit of Christmas

I realized that Christmas was upon us when I saw a sprig of holly over the list of prisoners hung on the wall of the cells under the Old Bailey.

I pulled out a new box of small cigars and found its opening obstructed by a tinselled band on which a scarlet-faced Santa was seen hurrying a sleigh full of carcinoma-packed goodies to the Rejoicing World. I lit one as the lethargic screw, with a complexion the colour of faded Bronco, regretfully left his doorstep sandwich and mug of sweet tea to unlock the gate.

'Good morning, Mr Rumpole. Come to visit a customer?'

'Happy Christmas, officer,' I said as cheerfully as possible. 'Is Mr Timson at home?'

'Well, I don't believe he's slipped down to his little place in the country.'

Such were the pleasantries that were exchanged between us legal hacks and discontented screws; jokes that no doubt have changed little since the turnkeys locked the door at Newgate to let in a pessimistic advocate, or the cells under the Coliseum were opened to admit the unwelcome news of the Imperial thumbs-down.

'My Mum wants me home for Christmas.'

'Which Christmas?' It would have been an unreasonable remark and I refrained from it. Instead, I said, 'All things are possible.'

As I sat in the interviewing room, an Old Bailey hack of some considerable experience, looking through my brief and inadvertently using my waistcoat as an ashtray, I hoped I wasn't on another loser. I had had a run of bad luck during that autumn season, and young Edward Timson was part of that huge south London family whose criminal activities provided such welcome grist to the Rumpole mill. The charge in the seventeen-year-old Eddie's case was nothing less than wilful murder.

'We're in with a chance though, Mr Rumpole, ain't we?'

Like all his family, young Timson was a confirmed optimist. And yet, of course, the merest outsider in the Grand National, the hundred-to-one shot, is in with a chance, and nothing is more like going round the course at Aintree than living through a murder trial. In this particular case, a fanatical prosecutor named Wrigglesworth, known to me as the Mad Monk, was to represent Beechers and Mr Justice Vosper, a bright but wintry-hearted Judge who always felt it his duty to lead for the prosecution, was to play the part of a particularly menacing fence at the Canal Turn.

'A chance. Well, yes, of course you've got a chance, if they can't establish common purpose, and no one knows which of you bright lads had the weapon.'

No doubt the time had come for a brief glance at the prosecution case, not an entirely cheering prospect. Eddie, also known as 'Turpin' Timson, lived in a kind of decaying barracks, a sort of high-rise Lubianka, known as Keir Hardie Court, somewhere in south London, together with his parents, his various brothers and his thirteen-year-old sister, Noreen. This particular branch of the Timson family lived on the thirteenth floor. Below them, on the twelfth, lived the large clan of the O'Dowds. The war between the Timsons and the O'Dowds began, it seems, with the casting of the Nativity play at the local comprehensive school.

Christmas comes earlier each year and the school show was planned about September. When Bridget O'Dowd was chosen to play the lead in the face of strong competition from Noreen Timson, an incident occurred comparable in historical importance to the assassination of an obscure Austrian archduke at Sarajevo. Noreen Timson announced, in the playground, that Bridget O'Dowd was a spotty little tart quite unsuited to play any role of which the most notable characteristic was virginity.

Hearing this, Bridget O'Dowd kicked Noreen Timson behind the anthracite bunkers. Within a few days war was declared between the Timson and O'Dowd children, and a present of lit fireworks was posted through the O'Dowd front door. On what is known as the 'night in question', reinforcements of O'Dowds and Timsons arrived in old bangers from a number of south London addresses and battle was joined on the stone staircase, a bleak terrain of peeling walls scrawled with graffiti, blowing empty Coca-Cola tins and torn newspapers. The weapons seemed to have been articles in general domestic use such as bread knives, carving knives, broom handles and a heavy screwdriver.

At the end of the day it appeared that the upstairs flat had repelled the invaders, and Kevin O'Dowd lay on the stairs. Having been stabbed with a slender and pointed blade he was in a condition to become known as the 'deceased' in the case of the Queen against Edward Timson. I made an application for bail for my client which was refused, but a speedy trial was ordered.

So even as Bridget O'Dowd was giving her Virgin Mary at the comprehensive, the rest of the family was waiting to give evidence against Eddie Timson in that home of British drama, Number One Court at the Old Bailey.

'I never had no cutter, Mr Rumpole. Straight up, I never had one,' the defendant told me in the cells. He was an appealing-looking lad with soft brown eyes, who had already won the heart of the highly susceptible lady who wrote his social inquiry report. ('Although the charge is a serious one this is a young man who might respond well to a period of probation.' I could imagine the steely contempt in Mr Justice Vosper's eye when he read that.)

'Well, tell me, Edward. Who had?'

'I never seen no cutters on no one, honest I didn't. We wasn't none of us tooled up, Mr Rumpole.'

'Come on, Eddie. Someone must have been. They say even young Noreen was brandishing a potato peeler.'

'Not me, honest.'

'What about your sword?'

There was one part of the prosecution evidence that I found particularly distasteful. It was agreed that on the previous Sunday morning, Eddie 'Turpin' Timson had appeared on the stairs of Keir Hardie Court and flourished what appeared to be an antique cavalry sabre at the assembled O'Dowds, who were just popping out to Mass.

'Me sword I bought up the Portobello? I didn't have that there, honest.'

'The prosecution can't introduce evidence about the sword. It was an entirely different occasion.' Mr Barnard, my instructing solicitor who fancied himself as an infallible lawyer, spoke with a confidence which I couldn't feel. He, after all, wouldn't have to stand up on his hind legs and argue the legal toss with Mr Justice Vosper.

'It rather depends on who's prosecuting us. I mean, if it's some fairly reasonable fellow . . .'

'I think,' Mr Barnard reminded me, shattering my faint optimism and ensuring that we were all in for a very rough Christmas indeed, 'I think it's Mr Wrigglesworth. Will he try to introduce the sword?'

I looked at 'Turpin' Timson with a kind of pity. 'If it is the Mad Monk, he undoubtedly will.'

When I went into Court, Basil Wrigglesworth was standing with his shoulders hunched up round his large, red ears, his gown dropped to his elbows, his bony wrists protruding from the sleeves of his frayed jacket, his wig pushed back and his huge hands joined on his lectern in what seemed to be an attitude of devoted prayer. A lump of cotton wool clung to his chin where he had cut himself shaving. Although well into his sixties he preserved a look of boyish clumsiness. He appeared, as he always did when about to prosecute on a charge carrying a major punishment, radiantly happy.

'Ah, Rumpole,' he said, lifting his eyes from the police verbals as though they were his breviary. 'Are you defending *as usual*?'

'Yes, Wrigglesworth. And you're prosecuting *as usual*?' It wasn't much of a riposte but it was all I could think of at the time.

'Of course, I don't defend. One doesn't like to call witnesses who may not be telling the truth.'

'You must have a few unhappy moments then, calling certain members of the Constabulary.'

'I can honestly tell you, Rumpole,' his curiously innocent blue eyes looked at me with a sort of pain, as though I had questioned the doctrine of the immaculate conception, 'I have never called a dishonest policeman.'

'Yours must be a singularly simple faith, Wrigglesworth.'

'As for the Detective Inspector in this case,' counsel for the prosecution went on, 'I've known Wainwright for years. In fact, this is his last trial before he retires. He could no more invent a verbal against a defendant than fly.'

Any more on that tack, I thought, and we should soon be debating how many angels could dance on the point of a pin.

'Look here, Wrigglesworth. That evidence about my client having a sword: it's quite irrelevant. I'm sure you'd agree.'

'Why is it irrelevant?' Wrigglesworth frowned.

'Because the murder clearly wasn't done with an antique cavalry sabre. It was done with a small, thin blade.'

'If he's a man who carries weapons, why isn't that relevant?'

'A man? Why do you call him a man? He's a child. A boy of seventeen!'

'Man enough to commit a serious crime.'

'*If* he did.'

'If he didn't, he'd hardly be in the dock.'

'That's the difference between us, Wrigglesworth,' I told him. 'I believe in the presumption of innocence. You believe in original sin. Look here, old darling.' I tried to give the Mad Monk a smile of friendship and became conscious of the fact that it looked, no doubt, like an ingratiating sneer. 'Give us a chance. You won't introduce the evidence of the sword, will you?'

'Why ever not?'

'Well,' I told him, 'the Timsons are an industrious family of criminals. They work hard, they never go on strike. If it weren't for people like the Timsons, you and I would be out of a job.'

'They sound in great need of prosecution and punishment. Why shouldn't I tell the jury about your client's sword? Can you give me one good reason?'

'Yes,' I said, as convincingly as possible.

'What is it?' He peered at me, I thought, unfairly.

'Well, after all,' I said, doing my best, 'it is Christmas.'

It would be idle to pretend that the first day in Court went well, although Wrigglesworth restrained himself from mentioning the sword in his opening speech, and told me that he was considering whether or not to call evidence about it the next day. I cross-examined a few members of the clan O'Dowd on the presence of lethal articles in the hands of the attacking force. The evidence about this varied and weapons came and went in the hands of the inhabitants of number twelve as the witnesses were blown hither and thither in the winds of Rumpole's cross-examination. An interested observer from one of the other flats spoke of having seen a machete.

'Could that terrible weapon have been in the hands of Mr Kevin O'Dowd, the deceased in this case?'

'I don't think so.'

'But can you rule out the possibility?'

'No, I can't rule it out,' the witness admitted, to my temporary delight.

'You can never rule out the possibility of anything in this world, Mr Rumpole. But he doesn't think so. You have your answer.'

Mr Justice Vosper, in a voice like a splintering iceberg, gave me this unwelcome Christmas present. The case wasn't going well but at least, by the end of the first day, the Mad Monk had kept out all mention of the sword. The next day he was to call young Bridget O'Dowd, fresh from her triumph in the Nativity play.

'I say, Rumpole. I'd be *so* grateful for a little help.'

I was in Pommeroy's Wine Bar, drowning the sorrows of the day in my usual bottle of the cheapest Château Fleet Street (made from grapes which, judging from the bouquet, might have been not so much trodden as kicked to death by sturdy peasants in gum boots) when I looked up to see Wrigglesworth, dressed in an old mackintosh, doing business with Jack Pommeroy at the sales counter. When I crossed to him, he was not buying the jumbo-sized bottle of ginger beer which I imagined might be his celebratory Christmas tipple, but a tempting and respectably aged bottle of Château Pichon Longueville.

'What can I do for you, Wrigglesworth?'

'Well, as you know, Rumpole, I live in Croydon.'

'Happiness is given to few of us on this earth,' I said piously.

'And the Anglican Sisters of St Agnes, Croydon, are anxious to buy a present for their Bishop,' Wrigglesworth explained. 'A dozen bottles for Christmas. They've asked my advice, Rumpole. I know so little of wine. You wouldn't care to try this for me? I mean, if you're not especially busy.'

'I should be hurrying home to dinner.' My wife, Hilda (She Who Must Be Obeyed), was laying on rissoles and frozen peas, washed down by my last bottle of Pommeroy's extremely ordinary. 'However, as it's Christmas, I don't mind helping you out, Wrigglesworth.'

The Mad Monk was clearly quite unused to wine. As we sampled the claret together, I saw the chance of getting him to commit himself on the vital question of the evidence of the sword, as well as absorbing an unusually decent bottle. After the Pichon Longueville I was kind enough to help him by sampling a Boyd-Cantenac and then I said, 'Excellent, this. But of course the Bishop might be a Burgundy man. The nuns might care to invest in a decent Mâcon.'

'Shall we try a bottle?' Wrigglesworth suggested. 'I'd be grateful for your advice.'

'I'll do my best to help you, my old darling. And while we're on the subject, that ridiculous bit of evidence about young Timson and the sword . . .'

'I remember you saying I shouldn't bring that out because it's Christmas.'

'Exactly.' Jack Pommeroy had uncorked the Mâcon and it was mingling with the claret to produce a feeling of peace and goodwill towards men. Wrigglesworth frowned, as though trying to absorb an obscure point of theology.

'I don't quite see the relevance of Christmas to the question of your man Timson threatening his neighbours with a sword . . .'

'Surely, Wrigglesworth,' I knew my prosecutor well, 'you're of a religious disposition?' The Mad Monk was the product of some bleak northern Catholic boarding school. He lived alone,

and no doubt wore a hair shirt under his black waistcoat and
was vowed to celibacy. The fact that he had his nose deep into
a glass of Burgundy at the moment was due to the benign influence of Rumpole.

'I'm a Christian, yes.'

'Then practise a little Christian tolerance.'

'Tolerance towards evil?'

'Evil?' I asked. 'What do you mean, evil?'

'Couldn't that be your trouble, Rumpole? That you really
don't recognize evil when you see it.'

'I suppose,' I said, 'evil might be locking up a seventeen-year-
old during Her Majesty's pleasure, when Her Majesty may very
probably forget all about him, banging him up with a couple
of hard and violent cases and their own chamber-pots for twenty-
two hours a day, so he won't come out till he's a real, genuine,
middle-aged murderer . . .'

'I did hear the Reverend Mother say,' Wrigglesworth was
gazing vacantly at the empty Mâcon bottle, 'that the Bishop
likes his glass of port.'

'Then in the spirit of Christmas tolerance I'll help you to
sample some of Pommeroy's Light and Tawny.'

A little later, Wrigglesworth held up his port glass in a reverent
sort of fashion.

'You're suggesting, are you, that I should make some special
concession in this case because it's Christmas time?'

'Look here, old darling.' I absorbed half my glass, relishing
the gentle fruitiness and the slight tang of wood. 'If you spent
your whole life in that high-rise hell-hole called Keir Hardie
Court, if you had no fat prosecutions to occupy your attention
and no prospect of any job at all, if you had no sort of occupation
except war with the O'Dowds . . .'

'My own flat isn't particularly comfortable. I don't know a
great deal about *your* home life, Rumpole, but you don't seem
to be in a tearing hurry to experience it.'

'Touché, Wrigglesworth, my old darling.' I ordered us a
couple of refills of Pommeroy's port to further postpone the
encounter with She Who Must Be Obeyed and her rissoles.

'But we don't have to fight to the death on the staircase,'
Wrigglesworth pointed out.

'We don't have to fight at all, Wrigglesworth.'

'As your client did.'

'As my client *may* have done. Remember the presumption of innocence.'

'This is rather funny, this is.' The prosecutor pulled back his lips to reveal strong, yellowish teeth and laughed appreciatively. 'You know why your man Timson is called "Turpin"?'

'No.' I drank port uneasily, fearing an unwelcome revelation.

'Because he's always fighting with that sword of his. He's called after Dick Turpin, you see, who's always duelling on the television. Do you watch the television, Rumpole?'

'Hardly at all.'

'I watch a great deal of the television, as I'm alone rather a lot.' Wrigglesworth referred to the box as though it were a sort of penance, like fasting or flagellation. 'Detective Inspector Wainwright told me about your client. Rather amusing, I thought it was. He's retiring this Christmas.'

'My client?'

'No. D.I. Wainwright. Do you think we should settle on this port for the Bishop? Or would you like to try a glass of something else?'

'Christmas,' I told Wrigglesworth severely as we sampled the Cockburn, 'is not just a material, pagan celebration. It's not just an occasion for absorbing superior vintages, old darling. It must be a time when you try to do good, spiritual good to our enemies.'

'To your client, you mean?'

'And to me.'

'To you, Rumpole?'

'For God's sake, Wrigglesworth!' I was conscious of the fact that my appeal was growing desperate. 'I've had six losers in a row down the Old Bailey. Can't I be included in any Christmas spirit that's going around?'

'You mean, at Christmas especially it is more blessed to give than to receive?'

'I mean exactly that.' I was glad that he seemed, at last, to be following my drift.

'And you think I might give this case to someone, like a Christmas present?'

'If you care to put it that way, yes.'

'I do not care to put it in *exactly* that way.' He turned his pale blue eyes on me with what I thought was genuine sympathy. 'But I shall try and do the case of R. *v.* Timson in the way most appropriate to the greatest feast of the Christian year. It is a time, I quite agree, for the giving of presents.'

When they finally threw us out of Pommeroy's, and after we had considered the possibility of buying the Bishop brandy in the Cock Tavern, and even beer in the Devereux, I let my instinct, like an aged horse, carry me on to the Underground and home to Gloucester Road, and there discovered the rissoles, like some traces of a vanished civilization, fossilized in the oven. She Who Must Be Obeyed was already in bed, feigning sleep. When I climbed in beside her she opened a hostile eye.

'You're drunk, Rumpole!' she said. 'What on earth have you been doing?'

'I've been having a legal discussion,' I told her, 'on the subject of the admissibility of certain evidence. Vital, from my client's point of view. And, just for a change, Hilda, I think I've won.'

'Well, you'd better try and get some sleep.' And she added with a sort of satisfaction, 'I'm sure you'll be feeling quite terrible in the morning.'

As with all the grimmer predictions of She Who Must Be Obeyed this one turned out to be true. I sat in Court the next day with the wig feeling like a lead weight on the brain, and the stiff collar sawing the neck like a blunt execution. My mouth tasted of matured birdcage and from a long way off I heard Wrigglesworth say to Bridget O'Dowd, who stood looking particularly saintly and virginal in the witness-box, 'About a week before this did you see the defendant, Edward Timson, on your staircase flourishing any sort of weapon?'

It is no exaggeration to say that I felt deeply shocked and considerably betrayed. After his promise to me, Wrigglesworth had turned his back on the spirit of the great Christmas festival. He came not to bring peace but a sword.

I clambered with some difficulty to my feet. After my forensic efforts of the evening before, I was scarcely in the mood for a legal argument. Mr Justice Vosper looked up in surprise and greeted me in his usual chilly fashion.

'Yes, Mr Rumpole. Do you object to this evidence?'

Of course I object, I wanted to say. It's inhuman, unnecessary, unmerciful and likely to lead to my losing another case. Also, it's clearly contrary to a solemn and binding contract entered into after a number of glasses of the Bishop's putative port. All I seemed to manage was a strangled, 'Yes.'

'I suppose Mr Wrigglesworth would say,' Vosper, J., was, as ever, anxious to supply any argument that might not yet have occurred to the prosecution, 'that it is evidence of "system".'

'System?' I heard my voice faintly and from a long way off. 'It may be, I suppose. But the Court has a discretion to omit evidence which may be irrelevant and purely prejudicial.'

'I feel sure Mr Wrigglesworth has considered the matter most carefully and that he would not lead this evidence unless he considered it entirely relevant.'

I looked at the Mad Monk on the seat beside me. He was smiling at me with a mixture of hearty cheerfulness and supreme pity, as though I were sinking rapidly and he had come to administer supreme unction. I made a few ill-chosen remarks to the Court, but I was in no condition, that morning, to enter into a complicated legal argument on the admissibility of evidence.

It wasn't long before Bridget O'Dowd had told a deeply disapproving jury all about Eddie 'Turpin' Timson's sword. 'A man,' the Judge said later in his summing up about young Edward, 'clearly prepared to attack with cold steel whenever it suited him.'

When the trial was over, I called in for refreshment at my favourite watering hole and there, to my surprise, was my opponent Wrigglesworth, sharing an expensive-looking bottle with Detective Inspector Wainwright, the officer in charge of the case. I stood at the bar, absorbing a consoling glass of Pommeroy's ordinary, when the D.I. came up to the bar for cigarettes. He gave me a friendly and maddeningly sympathetic smile.

'Sorry about that, sir. Still, win a few, lose a few. Isn't that it?'

'In my case lately, it's been win a few, lose a lot!'

'You couldn't have this one, sir. You see, Mr Wrigglesworth had promised it to me.'

'He had *what*?'

'Well, I'm retiring, as you know. And Mr Wrigglesworth promised me faithfully that my last case would be a win. He promised me that, in a manner of speaking, as a Christmas present. Great man is our Mr Wrigglesworth, sir, for the spirit of Christmas.'

I looked across at the Mad Monk and a terrible suspicion entered my head. What was all that about a present for the Bishop? I searched my memory and I could find no trace of our having, in fact, bought wine for any sort of cleric. And was Wrigglesworth as inexperienced as he would have had me believe in the art of selecting claret?

As I watched him pour and sniff a glass from his superior bottle, and hold it critically to the light, a horrible suspicion crossed my mind. Had the whole evening's events been nothing but a deception, a sinister attempt to nobble Rumpole, to present him with such a stupendous hangover that he would stumble in his legal argument? Was it all in aid of D.I. Wainwright's Christmas present?

I looked at Wrigglesworth, and it would be no exaggeration to say the mind boggled. He was, of course, perfectly right about me. I just didn't recognize evil when I saw it.

Rumpole and the Boat People

'You'll have to do it, Rumpole. You'll be a different man.'

I considered the possibilities. I was far from satisfied, naturally, with the man I was, but I had grown, over the years, used to his ways. I knew his taste in claret, his rate of consumption of small cigars, and I had grown to have some respect for his mastery of the art of cross-examination. Difficult, almost impossible, as he was to live with on occasions, I thought we could manage to rub along together for our few remaining years.

'A different man, did you say?'

Dr MacClintock, the slow-speaking, Edinburgh-bred quack to whom my wife, Hilda turns in times of sickness, took a generous gulp of the sherry she always pours him when he visits our mansion flat, (It's lucky that all his N.H.S. patients aren't so generous or the sick of Gloucester Road would be tended by a reeling medico, yellow about the gills and sloshed on amontillado.) Then he said,

'If you follow my simple instructions, Rumpole, you'll become a different man entirely.'

Being Horace Rumpole in his sixties, still slogging round the Old Bailey with sore feet, a modest daily hangover and an aching back was certainly no great shakes, but who else could I be? I considered the possibilities of becoming Guthrie Featherstone, Q.C., M.P., our learned Head of Chambers, or Claude Erskine-Brown, or Uncle Tom, or even Dr MacClintock, and retreated rapidly into the familiar flesh.

'All you have to do, old man, is lose two or three stone,' the doctor told me.

' "Old man"? ' I looked closely at the sherry-swilling sawbones and saw no chicken.

'Just two or three stone, Rumpole. That's all you have to

lose.' Hilda was warming to her latest theme, that there was too much Rumpole.

'It's a very simple diet, perfectly simple. I've got it printed here.' Dr MacClintock produced a card with the deftness of a conjurer. The trick was known as the vanishing Rumpole, and the rapid materialization of a thinner and more eager barrister.

'No fat, of course.' The doctor repeated the oath on the card. 'Because it makes *you* fat. No meat, too rich in protein. No bread or potatoes, too many calories. No pastries, puddings, sweetmeats or sugar. No biscuits. No salt on the food. Steer clear of cheese. I don't recommend fruit to my patients because of its acid qualities. Eggs are perfectly all right if hard-boiled. Not too many though, or you won't do your business.'

'My business in the courts?' I didn't follow.

'No. Your business in the lavatory.'

'Didn't you say,' Hilda put in encouragingly, 'that Rumpole could eat spinach?'

'Oh yes. As much spinach as he likes. And brown rice for roughage. Now you could manage a diet like that, couldn't you, Rumpole? Otherwise I can't be responsible for your heart.'

'I suppose I might manage it for a while.' The Rumpole ticker, I knew, had come to resent the pressure put on it during a number of hard-fought battles in front of the mad Judge Bullingham down the Bailey. 'Of course, it'd have to be washed down by a good deal of claret. Château-bottled. I could afford that with all this saving on pastries and puddings.'

'Oh, good heavens!' The quack held his sherry glass out for a refill. 'No alcohol!'

'You're asking me to give up claret?'

'No alcohol of any sort!'

'Certainly not, Rumpole.' Hilda was determined.

'But you might as well ask me to give up breathing.'

'It'll come quite easily to you, after a couple of days.'

'I suppose when you've been dead a couple of days you find it quite easy to give up breathing.'

'It's you that mentioned death, Rumpole.' The doctor smiled at me tolerantly. 'I haven't said a word about it. Now why not get your wife to take you away for a holiday? You could spare a couple of weeks at the seaside, surely? It's always easier to give things up when you're on holiday.'

Brown rice, spinach and a holiday were not an appetizing combination, but Hilda seemed delighted at the prospect.

'We could go down to Shenstone, Doctor. I've always wanted to go to Shenstone-on-Sea. My old friend Jackie Bateman, you know I've told you, Rumpole, Jackie Hopkins as was, we were at school together, runs a little business at Shenstone with her husband. Jackie's always writing begging me to come down to Shenstone. Apparently it's a dear little place and extremely quiet.'

'My partner, Dr Entwhistle keeps his boat at Shenstone.' Dr MacClintock seemed to think this fact might lend some glamour to the hole. 'It's quite a place for the boating community.'

'I don't boat,' I said gloomily.

'Better not, Rumpole,' the doctor was actually laughing. 'Better not take out a small dinghy. You might sink it! Shenstone sounds just the place for you to get a bit of rest. Pick a small hotel. A *temperance* hotel. That's all you'll be needing.'

That night, Hilda booked us in to the Fairview Private Hotel in Shenstone-on-Sea, and wrote off to Mrs Bateman, the former Miss Jackie Hopkins, announcing the glad tidings. I viewed the approaching visit with some dismay, tempered by the knowledge that it did seem to be becoming a minor Everest expedition for me to mount the shortest staircase. My bones ached, my head seemed stuffed with cotton wool and buttons were flying off me like bullets at the smallest unexpected move. Perhaps desperate measures were called for and a holiday *would* do me good. We set out for Shenstone armed with umbrellas, mackintoshes, heavy pullovers and, in my case, the *Complete Sherlock Holmes Stories*, Marjoribanks's *Life of Sir Edward Marshall Hall* and *The Oxford Book of English Verse* (I make it a rule not to read anything I haven't read before, except for *The Times* and briefs). We launched ourselves into the unknown as, up to the time of our departure, Mrs Jackie Bateman hadn't been heard from.

Shenstone-on-Sea, in the county of Norfolk, was to be seen, like most English pleasure resorts, through a fine haze of perpetual rain. However, the main feature of Shenstone-on-Sea

was undoubtedly the wind. It blew straight at you from the
Ural mountains, crossing some very icy steppes, parky portions
of Poland, draughty country round Dortmund and the flats of
Holland, on the way. In this cruel climate the inhabitants gathered, stowing spinnakers and splicing ropes with bluish
fingers, the wind blowing out their oilskins tight as a trumpeter's
cheeks and almost doffing their bobble hats. For Shenstone-on-
Sea was, as my Scottish medical man had said, quite the place
for the boat community.

Apart from watching the daily armada of small boats set out,
there was little or nothing to do at Shenstone. Hilda and I sat
in the residents' lounge at the Fairview Hotel, and I read or did
the crossword while she knitted or wrote postcards to other old
schoolfriends and we listened to the rain driven across the windows by the prevailing wind. On our arrival we telephoned
Jackie Bateman and got no reply. Then we called on her at the
address Hilda had, which turned out to be a shop on the harbour
called Father Neptune's Boutique, a place for the sale of bobble
hats, seamen's sweaters, yellow gum boots, tea mugs with the
words 'Galley Slave' written on them and such-like nautical
equipment. The Batemans, according to Hilda, owned this
business and had a flat above the shop. We called, as I have said,
but found the place silent and locked up, and got no answer
when we rattled the door handle.

Hilda wrote a note for her elusive schoolfriend, and put it
through the door. We were standing looking helplessly at the
silent shop, when someone spoke to us.

'She's moved. Gone away.'

A tallish, thin person clad in a Balaclava helmet and a belted
mackintosh, and sporting a large pair of field-glasses, came by
pushing a gaunt bicycle.

'Mrs Bateman's not here?' Hilda seemed slow to absorb the
information.

'I tell you. She moved away. After it happened. Well. They
reckoned she couldn't abide the place after that.'

'After what?' Hilda hadn't heard from Jackie Bateman since,
she now remembered, the previous Christmas, and seemed not
have been kept *au courant* with the major developments in her
friend's life.

'Why, after the accident. When her husband got drowned. Hadn't you heard?'

'No, we hadn't. Oh dear.' Hilda looked surprised and shocked. 'What a terrible thing.'

The tall man pushed his bicycle away from us and we were left staring through the rain at the harbour where the frail boats were again putting out full of those, it now seemed, in considerable peril on the sea.

That night I was pecking away at a minute quantity of fish, almost entirely surrounded by spinach, in our private hotel, and moodily sipping water (an excellent fluid no doubt, most useful for filling radiators and washing socks, but of absolutely no value as a drink) when Hilda said,

'She was devoted to him, you know.'

'Devoted to whom?'

'To Barney. To her husband Barney Bateman. Jackie was. She always said he was such a wonderful man, and a terrific sailor with a really good sense of humour. Of course, he had your problem, Rumpole.'

'What's that? Judge Bullingham?'

'Don't be silly! Of course, I never met Barney, but Jackie told me he was a big man.'

'You mean fat?'

'That's what I think she meant. Jackie was always afraid he was going to get too heavy for dinghy racing. And he simply refused to go on a diet!'

'Sensible fellow.'

'How can you say he was sensible, Rumpole? Don't you remember, poor Jackie's husband's dead.'

Did Mr Bateman's weight become so gross that he simply sank with all hands? As I gave the lining of my stomach the unusual shock of a cascade of cold water, I decided not to ask the question, but to try at the earliest opportunity to get a little free time from She Who Must Be Obeyed.

My chance came the next day when Hilda said that she had a cold coming on, and I would have to take the morning walk alone. I sympathized with Hilda (although I supposed that the natural state of an inhabitant of Shenstone must be a streaming nose and a raised temperature) and left carefully in the direction of the cliffs, as a direct route towards licensed premises would have raised a questioning cry from the window of the residents' lounge.

I struggled up a path in a mist of rain and came, a little way out of town, upon the thin man with the Balaclava helmet. He was staring through his powerful field-glasses out to sea. I gave him a moderately depressed 'good morning', but he was too engrossed in watching something far out on the grey water to return my greeting. Then I took the next turn, down to the harbour and the Crab and Lobster, a large, old-fashioned pub with a welcoming appearance.

It was clearly the warmest place in Shenstone and the place was crowded. In very little time the landlord had supplied me with a life-restoring bottle of St Émilion and a couple of ham rolls, and I sat among the boat people in a cheerful fug, away from the knife-edged wind and the whining children in life-jackets, among the polished brass and dangling lobster pots, looking at the signed photographs of regatta winners, all dedicated to 'Sam', whom I took to be the landlord. In pride of place among these pictures was one of a windswept but resolutely smiling couple in oilskins, proudly clutching a silver trophy with "love from Jackie and Barney, to Sam and all the crowd at the Lobster" scrawled across it. The man seemed considerably and cheerfully overweight, and the colour print showed his flaming red hair and bushy beard. Jackie, Hilda's schoolfriend, also looked extremely cheerful. She had clear blue eyes, short hair which must have been fair but was now going grey, and the sort of skin which showed its long exposure to force-nine gales. Such, I thought, were the women who flew round the world in primitive planes, crossed deserts or rode over No Man's Land on a bicycle. I bought Sam, the landlord, a large whisky and water, and in no time at all we were talking about the Batemans, a conversation in which a number of the regulars at the Crab and Lobster, also supplied with their favourite tipples, seemed anxious to join.

'One thing I could never understand about Jackie,' Sam said. 'I mean, she lost a wonderful personality like Barney Bateman,

and they thought the world of each other. Never a cross word
between the two of them!'

'And Barney was a man who always had a drink and a story
for everyone. Never fumbled or rang the wife when it came to
his round.' A red-faced man in an anorak whom the others
called Buster told me. 'As I say, I can't understand why after
being married to Barney, the winner of the Shenstone regatta
five years running, she ended up with a four-letter man like
Freddy Jason! Hope he's not a friend of yours, is he?'

'Jason.' The name was entirely new to me.

'Jackie married him just six months after Barney died. We
couldn't believe it.' A voluminous blonde bulging out of a
pair of jeans and a fisherman's jersey shouted, 'Of course, I've
never actually met Mr Jason. He's moved her up to Cricklewood.'

'Dreadful house,' said Buster. 'Absolutely miles from the
sea.'

'Well, it is Cricklewood.' The blonde lady seemed prepared to
excuse the house.

'Like I told you, Dora. I went there once when I was up in
London. On business.'

'What business, Buster? Dirty weekend?' the seafaring
woman addressed as Dora screamed, and after laughter from the
boat people, Buster continued.

'Never you mind, Dora! Anyway, I looked up Freddy Jason
in the book and rang Cricklewood. Finally Jackie came on the
phone. Well, you remember what Jackie *used* to be like? "Come
on over, Buster; stew's in the oven. We'll have a couple of
bottles of rum and a sing-up round the piano." Not a bit of it.
"Ever so sorry, dear. Freddy's not been all that well. We're not
seeing visitors."'

'Can you imagine that coming from Jackie Bateman? "We're
not seeing visitors!"' Dora bawled at me, as though I would be
bound to know. She was clearly used to conversation far out to
sea, during gale-force winds.

'What you're saying is, there was a bit of a contrast between the
two husbands?' I was beginning to get the sense of the meeting.
'At least she didn't repeat the same mistake; that's what most
people do.'

'Barney wasn't a mistake,' Dora hailed me. 'Barney was a terrific yachtsman. And a perfect gent.'

I didn't repeat all this information to She Who Must Be Obeyed. To do so would only have invited a searching and awkward cross-examination about where I had heard it. But when we were back in London and recovering from our seaside holiday, Hilda told me she had had an unexpected telephone call from Jackie Bateman, Hopkins as was, Jason, as she had now discovered she had become. Apparently the boat woman had got our note by some means, and she wanted to bring her new husband to tea on Sunday to get 'a few legal tips' from Rumpole of the Bailey.

Hilda spent a great deal of Saturday with her baking tins in celebration of this unusual visit, and produced a good many rock cakes, jam tarts and a large chocolate sponge.

'Not for you, Rumpole,' she said in a threatening fashion. 'Remember, *you're* on a diet.'

In due course, Jackie turned up looking exactly like her photograph, bringing with her a thin and rather dowdy middle-aged man introduced as Freddy, who could not have been a greater contrast to the previous yachtsman and gent. Jason was dark, mouse-coloured and not red-haired; his one contribution to the conversation was to tell us that going out in any sort of boat made him seasick, and we discovered that he was a retired chartered accountant, whose hobby was doing chess problems. When Hilda pressed rock cakes and chocolate sponge on him, he waved her confections aside.

'What's the matter?' I asked him gloomily. 'Not on a diet too, are you?'

'Freddy never has to go on a diet,' his wife said with some sort of mysterious pride. 'He's one of nature's thin people.'

'That's right,' Freddy Jason told us. 'I simply never never put on weight.' All the same, I noticed that he didn't do any sort of justice to Hilda's baking, and he took his tea neat, without milk or sugar.

After some general chat we came on to the legal motive for the party.

'It's awfully boring, but naturally Barney was insured, and

the insurance company paid out. That's how we were able to get married and buy the house. But now it seems that Chad Bateman, that's Barney's brother in New Zealand, has raised some sort of question about the estate. Look, can I leave you the letters? You see, we really don't know any lawyers we can trust.'

I had to say that I had only done one will case (in which I had been instructed from beyond the grave by a deceased military man) and that my speciality was violent death and classification of blood. However, I was prepared to get the opinion of Claude Erskine-Brown, the civil lawyer in our Chambers (civil lawyers are concerned with money, criminal practitioners with questions of life and death) and I would give Mrs Jason, whose clear-eyed and sensible look of perfect trust I found appealing, the benefit of his deliberations in due course.

Before I had time to keep my promise, however, something happened of a dramatic nature. Hilda's old schoolfriend Jackie was arrested, as we heard the next week on the television news, on a charge of the wilful murder of her late husband, Barney Bateman.

We heard no more of Jackie Jason, Bateman, Hopkins and her troubles for a considerable period. And then, one morning, as I was walking into my Chambers in a state of some depression brought about by having mislaid about a stone of Rumpole in the course of my prolonged fast, my clerk Henry uttered words which were music to my ears.

'There's a new case for you, Mr Rumpole. A murder, from a new firm of solicitors.'

It was good news indeed. A new firm of solicitors meant a new source of work, claret and small cigars, and of all the dishes that figure on the Criminal Menu, murder is still the main course, or *pièce de résistance*.

'It's an interesting case, Mr Tonkin was telling me.' Henry handed me the bulky set of papers.

'Tonkin?'

'Of Teleman, Tonkin and Bird. That's the new firm from Norfolk. He says the odd thing about this murder is, they never found the body.'

'No corpse?' Without a corpse the thing should not, I thought, present much difficulty, although like all cases it would probably be easier without a client also. I looked down at the brief in my hands and saw the title on it 'R. *v.* Jason'.

In due course, I read the papers and issued out into Fleet Street to find a taxi prepared to take me to Holloway prison for an interview with Jackie Jason and Mr Tonkin. Waiting on the curb, I was accosted by a tall figure wearing a bowler hat and an overcoat with a velvet collar, none other than our learned Head of Chambers, Guthrie Featherstone Q.C., M.P.

'Hullo there, Horace!'

'Sorry, Guthrie. I'm just off to Holloway. Got a rather jolly murder.'

'I know.'

'Henry told you, did he? Strange thing, when I married She Who Must Be Obeyed, I never thought she'd be much help in providing me with work. But she's turned up trumps! She had the good luck to go to an excellent school where one of her form mates grew up to be charged with an extremely interesting . . .'

'I know.' Guthrie repeated himself. 'Jackie Jason.'

'*How* do you know?' Was Featherstone, I wondered, a spare-time boat person? His reply quite wiped off my grin of triumph and added, I thought, new difficulties to our defence.

'Because I'm leading you, of course. It'll be a pleasure to have you sitting behind me again, Horace. Ah, there's a cab. Holloway prison, please.'

Because I never took silk and was not rewarded by the Lord Chancellor with a long wig and a pair of ceremonial knee breeches I am compelled, in certain cases, to sit behind some Queen's Counsel and, although I am old enough to be Featherstone's father, I must be his 'junior', and sit behind the Q.C., M.P. and listen, with what patience I can muster, to him asking the wrong questions. In the Shenstone-on-Sea murder, it would hardly be a pleasure. No doubt with his talent for agreeing with the Judge, Guthrie Featherstone could manage to lose even a corpseless case, in the nicest possible way.

'The evidence against us is pretty strong,' Featherstone said, as we sat together in the taxi bound for the ladies' nick. 'Two heads are better than one in a matter like this, Horace.'

'I didn't find that,' I told him, 'when I won the Penge Bungalow Murders, entirely on my own.'

'Penge Bungalow? Oh, I think you told me. That was one of your old cases, wasn't it? Well, people couldn't afford leading counsel in those days. It was before legal aid.'

So, Q.C.s have become one of the advantages of our new affluence, I was about to say, like fish fingers and piped music in Pommeroy's Wine Bar. However, I thought better of it and we reached the castellated turreted entrance to Holloway prison in silence.

I may be, indeed I am, extremely old fashioned. No doubt an army of feminists are prepared to march for women to have equal rights to long-term imprisonment, but I dislike the sight of ladies in the cooler. For a start, Holloway is a far less jovial place than Brixton. The lady screws look more masculine and malignant than gentleman screws, and female hands never seem made for slopping out.

When we got to the Holloway interview room, my new solicitor Tonkin rose to greet us. He was an upright, military-looking man with a ginger moustache and an M.C.C. tie.

'Mr Featherstone. Mr Rumpole. Good of you to come, gentlemen. This is the client.'

Jackie Jason was looking as tanned and healthy as if she'd just stepped off a boat on a sunny day into the Crab and Lobster. She smiled at me from a corner of the room and said, 'I'm so glad I could find you a legal problem more in your line, Horace.'

I looked at her with gratitude. No doubt it was Jackie who had had the wisdom to choose Rumpole for the defence, and her solicitor Tonkin who had been weak-minded enough to choose Featherstone as a leader.

'I think it would help if you were just to tell us your story in your own way,' Featherstone kicked off the conference. I was sure that it would help him; no doubt he'd been far too busy with his parliamentary duties to read the brief.

'Well, Barney and I,' Jackie started.

'That was the late Mr Barney Bateman?' Featherstone asked laboriously.

'Yes. We used to live at Shenstone-on-Sea. Well, we were boat people.'

'Mrs Jason doesn't mean far-eastern refugees,' I explained to my leader. 'She means those who take to the water in yellow oilskins and sailing dinghies, with toddlers in inflated life-jackets, and usually call out the lifeboat to answer their cries of distress.'

'Barney and I never had toddlers,' Jackie said firmly.

'Horace, if I could put the questions?' Featherstone tried to assert his leadership.

'And we were pretty experienced sailors.'

'Yes,' I said thoughtfully, 'of course you were. And yet your husband died in a yachting accident.'

'Just remind me . . . ' Featherstone continued to grope for the facts.

'We went out very early that day. We wanted to sail the regatta course without anyone watching.'

'You and your late . . . husband?' Featherstone was examining the witness.

'Barney and I.'

'You were on good terms?'

'Always. He was a marvellous man, Barney. Anyone'd tell you, anyone in the crowd in the Crab and Lobster at Shenstone. We were the best of pals.'

Dear old pals, jolly old pals. Everyone in the Crab and Lobster agreed with that. And yet one pal fell out of the boat and his body was never recovered.

'You say there was a sudden gust of wind?' Featherstone was making a nodding acquaintance with his brief.

'Yes,' Jackie told him. 'It came out of nowhere. Well, it will in that bit of sea. Barney was on his feet and the boom must have hit his head. It was all so unexpected. The boat went over and there I was in the drink.'

'And your husband?'

'Stunned, I suppose. By the boom, you see. I looked for him for ten minutes, swimming, and then, well, I clung to the boat. I couldn't get her righted, not on my own I couldn't. I waited almost half an hour like that and then the harbour motor boat came out. They'd got a phone call. Someone must have seen us.

I was lucky, really. There aren't many people around in Shenstone at six o'clock in the morning.'

'But if you and your husband were on perfectly good terms . . . ' Featherstone was frowning, puzzled, when Mr Tonkin gave him some unhelpful clarification.

'That's not really the point, is it, Mr Featherstone? It's the policy with the Colossus Mercantile that made them bring this prosecution.' He was referring to the subject of the correspondence that Jackie Jason had given me when she was still at liberty, so I knew a little about the Colossus policy. Featherstone looked blank. If he hadn't been a politician he would have said, 'All-night sitting last night. I never got round to reading the brief.' As it was, he said,

'Do just remind me . . . '

'Mrs Jason insured her first husband's life with the Colossus Mercantile just two weeks before the accident,' Tonkin explained. 'Before these inquiries got going she had remarried and collected the money.'

'How much was it? Just remind me,' Featherstone asked.

Mr Tonkin gave us the motive which had undoubtedly led to the prosecution of the yachtswoman.

'Just about two hundred thousand pounds.'

'You know I'm going to Norfolk today,' I reminded Hilda at breakfast some weeks later. 'It's Jackie's trial.'

'You will get her off, won't you, Rumpole? She's relying on you, you know.' Hilda said it as if the case presented no particular problem.

'I might get her off. I don't know about my friend.'

'You didn't tell me you were taking a friend with you.' Hilda looked at me with sudden suspicion

'Didn't I? I'm taking Guthrie Featherstone. It's a secret romance. We've been passionately in love for years, Guthrie and I.'

'Rumpole, I don't know why you deliberately say things you know will annoy me. Also, it's not in the least degree funny!'

'I thought it was a *little* funny.'

'This is a letter from Lucy Loman.' This time Hilda showed me a pale green envelope.

'Is it really? I thought it was your pools.'

'Do stop being silly, Rumpole! I was at school with "Lanky" Loman!' As I wondered if there were anyone that Hilda *hadn't* been at school with, she went on, 'She tells me her daughter Tessa has just divorced a bankrupt garage proprietor with a foul temper and a taste for whisky.'

'Sounds a reasonable thing to do.'

'The problem is that Tessa has remarried.'

'Has she indeed?'

'Yes. A bankrupt ex-launderette owner with a much worse temper and a taste for gin.'

'So there's been no real change?'

'No. People don't change, do they?'

I was beginning to find She Who Must Be Obeyed unusually depressing that morning, when she went on thoughtfully,

'When they change partners, they always go for the same again, only slightly worse.'

Was there some similar, but even more ferocious version of She waiting to entrap me the second time around? The thought was too terrible to contemplate. I prepared to take self and brief off to Liverpool Street. On my way out, I said,

'Well, if you're going to change husbands while I'm gone . . .'

'Please don't be silly, Rumpole. I've had to tell you that once already. I'm quite prepared to make do with you, provided you're a good deal thinner.'

Make do for the rest of our natural lives, I thought. Matrimony and murder both carry a mandatory life sentence.

In the train from Liverpool Street Featherstone looked at me in a docile and trusting manner, as though he were depending on his learned junior to get him and his client out of trouble.

'I suppose you've read the birdwatcher's evidence?' he started gloomily.

'Mr "Nosey-Parker" Spong? Saw the whole thing through a pair of strong opera-glasses? Yes, I've read it.'

'Odd he never went to the police straight away.'

'The whole timetable's odd. The police and the insurance company accept her story of an accident. Colossus Mercantile pays out, she collects her two hundred thousand, calls herself a widow, marries Mr Jason, a retired accountant, buys a small house in Cricklewood and then . . .'

'The long-lost brother turns up from New Zealand.'

'Mr Chad Bateman. Hungry for his brother's estate which our client won't get if she's a murderess. So he disputes the insurance payment and starts inquiries. Advertises for the long-lost birdwatcher and puts together a case.'

'Puts together far too good a case for my liking.'

A silence fell between us, and somewhere in East Anglia I said, 'Featherstone?'

'Yes, Horace?'

'I get the feeling sometimes that you don't like me very much.'

'Now, whatever could have given you that idea?' My learned leader looked pained.

'We don't see eye to eye always on the running of Chambers. I find your cross-examination feeble and your politics anaemic and I don't mind saying so. I do ask you, however, to win this case. If you don't I may be in for a very rough time indeed from She Who Must Be Obeyed. She doesn't like having her old school chums convicted of murder.'

'You've got to help me, Horace.' The man looked positively desperate, so I gave my learned leader the benefit of a full account of my conversation with the habitués of the Crab and Lobster on the day I broke into my diet. When I had finished, Featherstone didn't look any more cheerful.

'Does that tell us anything?'

'Oh yes. Three things to be precise.'

'What on earth?'

'That the Batemans never had a cross word. That Jackie's second husband doesn't like visitors and that Barney Bateman won the regatta five times.'

'I don't see how that helps.'

'You're right. It doesn't help at all.'

'Now who's being depressing, Horace?'

'I know,' I told him perfectly frankly. 'I find the whole business very depressing indeed.'

In due course, I found myself sitting in the ancient, panelled Norfolk courtroom, in a place of importance behind my undecided leader, with a jury of solid East Anglian citizens and old Piers Craxton, a reasonably polite Judge, sent to try us. Our opponent was a jovial local silk named Gerald Gaunt who, being for the prosecution and with a strongish case, looked a great deal less gloomy than the nervous artificial silk in front of me. The witness-box was occupied by a figure familiar to me from my visit to Shenstone, the birdwatcher whom I had last seen surveying the North Sea with a pair of strong field-glasses. Without his Balaclava helmet, he looked older and slightly less dotty than when I had first seen him.

'Your name is Henry Arthur Spong?' Gaunt asked the ornithologist in the witness-box.

'Yes it is.'

'Do you remember being out very early one morning in July two years ago?'

'Tell him not to bloody well lead!' I whispered in a vain attempt to keep my learned leader on his toes.

'Ssh, Rumpole. I don't like to interrupt. It creates a bad impression.' Featherstone sounded deeply embarrassed.

'Creates a damn sight worse impression to let him lead the witness.'

'I remember it clearly. It was quite light at six a.m. and the date was July the sixth, 'Mr Spong intruded on our private dialogue.

'How can he remember that?' I whispered to Guthrie Featherstone, and Mr Spong supplied the answer.

'I wrote a note in my diary. I saw a number of kittiwake and gannets and I thought I saw a Mediterranean shearwater. I have all that noted down in my birdwatcher's diary. I was looking out to sea through a pair of powerful field-glasses.'

'Did you happen to spot a boat?' Gaunt asked and I prodded Featherstone again.

'Don't let him lead!'

'Please, Rumpole! Leave it to me.'

'Mr Spong. Out of deference to my learned friend's learned junior, I will frame the question in a non-leading form.' Gerald Gaunt raised a titter in Court. 'Did you see anything unusual?'

'Yes.' Spong clearly knew what he was being asked about. 'I saw a boat.'

'Surprise, surprise!' I whispered to Featherstone, who tried not to hear me.

'I noticed it because . . .'

'Yes. Tell us why you noticed it.' Gaunt encouraged the birdwatcher.

'There were two people standing up in it. One, I thought, was a man. He had a red beard. The other was a woman.'

'What did they appear to be doing?'

'I would say, struggling together. I couldn't see all that clearly.'

'And then?'

'Then the man seemed to fall from the side of the boat.' Gaunt, as any good barrister would, allowed a substantial pause for that to sink in, and then he asked,

'Tell me, Mr Spong. Was there any wind at the time?'

'No wind at all. No. It had been gusty a little earlier, but at the time the man fell from the boat it was perfectly calm.' It wasn't a helpful answer, being clean contrary to our client's instructions.

'And after he fell?'

'The woman waited for about five minutes.'

'She didn't dive in after him?'

'No.'

I saw the Judge make a note and the jury looked at the woman in the dock with no particular sympathy.

'What did she do then?'

'She deliberately upset the boat.'

During Gaunt's next and even longer pause, not only the Judge but the reporters were writing hard and the jury looked even less friendly.

'What do you mean by that, exactly?'

'She stood on the side and then swung herself out, pulling on the side ropes. She seemed to me to capsize the boat deliberately.'

'And after it had capsized?'

'She went into the water, of course. Then I saw her clinging to the boat.'

'What did you do?'

'Well, I thought she might be in some danger, so I bicycled off to telephone the police.'

'To the harbour?'

'Yes. The harbour office was locked up. It was so early you see. It took me some time to wake anyone in the cottages.'

'Thank you, Mr Spong.'

Gaunt sat down, clearly delighted with his witness and Guthrie Featherstone rose to cross-examine. Tall and distinguished, at least he managed to *look* like a barrister.

'Mr Spong,' he started, in his smoothest voice. 'You knocked up a Mr Newbold in one of the cottages?'

'Yes, I did. I banged on the door, and he put his head out of the window.'

'What did you tell him?'

'I asked him to phone the police and tell them that there was a woman in trouble with a boat.'

'You didn't tell him anything else you'd seen?'

'No, I didn't.'

'And having told Mr Newbold that a woman was in trouble with a boat, you got on your bicycle and rode away?'

'Yes. That is correct.'

Not a bad exchange, for Featherstone. I whispered my instructions to him.

'Leave it there.'

'What?' Guthrie whispered back, turning his head away from the witness.

'Don't give him a chance to explain! Comment on it later, to the jury.'

The trouble with leaders is that they won't take their learned junior's advice. Featherstone couldn't resist trying to gild the lily.

'Why didn't you tell Mr Newbold or the police the whole story? About the struggle in the boat and so on?'

'Well, sir. I thought I saw a Mediterranean shearwater, which would be extremely interesting so far out of its territory. I got on my bike to follow its flight, but when I spotted it later from the cliffs, it was a great shearwater, which is interesting enough.'

I sighed with resignation. From a dedicated birdwatcher, the answer was totally convincing.

'Mr Spong. Did you think sighting shearwaters was more im-

portant than a possible murder?' Featherstone asked with carefully simulated anger and incredulity.

'Yes, of course I did.'

Of course he did. The jury could recognize a man dedicated to
his single interest in life.

'In fact, you only came forward when Mr Chad Bateman
arrived from New Zealand and advertised for you?'

'That is correct.'

'How much did he get paid?' I whispered the question
ferociously to my leader's back.

'Did you get paid for your information?' At least Featherstone
obeyed orders, sometimes.

'I was given no money.'

'Thank you, Mr Spong.' My leader folded his silk gown about
him and prepared to subside, but I stimulated him into a final
question.

'Don't sit down! Ask him what he got apart from money,' I
whispered, and my leader uncoiled himself. After a pause which
made it look as though he'd thought of the question himself he
said,

'Just one thing. Did you get rewarded in any other way?'

'I was offered a holiday in New Zealand,' Spong admitted.

'By the deceased's brother?'

'Yes.'

'Do you intend to take it?'

'Oh yes.' And Spong turned to the jury with a look of radiant
honesty. 'There are some extremely interesting birds in New
Zealand. But I must make this clear. It hasn't made the slightest
difference to my telling the truth in this Court.'

I looked at the jury. I knew one thing beyond reasonable
doubt. They believed the birdwatcher.

'Yes, thank you, Mr Spong.' Featherstone was finally able to
sit down and turn to me for some whispered reassurance.

'It was a disaster, old darling,' I told him, but admitted, 'not
entirely your fault.'

Later, Featherstone had another opportunity to practise the
art of cross-examination on the police officer in charge of the
case.

'Inspector Salter. The body of Barney Bateman was never

recovered?' he asked. Well, at least it was a safe question, the answer to which was not in dispute.

'No, sir.' The Inspector, who looked as though he enjoyed fishing from his own small boat, had no trouble in agreeing.

'Is that not an unusual factor, in this somewhat unusual case?' Featherstone soldiered on, more or less harmlessly.

'Not really, sir.'

'Why do you say that?'

'There are particularly strong currents off Shenstone, sir. We have warnings put up to swimmers. Unfortunately, there have been many drowning accidents where bodies have never been recovered.'

'Did you say "accidents", Inspector?'

'Oh Featherstone, my old sweetheart. Don't try to be too brilliant,' I whispered, I hoped inaudibly. 'Just plod, Featherstone. It suits your style far better.'

'We have had bodies lost in accidents, yes, sir,' Inspector Salter answered carefully. 'I'm by no means suggesting that *this* was an accident. In fact, the view of the police is that it was deliberate.'

The Judge interrupted mercifully to spare Featherstone embarrassment.

'Yes. Thank you, Inspector Salter. I'm sure we all understand what the police are suggesting here.'

'If your Lordship pleases.' There was another rustle of silk as Featherstone sat. I had warned him. He should plod, just plod, and never attempt brilliance.

During the luncheon break we went to see our client in the cells.

'Mrs Jason. I'm sure it's a nerve-racking business, giving evidence on a charge of murder.' Featherstone was doing his best to prepare our client for the ordeal to come. But Jackie gave him a far too cheerful smile.

'I've been in cross-Channel races with Barney. And round Land's End in a force-nine gale which took away our mast in the pitch dark. I don't see that Mr Gaunt's questions are going to frighten me.'

'There's just one thing.' I thought I ought to insert a word of warning. 'I think the jury are going to believe the birdwatcher. It would be nice if we didn't have to quarrel with too much of his evidence.'

'What do you mean, it would be nice?' Jackie looked at me impatiently. 'That man Spong was talking absolute nonsense.'

'Well, for instance, he said that you were standing up in the boat together? Now, what could you have been doing – other than fighting, of course?'

'I don't know.' Jackie frowned. 'What could we have been doing?'

'Well, perhaps,' I made a suggestion, 'kissing each other good-bye?'

'That's ridiculous! Why on earth did you say that? Anyway,' she looked at Featherstone, 'who'll be asking me the questions in Court?'

'I shall, Mrs Jason,' he reassured her, 'as your leading counsel. Mr Rumpole won't be asking you any questions at all.'

Our client looked as if the news came to her as a considerable relief. Featherstone's questions would be like a gentle following breeze, and Rumpole's awkward voice would not be heard. However, I had to warn her, and said,

'Gerald Gaunt's going to ask you some questions for the prosecution as well. You should be prepared for that, otherwise they're going to strike you like a force-nine gale amidships.'

'Don't worry, Mrs Jason.' Featherstone poured his well-oiled voice on the choppy waters of our conference. 'I'm sure you'll be more than a match for the prosecuting counsel. Now, let's go through your proof again, shall we?'

In the course of time, Featherstone steered Jackie through her examination in chief, more or less smoothly. At least he managed to avoid the hidden rocks and shallows, but more by ignoring their existence and hoping for the best than by expert navigation. Finally, he had to sit down and leave her unprotected and without an anchor, to the mercy of such winds as might be drummed up by the cross-examination of our learned friend, Mr Gerald Gaunt, Q.C., who rose, and started off with a gentle courtesy which was deceptive.

'Mrs Jason. Your husband was a swimmer?'

'Barney could swim, yes. The point was,' Jackie answered confidently, 'we were too far out to swim ashore.'

'Oh, I quite agree,' Gaunt smiled at her. 'And he always said, didn't he, that it was far safer to cling to the wreckage and wait to be picked up than attempt a long and exhausting swim against the current?'

'Any experienced sailor would tell you that.' Jackie spoke to him as to a novice yachtsman.

'And that's exactly what *you* did?'

'Yes,' Jackie admitted.

'Why didn't your husband?'

'As I told you. He must have been stunned by the boom as we went about.'

Gaunt nodded and then produced a document from his pile of papers.

'I have here the account which you gave to the insurance company at the time. You said "the accident took place between the eighth and ninth marker buoys of the regatta course".'

'Yes.'

'Halfway between?'

'About that.'

'With the wind from the quarter it was on that morning, you could have sailed between those two points without going about at all, could you not?'

The healthy-looking woman in the witness-box seemed somewhat taken aback by his expertise. After a small hesitation she said,

'Perhaps we could.'

'Then why didn't you?' Gaunt was no longer smiling.

'Perhaps we're not all as clever as you, Mr Gaunt. Perhaps Barney made a mistake.'

'Made a mistake?' Gaunt looked extravagantly puzzled. 'On a course where he'd raced and won five times?'

Jackie Jason was proving to be the worst kind of witness. She was over-emphatic, touchy and had treated the question as an insult. I could see the jury starting to lose faith in her defence.

'Anyway, you've never been out from Shenstone on the regatta course.' She raised her voice, making matters a good deal worse. 'I don't know what you know about it, Mr Gaunt!'

'Mrs Jason!' the Judge warned her. 'Just confine yourself to answering the questions. Mr Gaunt is merely doing his duty with his usual ability.'

'Mrs Jason.' Gaunt was quiet and courteous again. 'Did you tell your husband you'd taken out this large life insurance?'

The jury were looking hard at my client, as she did her best to avoid the question.

'I didn't tell him the exact amount. I ran our business affairs.'

'Which were in a terrible mess, weren't they?'

'Not terrible, no.' She answered cautiously, and our opponent fished out another devastating document.

'I have here the certified accounts for the shop Father Neptune's Boutique which you ran in Shenstone. Had a petition in bankruptcy been filed by one of your suppliers?'

'You seem to know all about it.' Again, the answer sounded angry and defensive.

'Oh yes, I do.' Gaunt assured her, cheerfully. 'And were the mortgage repayments considerably overdue on your cottage at Shenstone-on-Sea?'

'We only needed a bit of luck to pay off our debts.'

'And the "bit of luck" was your husband's death, wasn't it?'

It was a cruel question, but I knew her answer chilled the hearts of the jury. It came coldly, and after a long pause.

'I suppose it came at the right moment, from the business point of view.'

'I thought that she stood up to that reasonably well.'

Featherstone and I were removing the fancy dress in the local robing room and he turned to me, once again, for a reassurance that I failed to give.

'It was a disaster,' I said. 'Can't wait to chat. I'm off to London.'

'London?' Featherstone looked perplexed. 'We could have had dinner together and discussed my final speech.'

'Before your final speech, we ought to discuss whom we're going to call as a witness.'

'Witness? Have we got a witness?'

But I was on my way to the door.

'See you here in the morning. We'll talk about our witness.'

I left my puzzled leader and caught an Inter City train. I sat munching an illicit tea-cake as a railway guard, pretending to be an air hostess, came over the intercom, and announced that we were due on the ground at Liverpool Street approximately twenty minutes late, and apologized for the delay. (I waited to be told to fasten my seat belt because of a spot of turbulence around Bishop's Stortford.) What I was doing was strictly un-professional. We legal hacks are not supposed to chatter to witnesses in criminal matters, and Featherstone would have been deeply pained if he had known where I was going. And yet I was on a quest for the truth and justice for Jackie, although she, also, would not have thought my journey really necessary. We arrived at Liverpool Street station after half an hour's delay (Please collect all your hand baggage and thank you for flying British Rail), and I persuaded a taxi to take me to Cricklewood.

When we stopped at the anonymous surburban house, I was glad to see a light on in a downstairs room. Freddy Jason came to the door when I rang the electric chime. He was wearing an old sweater and a pair of bedroom slippers. He led me into a room where a television set was booming, and I noticed a tray decorated with the remains of a pork pie, French bread and cheese, and a couple of bottles of Guinness.

'Aren't you afraid,' I asked him, 'of putting on weight?'

'I told you. I don't.' He clicked the television set into silence.

'How long can you keep it up, I wonder?'

'Keep what up?'

'Being a thin person.'

He looked at me, the skinny, mousy ex-accountant and said, with real anxiety,

'How's the trial going? Jackie won't let me near the place. Is it going well?' He had a dry, impersonal voice like the click of a computer adding up an overdraft.

'It's going down the drain.'

He sat down then. He seemed exhausted.

'I warned her,' he said. 'I was afraid of that. What can I do?'

'Do? Come and give evidence for her!'

'I don't know.' Jason looked at me helplessly. 'What can I say? I didn't get to know Jackie until after Barney's accident. I don't think I'd be much help in the witness-box, do you?'

'It depends,' I said, 'on what you mean by help.'

'Well. Does Jackie want me to come?'

'Jackie doesn't know I'm asking you.'

'Well, then. I can't help.'

'Listen,' I said. 'Do you want your wife to do a life sentence in Holloway? *For a murder she didn't commit?*'

He looked deeply unhappy. A thin man who had become, however unwillingly, involved in a fat man's death.

'No,' he said. 'I don't want that.'

'Then you'd better come back on the Inter City to Norfolk. You might as well finish off your supper. I mean, you don't have to worry, do you? About your weight.'

When I got to the Court the next morning I found Featherstone and Mr Tonkin anxiously pacing the hall. I gave them what comfort I could.

'Cheer up, old darlings. Things may not be as bad as you think. Her husband's here. He'll have to give evidence.'

'Freddy Jason?' Tonkin frowned.

'What on earth can *he* do for us?' Featherstone asked.

'Well, he certainly can't make things any worse. He can say he didn't get to know Jackie until after the accident. At least we can scotch the idea that she pushed Barney out to marry another man.'

'I suppose he could say that.' Mr Tonkin sounded doubtful. 'You think we need this evidence, Mr Rumpole?'

'Oh yes. I'm sure we need it.' I turned to my leader. 'Featherstone. I have a certain experience in this profession. I did win the Penge Bungalow Murders alone and without a leader.'

'So you're fond of telling me.'

'In any case, the junior is accorded the privilege of calling at least one witness in a serious case, with the permission of his learned leader, of course.'

'*You* want to call Jason?' In fact, Featherstone sounded extremely grateful. If the witness turned out a disaster, at least I should get the blame.

'Would you leave him to me?' I asked politely.

'All right, Rumpole. You call him. If you think it'll do the

slightest good. At least you won't be whispering instructions to
me the whole time.'

When the Court had reassembled, and the Judge had been
settled down on his seat, found his place in his notebook, been
given a sharp, new pencil and put on his glasses, he looked at my
leader encouragingly and said,

'Yes, Mr Featherstone.'

'My Lord,' Featherstone said with a good deal of detachment,
'my learned junior, Mr Rumpole, will call the next witness.'

'Yes, Mr Rumpole?' His Lordship switched his attention to
my humble self.

For the first and last time in the Shenstone-on-Sea murder
trial, I staggered to my feet. The calm woman in the dock gave
me a little smile of welcome.

'Yes, my Lord,' I said. 'I will call the next witness. Call
Frederick Jason.'

'No!' Jackie was no longer smiling. As the usher went out to
fetch her husband I whispered to Tonkin to keep our client
quiet and tell her that the evidence I was about to call was vital
to her case. In fact, it was one of those rare defences which depended on nothing less than the truth.

Tonkin was busy whispering to the lady in the dock when her
pale and nervous second husband was brought into the Court and
climbed into the witness-box. He took the oath very quietly.

'I swear to God that the evidence I shall give shall be the truth,
the whole truth and nothing but the truth.'

It was then that I asked the question which I had been waiting
to put throughout the trial.

'Is your name Barney Bateman?'

The reactions were varied. The Judge looked shocked. Showing some tolerance towards an ageing junior who was undoubtedly past it, he said,

'Haven't you made a mistake, Mr Rumpole?'

Featherstone felt it was his turn to whisper disapproving
instructions and said,

'*Jason*, Rumpole. His name's Jason.'

My client remained silent. I asked the question again.

'I repeat. Is your name Barney Bateman?' Then the witness

looked, for the first time, at the prisoner with a sort of apology. She seemed, suddenly, much older and too tired to protest. I reflected that there is a strange thing about taking the oath, it sometimes makes people tell the truth. Anyway, we had at least found the corpse in the Shenstone murder. It was now speaking, with increasing liveliness, to the learned Judge.

'My Lord,' the witness said, 'you can't go on trying Jackie for murder. I'm still alive, you see.' He smiled then, and I got a hint of the old Barney Bateman. 'Still alive and living in Cricklewood.'

It took another couple of days, of course, for the whole story to be told and for the good citizens of East Anglia to find Jackie Bateman (as she always was) not guilty of the murder with which she had been charged. Featherstone and I were eventually released and sat opposite each other in the British Rail tea car. My leader looked at me with a contented smile.

'Well, Horace,' he said. 'I think that can be notched up among my successes.'

'Oh yes, Guthrie,' I agreed. 'Many congratulations.'

'Thanks. Of course one depends a good deal on one's learned junior. Two heads are better than one, Horace. That's what I always say.'

'Three heads. Don't forget Hilda's.'

'Your wife's, Horace?'

'You can't fool She Who Must Be Obeyed,' I said. 'She told me that people don't change, they keep on marrying the same husband. Jackie Bateman did exactly that.'

It was quite a touching story, really. I was right about what they were doing when the birdwatcher spotted them. Not fighting, of course, but kissing each other goodbye. It was only to be a temporary parting. Barney was to swim ashore, to some quiet little bit of beach. Then he shaved off his beard, went on a diet, dyed his hair and waited for his loving wife to collect the boodle. The murder trial was a nasty gust of wind, but she thought she'd sail through it. He knew she wasn't going to. So he *had* to tell the truth.

'They'll charge her with the insurance swindle,' my leader reminded me.

'Oh, I'm afraid they will,' I said, biting into another tea-cake. 'I think I'll do that case, Featherstone, if you don't mind – alone and without a leader.'

That night, still grateful to Hilda, I took her out for a celebration dinner at my favourite restaurant in the Strand. She looked at me, somewhat aghast as I placed my order.

'Potted shrimps, I think. With plenty of hot toast. Oh, and steak and kidney pud, potatoes, swedes and Brussels sprouts. After that, we might consider the sweet trolley and I'll have the wine list, please.'

'Rumpole! You *mustn't* eat all that,' said She Who Must Be Obeyed.

'Oh yes I must. You're married to Rumpole, you know. Not some skinny ex-chartered accountant. You're stuck with him and so am I. We can't alter him, can we? Jackie's case proved that. You can't just change people entirely to suit your own convenience.'

Rumpole
and the
Golden Thread

For Jacqueline Davis

Contents

Rumpole and the Genuine Article

I would like to dedicate this small volume of reminiscences to a much-abused and under-appreciated body of men. They practise many of the virtues most in fashion today. They rely strictly on free enterprise and individual effort. They adhere to strong monetarist principles. They do not join trade unions. Far from being in favour of closed shops, they do their best to see that most shops remain open, particularly during the hours of darkness. They are against state interference of any kind, being rugged individualists to a man. No. I'm not referring to lawyers. Will you please charge your glasses, ladies and gentlemen, and drink to absent friends, to the criminals of England. Without these invaluable citizens there would be no lawyers, no judges, no policemen, no writers of detective stories and absolutely nothing to put in the *News of the World*.

It is better, I suppose, that I raise a solitary glass. I once proposed such a toast at a Chambers party, and my speech was greeted by a studied silence. Claude Erskine-Brown examined his fingernails, our clerk, Henry, buried his nose in his Cinzano Bianco. Uncle Tom, our oldest inhabitant, looked as though he was about to enter a terminal condition. Dianne, who does what passes for typing in our little establishment at Equity Court in the Temple, giggled, it is true, but then Dianne will giggle at almost anything and only becomes serious, I have noticed, whenever I make a joke. A devout barrister known to me as Sam Bollard (of whom more, unfortunately, in the following pages) took me aside afterwards and told me that he considered my remarks to be in excessively bad taste, calculated to cause a breach of the peace and bring our Chambers into disrepute.

Well, where would he be, I asked him, should the carrying of house-breaking implements by night vanish from the face of the earth? He told me that he could manage very well with his civil practice and happily didn't have to rely on the sordid grubbing for a living round the Old Bailey which I appeared to enjoy. I left him, having regretted the fact that men with civil practices are often so remarkably un-civil when addressing their elders.

So, as the night wears on, and as my wife Hilda (whom I must be careful not to refer to as 'She Who Must Be Obeyed' – not, at any rate, when she is in earshot) sleeps in her hairnet, dreaming of those far-off happy days when she cantered down the playing fields of Cheltenham Ladies College cradling her lacrosse net and aiming a sneaky pass at her old friend Dodo Perkins; as I sit at the kitchen table filling a barrister's notebook with reminiscences (I see the bare bones of a nasty little manslaughter on the opposite page), I pour a glass of Château Thames Embankment (on special offer this week at Pommeroy's Wine Bar – how else would Jack Pommeroy get anyone to buy it?) and drink, alone and in silence, to those industrious lawbreakers who seem to be participating in the one growth industry in our present period of recession. I can safely write that here. Whoever may eventually read these pages, you can bet your life that it won't be Sam Bollard.

I have been back in harness a good three years since my abortive retirement. I had, as you may remember, upped sticks to join my son Nick and his wife Erica in Florida, the Sunshine State.*

She Who Must Be Obeyed apparently enjoyed life in that curious part of the world and was starting, somewhat painfully at first, to learn the language. I, as others have done before me, found that Miami had very little to offer unless you happened to be a piece of citrus fruit, and I began to feel an unendurable nostalgia for rain, secretaries rubbing their noses pink with crumpled paper handkerchieves on the platform at Temple Station and the congealed steak and mushroom pie for luncheon in the pub opposite the Old Bailey. I got bored with cross-examining the nut-brown octogenarians we met on the beach,

* See *Rumpole's Return*, Penguin Books, 1980.

and longed for a good up-and-downer with the Detective Inspector in charge of the case, or even a dramatic dust up with his Honour Judge Bullingham (otherwise known as the Mad Bull). I was a matador with nothing left to do but tease the cat. I needed a foeman worthy of my steel.

It was a nice problem of bloodstains which brought me home to real life at the Old Bailey, and a good deal of diplomatic skill and dogged endurance which eased me back into the peeling leather chair behind the desk in my old room in Equity Court. When I returned, our Head of Chambers, Guthrie Featherstone, Q.C., M.P. (S.D.P.), didn't actually unroll the red carpet for me. In fact, and in the nicest possible way, of course, he informed me that there was no room at the Inn, and would have left me to carry on what was left of my practice from a barrow in Shepherd's Bush Market, if I hadn't seen a way back into my old tenancy.

Well, that's all water under the bridge by now, and the last three years have gone much as the last what is it, almost half a century? That is to say they have passed with a few triumphant moments when the jury came back and said in clear and ringing tones, 'Not Guilty', and a few nasty ones when you have to bid goodbye to a client in the cells (what do you say: 'Win a few, lose a few', or 'See you again in about eight years'?). I have spent some enjoyable evenings in Pommeroy's Wine Bar, and my health has been no worse than usual, my only medical problem being a feeling of pronounced somnolence when listening to my learned friends making speeches, and a distinct nausea when hearing his Honour Judge Bullingham sum up.

So life was going on much as usual, and I was pursuing the even tenor of my way in Equity Court, when I was faced with a somewhat unusual case which caused a good deal of a stir in artistic circles at the time, it being concerned, as so many artistic and, indeed, legal problems are, with the question so easily put yet answered with such confusion, 'What is real and what is the most diabolical fake?'

I first had the unnerving feeling that I was drifting away from reality, and that many of my assumptions were being challenged, when Guthrie Featherstone, Q.C., M.P., knocked briefly on my door and almost immediately inserted his face, which wore an expression of profound, not to say haunted anxiety, into my room.

'Rumpole!' he said, gliding in and closing the door softly behind him, no doubt to block out eavesdroppers. 'I say, Horace, are you working?'

'Oh no, Featherstone,' I said, 'I'm standing on my head playing the bagpipes.' The sarcasm was intentional. In fact I was wrestling with a nasty set of accounts, carefully doctored by a delinquent bank clerk. As, like the great apes, my mathematical abilities stop somewhere short at 'one, two, three, many', I have a rooted aversion to fraud cases. Studying accounts leads me to a good deal of blood, tears and the consumption of boxloads of small cigars.

Quite undeterred by the sharpness of my reply, the recently committed Social Democrat moved soundlessly towards my desk and ran a critical eye over my blurred and inaccurate calculations.

'Well,' said Featherstone, 'fraud's a nice clean crime really. Not like most of your practice. No blood. No sex.'

'Do you think so, Featherstone?' I asked casually, the Q.C., M.P., having failed to grip my full attention. 'A bank cashier seems to have lost about half a million pounds. Probably his adding up was no better than mine.'

'Still, it's almost a respectable crime. Your practice has become quite decent lately. We may even see you prosecuting.'

'No thank you,' I said with the determined air of a man who has to draw the line somewhere.

'Why ever not?'

'I'm not going to use my skills, such as they are, to force some poor devil into a condemned Victorian slum where he can be banged up with a couple of psychopaths and his own chamber pot.' I gave my learned Head of Chambers Article One of the Rumpole Creed.

'All the same, you being comparatively quiet of late, Horace, has led the Lord Chancellor's office, I know, to look on these Chambers with a certain amount of, shall we say, "good will"?'

I looked at Featherstone. He was wearing an expression which I can only describe as 'coy'. 'Shall we? Then I'd better get up to something noisy.' I was joking, of course, but Featherstone became distinctly agitated.

'Please, Horace. No. I beg you. Please. You heard about the awful thing that happened to old Moreton Colefax?'

'Featherstone! I'm trying to add up.' I tried to be firm with the fellow, but he sat himself down in my client's chair and started to unburden himself as though he were revealing a dire plot he'd recently stumbled on involving the assassination of the Archbishop of Canterbury and the theft of the Crown Jewels.

'The Lord Chancellor told Moreton that he was going to make him a judge. But the rule is, you mustn't tell anyone till the appointment's official. Well, Moreton told Sam Arbuckle, and Arbuckle told Grantley Simpson and Grantley told Ian and Jasper Rugeley over in Paper Buildings, and Ian and Jasper told Walter Gains whom he happened to meet in Pommeroy's Wine Bar, and ...'

'What is this, Featherstone? Some sort of round game?' My attention was not exactly held by this complicated account.

'Not for Moreton Colefax, it wasn't,' Guthrie Featherstone chuckled, and then went serious again. 'The thing became the talk of the Temple and the upshot was, poor old Moreton never got appointed. So if the Lord Chancellor sends for a fellow to make him a judge, Horace, that fellow's lips are sealed. He just mustn't tell a soul!'

'Why are you telling me then?' I only asked for information, I wasn't following the fellow's drift. But the effect was extraordinary. Guthrie sprang to his feet, paling beneath his non-existent tan. 'I'm not telling you anything, Horace. Good heavens, my dear man! What ever gave you the idea I was telling you anything?'

'I'm sorry,' I said, returning to the calculations. 'I should have realized you were just babbling away meaninglessly. What are you, Featherstone, a sort of background noise, like Muzak?'

'Horace, it is vital that you should understand that I have said nothing to you whatsoever.' Featherstone's voice sank to a horrified whisper. 'Just as it is essential to preserve the quiet, *respectable* image of our Chambers. There was that difficult period we went through when the Erskine-Browns were *expecting*, rather too early on in their married lives.'*

'They weren't married.' I recalled the happy event.

'Well, exactly! And of course that all passed over quite satisfactorily. We had a marquee in the Temple Gardens, if you remember, for the wedding. I believe I said a few words.'

'A *few* words, Guthrie? That's hardly like you.'

The above somewhat enigmatic conversation was interrupted by the telephone on my desk ringing and, after a few deft passes by Dianne on the intercom in our clerk's room, my wife Hilda's voice came over the line, loud, clear, and unusually displeased.

'There's a young girl here, Rumpole,' She Who Must Be Obeyed was reading out the indictment over the phone. 'She is sitting in the kitchen, asking for you. Well, she's making her own cigarettes, and they smell of burnt carpets.'

'But any sort of breath of scandal now. At this historic moment in the life of our Chambers.' Looking, if possible, more ashen than ever, Guthrie was still burbling in the background. And he didn't look particularly cheered up when he heard me address the instrument in my hand along the following lines:

'Something sort of arty-tarty, is she, do you say, Hilda? A young girl who says she's in trouble. What kind of trouble? Well, perhaps I haven't got your vivid imagination, but I quite honestly can't ... Well, of course I'm coming home. Don't I always come home in the end?' I put down the telephone. Featherstone was looking at me, appalled, and started to say, in a voice of deep concern, 'I couldn't help overhearing.'

'Couldn't you?' Well I thought he might, if he were a man of tact, have filtered out of the room.

'Horace, is your home life completely satisfactory?' he asked.

'Of course it isn't.' I don't know what the man was thinking about. 'It's exactly as usual. Some girl seems to have aroused the wrath of She Who Must Be Obeyed.'

'Did you say ... some *girl*?'

'Friend of yours, Guthrie?'

'What?'

* See 'Rumpole and the Course of True Love' in *The Trials of Rumpole*, Penguin Books, 1979.

'I thought it might be someone you had your eye on, from the typing pool, perhaps. I mean, I remember when ...' But before I could call the Featherstone mind to remembrance of things past, he went on firmly, 'This is not a time for looking backwards, Horace. Let us look forward! To the fine reputation of this set of Chambers.'

He went to the door and opened it, but before he left the Rumpole presence he said, as though it were a full explanation, 'And do please remember, I haven't told you anything!'

I suppose that was true, in a manner of speaking.

As, from the sound of She Who Must Be Obeyed's voice, there appeared to be a bit of a cold wind blowing in Casa Rumpole (our so-called 'mansion' flat in the Gloucester Road, which bears about as much relation to a mansion as Pommeroy's plonk does to Château Pichon Longueville), I delayed my return home and wandered into my usual retreat, where I saw our clerk Henry there before me. He was leaning nonchalantly against the bar, toying with his usual Cinzano Bianco, taken with ice and a twist of lemon. I began to press him for information which might throw some faint light on the great Featherstone mystery.

'As a barrister's clerk, Henry,' I said, 'you might be said to be at the very heart of the legal profession. You have your finger on the Lord Chancellor's pulse, to coin a phrase. Tell me honestly, has the old fellow lost his marbles?'

'Which old fellow, sir?' Henry seemed mystified. It was an evening for mystification.

'The Lord Chancellor, Henry! Has he gone off his rocker?'

'That's not for me to say, is it?' Our clerk Henry was ever the diplomat, but I pressed on. 'Is his Lordship seriously thinking of making Guthrie Featherstone, Q.C., M.P., a Red Judge? I mean, I know our learned Head of Chambers has given up politics ...'

'He's joined the S.D.P.'

'That's exactly what I mean. But a *judge*!'

'Speaking entirely for myself, Mr Rumpole, and I have no inside information ...' Henry had decided to play it cautiously.

'Oh, come on. Don't be so pompous and legal, Henry.'

'I would say that Mr Featherstone would cut a fine figure on the Bench.' Our clerk had the sort of voice which could express nothing whatsoever, a genuinely neutral tone.

'Oh, he'd *look* all right,' I agreed. 'He'd fit the costume. But *is* he, Henry? That's what I want to know. *Is* he?'

'Is he *what*, Mr Rumpole?'

'He may *look* like a judge, but is he really the *genuine article*?'

So I left Henry, having hit, almost by chance I suppose, on one of the questions which troubled old Plato, led Bishop Berkeley to some of his more eccentric opinions, and brought a few laughs to Bertrand Russell and a whole trainload of ideas to A. J. Ayer. It was that little matter of the difference between appearance and reality which lay at the heart of the strange case which was about to engage my attention.

As I say, I didn't expect much of a welcome from She Who Must Be Obeyed when I put into port at 25B Froxbury Court, and I wasn't disappointed. I had brought a peace offering in the shape of the last bunch of tulips I had found gasping for air in the shop at the Temple tube station.

'Where did you find those, Rumpole?' my wife Hilda asked tersely. 'Been raiding the cemetery?'

'Is she still here?' I hoped to see the cause of Hilda's discontent, and entered the kitchen. The place was empty. The bird, whoever she might have been, had flown.

'By *she* I suppose you mean your girl?' Hilda followed me into the kitchen and tried to bring back life to the tulips with the help of a cut-glass vase.

'She's not "my girl".'

'She came to see you. Then she burst into tears suddenly and left.'

'People who come to see me often burst into tears. It's in the nature of the legal profession.' I tried to sound reassuring. But I was distracted by a strange sound, a metallic clatter, as though someone were throwing beer cans up at our kitchen window.

'Hilda,' I put the question directly. 'What on earth's that?' She took a look out and reported – as it turned out, quite accurately – what she saw. 'There's a small man in a loud suit throwing beer cans up at our window, Rumpole. Probably another of your friends!' At which my wife made off in the direction of our living room with the vase of tulips, and I proceeded to the window to verify the information. What I saw was a small, cunning-looking old cove in a loud check suit, with a yellow stock round his neck. Beside him was a girl in ethnic attire, carrying a large, worn holdall, no doubt of Indian manufacture. The distant view I had of her only told me that she had red hair and looked a great deal too beautiful to have any business with the elderly lunatic who was shying beer cans up at our window. As I stuck my head out to protest, I was greeted by the old party with a loud hail of 'Horace Rumpole! There you are at last!'

'Who are you?' I had no idea why this ancient person, who had the appearance of a superannuated racing tipster, should know my name.

'Don't you remember Blanco Basnet? Fellow you got off at Cambridge Assizes? Marvellous, you were. Just bloody marvellous! Hang on a jiff. Coming up!' At which our visitors made off for the entrance of the building.

The name 'Blanco Basnet' rang only the faintest of bells. I had a vague recollection of some hanger-on round Newmarket, but what had he been charged with? Embezzlement? Common assault? Overfamiliarity with a horse? My reverie was interrupted by a prolonged peal on the front door bell, and I opened up.

'Are you Basnet?' I asked the fellow as Hilda joined us, looking distinctly displeased.

'Course not. I'm Brittling.' He introduced himself. 'Harold Brittling. I was a close chum of old Blanco's, though. And when you got him off without a stain on his bloody character, we drank the night away, if you will recall the occasion, at the Old Plough at Stratford Parva. Time never called while the landlord had a customer. We swapped addresses, don't you remember? I say, is this your girl?' This last remark clearly and inappropriately referred to She Who Must Be Obeyed.

'This is my wife Hilda,' I said with as much dignity as I could muster.

'This is my girl Pauline.' Brittling introduced the beauty dressed in a rug at his side.

'I've met her,' Hilda said coldly. 'Is she your daughter?'

'No, she's my girl.' Brittling enlarged on the subject. 'Don't talk much, but strips down like an early Augustus John. Thighs that simply call out for an HB pencil. I say, Rumpole, your girl Hilda looks distinctly familiar to me. Met before, haven't we?'

'I think it's hardly likely.' Hilda did her best to freeze the little man with a glance. It was ineffective.

'Round the Old Monmouth pub in Greek Street?' Brittling suggested. 'Didn't you hang a bit round the Old Monmouth? Didn't I have the pleasure of escorting you home once, Hilda, when the Guinness stout had been flowing rather too freely?'

At which Brittling, with the girl in tow, moved off towards the sitting room, and I was left with the thought that either the little gnome was completely off his chump or there were hidden depths to She Who Must Be Obeyed.

When we followed him into our room, Brittling furnished some further information.

'You two girls have chummed up already,' he said. 'I sent Pauline to find you, Horace, as I was temporarily detained in the cooler.'

It was with some relief that I began to realize that Brittling had not paid a merely social call. He brought business. He was a customer, a member of the criminal fraternity, and probably quite a respectable little dud-cheque merchant. However, legal etiquette demanded that I spoke to him sharply. 'Look, Brittling,' I said, 'if you've come here for legal advice, you'll have to approach me in the proper manner.'

'I shall approach you in the proper manner, bearing bubbly! Perhaps your girl will go and fetch a few beakers from the kitchen. Then we can start to celebrate!'

At which he started to yank bottles of champagne out of Pauline's holdall, with all the éclat of a conjurer producing rabbits from a hat.

'Celebrate what?' I was puzzled. Nothing good seemed to have happened.

'The case in which I'm going to twist the tail of the con-o-sewers,' Brittling almost shouted. 'And you, my dear Horace, are going to twist the tail of the legal profession. Game for a bit of fun, aren't you?'

At this moment he released the wine, which began to bubble out over the elderly Persian-type floor covering. This, of course, didn't add a lot to Hilda's approval of the proceedings. 'Do be careful,' she said tartly, 'that stuff is going all over the carpet.'

'Then get the glasses, Hilda.' Brittling was giving the orders. 'It's not like you, is it, to hold up a party?'

'Rumpole!' Hilda appealed to me with a look of desperation, but for the moment I couldn't see the point of allowing all the champagne to be drunk up by the carpet. 'No harm in taking a glass of champagne, Hilda,' I said reasonably.

'Or two.' Brittling winked at her. To my amazement, she then went off to fetch the beakers. When Hilda was gone I pressed on with the interrogation of Brittling.

'Who are you, exactly?' I asked, as a starter. The question seemed to provoke considerable hilarity in the old buffer.

'He asks who I am, Pauline!' He turned to his companion incredulously. 'Slade Gold Medal. Exhibited in the Salon in Paris. Hung in the Royal Academy. Executed in the Bond Street Galleries. And once, when I was *very* hungry, decorated the pavement outside the National Portrait Gallery. And the secret is – I can *do* it, Horace. So can you. We're pros. Give me a box of Conté crayons and I can run you up a Degas ballet dancer that old Degas would have given his eye teeth to have drawn.'

'His name's Harold Brittling.' The girl, Pauline, spoke at last, and as though that settled the matter. Brittling set off on a survey of the room as Hilda came back with four glasses.

'Who is he?' she asked anxiously as she handed me a glass.

'An artist. Apparently. Hung in the Royal Academy.' That was about all I was able to tell her.

'Not over-pictured, are you? What's this objet d'art?' Brittling had fetched up in front of a particularly watery watercolour presented to Hilda by her bosom chum Dodo, an artwork which I wouldn't give house room to were the choice mine, which of course it wasn't.

'Oh, that's a study of Lamorna Cove, done by my old school

friend, Dorothy Mackintosh. Dodo Perkins, as was. She lives in the West Country now.'

' "Dodo" keeps a tea-shop in St Ives.' I filled in the gaps in Hilda's narrative.

'She has sent in to the Royal Academy. On several occasions. Do you like it, Mr ... ?' She actually seemed to be waiting anxiously for the Brittling verdict.

'Harold,' he corrected her. And, looking at her with particularly clear blue eyes, he added, in a way I can only describe as gallant, 'Do *you* like it, Hilda?'

'Oh, I think it's rather fine.' It was She, the connoisseur, speaking. 'Beautiful in fact. The way Dodo's caught the shadow on the rocks, you know.'

Brittling was sloshing the champagne around, smiling at Hilda, and actually winking at Pauline as he said, 'Then if you think it's fine and beautiful, Hilda, that's what it is to you. To you it's worth a fortune. The mere fact that to me it looks like a rather colourless blob of budgerigar's vomit is totally irrelevant. You pay for what you think is beautiful. That's what our case is all about, isn't it, Horace? What's the difference between a Dodo and a Degas? Nothing but bloody talent which I can supply!'

'Look here, Brittling ...' Although grateful for the glass full of nourishing bubbles, I thought the chap was putting the case against Dodo's masterpiece a little strongly.

'Harold,' he suggested.

'Brittling.' I was sticking to the full formality. 'My wife and I are grateful for this glass of ...'

'The Widow Cliquot. Non vintage, I'm afraid. But paid for with ready money.'

'But I certainly can't do any case unless you go and consult a solicitor and he cares to instruct me.'

'Oh I see.' Brittling was recharging all our glasses. 'Play it by the rules, eh?'

'Exactly.' I intended to get this prospective client under control.

'Then it's much more fun breaking them when the time comes,' said the irresponsible Brittling.

'I must make it quite clear that I don't intend to break any rules for you, Brittling,' I said. 'Come and see me in Chambers with a solicitor.'

'Oh, I walk along the Bois du Boulogne ... With an independent air ...' Brittling began to sing in a way which apparently had nothing whatever to do with matters in question.

'Oh come along, Harold.' The girl Pauline took the old boy's arm and seemed to be urging him towards the door. 'He's not going to take your case on.'

'Why ever not?' Brittling seemed puzzled.

'*She* doesn't like you. And I don't think *he* likes you much either.'

'You can hear them all *declare*, I must be a *millionaire*,' Brittling sang and then looked at me intently. 'Horace Rumpole may not like me,' he said at last, 'but he envies me.'

'Why should he do that?'

'Because of what he has to live with.' Brittling's magnificent gestures seemed to embrace the entire room. 'Pissy watercolours!'

And then they left us, as unexpectedly as they had come, abandoning the rest of the Veuve Cliquot, which we had with our poached eggs for supper. It wasn't until much later, when we were lying at a discreet distance in the matrimonial bed, that I happened to say to Hilda, by way of encouragement, 'I don't suppose we'll see either of them again.'

'Oh yes you will,' she announced, as I thought, tartly. 'You'll do the case. You won't be able to resist it!'

'I can resist Mr Harold Brittling extremely easily,' I assured her.

'But *her*. Can you resist *her*, Rumpole?' And she went on in some disgust, 'Those thighs that simply seem to be *asking* for an HB pencil. I don't know when I've heard anything quite so revolting!'

'All the same, old Brittling seems to enjoy life.' I said it quietly, under my breath, but She almost heard me.

'*What* did you say?'

'I said I don't suppose he's got a wife.'

'That's what I thought you said.' And Hilda, somewhat

mortified, snapped off the light, having decided it was high time we lost consciousness together.

To understand the extraordinary case of the Queen against Harold Brittling, it is necessary to ask if you have a nodding acquaintance with the work of the late Septimus Cragg, R.A. Before he turned up his toes, which I imagine must have been shortly before the last war, Septimus Cragg appeared to the public gaze as just what they expected of the most considerable British painter of his time. His beard, once a flaming red, later a nicotine-stained white, his long procession of English and European mistresses, his farmhouse in Sussex, his huge collection of good-looking children who suffered greatly from never being able to paint as well as their father, his public denunciations of most other living artists, and his frequently pronounced belief that Brighton Pavilion was a far finer manifestation of the human spirit than Chartres Cathedral – all these things brought him constantly to the attention of the gossip columnists, and perhaps made his work undervalued in his final years.

Now, of course, as I discovered when I started to do a little preparation for the defence of Harold Brittling, there has been a considerable boom in Craggs. The generally held view is that he was by far the finest of the British Post-Impressionists, and had he had the luck to be born in Dieppe, a port where a good deal of his life and a great many of his love affairs were celebrated, he might be mentioned in the same breath as such noted Frog artists as Degas and Bonnard. By now the art world will pay a great deal of hard cash for a Cragg in mint condition, particularly if it's a good nude. There's nothing that has the art world reaching for its cheque book, so it seems, as quickly as a good nude.

The rise in expert esteem of the paintings of Septimus Cragg was shown dramatically in the prices fetched in a recent sale at which Harold Brittling was seen to be behaving in a somewhat curious manner. The particular Cragg to come under the hammer was entitled 'Nancy at the Hôtel du Vieux Port, Dieppe', and it appeared to have an impeccable pedigree, having been put up for auction by a Miss Price, an elderly spinster lady who lived in Worthing and was none other than Septimus Cragg's niece. As the bidding rose steadily from fifty to fifty-six thousand pounds, and as the picture was finally knocked down to a Mrs De Moyne of New Haven, Connecticut, for a cool sixty thousand, Harold Brittling, sitting beside a silent and undemonstrative Pauline in the audience, could be seen giggling helplessly. On his way out of the auction, the beaming Brittling was fingered by two officers of the Fine Art and Antiques Department at Scotland Yard and taken into custody. Pauline was sent to enlist the immediate help of Horace Rumpole, and so earned the suspicious disapproval of She Who Must Be Obeyed.

Nancy, whoever she may have been, was clearly a generously built, cheerful young lady, who brought out the best in Septimus Cragg. He had painted her naked, with a mane of copper-coloured hair, standing against the light of a hotel bedroom window, through which the masts and funnels of the old port were hazily visible. In the foreground there was a strip of purplish carpet, a china basin and jug on a wash stand, and the end of a brass bed, over which a man's trousers, fitted with a pair of braces, were dangling negligently. I was looking at a reproduction of the work in question in my Chambers. I hadn't yet seen the glowing original; but even in a flat, coloured photograph, the picture gave off the feeling of a moment of happiness, caught for ever. I felt, looking at it, I must confess, a bit of a pang. There hadn't, I had to face it, been many such mornings in hotel bedrooms in Dieppe in the long life and career of Horace Rumpole, barrister-at-law.

'It's only a reproduction,' Brittling said. 'Doesn't do it a bit of justice.'

And Mr Myers, old Myersy, the solicitor's managing clerk, who has seen me through more tough spots down the Bailey than I've had hot dinners, who sat there with his overcoat pockets bulging with writs and summonses, puffed at his nauseating, bubbling old pipe and said, as though we were looking at a bit of bloodstained sweatshirt or a mortuary photograph, 'That's it, Mr Rumpole. Exhibit J. L. T. (One). That's the evidence.'

Brittling, it seemed, had at least partially come to his senses. He had decided to consult a solicitor and approach me in a more formal manner than the mere lobbing of beer cans at my kitchen window. He looked at the exhibit in question and smiled appreciatively.

'It's a corker, though, as a composition, isn't it?'

'How is it as a forgery? That's what you're charged with, you know,' I reminded him, to bring the conversation down from the high aesthetic plane.

'A smashing composition,' Brittling went on as though he hadn't heard. 'And if you saw the texture of paint, and the way the curtains are moving in the wind from the harbour! There's only one man who could ever paint the air behind a curtain like that.'

'So it's the genuine article!' Myers assured me. 'That's what we're saying, Mr Rumpole.'

'Of course it's genuine!' Brittling called on the support of Keats: ' "A thing of beauty . . . is a joy for ever:" '

I helped him with the quotation,

'Its loveliness increases; it will never
Pass into nothingness; but still will keep
A bower quiet for us, and a sleep
Full of sweet dreams, and health, and quiet breathing . . .

Quiet breathing in the Nick,' I reminded him somewhat brutally, 'if we don't keep our wits about us. Did you ever know Cragg?'

'Septimus . . . ?'

'Did you know him?' I asked, and Brittling embarked on a fragment of autobiography.

'I was the rising star of the Slade School,' he said. 'Cragg was the old lion, the king of the pack. He was always kind to me. Had me down to the farmhouse at Rottingdean. Full of his children by various mothers, and society beauties, waiting to have their portraits painted. There was such a lot of laughter in that house, and so many young people . . .'

' "Nancy at Dieppe".' I picked up the reproduction. The features were blurred against the light, but didn't there seem to be something vaguely familiar about the girl in the hotel bedroom? 'Do you recognize the model at all?'

'Cragg had so many.' Brittling shrugged.

'Models or girlfriends?'

'It was usually the same thing.'

'Was it really? And *this* one?'

'Seems vaguely familiar.' Brittling echoed my thoughts. I gave him my searching look, reserved for difficult clients. 'The sort of thighs,' I asked him, 'which simply call out for an HB pencil, would you say?'

Brittling didn't seem to resent my suggestion. In fact he turned to me and gave a small but deliberate wink. I didn't like that. Clients who wink at you when you as good as tell them that you think they're guilty can be most unsettling.

I was still unsettled as I undressed in the matrimonial bedroom in Froxbury Court. Hilda, in hairnet and bed jacket, was propped up on the pillows doing the *Daily Telegraph* crossword puzzle. As I hung up the striped trousers I thought that it was a scene which would never have been painted by Septimus Cragg. I was reflecting on the difference between my life and that of the rip-roaring old R.A. and I said, thoughtfully, 'It all depends, I suppose, on where your talents lie.'

'What does?' Hilda asked in a disinterested sort of way.

'I mean, if my talents hadn't been for bloodstains, and cross-examining coppers on their notebooks, and addressing juries on the burden of proof ... If I'd had an unusual aptitude for jotting down a pair of thighs in a hotel bedroom ...'

'You've seen *her* again, haven't you?' Hilda was no longer sounding disinterested.

'I might have been living in a farmhouse in Sussex with eight pool-eyed children with eight different mothers, all devoted to me, and duchesses knocking on my door to have their portraits painted. My work might have meant trips to Venice and Aix-en-Provence instead of London Sessions and the Uxbridge Magistrates Court! No, I didn't see her. She didn't come to the conference.'

'You want to concentrate on what you *can* do, Rumpole. Fine chance *I* ever have of getting invited to the Palace.'

'No need for the black jacket and pin stripes. Throw away the collar like a blunt execution. All you need is an old tweed suit and a young woman who's kind enough to wear nothing but a soulful expression. What's all that about the Palace?'

'They're making Guthrie Featherstone a judge, you know,' Hilda said, as though it were all, in some obscure way, my fault.

'Whoever told you that?'

I felt suddenly sorry for the old Q.C., M.P., and worried that the chump's chances might be blown by a lot of careless talk. For Hilda told me that she had met Marigold Featherstone somewhere near Harrods, and that whilst she had been looking for bargains, the future Lady Marigold had told her that she had acquired a suitable outfit with the 'Princess Di' look for a visit to the Palace on the occasion of our not very learned Head of Chambers being awarded a handle to his name. When Hilda, not a little mystified, had asked her what sort of handle they had in mind, Marigold had rushed off in the direction of Sloane Street, urging Hilda to forget every word she had said, forgetting, of course, that She Who Must Be Obeyed never forgets.

'You didn't tell anyone else this, did you?' I asked.

'Well, no one except Phillida Erskine-Brown. I happened to run into her going into Sainsbury's.'

'You did *what*?'

'And Phillida explained it all to me. If you get made a judge you're knighted as a matter of course, and have to go to Buck House and all that sort of thing. So that was why Marigold was buying a new outfit.'

I was appalled, quite frankly. Phillida Erskine-Brown is a formidable lady advocate, the Portia of our Chambers. As for her husband, as I explained to Hilda, 'Claude Erskine-Brown gossips about the judiciary in the way teenagers gossip about film actors. Star-struck is our Claude. Practically goes down on his knees to anything in ermine! And he pops into Pommeroy's whenever he gets a legal aid cheque. Let's just hope he doesn't get paid until poor old Featherstone's got his bottom safely on the Bench.'

'One thing is quite certain, Rumpole,' said Hilda, filling in a clue. 'There's no earthly chance of your ever getting a handle.'

A few weeks later I had slipped in to Pommeroy's Wine Bar for a glass of luncheon when Guthrie Featherstone came up to me and, having looked nervously over his shoulder like a man who expects to be joined at any moment by the Hound of Heaven, said, 'Horace! I came in here to buy a small sherry ...'

'No harm in that, Guthrie.' I tried to sound reassuring.

'And Jack Pommeroy, you know what Jack Pommeroy called me?' His voice sank to a horrified whisper. 'He called me *"Judge"*!'

'Well, you'll have to get used to it.' I couldn't be bothered to whisper.

Featherstone looked round, appalled. 'Horace, for God's sake! Don't you see what this means? It means someone's been talking.'

And then his glance fell on a table where Claude Erskine-Brown was knocking back the Beaujolais Villages with assorted barristers. Featherstone's cup of unhappiness was full when Erskine-Brown raised his glass, as though in congratulation.

'Look! Claude Erskine-Brown, raising his glass at me!' Featherstone pointed it out, rather unnecessarily, I thought.

'Just a friendly gesture,' I assured him.

'You remember poor old Moreton Colefax, not made a judge because he couldn't keep his mouth shut.' The Q.C., M.P., looked near to tears. 'It's all round the Temple.'

'Of course it's not. Don't worry.'

'Then why is Erskine-Brown drinking to me?'

'He thinks you *look* like a judge. Beauty, after all, Guthrie my old darling, is entirely in the eye of the beholder.' Curiously enough, when I said that, Guthrie Featherstone didn't look particularly cheered up.

In the course of time, however, Guthrie Featherstone, Q.C., M.P., did cheer up, considerably. He fulfilled his destiny, and took on that role which led him to be appointed head boy of his prep school and a prefect at Marlborough, because, quite simply, he never got up anyone's nose and there were no other likely candidates available.

At long last Guthrie's cheerfulness round the Sheridan Club and his dedication to losing golf matches against senior judges earned him his just reward. A man who had spent most of his life in an agony of indecision, who spent months debating such questions as whether we should have a coffee machine in the clerk's room, or did the downstairs loo need redecorating; a fellow who found it so hard to choose between left and right that he became a Social Democrat; a barrister who agonized for hours about whether it would be acceptable to wear a light grey tie in Chambers in April, or whether such jollifications should be confined to the summer months, was appointed one of Her Majesty's judges, and charged to decide great issues of life and liberty.

Arise, Sir Guthrie! From now on barristers, men far older than you, will bow before you. Men and women will be taken off to prison at your decree. You will have made a Lady out of Marigold, and your old mother is no doubt extremely proud of you. There is only one reason, one very good reason, for that smile of amiable bewilderment to fade from the Featherstone features. You may make the most awful pig's breakfast of the case you're trying, and they'll pour scorn on you from a great height in the Court of Appeal.

So Guthrie Featherstone, in the full panoply of a Red Judge at the Old Bailey, was sitting paying polite and somewhat anxious attention to a piece of high comedy entitled R. *v.* Brittling, starring Claude Erskine-Brown for the prosecution, and Horace Rumpole for the defence. As the curtain rose on the second day of the hearing the limelight fell on a Mr Edward Gandolphini, an extremely expensive-looking art expert and connoisseur, with a suit from Savile Row, iron-grey hair and a tan fresh from a short break in the Bahamas. In the audience Pauline was sitting with her embroidered holdall, listening with fierce concentration, and in the dock, the prisoner at the Bar was unconcernedly drawing a devastating portrait of the learned Judge.

'Mr Gandolphini.' Erskine-Brown was examining the witness with all the humble care of a gynaecologist approaching a duchess who had graciously consented to lie down on his couch. 'You are the author of *Cragg and the British Impressionists* and the leading expert on this particular painter?'

'It has been said, my Lord.' The witness flashed his teeth at the learned Judge, who flashed his back.

'I'm sure it has, Mr Gandolphini,' said Featherstone, J.

'And are you also,' Erskine-Brown asked most respectfully, 'the author of many works on twentieth-century painting and adviser to private collectors and galleries throughout the world?'

'I am.' Gandolphini admitted it.

'And have you examined this alleged "Septimus Cragg"?' Erskine-Brown gestured towards the picture which, propped on a chair in front of the jury, revealed a world of secret delight miles away from the Central Criminal Court.

'I have, my Lord.' Mr Gandolphini again addressed himself to the learned Judge. 'I may say it isn't included in any existing catalogue of the artist's works. Of course, at one time, I believe, it was thought it came from a genuine source, the artist's niece in Worthing.'

'Now we know that to be untrue,' said Erskine-Brown with a meaningful look at the jury, and thereby caused me to stagger, filled with extremely righteous indignation, to my feet.

'My Lord!' I trumpeted. 'We know nothing of the sort – until that has been found as a fact by the twelve sensible people who sit in that jury-box and *no one else*!'

'Very well,' said his Lordship, trying to placate everybody. 'Very well, Mr Rumpole. Perhaps he suspected it to be untrue. Is that the situation, Mr Gandolphini?'

Guthrie turned to the witness, smiling, but I wasn't letting him off quite so easily. 'My Lord, how can what this witness suspected possibly be evidence?'

'Mr Rumpole. I know you don't want to be difficult.' As usual Featherstone exhibited his limited understanding of the case. I considered it my duty to be as difficult as possible.

'May I assist, my Lord?' said Erskine-Brown.

'I would be grateful if you would, Mr Erskine-Brown. Mr Rumpole, perhaps we can allow Mr Erskine-Brown to assist us?'

I subsided. I had no desire to take part in this vicarage tea-party, with everyone assisting each other to cucumber sand-wiches. I thought that after one day on the Bench Guthrie had learnt the habit of getting cosy with the prosecution.

'Mr Gandolphini,' Erskine-Brown positively purred at the wit-ness, 'if you *had* known that this picture did not in fact come from Miss Price's collection, would you have had some doubts about its authenticity?'

'That question is entirely speculative.' I was on my feet again.

'Mr Rumpole.' Featherstone was being extremely patient. 'Do you want me to rule on the propriety of Mr Erskine-Brown's question?'

'I think the time may have come to make up the judicial mind, yes.'

'Then I rule that Mr Erskine-Brown may ask his question.' Guthrie then smiled at me in the nicest possible way and said, 'Sorry, Mr Rumpole.' The old darling looked broken-hearted.

'Well, Mr Gandolphini?' Erskine-Brown was still waiting for his answer.

'I had a certain doubt about the picture from the start,' Gandolphini said carefully.

'From the start ... you had a doubt ...' Featherstone didn't seem to be able to stop talking while he wrote a note.

'Take it slowly now. Just follow his Lordship's pencil,' Erskine-Brown advised the witness and, in the ensuing pause, I happened to whisper to Myersy, 'And you may be sure his pencil's not drawing thighs in Dieppe.'

'Did you say something, Mr Rumpole?' his Lordship asked, worried.

'Nothing, my Lord, of the slightest consequence,' I rose to explain.

'I say that because I have extremely acute hearing.' Featherstone smiled at the jury, and I could think of nothing better to say than, 'Congratulations.'

'I thought the painting very fine.' Gandolphini returned to the matter in hand. 'And certainly in the manner of Septimus Cragg. It is a beautiful piece of work, but I don't think I ever saw a Cragg where the shadows had so much colour in them.'

'Colour? In the shadows? Could I have a look?' The Judge tapped his pencil on the Bench and called, 'Usher.' Obediently the Usher carried the artwork up to his Lordship on the bench, and his Lordship got out his magnifying glass and submitted Nancy's warm flesh tints and flowing curves to a careful, legal examination.

'There's a good deal of green, and even purple in the shadows on the naked body, my Lord,' Gandolphini explained.

'Yes, I do see that,' said the Judge. 'Have you seen that, Mr Rumpole? Most interesting! Usher, let Mr Rumpole have a look at that. Do you wish to borrow my glass, Mr Rumpole?'

'No, my Lord. I think I can manage with the naked eye.' I was brought the picture by the Usher and sat staring at it, as though waiting for some sudden revelation.

'Tell us,' Erskine-Brown asked the witness. 'Is "Nancy" a model who appears in any of Cragg's works known to you?'

'In none, my Lord.' Gandolphini shook his head, almost sadly.

'Did Cragg paint most of his models many times?'

'Many, many times, my Lord.'

'Thank you, Mr Gandolphini.'

Erskine-Brown sat, apparently satisfied and I rose up slowly, and slowly turned the picture so the witness could see it. 'You said, did you not, Mr Gandolphini, that this is a beautiful painting.' I began in a way that I was pleased to see the witness didn't expect.

'It's very fine. Yes.'

'Has it not at least sixty thousand pounds' worth of beauty?' I asked and then gave the jury a look.

'I can't say.'

'Can you not? Isn't part of your trade reducing beauty to mere cash!'

'I value pictures, yes.' I could see that Gandolphini was consciously keeping his temper.

'And would you not agree that this is a valuable picture, no matter who painted it?'

'I have said ...' I knew that he was going to try and avoid answering the question, and I interrupted him. 'You have said it's beautiful. Were you not telling this jury the truth, Mr Gandolphini?'

'Yes, but ...'

>   ' "Beauty is truth, truth beauty," – that is all
>   Ye know on earth, and all ye need to know.'

I turned and gave the jury their two bobs' worth of Keats.

'Is that really all we need to know, Mr Rumpole?' said a voice from on high.

'In this case, yes, my Lord.'

'I think I'll want to hear legal argument about that, Mr Rumpole.' Featherstone appeared to be making some form of minor joke, but I answered him seriously. 'Oh, you shall. I promise you, your Lordship.' I turned to the witness. 'Mr Gandolphini, by "beauty" I suppose you mean that this picture brings joy and delight to whoever stands before it?'

'I suppose that would be a definition.'

'You suppose it would. And let us suppose it turned out to have been painted by an even more famous artist than Septimus Cragg. Let us suppose it had been done by Degas or Manet.'

'Who, Mr Rumpole?' I seemed to have gone rather too fast for his Lordship's pencil.

'Manet, my Lord. Edouard Manet.' I explained carefully. 'If it were painted by a more famous artist it wouldn't become more of a thing of beauty and a joy to behold, would it?'

'No ... but ...'

'And if it were painted by a less famous artist – Joe Bloggs, say, or my Lord the learned Judge, one wet Sunday afternoon ...'

'Really, Mr Rumpole!' Featherstone, J., smiled modestly, but I was busy with the con-o-sewer. 'It wouldn't become *less* beautiful, would it, Mr Gandolphini? It would have the same colourful shadows, the same feeling of light and air and breeze from the harbour. The same warmth of the human body?'

'Exactly the same, of course, but ...'

'I don't want to interrupt ...' Erskine-Brown rose to his feet, wanting to interrupt.

'Then don't, Mr Erskine-Brown!' I suggested. The suggestion had no effect. Erskine-Brown made a humble submission to his Lordship. 'My Lord, in my humble submission we are not investigating the beauty of this work, but the value, and the value of this picture depends on its being a genuine Septimus Cragg. Therefore my learned friend's questions seem quite irrelevant.'

At which Erskine-Brown subsided in satisfaction, and his Lordship called on Rumpole to reply.

'My learned friend regards this as a perfectly ordinary criminal case,' I said. 'Of course it isn't. We are discussing the value of a work of art, a thing of beauty and a joy forever. We are not debating the price of fish!'

There was a sound of incipient applause from the dcck, so I whispered to Myersy, and instructed him to remind Brittling that he was not in the pit at the Old Holborn Empire but in the dock at the Old Bailey. I was interrupted by the Judge saying that perhaps I had better pursue another line with the witness.

'My Lord,' I said. 'I think we have heard enough – from Mr Gandolphini.' So I sat and looked triumphantly at the jury, as though I had, in a way they might not have entirely understood, won a point. Then I noticed, to my displeasure, that the learned Judge was engaged in some sort of intimate *tête-à-tête* with the man Gandolphini, who had not yet left the witness-box.

'Mr Gandolphini, just one point,' said the Judge.

'Yes, my Lord.'

'I happen myself to be extremely fond of Claude Lorrain,' said Featherstone, pronouncing the first name 'Clode' in an exaggerated Frog manner of speaking.

'Oh, my Lord, I do *so* agree.' Gandolphini waxed effusive.

'Absolutely *super* painter, isn't he? Now, I suppose, if you saw a good, a beautiful picture which you were assured came from a reputable source, you might accept that as a "Clode" Lorrain, mightn't you?'

'Certainly, my Lord.'

'But if you were later to learn that the picture had been painted in the seventeenth century and not the eighteenth! Well, you might change your opinion, mightn't you?'

Featherstone looked pleased with himself, but the turn of the conversation seemed to be causing Gandolphini intense embarrassment. 'Well, not really, my Lord,' he murmured.

'Oh, I'm sorry. Will you tell us why not?' The learned Judge looked nettled and prepared to take a note.

Gandolphini hated to do it, but as a reputable art expert he had to say, 'Well. You see. Claude Lorrain *did* paint in the seventeenth century, my Lord.'

It was almost the collapse of the Judge's morale. However, he started to talk rather quickly to cover his embarrassment. 'Oh, yes. Yes, that's right. Of course he did. Perhaps some of the jury will know that ... or not, as the case may be.' He smiled at the jury, who looked distinctly puzzled, and then at the witness. 'We haven't all got *your* expertise, Mr Gandolphini.'

All I could think of to say was a warning to Mr Justice Featherstone to avoid setting himself up as any sort of con-o-sewer. Wiser counsels prevailed and I didn't say it.

For our especial delight we then had an appearance in the witness-box by Mrs De Moyne, a well-manicured lady in a dark, businesslike suit, with horn-rimmed glasses and a voice like the side of a nail file. Mrs De Moyne spoke with the assurance of an art lover who weighs up a Post-Impressionist to the nearest dollar, and gives you the tax advantage of a gift to the Museum of Modern Art without drawing breath. She gave a brief account of her visit to the auction room to preview the Cragg in question, of her being assured that the picture had a perfect pedigree, having come straight from the artist's niece with no dealers involved, and described her successful bidding against stiff competition from a couple of Bond Street galleries and the Italian agent of a collector in Kuwait.

Erskine-Brown asked the witness if she believed she had been buying a genuine Septimus Cragg. 'Of course I did,' rasped Mrs De Moyne. 'I was terribly deceived.' So Erskine-Brown sat down, I'm sure, with a feeling of duty done.

'Mrs De Moyne. Wouldn't you agree,' I asked as I rose to cross-examine, 'that you bought a very beautiful picture?'

'Yes,' Mrs De Moyne admitted.

'So beautiful you were prepared to pay sixty thousand pounds for it?'

'Yes, I was.'

'And it is still the same beautiful picture? The picture hasn't changed since you bought it, has it, Mrs De Moyne? Not by one drop of paint! Is the truth of the matter that you're not interested in art but merely in collecting autographs!'

Of course this made the jury titter and brought Erskine-

Brown furiously to his hind legs. I apologized for any pain and suffering I might have caused, and went on. 'When did you first doubt that this was a Cragg?' I asked.

'Someone rang me up.'

'*Someone?* What did they say?'

'Do you want to let this evidence in, Mr Rumpole?' The learned Judge was heard to be warning me for my own good.

'Yes, my Lord. I'm curious to know,' I reassured him. So Mrs De Moyne answered the question. 'That was what made me get in touch with the police,' she said. 'The man who called me said the picture wasn't a genuine Cragg, and it never had belonged to Cragg's niece. He also said that I'd got a bargain.'

'A bargain. Why?'

'Because it was better than a Cragg.'

'Did he give you his name?' It was a risky question, dangerous to ask because I didn't know the answer.

'He did, yes. But I was so upset I didn't pay too much attention to it. I don't think I can remember it.'

'Try,' I encouraged her.

'White. I think it had "white" in it.'

'Whiting? Whitehead?' I tried a few names on her.

'No.' Mrs De Moyne shook her head defeated. 'I can't remember.'

'Thank you, Mrs De Moyne.' When I sat down I heard a gentle voice in my ear whisper, 'You were wonderful! Harold said you would be.' It was the girl, Pauline, who had left her seat to murmur comforting words to Rumpole.

'Oh nonsense,' I whispered back, but then had to add, for the sake of truthfulness, 'Well, just a bit wonderful, perhaps. How do you think it's going, Myersy?'

The knowing old legal executive in front of me admitted that we were doing better than he expected, which was high praise from such a source, but then he looked towards the witness-box and whispered, 'That's the one I'm afraid of.'

The fearful object in Mr Myers's eyes was a small, grey-haired lady with wind-brightened cheeks and small glittering eyes, wearing a tweed suit and sensible shoes, who took the oath in a clear voice and gave her name as Miss Marjorie Evangeline Price, of 31 Majuba Road, Worthing, and admitted that the late Cragg, R.A., had been her Uncle Septimus.

'Do you know the defendant Brittling?' Erskine-Brown began his examination-in-chief, and I growled, '*Mister* Brittling,' insisting on a proper respect for the prisoner at the Bar. I don't think the jury heard me. They were all listening eagerly to Miss Marjorie Evangeline Price, who talked to them as though she were having a cup of afternoon tea with a few friends she'd known for years.

'He came to see me in Worthing. He said he had one of Uncle Septimus's paintings to sell and he wanted me to put it into the auction for him. The real seller didn't want his name brought into it.'

'Did Mr Brittling tell you why?'

'He said it was a businessman who didn't want it to be known that he was selling his pictures. People might have thought he was in financial trouble, apparently.'

'So did you agree to the picture being sold in your name?'

'I'm afraid it was very wrong of me, but he was going to give me a little bit of a percentage. An ex-schoolmistress does get a very small pension.' Miss Price smiled at the jury and they smiled back, as though of course they understood completely. She was, unhappily for old Brittling, the sort of witness that the jury love, a sweet old lady who's not afraid to admit she's wrong.

'Did you have any idea that the picture wasn't genuine?'

'Oh no, of course not. I had no idea of that. Mr Brittling was very charming and persuasive.'

At which Miss Price looked at my client in the dock and smiled. The jury also looked at him, but they didn't smile.

'And how much of the money did Mr Brittling allow you to keep?'

'I think, I'm not sure, I *think* it was ten per cent.'

'How very generous. Thank you, Miss Price.'

Erskine-Brown had shot his bolt and sat down. I rose and put on the sweetest, gentlest voice in the Rumpole repertoire. Cross-examining Miss Price was going to be like walking on eggs. I had to move towards any sort of favourable answer on tiptoe. 'Miss Price, do you remember your uncle, Septimus Cragg?' I started to move her gently down Memory Lane.

'I remember him coming to our house when I was a little girl. He had a red beard and a very hairy tweed suit. I remember sitting on his lap.'

His Lordship smiled at her – he was clearly pro-Price.

'Is that all you can remember about him?' I was still probing gently.

'I remember Uncle Septimus telling me that there were two sorts of people in the world – nurses and patients. He seemed to think I'd grow up to be a nurse.'

'Oh, really? And which was he?'

'My Lord, can this possibly be relevant?' Erskine-Brown seemed to think the question was fraught with danger, when I was really only making conversation with the witness.

'I can't see it at the moment, Mr Erskine-Brown,' the Judge admitted.

'Which did he say he was?' I went on, ignoring the unmannerly interruption.

'Oh, he said he could always find someone to look after him. I think he was a bit of a spoiled baby really.'

The jury raised a polite titter, and Erskine-Brown sat down. I looked as though I'd got an answer of great importance.

'Did he? Did he say that? Tell me, Miss Price, do you know who Nancy was?'

'Nancy?' Miss Price looked puzzled.

'This picture is of Nancy, apparently. In an hotel bedroom in Dieppe. Who was Nancy?'

'I'm afraid I have no idea. I suppose she must have been a' – she gave a small, meaningful pause – 'a friend of Uncle Septimus.'

'Yes. I suppose she must have been.' I pointed to the picture which had brought us all to the Old Bailey. 'You've never seen this picture before?'

'Oh no. I didn't ask to see it. Mr Brittling told me about it and, well, of course I trusted him, you see.' Miss Price smiled sweetly at the jury and I sat down. There's no doubt about it. There's nothing more like banging your head against a brick wall than cross-examining a witness who's telling nothing but the truth.

*

Later that afternoon the Usher came to counsel engaged on the case with a message. The learned Judge would be glad to see us for a cup of tea in his room. So we were received amongst the red leather armchairs, the Law Reports, the silver-framed photographs of Marigold and the Featherstone twins, Simon and Sarah.

The Judge was hovering over the bone china, dispensing the Earl Grey and petit beurres, and the Clerk of the Court was lurking in the background to make sure there was no hanky-panky, I suppose, or an attempt to drop folding money into the Judge's wig.

'Come along, Horace. Sit you down, Claude. Sit you down. You'll take a dish of tea, won't you? What I wanted to ask you fellows is ... How long is this case going to last?'

'Well, Judge ... Guthrie ...' said Erskine-Brown, stirring his tea. 'That rather depends on Rumpole here. He has to put the defence. If there *is* a defence.'

'I don't want to hurry you, Horace. The point is, I may not be able to sit next Monday afternoon.' The Judge gave a secret sort of a smile and said modestly, 'Appointment at the Palace, you know what these things are ...'

'Marigold got a new outfit for it, has she?' I couldn't resist asking.

'Well, the girls like all that sort of nonsense, don't they?' he said, as though the whole matter were almost too trivial to mention. 'It's not so much an invitation as a Royal command. You know the type of thing.'

'I *don't* know,' I assured him. 'My only Royal command was to join the R.A.F. Ground Staff, as I remember it.'

'Yes, Horace, of course. You old war-horse!' There was a pause while we all had a gulp of tea and a nibble of biscuit. 'How much longer are you going to be?' the Judge asked.

'Well, not long, I suppose. It's rather an absurd little case, isn't it? Bit of a practical joke, really. Isn't that what it is? Just a prank, more or less.' I was working my way towards a small fine should the old idiot Brittling go down; but to my dismay Mr Justice Featherstone looked extremely serious.

'I can't pretend that I find it a joke, exactly,' he said, in his new-found judicial manner.

'Well, I don't suppose that the shades of the prison house begin to fall around the wretched Brittling, do they? I mean, all he did was to pull the legs of a few so-called con-o-sewers.'

'And made himself a considerable sum of money in the process,' said Erskine-Brown, who was clearly anxious to be no sort of help.

'It's deceit, Horace. And forgery for personal profit. If your client's convicted I'm afraid I couldn't rule out a custodial sentence.' The Judge bit firmly into the last petit beurre.

'You couldn't?' I sounded incredulous.

'How could I?'

'Not send him to prison for a little bit of "let's pretend"? For a bit of a joke on a pompous profession?' I put down my cup and stood. My outrage was perfectly genuine. 'No. I don't suppose you could.'

Tea with the Judge was over, and I was about to follow Erskine-Brown and the learned Clerk out of his presence, when Mr Justice Featherstone called me back. 'Oh, Horace,' he said, 'a word in your ear.'

'Yes.'

'I've noticed you've fallen into rather a bad habit.'

'Bad habit?' What on earth, I wondered, was he about to accuse me of – being drunk in charge of a forgery case?

'Hands in pockets when you're addressing the Court. It looks so bad, Horace. Such a poor example to the younger men. Keep them out of the pockets, will you? I'm sure you don't mind me pulling you up about it?'

It was the old school prefect speaking. I left him without comment.

The hardest part of any case, I have always maintained, comes when your client enters the witness-box. Up until that moment you have been able to protect him by attacking those who give evidence against him, and by concealing from the jury the most irritating aspects of his personality. Once he starts to give evidence, however, the client is on his own. He is like a child who has left its family on the beach and is swimming, in a solitary fashion, out to sea, where no cries of warning can be heard.

I knew Harold Brittling was going to be a bad witness by the enormously confident way that he marched into the box, held the Bible up aloft and promised to tell the truth, the whole truth and nothing but the truth. He was that dreadful sort of witness, the one who can't wait to give evidence, and who has been longing, with unconcealed impatience, for his day in Court. He leant against the top of the box and surveyed us all with an expression of tolerant disdain, as though we had made a bit of a pig's breakfast of his case up to that moment, and it was now up to him to put it right.

I dug my hands as deeply as possible into my pockets, and asked what might prove to be the only really simple question.

'Is your name Harold Reynolds Gainsborough Brittling?'

'Yes, it is. You've got *that* perfectly right, Mr Rumpole.'

I didn't laugh; neither, I noticed, did the jury.

'You came of an artistic family, Mr Brittling?' It seemed a legitimate deduction.

'Oh yes,' said Brittling, and went on modestly, 'I showed an extraordinary aptitude, my Lord, right from the start. At the Slade School, which I entered at the ripe old age of sixteen, I was twice a gold medallist and by far the most brilliant student of my year.'

The jury appeared to be moderately nauseated by this glowing account of himself. I changed the subject. 'Mr Brittling, did you know the late Septimus Cragg?'

'I knew and loved him. There is a comradeship among artists, my Lord, and he was undoubtedly the finest painter of *his* generation. He came to a student exhibition and I think he recognized . . . well . . .'

I was hoping he wouldn't say 'a fellow genius'; he did.

'After that did you meet Cragg on a number of occasions?'

'You could say that. I became one of the charmed circle at Rottingdean.'

'Mr Brittling. Will you take in your hands Exhibit One.'

The Usher lifted Nancy and carried her to the witness-box. Harold Brittling gave me a look of withering scorn.

'This is a beautiful picture!' he said. 'Please don't call it

"Exhibit One", Mr Rumpole. "Exhibit One" might be a blunt instrument or something.'

The witness chuckled at this; no one else in Court smiled. I prayed to God that he'd leave the funnies to his learned Counsel.

'Where did that picture come from, Mr Brittling?'

'I really don't remember very clearly.' He looked airily round the Court as though it were a matter of supreme unimportance.

'You don't remember?' The Judge didn't seem able to believe what he was writing down.

'No, my Lord. When one is leading the life of an artist, small details escape the memory. I suppose Septimus must have given it to me on one of my visits to him. Artists pay these little tributes to each other.'

'Why did you take it to Miss Price and ask her to sell it?' I asked as patiently as possible.

'I suppose I thought that the dealers would have more faith in it if it came from that sort of source. And I rather wanted the old puss to get her little bit of commission.'

One thing emerged clearly from that bit of evidence: the jury didn't approve of Miss Price being called an 'old puss'. In fact, Brittling was going down with them like a cup of cold cod liver oil.

'Mr Brittling. What is your opinion of that picture?' Of course I wanted him to say that it was a genuine Cragg. Instead he closed his eyes and breathed in deeply. 'I think it is the work of the highest genius . . .'

'Slowly please . . .' The Judge was writing this art criticism down.

'Just watch his Lordship's pencil,' I advised the witness.

'I think it is a work of great beauty, my Lord . . . The painting of the curtains, and of the *air* in the room . . . Quite miraculous!'

'Did Septimus Cragg paint it?' I tried to bring Brittling's attention back to the case.

'It's a lovely thing.' And then the little man actually shrugged his shoulders. 'What does it matter who painted it?'

'For the purposes of this case, you can take it from me – it matters,' I instructed him. 'Now, have you any doubts that it is a genuine Cragg?'

'Only one thing gives me the slightest doubt.' Like all bad witnesses Brittling was incapable of a simple answer.

'What's that?'

'It really seems to be too good for him. It exists beautifully
on a height the old boy never reached before.'

'Did you paint that picture, Mr Brittling?' I tried to direct
his attention to the charge he was facing.

'Me? Is someone suggesting I did it?' Brittling seemed flattered
and delighted.

'Yes, Mr Brittling. Someone is.'

'Well, in all modesty, it really takes my breath away. You are
suggesting that I could produce a masterpiece like that!' And Mr
Brittling smiled triumphantly round the Court.

'I take it, Mr Rumpole, that the answer means "no".' The
Judge was looking understandably confused.

'Yes, of course. If your Lordship pleases.'

Featherstone, J. had interpreted Brittling's answer as a denial
of forgery. I thought that no further questions could possibly
improve the matter, and I sat down. Erskine-Brown rose to cross-
examine with the confident air of a hunter who sees his prey
snoozing gently at a range of about two feet.

'Mr Brittling,' he began quietly. 'Did you say you "laundered"
the picture through Miss Price?'

'He did *what*, Mr Erskine-Brown?' The Judge was not quite
with him.

'*Sold* the picture through Miss Price, my Lord, because it
seemed such an unimpeachable source.'

'Yes.' The witness didn't bother to deny it.

'Does that mean that the picture isn't entirely innocent?'

'Mr Erskine-Brown, all great art is innocent.' Brittling was outraged. It seemed that all we had left was the John Keats defence:

> 'Beauty is truth, truth beauty,' – that is all
> Ye know on earth, and all ye need to know.

'Then why this elaborate performance of selling the picture
through Miss Price?' Erskine-Brown raised his voice a little.

'Just to tease them a bit. Pull their legs ...' The worst was
happening. Brittling was chuckling again.

'Pull *whose* legs, Mr Brittling?'

'The art experts! The con-o-sewers. People like Teddy Gandolphini. I just wanted to twist their tails a little.'

'So we have all been brought here, to this Court, for a sort of a joke?' Erskine-Brown acted extreme amazement.

'Oh no. Not just a joke. Something very serious is at stake.' I didn't know what else Brittling was going to say, but I suspected it would be nothing helpful.

'What?' Erskine-Brown asked.

'My reputation.'

'Your reputation as an honest man, Mr Brittling?'

'Oh no. Far more important than that. My reputation as an artist! You see, if I did paint that picture, I must be a genius, mustn't I?'

Brittling beamed round the Court, but once again no one else was smiling. At the end of the day the Judge withdrew the defedant's bail, a bad sign in any case. Harold Brittling, however, seemed to feel he had had a triumph in the witness-box, and departed, with only a moderate show of irritation, for the Nick.

When I left Court – a little late, as we had the argument about bail after the jury had departed – I saw a lonely figure on a bench in the marble hall outside Number 1 Court. It was Pauline, shivering slightly, wrapped in her ethnic clothing, clutching her holdall, and her undoubtedly beautiful face was, I saw when she turned it in my direction, wet with tears. Checking a desire to suggest that the temporary absence of the appalling Brittling might come as something of a relief to his nearest and dearest, I tried to put a cheerful interpretation on recent events.

'Don't worry.' I sat down beside her and groped for a small cigar. 'Bail's quite often stopped, once a defendant's given his evidence. The jury won't know about it. Personally, I think the Judge was just showing off. Well, he's young, and a bit wet round the judicial ears.' There was a silence. Young Pauline didn't seem to be at all cheered up. Then she said, very quietly, 'They'll find Harold guilty, won't they?' She was too bright to be deceived and I exploded in irritation. 'What the hell's the matter with old Harold? He's making his evidence as weak as possible. Does he want to lose this case?'

And then she said something I hadn't expected: 'You know he does, don't you?' She put her hand on my arm in a way I found distinctly appealing.

'Please,' she said, 'will you take me for a drink? I really need one. I'd love it if you would.'

In all the circumstances it seemed a most reasonable request. 'All right,' I said. 'We'll go to Pommeroy's Wine Bar. It's only just over the road.'

'No we won't,' Pauline decided. 'We'll go to the Old Monmouth in Greek Street. I want you to meet somebody.'

The Old Monmouth, to which we travelled by taxi at Pauline's suggestion, turned out to be a large, rather gloomy pub with a past which was considerably more interesting than its present. Behind the bar there were signed photographs, and even sketches by a number of notable artists who drank there before the war and in the forties and fifties. There were also photographs of boxers, dancers and music hall performers, and many caricatures of 'Old Harry', the former proprietor, with a huge handlebar moustache, whose son, 'Young Harry', with a smaller moustache, still appeared occasionally behind the bar.

The habits of artists have changed. Perhaps they now spend their evenings sitting at home in Islington or Kew, drinking rare Burgundy and listening to Vivaldi on the music centre. The days when a painter started the evening with a couple of pints of Guinness and ended stumbling out into Soho with a bottle of whisky in his pocket and an art school model, wearing scarlet lipstick and a beret, on his arm have no doubt gone for ever. At the Old Monmouth pale young men with orange quiffs were engaged in computerized battles on various machines. There were some eager executives in three-piece suits buying drinks for their secretaries, and half a dozen large men loudly discussing the virtues of their motor cars. No one looked in the least like an artist.

'They all used to come here,' Pauline said, nostalgic for a past she never knew. 'Augustus John, Sickert, Septimus Cragg. And their women. All their women . . .'

'Wonder they found room for them all.' I handed her the rum

she had requested, and took a gulp of a glass of red wine which made the taste of Pommeroy's plonk seem like Château-Lafite. I couldn't quite imagine what I was doing, drinking in a Soho pub with an extraordinarily personable young woman, and I was thankful for the thought that the least likely person to come through the door was She Who Must Be Obeyed.

So I tossed back the rest of the appalling Spanish-style *vin ordinaire* with the sort of gesture which I imagine Septimus Cragg might have used on a similar occasion.

'It's changed a bit now,' Pauline said, looking round the bar regretfully. 'Space Invaders!' She gave a small smile, and then her smile faded. 'Horace ... Can I call you Horace?'

'Please.'

She put a hand on my arm. I didn't avoid it.

'You've been very kind to me. You and Hilda. But it's time you knew the truth.'

I moved a little away from her, somewhat nervously, I must confess. When someone offers to tell you the truth in the middle of a difficult criminal trial it's rarely good news.

'No,' I said firmly.

'What?' She looked up at me, puzzled.

'The time for me to know the truth is when this case is over. Too much of the truth now and I'd have to give up defending that offbeat little individual you go around with. Anyway,' I pulled out my watch, 'I've got to get back to Gloucester Road.'

'Please! Please don't leave me!' Her hand was on my arm again, and her words came pouring out, as though she were afraid I'd go before she'd finished. 'Harold said he loved Septimus Cragg. He didn't. He hated him. You see, Septimus had everything Harold wanted – fame, money, women, and a style of his own. Harold can paint brilliantly, but always like other people. So he wanted to get his own back on Septimus, to get his revenge.'

'Look. If you're trying to prove to me my client's guilty ...' I was doing my best to break off this dangerous dialogue, but she held my arm now and wouldn't stop talking.

'Don't go. If you'll wait here, just a little while, I'll show you how to prove Harold's completely innocent.'

'Do you really think I care that much?' I asked her.

'Of course you do!'

'Why?'

'Patients and nurses. Septimus said that's how the world is divided. We're the nurses, aren't we, you and I? We've *got* to care, that's our business. Please!'

I looked at her. Her eyes were full of tears again. I cursed her for having said something true, about both of us.

'All right,' I said. 'But this time I'll join you in a rum. No more Château Castanets. Oh, and I'd better make a telephone call.'

I rang Hilda from a phone on the wall near the Space Invader machine. Although there was a good deal of noise in the vicinity, the voice of She Who Must Be Obeyed came over loud and clear.

'Well, Rumpole,' she said, 'I suppose you're going to tell me you were kept late working in Chambers.'

'No,' I said, 'I'm not going to tell you that.'

'Well, what *are* you going to tell me?'

'Guthrie Featherstone put Brittling back in the cooler and I'm with the girlfriend Pauline. Remember her? We're drinking rum together in a bar in Soho and I really have no idea when I'll be back, so don't wait up for me.'

'Don't talk rubbish, Rumpole! You know I don't believe a word of it!' and my wife slammed down the receiver. If such were the price of establishing my client's innocence, I supposed it would have to be paid. I returned to the bar, where Pauline had already lined up a couple of large rums and was in the act of paying for them.

'What did you tell your wife?' she asked, having some feminine instinct, apparently, which told her the nature of my call.

'The truth.'

'I don't suppose she believed it.'

'No. Here, let me do that.' I felt for my wallet.

'It's the least I can do.' She was scooping up the change. 'You were splendid in Court. You were, honestly. The way you handled that awful Gandolphini, and the Judge. You've got what Harold always wanted.'

'What's that?'

'A voice of your own.' We both drank and she swivelled round on her bar stool to survey the scene in the Old Monmouth pub, and smiled. 'Look,' she said. 'It's here.'

'What?'

'All you need to prove Harold's innocent.'

I looked to a corner of the bar, to where she was looking. An old woman, a shapeless bundle of clothes with a few bright cheap beads, had come in and was sitting at a table in the corner. She started to search in a chaotic handbag with the air of someone who has no real confidence that anything will be found. Pauline had slid off her stool and I followed her across to the new arrival. She didn't seem to notice our existence until Pauline said, quite gently, 'Hullo, Nancy.' Then the woman looked up at me. She seemed enormously old, her face was as covered with lines as a map of the railways. Her grey hair was tousled and untidy, her hands, searching in her handbag, were not clean. But there was still a sort of brightness in her eye as she smiled at me and said, in a voice pickled during long years in the Old Monmouth pub, 'Hullo, young man. I'll have a large port and lemon.'

It is, of course, quite improper for a barrister to talk to a potential witness, so I will draw a veil over the rest of the evening. It's not so difficult to draw the aforesaid veil, as my recollection of events is somewhat hazy. I know that I paid for a good many rums and ports with lemon, and that I learnt more than I can now remember about the lives and loves of many British painters. I can remember walking with two ladies, one old and fragile, one young and beautiful, in the uncertain direction of Leicester Square tube station, and it may be that we linked arms and sang a chorus of the 'Roses of Picardy' together. I can't swear that we didn't.

I had certainly left my companions when I got back to Gloucester Road, and then discovered that the bedroom door was obstructed by some sort of device, probably a lock.

'Is that you, Rumpole?' I heard a voice from within. 'If you find her so fascinating, I wonder you bothered to come home at all.'

'Hilda!' I called, rattling at the handle. 'Where on earth am I expected to sleep?'

'I put your pyjamas on the sofa, Rumpole. Why don't you join them?'

Before I fell asleep in our sitting room, however, I made a telephone call to his home number and woke up our learned prosecutor, Claude Erskine-Brown, and chattered to him, remarkably brightly, along the following lines: 'Oh, Erskine-Brown. Hope I haven't woken you up. I have? Well, isn't it time to feed the baby anyway? Oh, the baby's four now. How time flies. Look. Check something for me, will you? That Mrs De Moyne. Yes. The purchaser. I don't want to drag her back to Court but could your officer ask if the man who rang her was called Blanco Basnet? Yes. 'Blanco'. It means white, you see. Sweet dreams, Erskine-Brown.'

After which, I stretched out, dressed as I was, on the sofa and dreamed a vivid dream in which I was appearing before Mr Justice Featherstone wearing pyjamas, waving a paintbrush, and singing the 'Roses of Picardy' until he sent me to cool off in the cells.

'You look tired, Rumpole.' Erskine-Brown and I were sitting side by side in Court awaiting the arrival of Blind Justice in the shape of Featherstone, J. The sledgehammer inside my head was quietening a little, but I still had a remarkably dry mouth and a good deal of stiffness in the limbs after having slept rough in Froxbury Court.

'Damn hard work, La Vie de Bohème,' I told him. 'By the way, Erskine-Brown, what's the news from Mrs De Moyne?'

'Oh, she remembered the name as soon as the Inspector put it to her. Blanco Basnet. Odd sort of name, isn't it?'

'Distinctly odd,' I agreed. But before he could ask for any further explanation the Usher called, 'Be upstanding', and upstanding we all were, as the learned Judge manifested himself upon the Bench, was put in position by his learned Clerk, supplied with a notebook and sharpened pencils, and then leant forward to ask me, with a brief wince at the sight of the hands in the Rumpole pockets, 'Is there another witness for the defence?'

'Yes, my Lord,' I said, as casually as possible. 'I will now call Mrs Nancy Brittling.'

As the Usher left the Court to fetch the witness in question I heard sounds, as of a ginger beer bottle exploding on a hot day, from the dock, to which Harold Brittling had summoned the obedient Myers.

Then the courtroom door opened and the extremely old lady with whom I had sung around Goodge Street made her appearance, not much smartened up for the occasion, although she did wear, as a tribute to the learned Judge, a small straw hat perched inappropriately upon her tousled grey curls. As she took the oath, Myers was whispering to me. 'The client doesn't want this witness called, Mr Rumpole.'

'Tell the client to belt up and draw a picture, Myersy. Leave me to do my work in peace.' Then I turned to the witness-box. 'Are you Mrs Nancy Brittling?'

'Yes, dear. You know that.' The old lady smiled at me and I went on in a voice of formal severity, to discourage any possible revelation about the night before.

'Please address yourself to the learned Judge. Were you married to my client, Harold Reynolds Gainsborough Brittling?'

'It seems a long time ago now, my Lordship.' Nancy confided to Featherstone, J.

'Did Mr Brittling introduce you to the painter Septimus Cragg at Rottingdean?'

'I remember *that*.' Nancy smiled happily. 'It was my nineteenth birthday. I had red hair then, and lots of it. I remember he said I was a stunner.'

'Who said you were a "stunner",' I asked for clarification, 'your husband or . . .?'

'Oh, Septimus said that, of course.'

'Of course.'

'And Septimus asked me to pop across to Dieppe with him the next weekend,' Nancy said proudly.

'What did you feel about that?' The old lady turned to the jury and I could see them respond to a smile that still had in it, after more than half a century, some relic of the warmth of a nineteen-year-old girl.

'Oh,' she said, 'I was thrilled to bits.'

'And what was Harold Brittling's reaction to the course of events?'

'He was sick as a dog, my Lordship.' It was an answer which found considerable favour with the jury, so naturally Erskine-Brown rose to protest.

'My Lord, I don't know what the relevance of this is. We seem to be wandering into some rather sordid divorce matter.'

'Mr Erskine-Brown!' I gave it to him between the eyebrows. 'My client has already heard the cell door bang behind him as a result of this charge, of which he is wholly innocent. And when I am proving his innocence, I will *not* be interrupted!'

'My Lord, it's quite intolerable that Mr Rumpole should talk to the jury about cell doors banging!'

'Is it really? I thought that was what this case is all about.'

At which point the learned Judge came in to pour a little oil.

'I think we must let Mr Rumpole take his own course, Mr Erskine-Brown,' he said. 'It may be quicker in the end.'

'I am much obliged to your Lordship.' I gave a servile little bow, and even took my hands out of my pockets. Then I turned to the witness. 'Mrs Brittling, did you go to Dieppe with Septimus Cragg, and while you were there together, did he paint you in the bedroom of the Hôtel du Vieux Port?'

'He painted me in the nude, my Lordship. I tell you, I was a bit of something worth painting in those days.'

Laughter from the jury, and a discreet smile from the learned Judge, were accompanied by a pained sigh from Erskine-Brown. I asked the Usher to take Exhibit One to the witness, and Nancy looked at the picture and smiled, happily lost, for a moment, in the remembrance of things past.

'Will you look at Exhibit One, Mrs Brittling?'

'Yes. That's the picture. I saw Septimus paint that. In the bedroom at Dieppe.'

'And the signature . . .?' Erskine-Brown had told the jury that all forged pictures carried large signatures, as this one did. But Nancy Brittling was there to prove him wrong.

'I saw Septimus paint his signature. And, we were so happy together, just for a bit of fun, he let me paint my name too.'

'Let his Lordship see.'

So the Usher trundled up to the learned Judge with the picture, and once again Guthrie raised his magnifying glass respectfully to it.

'It's a bit dark. I did it in sort of purple, at the edge of the carpet. I just wrote "Nancy", that's all.'

'Mr Rumpole,' Featherstone, J., said, and I blessed him for it. 'I think she's right about that.'

'Yes, my Lord. I have looked and I think she is. Mrs Brittling, do you know how your husband got hold of that picture?'

Once again, the evidence was accompanied by popping and fizzing noises from the dock as the prisoner's wife explained, with some gentle amusement, 'Oh yes. Septimus gave it to *me*, but when I brought it home to Harold he fussed so much that in the end I let him have the picture. Well, after a time Harold and I separated and I suppose he kept hold of it until he wanted to pretend he'd painted it himself.'

'Thank you, Mrs Brittling.' I sat down, happy in my work. The sledgehammer had quietened and I stretched out my legs, preparing to watch Erskine-Brown beat his head against the brick wall of a truthful witness.

'Mrs Brittling,' he began. 'Why have you come here to give this evidence? It must be painful for you, to remember those rather sordid events.'

'Painful? Oh, no!' Nancy looked at him and smiled. 'It's a pure pleasure, my dear, to see that picture again and to remember what I looked like, when I was nineteen and happy.'

The next morning I addressed the jury, and I was able to offer them the solution to the mystery of Harold Brittling and the disputed Septimus Cragg. I started by reminding them of one of Nancy's answers: ' "... he kept hold of it until he wanted to pretend he'd painted it himself." Harold Brittling, you may think, ladies and gentlemen of the jury,' I said, 'had one driving passion in his life – his almost insane jealousy of Septimus Cragg. Cragg became his young wife's lover. But worse than that in Brittling's eyes, Cragg was a great painter and Brittling was second rate, with no style of his own. So now, years after Cragg's death,

Brittling planned his revenge. He was going to prove that he could paint a better Cragg than Cragg ever painted. He would prove that this fine picture was his work and not Cragg's. That was his revenge for a weekend in Dieppe, and a lifetime's humiliation. To achieve that revenge Brittling was prepared to sell his Cragg in a devious way that would be bound to attract suspicion. He was prepared to get a friend of his named Blanco Basnet to telephone Mrs De Moyne and claim that the picture was not a genuine Cragg, but something a great deal better. He was prepared to face a charge of forgery. He was prepared to go to prison. He was prepared to give his evidence to you in such a way as to lead you to believe that he was the true painter of a work of genius. Don't be deceived, members of the jury, Brittling is no forger. He is a fake criminal and not a real one. He is not guilty of the crime he is charged with. He is guilty only of the bitterness felt for men of genius by the merely talented. You may think, members of the jury, as you bring in your verdict of "Not Guilty", that that is an understandable emotion. You may even feel pity for a poor painter who could not even produce a forgery of his own.'

As I sat down, the ginger beer bottle in the dock finally exploded and Brittling shouted, in an unmannerly way, at his defending counsel, 'You bastard, Rumpole!' he yelled, 'you've joined the con-o-sewers!'

'Good win, Horace. Of course, I always thought your client was innocent.'

'Did you now?'

The Judge had invited me in for a glass of very reasonable Amontillado after the jury brought in their verdict and, as the case was now over, we were alone in his room.

'Oh yes. One gets a nose for these things. One can soon assess a witness and know if he's telling the truth. Have to do that all the time in this job. Oh, and Horace ...'

'Yes, Judge?'

His Lordship continued in some embarrassment. 'That bit of a tizz I was in, about the great secret getting out. No need to mention that to anyone, eh?'

'Oh, I rang the Lord Chancellor's office about that. The day after we met in Pommeroy's,' I told him, and casually slipped my hands into my pockets.

'You *what*?' Featherstone looked at me in a wild surmise.

'I assured them you hadn't said a word to anyone and it was just a sort of silly joke put about by Claude Erskine-Brown. I mean, no one in the Temple ever dreamed that they'd make *you* a Judge.'

'Horace! Did you say that?'

'Of course I did.' He took time to consider the matter and then pronounced judgement. 'Then you got me out of a nasty spot! I was afraid Marigold had been a bit indiscreet. Horace, I owe you an immense debt of gratitude.'

'Yes. You do,' I agreed. His Lordship looked closely at me, and some doubt seemed to have crept into his voice as he said, 'Horace. *Did* you ring the Lord Chancellor's office? Are you telling me the truth?'

I looked at him with the clear eyes of a reliable witness. 'Can't you tell, Judge? I thought you had such an infallible judicial eye for discovering if a witness is lying or not. Not slipping a bit, are you?'

'What is it, Rumpole. Not flowers again?'

'Bubbly! Non vintage. Pommeroy's sparkling – on special offer. And I paid for it myself!' I had brought Hilda a peace offering which I set about opening on the kitchen table as soon as I returned to the matrimonial home.

'Where's that girl now?' she asked suspiciously.

'God knows. Gone off into the sunset with the old chump. He'll never forgive me for getting him acquitted, so I don't suppose we'll be seeing either of them again.'

The cork came out with a satisfying pop, and I began to fill a couple of glasses with the health-giving bubbles.

'I should have thought you'd had quite enough to drink with her last night!' Hilda was only a little mortified.

'Oh, forget her. She was a girl with soft eyes, and red hair, who passed through the Old Bailey and then was heard no more.'

I handed Hilda a glass, and raised mine in a toast.

> ' "Beauty is truth, truth beauty," – that is all
> Ye know on earth, and all ye need to know. '

I looked at She Who Must Be Obeyed and then I said, 'It isn't, is it, though? We need to know a damn sight more than that!'

Rumpole and the Golden Thread

There is no doubt about it, life at the Bar can have stretches of the hum and the drum. A long succession of petty thefts, minor frauds and unsensational indecencies, prolonged by the tedious speeches of learned friends and the leisurely summings up of judges who seemed to have nothing much to say and all the time in the world in which to say it, produced, after a month or six, a feeling of pronounced discontent. There was no summer that year, and precious little spring. The rain fell regularly on the Inner London Sessions, and on Acton, and on the Uxbridge Magistrates Court. Most members of the jury seemed to have bad colds, their noses were pink and they sucked Zubes in their box. The courtrooms smelled of lozenges and resounded to hacking coughs. The pound was falling and my spirits with it. I began to dream of sandy deserts, the cool shade of a sparkling oasis, almond eyes behind latticed windows, the call of the *muezzin* in the dusty pink of the evening, things which I had never seen and were unlikely to be found between Snaresbrook and Reading Crown Court. I took to remembering a neglected piece of James Elroy Flecker which had enraptured me during my schooldays, describing, as it did, the journey of a number of persons of the Middle Eastern persuasion to a place romantically called 'Samarkand'.

These verses were running through my head as I joined She Who Must Be Obeyed at the sink after supper one night (lamb chops, frozen peas and a bottle of Pommeroy's worst).

> 'Have we not Indian carpets, dark as wine,
>   Turbans and sashes, gowns and bows and veils,
>   And broideries of intricate design,
>   And printed hangings in enormous bales?'

As a matter of fact we hadn't. We were in the kitchen at 25B

Froxbury Court (our alleged mansion flat in the Gloucester Road), my good self and She Who Must Be Obeyed, and far from being clad in turbans and sashes, sipping sherbet and sniffing oriental perfumes, we were dressed in a pair of aprons and doing the washing up; that is to say, I was up to my elbows in the Fairy Liquid and Hilda was wielding a doughty dishcloth. The words kept going round in my head, and I gave Hilda a snatch or two of the magical East.

' "We are the Pilgrims, master;" ' I told her,

> 'we shall go
> Always a little further: it may be
> Beyond that last blue mountain barred with snow,
> Across that angry or that glimmering sea,
>
> White on a throne or guarded in a cave
> There lives a prophet who can understand
> Why men were born . . .'

'What are you talking about, Rumpole?' Hilda asked. I gave her the best answer possible . . .

> 'but surely we are brave,
> Who make the Golden Journey to Samarkand.'

'Rumpole! This plate's not washed up properly at all.' Hilda had been staring critically at it, now she dropped it back into the suds for me to do again.

' "Away, for we are ready to a man!" ' I told her,

> 'Our camels sniff the evening and are glad.
> Lead on, O Master of the Caravan:
> Lead on the Merchant-Princes of Bagdad.'

'I don't know why you always choose the washing. Why can't you dry?' said Hilda, who didn't seem keen on crossing the desert.

'Washing's more fun.' So it was, comparatively speaking.

'It's not much fun when you leave bits of gravy untouched by the mop, Rumpole!'

'What's it matter – a bit of yesterday's gravy never did anyone any harm. "Is not Baghdad, the beautiful? O stay!" '

'If a thing's worth doing it's worth doing properly,' said Hilda.

'Not much chance of adventure round here in Gloucester Road, is there, Hilda? Unless you count the choice between drying up the dishes or sloshing them about in a mess of bottled soap suds.'

'You're getting a little too old for adventure, Rumpole.' She was drying up a fork very thoroughly indeed.

'Oh yes. You know what I spent the last three weeks doing? A serious case of unpaid V.A.T. on plastic egg timers – in Sydenham!' Travels Rumpole East Away? Of course the answer was 'no', I realized, as I pulled out a coffee cup which seemed to have lost its handle in the stormy sink.

'You'd better get a tea towel and help with the rest of the drying. You've done quite enough damage already.'

At which point, and it is strange how things often happen in answer to some unspoken wish or silent prayer, the telephone on our kitchen wall gave urgent tongue. As Hilda answered it, I had no idea what sort of wish the genie of the telephone had come to answer, or how near to disaster its unseen voice would eventually bring me.

'Hello, 4052, Hilda Rumpole.' Hilda listened, then lowered the receiver with her hand over it and hissed at me in a voice pregnant with suspicion.

'Justitia, Rumpole. Who's *she*?'

'*She's* a sort of blind goddess, Hilda, who goes around lumbered with a sword and a blooming great pair of scales.' I took the instrument from her, and Hilda heard me say, 'Rumpole speaking ... Yes, Justitia International. I know your organization. Yes ... Who ...? Oh yes. He remembers *me*? I taught him at the crammers. Criminal practice.'

'Who is it, Rumpole?' But I was still in close conversation with the unseen caller. 'Well, yes. Just before the war, as a matter of fact. Down a sort of cellar in Fetter Lane ... Oh ... Well, I've read in *The Times* occasionally ... Got into some sort of trouble over there, has he? Lunch with you tomorrow? La Venezia in Fleet Street? I don't really see why not.'

I put down the telephone, and when I turned to Hilda I was smiling as though I could smell, on the wind blowing up from Gloucester Road tube station, the spice-laden breezes of Africa.

'What's the matter with you, Rumpole? You look remarkably

pleased with yourself!' As she put away the plates Hilda was frowning suspiciously. I found an open bottle and poured out a couple of glasses of Pommeroy's ordinary.

'Dodo's coming to stay next week, remember?' As I showed no immediate reaction she repeated the information. 'My old school friend, Dodo Mackintosh, will be here for a couple of days next week. You won't forget that, will you, Rumpole?'

I handed her a glass of wine. Life seemed to have improved for the better all round. 'Dodo descending on us, eh? That makes it even better.'

'Makes what better?' Hilda asked. I raised my glass and turned towards the East as I said, ' "We take the Golden Road to Samarkand!" '

Justitia International, as you may know, is an organization which attempts to see that trials are fair and justice done in even further away places with stranger-sounding names than the Uxbridge Magistrates Court. It exists on hope, an overdraft, and donations from such public-spirited citizens as still care if a foreign politician is hanged, or a Third World writer imprisoned after some trial which has been about as predictable as a poker game with a card sharper. To lands which will still receive them (a small and ever-shrinking number), Justitia will send English barristers to defend the oppressed; to other parts of the world observers are sent, who write reports about the proceedings. Such reports are filed away. Protests are sent. Sometimes letters are written to *The Times* and occasionally a prisoner is released or an injustice remedied. As I say, Justitia has no vast sums of money, so I thought it very decent of Amanda Pinkerton, the International Secretary, to take me out to lunch at a small trattoria in Fleet Street, where we sat over the remains of our spaghetti bolognaise and Chianti, studying an illustrated folder entitled 'Neranga Today'. I found Miss Pinkerton to be a large, energetic lady in her forties, given to wearing an assortment of coloured scarves and heavyweight costume jewellery, so she looked as if she had just returned from the bazaar.

' "Neranga," ' she read out to me, as though she were giving an elementary geography lesson to a class of backward and dyslexic ten-year-olds. ' "A lump of land carved out by the British, who called it New Somerset. Capital, Nova Lombaro. Deeply divided into two tribes, the Apu and the Matatu, who hate each other so much that if an Apu man marries a Matatu girl, both their families throw them out and they're cursed forever." '

'Same sort of thing that goes on in Surrey,' I suggested.

'Yes. Well . . .' Miss Pinkerton turned a page and we were met with the face of an African with horn-rimmed glasses, a cotton cap and robe, standing in front of a microphone, apparently addressing a meeting of UNESCO. 'The Prime Minister,' Miss Pinkerton explained. 'Dr Christopher Mabile, a member of the Matatu tribe, warriors and head hunters not so long ago. He's a Marxist. Educated by the Jesuit Fathers, who sent him to Balliol. Got his medical degree in Moscow and postgrad in Cuba. When the country got independence, he had to have a token Apu in his Cabinet. So he made David Mazenze Minister of Home Affairs.' She turned the page and showed me another photograph.

'Looks older than I remember,' I told her. 'Well, I suppose it's only to be expected.'

'David's one of the more peaceful Apus. The British locked him up for about ten years, but he never bore a grudge. Moderate socialist. Good friend to Justitia. Sound on land reform and contraception. Excellent Chairman of the Famine Programme. And . . .' her eyes became somewhat misty, 'he's got an absolutely *marvellous* voice.'

'But did he *do* it, do you think?' I asked. It seemed important.

Miss Pinkerton's mind, however, was clearly on other matters. 'It's a sort of thrilling voice! Of course, the Apu people absolutely *worship* David.'

The photograph was of an African with a noble head, short, grizzled hair, a strong neck and amused eyes. He was wearing an open-necked shirt and smoking a pipe. I thought back to a stuffy cellar off Fetter Lane, the offices of Pinchbeck and Swatling, legal crammers who could guarantee to force you through the Bar exams in about six months. It was there I had taught young David Mazenze the elements of our Criminal Law, which, together with Wordsworth, Shakespeare and Oxford marmalade, must be one of our most valuable exports.

It was a shortage of briefs, in the years after my return to civilian life from a somewhat inglorious career in the R.A.F. Ground Staff, which led me to take on part-time work at the crammers. I may not have taught much law, in the strict sense of the word, but I gave young David Mazenze and his fellow students from India, Fiji, Singapore and Godalming the basic speech to the jury, which should always refer to the 'Golden Thread' which runs through our justice – the immutable principle that everyone is innocent unless twelve good men and women and true are certain that the only possible answer is that they must be guilty. I also gave my class a lecture on my pre-war triumph in the Penge Bungalow Murders, a case which careful readers of these reminiscences will remember I won after a two-week hearing alone and without a leader. David Mazenze may not have emerged from my lessons the greatest academic lawyer in the world, but he knew something about bloodstains and how to cross-examine a policeman on his notebook, and he knew almost all there is to be known about the burden of proof.

When he went back to his native Neranga, David practised law, took up politics, and had that essential training for all successful African politicians – a fairly long term of imprisonment by the British. Then he was released, Neranga got its independence, and David Mazenze became the Apu representative in Dr Mabile's predominantly Matatu government. Each year he sent us a Christmas card, much decorated with snow and robins and holly, and best wishes to 'My old Mentor, Horace Rumpole and his Good Lady'. For a number of years, I am ashamed to say, I had forgotten to send one back.

I learned the basic facts of David Mazenze's case from Miss Pinkerton at that luncheon. The road to the capital of Neranga, Nova Lombaro, leads through many miles of scrubland and bush. One rainy night the fat and self-important Bishop Kareele, himself a remarkably devious politician, was being driven by a clergyman in a Mercedes along this road. They were stopped by an unknown African who waved the car down. As soon as they stopped the Bishop was shot, the clergyman ran into the bush and would live to give evidence.

Later the police raided David Mazenze's bungalow and found him calmly smoking his pipe and listening to the Fauré *Requiem*. He was arrested and refused bail by Chief Justice Sir Worthington Banzana, who was, quite coincidentally, a member of the Matatu tribe. As he was dragged from his house by the brutal officers of the law, David shouted a short sentence to his distracted wife, Grace. It consisted of the simple words, 'Horace Rumpole, Equity Court in the Temple.'

'But what I want to know is,' I told Miss Pinkerton, 'did he do in the dear old Bish?'

'We've had reports from reliable sources that Mabile's got David locked up in the most ghastly conditions! There may have been torture.'

Disturbing, no doubt, but hardly an answer to my question, which I repeated. 'But did our David *do* it?'

'I don't know whether we've actually *asked* him that.' Miss Pinkerton flipped vaguely through her file. 'Oh, here's Pam.' A secretary, a younger but equally eager version of Miss Pinkerton, who seemed to have bought her clothing at an army surplus store instead of an oriental bazaar, came into the restaurant at that moment in a state of high excitement.

'We've had a cable from Jonathan Mazenze,' Pam announced.

'David's younger brother,' Miss Pinkerton explained. 'He's been a tower of strength. What's it say, Pam?'

At which Pam pulled the cable from the pocket of her fatigues and read, ' "Barrister Rumpole will be allowed to represent David at trial. Visa being arranged. Greetings, Jonathan Mazenze." '

'We're in luck!' said Miss Pinkerton. 'Is there anything else you want to know?'

'Only one thing,' I said. 'What do they give a chap for murder, in those particular parts?'

'It's death, isn't it, Mandy?' Pam asked casually. I closed my eyes. I was back in the shadow of the gallows which fell, every day, over my conduct of the Penge Bungalow Murders and I didn't know whether I was still strong enough to face it.

'Oh yes.' Miss Pinkerton sounded almost cheerful. 'The

Prime Minister can't wait to hang David. You've got to save his life.'

So that was all I had to do. It was enough worry to be going on with, so I didn't think of the fact that should have concerned me most. If I had done so I might have wondered why Horace Rumpole, an elderly junior barrister, and not even an artificial silk, had been admitted so easily to the Nerangan Bar.

I was in the clerk's room next morning, sorting through the circulars, advertisements for life insurance and filing systems, together with *billets-doux* from Her Majesty's Customs and Excise and the Inland Revenue, which seem to constitute the bulk of my mail, and I happened to ask Henry, our clerk, in a casual sort of way, if he had any exciting work in store for me.

'Not according to my diary, Mr Rumpole.' Henry flipped through his book of engagements. 'There's a little murder down the Bailey. But that won't be for a few weeks.'

'Mysterious crime done with a broken Guinness bottle in a crowded pub in Kilburn. Routine stuff. Legal Spam!' I spoke of the 'little murder' with some contempt. 'It's a pity with all your talents as a clerk, Henry, that you can't find me something more exotic.'

'Perhaps you'd care to find your own exotica, if you're not satisfied with my clerking, Mr Rumpole!' Henry sounded distinctly nettled.

'I have done. A brief will be arriving, Henry, from Justitia International. I am defending the Minister of Home Affairs in the High Court of Neranga.' It sounded, as I said it, fairly impressive.

'You'll be away from Chambers?' I was afraid I detected a note of relief in Henry's voice, the clear inference being that it was not altogether a picnic clerking for Rumpole. 'Certainly I shall be away, Henry,' I reassured him. 'They will look round Innner London Sessions and they will find me gone. They will whisper, "Travels Rumpole East Away?"'

'You seem very cheerful about it, Mr Rumpole.' Dianne paused in her non-stop rattling of her typewriter.

'My camels sniff the evening, Dianne, and are glad,' I told

her, and then turned, more confidently, to Henry. 'She Who Must Be Obeyed's old school friend, Dodo Mackintosh, will be coming for a short stay next week and I will have to miss the jollifications. Adventure calls, Henry, and how can Rumpole be deaf to it?' I moved to the door, anxious to be on my way. 'Send a cable if there's anything urgent.'

'A cable?' Henry sounded as though he'd never heard of the device.

'Or at least a pigeon.' As I finally left the clerk's room, a grey and unremarkable barrister called Hoskins came in and nearly knocked me over. 'Look out, Rumpole,' he said. 'Where are you going?'

I passed on, declaiming,

> 'For what land
> Leave I the dim-moon city of delight?
> I make the Golden Journey to Samarkand.'

'It's too bad, Rumpole. You'll miss Dodo,' Hilda said a few evenings later.

'Hilda! Africa is waiting. The smoke-signals are drifting up from the hills and in the jungle, the tom-toms are beating. The message is, "Rumpole is coming, the Great Man of Law." What message am I to send back? "Sorry, visit cancelled owing to the arrival of Dodo Mackintosh in Gloucester Road"?'

'But why *you*, Rumpole?'

'There was something to be said for the old days of the Empire. Almost all African politicians were students in the Temple. Gandhi started it.'

'Was Gandhi *African*?' Hilda quibbled.

'Maybe not. But they returned to their native bush with an intimate knowledge of the ABC tea-rooms, Pommeroy's Wine Bar and the Penge Bungalow Murders.'

'You'll have to have shots.'

'Why, Hilda? I'm not going to a war.'

'Against tropical diseases. I'll send you round to Dr MacClintock [this was our Scottish quack who had once tried to psychoanalyse my alleged libidinous tendencies*] and I'll go to

---

* See *Rumpole's Return*, Penguin Books, 1980.

D. H. Evans in the morning and get three yards of butter muslin.'
'What on earth for?'
'Mosquitoes,' Hilda said darkly. 'We don't want to lose you
to the malaria, Rumpole. And for heaven's sake don't eat lettuce.'

I had forgotten – one forgets pain so quickly – about the delights
of long-distance air travel, which I have described, when I
suffered it between London and Miami, as offering all the joys
of the rush hour on the Bakerloo Line plus the element of fear.
There I was now, packed into an airless cigar-shaped tube which
hurtled through space playing selections from *The Sound of Music*
or showing an unwatchable film about little green men from outer
space. Now and again food, which after some careful processing
had been robbed of all taste, was pushed in front of me by ladies
in some type of paramilitary uniform, who had clearly been
trained by a period of supervising a recalcitrant pack of Brownies.
Eventually, with the aid of about four half-bottles of claret
(Château Heathrow), I fell into a sort of coma, shot through with
lurid and fearful considerations of the penalty for failure in the
David Mazenze case. I mean, how do you do a case of capital
murder? Death, if you ask a wrong question. Death, if you don't
object to the right bit of evidence. Death, round every legal
corner. How *can* you do it? Answer: do it like every other case.
Win it if you can. Win it, or else. As I began to doze, I spoke
to myself severely, 'Pull yourself together, Rumpole! There was
a death sentence when you did the Penge Bungalow Murders.
Your finest hour.' Penge ... Death ... We take the Golden Road
... to the Death Penalty.

Claret-induced sleep began to overtake me when I was woken
by the trumpet call of the Brownie supervisor.

'Wakey, wakey, sir! Don't we want our meal?'

The Customs Hall at Nova Lombaro's 'Mabile Airport',
named, of course, after the Prime Minister, was a large echoing
shed. Even at night it was breathlessly hot without air
conditioning. I was crumpled, sweating, exhausted and still
trembling in time to the engines and *The Sound of Music*. My
mouth was dry, and as I lugged my red bag in which my wig
and gown travelled, my battered suitcase and my briefcase to-

wards a customs officer apparently wearing the uniform of a Major-General in the Neranga Army, I smelled the dry, sweet smell of Africa and felt, weakened as I was by lack of sleep, sudden and irrational fear.

'Object of visit?' The customs officer looked at me with considerable contempt.

'Justice,' I murmured sleepily and he pointed at my suitcase. 'Open!'

I struggled with the battered and rusty fastenings and then the case flew open, disgorging what seemed to be about a mile of white muslin, bought for me by Hilda at D. H. Evans.

'Your dress?' the customs officer appeared to be giggling.

'No. My mosquito net. My wife got it for me.' After the muslin, a whole chemist's shop of pill bottles was revealed.

'Drugs? *Stupefiants*.' The official was understandably suspicious, particularly when he discovered a hypodermic syringe which Dr MacClintock had supplied for me to give myself some 'shots in case of tropical disease'.

'Certainly not! Just my wife's going-away present.'

I might have been in serious trouble, but an extremely elegant African, whom I judged to be about forty, came up; he was wearing a grey suit with a silkish sheen to it, carrying a crocodile-skin briefcase, and smoking a cigarette through an ivory holder. He was followed by a porter with a couple of matching suitcases and surrounded by the aura of an enormously elegant aftershave. He had clearly jetted in from some Third World jamboree, and after he had exchanged a few words with the customs man in their native tongue, not only was his luggage passed, but my own traps were chalkmarked as fit for importation into Neranga. My deliverer looked at me in some amusement and said, 'Horace Rumpole?'

'A piece of him,' I admitted.

'I'm agin you in the Mazenze case. Looking forward to seeing how you Old Bailey fellows handle a homicide.' At which he flipped out a wallet and gave me a card on which was engraved, with many flourishes, 'The Honourable Rupert Taboro. Attorney-General of the Independent State of Neranga.' 'Anything you need,' Taboro said, 'just ask for the Attorney-General.'

'Thank you very much.'

'Don't mention it, old fellow. After all, we learned friends have got to stick together.'

The law officer swanned off and I humped my bags out of customs and was immediately greeted by a young man in a white shirt and dark trousers who had a huge glittering smile of welcome ready for me.

'Mr Rumpole?'

I admitted it again.

'I am Freddy Ruingo, sir, instructing solicitor. You got through all the formalities?'

'Surprisingly.'

'Come on, I'll take you to the car. Then we go to the prison. Then we have a reception David's wife and brother give for you. You'll meet the leaders of our Apu People's Party.'

'It sounds,' I said, 'an evening packed with excitement.'

So we walked out into the hot African night, and heard the deafening racket set up by insects, howling dogs, the starting of reluctant cars and the scream of brakes at unseen accidents. Freddy Ruingo piled my luggage into the boot of a rusty old Jaguar, whose rear window was a hole surrounded by splintered glass. I sat beside Freddy, still feeling that I was in a sort of dream, as he drove, very fast, out of the town and down a long pot-holed road surrounded by darkness, along which, regardless of the danger to their lives from my instructing solicitor's driving, a stream of people – women with loads on their heads or carrying babies, men laughing and pushing bicycles – were walking in an endless procession.

'I can't understand why your Mr Mazenze hasn't got some smart British Q.C. to defend him,' I shouted over the rattling and roaring of the Jaguar.

'Oh, David believes in the very common man, Mr Rumpole,' Freddy Ruingo assured me. 'He just wanted some ordinary little lawyer like yourself. A perfectly lowly fellow.'

'Thank you very much!' I gasped as we ricocheted across a pot-hole.

'But someone typical of British justice. Quite incorruptible. Not draughty in this car, are you?'

'No!' In fact I was sweating and mopping my brow with the old red spotted handkerchief.

'Some clever Matatu chucked an assegai through the back window of my Jag. They fell out of the trees, those fellows,' Freddy said contemptuously.

None too soon we arrived at a long, low building in the middle of a collection of huts. It was, apparently, some District Police Headquarters, which was considered more secure than the prison in Nova Lombaro. After a considerable wait we entered the Superintendent's office and met another youngish African, wearing knife-edged grey flannel trousers, suede shoes and a blazer with brass buttons. He also sported what might well have been a rowing club tie. After he and Freddy had exchanged a few Nerangan greetings, this officer nodded in my direction and said, 'You've come to see David?'

'Let me introduce Mr Horace Rumpole. Barrister-at-law. Inner Temple.' Freddy did the honours. 'Superintendent Akimbu. Special Branch.'

'You see, we've got David at District Police Headquarters,' Superintendent Akimbu explained. 'We don't want him mixed up with the plebs in Lombaro jail. You want to visit our dungeons, Mr Rumpole?'

He was smiling, but I looked back at him with strong disfavour. I had been warned of this by Miss Amanda Pinkerton in the Fleet Street trattoria. Human rights, I had already begun to suspect, might count for very little in Neranga.

'I want to see my client, yes.'

The Superintendent rose to his feet. He was taller than I had expected, and very thin. 'It's an honour to meet you, Mr Rumpole. You know Croydon well?'

'Not too well, actually.' I was a little taken aback by the question.

'I did six months with your Special Branch in London. The Old Baptist's Head in Croydon. Wonderful draught Bass! Remember me to it. This way please.'

He led me out of a side door and down a passage to another door guarded by a policeman in khaki shorts, who was carrying an automatic rifle.

'We've got your client chained to the wall in here.' The Superintendent was still smiling. 'Better watch out for the rats, you know, and the water dripping from the ceiling!' He nodded to the policeman, who unlocked the door. We were greeted by the sound of some celestial music, which David Mazenze later told me was his favourite Fauré *Requiem*. 'Justitia International,' the Superintendent said as he left Freddy Ruingo and me with our client. 'Poor dears. They have such vivid imaginations.'

The room we had been shown into was large and airy. There were table lamps and a big electric fan, some of David Mazenze's own pictures hung on the walls and on a table were bottles of wine, a bowl of fruit and a gramophone, which was playing as we came in. There was a photograph of David's wife, Grace, and their children beside a pile of records. The man in the chair, smoking a pipe and listening to the music, hadn't moved as we came in, but now he stood up slowly, switched off the music and came towards us.

When I had known him he had been a young, rather over-eager African student. Now he was a grey-haired man who looked as if he had great reserves of physical energy and was a natural leader. His voice was low, melodious but compelling, and his manner was very gentle, as though he were used to getting his own way without being violently assertive.

'Dear old Horace Rumpole! What's your tipple? Bordeaux, if my memory serves me right?'

'I won't say no.'

'You too, Freddy?' I was looking round the room as David Mazenze set about opening what seemed to be a very reasonable bit of the château-bottled.

'Wait until they hear about this in Wormwood Scrubs!' I said.

'I have a few friends in the French Embassy,' David Mazenze handed me a glass.

'Your friends at Justitia however ...' I drank, and decided it was probably the best glass of Margaux to be had in Central Africa.

'Such good chaps. If not all that experienced politically.' David Mazenze smiled.

'They said I'd find you in the Château d'If. With rising damp and the bread and water just out of reach.'

'Even Dr Death wouldn't dare to do that to me.'

'Dr?'

'Le bon docteur Christopher Mabile. The Prime Minister whose culture is firmly founded on the Inquisition *and* the K.G.B.'

'Stirred up with some of the basic cannibalism of the Matatu tribe.' Freddy Ruingo had found a chair in a corner and was grinning at us over his claret glass.

'Forgive Freddy. He makes such primitive remarks! Tribalism is our curse, however. Just as the British class system is yours. Horace, do find yourself a pew, why don't you?' David Mazenze went back to his armchair, but I was wandering round the room looking at the titles of his books.

'P. G. Wodehouse.' I picked up a paperback.

'I think of England so often.' David Mazenze was puffing on his pipe. 'I long for your Cotswolds. If Dr Death ever lets me see them again. If I'm hanged, think of this, Horace. There is some corner of a Nerangan jail house that is forever Moreton-in-Marsh.' He took out his pipe and laughed. I thought that I had never seen a man facing a death sentence looking so confoundedly cheerful. I wondered if it was courage, or the certainty of innocence, or had he, perhaps, spent a day with the wine? It was time to get down to business, so I sat and started to undo the tape on my brief. David Mazenze waited politely for me to begin.

'The dead man. Bishop Kareele . . .' I thought that was as good a starting-point as any.

'A trouble-maker!' David Mazenze frowned slightly. 'As only an African bishop can be. He wanted the Prime Minister's job. He wanted my job. He was always causing trouble between my Apus and the Matatu people. I told you, Horace. Tribal hatred is the curse of our politics!'

'The evidence is that you threatened him,' I was turning over the statements. 'You quarrelled outside the Parliament building and you said to the Bishop, "I'll kill you."'

'All right, I quarrelled with the man.' David Mazenze shrugged. 'He quarrelled with everyone.'

'Death is fixed at around 9.30 p.m. on the 13th. That's when the shots were heard. Where were you then, exactly?'

He knocked out his pipe, got up and walked over to the window, where he stood looking out into the noisy darkness.

'Does it matter?'

'Of course it matters.' I hoped he remembered my basic training on alibis.

'I had a speech to make the next day. An important statement of policy at our Apu People's Party Congress. I went out in my car to drive around and think about it.'

'What time did you go out?' I lit a small cigar and began to make some notes.

'I've said in my statement. About 8.30.'

'What time did you get home?'

'After eleven. My wife Grace made some coffee and we listened to music. I always listen to music for half an hour before turning in.'

'What was the speech?'

'What?' He turned round to look at me, apparently surprised by the question.

'What were you going to say?'

'It was a plea for friendship between the Apu and the Matatu people. That we should all work together, for the good of Neranga.'

'Did you ever make it?'

'How could I? I was arrested.' He came and sat beside me. We were silent for a moment. Then he said, 'Well. How does it look to you?'

'Identification cases are always tricky. And I've known healthier alibis.' I suddenly felt very tired. The only thing I wanted to do was to clean my teeth, go to bed, pull the pillow round my ears and forget all about charges of capital murder.

'You won't win this on alibis,' David Mazenze said. 'You know what you'll have to rely on?'

'I would welcome suggestions.'

'On the Common Law of England! The Presumption of Innocence, you know what you taught me: the Golden Thread which goes through the history of the law. I like that phrase so very much.'

'You have a remarkable memory for what I told you at the crammers all those years ago.' I was flattered.

'A man is innocent until he's proved guilty. Better that ten guilty men should go free than one who is not guilty should be convicted, for to convict the innocent is ...' The words sounded particularly convincing in his dark velvet voice, and I joined in the chorus, 'To spit in the face of justice.'

'Do you still use that one, Horace' – the Apu leader was smiling nostalgically – 'in your speeches to the jury at the old London Sessions?'

'I must confess I do. From time to time. A jury in Neranga can't be much different.'

'Mr Rumpole.' Freddy Ruingo was about to say something, but the words of my favourite speech had banished exhaustion and started the adrenalin coursing through my veins. I stood and addressed the others as though they were the jury. 'The evidence calls for guesswork in this case, members of the jury,' I said and went on, warming to the occasion. 'Now you may pick the winner of the Derby by guesswork, but it is no way to bring in a verdict on a charge of *capital* murder against a fellow human being.'

'Steady on, Mr Rumpole.' Freddy Ruingo managed to get his word in. 'We have no jury.'

'No jury?' I was incredulous, appalled.

'You British abolished juries in murder cases when Neranga was still "New Somerset".' David Mazenze appeared to think it was something of a joke.

'*We* did that?' I was more appalled than ever.

'I must say, Dr Death followed your example quite enthusiastically,' Freddy admitted.

'No jury. And the Judge?'

'Worthington Banzana,' David Mazenze told me. '*Sir* Worthington. You remember that old judge, Horace? What did you say he always ordered for tea after death sentences?'

'Muffins. You mean Twyburne?'

'Exactly. Well, our Chief Justice is like your Mr Justice Twyburne.' He laughed. 'Only black!'

'And he is Dr Death's chicken. He will run for him, wherever he wants him to go.' Freddy Ruingo wasn't, I must admit, being particularly encouraging.

About half of my heavy task was done, and the day seemed to have already lasted several years, when we left the Police House and bumped off, along what appeared to be Neranga's single road, to the Mazenze residence. There the leading lights of the Apu People's Party, or A.P.P., were, Freddy assured me, assembled to do honour to the great white barrister who had dropped out of the skies by courtesy of Justitia International.

When we got to the bungalow the sound of old pop records was mixed with the noises of the night. It didn't seem that the Mazenze family, or the Apu leaders, were sitting wrapped in gloom, stricken by the danger that hung over their hero's head. Freddy and I squeezed our way past a crowd of young men and girls in the open doorway and went down a passage towards a big comfortable room with doors which opened on to a verandah. The room seemed full of people, women in brightly printed cotton frocks, men in shirts and trousers, dancing, or drinking, or arguing, with children running among their feet. As I entered, the gramophone was immediately switched off and the assembled company burst into a verse of 'For He's a Jolly Good Fellow'. I stood propped against the doorway, smoking a small cigar, and praying that I shouldn't fall asleep standing there, like a horse.

'Beer? Seven-Up? Scotch on the rocks?' said Freddy Ruingo, who was minding me.

I chose beer, which Freddy brought back in the form of a cold tin of Tuborg. He also brought a placid, middle-aged woman, whose hair was just starting to turn grey, and introduced her as David Mazenze's wife, Grace.

'Mrs Mazenze.' I shook her hand. She looked at me trustingly.

'It is kind you came to us.'

'Nice of you to ask me.'

'You came to save David, I mean.'

'I can't promise that, you know.'

I began to feel the awful burden on the defending lawyer, the need to work miracles.

'David remembers you so well. He has often talked about you. He has so much faith in you.'

'I'll do everything I can. But in the end a barrister's not much better than his case.' Mrs Mazenze was looking at me, hurt by my lack of complete confidence. 'You can't make bricks without straw,' I told her.

'I don't understand.' She shook her head and there were tears in her eyes.

'What we could do with is a bit of evidence.'

Before I could tell her what I thought were the gaps in the case, however, we were interrupted by a tall, thinnish young African, brightly dressed in his native costume. His features were sharper than David's, his eyes narrower and his nose thinner, and when he spoke, his voice was higher and less melodious.

'Don't you worry, Grace,' he said to her, 'no one can hurt David. David is one of the immortals.' He turned and held out a hand to me; it had a pale palm and curiously long fingers. 'Welcome to Neranga, Mr Rumpole. Welcome to the home of the Apu people. I am Jonathan Mazenze, David's little brother.'

'Little John?' I found myself looking up at him.

'Oh yes. And was my big brother delighted to see you, his old hero from his student days! He said you used to tease the judges. He said you used to pull their legs unmercifully.'

'Well, I did pull a few judicial legs, I suppose.' I was yawning modestly.

'And that you always dropped cigar ash down your stomach.'

'Did he remember that?' I brushed a deposit about the size of the eruption of Vesuvius off my shirt front. At which point a woman who had been handing round plates of food came up to speak to Grace, who excused herself and left us. Jonathan looked after her and then turned to me.

'What did you tell Grace we needed to win the case for David?'

'A witness or two would be a help,' I muttered.

'What sort of witness do you want, exactly?'

'Someone who saw David Mazenze at the time of the murder. He says he was just driving round aimlessly, composing his speech.'

Jonathan laughed, apparently at the simplicity of my requirements. 'You want some fellows who saw him? I can arrange it. How many fellows do you want, half a dozen?'

I was too tired not to let my anger show. 'No, you can't arrange it! I want a witness who'll stand up in Court and tell the truth.'

'How very British you are, Mr Horace Rumpole!' Jonathan smiled down on me now.

'That's why I'm here, you know. As a representative of British justice.'

Jonathan suddenly stopped smiling. He spoke quietly, but with great intensity. 'David doesn't need all that humbug,' he said. 'He needs the anger of the Apu people. If David is found guilty there are three thousand Apus with their guns hidden in the bush who will rescue him in one hour! That's how we win this case, don't you worry, old barrister!'

'Really? I prefer to rely on the way we do it down the Old Bailey,' I said, somewhat coldly.

'Dr Death's gone too far this time. The Apu people are on the move!'

'And I must be on the move too,' I told him. 'Which way is the gents?'

Going to the lavatory in foreign parts is, in my limited experience, to take your life in your hands, but the Mazenze facilities were clean and efficient. There was a pile of old numbers of the *New Statesman* and *New Society*, caricatures of David on the walls, and all the basic comforts. It may be that I dropped asleep for a moment or two, and when I emerged the music had stopped. I was in the long passage which led to what must have been a back door open to the night. I caught a glimpse of a very beautiful young girl in African dress looking in, asking what seemed to be an urgent question. Grace Mazenze, who was standing with her back to me, said something and then closed the door, shutting out the girl. I stood watching, and Grace went back to the living room. I followed her to find the room was empty. The doors on to the verandah were open and all the guests, together with Grace, seemed to have moved out into the darkness, from which came a sound of rhythmic shouting.

When I moved on to the verandah, I saw that the night was filled with people, and there were rows of white eyes, white teeth, white shirts, glimmering. Jonathan Mazenze was standing above the crowd with his fist raised, chanting, 'AH ...PU ... AH ... PU ... AH ... PU,' and the chorus of voices took up the chant.

'What's all this?' I asked Freddy Ruingo, who had manifested himself beside me. 'A party political broadcast on behalf of the Apu People's Party?'

By the time I got to the old Majestic Hotel in Nova Lombaro, which was to be my home during the trial in Neranga, I felt to a great degree disorientated in time and space. I found it hard to remember where I was, or when I got there, or what time it might be. So I stood, swaying gently, in a hotel lounge which cannot have changed much since it was used by the white businessmen, farmers and district officers of 'New Somerset'. Only now there was a large, and no doubt obligatory photograph of the Prime Minister behind the reception desk, where there once must have been one of the Queen.

I was giving instructions for my morning call to the somewhat confused African porter behind the desk, when I was vaguely conscious of a tall, grey-haired Englishman in an old tropical suit who was moving towards me with a couple of middle-aged orientals in tow.

'Six o'clock call, please,' I said to the porter. 'Room 51. Mr Rumpole. R ... U ... M ... P ... O ... L ... E.'

'Mr Rumbold, I presume,' said the Englishman, who must have heard me.

'Rumpole.'

'All hail! I was dining with Mr and Mrs Singapore here. We all call each other after our countries, as diplomats, don't we, Mrs Singapore? I'm Mr Old England. Arthur Remnant, British High Commissioner. This is our notable British barrister. Remind me of your name again.'

'Rumpole.' I wondered how long I could keep this up. Mr and Mrs Singapore were smiling at me as though I had said something funny.

'I must invite you to the High Commission,' said the man Remnant. 'Our problem is, the cook's so terribly anglophile that everything tastes of Bisto. I say, it must be exciting for you, doing a murder trial, out *here*.' His voice sank to an eerie whisper. 'Topping!'

'Ripping!' I said. I supposed it was expected of me.

'No, I mean "topping".' Remnant explained with a smile. 'Swinging. We're so Victorian in Neranga. Full of Baptist chapels, and plum jam and the death penalty. The Black Cap does add a bit of zest to a murder trial, doesn't it?'

'I don't suppose my client thinks so.' The High Commissioner was beginning to sicken me a little.

'Well, I suppose not. You know, I was amazed when they gave permission for you to come here.' He started to move away from me with the Singapores. 'Christopher Mabile's got something up his sleeve. Such a brilliant politician. We could do with *him* in Commonwealth Relations. Anyway, welcome, Rumbelow. We'll throw a little cocktail for you!'

'How very topping!' I said to his back. It was my last word of the evening.

At last I went upstairs and pulled off my tie, which seemed to have become, during that endless evening, unreasonably tight. I heard the sound of driving rain and turned to the window. The curtain was blowing back, heavy rain was splashing the sill and the carpet. I closed the window, and looked for a moment at the wet glass and out into the darkness. A few minutes later I was asleep.

It rained for the next three days. I sat in the hotel and ate large, indigestible meals that looked back to the days of New Somerset. Features of the menu were castle puddings doused in custard, and a large, trembling, pink blancmange. I studied weather reports, maps, and the characters of Nerangan politicians. I had a couple more inconclusive conferences with my client, who seemed anxious to discuss P. G. Wodehouse, my old cases, the short-comings of UNESCO, the role of barristers in the Third World and the lasting benefits of British rule in the New Neranga; anything, in fact, except the small question of his defence. When I mentioned the trial he would smile, spend a good deal of time lighting his pipe and, as soon as possible, turn on the Fauré *Requiem*.

Freddy Ruingo took me to see the scene of the crime. It looked exactly like any other part of that endless, overcrowded road to Nova Lombaro. We didn't get out of the car, but a crowd of wet, black, shining children milled round us, demanding cigarettes. The rain came through the back window of the Jaguar, which Freddy hadn't yet been able to get mended.

The fourth day of my stay in Neranga started with blinding sunshine. I got out of a taxi, sweating in a black jacket and striped trousers, and carried my briefcase and red robe bag up the steps of the white-pillared portico of the British-built High Court of Justice. The steps were crowded with people, some faces I remembered from the night of the party, many more strange to me. At the top of the steps, resplendent in his bright cottons, stood Jonathan Mazenze. He was smiling and seemed to be leading the low chanting of the people around him. The syllables emerging were not 'AH...PU...' this time. Listening hard I could have sworn they were 'RUM...POLE!' I lifted a hand in salutation and went into the building.

The robing room in the Nova Lombaro High Court was a good deal more comfortable than that at the Old Bailey. It was a high room, with cedarwood lockers and long mirrors. An attendant in a white uniform made me a cup of Nescafé as I changed my shirt and prepared to put on the blunt execution of a winged collar. It was then that I realized that my packing, for all the medicines and mosquito nets I had bought, was lacking in one vital commodity.

'Damn,' I said aloud. 'Where do you get a front collar stud in Africa?'

'Right here, my learned friend.' Mr Rupert Taboro, Attorney-General and prosecuting Counsel, had stolen up beside me and was holding out a leather stud-box. 'I had a gross of these little chaps flown in from Harrods,' he said. 'Be my guest.'

'That's remarkably civil of you.' I took a stud and fixed the collar.

'Merely in accordance with the best traditions of the Bar. I see young Jonathan Mazenze had his friends from Rent-an-Apu out there to greet you.'

'Yes. I found it rather encouraging,' I told him. 'The people cheering on my victory.'

'*Your* victory?' Taboro smiled tolerantly at me. 'Do you really think that's what they want?'

And, before I could ask him what the hell he meant, he had glided away about his business.

Apart from the fact that all the faces under the white wigs, except for mine, were black, the Court was set out exactly as it is in the Old Bailey. Only the big, slowly revolving wooden fans on the ceiling, and the Court attendants in white uniforms and small red fezes, were different from the buzzing air conditioning and black-gowned ushers in England. The public gallery, instead of containing one old man in a mackintosh and a party of schoolgirls, was crammed with loyal members of the Apu tribe, prepared, if anyone gave them half a chance, to cheer for the prisoner.

The only other white faces in the Court belonged to half a dozen reporters from European papers who had come to report on the trial of a well-known African politician; and were hoping, no doubt, to be able to describe a further collapse of justice in a Third World state.

I had sat, during the Attorney-General's opening, staring up at our learned Judge. Sir Worthington Banzana was a small, broad-shouldered, stocky man, whom I judged to be about seventy years old. He had been more or less silent during the early stages of the trial, and had noticeably refrained from welcoming a visitor from across the sea to the Nerangan Bar. In fact he had hardly glanced in my direction. So I took a few notes and tried to calm a bubbling and over-eager Freddy Ruingo, who kept moving from his seat in front of me to whisper to the prisoner in the dock. David Mazenze seemed strangely uninterested in the proceedings.

I glanced round the Court. I could see Mrs Grace Mazenze looking down at me with trusting anxiety from the public gallery. I turned away from her to look at the first prosecution witness, a plump young African in a crumpled suit, who was glistening with sweat as he answered the calm, reassuring questions of my learned friend, Mr Rupert Taboro.

'Are you Magnus Nagoma?'

'I am.'

'You are in government service?'

'I am Permanent Private Secretary to the Minister for Home Affairs.'

'The defendant is your boss?' Taboro glanced at the dock.

'He is, yes.'

'My boss . . .' The Chief Justice repeated in a deep and gravelly voice as he made a note.

'Do you remember a day last July when you went to meet your boss outside the Parliament building?' Taboro asked, smiling gently.

'I do, yes. He was there with Bishop Kareele. They were having an argument.'

'A heated argument?'

'Please don't lead!' I growled a warning from my seat.

'I hear my learned friend's objection.' Taboro smiled at the Judge, who looked at me for the first time. It was by no means a smile of friendliness. '*I* don't, I must confess.' He was tapping his pencil on his desk with suppressed irritation. 'Mr Rumpole! Is it no longer customary in England to stand on your hind legs if you wish to make an objection?'

I thought it right and proper to climb to my feet at this juncture. 'Then I wish to object, my Lord, to a leading question.'

'It was very heated this argument, yes.' The witness burst in on our argument uninvited, and the Chief Justice smiled at me for the first time. 'Too late, I think, Mr Rumpole,' he said, and I subsided. What we had was undoubtedly a black version of Judge Bullingham, the terror of the Old Bailey, but somewhat quicker off the mark than his English equivalent.

'Did the defendant say anything to the Bishop?' Taboro was pursuing the even tenor of his way.

'Yes. He said "I'll kill you."'

There was a stir in Court, the usual reaction to a piece of important and damaging evidence, and the Judge was careful to repeat the words as he wrote them down. ' "I'll kill you," ' he said.

'That's an old judicial trick,' I whispered to Freddy Ruingo, and then I suggested a little practical demonstration we might indulge in when I rose to cross-examine. The judicial pencil tapped again, and I was addressed from on high.

'Mr Rumpole,' said Sir Worthington menacingly. 'Please do not hesitate to rise if you have something to say.'

'I have nothing whatever to say, my Lord.' I rose to about halfway and then sank back in to my seat.

'Then it is customary to remain silent when seated. Did not your old pupil master teach you that? Was he not C. H. Wystan of the Inner Temple?'

I hadn't bargained for a Nerangan Chief Justice with an encyclopaedic knowledge of English barristers. He had even remembered the name of my sainted father-in-law, Daddy to She Who Must Be Obeyed, who had guided my first faltering steps in his own inexpert sort of way when I first went into Chambers.

'What happened then, Mr Nagoma?' Taboro went on when the judicial rebuke was over.

'We got into the Minister's car,' the witness answered.

'Just you and Mazenze?'

'Yes.'

'What did the defendant say?'

'He said, "Who will rid me of this turbulent priest?"'

'And by "turbulent priest", who did you take him to mean?' Taboro was taking no chances.

'He meant the Bishop.'

'Yes. Thank you, Mr Nagoma.' Taboro sat down smiling. I took off my wig, applied the red spotted handkerchief to the brow, replaced the wig and rose to cross-examine.

'Mr Nagoma ...' I started, and then, as arranged, Freddy tugged at my gown and whispered, 'This man is a Matatu. Naturally he is hostile to David.'

So I whispered angrily back, loudly enough for everyone in the Court to hear. 'Look, if you interrupt my cross-examination, I'll kill you!'

My Apu supporters in the public gallery took the point and laughed. The Chief Justice's pencil got to work again, and rapped the desk in an angry manner.

'Mr Rumpole. There is no jury here!' he reminded me.

'My Lord, I'm sorry we abolished that great institution.' I took the opportunity of denouncing a retrograde step.

'That was a jury trick you pulled quite shamelessly, Mr Rumpole. It was not worthy of a former pupil of Mr C. H. Wystan.'

Not worthy of Wystan, a man who knew nothing whatever about bloodstains! I controlled myself with difficulty. 'It was not a trick. It was a demonstration.' I told the Judge. 'I am about to put the question to the witness.'

'Put it then, Mr Rumpole. Without play-acting please!'

It was too early in the case to quarrel with the Judge, and there was – oh the pity of it! – no jury. I addressed myself to the witness. 'Were not the words used to the Bishop just as I've used them to my learned instructing solicitor, as a bit of meaningless abuse?' I asked Nagoma.

'I don't know that, sir.'

'Do you not? And do you not know what they were quarrelling about? "The freedom of religious instruction in the Schools Enabling Bill". Apparently the Bishop was putting up what is known as a filibuster and talking for hours to delay matters.'

Taboro half rose, and made a funny. 'I'm sure that is a process well known to my learned friend,' he said.

The Chief Justice and the police officers and about half of the public, who were, no doubt, of the Matatu tribe, had an excellent laugh at this gem. When the hilarity had died down, I asked another question.

'It was a moment of irritation at some unparliamentary behaviour, isn't that so?'

'Mr Rumpole.' The Judge was serious again. 'The witness was *outside* the parliament building. How can he answer?'

'He can answer this. Was it meant seriously?'

Mr Nagoma, bless his heart, hesitated for a long time before he said, 'I don't know. Quite honestly.'

'Yes. Thank you, Mr Nagoma.' I was grateful. 'And when he said, "Who can rid me of this turbulent priest?" you recognized the quotation, I imagine?'

'Quotation? No.' Mr Nagoma looked blank and the Chief Justice's disapproval was turned on him for a change.

'Oh really!' The pencil was thrown down on to the desk on

this occasion. 'It beats me how some of you fellows get into the Civil Service, let alone become Ministers' secretaries. Henry the Second said that of Thomas à Becket in the year – what year was it, Mr Rumpole?' For the first time he asked me a question which was not an attack.

'I don't immediately recollect.'

'Oh, I do. I recollect.' The wily old Judge had clearly known the answer all the time. 'It was 1170, I'm sure.'

But he had delivered himself into my hands. I looked hard at the foreign reporters, my only jury, and said loudly, 'And I'm sure Henry the Second was never charged with murder!'

I shouldn't have under-estimated Sir Worthington Banzana. He came back fighting with a smile and said, 'Although St Thomas à Becket, just like the unfortunate Bishop Kareele, found himself dead as mutton. Yes, Mr Rumpole?'

'No more questions, my Lord.'

I sat down and looked gloomily round the Court as Mr Nagoma left the witness-box with obvious relief, and a young clergyman, whose head seemed to emerge reluctantly from a dog collar several sizes too large for his neck, replaced him. The darling old Chief Justice, I thought, was beginning to make me feel almost nostalgic for Judge Bullingham, and the fog descending comfortably on Ludgate Circus, and Henry sending me out to do a little V.A.T. fraud with absolutely no danger of anyone being condemned to death. I had never thought that the Golden Road to Samarkand would prove such hard going.

It was at about this time that, on the other side of the world, Mr Myers, my favourite solicitor's clerk, or 'legal executive', as they are called today, stepped into our clerk's room in Chambers with a brief concerning the unfortunate killing in the Kilburn pub.

'Mr Rumpole in, is he?' Mr Myers asked Henry.

'I think he just slipped out for a moment to Central Africa. You wanted to see him, Mr Myers?'

'Fixed this little murder of his – down the Bailey for the 21st of the month. 10.30 start.' Myers put the brief on Henry's desk. 'He will be there, won't he, Henry?'

'I'll get him back for you by then. Leave it with me, Myersy,' Henry assured him.

'Central Africa! What's Mr Rumpole gone there for?'

'I rather gather his wife's got a visitor at home.'

'Oh, well then. That explains it.' Mr Myers went on his busy way and Henry turned to Dianne and said, 'We've got to get Mr Rumpole back for the 21st, Dianne. We can't have him out there forever, not sunning himself in the tropics. What did he say, send him a cable?'

Dianne sighed, got out her pencil and notebook, and prepared to take dictation.

Across that angry or that glimmering sea I was cross-examining the Reverend Kenneth Cuazango, the young clergyman who had been driving Bishop Kareele on the night of the murder. In spite of the huge fans, the courtroom was growing more stifling as the day wore on, and the Chief Justice had fallen into a temporary silence.

'You say that when you first heard shots you jumped out of the car and ran with your head *down*?'

'Yes.'

'So you didn't see the attacker at that time?'

'No. I told you, sir. I saw him through the windscreen.'

'When you reached your house – after a run of how long?'

'About three miles. That's all.'

'Did you telephone the police immediately?'

'Almost immediately, sir.'

'Almost immediately,' the Judge muttered as he wrote.

'What did you do first, when you got home?'

'I changed my clothes first. I was soaked to the skin.'

'Exactly!' I picked up a sheet of paper supplied by Freddy. 'I have a metereological report here. There was heavy rain that night, was there not, between the hours of nine and eleven o'-clock?'

'Didn't I say that?'

'No. I'm sorry, you didn't. And when it rains in Neranga it's not a gentle April shower, is it? It's a cataract!'

'Call it Noah's Flood?' The reverend young gentleman smiled.

'Why not? The windscreen was streaming with water, wasn't it? You couldn't possibly have identified my client!'

The Chief Justice, of course, couldn't resist an interruption. '*Could* you identify him?' He asked the witness, in a way that made the answer he wanted perfectly clear.

'I'm sure I could.' But the Bishop's chaplain didn't sound entirely convinced.

'I'm sure I could ...' The Judge wrote down the words, but not the doubt, and looked at me. 'You see, Mr Rumpole?'

'I see, my Lord. But *he* couldn't.'

'Isn't that the fact which *I* shall have to decide?' The Chief Justice gave me a wide, and I thought dangerous, smile.

It had been a long, hot and hard day, and I sat in the big, empty lounge of the Majestic Hotel drinking cold beer. (Wine seemed to be served only in the confines of the prison, and a glass of whisky would have absorbed almost my entire fee from Justitia International.) I was trying to remember a bit of old Wordsworth, partly because it would stop me thinking of the trial, but mainly because it gave me an obscure feeling of comfort.

> In the soothing thoughts that spring
> Out of human suffering;
> In the faith that looks through death,
> In years that bring the philosophic mind.

But before the mind could become too philosophical, I was brought back to the matter in hand by the sight of Mrs Grace Mazenze being directed by the porter across the waste land of the lounge towards my table. She sat down, refused my offer of refreshment and seemed reluctant to start talking. At last she said, 'That Judge, sir! He wants to hang David.' I took a swig of beer, having no particular comfort for her. 'You said you needed evidence,' she went on.

'Yes.'

'A witness?'

'Your brother-in-law offered me any amount of useless ones.'

'Jonathan! He wants to make an Apu martyr of David.' She spoke with a sudden vehemence. 'I want my David alive, though.'

'Are you sure you wouldn't like a drink?'

'Nothing, thank you.' There was another silence, and then she said, 'I have a witness for you. One who tells the truth.'

'The best sort,' I assured her.

'Only one thing is wrong. David wouldn't allow this one witness to come for him. Not if he knew. He would forbid it.'

'Why ever . . . ?' I was puzzled.

'This is a person of the Matatu people. David would never agree to such a witness.'

'It's the evidence that matters, for God's sake. Not the family background.'

'You may know very much law, Mr Rumpole, but you don't understand our country. Also, I'm afraid, David would not want this witness,' her voice sank almost to a whisper, 'for my sake.'

'For *your* sake?'

'This is something David try to keep a secret from me! Too late now for secrets. I think so.'

She opened a smart handbag she was carrying, a contrast to her bright African costume, and brought out a sheet of paper, covered with handwriting. I took it and looked at her. Then I read what had been written in primitive, badly spelled English and realized that bedtime would have to be indefinitely postponed.

An hour later I was sitting in David Mazenze's comfortably appointed cell in the District Police Headquarters. I was drinking wine, and thought he had probably drunk more than a bottle. He was playing music – not Fauré this time, but a Mozart piano concerto. I didn't show him the document I had read in the hotel, and some instinct stopped me telling him about it at once. So I sat for a minute in silence, staring into my glass.

'Don't look so down in the dumps, old fellow.' David Mazenze smiled at me.

'You may not have noticed, but the Chief Justice is against us.'

At which my client looked entirely unconcerned. 'A member of the Matatu tribe, and the Prime Minister's little chicken?' he said. 'Why shouldn't he be against an Apu leader? Everything is going as expected.'

'We've got to win this case.' I got up restlessly and went for a walk round the cell.

'Don't worry, old fellow. You're doing exactly what is needed.' My client, I thought, was trying to cheer me up.

'What's that?' I asked.

'Upholding the best traditions of British justice for the foreign papers. When we lose, everyone will know this Dr Death has no respect for the law. So our revolution will be perfectly justified.'

I switched off Mozart. What he was saying had suddenly become too important for even the most enticing distraction.

'Your *revolution*?'

David Mazenze refilled his glass and drank deeply. 'Our boys in the bush, Horace, yes. They will attack on the day I am convicted. No sentence will ever be carried out against David Mazenze. Now then, has that taken a bit of a weight off your mind?'

'Not really.'

I felt entirely lost, aimless and deceived. I asked the question that had been nagging at me since our last inconclusive conference.

'Tell me the truth,' I said. 'Are you saying that I was brought out here to lose this case?'

'Calm down,' David Mazenze said soothingly. 'You were brought out here to make your speech about the Golden Thread, Horace.'

'And then to *lose*?' I stood in front of him, no longer able to control my temper, exhausted by the long, apparently pointless day.

'It will be Dr Death who loses in the end, Horace. And the Judge. Some of our boys in the bush are likely to pass a motion of censure on that old Chief Justice Banzana.'

'I was brought out here to *lose*!' I shouted at him in my certainty. 'No wonder you didn't want an important Q.C.! Old Horace Rumpole is good enough to utter a few legal platitudes, and accept defeat gracefully. Is that it? Look, I was going to tell you ...'

'Tell me what, Horace?' He went to the gramophone and turned the music on again. He sat and closed his eyes, apparently bored by our conversation. It was then that I decided on a course which was, I must reluctantly admit, entirely unprofessional.

'No. I see it wouldn't do any good,' I said. 'Do you know what the Golden Thread that runs through British justice is?'

'Yes, Horace. I know that,' David Mazenze murmured through the Mozart.

'Rumpole presumes every case to be winnable until it's lost. I don't know any other way of doing them. And you can tell that to your "Boys in the Bush".'

'Thank you for coming to see me, Horace. I appreciate your efforts.'

But I had knocked on the door and the guard was letting me out. From then on I would have to do the Mazenze case alone and without a client.

The next morning I found my opponent adjusting his wig in front of the robing-room mirror. He was smoking a black Balkan Sobranie cigarette in his white ivory holder. I waved the scrap of paper I had been given by Mrs Grace Mazenze in his general direction.

'My learned friend!' said Taboro, in a pitying sort of way. 'His Lordship is giving you a bit of a bully ragging, I'm afraid.'

'Look, I should have served you with an alibi notice. Under British law.' I started, ignoring the commiserations.

'Under our law too.'

'If I show you a statement, would you object to my calling the witness?'

Rupert Taboro took my precious document and glanced at it. The only sign of his surprise was the lift of about half an inch in the angle of his cigarette holder. He handed the statement back to me with a smile of absolute friendliness.

'I shall raise no objection at all to this witness being called, at short notice. See you in Court, old fellow.' So he left me, as I was wishing to goodness that my Judge was as sympathetic as my prosecutor.

Freddy Ruingo came up to me in the crowded passage outside the Court and said he'd been talking to David Mazenze, and that our client had decided that, as the charge was beneath his contempt, he was not going to give evidence. 'So it's up to you now, sir. The great final speech on the presumption of innocence. Isn't that it?'

'Not quite yet.'

'Not?'

'We may have to go through certain legal formalities first.'

As I pushed my way on through the crowd, I met Grace standing by the door of the Court. She told me that my witness was there, and ready to give evidence.

'I will now call Mrs *Mabel* Mazenze.' The Chief Justice made a note, the reporters looked interested, Freddy turned to me with a look of almost comic dismay, Jonathan rose in his seat in the public gallery and my client shouted, 'No!' furiously from the dock. The Court attendant called for silence, but David was struggling with the warder in the dock and insisting that he would not have the witness called. In a moment's silence I heard the tap of the Judge's pencil.

'The defendant will be silent or I will have him taken down below and the trial will take place in his absence. Yes. Continue, Mr Rumpole.'

'Mrs Mabel Mazenze!' I heard the call outside the Court.

And then the young African girl came in and the Court was hushed; everyone was staring at her remarkable beauty. I remembered the glimpse I had had of her face, through an open door at the end of a passage, on that first night I had arrived in Neranga. She was in the witness-box now, holding up the Bible in a slim, brown hand.

'Are you Mabel Mazenze?' I asked her, when she had been sworn.

'Yes.'

'Mrs Mabel Mazenze. Are you a lady of the Matatu tribe?'

'Is she Matatu woman? Is that what you mean, Mr Rumpole?' the Chief Justice rumbled in the background.

'I was trying to put it a little more elegantly, my Lord.'

The Judge turned to the witness. 'Don't mind the elegance. You Matatu woman?'

'Yes, sir.' She gave him a glittering smile.

'And are you married to David Mazenze, the defendant in this case?'

I heard the Court buzz. The reporters were writing, Apu supporters in the public benches were looking shocked and puzzled. Rupert Taboro looked at the ceiling. Grace looked severely at the witness.

'The officer in charge has told us that your client's wife is called *Grace* Mazenze, Mr Rumpole.' The Chief Justice registered elaborate surprise. I obliged him by asking the witness, 'Did he also go through a ceremony of marriage with you, according to the tribal customs of the Matatu people, on the 8th of March, 1979?'

A door banged somewhere behind me. It was Jonathan Mazenze leaving Court.

'Yes, he did,' the witness agreed. 'David and I did. We kept it secret. Both our people would make us great mischief if they knew of it. And David having a wife of his own people also ...' Her voice trailed away as she looked round the Court, to meet hostile Apu eyes.

'The 8th of March this year was the anniversary of that ceremony. Where did David spend that evening?' I asked her.

'With me,' she answered clearly.

'Where was he between nine and eleven that rainy evening?'

'In my ... in our house, here in Nova Lombaro. He was with me from before nine o'clock.'

'When did he leave?'

'About quarter past eleven. He went to sleep in his bed at home with Grace as he had a big speech to make the next day. He thought with me he would not do so much sleeping.'

Mabel looked round the Court, smiling. There was some laughter, but not from the Apu spectators. Grace looked at her with a sort of solemn curiosity, as I asked, 'Has it been difficult for you to come here and give evidence?'

'I think my family never see me again when they know what I did with an Apu man,' Mabel answered seriously.

'*Why* have you come here to give evidence?'

'Only because I know David cannot have killed the old man. Only because of that.' She looked at the prisoner in the dock. He avoided her eye. 'And to save his life ...'

'Thank you, Mrs Mabel Mazenze.' I sat down and the Chief Justice asked the Attorney-General if he wished to cross-examine the witness. To my extreme surprise Rupert Taboro said that he had no questions to ask. I rose to my feet, determined to make the most of the situation.

'Perhaps my learned friend would help me. Does that mean that the prosecution accepts this witness's evidence?'

'It simply means, my Lord,' Taboro said in his most treacly voice, 'that we have no questions we wish to put.'

'I must insist . . .'

But the Chief Justice looked down on me and smiled mirthlessly. 'No good insisting, Mr Rumpole. In the end it will be a matter entirely for me!'

I wasn't able to deal with the Judge's remark until after the prosecutor's final speech, which was a fair and reasonable summary of the facts. After he had finished I made my own oration, and I must say it was one of my best, along familiar lines perhaps, but given a feeling of freshness by being made in unfamiliar surroundings. The Court was very quiet. My client was sitting in the dock with his head in his hands. Perhaps, I thought, he had given up hope, but I hadn't. I reached my peroration and I said:

'It is *not* a matter entirely for your Lordship.' And I said it fearlessly. 'It is a matter for our Common Law! And when London is but a memory and the Old Bailey has sunk back into the primeval mud, my country will be remembered for three things: the British Breakfast, *The Oxford Book of English Verse* and the Presumption of Innocence! That presumption is the Golden Thread which runs through the whole history of our Criminal Law – so, whether a murder has been committed in the Old Kent Road or on the way to Nova Lombaro, no man shall be convicted if there is a reasonable doubt as to his guilt. And at the end of the day, how can any Court be certain sure that that fearless young woman Mabel Mazenze has not come to tell us the plain and simple truth?'

When I had finished I sat down exhausted. My shirt was sticking to my back. I felt I had made a long journey, and I was now tired out, with nowhere further to go. Had I, I wondered for a low, despairing moment, made the great 'Golden Thread' speech for the last time? Was it some irony of fate, some obscure joke, that I should make it finally before a Court full of strange faces in the middle of Africa? I told myself that I had done all I could, that I had said every possible word in David Mazenze's defence, that the decision to call Mabel was inevitable.

But then I thought of the consequences of any mistake I might have made, and I found myself shivering in the stifling Court. Through all this the Chief Justice had been summing up, going through the facts of the case, and his voice seemed to be coming from a long way off. I forced myself to pay attention and, at first, I wished I hadn't.

'Neranga ranks high on the list of civilized countries,' the deep judicial voice was saying. 'We observe the rule of law. This is demonstrated by the fact that we have allowed a barrister in from England. He is a "junior" barrister. In England they have quite elderly "juniors", barristers as "long in the tooth", he will not mind my saying this, as Mr Horace Rumpole.'

There was some sycophantic laughter from parts of the Court, in which, I was sorry to see, my learned friend Mr Taboro joined.

'Mr Horace Rumpole has come to plead here,' the Judge went on, 'as a guest at our Bar. But he has told us nothing we didn't already know. We know that a man is innocent until he's proved guilty. That is the Golden Thread which runs through the law of Neranga. This law is also followed in Britain, I believe. The Court has the evidence of identification given by the Reverend Kenneth Cuazango. On the other hand, we have the positive evidence of Mabel Mazenze, the Matatu woman whom the defendant, a well-known member of the Apu tribe, has married as a second wife – a backward form of indulgence which is not in the best tradition of the New Neranga of Prime Minister Christopher Mabile. In these circumstances the Court is unable to feel that the prosecution has proved this case beyond reasonable doubt. Acting entirely on the principles of ancient Common Law, we pronounce on David Mazenze, whatever we may think of his morality, a verdict of "Not Guilty". Let the defendant be discharged.'

'Be upstanding in Court!' the attendant shouted.

We all stood and, as he left us, I bowed low, and with astonished gratitude, to the Chief Justice, Sir Worthington Banzana. I seemed to be bowing in the middle of an enormous silence. Then the Court began to empty quickly. I saw David Mazenze leaving the dock and, planning to meet him when he had received his congratulations, I turned to Freddy Ruingo.

'We did it, Freddy!' I smiled at him. 'We notched up a triumph, I'm sure you'll agree. We brought the Golden Thread to Samarkand!' But Mr Ruingo had made off and was dodging away among the crowd as though in some maze. The kindest word was spoken to me by my opponent, who came up smiling. 'Good win, my learned friend,' he said. 'Heartfelt congratulations.'

'Thank you. You were a great help.' I meant it. 'I'd better go and see my client.'

I moved away, but Taboro put a hand on my arm. 'I should warn you, old fellow. You may not find him particularly grateful.'

'I *did* save his life.' I looked at him, puzzled. But Taboro shook his head sadly. 'You also broadcast the fact that the leader of the Apu People's Party had got himself hitched to a Matatu woman. Not too good that, politically speaking. But then, I don't suppose you're tremendously interested in local politics. Oh, before you go,' – he held out a well-manicured hand – 'could I have my stud back, please?'

I took off my collar then and there and gave it to him. It seemed that I owed quite enough to Rupert Taboro.

I went up to the robing room to change, and met no one except the attendant in charge of wigs and gowns, who also seemed aloof, as though anxious to get me out of his domain as soon as possible. When I came downstairs the passage outside the Court was empty and silent.

I came out on to the steps of the Law Courts, and was hit in the face by the heat and blinding sunshine. And as I stood there blinking, two Nerangan policemen in khaki shorts with revolvers bumping against their hips, came running towards me. They grabbed my arms and hustled me, too astonished to protest, into a waiting police car. The engine roared, the tyres screeched on the burning road, and we were off, scattering chickens and children and the remnants of a crowd. It had happened at long,

long last. After an endless career in crime, I was under arrest.

Of course I always knew I'd end up in the Nick. It was my nightmare, a recurring dream from the days when I was a nipper. I could hardly close my eyes without hearing a voice somewhere saying, 'And the least sentence I can possibly pass on you is about a hundred years in the chokey.' Extraordinary thing, perhaps that's what made me take up the law. These thoughts were racing, in a confused fashion, through my head as I was hustled into the presence of Mr Akimbu, the blazered Superintendent of Police. He was holding a cable and looking at me with extreme hostility. 'Mr Rumpole. Will you please explain this cablegram which we have intercepted. Addressed to you, I think, at the Hotel Majestic.'

I took the document in question, looked at the signature and felt a flood of relief. Of course, I realized that the thing could have been phrased more happily.

'Please take your time – we have the whole night before us.'

The Superintendent's words were not particularly encouraging. I read him the message on the cable: ' "Murder fixed for 21st of this month at 10.30 a.m. Signed Henry." '

'What murder, Mr Rumpole? And who is your associate, "Henry"?'

Akimbu stood up and moved towards me. I felt a sense of pleasurable anticipation from the policemen by the door. The interrogation was about to begin.

'Good heavens. This is really very funny!' I smiled round the room, and got no reaction.

'Funny? You find murder "funny", Mr Rumpole?'

'No. No, of course not,' I assured him. 'But I see how you've been misled. It really is quite a joke.'

'Not a *real* murder?' The Superintendent frowned.

'No. No, of course. It *is* a real murder. A very real murder.' I heard myself babbling. I clearly had no talent for being interrogated.

'The 21st. That will be ...' The Superintendent examined a calendar on the wall. 'Ten days from now.' He turned on me triumphant.

'Ten days from now I shall be back in England. No need for you to worry.'

'Leaving the dirty side of the business, I suppose,' the Super-intendent almost sneered, 'to this Henry.'

At which moment an intercom buzzed on his desk. The Super-intendent answered with a Nerangan word, and a moment later a police officer opened the door to admit Arthur Remnant, Her Majesty's High Commissioner to the State of Neranga.

'There you are, Rumbold!' He came in smiling. 'You know what, my dear fellow, you need a good lawyer!'

I was booked back on the midnight plane. Earlier in the evening I was invited for cocktails at the High Commission. There was a fair sprinkling of guests – politicians, the Head of Nerangan Radio and his good lady, and some leading members of the Nerangan Bar, who smiled at me in a knowing sort of way but otherwise avoided my company. I stood under a portrait of the Queen and drank a reviving whisky and soda. Remnant looked at me as though it would take him a long time to get over the joke and said, 'It was a splendid result. Just what our brilliant Prime Minister always had in mind!'

'The Prime Minister wanted me to *win*?' I confess I wasn't following his drift.

'Just the way to please the International Monetary Fund, old fellow, and reassure Barclays Bank, and put Christopher Mabile in line for a "K" at the next Commonwealth Prime Ministers' Conference. You've probably earned him a bally knighthood, apart from the fact that you've seen off David Mazenze.'

'Seen him off? I was under the impression that I'd got him acquitted.' Never had a remarkable victory, I thought, been met with such a singular lack of acclaim.

'The Apus would never have let him hang,' Remnant explained patiently, as to a child. 'They'd have risen in their thousands – plenty of guns available in the bush, didn't they tell you? But they're a lazy people. Nothing in today's verdict to get them going. And they won't move a finger for a leader who married a Matatu woman.'

'Just a minute. I want to know . . .' But Remnant was moving away from me.

'What do you want to know, old fellow?'

'Who shot the Bishop?'

'The poor old Bishop! A politician who had outstayed his welcome. Of course, we'd know exactly what to do with him in England. Too bad there's no House of Lords in Neranga.'

'There you are, Mr Horace Rumpole.' I heard a deep and familiar voice behind me and turned to see a small, smiling Chief Justice. Beside him stood a man in bright African costume. The lights of the room reflected in his thick horn-rimmed glasses and made it impossible to see his eyes. I needed no introduction to tell me that I was in the presence of the Prime Minister, Dr Christopher Mabile, my former client's 'Dr Death'.

'Congratulations, Mr Rumpole.' The Prime Minister's voice was dry, academically precise. 'I hear you put up a first-rate show. You know the Chief Justice, of course. Your old sparring partner!'

They both looked at me as though I were a rare specimen who might soon become extinct.

'It has been a pleasure to have a British barrister among us,' the Prime Minister said. 'When are you leaving us?'

'Tonight.'

'Such a short visit! You should have stayed longer. Gone up country. We could have shown you some of our old tribal customs.'

'Thank you, Prime Minister,' I told him. 'I think I've seen them.'

It was only a week later, at breakfast in Froxbury Court, when I saw in *The Times* newspaper a photograph of a small part of the road to Nova Lombaro. The picture showed a battered car, riddled with bullets. The door was swinging open, and in the passenger seat was the crumpled, murdered body of David Mazenze, the former leader of the Apu People's Party, an organization which had now been taken over, so the story under the photograph informed the *Times* readers, 'by the deceased's younger brother, Mr Jonathan Mazenze'. The story ended, 'No arrest has yet taken place, according to the Attorney-General, Mr Rupert Taboro.' Neranga, quite clearly, was still a country which believed in the death penalty.

When I read the story out to Hilda all she said was, 'Mazenze ... Apu ... Rupert Taboro ... what extraordinary names.'

'Yes,' I said, 'almost as odd as Rumpole and Dodo Mackintosh.'

The world news was bad that day. Hilda's old school friend was still with us, sitting on the other side of the kitchen table, regarding me with pursed lips and an expression of disapproval.

'Wasn't it good of Dodo to stay on another week,' Hilda said, 'so you could see something of her?'

I gulped my coffee, got up and struggled into my jacket. 'Well, off to work!' I said as brightly as possible.

'You will be home early, won't you, dear? Dodo does like her game of three-handed whist, you know.'

I was on my way to the door, planning a leisurely aperitif at Pommeroy's Wine Bar.

'Anyway, where are you going today?' said She Who Must Be Obeyed.

'I'm going to the Old Bailey,' I answered her. 'Samarkand is definitely off.'

Rumpole and the Old Boy Net

To call the public school where I spent some of the worst years of my life 'minor' would be to flatter it. It was a small, poorly run penal colony on the Norfolk coast where the water habitually froze in the bogs and, on one remarkable occasion, we all believed, turned the glass of Milton, which contained the Headmaster's teeth, into a solid block of ice. Such education as was on offer had to be wrung out of reluctant masters whose own ambition was to rush from the classroom and huddle round the common room fire. It's true that Jimmie Jameson, a somewhat primitive type of Scottish Circuit Judge, had been to Linklaters, as, for a short spell when his parents were abroad, had old Keith from the Lord Chancellor's office. Apart from having once been asked to organize the Old Linklaters at the Bar*, I have never had much to do with my old school acquaintances, and having possessed the Old Linklater tie (I used it to secure a bulky set of books I was taking by train to a case in Chester about thirty years ago and haven't seen it since) has never helped me in the slightest degree on my way through life. Say 'I'm an Old Linklater' to most men of power and influence in this world, and their answer is most likely to be 'Mine's a Scotch.'

It is not so, of course, with the great public schools such as Eton, Harrow, Winchester and Lawnhurst. Having 'swung, swung together, with their bodies between their knees' at school, the ex-pupils of such places are liable to stick to each other for the rest of their natural lives. No sooner have they left school, but they meet up again in the Cabinet, or the House of Lords, or on the Board of the United Metropolitan Bank, or perhaps

* See 'Rumpole and the Fascist Beast' in *The Trials of Rumpole*, Penguin Books, 1979.

at an address in Barnardine Square which, as you may or may not know, is not a million miles from Victoria Station.

But I am going too fast. I should watch his Lordship's pencil, or my rapidly fading biro. All I wished to bring to your attention at the moment is the remarkable loyalty, as some would say, or the unspeakable clannishness, as others would hold, of the English public school system. Now I would ask you to turn, as my wife Hilda did on that gusty March morning at breakfast time in our mansion flat at 25B Froxbury Court, to the news pages of the *Daily Telegraph*. Hilda takes the *Telegraph*, although I prefer the Obituaries and the crossword in *The Times*. The *Telegraph* gives Hilda much that she needs, including detailed coverage of many scandalous events. On that particular morning the stories on offer in Hilda's favourite journal included one entitled, 'London Vice House Catered for Top People', and described the committal at the Central Criminal Court of a couple named Lee, on charges of blackmail and keeping a disorderly house.

'Can you understand it, Rumpole?'

'Understand what, Hilda?' I was spreading butter on my toast and couldn't see that the news item presented any form of intellectual challenge.

'These members of the aristocracy, top civil servants, and a vicar! Well really, haven't they got wives?' No doubt she was referring to the patrons of the Lee house in Barnardine Square.

'Life at the top isn't all roses, Hilda. Is that the marmalade gone to ground under your *Daily Telegraph*?'

'Well! Surely a wife's enough for anyone.'

'Quite enough,' I said, munching toast and Oxford marmalade.

'So why – run after other women?' Hilda seemed genuinely puzzled.

'I must confess, I'm baffled.' It was, I suppose, decidedly rum. I stood up, finishing my toast. Hilda looked at me critically, apparently finding that I might come last in any contest for the best-dressed barrister.

'Rumpole,' she said, 'come here. You've got marmalade on your waistcoat!' She fetched a damp teacloth from the kitchen sink and started to dab at me in a violent manner.

'I quite like marmalade on it,' I protested.

'You've got to be careful of your appearance now Guthrie Featherstone's been made a judge.'

'Out of respect to the dead?' I wasn't following her drift.

'Because you're going to take your rightful place, now Guthrie's gone, as Head of Chambers! Well, they said they'd come to a final decision, didn't they, when you got back from the jungle?'

'It wasn't the jungle, Hilda. It was the High Court of Neranga. Chief Justice Sir Worthington Banzana presiding.'

Hilda, however, pursued her own train of thought and disregarded the connection. 'There isn't another Q.C. to take Guthrie's place. You're the only candidate! I shall ask my friend Dodo Mackintosh to take on the catering at your first Chambers party. Marigold Featherstone will never have put on a do like it.'

I sighed. 'Those occasions are quite grim enough without Dodo's rock cakes.'

'Nonsense. Dodo's pastry's as light as a feather.' She stood back, apparently noticing some sartorial improvement in my good self. 'There now. You look more like a Head of Chambers! Someone fit to take the place Daddy once occupied!'

I beat it hastily to the door. Hilda hadn't noticed that, for the sake of greater comfort after my return from Africa, I had taken to wearing a delightful old pair of brown suede shoes with the dark blue suit I wore when I wasn't actually engaged in any of Her Majesty's Courts of Justice. Whilst I was working in Chambers I hoped that the Sovereign wouldn't notice my feet.

About an hour later I put my head round the door of the clerk's room in Equity Court and saw Henry checking the diary and Dianne busily decorating her fingernails with some preparation that smelled of model aeroplanes.

> 'This be the verse you grave for me:
> "Here he lies where he longed to be;
> Home is the sailor, home from the sea,
>   And the hunter home from the hill!"'

I announced.

'You're back then, Mr Rumpole.' Henry scarcely lifted his eyes from the diary.

'And not much thanks to you, Henry,' I said. 'That idiotic cable you sent me to Africa! I was almost dragged off to execution.'

'It was my duty to keep you informed, sir, about your position at the Old Bailey.'

'They thought I was going to *do* a murder. Not appear in one.'

'Oh really!' Dianne gave one of her silvery laughs. 'How dreadful!'

'Anyway,' said Henry, who didn't seem to appreciate the dire effects of his message. 'That murder's gone off. It won't be this term.'

'I came back ready for anything. Are you trying to tell me there's no work, Henry?' I started to open the various bills and circulars which had been awaiting my return.

'Oh, it's not as bad as that, sir. Mr Staines rang. He wanted a con. today, in the bawdy house case, R. *v.* Lee.'

My heart leapt up at the sight of what might be said to be a bit of a *cause célèbre*.

'Keep thy foot out of brothels, Henry! Such places are no doubt more entertaining to litigate about than to visit. Tell Stainey that I'm ready for him.' I did a quick sorting job on my correspondence. 'On Her Majesty's Service! Hasn't our gracious Queen anything better to do than to keep writing me letters?' I shed a pile of expendable mail and opened another envelope. 'What's this? A communication from L.A.C.! "Lawyers As Churchgoers – Moral Purpose in the Law – A Call to Witness for all Believing Barristers"!' I let that one follow the circulars. 'Brothel case, eh? Not much danger of finding a moral purpose in that, I suppose.'

At this point Claude Erskine-Brown came into our clerk's room, started to collect his letters, and looked up to see the traveller returned.

'Rumpole! We thought you'd gone native. We pictured you ruling some primitive tribe under a bong tree!'

'Most amusing, Erskine-Brown!' I gave him a rapidly disappearing smile. 'Well, now I suppose I've got to take over the extremely primitive tribe in these Chambers?'

I realized that She Who Must Be Obeyed would never let me

hear the last of it if I didn't claim my rightful place as Head, now that Guthrie Featherstone had been translated.

'We're deciding the Head of Chambers problem at the end of the month. When we have our meeting.' Erskine-Brown was always a stickler for formality.

'And after that I'll have to shoulder the cares of office. No one in Mr Justice Featherstone's old room, is there, Henry?'

'I don't think so, but . . .'

I had left him and was going up to take possession of the Captain's Quarters before he could finish his sentence. However, as I was mounting the stairs, Erskine-Brown came panting after me; apparently he had something to communicate in the deepest confidence.

'Horace. I think I should let you know. I've done it!'

'Then your only course is to plead guilty.' I gave him sound legal advice, but the fellow looked distinctly miffed.

'I have applied for silk, Rumpole,' he said with dignity. 'I think I've got a reasonable chance. Philly's right behind me.'

'I can't see her.' I looked behind him in vain.

'I mean,' he said, with some impatience, 'my wife is right behind me in my application for silk. "Claude Erskine-Brown, Q.C." How do you think it sounds?'

'Pretty encouraging, if you happen to be on the other side.' He looked displeased at that, so I went on brightly, 'Tell me, Claude. When is this Q.C. business likely to happen?'

'In about six weeks' time.'

'*After* the decision as to Head of Chambers?'

'Yes. I suppose so. After that.'

'Well, that's all right then. Best of British luck.'

I gave the man a reassuring slap on the shoulder. Of course, if he were to acquire a silk gown before the Chambers meeting, Claude would be entitled to that position which Hilda had set her heart on for me. As it was, I could see no way of stopping the 'Rumpole for Head of Chambers' bandwagon. I entered into my inheritance, Guthrie Featherstone's old room, and heard the sound of a woman in tears.

The woman in question was, in fact, no more than a mere slip of a girl. She was wearing dark clothes, had longish dark hair and, from what I could see of her face, she was extremely personable. At that moment she was in clear distress; her eyes were pinkish, she was dabbing at them with a small handkerchief which she had wound into a ball, and an occasional sob escaped her.

'I'm sorry.' I didn't quite know why I was apologizing; perhaps it was because I had intruded on private grief. 'Can I help at all?'

She looked up at me guiltily, as though I had caught her doing something wrong. 'I thought it was all right to come in here,' she excused herself. 'Doesn't this room belong to a judge who doesn't come here any more?'

'Bare ruin'd choirs, where late old Guthrie sang. Yes that's right.' I was overcome by curiosity. 'What's the trouble? Shoplifting? You look too young for a divorce.'

'I'm a b ... b ... barrister.' She sobbed again.

'Oh, bad luck!' I was sorry it seemed to be causing her such distress, and I offered her a large red-and-white spotted handkerchief as a back-up to the sodden ball of lace she was clutching.

'I'm Mrs Erskine-Brown's pupil. Thanks.' She dabbed her eyes again.

'Mrs Erskine-Brown, Phillida Trant that was, the Portia of our Chambers? Miss Trant now has a pupil? How time flies!' Much had happened, it seemed, during my absence in the tropics.

'She left me in a case after lunch at Tower Bridge. Well, there was a terrible argument about the evidence and I said I couldn't do it without my learned leader, Miss Trant, who was in a difficulty.'

'You should have plunged in – taken your chance,' I told her.

'And the Magistrate said, "What sort of difficulty?" and I said, "I think she's still at the hairdresser."'

I could understand our Portia's irritation with her tactless and inexperienced pupil. 'You forgot the most important lesson at the Bar,' I told her. 'Protect the private life of your learned pupil master – *or* mistress.'

'Now Mrs Erskine-Brown says I'm wet behind the ears and I'd better get a nice job in the Glove Department at Harrods. She says that they probably won't want another woman in

Chambers anyway.' She gave one final sniff, and handed me back my handkerchief.

'Got a name, I suppose?' I asked her.

'Fiona Allways.'

'Well, it's not your fault,' I comforted her.

'It's all I've ever wanted to *be*,' Fiona Allways explained. 'When the girls at school wanted to ride show-jumpers, I just stood in front of the mirror and made speeches in murder cases!'

I looked at her, made a decision and went to sit behind Featherstone's old desk.

'I've got a conference later. You could take a note of it, if you'd like to. Make yourself useful. No particular objection to prostitution, have you?' To my dismay she seemed to be about to cry again. 'Well, what on earth's the matter now?'

Miss Allways looked at me, fighting back her tears, and said, 'I suppose that's all you think I'm fit for!'

The police had been keeping observation on the Lees' large Victorian house in Barnardine Square for weeks. They had chronicled, in boring detail, the visits of a large number of middle-aged men of respectable appearance to that address and had seen girls arrive in the morning and leave at night.

On the day of the arrest, a particularly respectable middle-aged man arrived on the doorstep, rang the bell, and was heard to say in to the door speaker, 'I'm a caller. Come to visit a friendly house.' He was a man who would subsequently become unknown to the world as 'Mr X'. As the door was opened, police officers invaded the house and flushed out a large number of distinguished citizens in positions of unusual friendliness with certain youngish ladies. Mr X was asked for his name and address and subsequently gave a lengthy statement to the police. Both Mr Napier Lee, the owner of the premises, and his wife, Mrs Lorraine Lee, were present when the police raided. Mr Lee protested and said that an Englishman's home was, after all, his castle. Mrs Lee asked if the matter couldn't be dealt with in a civilized manner, and invited the officers to take a nice cup of Earl Grey tea. Now Mr and Mrs Lee were in conference with my learned self; also present were Mr Staines, our solicitor, and Miss Fiona Allways, who had so far recovered her spirits as to be able to take a note.

'Apart from the little matter of keeping a disorderly house,' I reminded the assembled company, 'there's an extremely unpleasant charge of blackmail.'

'Demanding money with menaces. I have explained that to the clients,' said Mr Staines.

'Neither Napier nor I can understand anyone saying that about us, can we, Nappy?' Mrs Lee sounded deeply hurt. 'All our clients are such awfully decent people. Public school, of course, and I do think that makes *such* a difference.'

This madame, I thought, would appear to be the most appalling old snob. I looked at my visitors. Mr and Mrs Lee were the sort of genteel, greying couple you might meet any day at the Chelsea Flower Show. He was wearing an elderly tweed suit, meticulously polished shoes, and what I later assumed to be an Old Lawnhurst tie. Mrs Lee was in a twinset and pearls, with a tweed skirt and brogues. Only Mr Staines, the solicitor, who affected striped suits and a number of rings, looked anything like a ponce.

'All our visitors are thoroughly good sorts, Mr Rumpole,' Mr Lee assured me. 'All out of the absolutely top drawer, not a four-letter man among them! And I'll tell you something else my lady and I have noticed, haven't we, Lorraine?'

'What's that, Nappy?' His wife smiled vaguely.

'Absolutely no side. I mean, they come into our home and behave just like one of us.'

'I'm sure they do,' I murmured.

'Napier was at Lawnhurst,' Mrs Lee told me proudly. 'Down for it from birth, weren't you, Nappy?'

'Oh yes. The guv'nor put me down for Lawnhurst at birth.'

We had had enough, I thought, of childhood reminiscences, and I spoke a little sharply. 'Mrs Lorraine Lee, Mr Napier Lee, it may be all very pleasant to sit here, over a cup of tea, and discuss the merits of the public school system, but you are charged with obtaining money by threats from a certain ...'

'Please, Mr Rumpole!' Mrs Lee held up her hand in a call for discretion.

'There's no need to name names, is there?' Mr Napier Lee asked anxiously.

'Not when it comes to a man in his position.' Mrs Lee was referring, deferentially, to the future 'Mr X'.

'Lawnhurst, New College Oxford, the Brigade of Guards and then the Ministry.' Mr Lee gave the man's curriculum vitae.

'Napier was destined for the Foreign Office if his guv'nor hadn't had a bit of bad luck in the City, weren't you Nappy?' Mrs Lee was now positively glowing with pride.

'Well, dear. I never had the "parlez-vous" for the Foreign Office.' Mr Lee smiled at his wife modestly. I was anxious to return to the case and picked up a couple of accounts from the brief.

'This gentleman in question seems, from time to time, to have paid your gas bills,' I reminded them.

'When business was slack, I'm not denying it, he helped us out, Mr Rumpole.' Mrs Lee smiled with extreme candour.

'And did you threaten to publish his little secret?' It was the sixty-four-thousand-dollar question, but the Lees rejected the suggestion with disdain.

'Oh no. He knew we'd never have done that. Didn't he, Nappy?' Mrs Lee appealed to her husband.

'Of course he knew. That would have been against the code, wouldn't it?'

'Sneaking! One does not sneak, does one?' Mrs Lee gathered up her handbag, as though to bring the proceedings to an end. 'Well Nappy,' she said, 'I really think that's all we can tell Mr Rumpole.'

'No, it's not,' I said firmly. 'You can tell me something else. How did you get into this business?' I asked Mrs Lee. 'Looking at you, a small cardigan shop in Cheltenham Spa might have seemed more appropriate.'

'Napier had a bit of bad luck in the City. Also his health wasn't quite up to it after the war.'

'Ticker a bit dicky. You know the sort of thing.'

'It was Nappy's war service.'

'Four years playing a long innings against Brother Boche.'

'And Napier had a dicky ticker.'

'Then I happened to run into a friend. Quite by chance,' Mr Lee told me. 'Well, we discussed the possibilities of a business along the lines of the one we're running now.'

'A friendly house!' Mrs Lee smiled. 'For the nicer sort of customer. People Nappy got to know on the "Old Boy Net".'

'And this fellow very decently came up with a spot of capital.'

'And was this helpful friend someone you'd known for a long time?'

'Oh yes. An old "mate", you understand. From way back. Of course, we'd drifted apart a bit, over the years.'

'An old school friend, perhaps?' I suggested.

'Oh, Napier couldn't possibly tell you that.' Mrs Lee pursed her lips.

'No. I couldn't tell you that,' Napier agreed.

'Against the code?' I wondered.

'The unwritten law,' Napier said. 'The sort of thing that just isn't done. It would be as unthinkable as ...' He searched for some suitable enormity. 'Well, as wearing brown suede shoes with a blue suit, for instance.' Then he looked down at my feet.

'Don't worry,' I said. 'I wasn't at Lawnhurst, you know.'

When the conference was over, I went into the clerk's room to say goodnight to the workers. There Henry told me, somewhat puzzled, that he had just had a telephone call from She Who Must Be Obeyed.

'Did she want me?' I wondered what I had done amiss.

'She seemed to want to speak to *me*, sir. On the subject of snacks.'

'*Snacks*, Henry?'

'Sausage rolls. Rolled-up asparagus. She said her friend, Mrs Mackintosh would provide us with little cheesy things, sir. I told her we weren't having the Chambers party until after the meeting, and then we'd be able to welcome our new Head of Chambers.'

'Head of Chambers! She Who Must Be Obeyed has set her heart on it. She won't take no for an answer. You follow me?' I looked hard and long at Henry. I wanted to be sure that the man was on my side in my bid for the leadership.

*

It was a sunny morning on the day the Lees' trial started, and I decided to take a slightly longer walk along the Embankment down to the Bailey. As the wind sent small white clouds chasing each other across the sky, and the seagulls came swooping in over Temple Gardens, I was put in mind of certain lines by the old sheep of the Lake District:

> Earth has not anything to show more fair:
> Dull would he be of soul who would pass by
> A sight so touching in its majesty ...

A sight not quite so touching in its majesty was likely to be his Honour Judge Bullingham. The Mad Bull had been picked by some practical joker on the Bailey staff to try the case of the frightfully nice bawdy house keepers. Did the Bull go to a public school? I wondered. I couldn't remember. Probably he went to some establishment where they played soccer with a cannon ball and learning to read was an optional extra.

I passed Ludgate Circus and turned up towards the dome of the Old Bailey. I was just about to cross the road and dive in through the swing doors, when I heard a panting sound at my elbow, and Hoskins, a fairly unmemorable barrister in our Chambers, was at my side.

'Rumpole,' said Hoskins, 'You've got back from Africa!'

'No, Hoskins. I'm still there, dispensing tribal justice in a loin cloth and a top hat. What're you talking about?'

'Just to let you know that I'm against you in the brothel case. Sam Ballard's leading me.'

'Who?' The name was unknown to me.

'Sam Ballard. The Q.C. from the North-East Circuit. You know, the one who's coming to practise in London. Haven't you been told?'

'Yes. You've just told me.' I was glad Hoskins was on the other side in our case and not helping me. His mind seemed to be wandering.

'But you haven't been told anything else about him?' Hoskins looked surprisingly embarrassed.

'No. What is there to tell?'

'You'll get on with him like a house on fire,' Hoskins assured me. 'He's Chairman of L.A.C., you know – "Lawyers As Churchgoers".'

Having climbed laboriously into the wig and gown (did I detect, still hanging in the horsehair, the dry scented smell of Africa?), I made my way to Judge Bullingham's Court attended by my small retinue consisting of Miss Fiona Allways and Mr Staines.

When I got to the courtroom door, I found a tall, somewhat stooping figure waiting for me. He was, I supposed, younger than he looked. He seemed the sort of man who had felt the weight of heavy responsibilities in the nursery: his brow was furrowed by a look of anxiety and his mouth was drawn down in an expression of almost permanent disapproval. He wore his black Court coat and striped trousers like a suit of mourning and, in all the circumstances, his silk Q.C.'s gown seemed something of a frivolity. His face was pale, and when he spoke his tone was slow and sepulchral. I suppose you could sum the matter up by saying that he was a character who might have been quite nice looking, when he was alive.

'Are you Horace Rumpole?' The question seemed to contain a lurking accusation.

'I suppose I must be.'

'Sam Ballard.' He introduced himself. 'I'm leading for the Crown. In "Lee". By the way, I passed Chambers this morning. In fact I dropped something in your tray.'

'Did you, Bollard?' I said airily. 'Can't say I noticed.'

'It was about a meeting of LAC.' He pronounced it as one word, like the place Sir Lancelot came from. 'I do hope you can find time to join us. We *should* value your contribution.'

' "Lawyers As Churchgoers"? I may have to give that a miss, Bollard. My doctor has advised me to avoid all excitement.'

'Ballard.'

'Yes, of course. I imagine your little get-together might put considerable strain on the ticker. Where do you meet? Pentonville Women's Institute? The whole orgy topped up by barn dancing and silent prayer?'

'Henry warned me about you, Rumpole.' The man was unsmiling.

'Henry?' I wondered why Henry had discussed my character with this lay reader.

'Henry the clerk. He said you had a sense of humour.'

'Only a mild one, Bollard. Nothing fatal. You've managed to keep free of it? What do you do? Jog a lot, I imagine.' He looked at me in silence for a long time and then said, more in sorrow than in anger, 'Some of our keenest members scoffed at the out-set.'

'I dare say they did.' Fascinating as this conversation was, duty called. I had to tear myself away, and moved towards the door of the Court. As I did so, I uttered a pious thought. 'Well, all I hope is that this little prosecution will be conducted in a thoroughly Christian spirit.'

'You can rely on me for that.'

I was almost through the door as I said, 'Perhaps you'll show a certain reluctance about casting the first stone.'

Far from showing any reluctance in the stone-throwing depart-ment, the lugubrious Ballard fired off a volley of moderately lethal rocks in the course of his opening speech to the jury.

There I sat facing Judge Bullingham, who glowered like a larger white (or rather purplish) Sir Worthington Banzana, and I looked round the Court to which I had come home from my travels. I saw the Lees, sitting calmly in the dock as though they had just been asked to drop in for a cup of tea. I glanced at the Press box which was more than usually full, R. *v.* Lee being, it seemed, a bit of a draw and likely to fill the Sunday papers for the next couple of weeks. Prominent among the journalists I saw a youngish girl in a boiler suit and glasses, who wore a button bearing the legend HOME COUNTIES TELEVISION. I thought that she was smiling at me and I smiled back, somewhat flattered, until I saw that the message was being beamed at Fiona Allways, who was sitting beside me, industriously writing down Ballard's rubbish. Then I closed my eyes, hoping to indicate to the jury that nothing the prosecution said could possibly be of the slightest interest. Steadily, remorselessly, the voice of the Ballard droned on.

'Decent men, family men, men who had earned the respect

of the community and were placed in positions of trust, found themselves tempted by this house, 66 Barnardine Square, Victoria. Some of you may know Victoria, members of the jury, you may know its brightly lit streets and British Railway Terminal. I'm sure none of you know the darker streets, where the market is in human flesh. Men left that particular house, members of the jury, with their consciences burdened with guilt and their wallets lightened. In the case of one of the witnesses I am about to call, the financial gain to those who exercised this appalling trade was considerably more. This is the subject of Count Two of the indictment, my Lord.'

I opened my eyes as the Judge weighed in with, 'Yes, Mr Ballard. I am sure the jury understand. The *blackmail*!' The Bull looked at the jury to remind them that this was a very grave charge indeed and then glowered at me as though it were all my fault.

I smiled back at Bullingham in a friendly fashion.

'Among the many respectable figures who fell to the temptations of 66 Barnardine Square . . .' Ballard went on, and I began to speculate, in a random sort of way, as to who the many respectable figures might be. Doctors? Politicians? Police officers? Lawyers? *Lawyers? Judges!* I looked at his Honour Judge Roger Bullingham with a wild surmise. I thought I must ask my clients. Of course, they'd never tell me. But a Bull in a knocking shop! The idea was almost too good to be true. I couldn't suppress a momentary gasp of merriment.

'Did you say something, Mr Rumpole?' The Bull cast a scowl in my direction.

'Nothing at all, my Lord!' I rose slightly and then sank into silence.

'I should remind everyone in Court that this is a most serious case.' The Judge made a pronouncement. 'The charges are extremely grave, and if the evidence as outlined by Mr Ballard is true . . . Of course, I haven't begun to make up my mind about it yet.'

'Haven't you, Bull?' I muttered to myself in the most *sotto* of possible *voce*s as his Lordship continued.

'Then all I can say is that the activities at this property in

Victoria were very wicked indeed. So we will have no laughter from anywhere in this Court.' After a meaningful look at counsel for the defence, the Judge smiled on the prosecution. 'Yes, Mr Ballard.'

'If your Lordship pleases.' My opponent bobbed a small bow to the learned Bull and then carried on with his work. 'Members of the jury,' he said. 'A suitable motto to be written up over the door of 66 Barnardine Square is that which Dante chose for his Inferno ...' I didn't think much of that for a legal reference. His Lordship probably thought that Dante was some-one who did conjuring tricks on television, but Ballard soldiered on with: ' "Abandon hope all ye who enter here." Because, of course, once he was in the door, and once the spiders got to know who he was, a fact which they took great pains to find out, the fly was trapped. He couldn't get away, and if he was a man who enjoyed a high and responsible position, he would pay anything, you may think, to buy the silence of this brazen woman and her procuring husband ...'

The jury looked at the couple in the dock. Napier Lee had his hand cupped over his ear and a gently pained expression as a result of what he was able to hear. At which point Ballard announced that he would call his first witness. I noticed that this announcement was not accompanied by any name, and then the Usher went out of Court and returned, after a longer lapse of time than usual, with a tall, distinguished-looking, grey-haired man wearing a dark suit, a striped shirt with a stiff white collar, and a Guards tie. He walked across the Court with the stiff-upper-lipped expression of an officer and gentleman marching out to face a firing squad. Once in the box he lifted the Bible, raised his eyes to heaven and repeated the oath as though it were his last will and testament. When he had finished he put the Good Book down carefully on the ledge in front of him, and turned to face the fusillade of Ballard's questions. Before he did so, I gave vent to a loud mutter of 'Name please.'

Triggered off by this perfectly normal request, Ballard made an application to the learned Judge.

'My Lord,' he started confidently, 'I would like to make the usual application in a blackmail case. I ask that this witness should be known simply as Mr X and that your Lordship directs that the ladies and gentlemen of the Press should not repeat his name under any circumstances.'

I glanced at the Press box and saw the young lady television reporter look up from her notebook and stare hard at the man in the witness-box. Meanwhile, the Judge was nodding his agreement. 'That seems to be a very proper order to make, in view of this gentleman's position,' he said. 'I imagine you have no objection, Mr Rumpole?'

I rose slowly to my feet, glowing with helpfulness.

'I would have no objection, my Lord, provided a similar concession is made for the benefit of my clients.'

'My Lord.' My words had clearly alarmed my learned friend. 'Perhaps we should continue with this in the absence of the jury, if there is to be an argument.' Well, he could bet his old hair shirt there was going to be an argument.

'Very well. Members of the jury.' Bullingham smiled in an ingratiating manner at the twelve good men and women and true. 'Unfortunately, legal matters arise from time to time which have to be resolved. Would you go to your room? We shouldn't have to detain you long.'

The jury filed out, grateful for a smoke and a cup of Old Bailey coffee. The boiler-suited girl in the Press box was writing furiously in her notebook. As the door closed on the last jury member the Bull fixed me with a malevolent eye.

'Now, Mr Rumpole,' he said. 'Did I hear a somewhat unusual argument with regard to the defendants in this case?'

'That they should be known as Mr and Mrs Y? Why not, my Lord?' I asked innocently. 'My learned friend talks about embarrassment. Mr and Mrs Napier Lee have been spattered over the front pages of every newspaper in England. "Alleged Vice Queen Arrested"; "The Darby and Joan Who Owned the House of Shame"; "Charged with Being the Top People's Madame" ... and so on. They have had to submit to a barrage of prejudicial publicity whilst this client of theirs can creep into Court under cover of a letter of the alphabet and preserve his precious respectability intact!'

'Mr Rumpole. There is no charge against this gentleman. He

is innocent of any crime!' His Lordship seemed to be turning a darker shade of purple.

'So are my clients innocent!' I did my bit to match the Judge's outrage. 'Until they're proven guilty. Or doesn't that rule still apply in your Lordship's Court?' I was regarded with a look of admiration from Miss Fiona Allways and the boiler-suited television lady, and a trumpet of indignation from the Bench.

'Mr Rumpole! This Court is entitled to some respect.'

'I am so full of respect to this Court, my Lord, that I give it credit for still applying the law of England – or has that been changed while I was out of the country? I merely ask for information.' I tried a charming smile, which was about as calming as a red rag to the Bull. He came charging to judgement. 'Your application that your clients' names should not be published is refused, Mr Rumpole,' he said. 'This case can be reported in full so far as they are concerned.'

'And they will no doubt be delighted to contribute to the pleasures of the great British Breakfast.' I bowed with great courtesy and sat. 'If your Lordship pleases.'

'Now, Mr Ballard.' The Judge turned to the more congenial matter of dealing with the prosecution. 'Your application for this witness to remain anonymous is made on good authority?'

'Certainly, my Lord. The Contempt of Court Act gives your Lordship power to order that the witness's name should never be published.'

'In perpetuity?' I grumbled from a seated position.

'My learned friend says, "In perpetuity?" and the answer would be "yes",' Ballard answered without hesitation.

'I suppose your argument would be,' the Judge suggested helpfully, 'that if this witness's secrets are exposed to the public, then in effect the blackmail threat would have been successful. Is that your argument, Mr Ballard?' Of course it was, once the Judge had told him.

'Yes, it is, my Lord. And your Lordship puts it so much better than I can.' At least Ballard's religious integrity didn't prevent a little grovelling on occasions.

'What's your answer to *that*, Mr Rumpole?' His Lordship turned to the defence.

'What blackmail?' I rose with apparent reluctance. 'What blackmail is your Lordship referring to? I merely ask for information.'

'We all know what this case is about,' Bullingham rumbled.

I responded with another burst of carefully simulated outrage. 'There hasn't yet been a word of evidence about blackmail,' I said. 'Nothing has been proved. Nothing! In my submission your Lordship cannot make a decision based on unproven allegations. And one more thing . . .'

'Yes, Mr Rumpole.' The Judge looked pointedly at the clock and sighed.

'One more principle of which this Court should be reminded. British justice is meant to take place in public. Justice is not to be seen cowering behind an initial.'

'Is that all, Mr Rumpole?' His Lordship sighed again.

It was all that was fit for mixed company, so I bowed with elaborate courtesy. 'If your Lordship pleases. With the greatest respect.' I bowed again. 'I think your Lordship has my argument.' I did a final gesture of mock subservience and sat down.

'Yes, Mr Rumpole. I think I have. I see it's nearly one o'clock, but I'll give judgement on this point now, so that the witness may have his lunch with some degree of peace of mind.' The Judge smiled at the silent figure in the witness-box, and continued. 'The defendants, through their counsel, seem particularly anxious that this gentleman's patronage of their alleged house of ill repute should become widely known to the public.'

Turning round I saw Mrs Lee, deeply wounded, shake her head. Bullingham continued with grim determination. 'If that were allowed it would be a blackmailer's charter. No victim would ever dare to go to the police. I am determined that this witness's high reputation shall be protected. He will give his evidence to the jury as "Mr X" *after* luncheon. Thank you, Mr Ballard.'

The Usher called us to our feet and the Judge left us. I told Stainey to inform the Lee family that I would visit them in the cells shortly and gathered up my papers. When I got outside the Court I saw Fiona Allways, my learned note-taker, in close conversation with the lady from the Press box. When she saw me,

Fiona said to her, 'See you, Izzy. See you here after lunch,' and joined me on my journey to the lifts.

'Who was that?' I asked by way of idle chatter.

'Isobel Vincent. She was a prefect when I was at Benenden. I hero-worshipped her rather,' Miss Allways admitted.

'Do girls have an "Old Boy Net" too?'

'Izzy works for Home Counties News,' Fiona Allways sounded deeply impressed. 'She's tremendously into Women's Liberation.'

'So am I!' I said as we waited for the lift.

'You?'

'All for Women's Liberation. Particularly the liberation of Mrs Lorraine Lee.'

The lift arrived and we stepped into it and sank towards the cells. As we did so Miss Allways was looking at me with the sort of admiration she had previously reserved for Izzy, the fearless television reporter.

'I say, Rumpole. You *were* splendid. Really fighting.'

'Let's say – going through the motions towards a graceful defeat.'

'Well, I think it's *jolly* unfair. Keeping his name a secret.'

'Do you, Fiona?'

She spoke with a passion which I found unexpected. 'I mean, those sort of places wouldn't exist at all, would they, if it weren't for the Mr Xs?' She looked at the papers I was clutching. 'The name's in your brief, isn't it? I suppose *you* know what his name is?'

'He signed his deposition. I know it, yes,' I admitted.

'So you could tell anybody . . . ?'

'Contempt of Court, Fiona,' I told her, 'should be a silent exercise, like meditation.'

The lift stopped and we got out in the basement. We passed the carefully preserved door of Old Newgate prison, rang for a screw and were finally admitted to the dungeon department of the Central Criminal Court.

'We don't want his name splashed around the papers, Mr Rumpole. We wouldn't want that.' I don't know what it was about Mrs Lorraine Lee, but she could make the dreary little interview room, with its plastic table and old tin which did for an ashtray, seem somehow cosy and refined. Both of the Lees were looking at me, more in sorrow than in anger. I was taking exercise, walking up and down the confined space as I smoked a small cigar, and Fiona was sitting at the table nonchalantly turning the pages of my brief.

'Damned painful for him to be asked to give his name, in *his* position,' Napier Lee agreed with his good lady.

'We abide by the code, you see,' Mrs Lee said. 'The unwritten law. All the chaps who come to our house know they can trust us.'

'The "Old Boy Net"!' I said with some asperity. 'Look, he's "sneaked" on you. Why not return the compliment?'

'That's not how it works, I'm afraid.' Mr Lee shook his head. 'Whatever he's done, we've got to do the decent thing.'

'We think the Judge is a perfect gentleman, don't we, Nappy?' Mrs Lee amazed me by saying.

'He understands the code, you see,' her husband agreed.

'He didn't want the poor fellow's name mentioned. That would've been terribly embarrassing.'

'And it would be terribly embarrassing, Mrs Lorraine Lee, if you and your husband got five years for blackmail!' I suggested. 'I mean, you might be as snug as bugs in the Nick, but what's going to happen to me? I just can't afford to lose cases, not at this particular point in my career. I'm just about to be elected to high office in my Chambers.' Then I turned on her and asked, 'Why just the gas bill?'

'What?' Lorraine seemed confused.

'Use a lot of gas, did you, at Barnardine Square?' I pressed my inquiries.

'Not particularly,' Napier Lee said. 'The bills used to lie out on the hall table and, well, he offered to pay one or two – out of kindness, really.'

'Just a tremendously decent gesture,' his wife agreed. 'It was over and above the call of duty.'

'*How* did he pay them, exactly?'

'Oh, he used to give us a cheque,' Mrs Lee told me.

'A cheque!' I was astonished. 'In a house of ill repute? Mr X is either very naïve or . . .'

'Or what?' Napier Lee was puzzled, as though the point had never occurred to him before.

'I don't know. And we may never have a chance to find out.' I stubbed out the cigar end and was preparing to leave them, when Mr Lee uttered a mild rebuke. 'We don't like it called a house of ill repute, Mr Rumpole. We call it a friendly house.'

My usual luncheon, when engaged on a case down the Bailey, consisted of a quickly snatched sandwich and a glass of stout in the pub opposite if I was in a hurry, or a steak pie washed down with *vin* extremely *ordinaire* in the same resort. Our visit to the cells had left us so little time, however, that Fiona Allways and I took the lift up to the Bar Mess, the eatery on the top floor. This is a place I habitually avoid. It is always full of barristers telling each other of the brilliant way they dealt with discovery of documents, or the coup they brought off in some hire-purchase claim in Luton. The large room was resonant with the sort of buzz and clatter that usually accompanies school dinners, and there was a marked absence of cheerful atmosphere.

My reluctance to mingle freely with the learned friends at the trough was justified by the fact that, when Fiona and I put down our ham salads at the long table, we found ourselves sitting opposite the lugubrious Ballard, who was peeling himself a chocolate biscuit.

'Hello, Ballard,' I said, making the best of things. 'Enjoyed the sermon.'

'Did you, Rumpole?' A shadow of a smile flitted across his face, and was promptly dismissed.

'Haven't had such a good time since our old school parson gave us three quarters of an hour on hell fire,' I assured him. 'Always eat here, do you?'

'Don't you use the Bar Mess?' Ballard seemed puzzled.

'As a matter of fact, no. I prefer the pub – you get the chance of rubbing shoulders with a few decent criminals.'

To my surprise, the Ballard smile returned, and his tone was unexpectedly friendly. 'Perhaps you'll take me to your pub sometime. I mean, we should get rather better acquainted,' he said.

'Should we?' I could see no pressing reason for this bizarre suggestion.

'Well, we're going to have to spend a good deal of time together.'

'Why? This case isn't going to go on for ever, is it? Talking of which . . .'

'Yes?'

'Sam. I might come along to one of those churchgoers' meetings of yours . . .' I, too, was having a go at the friendly approach.

'Really?' The man seemed gratified.

'I mean, there is a great deal to be said for introducing a little more Christian spirit into the law . . .'

'I'm so glad you think so.' Those who had seen St Paul on the road to Damascus no doubt looked a little like Ballard, Q.C., peering at Rumpole.

'Oh, I do,' I assured him. 'There is more joy in heaven, as I understand it, old darling, over one sinner that repenteth, and all that sort of thing.'

'That sort of thing, yes,' Ballard agreed.

'And if two sinners repenteth,' I was getting nearer to the nub, the heart of this unusual conversation. 'I mean, repent to the tune of pleading guilty to keeping a disorderly house, wilt thou not drop the blackmail charges, old cock?'

'No.' All smiles were discontinued. Ballard closed his teeth firmly on his chocolate biscuit.

'Did I hear you aright?' I said, with a good deal of sorrow.

'I said, "No." It's quite impossible.'

'Look here.' I wrestled patiently for the man's soul. 'Is that an entirely Christian attitude? Forgive them their trespasses, unto seventy times seven! Well, there's only one little count of blackmail.'

'No doubt they may be forgiven eventually. After a suitable period of confinement.' Ballard masticated unmercifully.

'The Mad Bull is quite capable of giving them five years for blackmail.' I pointed out the brutal facts of the matter.

'Is *that* what you call the learned Judge?' Ballard looked at me severely. 'I had thought in terms of seven, for blackmail. And the top sentence for keeping a disorderly house is six months.

Is that the reasoning behind your appeal to Christian principles, Rumpole?'

'You show a remarkably cynical attitude, for a churchgoer.' It pained me to find the man so worldly.

'As a churchgoer, I have a duty to protect public decency. I don't know what your particular morality is.'

'It mainly consists of getting unfortunate sinners out of trouble. You don't learn about that, apparently, in your scripture lessons.'

'Blessed are the blackmailers, for they shall walk out without a stain on their characters.' A hint of the smile returned. 'Is that your version of the Sermon on the Mount, Rumpole?'

' "Prisons are built with stones of law, brothels with bricks of religion." That's William Blake, not me. And I'll give you another quotation: "I come not to call the righteous, but the sinners to repentance." Matthew 8, verse 13.'

'How do *you* know that?' Ballard was clearly surprised.

'My old father was a cleric. And I'll tell you something. He hated Bible classes.'

A silence fell between us. Ballard was rolling the silver-paper wrapping of his chocolate biscuit between his fingers. 'It's a pretty odd sort of story, isn't it, for blackmail?' I said.

'It seems a painfully usual one to me.'

'Does it? If you were in a brothel, would you write out a couple of cheques on the NatWest, and sign them with your real name? Particularly if you're such a shy, retiring violet as your precious witness Mr X.'

Ballard looked at his watch. 'The Judge'll be coming back,' he said firmly.

The theological debate was over. Ballard left us and Fiona Allways looked at me in evident distress. 'Five years!' she said. 'They'd really get five years?'

I finished my Bar Mess light ale and gave her my learned opinion. 'You know what we need in this case? A witness who knows something about Mr X. No one's going to come rushing to our aid while his name's kept a deadly secret. There, Fiona old girl, is the rub.'

*

The gentleman in the Guards tie gave his damning evidence of blackmail to an attentive jury and an appreciative Bull, and it wasn't until later in the afternoon that I rose to cross-examine.

'You won't mind me calling you Mr X?' I started politely.

'No.'

'I thought you wouldn't. For how long were you a habitué of this house of ill repute?'

'Really, Mr Rumpole,' the Judge protested. 'Does that make the slightest difference?'

'Please answer the question.' I kept my eye on the witness. 'Unless my Lord rules against it, on a point of law.' My Lord didn't.

'I had been visiting there for about five years.'

'On your way home from directing the nation's affairs?' The question had the desired effect on his Lordship, who uttered a loud rebuke. 'Mr Rumpole!'

'Very well,' I said in my usual conciliatory fashion. 'On your way home from work. Before you got lost in the bosom of your family, it was your practice to visit 66 Barnardine Square?'

'Yes,' Mr X answered reluctantly.

'How did you first hear of this place of resort?'

'Hear of it?' The witness seemed puzzled by the question.

'Yes. Bit of gossip at the Club, was it? Or an advertisement in the *Times* personal column?'

There was a welcome little patter of laughter in Court. The Judge didn't join in. It took some time for Mr X to answer.

'I heard about it from a friend.'

'An *old* friend? I don't mean in years, but a friend of long standing?'

'Yes.'

'I really can't imagine what the relevance of these questions is.' Ballard rose to protest, and the Judge came to his assistance.

'Mr Rumpole. What *has* this got to do with it?' he asked wearily.

'My Lord.' I decided to go into a bit of an aria. 'I'm fighting this case in the dark, with my hands tied behind my back, against a prosecution witness who has chosen to shelter behind anonymity. I must be allowed to cross-examine him as I think fit. After all, it would greatly add to the costs of this case if it had to be reconsidered ... elsewhere.'

His Honour Judge Bullingham was no fool. He got the clear reference to the Court of Appeal, where his interventions might not look so attractive on the transcript of evidence as they sounded in the flesh. He thought briefly and then came out, in judicial tones, with 'I think we may allow Mr Rumpole to pursue his line, Mr Ballard.' Then he turned to me and said, 'It remains to be seen, of course, Mr Rumpole, if these questions will do your clients any good, in the eyes of the jury.'

So, having registered a sort of minor and equivocal success, I turned back to the witness. 'Was it a friend you had known from your schooldays, by any chance?' For that I got a reluctant agreement.

'You had kept up with him?' I went on.

'No. We met again after an interval of a good many years.'

'Where did you meet?'

'In a public house.'

'In the Victoria area?' I took a gamble and asked.

'Somewhere near there. Yes.'

'Meet a nice type of girl in that public house, do you?'

'Mr Rumpole!' The Bull was growing restive again and had to be dealt with.

'My Lord. I withdraw the question. What did your friend tell you?' I asked the witness.

'He told me that he'd been ill. And that he'd had a bit of bad luck in business. He said he had a house near Victoria Station and his wife and he were starting a business there.'

'A business ... in agreeable ladies?'

We were then treated to a long pause before Mr X said, 'Yes.'

So, with a good deal of the preparatory work done, I decided to be daring and ask a question to which I didn't know the answer – always a considerable risk in cross-examination.

'Did you offer to put a little much-needed capital into this business? I mean, the Court has kept your name a secret because you are so respectable, Mr X. Were you in fact an investor in a bawdy house?'

The jury looked so interested in the answer that Ballard rose to make an objection. 'My Lord,' he said. 'The witness should be warned.'

'I *do* know my job, Mr Ballard.' For the first time, Bullingham sounded a little testy with the prosecution. Then he turned to the witness and said, 'I should warn you that you are not bound to answer any question that might incriminate you. Now, do you wish to answer Mr Rumpole's question or would you prefer not to?'

There was a long pause during which perhaps Mr X's whole life flashed before his eyes, in slow motion. At long last he said, in the nicest possible way, 'I would prefer not to, my Lord.'

I looked hard at the jury, raised an eyebrow or two, and repeated, 'You would prefer not to?' As no answer came from the witness-box I tried another question. 'Can you answer this. How long ago was the meeting in the public house in Victoria?'

'About five years ago.' Mr X appeared to be back in answering mood.

'And was the public house the Barnardine Arms?'

'Yes.'

'And was the old school friend in question by any chance Mr Napier Lee, the male defendant in this case?' He had only to say, 'No,' politely, and I would have had to sit down with egg all over my silly face. However, my luck stayed in, and Mr X gave us a very quiet, 'Yes.'

'Speak up, Mr X,' I said.

'Yes, my Lord, it was. Mr Napier Lee.'

For some obscure reason, best known to Himself, God seemed to be on my side that day.

'So you met Mr Lee some five years ago,' I continued the cross-examination. 'And his wife, Mrs Lorraine Lee?'

'I met her shortly afterwards.'

'When you started to patronize their business?'

'Yes.'

'So ever since he was an inky school boy in the fourth form at Lawnhurst, Mr Napier Lee has known exactly who you were.'

'We met in Lower Five actually.'

'In Lower Five. Oh yes. I stand corrected. So he has had at least five years to blackmail you, if he wanted to.'

Mr X gave a puzzled look at the jury, but they looked as if they saw the point perfectly well. Then he answered, 'Yes.'

'And neither he nor his wife made any suggestion of this sort until six months ago?'

'That is right,' Mr X admitted.

'When you were asked to pay a couple of trivial little gas and electricity bills.' I opened my brief then, not a thing I find I have to do too often, and fished out copies of the documents in question. 'Bills for £45 and £37.53.' Mr X agreed. He seemed to have something of a head for figures.

'And you paid these bills for the Lees by cheque?'

'Yes.'

'Why on earth . . . ?' My eyebrows went up again, and I turned to the jury.

'Because, as I have told you, Mr Rumpole, they threatened to tell my employers about my visits to their . . . house unless I did so.'

'I don't mean *that*.' I showed a little well-calculated impatience. 'I mean why pay by *cheque*?'

'I . . . I don't know exactly . . .' Mr X faltered. The point seemed not to have occurred to him.

'Did you ever pay by cheque when you visited this house on any other occasion?'

'No.'

'Always in cash?'

'Of course.'

'Yes. Of course,' I agreed. 'Because you didn't want to leave a record of your name in connection with the Lees' "business".' I paused as meaningfully as I could, and then asked, 'But on the occasion of this alleged blackmail you *did* want to leave a record?'

'I told you . . . I don't know why I paid them by cheque.' Mr X was looking to Ballard for help. None was immediately forthcoming.

'Was it because you wanted evidence on which to base this unfounded allegation of blackmail against my clients?' I suggested.

'No!' Mr X protested vehemently, and then added, weakly, 'I suppose I just didn't think about it.'

'Thank you, Mr X!' I gave the jury a last meaningful look and then sat down with the feeling of a job well done. His Lordship leant forward and, in a quiet and reassuring tone of voice, did his best to repair the damage.

'Mr X. I suppose you paid the ... "girls" at this establishment in cash?' Bullingham's smile said, 'We're all men of the world here, now aren't we?'

'Yes, my Lord. I did,' Mr X answered, encouraged.

'Did it strike you as a different matter when you were paying the Gas Board and the Electricity Board?'

'Yes, my Lord.' The witness took the hint gratefully.

'You saw no particular harm in paying those two great authorities by cheque?' Bullingham suggested gently.

'No harm at all, my Lord.' Mr X was clearly feeling better.

'Very well, we'll rise now.' The Judge smiled at the jury, conscious of a job pretty well done. 'Shall we say, 10.30 tomorrow morning?'

That night Hilda and I were sitting at leisure in the living room of our 'mansion' flat at 25B Froxbury Court in the Gloucester Road. She Who Must Be Obeyed was knitting some garment. I have no idea what it was, except that it was long and pink and was no doubt destined for her old school friend Dodo Mackintosh, and I was smoking a small cigar, watching the tide go down in a glass of Pommeroy's very ordinary, when She asked me, not with the air of anyone who intended to listen too closely to the answer, 'Went the day well?' or words to that effect.

'You could describe it as a nightmare,' I confided in her, blowing out smoke.

'You mean it's not going well?'

'Well.' I gave one of my mirthless laughs. 'We've got a prosecutor who wears a hair shirt and seems to have done his pupillage with the Inquisition. The Mad Bull is madder than ever. The chief witness has this in common with the late Lohengrin – no one must ever ask him his name. And my clients think it's in the best public school tradition to get convicted of blackmail. There we are, all together at the Old Bailey,

Rolled round in earth's diurnal course,
With rocks, and stones, and trees ...

It's making my head ache.'

My glass seemed to have drained itself during this monologue. I rose to refresh it from the bottle.

'I mean in Chambers. The *Headship*, Rumpole! Is it going to be ours?' Hilda asked with some impatience.

'You have great legal ambitions, Hilda. I'm sorry, I can't bring you back the Lord Chief Justice's chain of office with a bottle of Pommeroy's Château Plonkenheim.' I raised my glass to her, in recognition of her fighting spirit, and drank.

'I'm not looking for Lord Chancellor, Rumpole,' Hilda told me patiently. 'Just Head of Daddy's old Chambers. Of course, I was brought up in the law.' There was a pause. She looked at me with some suspicion, her knitting needles clicked, and then she asked, 'There's no one more senior than you, is there? No one else they might appoint?'

'No one who has been longer in the bottle as an Old Bailey hack, no,' I reassured her.

'And no silks?' For a moment, Hilda stopped knitting, as though her fingers were frozen in suspense. I gave her encouraging news. 'Not as yet. Erskine-Brown's application doesn't come up till after the meeting.'

'Then it's in the bag, isn't it?' Hilda breathed a sigh of relief, and her knitting needles clicked again.

'Fear not, Hilda. So far as I can see, your election is assured.' I poured another glass to drink to her success. I must say, She Who Must Be Obeyed smiled with some satisfaction.

'Dodo's agreed to help me out at the party,' she told me. 'She does all sorts of dips.'

'Damned versatile, old Dodo,' I agreed, and then with a mind to see what, if anything, was going on in the world outside Froxbury Court, I switched on the small and misty television set we hire from Mr Mehta who keeps a shop full of electrical appliances on our corner of the Gloucester Road. Thanks to the wonders of science, I was immediately rewarded by the sight of Fiona Allways's friend Isobel Vincent, who was clutching a microphone, wearing her boiler suit, standing under the dome of the Old Bailey, and giving a waiting world much too much news of the events that had occurred in Court during that eventful day.

'The Top People's Disorderly House Case,' said Izzy. 'Home Counties News can reveal the fact that Mr X is in fact the very senior civil servant at the Foreign Office, Sir Cuthbert Pericles. He is just one of the men, highly placed in public life, who are believed to have visited the house in Barnardine Square. This is Isobel Vincent, Home Counties News, at the Old Bailey.'

I switched off the set, Isobel Vincent shrank to a small point of light and vanished, unhappily not off the face of the earth. I looked at Hilda, appalled. 'My God,' I said. 'What a disaster!'

'Whatever is it, Rumpole?' Hilda sighed. Again she was not over-interested.

'You were nearest the window, Hilda. Didn't you hear a loud noise,' I asked her, 'coming from Kensington?'

'What sort of noise?'

'His Honour Judge Bullingham,' I suggested, 'blowing up?'

The next day, his Honour was still in one piece, although sitting on the Bench breathing heavily and a darker purple than ever. I began to fear that we were about to witness one of the few recorded cases of spontaneous combustion. He was delivering a pretty decided judgement on Miss Isobel Vincent, who stood, still defiantly boiler-suited, in the well of the Court in front of him, about as apologetic as St Joan when called on to answer a nasty heresy charge before the Inquisition.

'In almost half a century's experience at the Bar and on the Bench, I have never known such a flagrant, wicked and inexcusable Contempt of Court!' Bullingham boomed. I must say I wasn't giving him my full attention. I was turning to the door hoping that at any minute Mr Staines, my instructing solicitor, might come into Court with the news I was hoping and praying for.

Meanwhile Isobel was still looking noble, Fiona Allways was trying to look at no one in particular, and the Judge was still carrying on. 'I have heard that your employers, Home Counties Television, had no idea that you were disobeying a Court Order.

That will be investigated. If anyone who has been in this Court, anyone at all, had anything to do with this matter ...' At this point his Lordship could be seen glaring at Horace Rumpole. 'They will be sought out and punished.'

And then the miracle happened. Old Stainey filtered back into Court and whispered the news that the man I was waiting for was without, and he wanted to know if I would call him first.

'Of course I'll call him first,' I whispered back. 'It shouldn't be long now. The Bull's running out of steam.'

'I will send the papers to the proper quarter in order that it may be decided what action shall be taken against this most foolish and wicked young woman ...' The Judge dismissed Isobel then, and she left the Court with her head held high and a look at Fiona which caused that young lady to blush slightly. Shortly thereafter the show was on the road again, and I was on my hind legs opening our defence to the jury.

'Members of the jury. It is my duty to outline to you the evidence the defence is going to call. I'm going to call a witness ...' – well, I hoped to God I was going to call a witness – 'who may be able to penetrate the pall of secrecy which has fallen over this case. Someone, perhaps, may have the bad manners and rotten taste to tell us the truth about the evidence. Someone may be able to cast aside the "Old Boy Net" and let the secret out. Ladies and gentlemen of the jury, I will now call ...' I paused long enough to stoop and whisper to old Staines, who was sitting in front of me, 'Whom the hell will I now call, Stainey?'

'Mr Stephen Lucas,' Mr Staines whispered back.

'I will now call Mr Simon ...' I started.

'Stephen!' Another whisper from Stainey.

'Mr Stephen Lucas.' I was confident at last.

'Very well, Mr Rumpole.' The Judge picked up his pencil with an air of resignation, and prepared to make a few jottings. And then a man came into Court, entered the witness-box as though he had a day full of far better things to do, and promised to tell us the truth, the whole truth and nothing but the truth. He was a smaller, fatter, more jovial type of person than Mr X, but when he spoke it was with the impatient confidence of someone who had spent many years in a trusted position in the corridors of power. He gave his name as Stephen Lucas.

'Are you a member of the Foreign Office Legal Department?' I asked him.

'Yes, I am.'

'And do you know the witness we have called "Mr X"? I have asked him to remain in Court so that you may identify him.'

The witness looked down at the man who was sitting in front of Ballard with as much detachment as if Mr X were something that had just arrived in his 'In tray'.

'Yes, I do,' he said.

'Are you a friend of his?'

'We meet, of course, in the Foreign Office,' Lucas said cautiously. 'I would say I've known him fairly well, and over a long period.'

'Of course. Do you remember having lunch with him at his Club about a year ago? Was that at his invitation?'

'Yes, it was.'

'What did he discuss, do you remember?'

'Well, we discussed a number of things, the work of my department and so on, and then he asked me some questions about the recent Contempt of Court Act. He seemed to want my opinion about it, as a lawyer. It's not really my subject, but I told him what I knew.'

'What aspect of the Act was our "Mr X" particularly interested in?'

'In the Court's power to order that the name of a witness in a blackmail case should be kept secret, perhaps for ever.' The witness paused. The jury were looking at him with interest and the Bull, I was pleased to see, was writing busily. Then Lucas went on with his story. 'I remember his saying that if you didn't want your name to come out in a particular scandal or something of that sort, all you would have to do would be to accuse someone of blackmail.'

'Mr Lucas, what made you remember this conversation?' I asked, to pre-empt a bit of Ballard's cross-examination.

'It was last night, when I heard Mr X's name on the television news. I thought it might have some bearing on this case.'

The Judge frowned, and I went on quickly to prevent any un-friendly comment from the Bench. 'Tell us, Mr Lucas. You say you've known Mr X for a long time. You weren't at school together, by any chance?'

'No. I wasn't at Lawnhurst,' Lucas admitted.

'Or at any public school?'

'No.'

Thank God, I thought, or we'd never have got a word out of him. I sat down and Ballard was up with his long black silk gown flapping with indignation.

'So, Mr Lucas, you would never have come here to give evidence if there hadn't been a flagrant Contempt of Court and Mr X's name had not appeared on the television news.'

'That's right.' Lucas seemed to be not in the least worried by the course of events.

'It's most unfortunate, I agree, Mr Ballard.' The Judge looked sadly at the prosecutor. 'But I don't see what I can do about it. I can't exclude this evidence.'

'Oh no, my Lord. But it *is* most unfortunate.' Ballard seemed to be regretting some huge historical disaster, like the Decline and Fall of the Roman Empire.

'Of course it is.' The Judge cast a meaningful glance at the Rumpole faction. 'But the harm's been done.' Whether it was harm or good, of course, depended on which side you were sitting.

Well, in due course the Lees gave evidence and denied the blackmail in a pained sort of way, and answered Ballard's passion-ate denunciations with excessively polite murmurs of dissent, as though they were regretfully declining the offer of more bread and butter. Later in the proceedings, my learned opponent gave the jury another two-hour sermon, during the course of which I was delighted to see them getting somewhat restive. And then, almost before I knew it, final speech time was round again.

'Mr X couldn't give up his visits to the friendly house in Barnardine Square, members of the jury,' I told them. 'But he was always terrified that the place might be raided and his name would come out in the ensuing scandal. So he hit on this some-what over-ingenious device: a couple of cheques, a sure proof that he had paid money to the Lees, could lay the basis for a

314   RUMPOLE AND THE GOLDEN THREAD

trumped-up blackmail charge that would keep his name a secret for ever! It was an elaborate plan, complicated, expensive and entirely futile. Just the sort of plan, you may think, that would occur to someone high in the government of our country. Why was it futile? Because Mr X need have had no fear. The Lees would never have betrayed his pathetic little secrets. You see, it was for them, as it never was for him, a question of morality. They had their code.'

At the end of it all the Judge summed up with surprising moderation. The jury stayed out for three hours, and mugs of tea were being served in the cells when we got down to discuss the result with Mr and Mrs Napier Lee.

'A great win on the blackmail, Mr Rumpole.' Mr Staines, at least, could always be relied on to say the right thing.

'Wasn't it, Stainey! Six months for the disorderly house, I'm afraid,' I said regretfully.

'I just hope "Custard" doesn't think we sneaked on him.' Mr Lee looked extremely worried.

'He knows we'd never do a thing like that!' Mrs Lorraine Lee was consoling him.

'Who the hell's "Custard"?' I felt I was losing my grip.

'Pericles. His name's Cuthbert, so we called him "Custard" at school.'

'I suppose that follows,' I admitted.

'*We* know we didn't break the code, Nappy. We've got that to comfort us,' Lorraine told her husband. And I thought that I'd add my own two pennyworth of consolation for them both.

'They'll probably send you to an open Nick,' I said. 'You might meet some of the chaps from school.'

'I never went to Lawnhurst,' Mrs Lee said regretfully.

'By Jove, that's a point.' Napier seemed suddenly depressed.

'Daddy had set his heart on Roedean for me. But it was a question of the readies,' Mrs Lee explained.

But Napier seemed to realize quite suddenly that he was about to be separated from his wife. 'It's boys only where I'm going, I suppose?' he said.

'I'm afraid so. No co-education.' I had to break it to him.

'Sorry, old girl. We'll be separated.' He held out his hand to his wife, and she took it.

'Not for long, Nappy,' she said. 'And we've had a marvellous offer for the freehold.'

'Not to mention the good will!'

'Then you've just got to bear it for six months,' I said as I moved to the door, the rest of the legal team following behind me.

'When a chap's been to Lawnhurst, Mr Rumpole,' Napier said, 'he can't really feel afraid of prison.'

When we left them, they were still holding hands.

Walking back to Chambers with Miss Fiona Allways, I could feel her deep embarrassment and fear of the subject which I knew perfectly well I would have to mention. There was a fine rain falling over Fleet Street then. The buses were roaring beside us, no one could hear what I had to say and, I hoped to goodness, no one had guessed Miss Allways's secret; otherwise hers might have been one of the shortest careers in the history of the legal profession.

'You'd better learn something quickly, Fiona,' I told her. 'If you want to be a barrister, keep the rules!'

'I don't know what you mean . . .' she started unconvincingly, and then blushed beneath her headscarf.

'Don't you?' I looked at her. 'Don't worry. I don't imagine Mzz Isobel Vincent is going to reveal her sources. She's all out for glorious martyrdom, and I bet she doesn't want to share her publicity with anyone.' We were turning into the Temple entrance, and I stopped, faced her, and said with all the power I could command, 'But you have to keep the rules! You can swear at them, argue your way round them, do your damnedest to change them, but if you break the rules yourself, how the hell are you going to help the other idiots out of trouble?'

Miss Allways looked at me for a long time, and I hoped to God I wasn't going to see her in tears ever again. 'I'll never get a place in Chambers now,' she said.

'I don't know. Perhaps you will. Perhaps you won't,' I said briskly and started to walk into our place of work. 'You can help me out on another little cause or matter.'

'Can I?' Miss Allways trotted behind me eagerly. I told her what I had in mind. 'Look up the cases on Contempt of Court, why don't you?' I suggested. 'We may be having to cope with the defence of Mzz Vincent, and we've got to keep the good Mzz out of chokey. Martyrs make me exceedingly nervous.'

When I got into the clerk's room, Henry told me that a Chambers meeting was about to take place – a forum, I instantly realized, for preliminary discussions on the Headship, at which the way would be smoothed for the Rumpole take-over at Number 3 Equity Court. So, in the shortest possible time, the ambitions of She Who Must Be Obeyed might be fulfilled. Before I went upstairs, Henry handed me a letter which, he said, had been delivered by hand as a matter of urgency. I stuffed it into my pocket and went upstairs to what had been Guthrie Featherstone's room, and would now, I thought, be my room in perpetuity.

As I got to the head of the stairs, I heard the buzz of voices and, for a moment, I was puzzled that the meeting should have started without my good self as the natural Chairperson and Master of Ceremonies. Then I supposed that they were merely chattering about the splendours and miseries of their days in various Courts. I advanced a couple of steps, threw open the door, entered the room, and then, it is no exaggeration to say, I was frozen in horror and dismay.

Of all the nasty moments in Macbeth's life, and they certainly came to him thick and fast after his encounter with the witches, I have always thought that by far the worst must have come when he went to take his old place at the dinner party and found that the ghost of Banquo had got there before him, and was glowering at the poor old Thane in a blood-bolter'd and accusing sort of way. So it was for me on the occasion of that Chambers meeting, only the person in the chair behind Guthrie's old desk, the man in the seat of honour directing the proceedings, was not Banquo but Sam Ballard, One of Her Majesty's Counsel and founder member of the Lawyers As Churchgoers Society.

'Come along, Rumpole, you're late.' This spectre spoke. 'And would you mind shutting the door.'

'Bollard.' I looked around the room which contained Claude
Erskine-Brown, Hoskins, Uncle Tom (our oldest inhabitant) and
five or six other assorted barristers. Mrs Phillida Erskine-Brown,
our Portia, was apparently away doing a long firm fraud in York.

'What's this?' I asked Ballard. 'A prayer meeting or something?
What on earth are you doing here?'

'Hasn't anyone told you?' The man, Ballard, seemed genuinely
puzzled. 'Featherstone, J., said he'd written you a note as soon
as he knew you were back from Africa.'

I pulled the letter Henry had given me from my pocket, and saw
it was embossed with the insignia of the Royal Courts of Justice.
I have kept the Featherstone letter in my Black Museum to this
day, together with other criminally used instruments of murder
and mayhem, so I can now give it to you verbatim. All you will
miss is Guthrie's haphazard and occasionally illegible handwriting.

'Dear old Horace, old boy,' the letter ran. 'Just a brief note
to introduce Sam Ballard, who was, in fact, my fag master at
Marlborough, and is now a silk with an excellent practice in the
Midlands.' As I read this I felt a faint hope: perhaps the wretched
Bollard would stay in the Midlands. 'But,' the letter went on,
'Sam came to us looking for a London home. All the other fellows
agreed and, as you were off in the jungle, we knew you'd have
no objection. Someone'll have to take over as Head of Chambers
as I'm detained "During Her Majesty's Pleasure". And Sam
Ballard is clearly a likely candidate. But I don't want to interfere,
at this distance, with the democratic process of my old set.
Marigold joins me in sending all our best wishes to you and Hilda.
May you soldier on for many years yet, old fellow. Guthrie
Featherstone.'

'Glad you could make it to the meeting, Rumpole.' Hoskins
was smiling at me.

'Are you?' I took a seat by the door.

'We thought Roger Bullingham might have put you in chokey,
Horace, on a little matter of Contempt of Court!' Claude was
having his little joke.

'Oh, Erskine-Brown, you're so amusing!'

'Well. Now we're all assembled ...' The Bollard throat was
being cleared in an ecclesiastical manner.

'Dearly beloved brethren,' I muttered.

'I suppose we should decide who is going to approach the Inn, as the new Head of this Chambers,' Ballard ploughed on regardless. 'Now I don't suppose it's a matter we should want to discuss in a public meeting.'

'What do you suggest we do, Bollard?' I asked. 'Go into a session of silent prayer, and then send puffs of smoke up from the clerk's room? Let's have it out, for God's sake.'

'Speaking for myself, I have been in these Chambers for a good many years,' Erskine-Brown weighed in.

'Not half as long as Rumpole!' Uncle Tom made the first pro-me remark. I thanked him for it silently.

'Rumpole's been here since the year dot, as far as I can remember,' Uncle Tom added, less helpfully.

'And although I've not yet been able to put on the knee breeches and silk gown, as you have, Ballard,' Erskine-Brown gave a modest grin, 'my application is in to the Lord Chancellor's office and I can't imagine there'll be any difficulty.'

'Don't count your chickens, old darling,' I warned him.

'Why? Have you heard anything?' I was relieved to see a look of anxiety on the Erskine-Brown face.

'There's many a slip,' I improvised, 'between the knee breeches and the hip.' This managed to get a lone chuckle from Uncle Tom.

'Of course, I'm a complete newcomer here,' Ballard started off again, very seriously.

'Yes, you are,' I agreed. 'They just dropped you in with today's *Times*.'

'But whoever heads these Chambers will, I hope, be able to take the position seriously.' Ballard gave me an aloof sort of look.

'Here endeth the first lesson,' I said.

'It's also terribly important that whoever heads us should be a barrister entirely *sans reproche*,' Claude suggested.

'Oh, *absolument*, Erskine-Brown,' I said.

'Our Chambers is riding high at the moment. One of our number has just been made up to the High Court Bench,' Claude went on.

'Oh, I agree.' Hoskins always agreed. 'We should remember

that this election is caused because Guthrie Featherstone has been made a judge.'

'The age of miracles is not dead.' I did a bit of agreeing myself.

'We must be careful to keep our high reputation,' Erskine-Brown said. 'It would be most unfortunate if we had a Head who could possibly be accused of sharp practice.' He gave a casual glance in my direction, and I asked him, 'What do you mean exactly, Erskine-Brown?'

'I don't think there should be any speculation arising out of the recent case at the Old Bailey,' Ballard was delighted to say. 'It's true a question of Contempt of Court *did* arise, but that issue still has to be decided. There has been no finding as to how the information was "leaked". Of course,' he also gave me a look, 'one hopes that the "leak" didn't come from any member of the legal profession.'

'Does one really hope that?' I asked, but Ballard ignored the question.

'So I would ask you all to put the regrettable matter of a flagrant Contempt out of your minds for the purposes of this decision. Wouldn't you agree that that is the fair approach?'

'Oh, Bollard,' I thought. 'How very clever!'

'Well now. Rumpole, as an old member of this set . . .'

'Of course he's old. Rumpole can't help being old!' Uncle Tom explained to the meeting.

'Have you anything to say?' Ballard asked.

'Why sentence of death should not be passed against me?' I said, and then addressed them all. 'Only this. Don't forget the claims of someone who has been associated with these Chambers for far, far longer than any of you, who grew up in these fly-blown rooms and on this dusty staircase, who doesn't aspire to silk, or judicial office, or even to appearing before the Uxbridge Magistrates, one whose whole ambition is centred on that meaningless title, "Head of Chambers"!'

'What's Rumpole talking about?' Uncle Tom asked no one in particular.

'He means himself,' said Claude.

'No, Erskine-Brown,' I assured him. 'I don't mean me.'

I was thinking, of course, of She Who Must Be Obeyed, whose

ambition to be married to the Head of her father's old Chambers was, thinking again of the old Scottish Tragedy, much like Lady Macbeth's bizarre longing to see her husband tricked out in Duncan's crown. When I got home to our mansion flat, She was ambling round a hot stove, and once again She asked me how it went.

'Half and half,' I told her.

'What?'

'The Lees got off the blackmail. Six months apiece on the disorderly house.'

'I don't mean in Court! I mean in *Chambers*.'

'Well, it's in Court that things happen, Hilda. People don't get sent to prison in Chambers. Well, not yet, anyway.'

'Oh, don't be so tiresome, Rumpole. I mean in the Chambers meeting! Has it been decided yet?'

It was time to attack an evening bottle of the ordinary claret with a corkscrew, and I did so without delay. Someone had to celebrate something.

'Well. Not finally,' I told her.

'But in principle, Rumpole. I mean, it's been decided in principle?'

'Yes. Yes, I think so.'

'The Chambers party's on the 29th. That's when they'll announce the decision, isn't it?'

'I shouldn't bother to go to that, Hilda.' I poured her a generous slurp. 'They're pretty grim occasions.'

'This won't be grim!' She assured me. 'It'll be a triumph, Rumpole. And nothing on earth is going to keep me away!'

Until the day of the Chambers party dawned, I avoided discussing the subject further with Hilda, and She remained determined to join in what she felt sure would be the jollifications. Not long before the party, our assorted barristers voted on the question of leadership, but for one reason or another I didn't bring home to Hilda the result of their decision. On the day in question, several large cardboard boxes, filled, so it seemed, with 'cocktail snacks', were brought by Hilda's friend, Dodo Mackintosh, round to the mansion flat, and I had to ferry them down to Chambers by taxi.

So, at the end of the day, we all assembled in the former Featherstone room, where Henry and Dianne had set up a bar on the desk, and had Dodo's delicacies set out on plates ready for handing round. Hilda was there, resplendent in what seemed to be a new rig-out, and there were a few other wives and girl-friends, although Mrs Phillida Erskine-Brown, whose practice seemed to be growing to gigantic proportions, was now away doing an arson in Swansea.

I hovered around, keeping within pouring distance of the bar, and I heard my wife in close conversation with the blasted Ballard. She seemed to be giving him a guided tour of Dodo's cookery, which he was consuming steadily without interrupting her flow of words.

'These are cheese-and-oniony, and those are the little sausage arrangements, if that's what you'd prefer,' I heard Hilda telling him. 'Of course, I'll be looking after these parties now. Marigold Featherstone was a sweet person, wasn't she? But I don't think she took a great interest in the canapés.' The same could not be said of Ballard. He took another couple of items from a plate, and Hilda went on talking. 'That's a little prawny sort of vol-au-vent arrangement. Frightfully light, isn't it? I do want these evenings to be a success for Rumpole!'

There was a scatter of applause then for Henry, who requested silence by bumping a glass on the desk, and Uncle Tom was called on to say a few moderately ill-chosen words.

'It falls to me,' he started, 'as the oldest member of Chambers, in the matter of years, to do honours here tonight.'

'Uncle Tom!' Hilda called out to him in high excitement. He stopped and gave her a look of some surprise. 'Mrs Rumpole?'

'Carry on then, Uncle Tom,' Hilda gave her permission grace-fully.

'Thank you. I remember Number 3 Equity Court years ago, when old C. H. Wystan was Head of Chambers.'

'Uncle Tom remembers Daddy!' Hilda announced to the world in general.

'Exactly. And Horace Rumpole and I used to hang about waiting for work. I used to practise approach shots with an old mashie niblick! It seemed my one legal ambition was to get my balls into the waste-paper basket in the clerk's room.'

This last sentence caused Miss Fiona Allways to choke on an asparagus roll, and have to be slapped on the back by Henry. Uncle Tom went on with his past history of Equity Court.

'Then the present Mr Justice Featherstone came to head us. Of course, he was then plain Guthrie Featherstone, Q.C., M.P. And now another chapter opens in our history . . .'

'Hear, hear!' Hilda applauded loudly.

'The man I have to introduce as our new Head, agreed on by a comfortable majority, is well known, not only in legal circles but in the Church . . .' Uncle Tom said, and in this puzzled She Who Must Be Obeyed. She looked at me, startled, and murmured, 'Rumpole religious?'

'He is a man deeply concerned with problems of morality,' Uncle Tom continued, warming to his work. 'I happened to be taking dinner with old Tuppy Timpson, ex-Canon of Southwark Cathedral, and he said, "Little bird told me about your new Head of Chambers. You've got a sound man there. And one who walketh in the ways of righteousness, even through the Valley of the Central Criminal Court."'

'The ways of righteousness!' Hilda was laughing. 'You ought to see him at breakfast, particularly when he's in a nasty temper!'

'Hilda!' I whispered to her, begging her to stop.

'Not much of the ways of righteousness then, Uncle Tom,' She said, but the oldest inhabitant was into his peroration.

'So let us raise a glass, ladies and gentlemen, to our new Head of Chambers. I give you our dear old Chambers, Number 3 Equity Court, coupled with the name . . .'

'Rumpole!' Hilda said loudly, but Uncle Tom was louder when he announced, 'The name of Sam Ballard, One of Her Majesty's Counsel. Long may he reign over us!'

They were all drinking to the Bollard health and all I could say was, 'Amen.' Then I turned to Hilda, and there were tears in her eyes.

'I'm sorry old girl.' I felt I should comfort her.

'You never told me!'

'I funked it.' It was perfectly true.

'Passed over again!' She dabbed her eyes with her handker-chief, sniffed and looked extremely bleak.

'Cheer up,' I said. 'It's not the end of the world. You know you're still a great advocate. Terrific in an argument. Who cares about being Head of Chambers?'

Henry had found a bottle of Pommeroy's special offer cham-pagne to toast our new leader, and I got my fingers round it. Hilda looked at me coldly, and then pronounced judgement.

'You're a failure, Rumpole!' she said.

'Then take a slurp of champagne, why don't you?' I filled our glasses. 'Let's drink to failure!'

But Hilda was looking across to where Ballard stood masticat-ing.

'He's eating *all* Dodo's little cheesy bits. The *cheek* of it!' she said. She sounded furious and I knew, with considerable relief, that She Who Must Be Obeyed was herself again.

Rumpole and the Female of the Species

It may be said by those who read these memoirs, particularly by those of the female persuasion, that Rumpole is in some ways unsympathetic to the aspirations of women. This may be because, in the privacy of my own thoughts and when writing late at night in the solitary confines of my kitchen, I refer to my wife, Hilda Rumpole, as 'She Who Must Be Obeyed'. It is true that I have given her this title, but Hilda's character, her air of easy command which might, if she had been born in other circumstances, have brought empires under her sway, and her undisputed government of our daily life at Froxbury Court, entitles her to no less an acclamation. Those who feel that I am not firmly on the female side in the Battle of the Sexes may care to consider my long struggle to get Miss Fiona Allways accepted as a member of our Chambers at Equity Court, and those who might think that I only engaged myself in this struggle to annoy the egregious Bollard and irritate Claude Erskine-Brown are guilty of a quite unworthy cynicism.

The dispute over the entry of Miss Allways into our close-knit group of learned friends arose during the time that our Chambers had a brief in the Pond Hill bank job. We were charged with the defence of Tony Timson.

I have written repeatedly elsewhere of the Timsons, the large family of South London villains who, many years ago, appointed me their Attorney-General and whose unending efforts have brought a considerable amount of work to Equity Court. Tony Timson belonged to the younger generation of the clan. He occupied a pleasant, semi-detached house on a South London estate with his wife, April, and their child, Vincent. His house was lavishly furnished with a large variety of video-recording machines, television sets, hi-fi equipment, spindriers, eye-line grills, ultraviolet-ray cookers, deep freezes and suchlike aids to gracious living. Many of these articles were said to be the fruit of Tony Timson's tireless night work.

When Inspector Broome called at the Timson house shortly after the Pond Hill bank job, he found the young master alone and playing 'Home Sweet Home' on a newly acquired electric organ. He also found five thousand pounds in crisp, new, neatly packaged twenty-pound notes in the gleaming Super Snow White Extra Deluxe model washing machine. Tony Timson was ripped from the bosom of his wife April and young Vincent, and placed within the confines of Brixton Prison, and I wondered if I should ultimately get the brief.

The appointment of Rumpole for the defence should, of course, have been a foregone conclusion. But the Timson Solicitor-General was Mr Bernard, and between that gentleman and Rumpole there was a bit of a cold wind blowing, owing to a tiff which had taken place one day at the Uxbridge Magistrates Court. I had arrived at this particular Palais de Justice a little late one day, owing to a tailback on the Piccadilly Line, only to discover that the gutless Bernard had allowed our client of the day to plead guilty to a charge of handling. He had thrown in the towel!

I hadn't actually been rude to Mr Bernard. I had merely improved his education by quoting Shakespeare's *Richard II*. 'O, villain, viper, damned without redemption!' I said to my instructing solicitor, 'Would you make peace? Terrible hell make war upon your spotted soul for this.' Mr Bernard, it seemed, hadn't appreciated the quality of the lines and there was, as I say, an east wind blowing between us. So I wasn't greatly surprised when Henry gave me an account of what happened when Bernard came into our clerk's room and gave Henry the brief in R. *v.* Timson. Henry said that he supposed that would be for Mr Rumpole.

'You suppose wrong, young man,' Mr Bernard said firmly.

'Do I?' Henry raised his eyebrows.

'The brief is clearly marked for the attention of Mrs Phillida Erskine-Brown,' Bernard pointed out, and Henry saw that it was so. 'I can put up with a good deal, Henry, from members of the so-called senior branch of our great profession,' Mr Bernard told him, 'but I will not be called a villainous viper in the clear hearing of the Clerk to the Uxbridge Magistrates Court.'

At which point Mrs Phillida Erskine-Brown, now an extremely successful lady barrister, entered the clerk's room and Henry handed her the papers.

'A wonderfully prepared brief, I don't doubt, like all Mr Bernard's work.' Phillida smiled with great charm at the glowing solicitor, and then asked tactfully, 'How's your daughter, Mr Bernard? Polytechnic going well still, is it?' Mrs Erskine-Brown, since the days when she was plain Miss Phillida Trant, hadn't got where she was by legal ability alone; she was expert at public relations.

'Three A's,' Mr Bernard was delighted to say. 'Thank you for asking.'

'And *still* keeping up her figure skating, I bet. Chip off the old block, wouldn't you say so, Henry? See you in Brixton, Mr Bernard.'

She flashed another smile and went on her way, whereupon Bernard told Henry that he always thought that Mrs Erskine-Brown had a real feeling for the law.

I had decided to improve the facilities in our mansion flat at Froxbury Court by erecting a shelf on our living-room wall to accommodate such necessities as *The Oxford Book of English Verse* (the Quiller-Couch edition), Professor Andrew Ackerman on *The Importance of Bloodstains in the Detection of Crime*, Archbold's *Criminal Pleading and Practice* – a little out of date, and a spare bottle or two of Château Thames Embankment of a fairly recent year. I celebrated my entry into the construction industry by buying what I think is known as a 'kit' of Easy-Do Convenience Shelving and a few basic tools, and in no time at all, such was my natural feeling for woodwork, I had the shelf up and triumphantly bearing its load.

When I showed the results of my labours to Hilda, she didn't immediately congratulate me, but asked, unnecessarily I thought, if I had 'plugged' the wall in accordance with the instructions that came in the 'Easy-Do' box.

'I never read the instructions to counsel before doing a murder,

Hilda,' I told her firmly. 'Rely on the facts, and the instinct of the advocate. It's never let me down yet in Court.'

'Well, I do notice you haven't been in Court very much lately.' Hilda took an unfair advantage.

'A temporary lull in business. Nothing serious,' I assured her.

'It's because you're rude to solicitors.' Hilda, of course, knew best. I didn't want to argue the matter further, so I told her that my new shelf was firm as a rock, and added an air of distinction to our living room.

'Are you sure it's straight?' Hilda asked. 'I think it's definitely at an angle.'

'Oh really, Hilda! It's because *you're* at an angle,' I said, I'm afraid a little impatiently. 'One small gin and tonic at lunchtime and you do your well-known imitation of the Leaning Tower of Pisa.'

'Well, if that's how you talk to solicitors,' Hilda was starting to tidy away my carpenter's tools and sweep up the sawdust, 'no wonder I've got you at home all day.' As I have remarked earlier, there is a good deal to be said in favour of She Who Must Be Obeyed, but she's hardly a fair opponent in an argument.

I left our improved home and went down to Chambers and, there being not much else to engage my attention before a five o'clock Chambers meeting, I took a little time off to instruct Miss Fiona Allways, who had proudly acquired a case entirely of her own, in the art of making a final speech for the defence. Picture us then, alone in my room, the teacher Rumpole standing as though to address the Court and the pupil Allways sitting obediently to learn.

'Soon this case will be over, members of the jury.' I gave her my usual peroration. 'In a little while you will go back to your jobs and your families, and you will forget all about it. At most it is only a small part of your lives. But for my client it is the *whole* of his life! And it is that life I leave with confidence in your hands, certain that there can be only one verdict in this case – "Not Guilty"! ... Sink down exhausted then, Fiona,' I told her, 'mopping the brow.' I sat and plied a large red spotted handkerchief. 'Good end to a final speech, don't you think?'

'Will it work just as well for me?' she asked doubtfully. 'I mean, my man's only accused of nicking six frozen chicken pieces from Safeways.'

'Goes just as well on any occasion!' I assured her.

And then Claude Erskine-Brown put his head round the door and told me that Ballard was upstairs and just about to start the Chambers meeting. Erskine-Brown then retired and Fiona looked at me in a despondent sort of manner.

'Is this when they decide,' she sounded desperately anxious, 'if they're going to let me stay on here?'

'Don't worry. I shall tell them . . .' I promised her.

'What?'

'Well, let me think. Something like, "The female of the species is more deadly than the male." Look on the bright side, Miss Allways. Perk up, Fiona. I've cracked far tougher Courts than that lot up there!'

I went to the door without any real idea of how to handle the case of Allways and then, as so often happens, thank God, inspiration struck. I turned back towards her.

'Oh, by the way,' I said. 'Just one question. You know old Claude, who just popped his head in here?'

'Mr Erskine-Brown?'

'He doesn't tickle your fancy, does he, by any chance? You don't find him devastatingly attractive?'

'Of course not!' Fiona managed her first smile of the day. 'He's hardly Paul Newman, is he?'

'No, I suppose he isn't.' I must confess the news came to me as something of a relief. 'Well, that's all right then. I'll see what I can do.'

Ballard had made a few changes, none of them very much for the better, in Featherstone's old room. Guthrie's comfortable chairs had gone, and his silver cigarette-box, his picture of Marigold and the children, his comforting sherry decanter and bone china tea service and his perfectly harmless watercolours. Ballard had few luxuries except a number of etchings of English cathedrals in plain, light oak frames, the corners of which protruded in a Gothic and ecclesiastical manner, and an old tin of ginger biscuits which stood on his desk, and which he never offered about.

'Sorry. Am I late for Evensong?' I asked cheerfully as I sat beside Uncle Tom. Ballard, without a glance in my direction, continued with the business in hand.

'We have to consider an application by Fiona Allways for a permanent seat in Chambers,' he said. 'Mrs Erskine-Brown, you were her pupil master.'

'Mistress,' I corrected him, but nobody noticed.

'It's an extremely tough life at the Bar for a woman,' Phillida spoke from the depths of her experience. 'I'm by no means sure that Allways has got what it takes. Just as a for instance, she burst into tears when left alone at Thames Magistrates Court.'

'I know exactly how she felt,' I said. 'That was never my favourite tribunal.'

'Of course. Rumpole's done a case with her.' Ballard looked at me in a vaguely accusing manner.

'She took a note for me once. Something about her I liked,' I had to admit. And when Hoskins asked me what it was, I said that she felt strongly about winning cases.

'Who is this fellow Allways?' Uncle Tom asked with an expression of mild bewilderment.

'This fellow's a girl, Uncle Tom,' I told him.

'Oh, good heavens. Are we getting another one of them?' Our oldest inhabitant grumbled, and Mrs Erskine-Brown brought the discussion up to date by saying, 'I really don't think that the mere fact that this girl is a girl should guarantee her a place at 3 Equity Court.'

'Philly's perfectly right.' Claude came in as a dutiful husband should. 'We shouldn't take in a token woman, like a token black.'

'Are we taking in a black woman, then?' Uncle Tom merely asked for clarity.

'Why not?' I said. 'I could've brought one back from Africa.'

'This is obviously a problem that has to be taken seriously.' Ballard spoke disapprovingly from the chair.

'Well, I think we should go for a well-established man. Someone who's got to know a few solicitors, who can bring work to Chambers,' Mrs Erskine-Brown suggested politically.

'Steady on, Portia old fellow,' I cautioned her. 'Whatever happened to the quality of mercy?'

'I honestly don't see what mercy has to do with it.'

'Dear God,' I was moved to say. 'It seems but yesterday that Miss Phillida Trant, white in the wig and a newcomer to the ladies' robing room, was accusing Henry of hiding the key to the lavatory, as a sexist gesture! Can it be that now you've stormed the citadel you want to slam the door behind you?'

'Really, Rumpole!' Ballard called me to order. 'You're not addressing a jury now. I don't think anyone could possibly accuse this Chambers of having the slightest prejudice against female barristers.'

'Of course not. Provided they settle somewhere else, no doubt we find them quite delightful,' I agreed.

'I believe I've told you all that I've applied for a silk gown.' Erskine-Brown was never tired of telling us this.

'And I'm sure you'll look extremely pretty in it,' I assured him.

'And from what I hear, quite informally of course...'

'In the bag, is it, Erskine-Brown?'

'That's not for me to say, but Philly is, of course, right behind me in this.'

'Absolutely,' his wife assured him. The Erskine-Browns were in a conjugal mood that day. And he rambled on, saying, 'So with two Q.C.s at the top, it would be a great pity if these Chambers became weak in the tail.'

'What would be a pity?' Uncle Tom asked me.

'If our tail got weak, Uncle Tom.'

'Of course it would.' It was a puzzling meeting for the old boy. Erskine-Brown didn't further enlighten him by saying, 'I'm not interested in the sex side, of course.' I noticed then that his wife was looking into the middle distance in a detached sort of way. 'But I just don't feel that Allways is the right person to carry on the best traditions of these Chambers.'

'I agree,' Hoskins agreed.

'So Fiona Allways can swell the ranks of the unemployed?' I asked with some asperity.

'Oh, come on, Rumpole. She's got a rich daddy. She's not going to starve.'

'Only miss the one thing she's ever wanted to do,' I grumbled, but Ballard was collecting the final views of the meeting. He asked Uncle Tom for his considered opinion.

'I remember a Fiona. Used to work in the List Office.' Uncle Tom wasn't particularly helpful. 'She wasn't black, of course. No, I'm against it.'

'Well, I think I've got the sense of the meeting. I shall tell Miss Allways that she'll have to look elsewhere.'

It was time for quick thinking, and I thought extremely quickly. The best way to confuse lawyers is to tell them about a law which they think they've forgotten.

'Just a moment.' I hauled a diary out of my waistcoat pocket.

'What is it, Rumpole?' Ballard sounded impatient.

'This isn't the third Thursday of the Hilary Term!' I said severely.

'Of course it isn't.' Erskine-Brown had not got my point, but I had, just in time. 'Well!' I said positively. 'We always decide questions of Chambers entry on the third Thursday of the Hilary Term. It was the rule of my sainted father-in-law's day. Guthrie Featherstone, Q.C., observed it religiously. Of course, if the new broom wants to make any *radical* changes . . . ? I looked at Ballard in a strict sort of way, and I must say he flinched.

'Well. No,' he said. 'I suppose not. Are you sure it's the rule?' He looked at Erskine-Brown, who couldn't say he remembered it.

'You were in rompers, Erskine-Brown, when this thing was first decided,' I told him impatiently. 'Our old clerk, Albert, said it was impossible otherwise, from a book-keeping point of view. I do think we should keep to the rules, don't you, Bollard? I mean, we can't have anarchy at Equity Court!'

'That's in four weeks' time.' Ballard was consulting his diary now.

'Exactly!'

Ballard put away his diary and came to a decision. 'We'll deal with it then. It shouldn't take long, as we've reached a conclusion.'

'Oh no. A mere formality,' I agreed.

'What are you playing at, Rumpole?' Mrs Erskine-Brown was looking at me with some suspicion.

'Nothing much, Portia,' I assured her. 'Merely keeping up the best traditions of these Chambers.'

The Pond Hill branch of the United Metropolitan Bank was held up by a number of men in stocking masks, who carried holdalls from which emerged a sawn-off shotgun or two and a sledgehammer for shattering the glass in front of the cashier. When the robbery was complete the four masked men ran to the getaway car, a stolen Ford Cortina, which was waiting for them outside the bank, and it was this vehicle, the prosecution alleged, that Tony Timson had been driving. On the way to the car one of the men stumbled and fell. He was seized upon by an officer on traffic duty, and later found to be a Mr Gerry Molloy – a remarkable fact when you consider the deep hostility which has always existed between the Timson family and the clan Molloy. Indeed, these two tribes have hated each other for as long as I can remember and I have already chronicled an instance of their feud.*

It seems that all the other men engaged on the Pond Hill enterprise were Molloys. They got away, so it was hardly to be wondered at that Mr Gerald Molloy decided to become a grass and involve a Timson when he told his story to the police.

In the course of time Mrs Erskine-Brown and her instructing solicitor went to Brixton to see their client but, as I later heard from him and from Mr Bernard, Tony Timson seemed to have only one thing on his mind as he walked into the interview room and said, 'Where's Mr Rumpole?'

Phillida Erskine-Brown, in her jolliest, 'we're all lads together' voice, merely said, 'Care for a fag, Tony?' Tony didn't mind if he did, and when Phillida had lit it for him, Bernard broke the bad news.

'This is Mrs Erskine-Brown, Tony,' he said. 'She's going to be your brief.'

'I see they've charged you with taking part in the robbery, not merely the receiving. Of course, they've done that on Gerry Molloy's evidence.' Phillida started off in a businesslike way, but

* See 'Rumpole and the Younger Generation' in *Rumpole of the Bailey*, Penguin Books, 1978.

Tony Timson was looking at his solicitor in a kind of panic and paying no attention to her at all.

'Mr Rumpole's always the Timsons' brief,' he said. 'You know that, Mr Bernard. Mr Rumpole defended my dad, and my Uncle Cyril and saw me through my Juvenile Court and my Borstal training...'

'Mr Rumpole can't have done all that well for you if you got Borstal training,' Bernard said reasonably.

'Well...' Tony looked at Phillida for support. 'Win a few, lose a few, you know that, missus?'

'Any reason why Gerry Molloy should grass on you, Tony?' Phillida tried to return to the matter in hand.

'Look. It's good of you to come here but...'

At which Phillida, no doubt in an attempt to reassure the client, lapsed into robbers' argot. 'You ever had a meet with him where any sort of bank job was ever mentioned?' she asked. 'Molloy says in the deps that he was the sledge, two others had sawn-offs in their holdalls, and you were the driver. He says you're pretty good on wheels, Tony.'

'This is highly embarrassing, this is.' Tony looked suitably pained at Phillida's personal knowledge of crime.

'What is, Tony?' She did her best to sound deeply sympathetic.

'You being a woman and all. It don't feel right, not with a woman.'

'Don't think of me as a woman, Tony,' she tried to reassure him. 'Think of me entirely as a brief.'

'It's no good.' Tony shook his head. 'I keep thinking of my wife, April.'

'Well, of course she's worried about you. That's only natural, seeing you got nicked, Tony.'

'I don't mean that. I mean I wouldn't want a woman like my April to take on my job, would I? Briefs, and us what gets ourselves into a bit of trouble down the Bailey and that. It's all man's work, innit?'

Well, that may come as a shrewd shock to all readers of those women's pages which I have occasionally glanced at in Fiona Allways's *Guardian*, but I'm told that it is exactly what Tony Timson said. As a consequence it was a rueful Phillida Erskine-

Brown who walked away from the interview room, across the yard where the screws exercised the alsatians and the trusties weeded the flower beds, towards the gate.

'The Timsons are such *old-fashioned* villains.' Mr Bernard apologized for them. 'They're always about half a century behind the times.'

'It's not your fault, Mr Bernard,' said Phillida miserably.

'You wait till my wife gets to hear about this! They're pretty hot on women's rights in the Hammersmith S.D.P.' Bernard was clearly deeply affronted.

'It's the client's right to choose.' Phillida was taking it on the chin.

'It's decent of you to be like that about it, Mrs Erskine-Brown. It's absolutely no reflection on you, of course. But . . .' Bernard looked deeply embarrassed. 'I'm afraid I'll have to take in a chap to lead you.'

They had arrived at the gatehouse and were about to be sprung, when Phillida Erskine-Brown looked at Mr Bernard and said she wondered who the chap would be exactly.

'It goes against the grain,' said Bernard, 'but we've really got no choice, have we?'

A good deal later that evening I was on my way home when I happened to pass Pommeroy's Wine Bar and, in the hope that they might be offloading cooking claret at a reasonable rate, I went in and saw, alone and palely loitering at the bar with an oldish sandwich and a glass of hock, none other than Claude Erskine-Brown. I saw the chance of playing another card in the long game of 'Getting Fiona into Chambers', and I engaged the woebegone figure in conversation, the burden of which was that Phillida was so enormously busy at the Bar that the sandwich might well have to do for the Erskine-Brown supper.

'Of course,' I said sympathetically. 'Your wife must be pretty hard pressed now she's taken the Timsons off me.'

'She doesn't get home in the evenings until Tristan's gone to bed,' Erskine-Brown told me, and I looked at him and said, 'Just as well.'

'Do you think so?' The man sounded slightly offended.

'Just as well young Fiona Allways isn't coming into Chambers,' I explained.

'You agree that we shouldn't take her?'

'In all the circumstances, well, perhaps I'd better not say anything.'

'*What* do you mean, Rumpole?' Erskine-Brown was puzzled.

'It might have raised all sorts of problems. I mean, it might have got too much for you to handle.'

'*What* might have got too much for me to handle?'

'It would create all sorts of difficulties, in the spring, and all that sort of thing. We don't want the delicate perfume of young Fiona floating round Chambers, do we?' I said, as casually as possible.

'Well, I don't suppose I'd've seen much of her.'

'Oh, but you would, you know.'

'Not as a silk.'

'You'd've been thrown together. Chambers meetings. Brushing past each other in the clerk's room. Before you knew where you were you'd be popping out for tea and a couple of chocky biscuits in the ABC.' I looked as gravely concerned as I knew how. 'Terribly dangerous!'

'Why on earth?' He still hadn't quite caught my drift.

'Well, you know exactly what these young lady barristers are, impressionable, passionate even, and enormously impressed with the older legal hack, especially one teetering on the verge of knee breeches and a silk gown.'

'You don't mean . . . ?' I could see that now he had perked up considerably.

'And she seems to find you extremely personable, Claude!' I laid it on thick. 'You put her in distinct mind, so she has told me, of a film actor – "Newman", could that be the name?' I asked innocently, and drained my glass. At which moment, Claude Erskine-Brown took off his spectacles and admired himself in one of the mirrors, decorated with fronds of frosty vegetation, that cover Pommeroy's walls. 'Ridiculous!' he said, but I could see that the old fish was well and truly hooked.

'Of course it's ridiculous,' I agreed. 'But on second thoughts, far better she doesn't get into Chambers. Wouldn't you agree?' I left him then, but as I went out of Pommeroy's, Erskine-Brown was still looking at himself shortsightedly in the mirror.

The next day Henry gave me the glad news that I was to be *leading* the extraordinarily busy Mrs Phillida Erskine-Brown in the Timson defence. It seemed that Mr Bernard had seen sense on the subject of our little disagreement at Uxbridge, but Henry told me, extremely severely, that he couldn't go on clerking for me if I called my instructing solicitor a 'viper' again. I asked him if he'd pass 'snake', assured him I wasn't serious, and then went up to seek out our new Head of Chambers in his lair.

I was going to play the next card in the Fiona Allways game. I knocked at the door, heard a cry of 'Who is it?' and found Ballard with a cup of tea and a ginger biscuit working on some massive prosecution involving a large number of villains who were all represented by different-coloured pencils.

'Oh. It's you.' Our leader didn't sound particularly welcoming. All the same I came in, pushed Ballard's papers aside and sat on the edge of his desk.

'Just thought I ought to give you a friendly warning,' I started confidentially.

'Isn't it you that needs warning? Henry tells me that you've taken to being offensive to Mr Bernard.'

I lit up a small cigar and blew out smoke. Ballard coughed pointedly.

'It doesn't do Chambers any good, you know, insulting a solicitor,' he told me. By way of an answer I closed my eyes and tried a vivid description.

'Fascinating character!' I began. 'Marvellous hair, burnished like autumn leaves. Tender white neck, sticking out of the starched white collar...'

'Mr Bernard?' Ballard was puzzled.

'Of course not!' I put him right. 'I was speaking of Miss Phillida Trant, now Mrs Erskine-Brown.' I brought out the packet of small cigars and offered it. 'You don't smoke, I suppose?'

'You know I don't.'

'What *do* you do, I wonder?' There was a short diversion as Ballard blew my ash off his depositions and then I said thought-fully, 'Gorgeous creature in many ways, our Portia.'

'With a most enviable practice, I understand,' Ballard agreed.
'Perhaps she's polite to solicitors.'

'Determined to rise to the absolute top.'

'I have the highest respect for Phillida, of course, but . . .'

'Devious.' I supplied the word. 'A brilliant mind, of course, but
devious!'

'Rumpole. What are you trying to tell me?' Ballard seemed
anxious to bring our dialogue to a swift conclusion.

'The way she got you to show your sexual prejudices at that
Chambers meeting!' I said with admiration.

'My *what* . . . ?'

'Your blind and Victorian opposition to women in the legal
profession. I believe she's writing a report on that to the Bar
Council. Plus ten articles for the *Observer*, in depth.'

'But Rumpole, she spoke *against* Allways.' Ballard was already
arguing weakly.

'What a tactician!' For the sake of emphasis, I gave Ballard a
brisk slap on the shoulder.

'She seemed totally opposed to the girl.'

I slipped off his desk and took a turn round the room. 'Just to
lead you on, don't you see? To get *you* to show your hand. You
walked right into it, Bollard. I can see the headlines now!
"Christian barrister presides over sexist redoubt!" "Bollard, Q.C.,
puts the clock back fifty years."'

'Ballard.' He corrected me without too much conviction and
said, 'I didn't take that attitude, surely.'

'You will have done!' I assured him, 'by the time our Phillida's
finished with you. Don't cross her, Bollard, I warn you. She has
the ear of the Lord Chancellor. I don't know if you were ever
hoping for some sort of minor judgeship . . .' I went to the door
and then turned back to Ballard. 'Of course, you have one thing
in your favour.'

'What's that?' He seemed prepared to clutch at a straw. It was
then that I played the ace. 'Our Portia seems to have taken
something of a shine to you,' I told him. '"Craggily handsome"
I think was the way she put it. I suppose there's just a chance you
might get round her. Try using your irresistible charm.'

I left him then. The poor old darling was looking like a person who has to choose between a public execution and a heady draught of hemlock.

Whatever may be said about the equality of the sexes, there is still something about the nature of women which parts the average man almost entirely from his marbles. Faced with most problems, both Erskine-Brown and Ballard might have proved reasonably resolute. When the question concerned a moderately personable young woman, they became as clay in the potter's hands. These thoughts passed through my mind as I lay in bed that night staring at the ceiling, while Hilda sat at the dressing table in night attire, brushing her hair before coming to bed.

'What are you thinking, Rumpole?' she asked. 'I know you, Rumpole. You're lying there *thinking* about something!'

'I was thinking,' I confessed, 'about man's attitude to the female of the species.'

'Oh, were you indeed?' Hilda sounded deeply suspicious.

'On the one hand the presence of a woman strikes him with terror!'

'Really, Rumpole, don't be absurd,' Hilda said severely.

'And fierce resentment.'

'Is *that* what you were thinking?'

'And yet he finds her not only indispensable, but quite irresistible. Faced with a whiff of perfume, for instance, he is reduced to a state bordering on imbecility.'

'Rumpole. Are you really?' Hilda's voice had softened considerably. The room became redolent with the smell of lavender water. Hilda was spraying on perfume.

> 'She is a woman, therefore may be woo'd;
> She is a woman, therefore may be won;'

I repeated sleepily.

I saw Hilda emerge from her dressing gown and make towards the bed. She said, 'Oh, Rumpole...' quite tenderly. But then sleep claimed me, and I heard no more.

One afternoon I turned up at the gates of Brixton Prison with my learned junior, Mrs Phillida Erskine-Brown, and there was

Mr Bernard waiting for us and replying to my hearty greeting in a somewhat guarded manner.

'Hail to thee blythe Bernard!' I said, and he replied, 'We're taking you in on the express wishes of the client, Mr Rumpole. Just for this case.'

I then became aware of a pleasant-looking young woman with blonde hair and a small, rather plump child who was sitting slumped in a pushchair, regarding me with a wary eye.

'Mr Rumpole.' The lady introduced herself. 'I'm April Timson. Tony's that glad that you're going to be his brief.'

My companion looked less than flattered, but I greeted our client's family warmly.

'Mrs Timson, good of you to say so. And who's this young hopeful?'

'That's our young Vince. Been in to see his dad,' said the child's proud mother.

'Delighted to meet you, Vincent,' I said, and managed to leave a thought with April which might pay off in the course of time. 'Let me know,' I said, 'the moment he gets into trouble.'

'Straight up, it's a sodding plant,' said Tony Timson, and then turned apologetically to my junior. 'Pardon my French.'

'Don't be so silly, Tony.' Phillida didn't like not being taken for one of the boys. We were sitting in a small glass-walled room in the interview block at Brixton, and I felt I had to question Tony further as to his suggested defence.

'What sort of a plant are you suggesting,' I asked. 'A floribunda of the Serious Crimes Squad or an exotic bloom cultivated by the Molloys?'

'That D.I. Broome. He's got no love for the Timsons,' Tony grumbled.

'Neither have the Molloys.'

'That's true, Mr Rumpole. That's very true.'

'A plant by the supergrass's family? I suppose it's possible.' I considered the suggestion.

'I'd say it's typical.'

'So some person unknown brought in the cash and popped it

into your Super Snow White Extra DeLuxe Easy-Wash?' I framed the charge.

'The jury may now wonder how Tony can afford all these luxuries out of window-cleaning,' Phillida suggested.

'It's not a luxury. My April says it's just something you got to have,' said Tony, the proud householder.

'You know how he affords these things, Portia?' I explained our case to one not expert in the Timson branch of the law. 'Tony's a minor villain. Small stuff. Let's have a look at his form.' I plucked a sheet of paper from my brief. 'Warehouse-breaking, shop-breaking, criminal damage to a set of traffic lights . . .'

'I misjudged a turning, Mr Rumpole,' Tony admitted. It was the item of which he seemed slightly ashamed. But there was more to come.

'Careless driving, dangerous driving, failure to report an accident,' I read out. 'Look here, old sweetheart. If I get you out of this, do promise not to give me a lift home.'

That same evening, Claude Erskine-Brown put his head round the door of my room, where Miss Fiona Allways was looking up a bit of law, and invited her to join him in a bottle of Pommeroy's bubbly. Naturally anxious to be on friendly terms with those who held her legal future in their hands, she accepted the invitation, and I am indebted to her for an account of what then took place.

Once ensconced at a corner table in the shadowy regions of the wine bar, Erskine-Brown took off his spectacles and sighed as though worn out by the cares of office.

'It can be lonely at the top, Fiona,' he said. 'I mean, you may wonder what it feels like to be on the verge of becoming a Q.C.' Perhaps he was waiting for her to say something, but as she didn't he repeated with a sigh, 'I'll tell you. Lonely.'

'But you've got Mrs Erskine-Brown.' Fiona was puzzled.

Claude gave her a sad little smile. 'Mrs Erskine-Brown! I seem to see so little of Phillida nowadays. Pressures of work, of course. No,' he went on seriously, 'there comes a time in this job when a person feels terribly alone.'

'I suppose so.' Fiona felt the topic was becoming exhausted.

'I envy you those happy, carefree days when you hop from Magistrates Court to Magistrates Court, picking up little crumbs of indecent exposure.'

'Frozen chicken,' Fiona corrected him.

'What?' Erskine-Brown looked puzzled.

'I was doing a case about frozen chicken pieces. It seemed quite a responsibility to me.'

As the subject had moved from himself Claude's attention wandered. He looked across to the bar and said, 'Is that old Rumpole over there?'

'Why?' Fiona asked, in all innocence. 'Can't you see without your glasses?'

In fact, and this Erskine-Brown didn't notice, perhaps because she was hidden in the mêlée at the bar, I had come into the joint with Phillida in order that we might refresh ourselves after a hard conference at Brixton. I said I hoped she had no hard feelings about me being taken in to lead her in the Timson affair. She confessed to just a few hard feelings, but was then sporting enough to buy us a perfectly reasonable bottle.

'Criminals and barristers, Portia,' I told her as Jack Pommeroy was uncorking the claret. 'Both extremely conservative professions . . .'

But before she had time to absorb this thought, Phillida was off like a hound on the scent towards a corner of the room. Again I have to rely on Miss Allways's account for what was going on at the distant table.

'And if ever you have the slightest problem,' Erskine-Brown was saying gently, 'of a legal nature, or anything else come to that, don't hesitate, Fiona. A silk's door is always open to a member of Chambers, however junior.'

'A member of Chambers?' Fiona repeated hopefully.

'I'm sure. I mean, some old squares are tremendously prejudiced against women, of course. But speaking for myself . . .' He put a hand on one of Fiona's which she had left lying about on the table. 'I have absolutely no objection to a pretty face around Number 3 Equity Court.'

'Haven't you, Claude?' Mrs Erskine-Brown had fetched up beside the table and spoke with considerable asperity.

'Oh, Philly.' Erskine-Brown hastily withdrew his hand. 'Are you going to join us for a drink? You know Fiona, of course . . .'

'Yes. I know Allways.' Phillida looked suspiciously at the gold-topped bottle. 'What is it? Somebody's birthday? No, I'm not joining you two. I'm going to go straight back to Chambers and write a letter.'

At which Phillida Erskine-Brown banged out of Pommeroy's, leaving her husband with a somewhat foolish expression on his face, and me with an entire bottle of claret.

Phillida, always as good as her word, did go back to her room in Chambers and started to write a lengthy and important letter to an official quarter. It was whilst she was doing this that there came a tap at her door, which she ignored, and then the devout Ballard entered uninvited. This time I have to rely on our Portia for a full account of what transpired, and when she told me, over a rather hilarious celebratory bottle about a month later, her recollection may have grown somewhat dim; but she swears that it was a Ballard transformed who came gliding up to her desk. He was wearing a somewhat garish spotted tie (in pink and blue, as she remembered it), a matching silk handkerchief lolled from his top pocket, and surrounding the man was a fairly overpowering odour of some aftershave which the manufacturers advertise as 'Trouble-starter'. He was also smiling.

'I saw your light on,' Ballard murmured. Apparently Phillida didn't find this a statement of earth-shaking interest and went on writing.

'Mrs Erskine-Brown,' Ballard tried again. 'You won't mind me calling you Phyllis?'

'If you want to, but it doesn't happen to be my name.' Phillida didn't look up from her writing.

'Burning the midnight oil?'

'It's only half past six.'

Although she had given him little encouragement, Ballard came and perched, no doubt as he thought, jauntily, on the corner of her desk and made what seemed to Phillida to be an entirely unnecessary disclosure. 'I've never married of course,' he said.

'Lucky you!' Phillida said with meaning as she went on with her work.

'I lead what I imagine you'd call a bit of a bachelor life in Dulwich. Decent-sized flat, though, all that sort of thing.'

'Oh, good,' Phillida said in as neutral a manner as possible.

'But I don't want you to run away with the idea that I don't like *women*, because I do like women ... very much indeed. I am a perfectly normal sort of chap in that regard,' Ballard assured her.

'Oh, jolly good.' Phillida was still busy.

'In fact, I have to confess this to you. I find the sight of a woman wigged and wearing a winged collar surprisingly, well, let's be honest about this, alluring.' There was a considerable pause and then he blurted out, 'I saw you the other day, going up the stairs in the Law Courts. Robed up!'

'Did you? I was on my way to do a divorce.' Phillida was folding her letter with grim determination.

'Well, I just didn't want you to be under any illusions.' Ballard stood and gave Phillida what was no doubt meant to be a challenging look. 'I'm thoroughly in favour of women, from every point of view.'

'I'm sure the news will come as an enormous relief to the women of the world!' She licked the envelope and stuck it down. What she said seemed to have a strange effect on Ballard and he became extremely nervous.

'Oh, I don't want it published in the papers!' he said anxiously. 'I thought I'd make it perfectly clear to you, in the course of private conversation.'

'Well, you've made it clear, Ballard.' Phillida looked him in the eye for the first time, and didn't particularly like what she saw.

'Please, "Sam",' he corrected her skittishly.

'All right, "Sam". You've made it terribly clear,' she repeated.

'Look. Some day when you're not in Court,' he was smiling at her again, 'why don't you let me take you out to a spot of lunch? They do a very decent set meal at the Ludgate Hotel.'

Phillida looked at him with amazement and contempt. She then got up and walked past him to the door, taking her letter. 'I've got to put this out to post,' was all she had to say to that.

I had gone back to our clerk's room to pick up some forgotten papers and was alone there, Henry and Dianne having left for some unknown destination, when Phillida came to put her letter in the 'Post' tray on Dianne's desk.

'What on earth happened, Portia?' I asked her. 'You left me to finish the bottle.'

'Has everyone in this Chambers gone completely out of their heads?' she replied with another question.

'Everyone?'

'Ballard just made the most disgusting suggestion to me.' She did seem extremely angry.

'Bollard did? Whatever was it?' I asked, delighted.

'He invited me to have the set lunch at the Ludgate Hotel. And as for my so-called husband . . .' Words failing her, she went to the door. 'Goodnight, Rumpole!'

'Goodnight, Portia.'

It was then that I looked down at the letter she'd just written. The envelope was addressed to 'The Lord Chancellor, The Lord Chancellor's Office, The House of Lords, London, s.w.1.'

A good deal, I thought, was going on under the calm surface of life in our Chambers at Equity Court. I was speculating on the precise nature of such movements with considerable pleasure as I started to walk to the Temple station. On my way I found Miss Fiona Allways waiting for a bus.

'I say,' she hailed me. 'Any more news about my getting into Chambers?'

'There is a tide in the affairs of women barristers, Fiona,' I told her, 'which, taken at the flood, leads God knows where.'

'What's that mean, exactly?'

'It means that they'll either let you in, or they'll throw *me* out.' I moved on towards Hilda and home. 'Best of luck,' I said, 'to both of us.'

His Honour Judge Leonard Dover was a fairly recent appointment to the collection of Old Bailey judges. He was a youngish man, in his mid forties perhaps, certainly young enough to be my son, had fate chosen to inflict such a blow. He wore rimless glasses and was a fairly rimless character. He was the sort of judge who has about as many laughs in him as a digital computer, and seemed to have been programmed by the Civil Service. Press all the right buttons – you know the type – and he gives you seven years in the Nick. I have often thought that if he were plugged into the mains, Judge Dover could go on passing stiff sentences for ever.

On my way into Dover's Court I had passed Mrs April Timson, made up to the nines and wearing a sky-blue trouser suit, come to celebrate her husband's day of fame. She accosted me anxiously.

'Tony says you've never let the Timsons down, Mr Rumpole.'

'Mrs Timson!' I greeted her. 'Where's young Vincent today? Otherwise engaged?'

'He's with my friend, Chrissie. She's my neighbour and she's minding him. What are our chances, Mr Rumpole?'

'Talk to you later,' I said, not caring to commit myself.

After the jury had been sworn in, Judge Dover leant towards them and said, in his usual unremarkable monotone, 'Nothing that I am going to say now must be taken against the defendant in any way . . .'

I stirred in my seat. Whatever was going on, I didn't like the sound of it.

'This is a case in which it seems there is a particular danger of your being approached . . . by someone,' Dover went on, sounding grave. 'That often happens in trials of alleged armed robbery by what is known as a "gang" of serious professional criminals.'

It was time to throw a spanner in his programming. 'My Lord,' I said firmly, and rose to the hind legs, but Dover was locked in conversation with the jury.

'You will be particularly on your guard, and purely for your assistance, of course, you will be kept under police observation.' He seemed to notice me at long last. 'What is it, Mr Rumpole? Don't you want this jury to be protected from interference?'

'I don't want the jury to be told this is a case concerning a serious crime before they've heard one word of evidence,' I said with all possible vehemence. 'I don't want hints that my client belongs to a gang of serious professionals when the truth may be that he's nothing but a snapper-up of unconsidered trifles. I don't want the jury nobbled, but nobbled they have already been, in my respectful submission, by your Lordship's warning.'

'Mr Rumpole! That's an extraordinary suggestion, coming from you.'

'It was made to answer an extraordinary statement coming from your Lordship.'

'What is your application, Mr Rumpole?' Judge Dover asked in a voice several degrees below zero.

'My Lord, I ask that a fresh jury be empanelled, who will have heard no prejudicial suggestions against my client.'

'Your application is refused.' I had pressed the wrong button and got the automatic print-out. There was nothing for it but to sit down looking extremely hard done by.

'Members of the jury.' The Judge turned back to them. 'I have already made it perfectly clear to you that nothing I have said contains any suggestion whatever against Mr Timson. Does that satisfy you, Mr Rumpole?'

'About as much as a glass of cold carrot juice, old darling,' I muttered to Phillida.

'I'm sorry, I didn't hear you, Mr Rumpole.'

'I said, I suppose it will have to, my Lord.' I rose in a perfunctory manner.

'Yes, Mr Rumpole,' the Judge said. 'I suppose it will.'

Back in the alleged mansion flat things weren't going too well either. Hilda, in the course of tidying up, found my old *Oxford Book of English Verse* on a chair (I had been seeking solace in the 'Intimations of Immortality' the night before), and she put it on my excellent shelf. No doubt she thumped it down a fair bit, for my elegant carpentry creaked and then collapsed, casting a good many books and a certain amount of wine to the ground. I have spoken already of the strength of my wife's character. Apparently she went out, purchased a number of rawlplugs and an electric drill and started a career as a handyman, the full effects of which weren't noticed by me for some time.

In Court, the prosecution was in the hands of Mr Hilary Onslow, a languid-looking young man whose fair curly hair came sprouting out from under his wig. In spite of his air of well-born indifference, he could be, at times, a formidable opponent. One of the earliest witnesses was the supergrass, Gerry Molloy, an overweight character with a red face and glossy black hair, who sweated a good deal and seemed about to burst out of his buttons.

'Mr Molloy. I want to come now to the facts of the Pond Hill bank raid.'

'The Pond Hill job. Yes, sir.' Gerry sounded only too eager to help.

'How many of you were engaged on that particular enterprise?'

'There was two with sawn-offs. One collector . . .'

'And you with the sledgehammer?' Onslow asked.

'I was the sledge man, yes. There was five of us altogether.'

'Five of you counting the driver?'

'Yes, sir.'

'Did you *see* the driver?'

'Course I did.' The witness sounded very sure of himself. 'The driver picked me up at the meet.'

'Had you seen him before?'

'Seen him before?' Molloy thought carefully, and then answered, 'No, sir . . .'

'Some weeks later did you attend an identification parade?' Onslow turned to me and asked languidly, 'Is there any dispute as to whom he picked out at the I.D.?'

'No dispute as to that. No,' I granted him.

'Thank you, Mr Rumpole.' The Judge gave me a faint look of approval.

'Delighted to be of assistance, my Lord,' I rose to say, and sank back into my seat as quickly as possible.

'Did you pick out the defendant, Mr Timson?' Onslow asked.

Tony Timson was staring at the witness from the dock. Gerry Molloy looked away to avoid his accusing eyes and met a glare from April Timson in the public gallery.

'Yes.' The answer was a little muted. 'I pointed to him. I got no hesitation.'

'Thank you, Mr Molloy.'

Hilary Onslow sat and crossed his long legs elegantly. I rose, full of righteous indignation, and looked at the jury in a pained manner as I cast my questions in the general direction of the witness-box.

'Mr Molloy. You have turned Queen's Evidence in this case?'

'Come again?' The answer was impertinent, so I put my voice up several decibels. 'Translated into everyday language, Mr Molloy, you are a grass. Not even a "supergrass". A common or garden ordinary bit of a grass.'

There was a welcome stir of laughter from the jury, immediately silenced by the computer on the Bench.

'Members of the jury,' Judge Dover reminded them, if they needed reminding, 'this is not a place of public entertainment. This witness is giving evidence for the prosecution,' he added, as though that covered the matter.

'You're giving evidence for the prosecution because you were caught.' I turned to the witness-box then. 'Not being a particularly efficient sledge, you tripped over your holdall in the street and missed the getaway car. You were apprehended, Mr Molloy, in the gutter!'

'They nicked me, yes,' Molloy admitted.

'And you have already been sentenced to two years for your part in the robbery?'

'I got a two, yes.'

'A considerable reduction because you agreed with the police to grass on your colleagues,' I suggested.

'I got under the odds, yes,' he agreed, less readily.

'Considerably under the odds, Mr Molloy, and for that you were prepared to betray your own family?'

'Come again?'

'Three of your colleagues were members of the clan Molloy.'

'They were Molloys, yes.'

'And only one Timson?'

'Yes.'

'And as the Montagues to the Capulets, I put it to you, so are the Timsons to the Molloys.'

'Did you say the "Montagues", Mr Rumpole?' The Judge seemed puzzled by a name he hadn't heard in the case before, so my literary reference was lost on the computer.

'I simply meant that the Molloys hate and despise the Timsons. Isn't that so, Mr Gerry Molloy?' I asked the witness.

'We never got on, no. It's traditional. Although . . .'

'Although what?'

'I believe my cousin Shawn's wife what he's separated from lives quite close to Tony Timson and his wife and . . .'

I interrupted a speech which I thought might somewhat blur the picture I had just painted. 'Apart from that, it's true, isn't it, that the Molloys are in a different league from the Timsons?'

'What league is that, Mr Rumpole?' Judge Dover looked puzzled.

'The big league, my Lord.' I helped him understand. 'You and your relations, according to your evidence, did the Barclays Bank in Penge, the Midland, Croydon, and the NatWest in Barking . . .' I was back with the witness.

'That's what I've said.' He was sweating more now, and two of his lower shirt buttons had gone off about their own affairs.

'Spreading your favours evenly round the money market. Have you ever known a Timson to be present at a bank robbery before, Mr Molloy?'

'Not as I can remember. But my brother Charlie was off sick and we was short of a driver.'

'Perhaps you were. Unhappily all your Molloy colleagues seem to have vanished.'

At which point my learned friend, Mr Hilary Onslow, felt it right to unwind his legs and draw himself to his great height. 'My Lord,' he said, 'I explained to the jury that determined efforts to trace the other participants in this robbery are still being made by the police . . .'

'If my learned friend wishes to give evidence, perhaps your Lordship would like him to go into the witness-box,' I said, and got the automatic judicial rebuke: 'Mr Rumpole. That comment was quite uncalled-for.'

'Steady on, Rumpole. Don't tease him.' Phillida whispered a bit of sound advice, so I said, with deep humility, 'So it was, my Lord. I entirely agree.' I turned back, with no humility at all, to Gerry Molloy. 'With your relations all gone to ground you had to have a victim, didn't you, to justify your privileged treatment as a grass?' The jury, who looked extremely interested, clearly saw the point. The witness pretended that he didn't.

'A victim?' He was playing for time, I gave him none.

'So you decided to pick one out of the despised Timsons and put him in the frame.'

'Put him in the *what*, Mr Rumpole?' The Judge affected not to understand. I hadn't time to teach him plain English.

'Put him in the driver's seat, where he certainly never was,' I suggested to the supergrass.

'He was there. I told you.' Gerry Molloy was growing indignant.

'Where did you meet?'

'One of the Molloy houses,' he said, after a pause.

'Which one?'

'I think it was Michael's . . . Or Vic's. I can't be sure.'

'Can't you . . . ?'

'It was Shawn's,' he decided.

'And having decided to frame Tony,' I went on quickly, 'was it some member of the Molloy family who planted a packet of stolen banknotes in the Timson home?'

'It couldn't have been him, could it, Mr Rumpole?' The Judge was looking back in his notes. 'This witness has been in custody ever since . . .'

'Since the robbery, yes, my Lord,' I agreed, and then asked Molloy, 'Did you receive visits in prison, before you made your statement?'

'A few visits, yes.'

'From your wife?'

'One or two.'

'And was it through her that the word was sent out to plant the money on Tony Timson?'

I made the suggestion for the benefit of the jury, but it deeply shocked Gerald Supergrass Molloy. 'I wouldn't ask my wife to do them sort of messages,' he said, deeply pained.

Back at home Hilda, swathed in an overall, was drilling the wall to receive a new consignment of 'Easy-Do' shelving in a completely professional manner. I was also plugging away in Court, asking a few pertinent questions of Detective Inspector Broome, the officer in charge of the case.

'Gerry Molloy made his statement two days after the robbery, at about 2.30 in the afternoon?' I suggested.

'2.35, to be precise.' The D.I. put me right.

'Oh, please. I'm sure my Lord would like you to be very precise. You went straight round to Tony Timson's house?'

'We did.'

'In a police car, with the siren blaring?'

'I think we had the siren on for some of the time. We were in a hurry.'

'And you were lucky enough to find him at home?'

'Well, he wasn't out doing window-cleaning, sir.'

There was a small titter from the jury. I interrupted it as soon as possible.

'My client opened the door to you at once?'

'Soon as we knocked. Yes.'

'No sort of interval while he tried to move the money to a more sensible hiding place, for instance?'

'Perhaps he was happy with it where it was.'

Before he got another laugh, I came in quickly with 'Or perhaps, Inspector, he had no idea that the money had been put there.'

'I don't know about that.'

'Don't you? One last matter. Was it Gerry Molloy who told you that Tony Timson was a dangerous member of a big-time robbery firm who might try and nobble the jury?'

'Molloy told us that, yes.' Inspector Broome was a little reluctant to answer.

'So a solemn warning was given by the learned Judge on the word of a self-confessed sledgehammer man who has already been convicted of malicious wounding, robbery and grievous bodily harm.'

'Yes.' The short answer came even more reluctantly from the Inspector.

'And doesn't that solemn warning give a quite unfair impression of Tony Timson?'

'Unfair, sir?' Broome did his best to look puzzled.

'You'd never put Tony Timson in for the serious crime award, would you? He's a small-time thief, who specializes in relieving householders of their home entertainment, video machines, teasmades and the like...'

'That would seem to be so, yes,' the Inspector admitted.

'So if I said to you that this robbery was quite out of Tony Timson's league, how would you translate that suggestion?'

'I would say it's out of his character, sir. Judging by past form.' So I sat down with some heartfelt thanks to Detective Inspector Broome.

At the end of the day I went with Phillida and Bernard to visit our client in the cells. He appeared pleased with our progress, but I hadn't yet an answer to what seemed to me the single important question in the case.

'The money in the washing machine, Tony,' I asked him. 'It must have been put there by someone. Does April go out much?'

'She takes young Vince round her friend's.'

'Her friend Chrissie?' The question seemed important to me, but Tony answered vaguely, 'I think that's her name. I don't know the woman.'

'Money found in the kitchen,' I said thoughtfully. 'I don't suppose you do much cooking, do you, Tony?'

'Oh, leave it out, Mr Rumpole!' Tony found the suggestion highly diverting.

'Never wash up?'

'Course I don't!' He could hardly suppress his laughter. 'That's April's job, innit?'

'I suppose it's only barristers who spend the evenings up to their wrists in the Fairy Liquid. Yes ... And of course you don't run young Vince's smalls through the washing machine?'

'Now would I be expected to do a job like that?' He looked to Mrs Erskine-Brown for support. 'Would I?'

'You mean, it would be a bit like having a woman defend you?' Phillida asked in a pointed sort of way. Tony Timson had the grace to look apologetic.

'I never meant nothing personal,' he said. 'It just doesn't seem natural.'

'Really.' Phillida was unappeased. 'As a matter of fact my husband is quite a good performer on the spindrier.'

'Poor bloke!' Tony was laughing again.

I interrupted the badinage. 'Let's take it that you leave such matters to April. When does she do the washing, Tony? On a Monday?'

'Suppose so.' He didn't sound particularly interested.

'The bank raid was on Monday. Gerry Molloy made his statement on Wednesday afternoon and the police were round at once. Whoever put it there didn't have much time.'

'I don't know,' and he added hopelessly, 'I just never go near the bleeding washing machine.'

I gathered up my brief and prepared to return to the free world.

'See you tomorrow, Tony,' I said. 'Come on, Portia. I think we've got what we wanted.'

When I left the Old Bailey that evening and stepped off the pavement, a small white sports car, driven with great speed and expertise, flashed past me, almost cutting me off somewhere past my prime, and, passing two or three slowly moving taxis on the inside, zipped off and was lost in the traffic. I caught sight of a blonde head behind the wheel and deduced that the driver was none other than that devoted housewife, Mrs April Timson.

I didn't sleep much that night. I was busy putting two and two together to make about five thousand nicker. Around dawn I drifted off and dreamt of washing machines and spindriers, and Ballard was bringing me a bouquet of roses and inviting me to lunch, and Fiona Allways had decided to leave the Bar and take up life as a coalminer, saying the pay was so much better.

So I arrived at the Old Bailey in a somewhat jaded condition. Having robed for the day's work, I went up to the canteen on the third floor and bought myself a black coffee and a slightly flaccid sausage roll. I wasn't enjoying them much when Erskine-Brown came up to me in a state of considerable distress, holding out a copy of *The Times* in a trembling hand. The poor fellow looked decidedly seedy.

'The silk list, Rumpole!' he stammered. 'Have you seen the new Q.C.s?'

'Haven't got beyond the crossword.' I opened the paper and found the relevant page. 'Well, here's your name. What are you worrying about?'

'*My* name?' Erskine-Brown asked bitterly.

'Erskine-Brown. *Mrs!*' I read the entry more carefully. 'Oh, I do see.' I felt for the man, my heart bled for him.

'She never warned me, Rumpole! I had no idea she'd applied. Had you?'

'No.' I honestly hadn't. 'Haven't you asked her about it?'

'She left home before the paper came. And now she's gone to ground in the ladies' robing room!' Then he asked with a faint hope, 'Do you think it might be some sort of misprint?'

I might have sat there for some time commiserating with Claude, but I saw a blonde head and a blue trouser suit by the tea-urns. I rose, excused myself to the still suffering, still junior barrister, and arrived alongside Mrs April Timson just in time to pay for her coffee.

'You're very kind, Mr Rumpole,' she said.

'Sometimes,' I agreed. She moved to a table. I went with her. 'Young Vincent well this morning, is he? Chrissie Molloy looking after him properly?'

'Chrissie's all right.' She sat and then looked up at me and spoke very quietly. 'Tony doesn't know she's a Molloy.'

I sat down beside her and took my time in lighting a small cigar. 'No. Mrs Timson,' I said. 'Tony doesn't know very much, does he?'

'We were at school together. Me and Chrissie. Anyway, she and Shawn Molloy's separated.'

'But still friends,' I suggested. 'Close enough for the Molloy firm to meet at Chrissie's house.' I blew out smoke and then asked, 'When did you know they were short of a driver?'

'I may have heard ... someone mention it.' She looked away from me and stirred her coffee. So I told her the whole story, as though she didn't know. 'Your husband wouldn't have been the slightest use in a getaway car, would he?' I said. 'He'd have had three parking tickets and hit a milk float before they'd got clear of the bank. You, on the other hand, I happen to have noticed, are distinctly nippy, driving through traffic.' A silence fell between us. It lasted until I said, 'What was the matter? Tony not ambitious enough for you?'

'Why ever should you think ...?' She looked up at me then. Whatever it was meant to be, the look was not innocent.

'Because of where you put the money,' I told her quietly. 'It was the one place in the house you knew your husband would never look.'

She had the nerve of an accomplished villain, had Mrs April Timson. She took a long swig of coffee and then she asked me what I was going to do.

'The real question is,' I said, 'what are *you* going to do?' And then I gave her my legal advice. 'Leave it out, April,' I said. 'Give it up, Mrs Timson. Keep away from it. It's men's work, you know. Let the men make a mess of it.' I paused to let the advice sink in, then I stood up to go. 'It was the first time, I imagine. Better make it the last.'

I got into Court some time before the learned computer took his seat on the Bench. As soon as Phillida arrived I gave her, believing it right to take my junior into my full confidence, my solution to the case, and an account of my conversation with April Timson.

She thought for a moment, and then asked, 'But why didn't Gerry Molloy identify *her*?'

'He was ashamed, don't you understand? He didn't want to admit that the great Molloys went out with a *woman* driver!'

'What on earth are we going to do?'

'We can't prove it was April. Let's hope they can't prove it was Tony. The jury don't much care for the mini-grass, and the Molloys *might* have planted the money.'

Hilary Onslow came in then, gave us a cheerful 'Good morning', and took his place. I spoke to Phillida in a whisper.

'Only one thing we can do, Portia. I'll just give them the speech about reasonable doubt.'

'No. *I* will . . .' she said firmly.

'What?' I wasn't following her drift.

'I'm *your* leader now. Don't you read *The Times*, Rumpole? I have taken silk!'

At which point the Usher shouted, 'Be upstanding,' and Judge Dover was upon us. He looked at the defence team, said, 'Yes, Mr Rumpole?' and then saw that Phillida was on her feet.

'Mrs Erskine-Brown. I believe that certain congratulations are in order?'

'Yes, my Lord. I believe they are,' said our Portia, and announced that she would now call the defendant.

Tony gave evidence. As he denied knowing anything about the money, or the whereabouts of the Pond Hill bank, or even the exact situation of his own washing machine, he was a difficult witness to cross-examine. Onslow did his best, and made a moderately effective final speech, and then I sat quietly and listened to Mrs Phillida Erskine-Brown, now my learned leader. I smiled as I heard her reach a familiar peroration.

'Members of the jury.' She was addressing them with carefully controlled emotion. 'Soon this case will be over. In a little while you will go back to your jobs and your families, and you will forget about it. At most it is only a small part of your lives, but for my client, Tony Timson, it is the *whole* of his life! And it is that life I leave with confidence in your hands, certain that there can be only one verdict in this case, "Not Guilty"!'

And then Phillida sank down in her seat exhausted, just as I had taught her to, as I had taught Fiona Allways, and anyone else who would care to listen.

'Good speech.' I congratulated Phillida as we came out of Court when the Timson case was over.

'Yes. It always was.'

'Portia of Belmont ... Phillida Erskine-Brown, née Trant ... and Fiona Allways ... the great tradition of female advocates should be carried on!' I lit a small cigar.

Phillida looked at me. 'It's not enough for you that we won Timson, is it? Not enough that you got the jury to disbelieve Gerry Molloy and think the money may have been planted. You want to win the Allways case as well.'

'Well,' I said reasonably, 'why shouldn't we take on Fiona?'

'Over my dead body!'

She moved towards the lifts. I followed her.

'But *why*?'

'She was making a play for Claude. I found them all over each other in Pommeroy's. That's when I got so angry I applied for silk.'

'Without telling your husband?' I asked sorrowfully.

'I'm afraid so.'

'I'd better come clean about this.' I took off my wig, and stood looking at her. She looked back at me, deeply suspicious. 'What've you been up to, Rumpole?'

'Well, I just wanted your Claude to look on Miss Allways with a warm and friendly eye. I mean, I thought that'd increase her chances of getting in, so . . .'

'You wanted Claude to *warm* to her . . .' Phillida's voice was rising to a note of outrage.

'I thought it might help. Yes,' I admitted.

'Rumpole! I suppose you told him that she fancied him.'

'Now, Portia. Would I do such a thing?' I protested.

'Very probably. If you wanted to win badly enough. I imagine you told him she thought he looked like Robert Redford.'

'No. I protest!' I was hurt. 'That is utterly and entirely untrue! I told him she thought he looked like a fellow called Newman.'

'And had Allways actually said that?' Phillida was still uncertain of the facts.

'Well, if you want me to be entirely honest . . .'

'It would make a change,' she said, unnecessarily, I thought.

'Well, no. She hadn't.'

And then, quite unexpectedly, our Portia smiled. 'Poor old Claude,' she said. 'You know what you were doing, Rumpole? You can't rely on a girl to get in on her own talents, can you? You have to manipulate and rely on everyone else's vanity. You were simply exploiting the male sex.'

'So now you know,' I asked her, 'will you vote for Fiona?'

'Tell me one good reason.'

'Ballard's against her.'

'I suppose that's one good reason. And because of you I've ended up a silk. What on earth can I tell Claude?' She seemed, for a delightful moment, overcome with guilt, and blushed very prettily, as though she had to admit the existence of a lover.

'Tell him,' I suggested, 'that the Lord Chancellor just thought there weren't enough women silks. So that's why you got it. He'll feel better if he thinks there's no damn merit about this thing.'

'I suppose so.' She looked a little disappointed as she asked me, 'Is that true?'

'Quite possibly,' I told her. After all, I hadn't undertaken to tell her the *whole* truth about anything.

When I got home that night, Hilda asked me if I had noticed anything. Suspecting that she had had a new hair-do or bought a new dress, I said that of course she was looking extremely pretty.

'Not me,' she said. 'Look at the walls.'

The shelf I had put up was not only firmly screwed and looking even better than usual, it seemed to have pupped and there were shelves all over the place, gamely supporting potted plants and glasses, telephone directories and bottles of plonk.

'What did you do, Hilda,' I asked her. 'Did you get a man in?'

'Yes,' she said. 'Me.'

It all ended once again with a Chambers party. The excuse for that particular shindig was the swearing-in at the House of Lords of Mrs Phillida Erskine-Brown as One of Her Majesty's Counsel. She made a resplendent figure as she came to split a few bottles of champagne with us in Ballard's room. Her handsome female face peeped out between the long spaniel's ears of her full-bottomed wig. She wore a long silk gown with a black purse on her back. There were lace cuffs on her tailed coat, and lace at her throat. Her black skirt ended with black stockings and diamond-buckled shoes. She carried her white gloves in one hand and a glass of Mercier (on offer at Pommeroy's) in the other. Just when matters were going with a certain amount of swing, Ballard took it upon himself to make a speech.

'In our great profession . . .' he was saying, and I muttered an, 'Amen.' 'We are sometimes accused of prejudice against the female sex.'

'Shame!' said Erskine-Brown.

'That may be true of some sets of Chambers, but it cannot be said of us at 3 Equity Court,' Ballard continued. 'As in many other things, we take the lead and set the example! Today we celebrate the well-deserved promotion of Mrs Phillida Erskine-Brown to the front row!'

'Philly looks very fine in a silk gown, doesn't she, Rumpole?' the proud husband said to me.

'Gorgeous!' I agreed.

'And we welcome a new member of our set. Young Fiona Allways,' Ballard concluded. All around me barristers were toasting the triumph of women.

'You know, between ourselves, Philly got it because it's the Lord Chancellor's policy to appoint more *women* Q.C.s,' Erskine-Brown told me confidentially.

'How appalling.' I looked on the man with considerable sympathy. 'You're a victim of sexual discrimination!'

'But Philly's made me a promise. Next year she's going to take some time off.'

'Good. I might get my work back.'

'We're going to have' – his voice sank confidentially – 'a little companion for Tristan.'

'Isolde?' I suggested.

'Oh, really, Rumpole!'

I moved away from him as I saw Phillida in all her glory go up to Fiona, who was wearing wide trousers which, coming to just below the knees, had the appearance of a widish split skirt.

'Well done, Allways!' Phillida gave the girl an encouraging smile. 'Welcome to Chambers.'

'Thank you, Mrs Erskine-Brown.' Fiona seemed genuinely pleased. But Phillida had stopped smiling.

'Oh, just one thing, Allways. No culottes!'

'Oh,' said Fiona. 'Really?'

'If you want to get on at the Bar, and it is a pretty tough profession,' Phillida told her, 'just don't go in for those sort of baggy trouser arrangements. It's just not on.'

'No. Remember that, Fiona,' I put my oar in. 'A fellow looks so much better in a skirt.'

Rumpole and the Sporting Life

'Rumpole,' said She Who Must Be Obeyed over breakfast one morning in the mansion flat. 'We're going to the Bar Races on Saturday, aren't we?' It was less a question than a statement of fact, less a statement of fact than a Royal command. It was no use protesting, for instance, that Rumpole has never been a racing man.

Claude Erskine-Brown, somewhat disappointed in his application for silk, had come to the conclusion that a more active part in the social life of the Bar might bring him to the attention of the powers that be. He joined the Bar Golfing Society, he put up for election to the Bar Council, and he decided that it would be just as well to be seen hobnobbing with those sporting judges who patronized the Bar Races. He decided to make up a party for this event, but Ballard, quite naturally, didn't approve of gambling, and Hoskins didn't want to lose his girls' school fees on a piece of fallible horseflesh. Accordingly, it was suggested that a party should be made up of the Erskine-Browns, Henry our clerk (who, being by far the wealthiest of us, undertook to supply three or four bottles of champagne), Uncle Tom, and the Rumpoles.

'We must go, Rumpole,' Hilda said as soon as she heard of the invitation. 'Daddy always went to the Bar Races.'

I had a distant memory of attending this annual point-to-point with C. H. Wystan when he was Head of Chambers. We journeyed down to the Cotswolds in his large and hearse-like motor, feasted on ham sandwiches and rock cakes, and the warmish hock flowed like cement. Once or twice, as I remember it, Hilda Wystan was in the party, and She would be in charge of the thermos and getting her father perched on his shooting stick in time to see the end of the Barristers' Handicap.

Over the course of the years fewer barristers have been able to find the spare currency to keep horses in livery, being hard pushed to keep their nearest and dearest in regular feed and stabling. The Barristers' Races have therefore shrunk to one event in an afternoon of races for adjacent hunts and military sportsmen, but a few alcoholic juniors with a taste for hunting still put their mounts, like nervous clients, to various jumps and hazards, and a great many judges and barristers and barristers' wives dress up in old caps and trilby hats, tweeds and green padded waistcoats, and consume, with icy fingers, large picnics from the boots of their motor cars and so join happily in the Sport of Kings.

'It'll be like the old days, won't it, Rumpole?' Hilda said as she daubed the ham sandwiches with mustard and wrapped them in greaseproof paper. 'And it'll do you so much good to have a day out in the countryside.' I was already marvelling at the English longing to journey vast distances to some damp and uncomfortable place and then, with none of the normal facilities such as knives and forks and dining-room furniture, eat a packed meal. I was busy storing as many bottles as possible of the Château Fleet Street into my red robe bag in the hope that I might, with their assistance, be able to keep out the cold.

We left London at a ridiculously early hour in the Erskine-Brown Volvo Estate. Phillida Erskine-Brown, Q.C., was wearing a sort of tweed cape and deerstalker, which gave her the curious appearance of a red-headed and personable female Sherlock Holmes. Claude, a great one for uniforms, was wearing the regulation padded waistcoat and green wellies. Uncle Tom sported an old hacking jacket with leather patches, and Henry wore a tweed suit with knife-edge creases, a sheepskin car coat and had, slung about his neck, a huge pair of racing binoculars. You have the complete picture when I tell you that Hilda was in a tweed two-piece with brogues and a Burberry, and I was in the old Sunday jacket, cavalry twill bags and everyday mac. When we had all assembled in the street outside Froxbury Court, I piled my bag of booze and Hilda's sandwiches into the hatch-back, as Henry rather quaintly called it, and it was tally ho and we were off to the races. A fine drizzle was falling then, and it went on falling for the rest of the day.

The point-to-point course was a fairly representative slice of the English countryside. There was a damp and distinct prospect of fields and hedgerows and a hillside on which the cars were parked and the bookies had set up their stands. The Mecca of the place, the large tent in which food and drink were supplied, had been pitched next to the saddling enclosure. I would have wished to spend most of the afternoon under canvas, but Hilda, encouraged by Phillida Erskine-Brown, who showed considerable sporting interest, insisted on trekking down to the rails to watch the finish of each race, and then climbing back to the bookies to put money on another loser.

My involvement with the sporting life, and the events which led to one of the most interesting murder cases of the Rumpole career (I put it not far below the Penge Bungalow affair in the list of my more engaging cases) started as we were watching the three o'clock race, in which members of the adjacent hunts contested the field with a few barristers. We were positioned near to the last fence as a bunch of riders, helmeted, goggled and pounding through a cloud of flying mud, approached the high brushwood and flung their horses at it.

'Into the last fence now and it's Number 13, Atlantic Hero, owned and ridden by the Honourable Jonathan Postern of the Tester Hunt in the pink and green colours,' the loudspeaker, crackling out a rasping commentary, informed us.

'Come on, Atlantic Hero! Don't hang about, Atlantic Hero!' Hilda was shouting lustily. For the first time in a long day it seemed that one of our party had backed a winner. What with the pounding of hooves and the shouts of the aficionados, I wasn't sure that Hilda's fancied animal could hear her. And then the last horse crashed through the brushwood, landed awkwardly, deposited its rider on the ground and galloped off as though happy to be out of the contest.

'And there's another one down,' the loudspeaker crackled. 'Number 11, Tricycle. Ridden by Maurice Fishbourne of the Tester Hunt.'

Two St John Ambulancemen with a stretcher were pounding

out to the fallen rider as the victory of Atlantic Hero was announced, and Hilda sent up a resounding cheer. I looked around and saw a handsome woman in her early thirties, dressed in the regulation headscarf and padded waistcoat, running towards the fallen rider. My attention was held, I suppose, because her face seemed vaguely familiar. Her mouth was open as she ran, as though in a silent scream. And then I saw the horseless rider sit up and stretch out his hand for a pair of gold-rimmed glasses. One lens had been shattered in his fall. He seemed a slight, unsportsmanlike character, who smiled a nervous apology at the ambulancemen and then stood, unsteadily, hooking on his glasses. At this the woman in the headscarf stopped running, her mouth closed, and she turned quickly and walked away in the general direction of the refreshment tent.

'First, Number 13, Atlantic Hero. Second, Number 8, Flash point. Third, Number 4, Ironside . . .' the loudspeaker told us.

'Come along, Rumpole, for heaven's sake! We've got to collect my winnings.' Hilda was triumphant.

'What did you have on it? One quid each way?' I asked her. 'We shall be able to retire to Biarritz.'

So our group started to plod up the hill, where the increasing rain was producing yet more mud. As we made our way to the old and reliable firm where Hilda proudly collected the fruits of 50p each way, Uncle Tom and Henry were discussing form for the 3.30, the Barristers' Handicap.

'His clerk tells me that Mr Lorrimer's not all that fit,' Henry was saying. 'He's been overworking on his Revenue cases.'

'Likely to fall at the first fence.' Uncle Tom marked his race card and then asked, 'Harley Waters, Q.C., in good condition, is he? Been taking his oats and all that?'

'Rather too liberally, his clerk informs me, sir. The fancy is,' Henry lowered his voice confidentially, 'Mr E. Smith on Decree Absolute.'

'Mr Smith in good form, is he?' Uncle Tom sounded anxious.

'Teetotal, according to his clerk.' Henry had no doubts. 'And he does press-ups in Chambers.'

When bets had been laid on various members of the Bar, we went into the tent where Hilda was determined to fritter away her winnings on loose living and self-indulgence. I was bringing up the rearguard with Erskine-Brown, when I heard a dry and elderly voice calling, 'There you are, Rumpole! Ah, Erskine-Brown ...' Claude immediately raised his hat and I turned to see the small, wrinkled, parchment-coloured face, inappropriately crowned by a jaunty bowler hat, of Mr Justice Twyburne, one of the old school of spine-chilling judges of the Queen's Bench, a man so old that he had been appointed before the age for retirement was inflicted on the Judiciary, and who stayed on – to the terror of unwary criminals and barristers alike.

'I haven't had you before me lately,' said this antique Judge. 'I suppose you don't get the *serious* crime nowadays.'

'I have been engaged elsewhere,' I said loftily and looked towards the bar as an avenue of escape. 'I must join my wife. She's spending the winnings.'

'Been having a little flutter here, have you? I don't see you as a gambling man, Rumpole?' The tent was full of horsy girls in well-fitting jods, and convivial farmers. It was my fate to be stuck with this daunting old codger.

'I suppose a person can't spend a lifetime in Old Bailey trials without getting a bit of a taste for games of chance,' I told him.

'What's that supposed to mean?' Mr Justice Twyburne clearly didn't like the analogy.

'Don't you ever feel that forecasting the results of cases is rather like sticking a pin in the *Sporting Life* with your eyes shut?' I asked him.

'The aim of an English criminal trial is to do justice,' the Judge said coldly. 'I don't see how you can possibly compare it to a horse race. Good day, Erskine-Brown.' He touched the rim of his bowler with a yellow-gloved hand, and went off to pass an adverse judgement on the animals in the saddling enclosure. When he had gone, Erskine-Brown looked at me as though I had failed to stand up during the National Anthem, or had been caught filling out my football pools while doing a case in the House of Lords.

'Rumpole!' he protested. 'Twyburne's our oldest Judge.'

'I know,' I answered him with some distaste. 'One of the few survivors who's ever passed a death sentence. They say he ordered muffins at his Club after those occasions.'

And then the rider of Atlantic Hero and the author of Hilda's good fortune came into the tent, recognizable to us by his green and pink silks and his white, mud-splattered riding breeches as well as the silver cup he was carrying. He was followed by a considerable retinue, including at least two pretty girls, a tall young man with longish hair and an amused expression and, bringing up the rear, the woman who had run with such distress towards the fallen rider.

As the crackling loudspeaker had told us, the victor of the three o'clock (the Adjacent Hunts Challenge Cup) was Jonathan Postern. I was watching as the Hon. Jonathan slapped his silver trophy down on the bar and shouted to one of the fresh-faced waitresses who had just served drinks to Hilda.

'Come on, sweetheart. Fill this jerry up with champers!'

'A loving cup – Jonno, how excessively brill!' one of the pretty girls chirruped as she held the arm of the winning rider. My attention was momentarily engaged by Hilda handing me a small rum. A bit of a disappointment, I thought. With her luck I expected her at least to fill my gum boots with champagne. As I sank my nose towards the rum, I heard the dulcet tones of Miss Fiona Allways greeting Hilda and the Erskine-Browns. She was dressed like most of the other girls in a padded waistcoat, green cord trousers, a sweater and the sort of man's flat cap which charladies used to wear.

'I see you're in uniform too, Fiona,' I greeted her. 'All you khaki figures, slogging through the mud to the encampment, put me in distinct mind of the retreat from Mons.'

'You were never at the retreat from Mons,' Erskine-Brown told Fiona, unnecessarily, I thought. 'Rumpole was in the R.A.F. Ground Staff. Weren't you, Rumpole?'

'All right. It puts me in mind of the Naafi at R.A.F. Dungeness after a heavy night,' I was saying, when the woman I had seen rushing to the fallen rider came up to greet Fiona. Then I knew why I had thought there was a familiar look to her.

'Hullo, Pimpsey,' the woman said.

'Oh, hi, Sprod,' Fiona answered.

'Disgusting to see you,' said the woman, and I made the some-what obvious comment, 'You two obviously know each other.'

'My big sister, Jennifer Postern. This is Rumpole, Mrs Rumpole,' Fiona introduced us.

'How riveting!' Jennifer turned to me. 'I've heard so much about you. Pimpsey says you got her into Chambers. By some miracle!'

'Well, it was one of my trickier cases,' I admitted.

'Oh, but Pimpsey says you win them all, because you're the most super barrister in the whole of England. Absolutely brill, thinks Pimpsey.'

'Did you come on your own, Fiona?' Claude had moved away from his wife and was asking Fiona a quiet and hopeful question.

'No. With my boyfriend, Jeremy Jowling. He's rather dull, but he *is* a solicitor. He's the one doing the serious drinking.'

We looked across to the group by Jonathan Postern. Jeremy Jowling appeared to be the longish-haired, amused young man who had just received a dark brown whisky. Hilda recognized her favourite rider's racing colours then and trumpeted loudly, 'Oh look. That's my gorgeous winner!'

'I say, your wife. Is she really the one you call "She Who Must . . ."' Jennifer whispered to me.

'No. She's the one I call "Mrs Rumpole",' I answered. Hilda was, after all, almost within earshot, but her attention was still on the young man in racing silks.

'Rumpole! That's the chap who won for me. On Atlantic Hero,' she told me once again. I looked at the winner and realized how remarkably handsome he was. He had close-cropped curly hair and a straight nose, putting me in mind of those Greek statues in which the eyelids are somehow heavy with exhaustion at maintaining the heroic pose. If Jonathan Postern looked like some minor antique deity, he was surrounded by his votive priestesses. As he drank from the huge silver cup, a number of girls kissed him, none of whom was his wife.

'Such a nice-looking young man. Do you know him?' Hilda said admiringly to Jennifer, who answered, 'He's my husband.'

'Oh, really? I do feel I should thank him personally.'

'Come on then. Why don't we whizz over?'

So our group moved over towards Jonathan Postern's celebration.

Hilda, flushed with her winnings and a small rum, engaged the hero in conversation at once.

'I just had to say "Well done". It does make a day at the races so much more thrilling when you're on a winner!'

'Were you? I can't say I saw you,' Jonathan answered, and then said, in a loud aside to one of the attendant maidens, 'Who are these amazing old wrinklies?'

'This is Mr and Mrs Rumpole, Jonno. And Mr Claude Erskine-Brown.' Fiona looked at him disapprovingly.

'Mr Rumpole's a *tremendous* legal eagle,' Jennifer Postern explained to her husband.

'My God! You're not one of the galloping barristers?' the Hon. Jonathan asked me.

'Hardly.'

'None of your lot got placed. Terribly bad luck.' He raised the chalice 'Care for a swig?'

'Thank you.'

I might have saved my thanks, for I never got a drink. At that moment the rider who fell, the man whose name the loudspeaker had given as Maurice Fishbourne, muddy and with his glasses broken, came into the tent and was peering round with a look of shortsighted amiability. Jonathan raised the cup and had a long refreshing drink, ignoring me.

'Thank you very much,' I muttered.

Jonathan lowered the cup and, still holding it, looked across at Fishbourne and called, 'Fishface!'

'He's cutting us dead!' one of the maidens said.

'He's being frightfully grand,' said another.

'Come on, Fish. Don't be weedy!' a red-haired girl in a hacking jacket shouted.

Fishbourne came towards them smiling in a hopelessly ingratiating way. Hilda, who was in a mood to greet anyone, greeted him. 'Good afternoon.'

'Oh, this is Maurice Fishbourne. He lives next to Jennifer and Jonno.' Fiona was keeping her head admirably in a difficult social situation.

'D ... delighted to meet you.' Fishbourne came towards us grinning weakly. His stammer seemed as much part of his character as his broken spectacles.

'How did you manage to stick on till the last fence, Fishy? Superglue?' Jonathan bayed at him, and the entourage laughed.

'He was hanging on to the mane. I saw him!' It was Jennifer Postern, joining in.

'C ... congratulations, Jonathan.' The man Fishbourne seemed to be perfectly civil.

'Oh, aren't you a lovely loser! If you want to ride something in the next race, why not try a bicycle?'

Once again the claque laughed at Jonathan Postern's sally, and once again Jennifer joined in.

'I'm not r ... riding in the next race.' Fishbourne smiled round at the laughing faces.

'Is Mummy taking you home to tea?' Again, to my surprise, it was Jennifer who asked the question. It didn't sound kindly meant.

'I'm driving Mother home, yes, Jennifer.' Fishbourne looked at her through his broken lens.

'Come on, Fishy. Have a slug of champers!' Jonathan Postern invited him.

'Oh ... Th ... thanks.' Fishbourne took the chalice.

'It's quite all right, only got all our germs in it,' one of the girls said.

Fishbourne smiled and started to drink. Jonathan knocked the bottom of the cup sending a wave of champagne over Fishbourne's face and down his neck. He emerged wet and still grinning to look round at his tormentors as though delighted to afford them all a little harmless fun.

At the next memorable breakfast we shared at Froxbury Court I noticed, in a state of considerable shock, that Hilda was reading *Country Life*. Not only did she read it to herself, she gave me a nugget from this strange periodical.

'"Lodge for sale on gentleman's estate, in wooded country near Tester."'

'Why are you reading that, Hilda?' I asked her. 'Were there no *Daily Telegraphs*?'

'"Three bedrooms, two receps, with access to good, rough shooting",' she went on. 'Doesn't that sound attractive, Rumpole?'

'I honestly think I have enough troubles in my life without you taking up rough shooting.'

'What did you say?'

'I said it might be more peaceful in Tooting. Or in Gloucester Road. Or round the Inner London Sessions, or the Old Bailey. I mean, there you can go out for a walk without being in imminent danger of a charge of buckshot or whatever it is.'

'Nonsense, Rumpole!' Hilda was flicking over glossy pages full of Georgian manor houses and sporting prints. 'That day at the Bar Races made me realize what we're missing.'

'Mud?' I suggested.

'The countryside, Rumpole! Now, if we sold our lease here . . .'

'We could buy a deer park, and a Palladian mansion. Fancy having your *Country Life* ironed by the butler?'

'Daddy always said that what a barrister needed was a place in the country,' Hilda said with quiet dignity.

'13 Acacia Road, Horsham. Wasn't that your Daddy's stately home?' I asked as I folded up *The Times*, preparing for my journey to the Temple.

'Can't you see us, Rumpole?' Hilda began to look distinctly dreamy. 'Sitting by a log fire, taking a glass of sherry, perhaps, as the sun sets over the home wood . . .'

'I see us with the boiler out, and all trains to London cancelled, and mud up to your elbows.' I stood up, gulping coffee. 'And out in the home wood there's bound to be someone killing something.'

Not long after that an elderly man called Figgis, who lived in a cottage in the woods on Jonathan Postern's Tester estate heard a shot and a woman's cry. He ran out of his overgrown garden and, just outside his tangled hedge, propped up against a fallen tree, he saw the dead body of the rider and owner of Atlantic Hero. Standing not a dozen yards away from him and holding a shotgun was Fiona's sister, Jennifer. Figgis asked her what had happened and her answer was one that was going to prove a serious problem to her defending counsel. 'I did it,' she said, and added, somewhat lamely, 'It was an accident.'

*

'Sprod wants you to defend her,' Fiona said.

'That's because you've been giving your sister a quite exagger-ated view of my abilities in matters of shotgun wounds, murder and sudden death,' I told her.

'Is it really possible to exaggerate your abilities?'

'Perhaps not,' I said modestly.

'Why shouldn't my sister have the best counsel available?'

She sat down in my client's chair. I lit a small cigar and looked at her. She had rushed back from Court to see me when she heard the news. Still in her stiff white collar and bands, she looked absurdly young, like a distressed choirboy.

'Friends,' I said.

'What?' She frowned, puzzled.

'One rule at the Bar, Fiona. Never appear for friends. Your judgement gets blurred. You care too much. You can't see the weaknesses in your own case. And if you lose, of course, they never, ever forgive you.'

'My sister's not your friend. Quite honestly, you hardly know her.'

'But I know you, Fiona.' I hoped I sounded gentle.

'Of course, but . . .'

'All the trouble I had to get you in here! I did it by some pretty ruthless manoeuvring, if you want to know the truth. And then to have to spend the rest of my life avoiding your eye in the clerk's room, ducking over to the other side of the road when I saw you walking back from the Bailey, and never feeling safe to pop into Pommeroy's for a strengthener in case I found you staring at me more in sorrow than in anger because I lost your sister's case. Life would be intolerable!'

'I do understand that,' she admitted. 'But . . .'

'But me no buts, Fiona,' I said firmly.

'I was only going to say, "But you're not going to lose it, are you?"'

So, in the course of time, and much against my better judge-ment, I found myself sitting in the corner of a railway carriage, studying a brief which contained a bundle of not uninteresting mortuary photographs. I was on my way to Tester Crown Court, to play my part in the case of the Queen against Jennifer Postern.

*

In London you hardly ever see death, I thought, as I looked from the photograph of the wounded body of Jonathan Postern to the fields and woodlands, the streams and bridges, the grey-stone houses and farm buildings of the Cotswold countryside. Once or twice in a lifetime, you may see an old age pensioner, perhaps, collapsed on a cold night in the tube, or a shape under a blanket and a small crowd as you drive past an accident.

In that peaceful landscape they saw death every day. They watched hounds tearing foxes to pieces or coursing hares. They hung up magpies and jays in the woods as a warning to others. No doubt at the end of the garden I saw from the passing train there was some retired naval man tearfully putting down his dog. Death is a routine event in the country. Well, I asked myself, what's a husband more or less in the shooting season?

And then we were in the outskirts of a grey, stony town. The train gasped to a standstill and I heard a porter calling, 'Tester! Change here for Deepside and Watching Junction.'

When I got outside the station, burdened, as usual on my travels, with my suitcase, briefcase and robe bag, I was hailed by the young man I had seen briefly in Jonathan Postern's entourage, and who had been pointed out as the boyfriend of Miss Fiona Allways.

'Horace Rumpole!' he was calling as he tried to stuff an ex-tremely large and melancholy-looking dog into the back seat of a battered sports car. 'Do hop in. I'm Jeremy Jowling, instructing you. Don't mind Agatha. She's a soppy old date really. Here, let me take your luggage.' As we put my travelling wardrobe into his boot, I fitted myself with some difficulty into the sports car. The front seat was covered with dog hairs and the Hound of the Baskervilles was breathing lugubriously down my neck.

'Where'd you like to go first,' young Jowling said as he forced himself into the driver's seat and switched on the engine. 'The Tester Arms or the prison?'

'Which is the least uncomfortable?' I asked him.

'I'd say the prison. Run you there, shall I? I must say it's all a G.M.B.U. . . . .'

'G.M.B.U.?' I asked, puzzled, as we roared off through the heart of Tester.

'Grand Military Balls-up,' he explained. 'Years since we had a murder in the Tester Hunt. Well, it'll get those dotty blood sports protestors going. Agatha! For God's sake don't kiss Mr Rumpole!'

I had, in fact, felt the slap of a warm tongue on the back of the neck. I leant forward and lit a small cigar. As he squeaked past a bus and slipped by as the light went red, I wondered how useful Fiona's swain would be in the coming trial.

'You're a partner?' I asked him.

'In Jowling and Leonard. My old man's firm, quite honestly. But he doesn't care for murder. So he handed this case on to me. "Well, my boy," he said. "You may as well start at the bottom . . ." You knew Jonathan Postern at all?'

'Only momentarily.'

'People round here had a tremendous lot of time for Jonno.'

'I'm sorry.' I meant it.

'What?'

'It's not what you need in a murder case, a well-liked corpse.'

'Well, you'd know about that, wouldn't you? Agatha. Don't kiss! I shan't tell you again. Only one trouble with Jonno Postern. He had a bad case of the M.T.F.s.'

'The *what*?' The young man seemed to need a simultaneous translation.

'Must Touch Flesh! Particularly the flesh of Debbie Pavier. Well, that's what the row was all about, wasn't it? A Grand Military Shout-up. I mean, if it hadn't been for that the constabulary might have taken Sprod's story about an accident, and no questions asked.'

'Debbie Pavier?' I asked. 'Was she the girl who was kissing him in the tent at the races?'

'One of them, yes. All the girls were crazy about Jonno.'

Tester prison was a smallish Victorian castle, not far from the centre of town. Jennifer Postern had been brought up from Holloway and we sat in a small, dark interview room and I rummaged in my brief and asked her questions. She seemed remarkably calm and self-possessed. She had none of the prison pallor I was used to in my clients, but seemed to bring into the stuffy little room a fresh breeze from the countryside.

'It was an accident,' she told me, as she had told the old man Figgis.

'Your housekeeper says you were quarrelling with your husband that afternoon.'

'Bit of a hangover. After some serious drinking the night before.'

'Do you remember saying something about "killing him"?'

'Isn't it the sort of thing one says?' Jennifer asked with a smile.

'Is it?'

'Well, don't you quarrel sometimes, with She Who . . .?'

'Happily, neither of us owns a shotgun.' I meant it. 'After the quarrel your husband went out?'

'Jonno wanted a walk, I suppose. To cool off.'

'And so did you?'

'Yes. I went out after he did.'

'And you took your twenty-bore with you?'

'You know something about guns?' For the first time, I thought, she looked a little worried.

'A little. Why did you take it?'

'I thought it might calm my nerves if I shot something.'

'Not the most tactful way of explaining your feelings to the jury.' I ground out the end of a small cigar on the tin ashtray on the table.

'I meant rough shooting. A rabbit, perhaps, or a pigeon or . . .'

'The gun was loaded when you met your husband in the wood?'

'Of course.'

'And the safety catch?'

'I put up a pheasant and I was about to have a shot, and then I remembered it was after February. Closed season for pheasants.' But not for husbands, I thought, but didn't say, as Jennifer went on, 'I must have forgotten to put the safety catch on again. I walked on a little.'

'Down the track in the wood?' I had another bundle of photographs in my brief, not of the mortuary but of rural scenes.

'Yes.'

'And then?'

She paused, seemed to be in some difficulty, and looked to the young solicitor for help. 'I've told Jeremy,' she said.

'Tell me.'

Her hesitation didn't last long. She took in a deep breath and said, 'I saw Jonno coming towards me.'

'He was still angry?'

'No, I don't think so. He looked perfectly calm, actually.'

'And you?'

'Oh, I was calm enough. I walked towards him. The track was rough, you know. Brambles. It needed clearing. And I must have tripped and . . . Well, that's how it happened.'

I looked at her in silence and then slapped my pockets. 'You don't have a small cigar about you?'

'No.' She was smiling and seemed relieved.

'Stupid of me. I must have left them in the car.' I turned to Jeremy Jowling. 'Your dog's probably guarding them with her fangs bared.'

'I'll whizz out and get them. Back in a jiff.'

Jeremy went obediently. I sat looking at Jennifer. 'He's one of your lot, isn't he?' I asked her when we were alone.

'Jeremy? Well, we knew his father, of course,' Jennifer answered vaguely.

'One of your lot,' I stood and spoke my mind to her. 'But I'm not. I don't wear green welly boots. I don't travel with a firearm and a bloody great mastiff in the back of my car. I'm even unfamiliar with your language – which seems to me to have been designed for the express purpose of saying nothing at all. I have landed in your midst, Mrs Postern, like a creature from outer space. You can speak to me as to a perfect stranger.'

'What do you want me to say?' She was smiling up at me with maddening politeness.

'Anything you think I ought to know.'

There was a pause. She continued to smile and then said, as she had always done, 'It was an accident.'

The Postern house was a long, grey Georgian manor in a small park which was bounded by the woods. The rough track I had seen in the photograph started at the edge of the parkland and passed the hedge which surrounded a small, tumbledown cottage. That afternoon I stood on the track near to a fallen tree, holding a shotgun in my hands. The weapon was the property of my instructing solicitor and I held it as though I were about to shoot a startled and unwary pheasant. Then I stumbled on the rough and overgrown ground and brought the gun up to point to Jeremy Jowling's chest, roughly the area in which Jonathan Postern had received the fatal charge of shot.

'I suppose it's possible,' I speculated. 'More likely I'd've shot your feet off, though.'

Jeremy took the gun from me gently.

> 'Never, never let your gun
> Pointed be at anyone.
> That it should unloaded be
> Matters not the least to me.'

'Come again?'

'You don't know that?' He sounded incredulous.

'No. We must have learnt different nursery rhymes.' Then an uncomfortable thought struck me. 'Jennifer Postern would've known it, though, wouldn't she? She must have learnt gun training on her Nanny's knee.' I was looking moodily at the ground, the trees and the bushes, the track that runs through the wood.

'Her father was a terrific shot. Runs in the family. What are you looking at?'

'The scene of the crime,' I told him. 'The *locus* in *quo*.'

'What do you do now?' Jeremy was interested to know. 'Crawl about on your hands and knees collecting bits of cigarette ash in an old envelope?'

'Not exactly. The *locus* in *quo* looks just like any old bit of the English countryside to me.'

I moved a little way along the track to a sign on a post, which bore the direction TO BADGER'S WOOD, and a picture of the appropriate animal.

'Where's that lead to?' I asked. 'More Postern country?'

'Fishbourne country, actually.'

'Who?'

'Maurice Fishbourne. Something of a weed with a good deal of money. Gets ragged a lot for trying to ride at point-to-points. Invariably hits the deck.'

'Fishface!' Yes, of course I remembered.

'You know him?'

'Hardly at all. He isn't a friend of the Posterns?'

'They can't stand him. No one can, actually. He's not P.L.U. exactly.'

'People Like Us?' I hazarded a guess.

'Well, he puts up those poncy little signs on his land and gets all his cash from laxatives: "Fishbourne's keep you regular."'

I was looking at the top windows of the cottage which were visible above the tangled hedge. 'I rely on medicinal claret myself,' I told him. And then I was startled by a raucous cry, coming from somewhere quite near us. It was a strangely sad sound, like the lament for some irreparable loss. 'What the hell's that?' I asked Jeremy. 'Someone in pain?'

'Not at all. That is a yell of pure randiness. Look, I'll show you.' He led me to a gap in the hedge and a gate into the untended cottage garden. And there, on the grass, was a rough coop in which a plump brown bird with a beady eye was imprisoned and letting people know about it. 'That's a calling bird. A cock pheasant,' Jeremy told me.

> 'A calling pheasant in a cage,
> Puts all Heaven in a rage,'

I suggested, and went on,

> 'The wanton boy that kills the fly
> Shall feel the spider's enmity.'

'Figgis, the old devil who lives here, keeps it to entice all the Postern pheasants into his front garden. Of course, when they get there he knocks them off from his front window with a shotgun. Cunning isn't it?'

'Did Jonathan Postern know he was being robbed?'

'I suppose he just let it go on. He couldn't get Figgis out of the cottage. Old Jonno was a bit of an innocent in spite of everything.'

I was looking at the cottage. A thin line of smoke was coming out of the chimney. 'Did you say "Figgis"?'

'I bet he's in there. Want to talk to him?'

'Talk to a prosecution witness?' I looked at Jeremy with deep disapproval. 'Not sporting, old fellow. Definitely not sporting.'

But as we moved away I saw a shape behind the blurred glass of a downstairs window. The prosecution witness was no doubt watching us with interest.

When I got to know the Tester Arms Hotel I realized how right Jeremy Jowling had been to take me straight to the prison. That evening I had what was known as the 'set meal': Pâté Maison in the form of liver ice-cream, a steak from the rump of some elderly animal lightly singed under the X-ray machine, a cheeseboard aptly named because the Cheddar tasted exactly like wood, and a bottle of chilled claret which made Pommeroy's plonk seem like Château-Lafite.

I didn't sleep well that night. It wasn't just the firewood in the mattress, or the intense cold, or the noise in the water pipes like a giant's indigestion. I had sat up until well after midnight reading the post mortem report of a certain Dr Overton, a local man no doubt and hitherto unknown to me, and looking again and again at the photographs of the wound. Thoughts about shotguns raced through my head all night, and in the dawn I ordered the cooked breakfast which was there in about an hour's time, cold as charity but better than dinner. At exactly nine o'clock I put through a call to the Forensic Department at St Cuthbert's Hospital in London and asked to speak to Professor Andrew Ackerman.

There are two people in England who know most of what there is to know about bloodstains: Horace Rumpole and Professor Andrew Ackerman. I have crossed swords with the good Prof across many a courtroom, one of the most recent occasions being in the case of a strange young man who fell in with an appalling religious sect. It was a case which turned on a nice point of blood, and I think I got one up on Ackerman on that occasion.[*] We are firm friends, however, and once a year Andrew Ackerman invites me to lunch at the Athenaeum, where we discuss various corpses of our acquaintance over a chop. My night thoughts on

* See *Rumpole's Return*, Penguin Books, 1980.

the Postern case had convinced me that what I now needed was a bit of help from the good Professor. By good fortune I got hold of him before he went down to the morgue, and the conversation we had about shotgun wounds was long and enthralling.

In due course young Jeremy Jowling came up to my room to fetch me for the *corrida* and, as I buttoned myself into the black jacket and waistcoat, I asked him if he'd read Dr Overton's report.

'I've glanced at it,' Jeremy said.

I was tying up my brief. 'Sure of himself, our Dr Overton. Perhaps a little too sure of himself for an *experienced* pathologist. Know anything about him?'

'Never heard of him. Gravely usually does all the stiffs for the Home Office.'

'How interesting!' I was checking the robes, and fitting the thick bundle of papers into my briefcase.

'What're our chances?' Jeremy Jowling asked with a small show of nerves.

'Speaking as a sporting man – you'd like to know the odds?'

'Any better than evens?'

'It's not exactly an easy defence,' I admitted. 'But she's a woman. She was probably badly treated by her husband. All we need is a sympathetic judge.'

And then young Jeremy Jowling dropped his bombshell. 'We've got a fellow called Mr Justice Twyburne,' he said, as though he were referring to the state of the weather. I must confess that the Rumpole jaw dropped.

'What do you think?' He must have noticed my dismay.

'I think – the odds have lengthened considerably.'

'Why? What's he like then?'

I sat down, recovered my breath, lit a small cigar to steady my nerves and asked young Jowling if he remembered Martin Muschamp.

'No . . .'

'One of the last death penalty cases. He went out with a gang, and was tried for shooting a copper. Twyburne summed up dead against him. Couple of years later another boy confessed and Marty Muschamp was cleared by a Home Office Inquiry.'

'That was all right then,' Jeremy suggested.

'Oh, lovely for everyone. Except for Martin Muschamp. He'd already been hanged.' I got up and went to the door. 'Don't worry too much. We don't do that sort of thing any more.'

Mervyn Harmsway was a pleasant, middle-aged prosecutor, who, so I was told, had a pretty Queen Anne house in Tester, and an impressive collection of Crown Derby. He opened the case perfectly fairly in the chilly atmosphere of Twyburne's Court, and the old Judge, more paper-coloured than ever, listened without expression.

The Court was full. I recognized a few faces, including the pretty girls who had kissed Jonno at the point-to-point. Fiona was in mufti on the bench behind me, and her sister smiled at her, apparently unworried, from the dock. The solid-looking county jury listened to Harmsway as though they were determined not to let anyone know what they were thinking.

'That is all I have to say in opening this sad case, members of the jury,' Harmsway finished. 'And now, with the assistance of my learned friend Mr Gavin Pinker, I hope to fairly put the evidence before you.'

'You are causing me a great deal of pain, Mr Harmsway.' A dry voice came from the Bench.

'I'm sorry, my Lord?' Harmsway looked puzzled.

'Please. Don't split them.' The Judge was looking extremely pained.

'Don't split what, my Lord?'

'Your infinitives!' his Lordship cracked back. 'This is a distressing case, in all conscience. Do we have to add to the disagreeable nature of the proceedings the sound of you tormenting the English language? You hope to put the evidence fairly.'

'Yes, my Lord.' Harmsway looked cowed.

'Then why don't you start to do it?' Twyburne asked testily.

'My learned friend, Mr Pinker, will call the first witness.'

Poor old Harmsway subsided, deflated, to his seat. His junior, Gavin Pinker, who seemed made of sterner stuff, rose and announced that he would now call Mrs Marian Hempe. As the Posterns' dear old housekeeper waddled into the witness-box and took the oath, Harmsway whispered to me bitterly, 'What a charming Judge!'

'Don't worry, old darling,' I comforted him. 'Twyburne's quite impartial. He'll be just as ghastly to me.' And then I turned my attention to the dialogue between Mrs Hempe and Mr Gavin Pinker.

'Mrs Hempe. How long have you worked for the Posterns?' Pinker started quietly.

'Ten years now, for Master Jonathan. And his father before him.'

'You don't live in?'

'I comes on my bicycle. They drive me home if it's a late dinner.'

'On the afternoon that Jonathan Postern died ... did you hear anything going on, between him and his wife?'

'Yes. They was quarrelling, like. In the sitting room. I could hear voices.'

'Whose voices?'

'Both, I reckon.'

'Could you hear any words?'

'I hear two words.'

'What were they?'

'"Kill you" – I heard that said. Loud. By her.'

'By Mrs Postern.' Pinker paused to let the evidence sink in. 'And after that?'

'Then I see Mr Postern go out. He walked towards the woods.'

'What happened then?'

'Mrs Postern stayed indoors. Then *she* went out.'

'How long did she stay out?'

'I don't rightly know. Ten minutes, quarter of an hour perhaps. Then she came back and got it.'

'Got what?'

Mrs Hempe pursed her lips as though about to have to mention some indelicacy, looked at the jury and said, 'Her shotgun.'

'Did you see her get it?' Pinker asked.

'No. But I see her go out with it under her arm. She went back towards the woods again.'

'That is the direction Mr Postern had taken?'

'Yes.'

'What happened next? Just tell the jury.'

'I heard a shot from the wood,' Mrs Hempe just told the jury.

'From the way they'd both gone.'

'Yes.'

'Thank you, Mrs Hempe.'

Gavin Pinker consulted Harmsway, who took the view that Mrs Hempe had done all that could be expected of her to scupper the defence, and I rose to cross-examine. I knew I would get nowhere at all by calling Mrs Hempe a liar, so I began to investigate the points that interested me, hoping to get the cooperation of the good Mrs Hempe.

'You heard *one* shot?' I asked her.

'No. I heard others.'

'You heard others. When?'

'I heard some shooting from the wood. That was before Mrs Postern went out.'

'But after *Mr* Postern went out?'

'Yes?'

'After *Mrs* Postern went out, how many shots did you hear?'

'Just one.'

'Are you sure of that?'

'I'll take my Bible oath to it.' Mrs Hempe sounded nettled.

'Just *one* shot and that is all?'

'It was enough, wasn't it?'

The jury nodded in sympathy with the witness. I hurried on to another topic. 'Now, you heard these words, "Kill you". You've sworn that was all you heard her say?'

'That's right.'

I took my courage in my hands and launched an extremely dangerous question. 'You didn't hear her say, "*I'll* kill you", for instance?' I suggested, and held my breath until the witness gave me a hesitant and reluctant, 'No.'

'So she might possibly have been warning him that someone else might kill him?'

'I suppose so,' Mrs Hempe sounded extremely grudging. 'But she was the only one there, wasn't she?'

'Exactly.' Twyburne was no longer able to restrain himself.

'Are you suggesting that someone else might have killed him, Mr Rumpole?'

'My Lord. I was merely exploring the possibilities.' I gave the old darling my most charming smile and sat down.

Sometime during that morning I glanced up at the public gallery and saw the face of Maurice Fishbourne staring down at me through a new pair of spectacles. Mr Figgis from the cottage in the woods near the Postern house was in the witness-box. He was a grizzled, stooping man in his late sixties, I judged, wearing an old torn tweed jacket. He was imperfectly shaved, and his shirt looked as though it hadn't been washed for some time. He was an old man who lived alone. Harmsway took him through his evidence-in-chief and then I rose to cross-examine.

'When did you first see Mrs Postern on that day?'

'When she was holding the shotgun. Standing about ten yards off him.' Figgis was only too anxious to repeat his evidence.

'Eventually you took the gun off her and broke it open?'

'I did, yes.'

'How many cartridges had been fired?'

'Just the one.' Figgis seemed to think the evidence damning, but I blessed him silently for it.

'Just the one,' I repeated for the jury. 'You ejected the spent cartridge?'

'Yes.'

'And did you go with her back to the house where she telephoned the police?'

'I did.' The old man seemed proud of the important part he played in these stirring events.

'And was her gun in your possession until the police arrived?'

'Yes.'

'I'm much obliged.' I gave the jury another look. 'Now, when you first saw Mrs Postern, what did she say, *exactly*?'

'She said, "*I* did it. It was an accident."'

'She said, "*I* did it." Might it not have been, "I *did* it"?'

'Is there a dispute as to what your client said, Mr Rumpole?' Twyburne was irritated at what he clearly thought was a quibble.

'No dispute as to what she said, my Lord. I am only interested to discover where the emphasis was put.'

'*You* may be interested in that, Mr Rumpole. It remains to be seen in the fullness of time whether the point interests the jury.' Twyburne looked at the jury and sighed heavily. The solid citizens continued to give nothing away.

'It may be a question of some importance, my Lord.'

'The words are there.' And then Twyburne delivered himself into my hands. 'How they were said seems to be a matter of unimportant insignificance,' he said weightily.

'May I suggest that it might be better to say, "of insignificance", my Lord.' I was extremely polite.

'What?' The Judge looked as puzzled as Harmsway had been on a similar occasion.

'"Unimportant insignificance" might be a bit of a tautology, might it not? Something of a torment to the English language,' I suggested innocently. The barristers in Court seemed too stunned to laugh. There was a moment's appalled silence when it seemed that the Judge might be prepared to commit me for Contempt of Court. Then he said quietly, 'Ask your question, Mr Rumpole.'

'Thanks awfully.' Harmsworth gave me a whisper of gratitude, and I whispered back, 'Don't mention it.' Then I asked Figgis again if he could remember how Jennifer Postern had emphasized the words of her admission.

'She said, "*I* did it,"' he decided, after a good deal of thought.

'Now I wonder why she said that,' I speculated. 'There was no one *else* about who could have done it, was there?'

'Not as I could see.'

'Not that you could see.' I gave the jury time to think about that answer and then attacked another subject.

'Mr Figgis. Do you keep a calling pheasant?'

'I don't know what you mean,' he protested.

'Oh, I think you do. A cock bird in a cage whose cries invite numerous lady pheasants to visit your front garden when you knock them off from your downstairs window. So far as I can gather, you must have pheasant for breakfast, dinner and tea.'

That got a small laugh from the jury. Figgis smiled modestly. 'Maybe I does a bit of that,' he admitted.

'Mr Rumpole. This witness is not on trial for poaching.' Twyburne was getting edgy. 'Has this evidence the slightest relevance to this case?'

'No doubt the jury will tell us that, my Lord. In the fullness of time.' I turned back to the witness before the Judge could get at me again. 'On the day you have been telling us about . . .'

'The day I see Mr Postern dead?'

'That's it. What had you been doing that afternoon?'

'I was in my cottage.'

'And as usual you were doing a bit of shooting, were you?'

'I may have been . . .' His answer was extremely reluctant.

'And your cottage is not more than fifteen yards from the scene of this alleged crime?'

'Mr Rumpole!' The Judge came to Figgis's rescue. 'May I remind you that your client admitted shooting her husband with a shotgun and shotgun wounds and pellets were found in her husband's body.'

'Your Lordship may remind me of that, but I can assure you I haven't forgotten it. Thank you, Mr Figgis.' I smiled politely at the Judge, the witness, the jury and anyone else I could think of and sat down. Harmsway announced that he had no further questions for the witness.

'Very well.' Mr Justice Twyburne looked at the clock, and gave a small, wintry smile at the jury. 'Members of the jury. This may be a convenient moment for you to obtain some refreshment. Be back at ten past two, please.'

So the Judge rose. As I was about to leave, Fiona came up to me and asked if I was coming down to see 'Sprod'.

'I don't think so,' I told her. 'Not till she's ready to tell me what happened.'

At which moment the Judge's clerk came up to me and said he had a message from his master.

'Am I under arrest?'

'On the contrary, sir. You're invited to lunch in the lodgings.'

'This case is full of surprises.'

'The car's outside. We travel in robes, sir.'

On my way out to the Judge's Rolls, I saw Maurice Fishbourne. He was standing on the pavement outside the Court, and he seemed about to speak to me, but then he changed his mind and turned away.

The invitation to take lunch in the Judges' 'lodgings', referred to above, may require some explanation for those not deeply versed in legal matters. In the olden days judges, barristers and their respective clerks and hangers-on, used to roll up in large coaches on circuit from one Assize town to the other, emptying the jails and usually despatching their inhabitants to some further proceedings beyond the grave. Each town had to provide fitting accommodation for the judges' regular visits. A house was set aside, provided with silver, decanters, wine and servants, bed linen and firewood and all appropriate comforts by the municipality, and was known as the 'Judges' lodging'.

Although the same enlightened planner (his name now escapes me) who abolished the greater part of the railways also cut out the circuit system – as though it were a rather slow branch line from Ashby de la Zouch – Red Judges, Judges of the Queen's Bench, still go on tour and sit to try criminal cases in provincial centres and once there, become prisoners in their own lodgings. They are waited on by elderly retainers, they have no worries about queueing at Tesco's, and they find it difficult to go to the pictures without a police escort. I have often wondered what would induce anyone to sentence themselves to such long terms of confinement.

The lodgings, of course, are usually large and pleasant old houses, and the one at Tester was no exception. It was of a warm red brick, much decorated by honeysuckle and clematis and surrounded by a carefully manicured lawn. We had travelled there with a couple of policemen on motorbikes as outriders and I resisted a strong temptation to wave in a royal fashion to a little crowd of women at a bus stop. We left our wigs on the hall table, where they lay like dead and dirty white birds while we ate in our robes. Twyburne sat at the head of the table, Rumpole for the defence on his right, and Harmsway and Pinker on his left. The lunch, which was plain but excellent, passed without any particular embarrassment, except that Twyburne ignored me and addressed all his remarks to the prosecution team. As the butler served coffee and put the decanter of port on the table, Twyburne was finishing a well-used anecdote.

'"He sat beside me in the cinema, sir," said the girl in the indecency case, "and put his hand up my skirt." "Very well," said the old Recorder, with his eye on the clock at lunchtime, "I suggest we leave it there until five past two."'

Twyburne's shoulders heaved and he laughed soundlessly at this. Pinker and Harmsway burst into almost uncontrollable mirth, and the Judge pushed the decanter in their direction. I was not laughing, and perhaps it was because he felt some sort of a challenge that the Judge turned to me for the first time.

'Well now. No more arguments about grammar this afternoon, eh, Rumpole?' he said.

'Possibly not.' I was making no promises.

'All the same, you stood up to me pretty well.' Twyburne was smiling in a patronizing sort of way. 'That's what we need in our job. Guts and determination to stick to an argument.'

'Even if it's wrong?' I asked him.

'Mistakes can usually be put right.' He took an apple from a dish in front of him and began to peel it slowly and with great accuracy. Still angry at being ignored over the last half-hour, I said, 'I suppose not in the death penalty days.'

'Oh, you're thinking of the young fellow who went out on the robbery. Case where they shot a policeman?' Twyburne spoke vaguely, as though it were a minor matter that had happened a long time ago.

'Martin Muschamp,' I reminded him firmly.

'Muschamp. Yes. Nothing else I could have done about that. I summed up the evidence – it was pretty damning, of course – and I left the matter to the jury.' He had finished peeling the apple now, and divided it into neat quarters.

'So it was just the luck of the draw, really?' I asked him.

'All this argument about the death penalty. We managed to take it in our stride. Did our duty. We didn't enjoy it, of course. Lot of nonsense talked about judges eating muffins after death sentences. Well, you couldn't get muffins in the Army and Navy Club.' He looked at me and seemed to be waiting for a comment, or an apology. I didn't oblige him. 'All you could do was sum up and leave the matter to the jury.' There was a new note in his voice now. It was no longer the voice of a Judge, but of an advocate, pleading for something. At last he said, 'Nothing else I could do, was there?'

I had a sudden feeling that Mr Justice Twyburne wanted to be forgiven, but who was I to forgive him? The only answer I had was, 'I don't know.'

A long silence followed and ended when Twyburne popped a quarter of the apple in to his mouth, chewed it and asked, 'Are you a gardener, Rumpole?'

'I'm afraid not.' I was no use to him.

'Excuse me, Judge, where . . .?' Harmsway asked, and when the Judge told him it was on the right just outside the door, he left, followed by his learned junior.

'I'm a rose man myself,' the Judge told me when we were left alone. 'Of course, it's been difficult to get round all the pruning since my wife died. Come and look at this.' Twyburne got up and went to the sideboard. I knew now, without a doubt, that he wanted me to feel pity for him. He took a silver-framed photograph off the long stretch of mahogany. I was looking at two little girls in the garden.

'The Mrs Sam Macreadys are flowering well, don't you think? And that's two of the grandchildren. I've got six now, altogether. This one's the budding show-jumper.'

He put the photograph down slowly and looked at me. He seemed very tired and enormously old. 'I think I summed up Muschamp quite fairly,' he said.

'Didn't you tell the jury they might well not believe a word of his evidence?' I wasn't letting him off.

'That was my personal opinion. They were quite free to come to their own conclusion, wouldn't you agree?'

I said nothing. I didn't want to give him what he wanted from me, not even a crumb of comfort. We stood facing each other in silence for a moment, and then Harmsway came back from the lavatory.

'So kind of you, Judge,' he said. 'Such an agreeable luncheon.'

*

When we had made our royal progress back to Court I cross-examined Detective Inspector Clover, the comfortable, rubicund local officer in charge of the case. I took hold of Exhibit One, which was Jennifer Postern's shotgun, and held it up for his inspection. I put my questions gently. I was saving all my strength for the coming battle with Dr Overton, the pathologist.

'This was the gun that fired the shot. You're satisfied of that, Inspector?'

'Quite satisfied, sir.'

'It was, of course, immediately submitted to the ballistics expert, Mr Collinson, whose evidence has been read. You know his view is that only one barrel had been fired within the hours before he saw it?'

'Yes.'

'And you found one cartridge case and one only at the scene of the crime?'

'Yes.'

'So your view of this case, after the most thorough inquiries by the police, is that Mrs Postern fired one shot at her husband and one shot only?'

The good Inspector turned to the Judge and gave me what I wanted. 'That is absolutely clear, my Lord,' he said.

'Absolutely clear.' I looked at the jury, willing them to remember what he'd said, and then I let the Inspector go.

Dr Overton was young and extremely pleased with himself. He stood in the witness-box, with his reports and the mortuary photographs spread out in front of him, and lectured us as though we were a collection of housewives taking a course in elementary pathology on the University of the Air. He smiled at the jury after every answer and, when addressed by the Judge, he bowed like an over-eager hall porter working his way up to a generous tip. He wore a neat blue suit, his hair came over the tops of his ears, and he sported a small moustache. As Harmsway took him through his evidence, I stirred in my seat restlessly. I couldn't wait for my turn to cross-examine.

'Dr Overton, have you investigated previous cases of death by shotgun wounds?' I began, when my opportunity came at last.

'I think one.' He smiled modestly at the jury.

'Just one. And have you been called on to give evidence in a murder trial before?'

'Well, no. Not, actually . . .'

'Congratulations on your debut.' I gave him a smile for which he wasn't grateful. 'Why was it that you were called in to perform the post mortem in this most important case? Is not Dr Gravely the most experienced and aptly named Home Office pathologist for the Tester district?'

'Dr Gravely was away at a conference in Scarborough. I was called in at short notice.'

'And saw your big chance?'

'His big chance of *what*, Mr Rumpole?' Twyburne didn't like my tone with the young doctor.

'Perhaps your big chance of ingratiating yourself with the local police by agreeing with their conclusions?' I suggested.

'I did agree with their conclusions, yes.'

'And with their view that Jonathan Postern's body had received the impact of one, and only one, shotgun wound.'

'That was my conclusion.' The doctor gave the Judge another small bow, and Twyburne gave him a shadowy smile of approval.

'From which we may draw the inference that it was the shot from Mrs Postern's gun which caused his death, either deliberately, or by accident?'

'Yes.' Dr Overton felt it was quite safe to agree.

'Shotgun pellets enter the body at one central point surrounded by an area of scatter?'

'That's true.'

'And the area of scatter is larger if the gun has been fired from a greater distance.' Elementary, of course, but I wanted also to give the jury a lesson in first principles.

'I agree.' Dr Overton was clearly feeling that he was emerging from my cross-examination unscathed. I was doing my best to lure him into a false sense of security. 'I'm glad you do. Take Photograph Three, if you will.'

The witness, the Judge and the jury opened the volume of mortuary photographs.

'You have made a pencil circle round the entry hole which you consider fatal. It's the right side of the chest in the jury's photograph.'

'I see that, yes.'

'That is where you consider the fatal shot entered?'

'I'm sure of it.'

'Absolutely positive?'

'I have no doubts whatever on the subject, Mr Rumpole.' For a moment I felt sorry for the young doctor – he was so sure of everything. I hardened my heart and said, 'There is another, smaller wound to the left, and a little above that, is there not? Perhaps you would like to borrow my glass?' I held out a magnifying glass, but the doctor scorned its assistance.

'No. I can see perfectly well, thank you.'

'Is that the darker spot on the photograph? Just show us where you're looking.' Twyburne was following carefully. Dr Overton held up his photograph and pointed and then gave another little bow.

'Yes. At about two o'clock from the pencil circle, members of the jury,' said the Judge. The jury found it and some nodded.

'What did you take *that* to be?' I asked the witness.

'I took that to be part of the scatter,' the doctor said very positively, hoping that would settle the matter. It didn't.

'Could it not be the central wound of a second shot, fired, perhaps, from some yards further away?' I suggested. I was rewarded by a considerable pause and when Dr Overton spoke again it was with rather less confidence. 'I suppose that's a possibility.'

'It wasn't a minute ago, was it, Dr Overton?'

'*Just* a possibility, my Lord,' the witness appealed to the Judge, but got no help.

'So when you told us you were absolutely certain there was only one shot, you were giving this jury an opinion which was not entirely reliable.' I saw the jury looking fairly sternly at the witness.

'I see no reason to suppose that there was more than one shot.' Dr Overton tried a retreat to his previously held position.

'But it's a *possibility*!'

'Yes,' he had to admit.

'What would turn that possibility into a probability, Dr Overton?'

'Well, I suppose if there was some strong additional evidence.' He made a concession which he clearly believed was safe.

'And you say there is *none*?'

'Not so far as I know, my Lord.' Another small bow to the Judge was received in sepulchral silence by Twyburne.

'What this jury has to consider, Dr Overton, is the extent of your knowledge. How many pellets, on an average, are there in a twenty-bore shotgun cartridge?' I had the satisfying feeling that I had fired him a question he wasn't prepared for. The doctor frowned, and answered with extreme care, 'I would say . . . about an ounce of shot.'

'Well done. Very promising.' Now I was being the teacher. 'And so how many pellets are there in an ounce of shot?'

'How many pellets?' he frowned.

'Are you hard of hearing, Dr Overton?'

'Not in the least.'

'Then could you force yourself to tell this jury the answer to my question.'

'I think, my Lord,' he said with a small bow of apology now, 'I would have to look that up.'

It was time for a bit of carefully controlled indignation, and I said, 'It didn't occur to you to look it up before you came here to give so-called expert evidence against a lady of unblemished character on a charge of murder?'

'No,' was the only answer possible.

'Then let us see if you remember this. When you carried out your post mortem examination you found a large number of shotgun pellets in the body, did you not?'

'A very large number indeed.' He seemed pleased by the fact; so was I.

'I'm obliged. Did you count them?'

'May I look at my notes?' But Dr Overton was now looking at Inspector Clover, sitting in the well of the Court, for help.

'Look at anything you like,' I said, 'except the Inspector in charge of the case. He's not going to be able to help, you know.'

'Mr Rumpole!' I heard a dry voice from the Bench and

apologized at once, of course. 'Your Lordship objected to that observation? Then I will withdraw it and we can get on with something more interesting. How many pellets did you find in the deceased's body, Dr Overton?'

'About four hundred and eighty, my Lord . . .' he said, and the Judge made a careful note.

'And there may have been others you didn't find?'

'There may well have been.'

'Now let me tell you something, doctor, which may be a help to you if you ever come to give evidence in a murder trial again. Your average cartridge for a twenty-bore shotgun contains two hundred and fifty pellets.'

'Well, I must accept that, of course.' The doctor couldn't very well do anything else. It was all in Ackerman.

'So does not the presence in the deceased's body of almost double that number of pellets indicate to you that there were probably two shots?'

The silence seemed endless. The Judge sat with his pencil poised over his notebook. In the dock Jennifer Postern looked as though the answer concerned her not at all. Then Dr Overton said, 'It might do so . . .'

'Might it not?' I came down on the answer quickly. 'And if Mrs Postern only fired one shot, might not some *other* person have fired the other?'

'Surely that is a conclusion for the jury, Mr Rumpole,' Twy-burne suggested, but this time it was not a rebuke.

'My Lord, it will be my submission that it is the *only* con-clusion. Thank you, Dr Overton.' I started to sit down, then changed my mind. 'Oh, doctor, before you go . . .' Dr Overton was leaving the witness-box with considerable relief. He paused dis-concertedly as I held up the small volume which had been my inspiration for the day. 'If you intend to continue in your present line of work, I would recommend a study by Professor Andrew Ackerman on *Gunshot Wounds in Forensic Medicine*. Such a useful little volume, and quite easy reading for the beginner.'

'Of course, that cross-examination was wonderful enter-tainment, Rumpole.' Miss Allways had come up to me after the

Judge left Court, and I was packing up my brief for another evening of quiet contemplation.

'One of my best, Fiona,' I said with becoming modesty. 'Perhaps my very best of a medical witness. Luckily I couldn't warm to Dr Overton.'

'But where does it get my sister?' Fiona asked.

'Just possibly, off.'

She frowned, as though she couldn't see it personally. 'Sprod says it was an accident. Are you suggesting that there were two accidents?'

'No, Fiona. Only one accident.'

'What are you getting at?'

'Your sister's not too keen on the truth coming out in this case, is she, Fiona? Tell her I'll be down to the cells to see her first thing tomorrow morning.'

'Why not tonight?'

'Not tonight. No. I'm going back to the Tester Arms. I've got to see somebody else first.'

I had seen Fishbourne hanging about in the back of the Court when I was talking to Fiona, which is why I had announced my evening's plans in as loud a voice as possible. But when I turned away from her he had gone and I couldn't find him in the corridor or waiting for me outside the building. So I went back to the hotel, had a bath to wash away the courtroom atmosphere and changed into an old pair of grey flannels and a tweed jacket that had seen better days. No one rang to say that I had a visitor and, as I struggled through the appalling grapefruit segments, battery hen and frozen veg, no one came up to my table.

Only as I sat in the residents' lounge, with a bottle of less than average claret and a small cigar, was my patience rewarded. He was coming towards me through a maze of deserted coffee tables.

'Thank you for coming, Mr Fishbourne,' I said. 'Do please sit down.'

He sat, refused a drink, and looked at me as though desperate for good news. 'Y . . . y . . . you can't get her off, can you?' he said.

'Suppose you tell me the answer to that, Mr Fishbourne.'

'I mean, I d ... don't see how you can. She said she did it.'

'What she said was, "*I* did it,"' I reminded him. 'Who else did she think might have done it, do you suppose?'

He looked at me then, I was glad to see, with considerable surprise. My suggestion, it seemed was one that hadn't occurred to him before.

'It couldn't possibly've been me.' He spoke quite calmly, without indignation or protest.

'*Couldn't?*'

'I d ... didn't see him. I'd gone up to London. Quite unexpectedly. I had a call from our solicitors and I went up just after lunch. All sorts of people saw me.'

I had no doubt they had, and felt a surge of relief. 'That's what we call an alibi in the trade,' I told him. 'Our first bit of luck in this case. But you know why Postern came to see you, don't you? I mean, it wasn't to criticize your riding abilities.'

'N ... n ... no. It wasn't for that.' He was looking at me, deciding to trust me. Then he accepted a glass of wine and started to tell me the whole story.

'How did you guess?' Jennifer Postern asked me when we met, early the next morning, in the cells under Tester Court. We had been given thick mugs of tea by the lady dock officer, and I felt easier in my mind than I had since the trial began.

'I saw you when Fishface fell at the last fence,' I told her. 'I thought you were his wife. Then you laughed at him with the others, so I knew you were hiding something. I suppose Jonathan found out about you and Maurice Fishbourne.'

'It's such a mess.' For the first time, she lost her extraordinary composure. She bowed her head, her hands were over her face and her shoulders shaking. Then she made a great effort, looked up, and said, 'What do you want me to do?'

'Why not try telling the truth? Sometimes people win cases like that. What do you say – shall we give it a try?'

So, when the Court assembled, I called Jennifer Postern into the witness-box, and she swore to tell the truth, the whole truth and nothing but the truth.

'Mrs Postern,' I went straight to the heart of the case, 'the afternoon your husband died you had a quarrel. What was that quarrel about?'

'About Maurice Fishbourne.'

Twyburne looked up at a new name; the jury were puzzled. I explained with a question, 'He is your next-door neighbour?'

'Yes.'

'What did you tell your husband?'

'I told Jonno that I loved Maurice and if he would divorce me we hoped to marry. I had been unhappy with my husband for a long time.' Now she had made up her mind to tell her story, Jennifer spoke simply and convincingly.

'Had Jonathan Postern been violent to you?'

'Yes. Quite often.'

'And so, on the afternoon you quarrelled ...?'

'Jonno said he'd go over and see Maurice and tell him never to see me again. He threatened to beat Maurice up. I knew Maurice could have a violent temper and that he hated Jonno. I think I shouted at my husband that if he went, Maurice might kill him.'

'Was Mrs Hempe in the house when you shouted that?'

'She was, yes.'

'And might have heard part of it?'

'Yes. Easily.'

'Had Maurice told you he might kill your husband?'

'When he heard how Jonno had treated me. Yes.'

'Did you take these threats seriously?'

'I knew that Maurice was a very determined man. He has a very strong will.'

'Let's come to the time when your husband left the house.'

'Jonno said he was going out to cool off, but after a while I thought he'd gone to Maurice's, so I decided to follow him. I got as far as the track by Figgis's cottage and I saw Jonathan. There was blood ...' She paused, seemed unable to go on, and then controlled herself. 'I saw that he was dead.'

'What did you think?'

'Of course I thought that Maurice had done it.' She looked at the jury. 'It was just by Maurice's wood. I thought he'd met

Jonathan there and they quarrelled and ...' For a moment her voice faded.

'And?'

'I knew Maurice wouldn't be able to get away with it.' She was summoning up reserves of strength. 'I thought he'd be convicted of murdering Jonathan. Oh, I was in a sort of panic, I suppose.'

'So what did you decide to do?' I asked her very quietly.

The Court and the jury were totally silent, almost breathless with attention as Jennifer answered, 'I decided to pretend I'd shot Jonathan. By mistake. In an accident. I went back to the house and got my shotgun. When I got to the wood again Jonathan was still there. I put in one cartridge and I fired.' Now she'd said it, the witness looked enormously relieved.

'One shot only?'

'Yes, only one.'

'Into his dead body?'

Jennifer's answer was hardly above a whisper. 'Yes.'

In the course of time my task was done, and I sat listening to Mr Justice Twyburne summing up to the jury. He spoke quietly: at times we had to strain our ears to hear him. With his lined face and thin neck emerging from a stiff collar that seemed too big for him, he looked like an aged tortoise. He was a lonely old Judge who refused to retire and who had come to me, of all people, for reassurance. And then he looked at me, and I gave his words my full attention.

'Members of the jury,' the Judge was saying, 'contrary to the views of *some people*, a British criminal trial cannot be compared in any way to a horse race.' He turned back to the jury. 'You do not get the result by closing your eyes and sticking a pin into the list of runners. If you are sure that, for whatever reason, Mrs Postern deliberately shot at her husband with the intention of killing him or doing him serious harm, why then you must convict her. But if you think that the account she gave you might be true, I say *might* be true, then she is entitled to be acquitted. There is some support for Mrs Postern's story, is there not, in the medical evidence?' Twyburne paused, searching for a place in his notebook. I was filled with amazement, as I slowly realized we were getting a fair, even a favourable summing up. I wondered for a moment if we had Martin Muschamp to thank for it. Then Twyburne went on to the jury, 'You have to consider the possibility that, in an accident caused by the man Figgis shooting from the window of his cottage, Mr Postern met his death on that woodland track. That Mrs Postern, coming on the body, assumed her lover to have been responsible, and took extraordinary steps to cover up what she thought had been a crime. This is not a Court of morals, members of the jury, and it is not a racetrack. What we are concerned with is certainty, and the truth.'

Hilda had the television on as I let myself into Casa Rumpole at Froxbury Court. It was booming news from Tester Assizes, and telling a waiting world that Jennifer Postern had been acquitted.

'Well, Rumpole,' said Hilda. 'I suppose you think you've done something frightfully clever.'

She was standing by the mantelpiece, on which she had put the photograph of a gentleman's lodge near Tester, cut carefully out of *Country Life*. Hilda was still hankering, quite clearly, for rural living and membership of the County set.

'No.' I told her, 'I think I've done something absolutely "brill".'

I went into the kitchen, opened a well-earned bottle of Pommeroy's plonk, and brought my wife a brimming glassful. Then I raised my own beaker in a toast. 'To Jennifer Postern,' I said. 'A wonderful woman in some ways. She took the most extraordinary risks to protect the man she loved.'

'Fiona's sister?' Hilda was frowning.

'Yes. Doesn't look all that much like Fiona.' I was staring at the cutting on the mantelpiece. 'Far more beautiful, don't you think? Fine-looking woman. We'll be able to see a good deal of her if we take that gentleman's lodge arrangement near Tester you're always talking about. Jennifer promises to give me shooting lessons.'

'Shooting lessons? *You*, Rumpole?' She was clearly worried.

'Oh yes. We plan to spend a good deal of time together. You'll be kept busy, I suppose, bottling fruit.'

Hilda went to the mantelpiece. She looked thoughtful.

'Rumpole. I've been thinking. It's really very convenient for us, this flat in the Gloucester Road.'

'Yes, but . . .'

'We can always have days out in the country.'

'I suppose that's true, but . . .'

'I think I've decided against Tester.'

She Who Must Be Obeyed took the advertisement, crumpled it up and threw it into the waste-paper basket.

'Well, Hilda,' I said. 'It's entirely your decision, but perhaps it'll be better for our health, living quietly in London.'

Rumpole and the Last Resort

I have almost caught up with myself. Decent crime has not been too thick on the ground recently, and time has been hanging a little heavily on the Rumpole hands. I have had a good deal of leisure to spend on these chronicles of the splendours and miseries of an Old Bailey hack and, although I have enjoyed writing them, describing and remembering is something of a second-hand occupation. I am happiest, I must confess, with the whiff of battle in my nostrils, with the Judge and the prosecuting counsel stacked against me, with the jury unconvinced, and everything to play for as I rear to my hind legs and start to cross-examine the principal witness for the Crown. There has been a notable decrease in the number of briefs in my tray in Chambers of late, and I have often set out for Number 3 Equity Court with nothing but the *Times* crossword and the notebook in which I have spent otherwise undemanding days recalling old murders and other offences. A barrister's triumphs are short-lived: a notable victory may provide gossip round the Temple for a week or two; a row with the Judge may be remembered a little longer; but those you have got off don't wish to be reminded of the cells where they met you, and those whose cases you have lost aren't often keen to share memories. By and large, trials are over and done with when you pack up your robes and leave Court after the verdict. For that reason it has been some satisfaction to me to write these accounts, although the truth of the matter is, as I have already hinted, that I haven't had very much else to do.

So up to date have I become that I can recount no more cases of sufficient interest and importance which have engaged my talents since my unexpected return from retirement. All I have left to do is something new to me – that is, to write about a case as I am doing it, in the hope that it will turn out to be sufficiently

unusual to be included among these papers which will form some
sort of memorial to the transient life of Horace Rumpole,
barrister-at-law. I am soon to go into Court with one of my
dwindling number of briefs, as counsel for the defence of a young
businessman named Frank Armstrong, Chairman and Managing
Director of Sun-Sand Holidays Ltd, an organization which sup-
plies mobile homes to holidaymakers in allegedly desirable sites
in the West Country, the Lake District and other places which
have every known inconvenience, including being much too far
away from Pommeroy's Wine Bar. The case itself may have some
points of interest, including the mysterious mobility of Sun-Sand
Mobile Homes, and the period about which I am writing contains
another minor mystery, that is to say, the disappearance of a Mr
Perivale Blythe, solicitor of the Supreme Court, a fellow who,
so far as I am concerned, is fully entitled to disappear off the
face of the earth, were it not for the fact that he has, for longer
than I care to remember, owed me money.

One of the many drawbacks of life at the Bar is the length of
time it takes to get paid for services rendered. As the loyal punter
may not appreciate, he pays the solicitor for the hire of a
barrister and, in theory at any rate, the solicitor passes the loot
on to the member of the Bar, the front-line warrior in the
courtroom battle, with the greatest possible despatch. In many
cases, unhappily, the money lingers along the line and months,
even years, may pass before it percolates into the barrister's bank
account. There is really nothing much the average advocate can
do about this. In the old days, when barristering was regarded
as a gentlemanly pursuit for persons of private means, rather
like fox-hunting or collecting rare seaweed, the rule grew up that
barristers couldn't sue for their fees, on the basis that to be seen
suing a solicitor would be as unthinkable as to be found dancing
with your cook.

So it was not only a decline in the number of briefs bearing
the Rumpole name, but a considerable slowing down in the
paying process, which caused my account at the Temple branch
of the United Metropolitan Bank to blush an embarrassing red.
One day I called in to cash a fifty-pound cheque, mainly to
defray the costs of those luxuries Hilda indulges in, matters such

as bread and soap powder, and I stood at the counter breathing a silent prayer that the cashier might see fit to pay me out. Having presented my cheque, I heard the man behind the grille say, to my considerable relief, 'How would you like the money, sir?'

'Oh, preferably in enormous quantities.' Of course it was a stupid thing to say. As soon as the words had passed my lips, I thought he'd take my cheque off to the back of the shop and discover the extent of the Rumpole debt. Why was he reading the thing so attentively? The art of cheque-cashing is to appear totally unconcerned.

'How would I like the money?' I said rapidly. 'Oh, I'll take it as it comes. Nothing fancy, thank you. Not doubloons. Or pieces of eight. Just pour me out a moderate measure of pounds sterling.'

To my relief the notes came out on a little wheel under the glass window. I scooped up the boodle and told myself that the great thing was not to run. Break into any sort of jog trot on the way to the door and they check up on the overdraft at once. The secret is to walk casually and even whistle in a carefree manner.

I was doing exactly that when I was stopped with a far from cheery good morning by Mr Medway, the Assistant Manager. I should have made a dash for it.

'Paying in or drawing out today, are we?' Medway looked at the money in my hand. 'Oh. Drawing out, I see. Could you step into my office, sir?'

'Not now. Got to get to Court. A money brief, of course.' I was hastily stuffing the notes into my pocket.

'Just a moment of your time, Mr Rumpole.' Medway was not to be put off. Within a trice I found myself closeted with him as I was grilled as to my financial position.

'Gone right over the limit of our overdraft, haven't we, Mr Rumpole?' The man smiled unpleasantly.

'My overdraft? A flea bite, compared with what you chaps are lending the Poles.'

I searched for a packet of cigars, feeling that I rather had him there.

'I don't think the Poles are making out quite so many cheques in favour of Jack Pommeroy of Pommeroy's Wine Bar.'

'Those are for the bare necessities of life. Look here, Medway. A fellow's got to live!'

'There's bound to come a time, Mr Rumpole, when that may not be necessary at the expense of the United Metropolitan Bank.' A peculiarly heartless financier, this Medway.

'"The Bank with the Friendly Ear".' I quoted his commercial, lit the cigar and blew out smoke.

'There comes a time, Mr Rumpole, when the United Metropolitan goes deaf.'

'That little overdraft of mine. Peanuts! Quite laughable compared to my outstanding fees.' It was my time to bring out the defence. 'My fees'll come in. Of course they will. You know how long solicitors keep owing us money? Why, there's one firm who still hasn't paid me for a private indecency I did for them ten years ago. No names, of course, but . . .'

'Is that Mr Perivale Blythe?' Medway was consulting my criminal record. 'Of Blythe, Winterbottom and Paisley?'

'Yes. I believe that's the fellow. Slow payer, but the money's there, of course.'

'Is it, Mr Rumpole?' Medway was a banker of little faith. 'Every time we've had one of these little chats, you've told me that you're owed a considerable amount in fees by Mr Perivale Blythe.'

'Can't remember how much, of course. But enough to pay off my overdraft and make a large contribution to the National Debt.' I stood up, anxious to bring this embarrassing interview to a conclusion. 'Must be scooting along,' I said. 'Got to earn both of us some money. Engaged in Court, you know.'

'My advice to you, Mr Rumpole,' Medway said darkly, 'is to take steps to make this Mr Perivale Blythe pay up. And without delay.'

'Of course. Get my clerk on to it at once. Now don't you worry, Medway.' I opened the door on my way to freedom. 'Having the Poles in next, are you? Hope you give them a good talking to.'

When I had told Medway that I had an engagement in Court it was a pardonable exaggeration. In fact I had nothing much to do but settle into my room at 3 Equity Court and write these memoirs. I had found the *tête-à-tête* in the bank somewhat depressing and I was in a low mood as I turned into the Temple and approached the entrance of our Chambers. There I met our demure Head, Sam Ballard, Q.C., who was standing on the step in conversation with a young man with dark hair, soft eyes and an expression of somewhat unjustified self-confidence which reminded me of someone. Ballard greeted me with 'Hullo there, Rumpole. How are you?'

'"Tir'd with all these, for restful death I cry,"' I told him candidly.

> 'As to behold desert a beggar born,
> And needy nothing trimm'd in jollity,
> And purest faith unhappily forsworn,
> And gilded honour shamefully misplac'd . . .'

'What's this talk of death, Rumpole?' Ballard was brisk and disapproving. 'You know young Archie Featherstone, don't you? Mr Justice Featherstone's nephew.' He introduced the young man, who smiled vaguely.

'My God. More Featherstones!' I was amazed. '"What! will the line stretch out to the crack of doom?"'

'I'm sure he'd like your advice about starting out at the Bar.'

'My advice is, "Don't",' I told the young man.

'Don't?' he repeated, pained.

'Don't slog your heart out. Don't tramp for years round some pretty unsympathetic Courts. What'll you have to show at the end of it? You're up to your eyes in debt to the United Metropolitan Bank and they'll grudge you such basic nourishment as a couple of dozen non-vintage Château Thames Embankment.'

'Young Featherstone would love to get a seat in our Chambers, Rumpole.' Ballard had clearly not followed a word I'd said. 'I've told him that at the moment there's just not the accommodation available.'

'At the moment?' Was the man expecting a sudden departure from our little band of barristers?

'Well, I don't suppose you'll be in your room for ever.' Ballard didn't sound too regretful. 'The time must come when you take

things a little more easily. Henry was saying how tired he thought
you looked.'

'"Tir'd with all these, for restful death I cry ..."' I repeated, and I looked at Ballard, remembering, '"And gilded
honour shamefully misplac'd". Oh yes, Ballard. The time's got
to come. Cheer up, young Featherstone,' I told him. 'You'll soon
be able to take over my overdraft.'

I left them there and went to report to the clerk's room. When
I got there I found Henry in position at his desk and Dianne
rattling her typewriter in a corner.

'Henry, how much does Perivale Blythe owe me in fees?' I
asked at once.

'Two thousand, seven hundred and sixty-five pounds, ninety-
three pence, Mr Rumpole,' Henry said, as if he knew it all by
heart.

'You tell me of wealth undreamed of by the United Metropolitan Bank. It's a debt stretching back over a considerable time,
eh, Henry?'

'Stretching back, Mr Rumpole, to the indecency at Swansea in
April, 1973.' Henry confirmed my suspicions.

'You have, I suppose, been on to him about it, Henry?'

'Almost daily, Mr Rumpole.'

'And what has this blighter Blythe to say for himself?'

'The last time his secretary told us a cheque was in the post.'

'Not true?' I guessed.

'Not unless it evaporated mysteriously between here and
Cheapside.'

'Get after him, Henry, like a terrier. Get your teeth into the
man Blythe, and don't let him go until he disgorges the loot.'

I looked at Henry's desk and my eyes were greeted with the
unusual and welcome sight of a brief bearing the Rumpole name.
'Is that a set of papers for me you're fingering?' I asked with
assumed indifference.

'Mr Myers brought it in, sir. It's a case at the Bailey.' Henry
confirmed the good news.

'God bless old Myersy. A man who pays up from time to time.'
I looked at the brief. 'What is it, Henry? Murder? Robbery?
Sudden death?'

'Sorry, Mr Rumpole.' Henry realized that I would be disappointed. 'It seems to be about Sun-Sand Mobile Homes.'

When I went up to my room to familiarize myself with the brief Henry had given me, I threw my hat, as usual, on to the hatstand; but, the hatstand not being there, the Rumpole headgear thudded to the ground. Of course, I knew what had happened. Erskine-Brown had always coveted the old hatstand that had stood in my room for years and, when he had a big conference, he put it in his room to impress the clientele. Before I started work I crept along the passage, found Erskine-Brown's room empty and purloined the old article of furniture back again. Then I sat down, lit a small cigar, and studied the facts in the case of R. v. Armstrong.

The trouble had started at a Sun-Sand holiday site in Cornwall. A family returned from a cold, wet day on the beach and had their mobile holiday home towed away before they could get at their high tea. Other punters were apparently sold holidays in mobile homes which were said to have existed only in the fertile imagination of my client, Frank Armstrong.

In due course police officers – Detective Inspector Limmeridge and Detective Sergeant Banks – called on Sun-Sand Holidays in North London. The premises were small and unimposing but the officers noticed that they were elaborately equipped with all the latest gadgets of computer technology. The young chairman of the company was there, busily pressing buttons and anxiously watching figures flash and hearing the bleeps and hiccoughs of such machines at work. When arrested, Mr Armstrong was given permission to telephone his solicitor, but when he did so he found that the gentleman in question had just slipped out of the office.

Eventually Frank Armstrong was allowed bail and turned up in my room at Chambers with old Myers, the solicitor's clerk (or legal executive, as such gentlemen are now called), whom I would rather have with me on a bad day at the Bailey than most of the learned friends I can think of. I had asked Miss Fiona Allways to join us and generally help with the sums.

'My brother Fred and I, we was born into the modern world,

Mr Rumpole,' said Frank. 'And what is the name of the game, in the world today?'

'Space Invaders?' I hazarded a guess. My client looked at me seriously. In spite of a sharp business suit, his Gaucho moustache, longish hair, gold watch and bracelet, Playboy Club tie and the manner of a tough young businessman, Frank Armstrong looked younger than I had expected, and both pained and puzzled by the turn of events.

'The name of the game is leisure interests and computer technology,' he told me seriously. 'You won't believe this, Mr Rumpole. You will not believe it.'

'Try me.'

'Our old dad kept a fruit barrow in the Shepherd's Bush Market.'

'Not incredible,' I assured him.

'Yes, indeed. Well, he made a few bob in his time and when he died my brother and I divided the capital. Fred went into hardware, right?'

'Ironmongery?'

'You're joking,' Frank said. 'Fred joined the microchip revolution. Looking round your office now, Mr Rumpole, I doubt it's fully automated. There are delays in sending your bills out, right?'

'Sometimes I think my bills are sent out by a carrier pigeon with a poor sense of direction,' I admitted.

'Trust in the computer, Mr Rumpole, and you'd have so much more time, leisure-wise. That's the . . .'

'Name of the game?' I hazarded.

'Yes, indeed. That's why I saw my future definitely in the leisure industry.'

'"Leisure industry". Sounds like a contradiction in terms.'

Frank didn't hear my murmur. He was clearly off on a favourite subject. 'Who wants hotel expenses these days? Who needs porters, tips, waiter service? All the hassle. The future, as I see it, is in self-catering mobile homes set in A3 and B1 popularity, mass appeal holiday areas. That's the vision, Mr Rumpole, and it's got me where I am today.'

'On bail, facing charges of fraud and fraudulent conversion,' I reminded him.

'Mr Rumpole. I want you to believe this . . .'

'Try me again.'

'I just don't understand it. I want to tell you that very frankly. I was doing my best to run a go-ahead service industry geared to the needs of the eighties. What went wrong exactly?' Frank asked plaintively. I got up, stretched the legs and lit a small cigar.

'I imagine a close study of the accounts might tell us that,' I said. 'By the way, that's one of the reasons I've asked you to give Miss Allways a little brief. She's got a remarkable head for figures.'

'And quite a figure for heads, I should think.' Frank gave our lady barrister one of his 'Playboy Club' leers and laughed. Fiona froze him with a look.

'Pardon me, Miss Allways. Probably out of place, right?' Our client apologized and Miss Allways ignored him and rattled out some businesslike instructions to old Myers. 'I'd like the accounts sent down to Chambers as soon as possible,' she said. 'There's a great deal of spadework to be done.'

'This is where we're in a certain amount of difficulty.' Myers coughed apologetically.

'Surely not?'

'You see, the accounts were all given to Mr Armstrong's previous solicitor. That was the firm that acted for his father back in the fruit barrow days and went on acting till after our client's arrest.'

'It's perfectly simple.' Fiona was impatient. 'You've only got to get in touch with the former solicitors.'

'Well, not quite as simple as all that, Miss Allways. We've tried writing but we never get an answer to our letters and when we telephone, well, the gentleman dealing with the matter always seems to have just slipped out of the office.'

'Really? What's the name of the firm?' Miss Allways asked, but I was ahead of her. 'Don't tell me, let me guess,' I said. 'What about Blythe, Winterbottom and Paisley?'

'Well,' our client admitted dolefully. 'This is it.'

At the end of the day I called into Pommeroy's Wine Bar and the first person I met was Claude Erskine-Brown on his way out. Of course I went straight into the attack.

'Erskine-Brown,' I said accusingly. 'Hatstand-pincher!'

'Rumpole. That's a most serious allegation.'

'Hatstand-pinching is a most serious crime,' I assured him.

'You don't need a hatstand in your room, Rumpole. Criminals hardly ever wear hats. I happened to have a conference yesterday with three solicitors all with bowlers.'

'That hatstand is a family heirloom, Erskine-Brown. It belonged to my old father-in-law. I value it highly,' I told him.

'Oh, very well, Rumpole. If that's the attitude.' He was leaving me.

'Goodnight, Erskine-Brown. And keep your hands off my furniture.'

As I penetrated the interior, I saw our clerk Henry, who is, far more effectively than the egregious Bollard, the true Head of our Chambers and ruler of our lives, in the company of the ever-faithful Dianne. I asked him to name his poison, which he did, in an unattractive manner, as Cinzano Bianco and lemonade.

'Dianne?' I included her in the invitation.

'I'll have the same.' She looked somewhat meltingly at Henry. 'It's what we used to have in Lanzarotte.'

'Did you really? Well, I won't inquire too deeply into that. And a large cooking claret, Jack, and no doubt you'd be happy to cash a small cheque?' I asked the host as he came past pushing a cloth along the counter.

'Well, not exactly happy, Mr Rumpole.' Pommeroy was not in one of his sunnier moods.

'Come on, you've got nothing to worry about. You haven't lent a penny to Poland, have you? This is a much safer bank than the United Metropolitan. Oh, give yourself one while you're about it,' I said, as Jack moved reluctantly to get the drinks and the money. Then I turned to my clerk in a businesslike manner. 'Now then, Henry, about this abominable Blythe. Not surfaced, by any stretch of the imagination?'

'No, Mr Rumpole. Not as yet, sir.'

'Not as yet. Lying in his hammock in some South Sea Island, is he, fondling an almond-eyed beauty and drinking up our brief fees and refreshers?'

'I've made inquiries around the Temple. Mr Brushwood in

Queen Elizabeth's Buildings had the same problem, his clerk
was telling me. Blythe owed well into four figures, and they
couldn't find hide nor hair of him, sir.'

'But poor old Tommy Brushwood is ...' The claret had come
and I resorted to it.

'No longer with us. I know that, sir. And as soon as he'd gone,
Blythe called on Mr Brushwood's widow and got her to give him
some sort of release for a small percentage. She signed as executor,
not quite knowing the form, I would imagine. Cheers, Mr
Rumpole.'

'Oh, yes. Cheers everso.' Dianne smiled at me over the fizzy
concoction.

'But Henry, why has this Blythe not been reported to the Law
Society? Why hasn't he been clapped in irons,' I asked him, 'and
transported to the colonies?'

'All the clerks have thought of reporting him, of course. But
if we did that we'd never get paid, now would we?'

'Despite that drink you indulge in, which has every appearance
of chilled Lucozade, I believe you still have your head screwed
on, Henry. I have another solution.'

'Honestly, Mr Rumpole? I'd be glad to hear it.'

'We need Blythe as a witness in the Sun-Sand Mobile Homes
case.'

'R. *v.* Armstrong?'

'Your memory serves you admirably. We'll get Newton the
Private Dick to find Blythe so he can slap a subpoena on him.
If "Fig" Newton can't find the little horror, no one can. Isn't
that all we need?'

'I hope so, Mr Rumpole,' Henry said doubtfully. 'I really hope
so.'

Ferdinand Ian Gilmour Newton, widely known in the legal
profession as 'Fig' Newton, was a tall, gloomy man who always
seemed to be suffering from a heavy cold. No doubt his work,
forever watching back doors, peering into windows, following
errant husbands in all weathers, was responsible for his pink
nostrils and the frequent application of a crumpled handkerchief.
I have known 'Fig' Newton throughout my legal career. He

appeared daily in the old-style divorce cases, when his evidence
was invariably accepted. Since the bonds of matrimony can now
be severed without old 'Fig' having to inspect the sheets or
observe male and female clothing scattered in a hotel bedroom,
his work has diminished; but he can still be relied upon to serve
a writ or unearth an alibi witness. He seems to have no interests
outside his calling. His home life, if it exists at all, is a mystery.
I believe he snatches what sleep he can while sitting in his battered
Cortina watching the lights go on and off in the bedroom of a
semi-detached, and he dines off a paper of fish and chips as he
guards the door of a debtor who has gone to earth.

'Fig' Newton called at the offices of Blythe, Winterbottom
and Paisley early one morning and asked to see Mr Perivale
Blythe. He was greeted by a severe-looking secretary, a lady
named Miss Claymore, with spectacles, a tweed skirt and
cardigan, and a Scots accent. Despite her assuring him that
Perivale Blythe was out of the office and not expected back that
day, the leech-like 'Fig' sat down and waited. He learned nothing
of importance, except that round about noon Miss Claymore
went into an inner office to make a telephone call. The detective
was able to hear little of the conversation, but she did say something about the times of trains to Penzance.

When Miss Claymore left her office, 'Fig' Newton followed
her home. He sat in his Cortina in Kilburn outside the Victorian
building, divided into flats, to which Miss Claymore had driven
her small Renault. He waited for almost two hours, and when
Miss Claymore finally emerged she had undergone a considerable
change. She was wearing tight trousers of some satin-like material
and a pink fluffy sweater. Her feet were crammed into high-
heeled gold sandals and she was without her spectacles. She got
into the Renault and drove to Soho, where she parked with
considerable daring halfway up a pavement, and went into an
Italian restaurant where she met a young man. 'Fig' Newton
kept observation from the street and was thus unable to share
in the lasagne and the bottle of Valpolicella, which he carefully
noted down. Later the couple crossed Frith Street and entered
a Club known as the 'Pussy Cat A-Go-Go', where particularly
loud music was being played. 'Fig' Newton was later able to

peer down into the basement of this Club, where, lit by sporadic, coloured lights, Miss Claymore was dancing with the same young man, whom he described as having the appearance of a young business executive with features very similar to those of our client.

On the evening that Mr Perivale Blythe's secretary went dancing, I was reading on the sofa at 25B Froxbury Court, smoking a small cigar and recovering from a hard day of writing this account in my Chambers. Suddenly, and without warning, my wife, She Who Must Be Obeyed, dropped a heavy load of correspondence on to my stomach.

'Hilda,' I protested. 'What are these?'

'Bills, Rumpole. Can't you recognize them?'

'Electricity. Gas. Rates. Water rates.' I gave them a glance. 'We really must cut down on these frivolities.'

'All gone red,' Hilda told me.

'It's only last month's telephone bill.' I looked at a specimen. 'We should lay that down for maturing. You don't have to rush into paying these things, you know. Mr Blythe hasn't paid me much of anything since 1972.'

'Well, you'd better tell Mr Perivale Blythe that the London Electricity Board aren't as patient as you are, Rumpole,' She said severely.

'Hilda. You know we can't sue anyone for our fees.'

'I can't think why ever not.' My wife has only a limited understanding of the niceties of legal etiquette.

'It wouldn't be a gentlemanly thing to do,' I explained. 'Against the finest traditions of the Bar.'

'Perhaps it's a gentlemanly thing to sit here in the dark with the gas cut off and no telephone and nasty looks every time you go into the butcher's. All I can say is, you can sit there and be gentlemanly on your own. I'm going away, Rumpole.'

I looked at Hilda with a wild surmise. Was I, at an advanced age, about to become the product of a broken home? 'Is that a threat or a promise.' I asked her.

'What did you say?'

'I said, "Of course, you'll be missed,"' I assured her.

'Dodo's been asked to stay with a friend in the Lake District, Pansy Rawlins, whom we were both at school with, if you remember.'

'Well, I don't think I was there at the time.'

'And Pansy's lost her husband recently.'

'Careless of her,' I muttered, moving the weight of the bills off me.

'So it'll be a bachelor party. Of course, when Dodo first asked me I said I couldn't possibly leave *you*, Rumpole.'

'I am prepared to make the supreme sacrifice and let you go. Don't worry about me,' I managed to say bravely.

'I don't suppose I shall, unduly. But you'd better worry about yourself. My advice to you is, find this Colindale Blythe.'

'*Perivale*, Hilda.'

'Well, he sounds a bit of a twister, wherever he lives. Find him and get him to pay you. Make that your task.' She looked down at me severely. 'Oh, and while I'm away, Rumpole, try not to put your feet on the sofa.'

Today I arrived in good time at the Old Bailey. I like to give myself time to drink in the well-known atmosphere of floor polish and uniforms, to put on the fancy dress at leisure and then go down to the public canteen for a cup of coffee and a go at the crossword. I needed to build up my strength particularly this morning, as Henry had let me know the name of our Judge the evening before. I therefore ordered a particularly limp sausage roll with the coffee, and I had just finished this and was lighting a small cigar, when Myers appeared carrying Newton's latest report, accompanied by Miss Fiona Allways, wigged and gowned and ready for the fray. Since the curious sighting of Blythe's secretary tripping the light fantastic at the Pussy Cat A-Go-Go, 'Fig' had kept up a patient and thorough search for the elusive Perivale Blythe, with no result whatsoever.

'I still think Blythe's an essential witness.' Fiona was sticking to her guns.

'Of course he is,' I agreed.

'We just need more time for Newton to make inquiries. Can't we ask for an adjournment?' Myers suggested hopefully.

'We can ask.' I'm afraid my tone was not particularly encouraging.

'Surely, Mr Rumpole, any reasonable judge would grant it.'

Perhaps Myers was right; but it was then that I had to remind him that we'd been landed with his Honour Judge Roger Bullingham. I stood up in front of him, with the jury out of Court and Ward-Webster, our young and eager prosecutor, relaxing in his seat, and asked for an adjournment in no less than five distinct and well-considered ways. It was like trying to shift a mountain with a teaspoon. Finally his Honour said, in a distinctly testy tone of voice,

'Mr Rumpole! For the fifth time, I'm not adjourning this case. So far as I can see the defence has had all the time in the world.'

'Your Lordship may know how long it takes to find a solicitor.' I tried the approach jovial. 'If your Lordship remembers his time at the Bar.' The joke, if it can be dignified with such a title, went down like a lead balloon.

'Mr Rumpole, neither your so-called eloquence nor your alleged pleasantry are going to make me change my mind.' Bullingham was beginning to irritate me. I raised the Rumpole voice a couple of decibels. 'Then let me tell you an indisputable fact. For years my client's business life was in the hands of Mr Perivale Blythe.'

'Your client's business life, such as it was, was in his own hands, Mr Rumpole.' The Judge was unimpressed. 'And it's about time he faced up to his responsibilities. This case will proceed without any further delay. That is my final decision.'

There is a way of saying 'If your Lordship pleases' so that it sounds like dumb insolence. I said it like that and sat down.

'You did your best, sir,' Myers turned and whispered to me. Good old Myersy. That's what he always says when I fail dismally.

For the rest of the day I sat listening to prosecution evidence. From time to time my eyes wandered around the courtroom and, on one such occasion, I saw a severe-looking female in spectacles sitting in the front of the Public Gallery, taking notes.

It was a long day in Court. When I got back to the so-called mansion flat, I noticed something unusual. She Who Must Be

Obeyed was conspicuous by her absence. I called, 'Hilda!' in various empty rooms and then I remembered that she had gone off, in none too friendly a mood, to stay with her old school chums, Dodo and Pansy, in the Lake District. So I poached a couple of eggs, buttered myself a slice of toast and sat down to a bottle of Pommeroy's plonk and this account. Now I am up to date with my life and with events in the Sun-Sand Mobile Holiday Home affair. Tomorrow, I suppose, will bring new developments on all fronts. The only thing that can be said with any certainty about tomorrow is that I shan't become any younger, nor will Judge Bullingham prove any easier to handle. Now the bottle's empty and I've smoked the last of my small cigars. The washing up can take care of itself. I'm going to bed.

THE NARRATIVE OF MISS FIONA ALLWAYS

I should never have taken this on. From the first day I met him in Chambers, after I had received a severe ticking-off from Mrs Erskine-Brown, Q.C., Rumpole was extremely decent to me. I'm still not absolutely sure how he managed to persuade the men at 3 Equity Court to take me on, but I have a feeling that he did something pretty devious for my sake. I took a note from him in quite a few of his cases and he was able to winkle a junior brief in R. v. Armstrong for me out of his instructing solicitor. So you see, although a lot of people found him absolutely impossible, and he could say the most appalling things quite unexpectedly, Rumpole was always extremely kind to me and, above all, he saved my sister Jennifer from doing a life sentence for murder.

So you can imagine my feelings about what happened to Rumpole in the middle of the Armstrong trial. Well, you'll have to imagine them, I'm afraid to say, because although I never got less than B + for an essay at school, and although I can get a set of facts in order and open a case fairly clearly at Thames Mags Court now, I'm never going to have Rumpole's talent for emotional speeches. All I can say is that the day R. v. Armstrong was interrupted, as it was, was a day I hope I never have to live through again. What I'm trying to say is, my feelings of gratitude to old Rumpole made that a pretty shattering experience.

All the same, I do realize that the records of one of Rumpole's more notable cases should be complete, and that's why I've agreed to give my own account of the closing stages of the Armstrong trial. I suppose my taking this on is the least I can do for him now. So, anyway, here goes.

I have to say that I never particularly liked our client, Frank Armstrong. He had doggy eyes and a good deal of aftershave and I got the feeling that he was trying to make some sort of a pass at me at our first conference; and that sort of thing, so far as I am concerned, is definitely not on. When he came to give evidence I think Rumpole soon realized that Armstrong wasn't going to be a particularly impressive witness, and he looked fairly gloomy as we sat listening to our client being cross-examined by Ward-Webster, who was doing a pretty competent job for the prosecution. I took a full note and, looking at it now, I see that the moment came when the witness was shown the photograph of the Sun-Sand Mobile Home site in Cornwall, and Judge Bullingham, who didn't seem to like Rumpole, turned to the jury and said, 'Hardly looks like the Côte d'Azur, does it, members of the jury? It looks like an industrial tip.'

'Looking in the other direction, there's a view of the sea, my Lord.' I remember our client sounding distinctly pained.

'What, between the crane and the second lorry?' Bullingham was still smiling at the jury.

'A great deal of our patrons' time is spent on the beach,' Armstrong protested.

'Perhaps they want a quiet night!' the Judge suggested, and the jury laughed.

'Mr Armstrong. Do you agree that on no less than fifty occasions holidays on the site in Cornwall turned out to have been booked in non-existent mobile homes?' Ward-Webster went on with his cross-examination.

'Yes indeed, but ...' the witness was sounding particularly hopeless.

'And that your firm was paid large deposits for such holidays?' Ward-Webster went on.

'Well, this is it, but ...'

'And on one occasion at least a mobile home was actually

removed from an unhappy mother just as she was about to enter it?'

'It was one of those things . . .'

'Instead of mother running away from home, the home ran away from mother?'

I remember that the Judge made his joke at that point, and Rumpole muttered to me, 'Oh well done, Bull. Quite the stand-up comic.'

'And that letters of protest from the losers and their legal advisers remained unanswered?' Ward-Webster went on when the laughter died down.

'If there were complaints, the information should have been fed into the office computer.'

'Perhaps the people in question would rather have had their money back than have their complaints consumed by your computer.'

'Quite frankly, Mr Ward-Webster, our office at Sun-Sand Holidays is equipped with the latest technology.' Our client sounded deeply offended. At this the Judge told him that it was a pity it wasn't also equipped with a little old-fashioned plain dealing.

Of course, Rumpole objected furiously and said that was the point the jury had to decide. My note reminds me that the Judge then smiled at the jury and said, 'Very well, members of the jury, you will have heard Mr Rumpole's objection. Now, shall we get on with the trial?'

'Mr Armstrong, are you telling us that these events are due to the inefficiency of your office?' Ward-Webster was only too glad to get on with it.

'My office is not in the least inefficient. My brother's business is computer hardware and . . .'

It was at about this point in the evidence that I saw Rumpole closely studying the report of Mr Newton, the inquiry agent.

'What's the relevance of that, Mr Armstrong?' Ward-Webster was asking.

'My brother supplies our office equipment,' our client told him proudly.

'Mr Ward-Webster,' said the Judge. 'This family story is no

doubt extremely fascinating, but has it really anything to do with the case?'

'I agree, my Lord. And I will pass to another matter . . .'

While this was happening, Rumpole asked me in a whisper if I thought that our client had ever danced with Blythe's secretary. I told him that I had no idea. In fact, I couldn't see the point of the question. But Rumpole leaned forward and asked Mr Myers, of our instructing solicitor's office, to get Mr Newton down to the Old Bailey during the lunch adjournment.

Mr Newton came and we met him with our client in the public canteen. He took a look at Frank Armstrong and said that Blythe's secretary's dancing partner did look like our client but he was sure that he wasn't the same man. Rumpole, who seemed to have a great deal of confidence in this detective whom he always called 'Fig' Newton, seemed to accept this and asked Frank Armstrong if he had a photograph of his brother.

'Yes, indeed.' Frank Armstrong got out his wallet. 'Taken in Marbella. The summer before last.' He handed a photograph to Newton.

'That's the gentleman,' Mr Newton said. 'No doubt about it.'

'Fred's been dancing!' Rumpole laughed. 'Where is he now?'

'In the Gulf. Dubai. So far as I know. He's been asked to develop a computer centre,' Frank Armstrong answered vaguely.

'How long did you think he'd been away?'

'Six months. All of six months.'

'Since before you were arrested?' Rumpole was puzzled. 'You see, Newton saw him a couple of weeks ago in London.'

'Mr Rumpole, I don't know what you're getting at. I'm sure Fred would help me if he possibly could,' Mr Armstrong said.

'You've never quarrelled?'

'Only one little falling out, perhaps. When he wanted to buy the land in Cornwall.'

'Did he offer you much money?' That seemed to interest Rumpole.

'Enormous! Stupid sort of price, I called it. But I wasn't selling. Bit unbrotherly of me perhaps, but I wanted to build up my empire.'

'Perhaps Fred wanted to build up his,' Rumpole said, and

then he turned to us and gave orders. He seemed, at that moment, quite determined and in charge of the case.

'There's a lot to be done,' he said. 'Newton's got to find brother Fred.'

'In Dubai?' Mr Newton protested.

'Keep a watch on the office of Sun-Sand Holidays after hours, late at night, early in the morning. Blythe, too. We *have* to get hold of Blythe. You may have to go to Cornwall,' he told Newton.

'I suppose you want all that before two o'clock?' Mr Myers was used to Rumpole's moments of decision.

'No. No, Myersy. Come on, Fiona. This time I've got to get the Mad Bull to give us an adjournment, or die in the attempt!'

So much of what Rumpole said that day sticks in my memory – that last sentence is one I shall never forget, as long as I live.

Of course, when Rumpole got to his feet after lunch Judge Bullingham was as unreceptive as ever.

'So what is the basis of this application, which you are now making for the fifth time since the start of this case?' the Judge asked, and when Mr Mason, the Clerk of the Court, rose to remind him of something, he was delighted to correct himself. 'Is it? Oh, thank you, Mason. For the *sixth* time, Mr Rumpole!'

'The basis should be clear, even to your Lordship,' Rumpole said; it was pretty typical of him, actually. 'It is vital that justice should be done to the gentleman I have the honour to represent.'

'Mr Rumpole. This case has been committed for six months. If Mr Blythe could have helped you he'd have come forward long ago.'

'That's an entirely unwarranted assumption! Perivale Blythe may have other reasons for his absence.'

'It seems you know very little about Mr Blythe. May I ask, have you a proof of his evidence?'

'No.'

'No?' The Judge raised his voice angrily.

'No, I haven't.' I remember Rumpole spoke casually and I remember he sounded quieter than usual.

'So you have no idea what this Mr Blythe is going to say?'

'No, but I know what I'm going to ask him. If he answers truthfully, I have no doubt that my client will be acquitted.'

'A pious hope, Mr Rumpole!' The Judge was smiling at the jury now.

'Of course, if your Lordship wishes to exclude this vital evidence, if you have no interest in doing justice in this case, then I have little more to say ...' His voice was really tired and quiet by then, and I wondered if he was going to give up and sit down, but he was still on his feet.

'Well, I have a lot more to say. As you should know perfectly well, Mr Rumpole, getting through the work at the Old Bailey is a matter of considerable public importance ...'

'Oh, of course. Far more important than justice!' Rumpole's voice was still faint and I thought he looked pale.

'In my view these constant applications by the defence are merely an attempt to put off the evil hour when the jury have to bring in a verdict,' the Judge went on, quite unnecessarily I thought. 'It's my duty to see that justice is done speedily. Mr Rumpole, I believe you have a taste for poetry. You will no doubt remember the quotation about the "law's delays".'

'Oh yes, my Lord. It comes in the same passage which deals with "the insolence of office". My Lord, if I might say ...'

'Mr Rumpole!' the Judge barked at him. 'This application for an adjournment is refused. There is absolutely nothing you could say which would persuade me to grant it.'

Then Rumpole seemed to be swaying slightly. He raised a finger to loosen his collar. His voice was now hoarse and almost inaudible.

'Nothing, my Lord?'

'No, Mr Rumpole. Absolutely nothing!' The Judge had reached his decision. But Rumpole was swaying more dangerously. Judge Bullingham watched, astonished, and the whole Court was staring as Rumpole collapsed, apparently unconscious. The Judge spoke loudly over the gasps of amazement.

'I shall adjourn this case.' Judge Bullingham rose, and then bent to speak to Mr Mason, the Clerk of the Court. 'Send for Matron!' he said.

In a while, when the Court had cleared, Mr Myers, the Usher and I managed to get Rumpole, who seemed to have recovered a certain degree of consciousness, out into the corridor and sit him down. He was still looking terribly grey and ill and the Usher went off to hurry up Matron.

'Always thought I'd die with my wig on,' Rumpole just managed to murmur.

'Did he say die?' A woman in glasses, whom I had noticed in Court, asked the Usher and, when he nodded at her, walked quietly away. I took his wig off then and stood holding it. 'Nonsense, Rumpole.' I tried to sound brisk. 'You're not going to die.'

'Fiona.' His voice was now a sort of low croak. I had to bend down to hear what came out like a last request. 'Air ... Miss Allways ... Must have air. Take me ... Take me out ...'

He was pulling feebly at his winged collar and bands. I managed to get them undone and then he rose to his feet and stood swaying. He looked absolutely ghastly. Mr Myers was supporting him under one arm. 'Just a breath of air ... Want to smell Ludgate Circus ... Your little runabout, Fiona ... Is it outside? Can't spend my last moments outside Bullingham's Court.'

I suppose I shouldn't have done it, but he looked so pathetic. He whispered to me about not being taken to some hospital full of bedpans and piped Capital Radio, and promised that his wife would send for their own doctor – he could at least die with dignity. Myers and I helped him out to my battered Deux Chevaux and I drove Rumpole to his home.

It took a long time to help him up the stairs and into his flat, but he seemed happy to be home and managed a sort of fleeting smile. His wife wasn't there but he muttered something about her having only just slipped out – said that she'd be back in a moment from the shops and that Dr MacClintock would look after him – for so long, he murmured, as anything could be done. At least, I told him, I'd help him into bed. So we moved towards the bedroom, but at the door he seemed to have second thoughts.

'Perhaps ... Better not. She Who Must Be Obeyed ... Bound to stalk in ... Just when I've lowered the garments ... Gets some ... funny ideas ... does She.'

All the same, I helped him as he staggered into the bedroom

and I hung his wig and gown, which I was carrying, over the bedrail as he lay down, still dressed. It was very cold in the mansion flat and I thought that the old couple must be extremely hardy. I covered Rumpole with the eiderdown and he was babbling, apparently delirious.

'Ever thought about ... the hereafter, Fiona?' I heard him say. 'Hereafter's all right. Until Bollard gets there ... He's bound to make it ... Have to spend all eternity listening to Bollard ... on the subject of "Lawyers for the Faith" ... Difficult to make an excuse ... and slip away. He'll have me buttonholed ... in the hereafter. Go along now ...'

'Are you sure?' I hated to leave him but I knew that our wretched client had been taken down to the cells when the trial was interrupted.

Someone would have to go and get him released until he was needed again.

'And bail,' Rumpole was muttering very faintly, echoing my thoughts. 'Ask bail ... from the dotty Bull. For Frank. Suppose Bullingham'll be turning up there too ... in the hereafter. Apply for bail ... Fiona.'

'I'll ring you later,' I promised as I moved to the door.

'Later ... Not too late ...' Rumpole closed his eyes as I went out of the door; he was quite motionless, apparently asleep.

Judge Bullingham was looking at me, smiling, apparently deeply sympathetic, when I applied for bail. Mr Mason, the Court Clerk, later told me that the Judge had taken something of a 'shine' to me and was considering sending me a box of chocolates. Life at the Bar can be absolute hell for a girl sometimes.

'Bail? Yes, of course, Miss Allways. By all means,' said the Judge. 'On the same terms. And what is the latest news of Mr Rumpole?'

'He is resting peacefully, my Lord,' I told him truthfully.

'Peacefully.' The Judge sounded very solemn. 'Yes, of course. Well, that comes to all of us in time. Nothing else for this afternoon, is there, Mason?'

The Judge went home early. But in the Old Bailey, round the other London Courts and in the Temple the news spread like wildfire. Rumpole had collapsed, the stories went, it was all over and the old boy had gone home at last. I heard that in the cells villains, with their trials due to come up, cursed because they wouldn't have Rumpole to defend them.

Some said he'd died with his wig on, others told how he'd been suddenly taken away before the Matron could get at him. Quite a lot of people, from Detective Inspectors to safe-blowers, said that, if he had to go, Rumpole would have wanted it to come as it did, when he was on his feet and in the middle of a legal argument.

When I got back to Chambers I found a crowd gathered in our clerk's room. Henry had been trying the phone in Rumpole's flat over and over again and getting no reply.

'No reply from Rumpole's flat!' said Hoskins, a rather dreary sort of barrister who's always talking about his daughters.

'Probably no one at home,' Uncle Tom, our oldest inhabitant, hazarded a guess.

'That would appear to be the natural assumption, Uncle Tom.' Erskine-Brown was as sarcastic as usual.

'Surely, we've got absolutely no reason to think ...' Hoskins said.

'I agree. All we know is that Rumpole suffered some sort of a stroke or a seizure,' Ballard told them.

'Rumpole often said Judge Bullingham had that effect on him,' Uncle Tom said.

'And that he's clearly been taken somewhere,' Erskine-Brown added.

'"Taken somewhere" expresses it rather well.' Uncle Tom shook his head. '"Taken somewhere" is about the long and short of it.'

Then I told them I'd taken Rumpole home where his wife would be able to get their own doctor to look after him. In the pause that followed Henry gave me the good news that he had got me a porn job in Manchester and I'd have to travel up overnight.

'A porn job!' Our Head of Chambers looked shocked. 'I'd've thought this was hardly the moment for that sort of thing.'

'Mr Rumpole would want Chambers to carry on, sir, I'm sure. As usual,' Henry said solemnly.

'Poor old fellow. Yes,' Uncle Tom agreed. 'Well. One thing to be said for him. He went in harness.'

'I don't really think it's the sort of subject we should be discussing in the clerk's room,' Ballard decided. 'No doubt I shall be calling a Chambers meeting, when we have rather more detailed information.'

As they went, I lingered long enough to hear Dianne, our rather hit-and-miss typist, give a little sob as she pounded her machine.

'Oh, please, Dianne,' Henry protested. 'Didn't you hear what I said to Mr Ballard? Chambers must go on. That would have been *his* wishes.'

So I went to Manchester and read a lot of jolly embarrassing magazines in a dark corner of the railway carriage. Meanwhile Mr Newton, the inquiry agent, was still keeping a watch on the offices of Sun-Sand Holidays every night. Of course, I saw his reports eventually and it seemed that the office was visited, late at night and in a highly suspicious manner, by our client's brother Fred, who spent a long time working on the computers.

And there were other developments. Archie Featherstone, the Judge's nephew, was still very anxious to get into our Chambers and, when there was no news of Rumpole's recovery, I suppose the poor chap felt a bit encouraged in a horrible sort of way.

Perhaps I can understand how he felt because, although I never liked Archie Featherstone much (he'd danced with me at some pretty gruesome ball and his way of dancing was to close his eyes, suck in his teeth, and bob up and down in the hope that he looked like Mick Jagger, which he didn't), I knew jolly well what it was like to be desperate to get a seat in Number 3 Equity Court.

It was while I was still in Manchester that Henry received a telemessage about Rumpole and immediately took it up to our Head of Chambers. Sometime later, when I bought him his usual Cinzano Bianco in Pommeroy's Wine Bar, Henry gave me a full account of how his meeting with Ballard went. First of all our Head read the message out aloud very carefully and slowly, Henry told me.

'"Please let firm of Blythe, Winterbottom and Paisley know

sad news. Deeply regret Rumpole gone up to a Higher Tribunal. Signed Rumpole."' Ballard apparently looked puzzled. 'What *is* it, Henry?'

'It's a telemessage, sir. Telegrams having been abolished, *per se*,' Henry explained.

'Yes, I know it's a telemessage. But the wording. Doesn't it strike you as somewhat strange?'

'Mr Rumpole was always one for his joke. It caused us a good deal of embarrassment at times.'

'But presumably this can't be signed by Rumpole. Not in the circumstances.' Ballard was working on the problem. 'On any reasonable interpretation, the word "Rumpole", being silent so far as sex is concerned, must surely be construed as referring to *Mrs* Rumpole?' He was being very legal, Henry told me, and behaving like a Chancery barrister.

'That's what I assumed, sir,' said Henry. 'Unfortunately I can't get through to the Gloucester Road flat on the telephone. It seems there's a "fault on the line".'

'Have you tried calling round?'

'I have, sir. No answer to my ring.'

'Well, of course, it's a busy time in any family. A busy and distressing time.' But Ballard was clearly worried. 'Does it strike you as rather odd, Henry?'

'Well, just a bit, sir.'

'As Head of Chambers I surely should be the first to be informed of any decease among members. Am I not entitled to that?'

'In the normal course of events, yes.' Henry told me he agreed to save any argument.

'In the normal course. But this message doesn't refer to me, or to his fellow members, or even to the Court where he was appearing when he was stricken down. This Blythe, Sidebottom and ...'

'Winterbottom, sir. And Paisley.'

'Was it a firm to which old Rumpole was particularly attached?'

'I don't think so, Mr Ballard. They owed him money,' Henry said he told him frankly.

'They owed him money! Strange. Very strange.' Ballard was

thoughtful, it seems. 'From the way he was talking the other day, I think the old fellow had a queer sort of premonition that the end was pretty close.' And then our Head of Chambers went back to the document Henry had given him. 'All the same, Henry. There is something hopeful in this telemessage.'

'Is there, sir?'

'I mean the reference to a "Higher Tribunal". You know, I'm afraid I'd always found Rumpole a bit of a scoffer. I couldn't get him interested in "Lawyers As Churchgoers". He wouldn't even come along to one meeting of LAC! But his wife's message says he was thinking in terms of a "Higher Tribunal". It suggests he found faith in the end, Henry. It must have been a great comfort to him.'

As I say, Henry told me this after I got back from Manchester, when I was buying him a drink in Pommeroy's Wine Bar. As we were talking I noticed that the frumpy sort of woman in glasses, the one who'd been listening to the Armstrong trial, was doing her best to overhear our conversation. She carried on listening when Jack Pommeroy slid his counter cloth up to us and said to Henry,

'I say. Has old Rumpole really had it? I've got about twenty-three of his cheques!'

'My clerk's fees aren't exactly up to date either,' Henry said. 'You'll miss him round here, won't you, Jack?'

'Well, he did use to pass some pretty insulting remarks about our claret. Called it Château Thames Embankment!' Jack Pommeroy looked pained. 'Didn't exactly help our business. And when he wasn't paying cash . . .'

I wasn't really listening to him then. I was watching the woman in glasses. She was talking into the telephone on the wall and I distinctly heard her say, 'True? Yes, of course it's true.'

Mr Newton, the inquiry agent, later pointed her out to me as Blythe's secretary, whom he had once seen dancing in Soho wearing, incredibly enough, pink satin trousers.

Oddly enough I won my case in Manchester. My solicitor told me that an elderly man on the jury had been heard to say that if a nice girl like me read those sort of magazines there couldn't be much harm in them. It seems I'm to get a lot more dirty books from Manchester! Anyway, I was back in time for the Chambers meeting and all of us, except for Mrs Erskine-Brown who was apparently doing something extremely important in Wales, assembled in Ballard's room. I was taking the minutes so I can tell you more or less exactly what happened. It started when Ballard read out the telemessage again in a very sad and solemn sort of way.

'Bit rum, isn't it? What's he mean exactly, "Higher Tribunal"?' Uncle Tom said.

'I have no doubt he means that Great Court of Appeal before which we shall all have to appear eventually, Uncle Tom,' Ballard explained.

'I never got to the Court of Appeal. Never had a brief to go there, as a matter of fact. Probably just as well. I wouldn't've been up to it.' Uncle Tom smiled round at us all.

'Knowing Rumpole,' said Erskine-Brown, 'there must be a joke there somewhere.'

'It must have been sent by Mrs Rumpole. Poor Rumpole is clearly not in a position to send "telemessages",' our Head of Chambers told us.

'Not in a position? Oh. See what you mean. Quite so. Exactly.' Uncle Tom got the point.

'Now, of course, this sad event will mean consequent changes in Chambers.' Ballard moved the discussion on.

'So far as the furniture is concerned. Yes.' Erskine-Brown opened a favourite subject. 'I don't suppose anyone will have any particular use for the old hatstand which stood in Rumpole's room.'

'His *hatstand*, Erskine-Brown?' Ballard was surprised.

'I happen to have conferences, from time to time, with a number of solicitors. Naturally they have hats. Well, if no one else wants it . . .'

'I don't think there'll be a stampede for Rumpole's old hatstand,' Uncle Tom assured him.

'I was thinking that there ought to be a bit more work about,' Hoskins said. 'I mean, I suppose Henry can hang on to some of Rumpole's solicitors. Myers and people like that. Now the work may get spread around a bit.'

'I'm not sure I agree with Hoskins.' Erskine-Brown was doubtful. 'There's some part of Rumpole's work which we might be glad to lose. I mean the sort of thing you were doing in Manchester, Allways.'

'You mean porn?' I asked him brightly.

'Obscenity! That's exactly what I do mean. Or rape. Or indecent assault. Or possessing house-breaking instruments by night. I mean, this may be our opportunity, sad as the occasion is, of course, to improve the image of Chambers. I mean, do we *want* dirty-book merchants hanging about the clerk's room?'

'Speaking for myself,' Ballard agreed, 'I think there's a great deal in what Erskine-Brown says. If you're not *for* these moral degenerates, in my view, you should be *against* them. I'd like to see a great deal more prosecution work in Chambers.'

'Well, you are certain of the money, with prosecutions.' Hoskins was with him. 'Speaking as a man with daughters.'

'There is a young fellow who's a certainty for the Yard's list of prosecutors,' Ballard said. 'I think I've mentioned young Archie Featherstone to you, Erskine-Brown?'

'Of course. The Judge's nephew.'

'It may be, in the changed circumstances, we shall have a room to offer young Archie Featherstone.'

'He won't be taking work from us?' Hoskins was more than a bit nervous at the prospect.

'In my opinion he'll be bringing it in,' Ballard reassured him, 'in the shape of prosecutions. Now, there are a few arrangements to be discussed.'

'I hope "arrangements" doesn't mean a crematorium,' Uncle Tom said mournfully. 'I always thing there's something terribly depressing about those little railway lines, passing out through the velvet curtain.'

'Of course, it is something of an event. I wonder if we'd get the Temple Church?' Hoskins seemed almost excited.

'Oh, I imagine not.' Erskine-Brown was discouraging. 'And, of course, we've seen nothing in the *Times* Obituaries. I'm afraid Rumpole never got the cases which made legal history.'

'I suppose they might hold some sort of memorial service in Pommeroy's Wine Bar,' Uncle Tom said thoughtfully. Our Head

of Chambers looked a bit disapproving at that, as it didn't seem
to be quite the right thing to say on a solemn occasion.

'I think we should send a modest floral tribute,' he suggested.
'Henry can arrange for that, out of Chambers expenses. Everyone
agreed?' They all did, and Ballard went on, 'In view of the fact
that at the eleventh hour he appeared to be reconciled to the
deeper realities of our brief life on earth, you might all care to
stand for a few minutes' silence, in memory of Horace Rumpole.'

So we all stood up, just a bit sheepishly, and bowed our heads.
The silence seemed to last a long time, like it used to in Poppy
Day services at school.

As I have been writing up this account for the completion of
Rumpole's papers, I have got to know Mrs Rumpole and, in the
course of a few teas, come to get on with her jolly well. As we
all knew in Chambers, Rumpole used to call her She Who Must
Be Obeyed and always seemed to be in tremendous awe of her,
but I didn't find her all that alarming. In fact she always seemed
grateful for someone to talk to. She told me a lot about the old
days, when her father, C. H. Wystan, was Head of Chambers,
and of how Rumpole always criticized him for not knowing
enough about bloodstains; and she described how Rumpole proposed to her at a ball in the Temple, when he'd had, as she
described it, 'quite enough claret cup to be going on with'. During
one of our teas (she took me, which was very decent of her, to
Fortnum's) she described the visit she had received at her flat
in the Gloucester Road shortly before Mr Myers restored R. *v.*
Armstrong for a further hearing before Judge Bullingham.

One afternoon there came a ring, so it seemed, at the door
bell of the Rumpole mansion flat. Mrs Rumpole – I'll call her
'Hilda' from now on since we've really become quite friendly –
opened the door to see a small, fat, elderly man (Hilda described
him to me as toad-like), who had a bald head, gold-rimmed
spectacles and the cheek to put on a crêpe armband and a black
tie. As he sort of oozed past her into her living room, he looked,
Hilda told me, like a commercial traveller for a firm of undertakers. She wasn't entirely unprepared for this visit, however.
The man had rung her earlier and explained that he was Mr

Perivale Blythe, a solicitor of the Supreme Court and anxious to pay his respects to the Widow Rumpole.

When he had penetrated the living room, Mr Blythe sat on a sofa with his briefcase on his knee and began to talk in hushed, respectful tones, Hilda told me.

'I felt I had to intrude,' he said softly. 'Even at this sad, sad moment, Mrs Rumpole. I do not come as myself, not even as Blythe, Winterbottom and Paisley, but I come as a representative, if I may say so, of the entire legal profession. Your husband was a great gentleman, Mrs Rumpole. And a fine lawyer.'

'A fine lawyer?' Hilda was puzzled. 'He never told me.'

'And, of course, a most persuasive advocate.'

'Oh, yes. He told me *that*,' Hilda agreed.

'We all join you in your grief, Mrs Rumpole. And I have to tell you this! There are no smiling faces today in the firm of Blythe, Winterbottom and Paisley!'

'Thank you.' Hilda did her best to sound grateful.

'Nor anywhere, I suppose, from Inner London to Acton Magistrates. He will be sorely missed.'

'I have to tell you what will be sorely missed, Mr Blythe,' Hilda said then, and said it in a meaningful kind of way.

'What, Mrs Rumpole?'

I think she said she stood up then and looked down on her visitor's large, pale, bald head, 'All those fees you owe him. Since the indecency case, I believe, in 1973.'

Blythe was clearly taken aback. He cleared his throat and began to fiddle nervously with the catch on his briefcase. 'You have heard a little about that?'

'I've heard a lot about it!'

'Well, of course, a great deal of that money hasn't been completely recovered from the clients. Not in full. But I'm here to settle up,' he assured her. 'I imagine you're the late Mr Rumpole's executor?'

He opened his briefcase; Hilda looked into it and noticed a cheque book. Blythe got out a document and shut the briefcase quickly.

'Of course I'm his executor,' Hilda told him.

'Then no doubt you're fully empowered to enter into what

I think you'll agree is a perfectly fair compromise. Now, the sum involved is . . .'

'Two thousand, seven hundred and sixty-five pounds, ninety-three pence,' Hilda said quickly. She has a jolly good memory.

'Quite the businesswoman, Mrs Rumpole.' The beastly Blythe smiled in a patronizing manner. 'Now, would an immediate payment of . . . let's say ten per cent, be a nice little arrangement? Then it'll be over and done with.'

'Mr Blythe. I have to face the butcher!' Hilda told him.

'Yes, of course, but . . .' Blythe didn't seem to understand.

'And the water rates. And the London Electricity Board. And the telephone has actually been cut off during my visit to the Lake District. I can't offer them a nice little arrangement, can I?'

'Well. Possibly not,' Blythe admitted.

'But I will offer *you* one, Mr Perivale Blythe,' Hilda said firmly.

'Well, that's extremely obliging of you . . .' Blythe took out his fountain pen.

And then Hilda spoke to him along the following lines. It was undoubtedly her finest hour. 'I will offer you this,' she said. 'I won't report this conversation to the Law Society, although this year's President's father was a close personal friend of *my* father, C. H. Wystan. I will not take immediate steps to have you struck off, Mr Blythe, just provided you sit down and write out a cheque for two thousand, seven hundred and sixty-five pounds, ninety-three pence, in favour of Hilda Rumpole.'

The effect of this on the little creep on the sofa was apparently astonishing. For a moment his mouth sagged open. Then, in desperation, he patted his pockets. 'Unfortunately forgot my cheque book,' he lied. 'I'll slip one in the post.'

'Look in your briefcase, Mr Blythe. I think you'll find your cheque book there.' Hilda's words of command were interrupted by the sound of a ring at the door. As she went to open it she said, 'Excuse me. And don't try the window, Mr Blythe. It's really a great deal too far for you to jump.'

No doubt about it, she was a woman born to command. When she was out of the room, Blythe, with moist and trembling fingers, wrote out a cheque for the full amount. She returned with a tall, lugubrious figure who was scrubbing the end of his nose with a crushed pocket handkerchief.

'Thank you, Mr Blythe,' Hilda said politely as she took the cheque. 'And now there's a gentleman to see you.'

At which the new arrival whisked a paper out of his pocket and put it into the hand of the demoralized Perivale Blythe.

'"Fig" Newton!' he said. 'Whatever's this?'

'It's a subpoena, Mr Blythe,' Mr Newton explained patiently. 'They want you to give evidence in a case down the Old Bailey.'

The case was, of course, R. *v.* Armstrong. On the morning when it started again I sat in Rumpole's place, the only defending barrister. When the jury was reassembled the Usher called for silence and his Honour Judge Bullingham came into Court, looked towards me, noticed the gap that used to be Rumpole, and clearly decided that it would be in order to say a few words of tribute to the departed. They took the form of a speech to the jury in which his Lordship sounded confidential and really jolly sincere. 'Members of the jury,' he said, and they all turned their faces solemnly towards him. 'Before we start this case, there is something I have to say. In our Courts, warm friendships spring up between judges and counsel, between Bench and Bar. We're not superior beings as judges; we don't put on "side". We are the barristers' friends. And one of my oldest friends, over the years, was Horace Rumpole.' Both Ward-Webster for the prosecution and I looked piously up to the ceiling. We carefully hid our feelings of amazement.

'During the time he appeared before me, in many cases, I can truthfully say that there was never a cross word between us, although we may have had trivial disagreements over points of law,' Bullingham went on. 'We are all part of that great happy family, members of the jury, which is the Criminal Court.'

It was at that moment that I heard a sound beside me and smelt the familiar shaving soap and small cigar. The Judge and the jury were too busy with each other to notice, but Ward-Webster and almost everyone else in Court were looking towards us in silent stupefaction. Rumpole was, I must say, looking in astonishingly fine condition, pinker than usual and well rested. He was obviously enjoying the Judge's speech.

'Mr Horace Rumpole was one of the old brigade.' By now Judge Bullingham was clearly deeply moved. 'Not a leader, perhaps, not a general, but a reliable, hard-working and great-hearted old soldier of the line.'

Of course, Rumpole could resist it no longer. He got slowly to his feet and bowed deeply, saying, 'My Lord.' The jury's faces swivelled towards him. Bullingham looked away from the jury-box and into the Court. If people who see ghosts go dark purple, well, that's how Bullingham looked.

'My Lord,' Rumpole repeated, 'I am deeply touched by your Lordship's remarks.'

'Mr Rumpole ... Mr Rumpole ...?' The Judge's voice rose incredulously. 'I heard ...'

'Greatly exaggerated, my Lord, I do assure you.' Of course, Rumpole had to say it. 'May I say what a pleasure it is to be continuing this case before your Lordship.'

'Mason. What's this mean?' Bullingham leant forward and whispered hoarsely to the Clerk of the Court. We heard Mr Mason whisper back, 'Quite honestly, Judge, I haven't a clue.'

'Mr Rumpole. Have you some application?' The Judge was looking at Rumpole with something like fear. Perhaps he thought he was about to call someone from the spirit world.

'No application.' Rumpole smiled charmingly. 'Your Lordship kindly adjourned this case, if you remember. It's now been re-stored to your list. Our inquiries are complete and I will call Mr Perivale Blythe.'

After the sensation of Rumpole's return from the tomb, where Bullingham quite obviously thought he'd been, I'm afraid to say that the rest of R. *v.* Armstrong was a bit of an anti-climax. Perivale Blythe padded into the witness-box, took the oath in a plummy sort of voice, and I have the notes of Rumpole's examination-in-chief.

'Mr Blythe,' the resurrected old barrister asked. 'After their father's death, did you act for the two Armstrong brothers, my client Frank and his brother Frederick?'

'Yes, I did,' Blythe agreed.

'And did Fred supply the computers set up in the offices of Sun-Sand Holidays, my client Frank Armstrong's firm?'

'I believe he did.' Blythe sounded uninterested.

'Mr Blythe, would you take the photograph of the Cornish holiday site?'

As the usher took the photograph to the witness-box, Bullingham staged a bit of a comeback and said, 'The industrial area, Mr Rumpole?'

'Exactly, my Lord.' Rumpole bowed politely. 'Do you know what that industry is, Mr Blythe?'

'Tin mines, my Lord. I rather think.' Once again, Blythe sounded deliberately unconcerned.

'You *know*, don't you? Didn't you visit that site on behalf of your client Mr *Frederick* Armstrong?'

'I did. He was anxious to buy his brother Frank's site.'

'Because he knew tin would also be discovered there.'

'Yes, of course.' And then Blythe forgot his lack of interest. 'I don't believe he told his brother that.'

'I don't believe he did.' Rumpole was after him now. 'And when his brother refused, didn't Fred take every possible step to ruin his brother Frank's business, no doubt by interfering with the computers that he'd installed so that they constantly gave misleading information, booked non-existent holiday homes and gave false instructions for caravans to be towed away?'

'I never approved of that, my Lord. I am an officer of the Court. I wouldn't have any part of it.' Perivale Blythe was sweating. He patted his bald head with a handkerchief and protested his innocence. I'd say he made a pretty unattractive figure in the witness-box.

'Although you knew about it. Come, Mr Blythe. You must have known about it to disapprove.' Rumpole pressed his advantage but the Judge, back to his old form, was getting restless. 'Mr Rumpole! I take the gravest objection to this in examination-in-chief. It is quite outrageous!'

'A trivial objection, surely?' Rumpole gave a sweet smile. 'Your Lordship has told the jury we only have trivial disagreements.'

'You are putting an entirely new case to this witness, so far as I can see, on no evidence.'

'Oh, there will be evidence, my Lord.'

'I hope my learned friend doesn't intend to *give* that evidence?' Ward-Webster rose to his feet to object for the prosecution.

'I hope that my learned friend doesn't wish to conceal from the jury the fact that Detective Inspector Limmeridge arrested Frederick Armstrong when he had entered his brother's office by night and was reprogramming the computers. There has been a charge of Perverting the Course of Justice,' Rumpole said, looking hard at the jury. 'In fact, Mr Newton has given the results of all his observations to the officer in charge of the case.'

'Is that right, Mr Ward-Webster?' Bullingham asked incredulously.

'So I understand, my Lord.' Ward-Webster subsided.

'I shall be recalling the Detective Inspector, my Lord,' Rumpole said triumphantly, 'as a witness for the defence.'

Well in the end, of course, the jury saw the point. Brother Fred had set out to ruin brother Frank's business by interfering with the computers so that they sold non-existent holidays, or removed existing caravans. With Frank in prison Fred could have got hold of the Cornish mobile home site and a great deal of tin. It wasn't one of Rumpole's greatest cases, but a jolly satisfying win. Horace Rumpole has taught me a lot about criminal procedure, but I don't think I'd ever dare try his way of getting an adjournment.

Well, I've written my bit. I hope it's all right and that someone will check it through for grammar. It tells what happened so far as I knew it at the time, or almost as far as I knew it.

(Signed) Fiona Patience Allways, barrister-at-law.

3 Equity Court

Temple

London, E.C.4

I'm extremely grateful to my learned friend, Miss Fiona Allways, for dealing with that part of the story. It had been necessary, as I expect you have guessed, to take her into my confidence (a little earlier than she divulges in her account) when

I decided to lie doggo, to feign death and lure the wretched Perivale Blythe out of hiding. Of course I saw Hilda as soon as she got back from her 'bachelor holiday' in the Lake District and I had to let her in on the scheme. But I must say, She was something of a sport about the whole business and the way she dealt with the appalling Blythe, much of which I heard from a point of vantage near our bedroom door, seemed to me masterly. When She Who Must Be Obeyed is on form, no lawyer can possibly stand up to her.

On the whole the incident gave me enormous pleasure. One of the many drawbacks of actually snuffing it will be that you can't hear the things people say about you when they think you're safe in your box. I enormously enjoyed Fiona's account of the Chambers meeting and the silent prayer which marked my passing – just as I will never let Judge Bullingham forget his funeral oration.

Oh, and one other marvellous moment: Hilda and I were sitting at tea one afternoon when I was out of circulation and a ring came at the door bell. Some boy was delivering Hilda a socking great wreath from Chambers, compliments of Sam Ballard and all the learned friends. The deeply respectful note to Hilda explained that the tribute was sent to her home as they didn't quite know when the interment was due to take place.

After I had won Frank Armstrong's case I walked up to Chambers and called on our learned Head. For some reason my appearance in the flesh seemed to irritate the man almost beyond endurance.

'Rumpole,' he said, 'I think you've behaved disgracefully.'

'I don't know why you should say that,' I told him. 'Isn't there a Biblical precedent for this sort of thing?'

'I suppose you're very proud of yourself,' Ballard boomed on.

'Well, it wasn't a bad win.' I lit a small cigar. 'Got the Sun-Sand Mobile Homes owner away and clear. Made the world safe for a few more ghastly holidays.'

'I am not referring to your case, Rumpole. You caused us all . . . You caused me personally . . . a great deal of unnecessary grief!'

'Oh, come off it, Bollard. I understand you couldn't wait to relet my room to young Archie Featherstone.

A little month; or ere those shoes were old
With which you follow'd poor old Rumpole's body,
Like Niobe, all tears . . .'

I gave him a slice of *Hamlet* which he didn't appreciate.

'We had to plan for the future, Rumpole. Deeply distressed as we all were . . .'

'Deeply distressed indeed! I hear that Uncle Tom suggested a memorial service in Pommeroy's Wine Bar.'

Ballard had the decency to look a little embarrassed. 'I never approved of that,' he said.

'Well, it's not a bad idea. And I happen to be in funds at the moment. Why don't I invite you all to a piss-up at Pommeroy's?'

Ballard looked at me sadly. 'And I thought you had finally found faith!' he said. 'That's what I can never forgive.'

In due course the learned friends assembled in Pommeroy's at the end of a working day. I had invited Hilda to join us. We were on friendly terms at the time and, as a result of Blythe's cheque, her bank balance was in a considerably more healthy state than mine. So I got Jack Pommeroy to dispense the plonk with a liberal hand and during the celebrations I heard She Who Must Be Obeyed talking to our Head of Chambers.

'It was very naughty of Rumpole, of course,' She said, 'but there was just no other way of getting his fees from that appalling man, Perivale Blythe.'

'Mrs Rumpole. Can I get this clear? You were a knowing party to this extraordinary conspiracy?'

'Oh yes.' And Hilda sounded proud of it.

'I'll have you after my job, Mrs Rumpole,' Henry said. 'I couldn't get Mr Blythe to pay up. Not till we got this idea.'

'Henry! You're not saying *you* knew?'

'I'm not saying anything, Mr Ballard,' Henry answered with a true clerk's diplomacy. 'But perhaps I had an inkling.'

'Allways! You took Rumpole home. You must have thought . . .' Ballard clearly guessed that he was on to an appalling conspiracy.

'That he'd died?' Fiona smiled at him. 'Oh, I can't see how anyone could think that. He'd never die in the middle of a case, would he?'

'It was exactly the same when we believed he'd retired,' Uncle Tom told the world in general. 'Rumpole kept popping back, like a bloody opera singer!'

At which point I felt moved to address them and banged a glass on the bar for silence.

'Well, my learned friends!' I said in my final speech. 'Since no one else seems inclined to, it falls on me to say a few words. After the distressing news you have heard, it comes as a great pleasure to welcome Horace Rumpole back to the land of the living. When he was deceased he was constantly in your thoughts. Some of you wanted his room. Some of you wanted his work. Some, I know, couldn't wait to get their fingers on the old boy's hatstand. You are all nonetheless welcome to drink to his long life and continued success in a glass of Château Thames Embankment!'

I must say that they all raised their glasses and drank with every appearance of enjoyment. Then I went over to Jack Pommeroy and asked him to bring out, from behind the bar, the tribute from Ballard which I had concealed there before the party began.

'Bollard,' I said as I handed it to him, 'this came to my home address. I'm afraid you went to some expense over the thing. Never mind. As I shan't be needing it now, keep it for one of your friends.'

So, at the end of the day, Sam Ballard was left holding the wreath.

Rumpole's Last Case

To all the friends, learned and otherwise, I made down the Old Bailey and especially to the criminal defenders Jeremy Hutchinson who, like me, has done his last case and Geoffrey Robertson who certainly hasn't.

Contents

Rumpole and the Blind Tasting

'Rumpole! How could you drink that stuff?'

'Perfectly easy, Erskine-Brown. Raise the glass to the lips, incline the head slightly backwards, and let the liquid flow gently past the tonsils.' I gave the man a practical demonstration. 'I admit I've had a good deal of practice, but even you may come to it in time.'

'Of course you *can* drink it, Rumpole. Presumably it's *possible* to drink methylated spirits shaken up with a little ice and a dash of angostura bitters.' Erskine-Brown smiled at me from over the edge of the glass of Côte de Nuits Villages '79, which he had been ordering in his newly acquired wine-buff's voice from Jack Pommeroy, before he settled himself at the bar; I couldn't help noticing that his dialogue was showing some unaccustomed vivacity. 'I fully appreciate that you *can* drink Pommeroy's Very Ordinary. But the point is, Rumpole, why should you want to?'

'Forgetfulness, Erskine-Brown. The consignment of a day in front of his Honour Judge Bullingham to the Lethe of forgotten things. The Mad Bull,' I told him, as I drained the large glass of Château Fleet Street Jack Pommeroy had obligingly put on my slate until the next legal aid cheque came in, 'constantly interrupted my speech to the Jury. I am defending an alleged receiver of stolen sugarbowls. With this stuff, not to put too fine a point on it, you have a reasonable chance of getting blotto.'

It is a good few years now since I adopted the habit of noting down the facts of some of my outstanding cases, the splendours and miseries of an Old Bailey hack, and those of you who may have cast an eye over some of my previous works of reminiscence may well be muttering '*Plus ça change, plus c'est la même chose'* or words to the like effect. After so many cross-examinations, speeches to the Jury, verdicts of guilty or not guilty, legal aid cheques long-awaited and quickly disposed of down the bottomless pit of the overdraft at the Caring Bank, no great change in the Rumpole fortunes had taken place, the texture of life remained much as it always had been and would, no doubt, do so until after my positively last case when I sit waiting to be called on in the Great Circuit Court of the Skies, if such a tribunal exists.

Take that evening as typical. I had been involved in the defence of one Hugh Snakelegs Timson. The Timsons, you may remember, are an extended family of South London villains who practise crime in the stolid, hard-working, but not particularly successful manner in which a large number of middle-of-the-road advocates practise at the Bar. The Timsons are not high-fliers; not for them the bullion raids or the skilled emptying of the Rembrandts out of ducal mansions. The Timsons inhabit the everyday world of purloined video-recorders, bent log-books and stolen Cortinas. They also provide me and my wife, Hilda (known to me, quite off the record, and occasionally behind the hand, as She Who Must Be Obeyed), with our bread and butter. When prospects are looking bleak, when my tray in the clerk's room is bare of briefs but loaded with those unpleasant-looking buff envelopes doshed out at regular intervals by Her Majesty the Queen, it is comforting to know that somewhere in the Greater London area, some Timson will be up to some sort of minor villainy and, owing to the general incompetence of the clan, the malefactor concerned will no doubt be in immediate need of legal representation.

Hugh Snakelegs Timson was, at that time, the family's official fence, having taken over the post from his Uncle Percy Timson,* who was getting a good deal past it, and had retired to live in Benidorm. Snakelegs, a thin, elegant man in his forties, a former winner of the Mr Debonair contest at Butlin's Holiday Camp, had earned his name from his talent at the tango. He lived with his wife, Hetty, in a semi-detached house in Bromley to which

* See 'Rumpole and the Age for Retirement' in *The Trials of Rumpole*, Penguin Books, 1979.

Detective Inspector Broome, the well-known terror of the Timsons, set out on a voyage of discovery with his faithful Detective Sergeant Cosgrove. At first Inspector 'New' Broome had drawn a blank at the Timson home; even the huge coffin-shaped freezer seemed to contain nothing but innumerable bags full of frozen vegetables. The eager Inspector had the bright idea of thawing some of these provisions however, and was rewarded by the spectacle of articles of Georgian silver arising from the saucepans of boiling peas in the manner of Venus arising from the Sea.

The defence of Hugh Snakelegs Timson had not been going particularly well. The standard receiver's story, 'I got the whole lot from a bloke in a pub who was selling them off cheap, and whose name I cannot for the life of me recall', was treated with undisguised contempt by his Honour, Judge Roger Bullingham, who asked, with the ponderous cynicism accompanied by an undoubted wink at the Jury, of which he is master, if I were not going to suggest that there had been a shower of sugar-sifters, cream jugs and the like from the back of a lorry? Anyway, if got innocently, why was the silverware in the deep-freezer? I told the Jury that an Englishman's freezer was his castle and that there was no reason on earth why a citizen shouldn't keep his valuables in a bag of Bird's Eye peas at a low temperature. Indeed, I added, as I thought helpfully, I had an old aunt who kept odd pound notes in the tea-caddy, and constantly risked boiling up her savings in a pot of Darjeeling. At this the Mad Bull went an even darker shade of purple, his neck swelled visibly so that it seemed about to burst his yellowing winged collar, and he told the Jury that my aunt was 'not evidence', and that they must in reaching a decision 'dismiss entirely anything Mr Rumpole may have said about his curious family', adding, with a whole battery of near-nudges and almost-winks, 'I expect our saner relatives know the proper place for their valuables. In the bank.'

At this point the Bull decided to interrupt my final speech by adjourning for tea and television in his private room, and I was left to wander disconsolately in the direction of Pommeroy's Wine Bar, where I met that notable opera buff and wine

connoisseur, half-hearted prosecutor and inept defender, the
spouse and helpmeet of Phillida Erskine-Brown, Q.C. Phillida
Trant, as was, the Portia of our Chambers, had put his nose
somewhat out of joint by taking silk and leaving poor old Claude,
ten years older than she, a humble Junior. So there I was, raising
yet another glass of Château Thames Embankment to my lips
and telling Claude that the only real advantage of this particular
vintage was that it was quite likely to get you drunk.

'The purpose of drinking wine is not intoxication, Rumpole.'
Erskine-Brown looked as pained as a prelate who is told that his
congregation only came to church because of the central heating.
'The point is to get in touch with one of the major influences of
western civilization, to taste sunlight trapped in a bottle, and to
remember some stony slope in Tuscany or a village by the
Gironde.'

I thought with a momentary distaste of the bit of barren soil,
no doubt placed between the cowshed and the *pissoir*, where the
Château Pommeroy grape struggled for existence. And then,
Erskine-Brown, long-time member of our Chambers in Equity
Court, went considerably too far.

'You see, Rumpole,' he said, 'it's the terrible nose.'

Now I make no particular claim for my nose and I am far from
suggesting that it's a thing of beauty and a joy forever. When I
was in my perambulator it may, for all I can remember, have had
a sort of tip-tilted and impertinent charm. In my youth it was no
doubt pinkish and healthy-looking. In my early days at the Bar
it had a sharp and inquisitive quality which made prosecution
witnesses feel they could keep no secrets from it. Today it is
perhaps past its prime, it has spread somewhat; it has, in part at
least, gone mauve; it is, after all, a nose that has seen a considerable quantity of life. But man and boy it has served me well, and
I had no intention of having my appearance insulted by Claude
Erskine-Brown, barrister-at-law, who looks, in certain unfavourable lights, not unlike an abbess with a bad period.

'We may disagree about Pommeroy's plonk,' I told him, 'but
that's no reason why you should descend to personal abuse.'

'No, I don't mean *your* nose, Rumpole. I mean the wine's nose.'

I looked suspiciously into the glass; did this wine possess

qualities I hadn't guessed at? 'Don't babble, Erskine-Brown.'

'"Nose", Rumpole! The bouquet. That's one of the expressions you have to learn to use about wine. Together with the "length".'

'Length?' I looked down at the glass in my hand; the length seemed to be about one inch and shrinking rapidly.

'The "length" a great wine lingers in the mouth, Rumpole. Look, why don't you let me educate you? My friend, Martyn Vanberry, organizes tastings in the City. Terrifically good fun. You get to try about a dozen wines.'

'A dozen?' I was doubtful. 'An expensive business.'

'No, Rumpole. Absolutely free. They are blind tastings. He's got one on tomorrow afternoon, as it so happens.'

'You mean they make you blind drunk?' I couldn't resist asking. 'Sounds exactly what I need.' At that moment the promise of Martyn Vanberry and his blind tastings were a vague hope for the future. My immediate prospects included an evening drink with She Who Must Be Obeyed and finishing my speech for Snakelegs to the Jury against the Mad Bull's barracking. I emptied Pommeroy's dull opiate to the drains and aimed Lethe-wards.

It might be said that the story of the unknown vendor of Georgian silver in the pub lacked originality, and that the inside of a freezer-pack was not the most obvious place for storing valuable antiques, but there was one point of significance in the defence of Hugh Snakelegs Timson. Detective Inspector Broome was, as I have already suggested, an enthusiastic officer and one who regarded convictions with as much pride as the late Don Giovanni regarded his conquests of the female sex. No doubt he notched them up on his braces. He had given evidence that there had been thefts of silver from various country houses in Kent, but all the Detective Inspector's industry and persistence had not produced one householder who could be called by the Prosecution to identify the booty from the freezer as his stolen silverware. So where, I was able to ask, was the evidence that the property undoubtedly received by Snakelegs had been stolen? Unless the old idea that the burden lay on the Prosecution to prove its case had gone out of fashion in his Lordship's court (distant rumblings as of a volcano limbering up for an eruption from the Bull), then perhaps, I ventured to suggest, Snakelegs was entitled to squeeze his way out of trouble.

Whether it was this thought, or Judge Bullingham's frenzied eagerness to secure a conviction (Kane himself might have got off his murder rap if he'd only been fortunate enough to receive a really biased summing up), the Jury came back with a cheerful verdict of not guilty. After only a brief fit of minor apoplexy, and a vague threat to bring the inordinate length of defending counsel's speeches to the attention of the legal aid authorities, the Bull released the prisoner to his semi-detached and his wife Hetty. I was strolling along the corridor, puffing a small cigar with a modest feeling of triumph, when a small, eager young lady, her fairly pleasing face decorated with a pair of steel-rimmed specs and a look of great seriousness, rather as though she was not quite certain which problem to tackle first, world starvation or nuclear war, came panting up alongside.

'Mr Rumpole,' she said, 'you did an absolutely first-class job!'

I paused in my tracks, looked at her more closely, and remembered that she had been sitting in Court paying close attention throughout *R. v. Snakelegs Timson*.

'I just gave my usual service.'

'And I,' she said, sticking out her hand in a gesture of camaraderie, 'have just passed the Bar exams.'

'Then we don't shake hands,' I had to tell her, avoiding physical contact. 'Clients don't like it you see. Think we might be doing secret deals with each other. All the same, welcome to the treadmill.'

I moved away from her then, towards the lift, pressed the button, and as I waited for nothing very much to happen she accosted me again.

'You don't stereotype that much, do you, Mr Rumpole?' She looked as though she were already beginning to lose a little faith in my infallibility.

'And you don't call me *Mister* Rumpole. Leave that to the dotty Bull,' I corrected her, perhaps a little sharply.

'I thought you were too busy fighting the class war to care about outdated behaviour patterns.'

'Fighting the *what*?'

'Protecting working people against middle-class judges.'

The lift was still dawdling away in the basement and I thought it would be kind now to put this recruit right on a few of the basic principles of our legal system. 'The Timsons would hate to be called "working people",' I told her. 'They're entirely middle-class villains. Very Conservative, in fact. They live by strict monetarist principles and the free market economy. They're also against the closed shop; they believe that shops should be open at all hours of the night. Preferably by jemmy.'

'My name's Liz Probert,' she said, failing to smile at the jest I was not making for the first time. At this point the lift arrived. 'Good day Mizz' – I took her for a definite Mizz – I said, as I stepped into it. Rather to my surprise she strode in after me, still chattering. 'I want to defend like you. But I must still have a lot to learn. I never noticed the point about the owners not identifying the stolen silver.'

'Neither did I,' I had to admit, 'until it was almost too late. And you know why they didn't?' I was prepared to tell this neophyte the secrets of my astonishing success. That, after all, is part of the Great Tradition of the Bar, otherwise known as showing off to the younger white-wigs. 'They'd all got the insurance money, you see, and done very nicely out of it, thank you. The last thing they wanted was to see their old sugarbowls back and have to return the money. Life's a bit more complicated than they tell you in the Bar exams.'

We had reached the robing-room floor and I made for the Gents with Mizz Probert following me like the hound, or at least the puppy, of heaven. 'I was wondering if you could possibly give me some counselling in my career area.'

'Not now, I'm afraid. I've got a blind date, with some rather attractive bottles.' I opened the door and saw the gleaming porcelain fittings which had been in my mind since I got out of Court. 'Men only in here, I'm afraid,' I had to tell Mizz Probert, who still seemed to be at my heels. 'It's one of the quaint old traditions of the Bar.'

*

The surprisingly rapid and successful conclusion of the *Queen* v. *Snakelegs* had liberated me, and I set off with some eagerness to Prentice Alley in the City of London, and the premises of Vanberry's Fine Wines & Spirits Ltd, where I was to meet Claude Erskine-Brown, and sample, for the first time in my life, the mysterious joys of a blind tasting. After my credentials had been checked, I was shown into a small drinks party which had about it all the gaiety of an assembly of the bereaved, when the corpse in question has left his entire fortune to the Cats' Home.

The meeting took place in a brilliantly lit basement room with glaring white tiles. It seemed a suitable location for a post-mortem, but, in place of the usual deceased person on the table, there were a number of bottles, all shrouded in brown-paper bags. It was there I saw my learned friend, Erskine-Brown, already in place among the tasters, who were twirling minute quantities of wine in their glasses, holding them nervously up to the light, sniffing at them with deep suspicion and finally allowing a small quantity to pass their lips. They were mainly solemn-looking characters in dark three-piece suits, although there was one female in a tweed coat and skirt, a sort of white silk stock, sensible shoes and a monocle. She looked as though she'd be happier judging hunters at a country gymkhana than fine wines, and she was, so Erskine-Brown whispered to me, Miss Honoria Bird, the distinguished wine correspondent of the *Sunday Mercury*. Before the tasting competition began in earnest we were invited to sample a few specimens from the Vanberry claret collection. So I took my first taste and experienced what, without doubt, was a draft of vintage that hath been 'Cool'd a long age in the deep-delved earth, Tasting of Flora and the country green, . . .' And it was whilst I was enjoying the flavour of Dance, and Provençal song, and sunburnt mirth, mixed with a dash of wild strawberries, that a voice beside me boomed, 'What's the matter with you? Can't you spit?'

Miss Honoria Bird was at my elbow and in my mouth was what? Something so far above my price range that it seemed like some new concoction altogether, as far removed from Pommeroy's Very Ordinary as a brief for Gulf Oil in the House of

Lords is from a small matter of indecency before the Uxbridge Magistrates.

'Over there, in case you're looking for it. Expectoration corner!' Miss Bird waved me to a wooden wine-box, half-filled with sawdust into which the gents in dark suitings were directing mouthfuls of purplish liquid. I moved away from her, reluctant to admit that the small quantity of the true, the blushful Hippocrene I had been able to win had long since disappeared down the little red lane.

'Collie brought you, didn't he?' Martyn Vanberry, the wine merchant, caught me as I was about to swallow a second helping. He was a thin streak of a chap, in a dark suit and a stiff collar, whose faint smile, I thought, was thin-lipped and patronizing. Beside him stood a pleasant enough young man who was in charge of the mechanics of the thing, brought the bottles and the glasses and was referred to as Ken.

'Collie?' The name meant nothing to me.

'Erskine-Brown. We called him Collie at school.'

'After the dog?' I saw my Chambers companion insert the tip of his pale nose into the aperture of his wine glass.

'No. After the Doctor. Collis-Brown. You know, the medicine? Old Claude was always a bit of a pill really. We used to kick him around at Winchester.'

Now I am far from saying that, in my long relationship with Claude Erskine-Brown, irritation has not sometimes got the better of me, but as a long-time member of our Chambers at Equity Court he has, over the years, become as familiar and uncomfortable as the furniture. I resented the strictures of this public-school bully on my learned friend and was about to say so when the gloomy proceedings were interrupted by the arrival of an unlikely guest wearing tartan trousers, rubber-soled canvas shoes of the type which I believe are generally known as 'trainers', and a zipped jacket which bore on its back the legend MONTY MANTIS SERVICE STATION LUTON BEDS. Inside this costume was a squat, ginger-haired and youngish man who called out, 'Which way to the anti-freeze? At least we can get warmed up for the winter.' This was a clear reference to recent scandals in the wine trade, and it was greeted, in the rarefied air of

Vanberry's tasting room, with as much jollity as an advertisement for contraceptive appliances in the Vatican.

'One of your customers?' I asked Vanberry.

'One of my best,' he sighed. 'I imagine the profession of *garagiste* in Luton must be extremely profitable. And he makes a point of coming to *all* of our blind tastings.'

'Now I'm here,' Mr Mantis said, taking off his zipper jacket and displaying a yellow jumper ornamented with diamond lozenges, 'let battle commence.' He twirled and sniffed and took a mouthful from a tasting glass, made a short but somehow revolting gargling sound and spat into the sawdust. 'A fairly unpretentious Côte Rotie,' he announced, as he did so. 'But on the whole 1975 was a disappointing year on the Rhône.'

The contest was run like a game of musical chairs. They gave you a glass and if you guessed wrong, the chair, so to speak, was removed and you had to go and sit with the girls and have an ice-cream. At my first try I got that distant hint of wild strawberries again from a wine that was so far out of the usual run of my drinking that I became tongue-tied, and when asked to name the nectar could only mutter 'damn good stuff' and slink away from the field of battle.

Erskine-Brown was knocked out in the second round, having confidently pronounced a Coonawarra to be Châteauneuf du Pape. 'Some bloody stuff from Wagga, Wagga,' he grumbled unreasonably – on most occasions Claude was a staunch upholder of the Commonwealth, 'one always forgets about the colonies.'

So we watched as, one by one, the players fell away. Martyn Vanberry was in charge of the bottles and after the contestants had made their guesses he had to disclose the labels. From time to time, in the manner of donnish quiz-masters on upmarket wireless guessing-games, he would give little hints, particularly if he liked the contender. 'A churchyard number' might indicate a Graves, or 'a macabre little item, somewhat skeletal' a Beaune. He never, I noticed, gave much assistance to the *garagiste* from Luton, nor did he need to because the ebullient Mr Monty Mantis had no difficulty in identifying his wines and could even make a decent stab at the vintage year, although perfect accuracy in that regard wasn't required.

Finally the challengers were reduced to two: Monty Mantis and the lady with the eyeglass, Honoria Bird or Birdie as she was known to all the pin-striped expectorating undertakers around her. It was their bottoms that hovered, figuratively speaking, over the final chair, the last parcelled bottle. Martyn Vanberry was holding this with particular reverence as he poured a taster into two glasses. Monty Mantis regarded the colour, lowered his nose to the level of the tide, took a mouthful and spat rapidly.

'Gordon Bennett!' He seemed somewhat amazed. 'Don't want to risk swallowing that. It might ruin me carburettor!'

Martyn Vanberry looked pale and extremely angry. He turned to the lady contestant, who was swilling the stuff around her dentures in a far more impressive way. 'Well, Birdie,' he said, as she spat neatly, 'let me give you a clue. It's not whisky.'

'I think I could tell that.' She looked impassive. 'Not whisky.'

'But think ... just think ...' Vanberry seemed anxious to bring the contest to a rapid end by helping her. 'Think of a whisky translated.'

'*Le quatre-star Esso?*' said the *garagiste*, but Vanberry was unamused.

'White Horse?' Birdie frowned.

'Very good. Something Conservative, of course. And keep to the right!'

'The right bank of the river? St Emilion. White Horse? Cheval Blanc . . .' Birdie arrived at her destination with a certain amount of doubt and hesitation.

'1971, I'm afraid, nothing earlier.' Vanberry was pulling away the brown paper to reveal a label on which the words Cheval Blanc and *Appellation St Emilion Contrôlée* were to be clearly read. There was a smatter of applause. 'Dear old Birdie! Still an unbeatable palate.' It was a tribute in which the Luton *garagiste* didn't join; he was laughing as Martyn Vanberry turned to him and said, icily polite, 'I'm sorry you were pipped at the post, Mr Mantis. You did jolly well. Now, Birdie, if you'll once again accept the certificate of *Les Grands Contestants du Vin* and the complimentary bottle which this time is a magnum of Gevrey Chambertin Claire Pau 1970 – a somewhat underrated vintage. Can you not stay with us, Mr Mantis?'

But Monty Mantis was on his way to the door, muttering about getting himself decarbonized. Nobody laughed, and no one seemed particularly sorry to see him go.

There must be no accounting, I reflected on this incident, for tastes. One man's anti-freeze may be another's Mouton Rothschild, especially if you don't see the label. I was reminded of those embarrassing tests on television in which the puzzled housewife is asked to tell margarine from butter, or say which washing powder got young Ronnie's football shorts whitest. She always looks terrified of disappointing the eager interviewer and plumping for the wrong variety. But then I thought that as a binge, the blind tasting at Vanberry's Fine Wines had been about as successful as a picnic tea with the Clacton Temperance Society and the incident faded from my memory.

Other matters arose of more immediate concern. One was to be of some interest and entertainment value. To deal with the bad news first: my wife, Hilda, whose very name rings out like a demand for immediate obedience, announced the imminent visit to our mansion flat (although the words are inept to describe the somewhat gloomy and cavernous interior of Casa Rumpole) in Froxbury Court, Gloucester Road, of her old school-friend Dodo Mackintosh.

Now Dodo may be, in many ways, a perfectly reasonable and indeed game old bird. Her watercolours of Lanworth Cove and adjacent parts of Cornwall are highly regarded in some circles, although they seem to me to have been executed in heavy rain. She is, I believe, a dab hand at knitting patterns and during her stays a great deal of fancy work is put in on matinée jackets and bootees for her younger relatives. Hilda tells me that she was, when they were both at school, a sturdy lacrosse player. My personal view, and this is not for publication to She Who Must Be Obeyed, is that in any conceivable team sent out to bore for England, Dodo would have to be included. As you may have gathered, I do not hit it off with the lady, and she takes the view that by marrying a claret-drinking, cigar-smoking legal hack who is never likely to make a fortune, Hilda has tragically wasted her life.

The natural gloom that the forthcoming visit cast upon me was somewhat mitigated by the matter of Mizz Probert's application to enter 3 Equity Court, which allowed me a little harmless fun at the expense of Soapy Sam Bollard (or Ballard as *he* effects to call himself), the sanctimonious President of the Lawyers As Christians Society who, in his more worldly manifestation, has contrived to become Head of our Chambers.

Sometime after the end of *Regina* v. *Snakelegs* (not a victory to be mentioned in the same breath as the Penge Bungalow Murders, in which I managed to squeeze first past the post *alone and without a leader*, but quite a satisfactory win all the same), I wandered into the clerk's room and there was the eager face of Mizz Probert asking our clerk, Henry, if there was any news about her application to become a pupil in Chambers, and Henry was explaining to her, without a great deal of patience, that her name would come up for discussion by the learned friends in due course.

'Pupil? You want to be a pupil? Any good at putting, are you?' This was the voice of Uncle Tom – T. C. Rowley – our oldest member, who hadn't come by a brief for as long as any of us can remember, but who chooses to spend his days with us to vary the monotony of life with an unmarried sister. His working day consists of a long battle with *The Times* crossword – won by the setter on most days, a brief nap after the midday sandwich, and a spell of golf practice in a corner of the clerk's room. Visiting solicitors occasionally complain of being struck quite smartly on the ankle by one of Uncle Tom's golf balls.

'Good at putting? No. Do you have to be?' Mizz Probert asked in all innocence.

'My old pupil master, C. H. Wystan,' Uncle Tom told her, referring to Hilda's Daddy, the long-time-ago Head of our Chambers, 'was a terribly nice chap, but he never gave me anything to do. So I became the best member at getting his balls into a waste-paper basket. Awfully good training, you know. I never had an enormous practice. Well, very little practice at all quite honestly, so I've been able to keep up my golf. If you want to become a pupil this is my advice to you. Get yourself a mashie niblick . . .'

As this bizarre advice wound on, I left our clerk's room in order to avoid giving vent to any sort of unseemly guffaw. I had a conference with Mr Bernard, the solicitor who appeared to have a retainer for the Timson family. The particular problem concerned Tony Timson, who had entered a shop with the probable intention of stealing three large television sets. Unfortunately the business had gone bankrupt the week before and was quite denuded of stock, thus raising what many barristers might call a nice point of law – I would call it nasty. Getting on for half a century knocking around the Courts has given me a profound distaste for the law. Give me a bloodstain or two, a bit of disputed typewriting or a couple of hairs on a cardigan, and I am happy as the day is long. I feel a definite sense of insecurity and unease when solicitors like Mr Bernard say, as he did on that occasion, 'Hasn't the House of Lords had something to say on the subject?'

Well, perhaps it had. The House of Lords is always having something to say; they're a lot of old chatterboxes up there, if you want my opinion. I was saved from an immediate answer by Mizz Probert entering with a cup of coffee which she must have scrounged from the clerk's room for the sole purpose of gaining access to the Rumpole sanctum. I thanked her and prepared to parry Bernard's next attack.

'It's the doctrine of impossible attempt of course,' he burbled on. 'You must know the case.'

'Must I?' I was playing for time, but I saw Mizz Probert darting to the shelves where the bound volumes of the law reports are kept mainly for the use of other members of our Chambers.

'I mean there have been all these articles in the *Criminal Law Review*.'

'My constant bedtime reading,' I assured him.

'So you do *know* the House of Lords decision?' Mr Bernard sounded relieved.

'Know it? Of course I know it. During those long evenings at Froxbury Court we talk of little else. The name's on the tip of my tongue . . .'

It wasn't, of course, but the next minute it was on the law report which Mizz Probert put in front of me. '"*Swinglehurst against the Queen ...*" Of course. Ah, yes. I've got it at my fingertips, as always, Mr Bernard. "*Doctrine of impossible attempts examined – R.* v. *Dewdrop and Banister distinguished*".' I read him a few nuggets from the headnote of the case. 'All this is good stuff, Bernard, couched in fine rich prose ...'

'So how does that affect Tony Timson trying to steal three non-existent telly sets?'

'How does it?' I stood then, to end the interview. 'I think it would be more helpful to you, Mr Bernard, if I gave you a written opinion. I may have to go into other authorities in some depth.'

So it became obvious that, as far as I was concerned, Mizz Liz Probert would be a valuable, perhaps an indispensable, member of Chambers. When I asked her to write the opinion I had promised Bernard, she told me that she had been the top student of her year and won the Cicero scholarship. With Probert's knowledge of the law and my irresistible way with a jury, we might, I felt, become a team which could have got the Macbeths off regicide.

A happy chance furthered my plans. Owing to the presence on the domestic scene of Dodo Mackintosh (not the sort of spectacle a barrister wishes to encounter early in the mornings), I was taking my breakfast in the Taste-Ee-Bite, one of the newer and more garish serve-yourself eateries in Fleet Street. I was just getting outside two eggs and bacon on a fried slice, when Soapy Sam Bollard plonked himself down opposite me with a cup of coffee.

'Do you read the *Church Times*, Rumpole?' he started improbably, waving a copy of that organ in the general direction of my full English breakfast.

'Only for the racing results.'

'There's a first-class fellow writing on legal matters. This week's piece is headed VENGEANCE IS MINE. I WILL REPAY. This is what Canon Probert says ...'

'Canon who?'

'Probert.'

'That's what I thought you said.'

'Society is fully entitled to be revenged upon the criminal.'

Ballard gave me a taste of the Canon's style. 'Even the speeding motorist is a fit object for the legalized vengeance of the outraged pedestrian.'

'What does the good Canon recommend? Bring back the thumb-screw for parking on a double yellow line?'

'"Too often the crafty lawyer frustrates the angel of retribution",' Ballard went on reading.

'Too often the angel of retribution makes a complete balls up of the burden of proof.'

'You may mock, Rumpole. You may well mock!'

'Thank you.'

'What we need is someone with the spirit of Canon Probert in Chambers. Someone to convince the public that lawyers still have a bit of moral fibre.' Ballard's further mention of this name put quite a ruthless scheme into my head. 'Probert,' I said thoughtfully, 'did you say Probert?'

'Canon Probert.' Ballard supplied the details.

'Odd, that,' I told him. 'The name seems strangely familiar . . .'

Later, when Mizz Probert handed in a highly expert and profound legal opinion in the obscure subject of impossible attempt, often known in the trade as 'stealing from an empty purse', I had a few words with her on the subject of her parentage.

'Is your father,' I asked, 'by any chance the Canon Probert who writes for the *Church Times*?' And then I gave her an appropriate warning: 'Don't answer that.'

'Why ever not?'

'Because our Head of Chambers is quite ridiculously prejudiced against women pupils whose fathers aren't canons who write for the *Church Times*. You may go now, Mizz Probert. Thank you for the excellent work.' She left me then. Clearly I had given her much food for thought.

So, in due course, a meeting was called in Sam Ballard's room to consider the intake of new pupils into Chambers. Those present were Rumpole, Erskine-Brown and Hoskins, a grey and somewhat fussy barrister, much worried by the expensive upbringing of his numerous daughters.

'Elizabeth Probert,' Ballard, Q.C., being in the Chair, read out the next name on his list. 'Does anyone know her?'

'I have seen her hanging about the clerk's room,' Erskine-Brown admitted. 'Remove the glasses and she might have a certain elfin charm.' Poor old Claude was ever hopelessly susceptible to a whiff of beauty in a lady barrister. 'I wonder if she could help me with my County Court practice . . .'

'That's all you think about, Erskine-Brown!' Hoskins sounded disapproving. 'Wine, women and your County Court practice.'

'That is distinctly unfair!'

'So far as I remember your wife didn't care for Fiona Allways.' Hoskins reminded him of his moment of tenderness for a young lady barrister now married to a merchant banker and living in Cheltenham.

'Yes. Well. Of course, Phillida can't be here today. She's got a long firm fraud in Doncaster,' Claude apologized for his wife.

'She might not take to anyone who looked at all elfin without her glasses.' Hoskins struck a further warning note.

'It was just a casual observation . . .'

'And I'm not sure we want any new intake in Chambers. Even in the form of pupils. I mean, is there enough work to go round? I speak as a member with daughters to support,' Hoskins reminded us.

'Thinking the matter over' – Erskine-Brown was clearly losing his bottle – 'I'm afraid Philly might be rather against her.'

It was then that I struck my blow for the highly qualified Mizz. 'I would be against her too,' I said, 'if it weren't for the name. Ballard, isn't that canon you admire so tremendously, the one we all read in the *Church Times*, called Probert?'

'You mean she's some relation?' Ballard was clearly excited.

'She hasn't said she isn't.'

'Not his daughter.' By now he was positively awe-struck.

'She hasn't denied it.'

Then Ballard looked like one whose eyes had seen his and my salvation. 'Then Elizabeth Probert comes from a family with enormously sound views on the religious virtue of retribution as part of our criminal law. I see her as an admirable pupil for Rumpole!'

'You think he might teach her some of his courtroom antics?'
Erskine-Brown sounded sceptical.

'I think she might' – Ballard spoke with deep conviction –
'just possibly save his soul!'

So it came about that I was driven to my next conference at
Brixton Prison in a very small runabout, something like a swaying
biscuit box, referred to by Mizz Probert as her *Deux Chevaux*,
and I supposed there was something to be said for having a pupil
on wheels. Apart from the matter of transport, there was nothing
particularly new or unusual about the conference in question,
for I had once again been summoned to the aid of Hugh Snakelegs Timson who had, once again, been found in possession of
a quantity of property alleged to have been stolen. Once again,
D.I. Broome and D.C. Cosgrove had called at the Bromley
semi to find the Cortina parked out in the street, and the lock-up
garage full of cases of a fine wine, none other than St Emilion
Château Cheval Blanc 1971.

'Hugh Timson seems to be always getting into trouble.' Mizz
Probert was steering us, with a good deal of dexterity, round the
Elephant and Castle.

'I suppose he takes the usual business risks.'

'Have you ever found out the root of the problem?'

'The root of the problem would seem to be Detective Inspector
Broome who's rapidly becoming the terror of the Timsons.'

'I bet you'll find that he comes from a broken home.'

'Inspector Broome? Probably.'

'No. I meant Hugh Timson. In an inner-city area. With an
anti-social norm among his peer group, most likely. He must
always have felt alienated from society.'

Was Mizz Probert right, and is it nurture and not nature that
shapes our ends? I suppose I was brought up in appalling conditions, in an ice-cold vicarage with no mod cons or central
heating. My old father, being a priest of the Church of England,
had only the sketchiest notion of morality, and my mother was
too occupied with jam-making and the Women's Institute to
notice my existence. Is it any real wonder that I have taken to
crime?

When we had met Mr Bernard at the gates of Brixton and settled down with the ex-Mr Debonair in the interview room, I thought I would put Mizz Probert's theories to the test. 'Come from a broken home, did you?' I asked Snakelegs.

'Broken home?' The client looked displeased. 'I don't know what you mean. Mum and Dad was married forty years, and he never so much as looked at another woman. Hetty and I, we're the same. What you on about, Mr Rumpole?'

'At least you were born in an inner-city area.'

'My old dad wouldn't have tolerated it. Bromley was really nice in those days. More green fields and that. What's it got to do with my case?'

'Not much. Just setting my pupil's mind at rest. Why was your garage being used as a cellar for fine wines?'

'Bit of good stuff, was it?' Snakelegs seemed proud of the fact.

'Didn't you try it?'

'Teetotal, me. You know that.' The client sounded shocked. 'Although the wife, she will take a drop of tawny port at Christmas. Not that I think it's right. It's drink that leads to crime. We all know that, don't we, Mr Rumpole?'

'So *how* . . .?'

'Well, I got them all a bit cheap. Not for myself, you understand. They'd be no good for Hetty and me. But I thought it was a drop of stuff I might sell on to anyone having a bit of a wedding – anything like that.'

'And *where* did you get it? The Judge might be curious to know.' I felt a sudden weariness, such as whoever it was among the ancient Greeks who had just pushed a stone up a hill, and seen it come rolling down again for the three-millionth time, must have felt. It was one thing to win a case because the prosecution evidence wasn't strong enough for a conviction. It was another, and far more depressing matter, to be putting forward the same distinctly shop-worn defence throughout a working life. I just hoped to God that Snakelegs wasn't going to babble on about a man in a pub.

'Well, there was this fellow what I ran into down the Needle Arms . . . What's the matter, Mr Rumpole?'

'Please, Snakelegs' – my boredom must have become evident – 'can't we have some sort of variation? Judge Bullingham's getting tremendously tired of that story.'

'Bullingham?' Snakelegs was understandably alarmed. 'We're not getting him again, are we?'

'Not if I can help it. This character in the Needle Arms – not anyone whose name you happen to remember?' I lit a small cigar and waited in hope.

'Afraid I can't help you there, Mr Rumpole.'

'You can't help me? And he sold you all these crates of stuff. Who's got the list of exhibits?' Mizz Probert handed it to me immediately. 'Cheval Blanc. St Emilion . . .'

'No. That wasn't the name. It was more like, something Irish . . .' Snakelegs looked at me. 'What's our chances, Mr Rumpole?'

'Our chances?' I gave him my considered opinion. 'Well, you've heard about snowballs in hell?'

'You saw me right last time.'

'Last time the losers didn't come forward to claim their property.'

'Because of the insurance.' Liz filled in the details.

'Mizz Probert remembers. This time the loser of the wine is principal witness for the Prosecution.'

'Martyn Vanberry.' Bernard was looking at the prosecution witness statements. First among them was indeed the proprietor of Vanberry's – purveyors of fine wines, Prentice Alley in the City of London – not a specially attractive character, the highly respectable public-school bully.

Back in the *Deux Chevaux*, I felt a little guilty about disillusioning Liz Probert and depriving Snakelegs of an unhappy childhood. I complimented her on her runabout and asked if it weren't by any chance a present from her father, the Canon. It was then that she told me that her father was, in fact, the leader of the South-East London Council widely known as Red Ron Probert. He was a man, no doubt, whose own article of religion was the divine right of the local Labour Party to govern that area of London, and he frequently appeared on television chat-shows to speak up for minority rights. His ideal voter was apparently an immigrant Eskimo lesbian, who strongly supported the I.R.A.

'Is there anything wrong with Ron Probert being my father?'

'Nothing at all provided you don't chatter about it to our learned Head of Chambers. Do you think you could point this machine in the general direction of Luton? I'm going to take a nap.'

'What are we doing in Luton?'

'Seeing a witness.'

'I thought we weren't allowed to see witnesses.'

'This is an expert witness. We're allowed to see them.'

Luton is not exactly one of the Jewels of Southern England. American tourists don't brave the terrorists to loiter in its elegant parks or snap each other in the Cathedral Close, but its inhabitants seem friendly enough and the first police officer we met was delighted to direct us to the Monty Mantis Service Station. It was a large and clearly thriving concern, selling not only petrol but new and secondhand cars, cuddly toys, garden furniture, blow-up paddling pools, furry dice and anoraks. The proprietor remembered my face from Vanberry's, and when I gave him a hint of what we wanted, invited us into his luxuriously appointed office, where we sat on plastic zebra-skin covered furniture, gazing at pictures of peeing children and crying clowns, while he poured us out a couple of glasses of Cheval Blanc from his own cellar, so that I might understand the experience. When I made my delight clear, he said it was always a pleasure to meet a genuine enthusiast.

'And you, Mr Mantis,' I ventured to ask him, 'I've been wondering how *you* became so extraordinarily well informed in wine lore. I mean, where did you get your training?'

'Day trip to Boulogne. 1963. With the Luton Technical.' He refilled our glasses. 'Unattractive bunch of kids, we must have been. Full of terminal acne and lavatory jokes. Enough to drive "sir" what took us into the funny farm. We were all off giving him the slip. Trying to chase girls that didn't exist, or was even fatter and spottier than the local talent round the Wimpy. Anyway, I ended up in the station buffet for some reason, and spent what I'd been saving up for an unavailable knees' trembler, if you'll pardon my French, Miss Probert. I bought a half bottle. God knows what it was. *Ordinaire de la Gare*, French railways perpetual standby. And there was I, brought up on Tizer and Coke that tastes of old pennies, and sweet tea you could stand the spoon up in, and it came as a bit of a revelation to me, Mr Rumpole.'

'Tasting of Flora and the country green . . . Dance, and Provençal song, and sunburnt mirth! . . .'

'Shame you can't ever talk about the stuff without sounding like them toffee noses round Vanberry's. Well, I bought four bottles and kept a cellar under my bed and shared it out in toothmugs with a chosen few. Then when I started work at the garage, I didn't go round the pub Friday nights. I began investing . . .'

'And acquired your knowledge?'

'I don't know football teams, you see. Haven't got a clue about the Cup. But I reckon I know my vintages.'

'Such as the Cheval Blanc 1971.' I sampled it again.

'All right, is it?'

'It seems perfectly all right.'

'You're sure you won't, Miss Probert?'

'I never have.'

Liz Probert, I thought, a hard worker, with all the puritanism of youth.

'This is better, perhaps' – I held my glass to the light – 'than the Cheval Blanc round Vanberry's?'

Monty Mantis looked at me then and began to laugh. It was not unkind, but genuinely amused laughter, coming from a man who no doubt knew his wines.

Our clerk, Henry, is a star of his local amateur dramatic society, and is famous, as I understand it, for the Noël Coward roles he undertakes. Henry's life in the theatre has its uses for us as a fellow Thespian is Miss Osgood, who, when she is not appearing in some role made famous by the late Gertrude Lawrence, is in charge of the lists down the Old Bailey. Miss Osgood can exercise some sort of control on which case comes before which judge, and when the wheel of fortune spins to decide such matters, she can sometimes lay a finger on it. I had fortunately hit on a time when Henry and Miss Osgood were playing opposite each other in *Private Lives* and I asked our clerk to use his best endeavours with his co-star to see that *R. v. Snakelegs Timson* did not come up for trial before Judge Bullingham. On the night before the hearing, Henry rang Froxbury Court to give me the glad news that the case was fixed to come on before a judge known to his many friends and admirers as Moley Molesworth.

'A wonderful judge for us,' I told Bernard and Liz Probert as we assembled at the door of the Court the next morning. 'I'll have Moley eating out of my hand. Mildest-mannered chap that ever thought in terms of probation.'

'For receiving stolen wine?' Bernard sounded doubtful.

'Oh, yes. I shouldn't be at all surprised. Community service is his equivalent of dispatching chaps to the galleys.'

But just when everything seemed set fair, a cloud no bigger than a man's hand blew up in the shape of Miss Osgood, who came to announce that his Honour Judge Molesworth was confined to bed with a severe cold and would not, therefore, be trying Snakelegs.

'A severe cold? What's the matter with the old idiot, can't he wrap up warm?'

'It's all right, Mr Rumpole. We can transfer you to another Court immediately.' Miss Osgood smiled with the charm of the late Gertrude Lawrence. 'Judge Bullingham's free.'

Why is it that whoever dishes out severe colds invariably gives them to the wrong person?

'Mr Rumpole. Do you wish to detain this gentleman in the witness-box?'

The Bull had clearly recognized Snakelegs, and remembered the antiques in the frozen peas. He looked with equal disfavour at the dock and at defending counsel. It was only when his eye lit upon young Tristram Paulet for the Prosecution, or the chief prosecution witness, Martyn Vanberry, who was now standing, at the end of his evidence-in-chief, awaiting my attention, that he exposed his yellowing teeth in that appalling smirk which represents Bullingham's nearest approximation to moments of charm.

'I have one or two questions for Mr Vanberry,' I told him.

'Oh' – his Lordship seemed surprised – 'is there any dispute that your client, Timson, had this gentleman's wine in his possession?'

'No dispute about that, my Lord.'

'Then to what issue in this case can your questions possibly be directed?'

I was tempted to tell the old darling that if he sat very quietly and paid close attention he might, just possibly, find out. Instead, I said that my questions would concern my client's guilt or innocence, a matter which might be of some interest to the Jury. And then, before the Bull could get his breath to bellow, I asked Mr Vanberry if the wine he lost was insured.

'Of course. I had it fully insured.'

'As a prudent businessman?'

'I hope I am that, my Lord,' Vanberry appealed to the Judge, who gave his ghastly smile and murmured as unctuously as possible, 'I'm sure you are, Mr Vanberry. I am perfectly sure you are.'

'And how long have you been trading as a wine merchant in Prentice Alley in the City of London?' I went on hacking away.

'Just three years, my Lord.'

'And done extremely well! In such a short time.' The Bull was still smirking.

'We have been lucky, my Lord, and I think we've been dependable.'

'Before that, where were you trading?' I interrupted the love duet between the witness and the Bench.

'I was selling pictures. As a matter of fact I had a shop in Chelsea; we specialized in nineteenth-century watercolours, my Lord.'

'The name of the business?'

'Vanberry Fine Arts.'

'Manage to find any insurance claims for Vanberry Fine Arts . . .?' I turned to whisper to Bernard, but it seemed he was still making inquiries. Only one thing to do then, pick up a blank sheet of paper, study it closely and ask the next question looking as though you had all the answers in your hands. Sometimes, it was to be admitted, the old-fashioned ways are best.

'I must put it to you that Vanberry Fine Arts made a substantial insurance claim in respect of the King's Road premises.'

'We had a serious break-in and most of our stock was stolen. Of course I had to make a claim, my Lord.' Vanberry still preferred to talk to his friend, the Bull, but at least he had been forced by the information he thought I had to come out with some part of the truth.

'You seem to be somewhat prone to serious break-ins, Mr Vanberry,' I suggested, whereupon the Bull came in dead on cue with, 'It's the rising tide of lawlessness that is threatening to engulf us all. You should know that better than anyone, Mr Rumpole!'

I thought it best to ignore this, so I then called on the Usher to produce Exhibit 34, which was, in fact, one of the bottles of allegedly stolen wine.

'You're not proposing to sample it, I hope, Mr Rumpole?' The Bull tried heavy sarcasm and the Jury and the prosecution counsel laughed obediently.

'I'm making no application to do so at the moment,' I reassured him. 'Mr Vanberry. You say this bottle contains vintage claret of a high quality?'

'It does, my Lord.'

'Retailing at what price?'

'I think around fifty pounds a bottle.'

'And insured for . . .?'

'I believe we insured it for the retail price. Such a wine would be hard to replace.'

'Of course it would. It's a particularly fine vintage of the . . . What did you say it was?' The Bull charged into the arena.

'Cheval Blanc, my Lord.'

'And we all know what you have to pay for a really fine Burgundy nowadays, don't we, Members of the Jury?'

The Members of the Jury – an assortment of young unemployed blacks, puzzled old-age pensioners from Hackney and grey-haired cleaning ladies – looked at the Judge and seemed to find his question mystifying.

'It's a claret, my Lord. Not a Burgundy,' Vanberry corrected the Judge, as I thought unwisely.

'A claret. Yes, of course it is. Didn't I say that? Yes, well. Let's get on with it, Mr Rumpole.' Bullingham was not pleased.

'You lost some fifty cases. It was insured for six hundred pounds a case, you say?'

'That is so.'

'So you recovered some thirty thousand pounds from your insurers?'

'There was a considerable loss . . .'

'To your insurance company?'

'And a considerable profit to whoever dealt with it illegally,' the Bull couldn't resist saying, so I thought it about time he was given a flutter of the cape: 'My Lord. I have an application to make in respect of Exhibit 34.'

'Oh, very well. Make it then.' The Judge closed his eyes and prepared to be bored.

'I wish to apply to the Court to open this bottle of alleged Cheval Blanc.'

'You're not serious?' The Bull's eyes opened.

'Your Lordship seemed to have the possibility in mind . . .'

'Mr Rumpole!' – I watched the familiar sight of the deep purple falling on the Bullingham countenance – 'from time to time the weight of these grave proceedings at the Old Bailey may be lifted when the Judge makes a joke. One doesn't do it often. One seldom can. But one likes to do it whenever possible. I was making a *joke*, Mr Rumpole!'

'I'm sure we're all grateful for your Lordship's levity,' I assured him, 'but I'm entirely serious. My learned pupil, Mizz Probert, has come equipped with a corkscrew.'

'Mr Rumpole!' – the Judge was exercising almost superhuman self-control – 'may I get this quite clear. What would be your purpose in opening this bottle?'

'The purpose of tasting it, my Lord.'

It was then, of course, that the short Bullingham fuse set off the explosion. 'This is a court of law, Mr Rumpole,' he almost shouted. 'This is not a bar-room! I have sat here for a long time, far too long in my opinion, listening to your cross-examination of this unfortunate gentleman who has, as the Jury may well find, suffered at the hands of your client. But I do not intend to sit here, Mr Rumpole, while you drink the exhibits!'

'Not "drink"' – I tried to calm the Bull – '"taste", my Lord. And may I say this: if the Defence is to be denied the opportunity of tasting a vital exhibit, that would be a breach of our fundamental liberties! The principles we have fought for ever since the days of Magna Carta. In that event I would have to make an immediate application to the Court of Appeal.'

'The Court of Appeal, did you say?' I had mentioned the only institution which can bring the Bull to heel – he dreads criticism by the Lords of Appeal in Ordinary which might well get reported in *The Times*. 'You would take the matter up to the Court of Appeal?' he repeated, somewhat aghast.

'This afternoon, my Lord.'

'That's what you'd do?'

'Without hesitation, my Lord.'

'What do you say about this, Mr Tristram Paulet?' The Judge turned for help to the Prosecution.

'My Lord. I'm sure the Court would not wish my learned friend to have any cause for complaint, however frivolous. And it might be better not to delay matters by an application to the Court of Appeal.' Paulet is one of Nature's old Etonians, but I blessed him for his words which were also welcomed by the Bull. 'Exactly what was in *my* mind, Mr Tristram Paulet!' the Judge discovered. 'Very well, Mr Rumpole. In the quite exceptional circumstances of this case, the Court is prepared to give you leave to taste . . .'

So, in a sense, the party was on. Mizz Probert produced a corkscrew from her handbag. I opened the bottle, a matter in which I have had some practice, and asked the Judge and my learned friend, Mr Paulet, to join me. The Usher brought three of the thick tumblers which are used to carry water to hoarse barristers or fainting witnesses. While this operation was being carried out, my eye lighted on Martyn Vanberry in the witness-box – he looked suddenly older, his expensive tan had turned

sallow, and I saw his forehead shining with sweat. He opened his
mouth, but no sound of any particular significance emerged.
And so, in the ensuing silence, Tristram Paulet sniffed doubtfully
at his glass, the Bull took a short swig and looked enigmatic, and
I tasted and held the wine long enough in my mouth to be
certain. It was with considerable relief that I realized that the
label on the bottle was an unreliable witness, for the taste was all
too familiar – that of Château Thames Embankment 1985, a
particularly brutal year.

   'Rumpole's got a pupil.'

   'I hope he's an apt pupil.'

   'It's not a he. It's a she.'

   'A she. Oh, really, Rumpole?' Dodo Mackintosh clicked her
knitting needles and looked at me with deep suspicion.

   'A Mizz Liz Probert . . .'

   'You call her Liz?' The cross-examination continued.

   'No. I call her Mizz.'

   'Is she a middle-aged person?'

   'About twenty-three. Is that middle-aged nowadays?'

   'And is Hilda quite happy about that, do you think?' Dodo
asked me, and not my wife, the question.

   'Hilda doesn't look for happiness.'

   'Oh. What does she look for?'

   'The responsibilities of command.' I raised a respectful glass
of Château Fleet Street at She Who Must Be Obeyed. There was
a brief silence broken only by the clicking of needles, and then
Dodo said, 'Don't you want to know what this Liz Probert is
like, Hilda?'

   'Not particularly.'

It was at this moment that the telephone rang and I picked it
up to hear the voice of a young man called Ken Eastham, who
worked at Vanberry's. He wanted, it seemed, to ask my legal
advice. I spoke to him whilst Hilda and her old friend, Dodo
Mackintosh, speculated on the subject of my new pupil. When
the call was over, I put down the telephone after thanking Mr
Eastham from the bottom of my heart. It's rare, in any experience,
for anyone to care enormously for justice.

'Well, Rumpole, you look extremely full of yourself,' Hilda said as I dialled Mr Bernard's number to warn him that we might be calling another witness.

'No doubt he is full of himself' – Dodo put in her two penn'orth – 'having a young pupil to trot around with.'

'Dodo's coming down to the Old Bailey tomorrow, Rumpole,' Hilda warned me. 'She's tremendously keen to see you in action.'

In fact Dodo Mackintosh's view of Rumpole in action was fairly short-lived. She arrived early at my Chambers, extremely early, and Henry told her that I was still breakfasting at the Taste-Ee-Bite in Fleet Street. Indeed I was then tucking into the full British with Mizz Probert, to whom I was explaining the position of the vagal nerve in the neck, which can be so pressed during a domestic fracas that death may ensue unintentionally. (I secured an acquittal for Gimlett, a Kilburn grocer, armed with this knowledge – the matter is described later in this very volume.) At any rate I had one hand placed casually about Mizz Probert's neck explaining the medical aspect of the matter when Dodo Mackintosh entered the Taste-Ee-Bite, took in the scene, put the worst possible construction on the events, uttered the words 'Rumpole in action! Poor Hilda' in a tragic and piercing whisper and made a hasty exit. This was, of course, a matter which would be referred to later.

I did not, as I think wisely, put Snakelegs Timson in the witness-box, but I had told Mr Bernard to get a witness summons delivered to the wine correspondent of the *Sunday Mercury* and took the considerable risk of calling her. When she was in the box I got the Bull's permission to allow her to taste a glass of the wine which the Prosecution claimed was stolen Château Cheval Blanc, although I had it presented to her in an anonymous tumbler. She held it up to the light, squinted at it through her monocle and then took a mouthful, which I told her she would have to swallow, however painful she found it, as we had no 'expectoration corner'. At which point Tristram Paulet muttered a warning not to lead the witness.

'Certainly not! In your own words, would you describe the wine you have just tasted?'

'Is it worth describing?' Miss Bird asked, having swallowed with distaste.

'My client's liberty may depend on it,' I looked meaningfully at the Jury.

'It's a rough and, I would say, crude Bordeaux-type of mixed origins. It may well contain some product of North Africa. It's too young and drinking it would amount to infanticide had its quality not made such considerations irrelevant.'

'Have you met such a wine before?'

'I believe it is served in certain bars in this part of London to the more poorly paid members of the legal profession.'

'Would you price it at fifty pounds a bottle?' this poorly paid member asked.

'You're joking!'

'It is not I that made the joke, Miss Bird.'

I could see Vanberry, who was looking even more depressed and anxious than he had the day before, pass a note to the prosecuting solicitor. Meanwhile, Birdie gave me her answer. 'It would be daylight robbery to charge more than two pounds.'

'Yes. Thank you, Miss Bird. Just wait there, will you?' I sat down and Tristram Paulet rose to cross-examine, armed with Vanberry's note.

'Miss Bird. The wine you have tasted came from a bottle labelled Cheval Blanc 1971. I take it you don't think that is its correct description.'

'Certainly not!' The admirable Birdie would have none of it.

'At a blind tasting which took place at Mr Vanberry's shop, did you not identify a Cheval Blanc 1971?' There was a considerable pause after this question, during which Miss Bird looked understandably uncomfortable.

'I had my doubts about it,' she explained at last.

'But did you not identify it?'

'Yes. I did.' The witness was reluctant, but Paulet had got all he wanted. He sat down with a 'thank you, Miss Bird', and

I climbed to my hindlegs to repair the damage in re-examination.

'Miss Bird, on that occasion, were you competing against a Mr Monty Mantis, a garage owner of Luton, in the blind-tasting contest?'

'Yes. I was.'

'Did he express a poor opinion of the alleged Cheval Blanc?'

'He did.'

'But were you encouraged by Mr Martyn Vanberry to identify it as a fine claret by a number of hints and clues?'

'Yes. He was trying to help me a little.' Miss Bird looked doubtfully at the anxious wine merchant sitting in the well of the Court.

'To help you to call it Cheval Blanc?' I suggested.

'I suppose so. Yes.'

'Miss Bird. What was your opinion of Mr Monty Mantis?'

'I thought him a very vulgar little man who probably had no real knowledge of wine.' She had no doubt about it.

'And, thinking that about him, were you particularly anxious to disagree with his opinion?'

There was a pause while the lady faced up to the question and then said with some candour, 'I suppose I may have been.'

'And you were anxious to win the contest?' Paulet rose to make an objection, but I ploughed on before the Bull could interrupt. 'As Mr Vanberry was clearly helping you to do?'

'I may have wanted to win. Yes,' Miss Bird admitted, and Paulet subsided, discouraged by her answer.

'Looking back on that occasion, do you think you were tasting genuine Cheval Blanc?' It was the only important question in the case and Bullingham and Martyn Vanberry were both staring at the expert, waiting for her answer. When it came it was entirely honest.

'Looking back on it, my Lord, I don't think I was.'

'And today you have told us the truth?'

'Yes.'

'Thank you, Miss Honoria Bird.' And I sat down, with considerable relief.

With Honoria Bird's evidence we had turned the corner. Young Ken Eastham, who had rung me at home, went into the witness-box. He told the Court that Vanberry had a few dozen of the Cheval Blanc, and then a large new consignment arrived from a source he had not heard of before. Martyn Vanberry asked him to set the new bottles apart from the old, but he had already unpacked some of the later consignment, and put a few bottles with the wine already there. Later, almost all the recently delivered 'Cheval Blanc' was stolen, and Martyn Vanberry seemed quite unconcerned at the loss. Subsequently, and by mistake he thought, one of the new bottles of 'Cheval Blanc' must have been used for the blind tasting. When I asked Mr Eastham why he had agreed to give this evidence he said, 'I've done a long training in wine, and I suppose I love the subject. Well, there's not much point in that is there, if there's going to be lies told on the labels.'

'Mr Rumpole' – his Honour Judge Bullingham was now interested, but somewhat puzzled – 'I'm not absolutely sure I follow the effect of this evidence. If Mr Vanberry were in the business of selling the inferior stuff we have tasted, and Miss Honoria Bird has tasted, as highly expensive claret surely the deceit would be obvious to anyone drinking . . .?'

'I'm not suggesting that the wine was in Mr Vanberry's possession for drinking, my Lord.' I was doing my best to help the Bull grasp the situation.

'Well, what on earth did he have it for?'

Of course Vanberry had fixed the burglary at his wine shop just as he had fixed the stealing of his alleged Victorian watercolours, so that he could claim the insurance money on the value of expensive Cheval Blanc, which he never had. No doubt, whoever was asked to remove the swag was instructed to dispose of it on some rubbish tip. Instead it got sold round the pubs in Bromley, where Snakelegs bought it, and was tricked, without his knowledge, into a completely honest transaction, because it was never, in any real sense of the word, stolen property. So I was able to enlighten Bullingham in the presence of the chief prosecution witness, who was soon to become the defendant, in a case of insurance fraud: 'Mr Vanberry didn't ever have this wine for anyone to drink, my Lord. He had it there for someone to steal.'

When the day's work was done I called into the Taste-Ee-Bite again and retired behind the *Standard* with a pot of tea and a toasted bun. At the next table I heard the monotonous tones of Soapy Sam Bollard, Q.C., our Head of Chambers. 'Your daughter's really doing very well. She's with Rumpole, a somewhat elderly member of our Chambers. Perhaps it's mixing with the criminal classes, but Rumpole seems somewhat lacking in a sense of sin. A girl with your daughter's background may well do him some good.'

I could recognize the man he was talking to as Red Ron Probert, Labour Chairman of the South-East London Council. Ballard, who never watches the telly, was apparently unable to recognize Red Ron. Liz's father, it seemed, had come to inquire as to his daughter's progress and our Head of Chambers had invited him to tea.

'I didn't realize who you were at first,' Ballard droned on. 'Of course, you're in mufti!'

'What?' Red Ron seemed surprised.

'Your collar.'

'What's wrong with my collar?'

'Nothing at all,' Ballard hastened to reassure him. 'I'm sure it's very comfortable. I expect you want to look just like an ordinary bloke.'

'Well, I am an ordinary bloke. And I represent thousands of ordinary blokes . . .' Ron was about to deliver one of his well-loved speeches.

'Of course you do! I must say, I'm a tremendous admirer of your work.'

'Are you?' Ron was surprised. 'I thought you lawyers were always Right . . .'

'Not always. Some of them are entirely wrong. But there are a few of us prepared to fight the good fight!'

'On with the revolution!' Ron slightly raised a clenched fist.

'You think it needs *that*' – Ballard was thoughtful – 'to awaken a real sense of morality . . .?'

'Don't you?'

'A revolution in our whole way of thinking? I fear so. I greatly fear so.' Ballard shook his head wisely.

'Fear not, Brother Ballard! We're in this together!' Red Ron rallied our Head of Chambers.

'Of course.' Ballard was puzzled. 'Yes. Brother. Were you in some Anglican Monastic Order?'

'Only the Clerical Workers' Union.' Red Ron laughed at what he took to be a Ballard witticism.

'Clerical Workers? Yes, that, of course.' Ballard joined in the joke. 'Amusing way of putting it.'

'And most of them weren't exactly monastic!'

'Oh dear, yes. There's been a falling off, even among the clergy. I really must tell you . . .'

'Yes, Brother.' Red Ron was prepared to listen.

'Brother! I can't really . . . I should prefer to call you Father. It might be more appropriate.'

'Have it your own way.' Ron seemed to find the mode of address acceptable.

'Father Probert,' Ballard said, very sincerely, 'you have been, for me at any rate, a source of great inspiration!'

I folded my *Standard* then and crept away unnoticed. I felt no need to correct a misunderstanding which seemed to be so gratifying to both of them, and had had such a beneficial effect on Mizz Probert's legal career.

That night I carried home to Froxbury Court a not unusual treat, that is to say, a bottle of Pommeroy's Château Thames Embankment. I was opening it with a feeling of modified satisfaction when Hilda said, 'You look very full of yourself! I suppose you've won another case.'

'I'm afraid so.' I had the bottle open and was filling a couple of glasses: 'Oh, for a draught of vintage! that hath been Cool'd a long age in the deep-delved earth, . . .' And then I tasted the wine and didn't spit. 'A crude Bordeaux-type of mixed origins. On sale to the more poorly paid members of the legal profession.' I couldn't help laughing.

'What've you got to laugh about, Rumpole?'

'Bollard!'

'Your Head of Chambers.'

'He met Mizz Probert's father. Red Ron. And he still thought he was some Anglican Divine. He went entirely by the name on the label . . .' I lowered my nose once more to the glass. '"Tasting of Flora and the country green . . ."' Isn't it remarkably quiet around here? I don't seem to hear the fluting tones of your old childhood chum, Dodo Mackintosh.'

'Dodo's gone home.'

'Dance, and Provençal song, and sunburnt mirth.'

'She's disgusted with you, Rumpole. As a matter of fact, I told her she'd better go.'

'You told Dodo that?' She Who Must Be Obeyed was usually clay in Miss Mackintosh's hands.

'She said she'd seen you making up to some girl, in a tea-room.'

'That's what she said?'

'I told her it was absolutely ridiculous. I really couldn't imagine a young girl wanting to be made up to by you, Rumpole!'

'Well. Thank you very much.' I refilled the glass which had mysteriously emptied:

> 'O for a beaker full of the warm South,
>   Full of the true, the blushful Hippocrene,
>   With beaded bubbles winking at the brim,
>   And purple-stained mouth . . .'

'She said you were in some sort of embrace. I told her she was seeing things.'

> 'That I might drink, and leave the world unseen,
>   And with thee fade away into the forest dim:
>
> Fade far away, dissolve, and quite forget
>   What thou among the leaves hast never known,
>   The weariness, the fever and the fret . . .'

I must say the words struck me as somewhat comical. At the idea of my good self and She dancing away into the mysterious recesses of some wood, the mind, as they say, boggled.

Rumpole and the Old, Old Story

Those of you who may have followed these memoirs which I have scribbled down from time to time (in the privacy of my Chambers during temporary lulls in business – I would not wish She Who Must Be Obeyed to have a sight of them and she studiously avoids any knowledge of their publication) will know that from time to time there is a bit of an East wind blowing around our homestead in Froxbury Court. Sometimes, in fact, the icy winds of Hilda's discontent could best be described as a blizzard, and then, if I can't organize a case in a distant town, I leave almost at dawn to breakfast in the Taste-Ee-Bite in Fleet Street and return as late as possible after a spot of bottled courage in Jack Pommeroy's Wine Bar, although this last expedient never seems to do much to warm up the domestic hearth.

Usually these moments of high drama subside. She Who Must Be Obeyed gives a few brief words of command, all hands snap to it, and the Rumpole marriage sails for a while into somewhat calmer waters. There was a time, however, and not too long ago at that, when the old tramp-steamer, with its heavy load of memories of my various delinquencies and its salt-stained smoke-stack, seemed to be heading for the rocks. My wife Hilda and I actually came, on one occasion, to the parting of the ways. I cannot decide whether to look back at that dramatic period of my life with nostalgia or regret. I can tell you that it came when I was most intellectually stretched, grappling as I was with one of my most important cases: the curious affair of the alleged attempted murder of Captain Arnold Gleason at the Woodland Folk Garden Centre. And, lest the readers should suspect the presence of some 'other' woman in the case, let me say at once that I have no reputation as a Lothario, that Mizz Liz Probert, about whom my wife's best friend, Dodo Mackintosh, nursed some unworthy suspicions, had not yet appeared at our Chambers, and neither of the two ladies for whom I have in the past entertained some tender feelings, that is to say, Bobby O'Keefe, once of the Women's Auxiliary Air Force, and a young woman named Kathy Trelawny, whom I defended on a drugs charge, had anything to do with the case.* Hilda and I, in fact, severed relations as the direct result of a joke.

We are not great diners-out. By the time I get home from Pommeroy's and remove the winged collar and put on the carpet slippers, preparatory to an evening's work on robbery or sudden death, a scrambled egg or, at best, a grilled chop, is about all we run to. On the night in question, however, Marigold Featherstone, wife of our old Head of Chambers, Sir Guthrie Featherstone, now translated to the Bench – an ermine- and scarlet-clad figure who had everything it takes to be a justice of the Queen's Bench Division except for the slightest talent for making up his mind – had given us a couple of tickets they couldn't use for the Scales of Justice annual dinner at the Savoy. Gatherings of lawyers at the trough are usually to be avoided like the plague, but Hilda was dead set on being among those present on this occasion and, in view of the opportunity offered of hacking away at the Savoy Hotel claret, I didn't oppose her wishes too strenuously. So she got my old soup and fish out of mothballs, cleaned the stains off the jacket with some pungent chemical, renewed a few essential buttons on the dress trousers, and we found ourselves ensconced at a table presided over by another scarlet judge, this time of a somewhat malign and Welsh variety, known as Mr Justice Huw Gwent-Evans, together with his spouse, Lady Gwent-Evans; Claude Erskine-Brown and his better half, Phillida Erskine-Brown, née Trant, the Portia of our Chambers; mixed with an assortment of younger barristers with their wives or live-in companions.

As dinner drew to an end, I discovered that my glass had been refilled at such regular intervals that I was seeing the whole

* See 'Rumpole and the Alternative Society' in *Rumpole of the Bailey*, Penguin Books, 1978.

proceedings lit by a kind of golden glow. I also saw, somewhat to my surprise, that She Who Must Be Obeyed was in animated conversation with the Welsh Judge who was regarding her with admiration, his small eyes bright with enjoyment at her lengthy reminiscences of life in the distant days when her Daddy, C. H. Wystan, ruled our Chambers at Equity Court. At long last the proceedings wound to an end and Mr Justice Gwent-Evans pulled out his gold repeater and said, with every appearance of disappointment, 'Good heavens, is that the time? I hate to break up such an extraordinarily enjoyable evening but . . .'

'The learned Judge is looking at the time.' My voice sounded, from where I sat, pleasantly resonant. I had the cue for one of my best stories, one which has never failed, in my long experience, to set the table on a roar.

'I well remember when old Judge Quentin Starkie at Inner-London Sessions looked at the time. It was during an indecent assault, sort of thing that always went on in the cinemas round Bethnal Green. This girl was giving evidence . . .' I was conscious of not playing to a particularly good audience. Indeed, Lady Gwent-Evans appeared to dread the outcome of the anecdote. Erskine-Brown stifled a yawn. Phillida looked at me tolerantly, although I knew that the outcome of the story would be no surprise to her. Hilda was stony-faced and the Judge cleared his throat in a warning manner. In spite of all discouragement I carried on, giving my well-known imitation of the witness's fluting tones: '"So he put his hand up my skirt, my Lord. This bloke sitting beside me in the one and nines."' Now I mimicked old Judge Starkie's low growl: '"Put his hand up your skirt, did he?"' And then his Honour looks at the clock and finds it's dead on lunchtime. '"Put his hand up your skirt? Well, I suggest we leave it there until ten past two!"'

One of the wives laughed loudly, the other young barristers seemed more moderately amused. Phillida did her best, and there was a weary titter from Claude, but no smiles from the Judge's wife or Hilda. The Welsh wizard looked as though he had just witnessed an act of adultery in Chapel. Erskine-Brown broke the ensuing silence with a somewhat pointless remark: 'They don't have them nowadays.'

'Indecent assaults in flick houses? Of course they do. Why, only the other day at Uxbridge . . .'

'No. I mean one and ninepennies . . .'

'Perhaps you're right. Let's say it's a joke from my distant past. Not a bad story, though, whenever it happened.'

The Judge rose to his feet in determined manner and asked his wife if she were ready to go; she told him that she'd been ready for some time. 'Delighted to meet *you*, Mrs Rumpole. Quite delightful,' the Judge said before he left us. 'I do hope we meet you again soon.' I noticed that I was not included in his eager anticipation of any future get-together.

'Telling that disgusting story about the girl in the Odeon!' Hilda sat in the taxi travelling down the Mall, leaving as much unoccupied seat between us as possible. The temperature had dropped to a point at which your fingers would fall off if you stayed out in it too long.

'It wasn't the Odeon,' I ventured to correct her. 'It was the Regal Cinema, Bethnal Green.'

'And you told it for the hundredth time! You must be getting senile.'

'Old jokes are always welcome. Like old poetry, old wine, old . . .' But she interrupted my speech. 'The Judge didn't know where to look.'

'Mr Justice Gwent-Evans bores for Wales,' I told her. 'A man with about as many laughs in him as a post-mortem.'

'He was a perfect gentleman, which is more than can be said for you, Rumpole. Fancy telling a blue joke with the Judge's wife sitting right beside you!'

'It was the Savoy Hotel, Hilda, not the Chapel in the valley.' At this point our taxi rattled to a halt by a traffic light.

'Wherever it was you made a fine fool of yourself tonight, Rumpole!'

And then, I suppose, something snapped, and the habit of years was broken. I knew it as I opened the taxi door and felt, as

I stepped out into the night, like the Count of Monte Cristo when he made his final and perilous escape from the Château D'If. I had at last found freedom. The world was in front of me; behind was Hilda's voice saying, 'What on *earth* are you doing, Rumpole?'

'Saying goodbye,' I told her, as I walked on across St James's Park and never, for one moment, turned back.

The reader will be no doubt relieved to turn from the painful and somewhat sordid world of married life to the more salubrious atmosphere of crime and criminals. Captain Arnold Gleason, ex-soldier and ex-golf club secretary, had become a partner in the Woodland Folk Garden Centre, just outside the large country town of Worsfield, some fifty miles to the West of London. Although he was a man in his sixties, with a prominent stomach and little hair, Captain Gleason must have had some charm for he had married Amanda Gleason, a red-haired beauty some thirty years his junior. He also had a partner, a handsome and youngish member of the Council for the Preservation of Rural England, the Friends of the Earth and such-like organizations dedicated to the saving of hedgerows and the protection of the badger, with a name like the hero of a Victorian novelette, Hugo Lutterworth. When I tell you that, from time to time, Mr Lutterworth and Mrs Gleason were seen kissing in the greenhouses, you will readily understand that the scene at the Woodland Folk Garden Centre was set for a triangular drama and a nasty accident.

The accident came about when Captain Gleason got into his Volvo Estate car to leave the Garden Centre. He drove carefully, as was apparently his practice, out of the Garden gates and started down a steepish hill which led to a junction with the main road to Worsfield. As the car descended, it became out of control as the braking system had clearly failed. With considerable presence of mind, the Captain steered into an area half-way down the hill used by the Garden Centre for assorted statues. He crashed into a sundial, ricocheted off a couple of heavy cherubs and finally came to rest among the gnomes. Captain Gleason mercifully escaped with nothing more than a mild concussion, a cut fore-

head, a number of bruises and a considerably battered Volvo
Estate. Subsequent inquiries by the industrious Detective In-
spector Rolph of the Worsfield force led to the arrest of young
Hugo Lutterworth on a charge of attempted murder.

Lutterworth had one small piece of luck. His solicitor, a grey-
haired and generally harmless Mr Dennis Driscoll, knew absolutely nothing about crime. He had however met Mr Bernard,
one of my regular customers, and the long-time representative of
the Timson family, over a matter of conveyancing. They struck
up a friendship, and when Mr Driscoll happened to mention
that he had an attempted murder on his hands, Bernard wisely
replied, 'Then Rumpole's your man,' or uttered words to the
like effect. I suppose if Captain Gleason had crashed into a lorry
on the main road and thereby met his end, there would have
been talk of taking in some querulous Q.C., some artificial silk to
lead me (and this, despite the success I scored, some years ago
now, in the Penge Bungalow Murders, alone and without a
leader). As it was such a peculiarly unsuccessful attempt, I was
allowed to handle the matter on my own.

The first time I saw Hugo Lutterworth was in a cell in Worsfield Gaol, a small Victorian prison with no proper interviewing
facilities. He was a fine-featured young man with an aureole of
fair hair, so that he looked like Sir Galahad, or Lancelot or any
of the rather over-sensitive chaps from the Table Round in a
Pre-Raphaelite painting. Mr Driscoll asked me what I thought
the chances of a conviction were, bearing in mind that the evidence clearly showed that the brakes in Captain Gleason's Volvo
Estate had been tampered with. What I thought was that, even if
the Prosecution were conducted by a first-year law student with
a serious speech impediment, we were likely to be defeated.
What I said was, 'I think we face ... certain difficulties. You
and Captain Gleason,' I asked Lutterworth, 'were partners in
the Garden Centre business?'

'I drew up the partnership agreement' – Driscoll was fumbling
among his papers, happy to be back in a branch of the law he
understood – 'I think I've got it here.'

'Never mind about that now, Mr Driscoll.' I turned to Hugo

to ask him the four-thousand-dollar question: 'And you were clearly having a bit of a walk-out with Gleason's wife?'

'I don't want Amanda's name mentioned.' The man was clearly keen on a place in a stained-glass window.

'*You* may not, old darling, but the Prosecution are going to mention it every ten minutes. Listen! Someone surely drained the fluid from the brakes in Gleason's car. There's no dispute about that.'

'No dispute at all,' Driscoll agreed.

'Well, what we want to know is, was that someone you?' It was clearly a tactless question. Hugo turned from me to ask Mr Driscoll if Amanda Gleason was all right.

'No one tampered with *her* brakes,' I was able to reassure him.

'She hasn't been questioned, has she? Not . . . not arrested?'

'There's no statement from Mrs Gleason among the prosecution documents.'

'They're not going to arrest her?'

'Not . . . as far as we know.'

'Can't we find out?'

'I suppose Mr Driscoll could have a word with the prosecution solicitor,' I suggested. 'Just in an idle chat on the phone, couldn't you, Driscoll? See if there's any intention of proceeding against Mrs Gleason for any offence . . .'

'I can't decide anything until I know about Amanda,' Hugo Lutterworth told us, and I wondered, idly but aloud, what offence he thought she might be charged with.

'I'd rather not say anything' – my client looked nobly resolute – 'not till I'm sure Amanda's safe. Do you understand?'

'No, Mr Lutterworth' – I was beginning to lose patience with all this nobility – 'I'm not at all sure that I do understand. This isn't *Gardeners' Question Time*, you know. I didn't come all this way for a nice chat about the herbaceous border. We're here to discuss matters of life and death.'

And then he gave me an answer which struck a kind of chill into the air of the over-centrally-heated cell. 'Gardening is really a matter of life and death,' he told us. 'Things either do well, or you just have to pull them up and throw them on the bonfire.

There's no room for mercy in gardening.' When we left our client he was going to consider taking us into his confidence once he had established that his precious Amanda Gleason was in the clear; but I thought that if he talked as ruthlessly about Captain Gleason's 'accident' as he had about gardening I might be saying goodbye to Sir Lancelot for about five years.

While we were in Worsfield I asked Mr Driscoll to show me the scene of the crime. The Garden Centre was surprisingly large and seemed well cared for. The slope in front of the gates was fairly steep, and led down to the busy junction where heavy lorries were frequently passing. My instructing solicitor took in all these facts and said, 'It's so out of Lutterworth's character.'

'Know him well, do you?'

'Oh, for years. And his father too. You know I always thought Hugo was almost painfully honest. That's why he needed a bit of protection in the partnership agreement.'

'Old Sir Lancelot was probably pretty honest,' I told him, 'until he started messing around with Queen Guinevere.'

'I suppose if Hugo gets sent away, Gleason'll have to sell this place.' We had wandered into the gates of the Garden Centre and were standing in the Cheap and Cheerful Shrub Department. 'One of those horrible great supermarkets has been after this site for years. Hugo was dead against selling. He'd built up the business, really. And he lived for his flowers. I say, we had better go, this is rather embarrassing.'

Mr Driscoll was looking out towards the hardy perennials. I saw an elderly, ill-tempered-looking man, walking with a stick. Beside him was a red-haired beauty, pale and with that rather self-conscious air of spirituality which makes Pre-Raphaelite pictures so irritating. She walked with her arm in his; Queen Guinevere was making a fuss of King Arnold. Domestic harmony seemed to have been restored.

I am running ahead of myself. My pre-trial visit to Worsfield Gaol occurred after my separation from Mrs Horace Rumpole. I had walked away from the taxi across the park with a lightness of step and a curious feeling of elation which I hadn't felt, perhaps, since the Jury brought in their not guilty verdict in the Penge Bungalow Murders. As I walked past the sleeping pelicans and towards Big Ben and shivered slightly in the night air, I began to consider the question of lodgings for the night. At first, in my enthusiasm, I considered the Savoy, but I soon remembered that very few people are able to stay at that inn on legal aid. So I turned my footsteps towards what I now regarded as my real home, Equity Court in the Temple, London E.C.4.

I had no doubt that my separation from Hilda was then permanent. What is a man, after all, but his old jokes, and to be matched with a wife who spurned them seemed to me a fate considerably worse than death. As I walked I repeated some lines by Percy Bysshe Shelley not, for some reason, known to Sir Arthur Quiller-Couch or included in my old India-paper edition of *The Oxford Book of English Verse*. Rather an irritating young man in many ways, Percy Bysshe, and unable to hold a candle to the Great Wordsworth, but he had some telling phrases on the subject of marriage, the 'beaten road' he called it:

> Which those poor slaves with weary footsteps tread,
> Who travel to their home among the dead
> By the broad highway of the world, and so
> With one chained friend, perhaps a jealous foe,
> The dreariest and the longest journey go.

My own journey was to freedom and Equity Court, and then I remembered a few minor drawbacks about the place. Our Head of Chambers, Soapy Sam Ballard, Q.C., was intent on declaring the place a smoke-free zone, banning all cheroots, panatellas, whiffs and fags, so that our Chambers might, as he put it, stand shoulder to shoulder with the Clean Air Brigade. He was also constantly reminding us that the lease specified that our home from home should be used 'for business purposes only', and not for any form of domestic life. A fellow named Jeffrey Mungo had recently been evicted from his Chambers in Lincoln's Inn for using them as a bedsitter. Despite this terrible warning, I thought I could probably settle fairly comfortably into my room at Equity Court, and Ballard would be none the wiser.

It cannot be said, however, that the suspicions of our Head of Chambers were not aroused. At our next Chambers meeting when we assembled to discuss the vital questions of the hour (Dianne's request for a rise in salary to keep up with the increased cost of nail varnish and women's magazines, or the escalating consumption of Nescafé), Ballard's desk was littered with a number of exhibits: Item One, a yellowish shaving-brush, still damp; Item Two, one tub of shaving soap; Item Three, one safety-razor (Gillette) and a slightly rusted blade. As those present gazed upon these articles in some bewilderment, Ballard opened the proceedings on a solemn note.

'Standards in Chambers,' he told us, 'must be kept up. We must give the impression of a tight and happy ship to the solicitors who visit us . . .'

'Aye, aye, Cap'n!' I felt it was appropriate to mutter.

'I was hearing of a set in Lincoln's Inn, where they had trouble with a tenant *cooking* in his room.' Ballard ignored my interruption and then Uncle Tom (T. C. Rowley, our oldest and briefless inhabitant) gave us a passage from his memoirs: 'Old Maurice MacKay had a pupil from Persia, I recollect. This fellow gave a birthday party and roasted half a sheep in the middle of Maurice's Turkey carpet.' Whereupon Ballard, feeling perhaps, that the case might be diverted into other channels, called our attention to the exhibits. 'These things' – he glanced at them with distaste – 'were found in the upstairs lavatory when the cleaning lady arrived this morning. The discovery was immediately reported to our clerk, Henry, who took them into his custody. Does anyone lay claim to them? They seem to be articles of antique shaving-tackle.'

'Well, they're certainly not mine,' Portia assured us.

'Of course they didn't have takeaway dinners in those days . . .' Uncle Tom rambled on. 'He ended up as a Prime Minister somewhere.'

'Who did?' Erskine-Brown asked.

'Old Maurice MacKay's pupil. The one who cooked the sheep . . .'

'Rumpole' – Ballard reasserted his command – 'do you know anything about these objects?'

'Oh, I never plead guilty, my Lord. Sorry I can't join in the fun, got to get down to a little place in the country.' I rose to leave the meeting.

'Your weekend cottage, Rumpole?' Uncle Tom asked.

'No. Worsfield Gaol.'

I had been summoned to a second conference with Hugo Lutterworth, who had, it seemed, something to impart. Mr Driscoll had been assured there was no prosecution of Mrs Amanda Gleason intended, but she had, a fact we didn't know at the time, visited Lutterworth in prison. When I called on him, he immediately told me that he had no further need of my services. As you can see, it was not a period of unmitigated success in the Rumpole career.

'You're giving me the sack?' I couldn't help it, my spirits were a little dashed.

'It's just I don't see what you can do for me. It was my fault, you see. Entirely my fault. I know that perfectly well.'

'Couldn't you think of me as an endangered species?'

'What?' Lutterworth was puzzled.

'*Avocatus minimus volubilis*, the lesser-booming barrister.' I lit a comforting small cigar. 'We're being flushed out of our natural habitats in Crown Courts and before the Magistrates. Batty bureaucrats are going to take away our right to juries and shift the burden of proof and leave us defenceless. Soon we'll be replaced by a couple of chartered accountants and a good computer. If you care for conservation at all, Mr Lutterworth, help save the barrister.' My client looked seriously concerned – not much of a sense of humour in Sir Lancelot. 'Do one thing for me. Let me cross-examine the prosecution witnesses. Let's just see if they've got a case.'

'No harm in that, Hugo.' Mr Driscoll advised him.

'All right.' Hugo Lutterworth thought it over and appeared to be prepared to do something to save the Rumpole from extinction. 'But I can't go into the witness-box and give evidence. I can't say anything that might implicate Amanda.'

So I would be fighting a hopeless battle with one hand tied

behind my back. Things did not go entirely smoothly either, in my stay at Equity Court. I had settled down moderately comfortably, and, much to my surprise, there was no message or telephone call from Mrs Hilda Rumpole, and I certainly did not lift the telephone to her. Well, I had little enough time on my hands, what with visits to Worsfield and fending off the unwelcome attentions of our Head of Chambers.

Soapy Sam Ballard, strolling down Fetter Lane, happened to glance into the window of Sam Firkin's barber-shop, where he saw Rumpole well-lathered, reclining in a chair and receiving the attention of Sam's cut-throat razor, to be followed by a hot towel and a dash of astringent lotion. From this glimpse he deduced, as Erskine-Brown told me much later, that I must either be in funds to enjoy the luxury of having myself shaved, or, and this seemed to him the more likely explanation, I had lost my shaving-tackle when our cleaning lady, Mrs Slammery, found it apparently abandoned in Chambers' upstairs lavatory.

Resolved to make further inquiries, Ballard called late at Chambers and was rewarded, again my informant is my learned friend, Claude Erskine-Brown, with a glimpse of a bedroom slipper and, above it, a portion of flannel-pyjama'd leg disappearing up a darkened stairway. He went in hot pursuit and beat on Rumpole's locked door, calling out my name repeatedly but answer came there none. One morning he arrived at Chambers early and asked Mrs Slammery, who was sweeping the doorstep, if she had seen me, but she was unable to help in his inquiries. I then turned up, full of bacon and eggs from the Taste-Ee-Bite.

'Rumpole,' Ballard pounced on me. 'What on earth are you doing?'

'Arriving at work,' I assured him, 'as I have been these last forty years.' Not satisfied with this answer he pursued me up to my room and began a minute examination of the broken-springed couch in the corner under the bookcase.

'I see you make yourself quite at home here, Rumpole.' He did his best to sound sarcastic. 'A person could easily sleep on that old Chesterfield.'

'Of course. Care for forty winks?'

'Filthy ash-tray.' He examined the object in question.

'Mrs Slammery hasn't flipped her magic duster yet.'

'I think I'd better warn you. I'm proposing that Chambers becomes a smoke-free zone, in accordance with present-day medical advice.'

'You're what?' I assumed surprise, although, of course, I had wind of Ballard's great plan from Erskine-Brown.

'It's not enough to abstain oneself. It's the other fellows' poison getting up your nostrils.'

'You want to ban smoking in Chambers?' I had to be sure of the prosecution case.

'That is my intention.'

'You can't do that!'

'I imagine the proposal will command pretty general support.'

'It's entirely illegal . . .' I peered back into the distant days at Keble when I had been up on *Constitutional Law in a Nutshell*.

'*What?*' Ballard appeared somewhat taken aback.

'It would be against our ancient rights of freedom, those great principles of justice our fathers fought and bled for. It would be clean contrary to Magna Carta.'

'I bow to your superior knowledge of history, Rumpole. Could you just remind me which clause in Magna Carta deals with smoking?'

'No freeman shall be taken or imprisoned, or destrained on or exiled or denied the comfort of the occasional cheroot . . . unless by the lawful judgement of his peers!' I gave him the sonorous quotation he asked for. 'I know you're remarkably ignorant of the common law of England, Bollard . . . however encyclopedic your knowledge of the Rent Laws and the Factory Acts.'

'Ah! Talking of which . . .'

'Of what?'

'The Factory Acts.'

'Do we have to?'

'I think we do. These Chambers, Rumpole . . .'

'To which you are a comparative newcomer,' I was at pains to remind him.

'. . . are designated as a place of work. This is not a doss-
house. As your Head, I'm not in the business of running a hotel
or some sort of Salvation Army hostel!'

'*What* are you suggesting?' I appeared not to follow his drift.

'I'm simply suggesting that you've been living in here,
Rumpole. Sleeping rough.' He darted to a cupboard and pulled
the door open, finding nothing but a few books and an umbrella.
'Last night I saw a pyjama leg!'

'I expect you did – on retiring for the night.'

'When I came in here. Late. After dining in Hall with Mr
Justice Gwent-Evans. I called into Chambers and I distinctly
saw a leg in pyjamas . . . beating a hasty retreat towards *your*
room, Rumpole!'

He ended triumphantly, but I only looked at him in a sorrowful
and pitying fashion. 'Lay off it, Bollard,' I said.

'It's a matter I intend to pursue, for the benefit of the other
tenants.'

'Please! Lay off the booze. That's what I mean. Keep off the
sauce. Cut down on the quaffing! I know what you Benchers get
up to at the High Table in Hall. No wonder you've started
seeing things!'

'*Things?*' Now he was struggling to follow *my* drift.

'Pyjama legs now' – I ostentatiously lit a small cigar – 'in a
little while it will be elephants. And pink mice crawling up the
curtains. Look, why don't you lie down quietly, sleep it off
before you go blundering across the road and make a complete
pig's breakfast of a Planning Appeal?'

At this Ballard coughed, equally ostentatiously, and moved
towards the door.

'I'm absolutely firm on my principles,' he said. 'This is not
the end of the inquiry. Remember Mungo.'

'Mungo?' I pretended ignorance of the Lincoln's Inn squatter.

'He tried to save money by moving into his Chambers. He was
found heating tins of Spaghetti Bolognese on the electric fire.
Jeffrey Mungo has been given three months' notice to quit!'

'Cut down on the port, Bollard.' I looked at him sadly. 'May
you find the strength to kick the habit. I shall pray for you.'

So the first attack by our Head of Chambers was repelled. Some nights later I was seated at my desk by the roaring electric fire as usual of an evening, dining on Château Fleet Street and a takeaway curry, tastefully served on a silver-paper dish from the Star of India, half-way up Chancery Lane. I was reading *The Oxford Book of English Verse*, and had reached what to my mind is one of the old sheep of the Lake District's finest, a sonnet I really had no need to read, as I had its inspiring lines by heart.

> It is not to be thought of that the Flood
> Of Rumpole's freedom, which, to the open sea
> Of the world's praise, from dark antiquity
> Hath flowed, 'with pomp of waters unwithstood' . . .
> should perish.

Then there was a knock on the door; I hastily covered my oriental dinner and *The Oxford Book* with a brief, and Mrs Phillida Erskine-Brown marched in. She had been working late and was wearing her glasses. 'Ballard knows all about it,' she said, coming to the point at once.

'Ballard knows all about what?'

Phillida lifted the statement of evidence and exposed my half-eaten dinner. 'You. Eating these takeaway curries in Chambers.'

'How on earth? . . .'

'Really, Rumpole. After nearly half a century of mixing with criminals you might have picked up a few tips. At least don't leave the evidence scattered around your waste-paper basket. Mrs Slammery's been finding Star of India placky bags around the place for days.'

'I don't see that it proves a thing. Is there anything wrong with a fellow, exhausted after a long case, taking a mouthful of Chicken Bindaloo on his way home?'

'But you're not.'

'Not what?'

'Not on your way home.'

'Perhaps . . . not exactly.' There was no doubt she had hit upon a weak spot in my defence, and our Portia was now staring at me over the top of her glasses, barking questions in the way I had, long ago, taught her to deal with a hostile witness. My lessons had clearly been well learnt.

'What do you mean, *not exactly*? You're either on your way home or you're not. Or do you make a vague shot at Froxbury Court and sometimes miss?'

'Not exactly . . .'

'Rumpole, do *try* and answer the question.' She sighed with that weary patience I often adopt in Court. 'I put it to you, you're living in Chambers!'

'Not exactly living . . .'

'*The Oxford Book of English Verse* – isn't it your regular bed-side reading?' And when I merely shrugged my shoulders, she pressed the point home. 'Why don't you answer? Are you afraid you might be incriminated?'

'I like a spot of Wordsworth before dropping off. Nothing wrong with that, is there, Portia?'

'Nothing at all. So *The Oxford Book of English Verse* is to be found on your bedside table. In the Gloucester Road?'

'Of course.' At which she pulled another mean Courtroom trick, rolled back the brief on my desk further and revealed my favourite anthology.

'Then what's it doing here? Rubbing shoulders with *Bloodstains I Have Known* by Professor Ackerman and an out-of-date *Archbold on Crime*?'

'I brought it here . . . to prepare a final speech in a case.' Quick thinking you'll agree, but she was on to me like a terrier.

'Which case?'

'Which what?'

'Case! Am I not speaking clearly?'

'An attempted murder. My client's an excellent gardener and a remarkably unsuccessful murderer. I have to address the Jury . . .'

'No, you haven't! That case doesn't start until next week.'

'How do you know?'

'Because I'm prosecuting. The game's up, Rumpole!'

'All right, guv.' I was, I confess it, beaten. 'You've got me bang to rights.'

'Oh, Rumpole. You know perfectly well criminals don't *say* that any more.' At that, she sat down, exhausted by her forensic brilliance, in my client's chair.

'A fellow is entitled to his own anecdotes for God's sake,' I started to explain. 'I mean, where would I be without my anecdotes?'

'Hilda took exception to one of them?' She guessed the terrible truth.

'An excellent story. You remember I told it at the Scales of Justice dinner. Went down rather well, I thought.'

'Did you? And what did Hilda have to say about it?'

'I prefer not to remember. I believe the word "senile" featured in her address to the Court. I opened the cab door and found freedom.'

'You'll have to go back sometime.' And she added thoughtfully, 'Anyway, you can't stay here. After the Jeffrey Mungo case, Ballard'll have you evicted for breaking the terms of the lease!'

'Mungo cooked Spaghetti Bolognese.'

'And you import curry; I'd say the offence is a great deal worse. They're on to you, Rumpole. Stay here another night and you'll lose your tenancy.' She looked at me with a sort of amused desperation. 'What *are* we going to do about you?' She sighed and made up her mind. 'Oh well. I suppose there's nothing else for it. Just till you find somewhere else, you understand . . .'

So it came about that I took up residence in a spare bedroom in the Erskine-Browns' agreeable house in Canonbury Square. I was, although I say it myself, no trouble at all to Claude and Phillida. For instance, I always did my own breakfast, manning the cooker to produce my own bacon, eggs and fried slice, whilst the family gloomily digested muesli (stuff which looked as though it were manufactured to line birdcages) and fat-free yoghurt. In the evenings I entertained my hosts with an anthology of my best anecdotes, together with a complete account of my cross examination of the pathologist in the Penge Bungalow Murders, a triumph of which I have almost total recall. I must say that the Erskine-Browns were kind and generous hosts; the same could not be said of their issue, children operatically named Tristan and Isolde. This couple of mere infants, no more than nine and seven years old respectively, were amazingly puritanical, and on the whole as censorious of Rumpole as Soapy Sam Ballard at his most disapproving.

One morning I was at the cooker in a dressing-gown, smoking a small cigar, and blowing out a slight fire caused by some leaping bacon fat on the grill. Portia was deep in a brief and Erskine-Brown had just had *Opera* magazine hot from the press, and the children were dressed for school when Tristan said, 'I can't understand why people have to smoke.'

'I can't understand why people have to chew gob-stoppers!' I was quick with my reply.

'I never chew gob-stoppers. They're bad for your teeth.'

'For one so young, you seem remarkably careful of your health. Let me tell you, Tristan, and you too, Isolde, if you'd care to listen, there's no pleasure on earth that's worth sacrificing for the sake of an extra five years in the geriatric ward of the Sunset Old People's Home, Weston-Super-Mare.'

'My teacher says they're going to make all smoking illegal,' young Isolde announced. 'They're going to send you to prison for it.' I wondered if Portia had given birth to a couple of prosecuting counsel when the child continued, 'My teacher says you shouldn't be allowed to smoke, even if you're all by yourself, sitting in a field in *the open air*.'

'Why ever not?'

'You might set yourself on fire with the matches; they'd have to cure your burns on the National Health.' Tristan supplied the answer with considerable satisfaction. Then Erskine-Brown rose to take his infants off to school. As they left the room, Isolde made a remark to her father which caused the fried slice to turn somewhat sour in my mouth and make me feel but a temporary visitor to Islington. 'Daddy,' I heard her piping up, 'how long is that man going to live here?'

In search of an answer to the same question, I heard much later, Phillida visited She Who Must Be Obeyed in Froxbury Court. She found Hilda with her feet up in an unusually tidy

flat, listening to *The Archers* (a programme which used to cause
some controversy between us) and tried to effect a reconciliation.
It seems she told Hilda that I was missing her greatly, whereupon
my wife said that she was hardly missing me at all, and thanked
Phillida for her courage in putting up with me. So much for the
gratitude of a woman to whom I had continually returned home
at a more or less regular hour from Pommeroy's Wine Bar for
the last forty years. No wonder I had chosen freedom.

A few nights before *R.* v. *Lutterworth* started, I came home
late from Chambers and let myself in quietly, thinking Tristan
and Isolde might have been mercifully asleep. The kitchen door
was open a crack and I thought I heard the sound of voices.
Phillida and Claude were no doubt sampling a rather cheeky
little Bergerac he had got in a job-lot from an old school-friend
in the wine trade. I paused by the door and heard Phillida say,
'You've got to talk to him, Claude. She doesn't want him back!
He might be with us for ever.'

'You invited him to stay. You ought to talk to him.' Claude
Erskine-Brown was showing his usual courage. 'Go on, Philly.
Be a man!'

'I'm not a man,' Phillida said, and there was clearly force in
her argument. 'You're the man, remember?'

A fellow can't help feeling a bit of a pang, when he hears he's
not a welcome guest in the house of a lady to whom he's taught
all she ever knew of the subject of cross-examination, and I trod
the cold stairway up to bed a little sadly.

So I was still a wanderer, with a temporary billet *à côté de chez*
Erskine-Brown, when our Portia rose to open the case of *R.* v.
Lutterworth to the Jury.

'It's the old, old story,' she told them. 'A young and attractive
wife, married to an elderly husband who had, perhaps, lost some
of his charm for her over the years. So she allowed herself to
drift into a love affair with her husband's partner, that no doubt
physically more attractive young man, Hugo Lutterworth, the
defendant in this case. Lutterworth is here today because he was
not content with mere sex! He wanted his partner, Captain
Gleason, out of the way so that he could enjoy his business *and*

his wife, without having to share them with anybody. Members of the Jury, it's difficult for us, who no doubt have stable homes and contented marriages, to understand the lengths to which some unhappy people will go in inflicting pain and suffering on others.'

Mrs Erskine-Brown, Q.C., was no doubt at her most eloquent, but I wasn't listening to her. I was gazing in fascinated horror at the Bench above me. There, chosen to preside over the Court, was the Welsh wizard, Mr Justice Huw Gwent-Evans, the Chapel guru who had failed to laugh at my joke in the Savoy Hotel, and there beside him, equally unamused, sat She Who Must Be Obeyed, my wife, Hilda, staring down at me apparently prepared to judge Rumpole, come to an unfavourable verdict and impose the severest penalty known to the law.

Among Phillida Erskine-Brown's early witnesses was a Garden Centre worker named Daphne Hapgood, a chunky, red-headed young daughter of the soil, whose nails were broken with much potting up. She testified to having seen Hugo Lutterworth bestowing a passionate kiss on Mrs Gleason in a greenhouse (people who live in glasshouses shouldn't kiss their employers' wives), evidence which shocked the Judge and She Who Must Be Obeyed equally. She also described seeing Lutterworth doing some work on the Volvo Estate, bending over it with the bonnet open, on the day before it crashed. She added that it was not unusual for Hugo to work on the cars, being apparently as handy with sparking plugs as he was with seedlings. Through all this evidence I noticed that Amanda Gleason couldn't resist looking distressed and lovingly at Hugo in the dock, bestowing upon him long glances which he, unfortunately, returned in a way which was doing us no good at all with the Jury.

'Did you ever hear Captain Gleason ask Hugo Lutterworth to look at his car for him?' I asked Daphne when I rose to cross-examine.

'I can't remember. He may have done.'

'May have on this particular occasion?'

'I suppose it's possible.'

'Thank you.'

'Is that all, Mr Rumpole?' The Judge seemed surprised. 'You're not challenging the evidence about the intimate conduct between your client and his partner's wife?'

'Oh, no, my Lord. That's admitted.'

'So this man' – the Welsh wizard was working himself up to a denunciation from the pulpit – 'admits kissing Mrs Gleason in full view of the Garden Centre workforce. He seems to have had a very tenuous grasp on morality.'

'This judge,' I whispered to Mr Driscoll, 'is suffering from a bad case of premature adjudication.'

'Did you say something, Mr Rumpole?' His Lordship was looking at me suspiciously, and I could see that my lady wife was not too pleased either. 'In due course there will be a full explanation,' I told him.

I hoped there would, but at the minute I had no particular idea what it was going to be. Happily the moment for luncheon had arrived and the Judge, showing that he had remembered more of my well-known anecdote than he cared to admit, said, 'Very well, Members of the Jury, we'll leave it there until . . .'

'Ten past two, my Lord?' I suggested. At which Sir Huw Gwent-Evans rose without another word and, ignoring my signals, She Who Must Be Obeyed swept out after him.

Later, after I had hung about for a while in the marble-paved hallway of the Worsfield Court, I saw Hilda advancing upon me in the company of Posnett, the Judge's clerk.

'Hilda!' I found myself, for once in my life, almost at a loss for words. 'What on earth . . .?'

'The Judge invited me down to luncheon and to hear a bit of your case, Rumpole. You may remember how well *I* got on with Mr Justice Gwent-Evans at the Savoy.'

Of course judges did ask distinguished visitors down to lunch in their lodgings, and they did ask such people – sheriffs, lords-lieutenant of the county and their good ladies, persons of that ilk – to sit beside them on the Bench during particularly fascinating cases. But persons of the ilk of She Who Must Be Obeyed? I suppose I found it hard to believe that the Judge had taken *such* a shine to her.

'Well, you might have let me know. It came as something of a shock to me, seeing you in the seat of judgement.'

'How could I let you know, Rumpole? I keep looking round the flat and you're nowhere to be found.'

'The Judge is just coming, Mrs Rumpole,' the Clerk said and started to withdraw from the presence.

'Oh, thank you, Posnett. I'll be waiting here. That's Posnett, the Judge's clerk. Quite a sweetie,' she explained to me, as though I were a child in matters concerning the legal profession. Then she said, 'Oh, by the way. That case of yours. Have you noticed the way Mrs Gleason keeps looking at your client? Quite an exhibition, isn't it? Don't you think she's really making it *too* obvious?'

The scarlet judge appeared with his clerk, Posnett, in attendance, and She was spirited off with them into the municipal Daimler to lunch in his lodgings. But what had happened was something of a miracle, a bit of a turn up for the book. What She had said had given me an entirely new view of the case; in fact She had come up with some sort of a legal inspiration. I went off in search of Driscoll and asked to see the original partnership agreement which came into existence when Gleason and Lutterworth got together to buy the Woodland Folk Garden Centre.

Hilda did not return to Court in the afternoon, and took no further part in the case. We heard evidence about the brakes on the Volvo Estate car having been cut, and when I suggested that it was a strange criminal who left such clear evidence of his crime, the Judge went so far as to suggest that the criminal clearly expected the runaway car to be mashed up by a passing lorry on the main road, so that the damage might have been obscured in the resulting mess. Whatever friends I had in the world, they clearly did not include Mr Justice Gwent-Evans. An officer then gave evidence that Hugo's fingerprints had been found near the area of the braking system. I managed to slip in a request for further investigations to see if the prints of anyone else who was connected with the Garden Centre could be found, and counsel for the Prosecution agreed readily. No doubt she wanted to propitiate me so that I would move out of her matrimonial home.

When I got back to Chambers I found a small handbill on my tray, which was the only message I had, and went to my room to bone up on the laws of partnership. Before I got down to work I read the handbill, which ran, as I remember, somewhat as follows:

> LAWYERS AS CHRISTIANS:
> THE SUFFRAGEN BISHOP OF SIDCUP
> WILL GIVE AN ADDRESS ON
> 'THE CHRISTIAN APPROACH TO THE RENT ACTS'.
> EVERYONE INTERESTED CORDIALLY INVITED.
> SHERRY AND SANDWICHES WILL BE SERVED
> AFTER THE DISCUSSION.
> SAMUEL BALLARD, Q.C., PRESIDENT.

Something about the connection between Soapy Sam Bollard and sherry had put a thought in my head, and then the door opened and Erskine-Brown was upon me.

'I wanted to have a word with you' – he perched uncomfortably on the arm of my client's chair – 'Philly's idea really.'

'A short word. I'm studying the law of partnership, in depth.'

'Of course, it has been tremendous *fun* having you to stay with us, for a short while. Just till you get fixed up.'

'Enjoyed some of the old stories, eh?' I lit a small cigar. 'Better than watching television. I've got plenty of them, for the long winter evenings.'

'Good.' Erskine-Brown sounded unenthusiastic. 'Philly and I would love that.'

'Well then. Does that solve your problem?'

'*Our* problem, yes ... But not Hilda's.'

'Hilda's?'

'Philly went to see her. She's most terribly upset.'

'Your wife's upset?' I was puzzled. 'She seemed quite bobbish in Court.'

'No. Hilda's, well, terribly down and lonely. She wants you

back desperately, Rumpole. We were both, well, rather sad about it.'

I looked pityingly at Erskine-Brown. Then I got up and slapped him heartily on the back. 'Claude. I have good news for you!'

'You're going back to Hilda?' The man appeared to have some hope.

'No. Set your mind at rest. Hilda's bright as a button. Happy as the day is long. She's chummed up with a peculiarly nauseating brand of Welsh judge and she's having an exotic social life round the Worsfield Assizes. She wanted me to tell you that she's enormously grateful to you and Portia for having me and long may the arrangement continue. Now, is that good news for you?' Erskine-Brown didn't answer. 'It isn't, is it?' Erskine-Brown still didn't answer. 'In fact, it's somewhat dashed your hopes? You really want to give me the order of the Imperial Elbow, don't you? Say no more! I can take a hint, Erskine-Brown. I can tell, when your children simulate terminal bronchitis every time I walk into a room, that it's time I was moving on. Only one thing. You'll have to help me to another billet.'

'How am I expected to do that?' the poor fellow asked weakly.

'Let me tell you, old cock. It's perfectly simple. All you have to do is to go to this shindig.' I let him have the handbill for nothing. 'The Bishop of Sidcup on "The Christian Approach to the Rent Acts".'

'But that night I've got tickets for *Rigoletto*,' he protested.

'*Rigoletto* will still be around in a hundred years' time,' I assured him. 'This is your one opportunity to hear the Bishop of Sidcup on this fascinating subject. Roll up, Claude! Be among those present on the night! Join Soapy Sam Bollard, our slithery Head of Chambers, and partake liberally of the sherry and sandwiches. Particularly the sherry . . .'

'Why on earth should I?'

'Because if you do this properly, old darling, I can fold my tent, take the Golden Road back to Chambers and stay here undisturbed. Now, this is all I'm asking you to do . . .' And I began to fill him in with the details of my plan.

*

The next day Captain Gleason went into the witness-box, a bulky figure in a double-breasted blue suit and a regimental tie; he seemed such an unlikely consort for the beautiful red-head in the well of the Court that it came as no surprise when she hardly looked at him. Phillida was winding to the end of her ex-amination-in-chief when she asked the Captain when he became doubtful about his wife's relationship with Hugo Lutterworth.

'I had been suspicious of my wife and Hugo for some time. About a year ago I came back from a regimental dinner in London and discovered them in a . . . compromising position.' Gleason spoke quietly, sounding the most forbearing husband. 'I decided to forgive them both. Of course, I had no idea that my partner would . . . try to get rid of me.'

'We have heard evidence that your wife visited Lutterworth in prison.'

'I heard that. Yes.' The Captain shook his head sadly.

'In spite of that, what is your present attitude towards your marriage?'

'I'm still prepared to give it another chance.'

'In spite of an attempt that may have been made on your life?'

'Yes. In spite of that.'

You could almost hear the purr of approval from the Jury as Phillida thanked him and sat down. The Judge added his thanks and then the Captain asked if he might sit during my questions as he had a little heart trouble.

'Of course, Captain Gleason,' the Welsh judge cooed at him. 'A glass of water? Usher, bring Captain Gleason a glass of water. Are you sure you feel quite well, Captain Gleason? You just sit there and take it quite easily. You won't be long, will you, Mr Rumpole?'

'Not very long, my Lord. And I'll try and adopt my best bedside manner.' I turned to Gleason and started quietly, 'Captain Gleason. Did my client, Hugo Lutterworth, look after the cars from time to time?'

'He did. Yes.'

'If they needed a service, or some adjustment, used he to do it?'

'He said he didn't trust garages.'

'The day before, let us use a neutral expression and call it the "accident", had you told him your estate car wasn't running very smoothly and asked him to have a look at it?'

'I can't remember.'

'Can you not?' I spoke more crisply, with a little vinegar in the honey. 'Did Mr Lutterworth tell you he'd adjusted the points, or the plugs? Something of that nature?'

'He may have done.' The answer came after a pause.

'So you *may* have asked him to look at your car?'

'It's possible. I haven't got much of a talent with mechanical objects.' Captain Gleason smiled at the Judge, who smiled back in a thoroughly understanding manner. Clearly they were both useless when it came to carburettors.

'You weren't in army transport?'

'No.'

'You were in the Catering Corps?'

'What about it?' The witness sounded defensive.

'Nothing at all. I'm sure you were a very gallant caterer. So you never attended to your car yourself?'

'Never.' The evidence was, happily, quite positive.

'Never even opened the bonnet?'

'Never. I got it filled up at the garage.'

'Hugo Lutterworth did the rest?'

'Did rather too much, on that particular occasion.' There was an unsettling rattle of sympathetic laughter from the Jury, in which his Lordship was pleased to join. I wiped the smile off his face when I asked, 'You say that, Captain Gleason. But looking back on it, wouldn't you agree that my client has done you a simply enormous favour?'

'I have no idea what you mean!' Gleason appeared startled and looked to the Judge for help.

'Neither have I, Mr Rumpole.' The Judge seemed all too willing to come to the witness's aid.

'You know exactly what I mean, Captain! Had you not had a very tempting offer for the Garden Centre site from a chain of immense supermarkets? Might not your greenhouses have become promenades for the purchase of everything from butterscotch to bedsteads . . .?'

'My Lord, I can't see how my business affairs can possibly be relevant.'

'Neither can I at the moment. Mrs Erskine-Brown, do you object to the question?'

'No, my Lord. Not at this stage.'

'Thank you, Portia. I'll be moving out soon,' I rewarded her with a whisper. 'Well, Captain Gleason?'

'We have had an offer for the site. Yes,' he answered with the utmost caution.

'And Mr Lutterworth was determined not to sell?'

'That's what he said.'

'Because he believes in flowers and badgers and butterflies and woodland folk. All that sort of thing. But you wanted to sell and make a thumping great profit?'

'I was in favour of the Arcadia Stores offer. Yes.' The Captain was still being very cautious.

'Captain Gleason. I would like the Court to see the partnership agreement between yourself and my client . . .' Driscoll handed copies of the agreement to the Usher, who started distributing them to the Judge, Jury and the witness. 'Mr Rumpole. How can that possibly be relevant to this charge?' His Lordship was displeased, and I started to launch into a legal argument which I had prepared with the aid of Mr Driscoll, who knew about partnership agreements. 'It goes right to the heart of the matter! It is the simple solution to what your Lordship and the Jury may have found an extremely puzzling case.'

'I can't speak for the Jury, of course. But I haven't found it in the least puzzling.'

'Not puzzling?' I did my best to sound extremely surprised. 'An alleged criminal who does everything in the presence of witnesses. A case of attempted murder which is so bungled that the victim suffers nothing but a few minor cuts and bruises? I should have thought that might have caused a certain amount of bewilderment, even to your Lordship.'

The Judge struggled with his irritation and suppressed it. Then he asked, '*Why* do you say I should look at this document?'

'Because I understand my learned friend has no objection.'

Once again I whispered my bribe to Phillida, 'I'll be out of your place by Thursday!'

'My Lord. We wouldn't wish to shut out any document which might possibly have some relevance.' She rose, I must say, splendidly to the occasion.

'Look at it, will you?' I asked the witness before the Judge could draw another breath. 'The Jury have their copies. "Whereas . . ." Skip all the waffle. Just look at Paragraph 12. Read it out, will you?'

' "If either of the said partners shall perform an act which is prejudicial to the interests of the partnership or shall be convicted of a criminal offence . . ." ' Gleason started to read as quietly as possible.

' "*Or shall be convicted of a criminal offence,*" ' I gave the Court the sentence at full volume. ' "All his rights in the partnership property and income and all other benefits due to him from the said partnership shall revert immediately to the other partner who shall, from the date of the said act or offence, be solely entitled to all the partnership assets." ' I lowered the agreement and looked at the witness, smiling. 'Congratulations. You've done extremely well out of this little case, haven't you, Captain Gleason?'

'I take the greatest exception to that!' The Captain rose to attention and almost shouted. He seemed to have momentarily recovered his health.

'Do you?' I hope I sounded mildly surprised. 'All you had to do was crash your car into the bird baths. Get a few superficial cuts and bruises, and you became solely entitled to the Woodland Folk Garden Centre, which you could then flog to the supermarket and make yourself a fortune.'

'Mr Rumpole. That *isn't* all he had to do.' A remarkable display of judicial bad temper was brewing up on the Bench.

'Oh, I'm grateful to your Lordship.' I tried to pour oil on the troubled judge. 'Your Lordship has got my point, of course. There was one other thing you had to do, wasn't there, Captain Gleason? You had to get the unfortunate Hugo Lutterworth convicted of a crime. But after that little formality – once the Jury came back and found my client guilty of attempted murder – you'd be laughing all your way to your newly bought holiday home on the Costa del Sol.'

There was a decided change in the atmosphere in Court. The Jury were looking with interest and some suspicion at Captain Gleason. Even the Judge was silent. Mrs Gleason was now looking at her husband, with some anxiety, and my client was beginning to look less blissfully unconcerned.

'I haven't got a house on the Costa del Sol,' was the only answer the Captain could manage.

'Oh, I'm sorry. Formentera? No matter. I still congratulate you. You've come into a fortune.'

Captain Gleason looked helplessly down at the partnership agreement. 'I don't know how that clause got in there . . .'

'Let me tell you. My client's solicitor, Mr Driscoll here, drew up the agreement. He didn't altogether trust you, did he? I don't know what it was. Some rumours about how you came to leave the Army? A story about the accounts when you were secretary of a golf club in Surrey? He put that in to protect Mr Lutterworth, and you remembered it when you wanted to get rid of him. Isn't that the truth *Captain* Gleason?'

'My Lord. Mr Rumpole is attacking my client's character!' Phillida threw self-interest to the winds and objected at last.

'Attack his character?' I protested. 'God forbid. I'm sure the Captain is as honest a man as ever perverted the course of justice.'

'Mr Rumpole! Will you please make your suggestion against this witness absolutely clear.' The Judge was still no Rumpole fan.

'With the greatest of pleasure.' I turned to the witness. 'You needed a way to get Lutterworth out of the partnership. I suspect your wife also wanted to get rid of him. They'd had a brief affair, but that was all over, at least so far as she was concerned.' There was a sound behind me, my client calling out some sort of protest, but I was doing too well to bother about Sir Lancelot's romantic susceptibilities. 'And you knew the terms of the partnership agreement. All you had to do was to stage the attempted murder of yourself and make it look as though Mr Lutterworth had done it. So you asked him to look at the points in your car. He'd done that often enough before, hadn't he, without trying to kill you?'

'I told you he'd done it before, yes.' Captain Gleason was swaying slightly and his speech was less clear.

'Mr Rumpole. Aren't you forgetting something?' It was his Lordship's last stand on behalf of the witness.

'Am I, my Lord? Remind me.'

'*Someone* cut this gentleman's brake cables.'

'Of course. You did that, Captain Gleason, didn't you?'

'Oh yes? And risk killing myself . . .' The Captain was trying to laugh; it was a somewhat grisly sound.

'Not much of a risk, was it? A short run down the drive and a crash into the statuary. No real risk – for a driver who knew exactly what had happened to his brakes?'

There was a long silence, but answer came there none. At last Captain Gleason swayed and fell crumpled at the side of the witness box. Amanda cried out and ran to kneel beside him: Queen Guinevere was showing her unaccountable love for the crotchety and dishonest old King Arnold. The Court Clerk and a police officer were opening Gleason's collar.

'We'll adjourn now.' The Judge decided to leave the field of battle. Mr Driscoll, a kindly fellow, was looking across at the fallen witness. 'Is he all right?'

'Oh, I think the Captain will survive,' I reassured him. 'He's survived most things.'

After that cross-examination the case was downhill all the way. Further investigation revealed Captain Gleason's prints on the brake cables. He was an incompetent crook, but then the ones with any talent rarely come our way. Hugo Lutterworth would clearly never forgive me for my revelations, but he agreed to give evidence and was finally acquitted. There was still one other matter which I had to bring to a successful conclusion.

Claude Erskine-Brown, no doubt driven by a longing to clear Rumpole from his domestic hearth, did his work well. At the

Lawyers As Christians meeting, he saw Ballard was suitably plied with sherry; indeed after the first two or three, Soapy Sam appeared to be cooperating with enthusiasm. When they finally emerged into the Temple car park, the Bollard walk was not altogether steady, nor his speech entirely clear. I have done my best to reconstruct their dialogue from what Claude told me later, but it seems to have gone somewhat as follows.

'The thing about the Bishop of Sidcup,' Ballard spoke with resonant emphasis, 'is that he knows *exactly* where he stands.' Already our Head of Chambers was fumbling for his car keys, preparing to motor home.

'Yes. But do *you*?' Claude asked.

'What?'

'Know where you stand? A bit unsteadily, if you ask my opinion. I mean' – he looked suspiciously at Ballard's sleek black Granada – 'you're not going to drive that thing, are you?'

'Of course I am. Back to Waltham Cross.'

'How many sherries did you have, Ballard?'

'Three. No more than three, Erskine-Brown.'

'Half a dozen at least. Way over the limit! I mean, do get in and drive! But if you ever want to be a judge . . .'

'What?' A Bollard nerve had been touched. Of course he wanted to be a judge.

'Drunk driving! The Lord Chancellor's going to cross you off his list of possibles. And in front of the Waltham Cross Magistrates, fellow in Arbuthnot's Chambers was telling me, it's automatic prison on a breathalyzer, a month inside! "Stamp out this menace!" You know the sort of thing you get from a bench of teetotallers.'

'But I've missed the eleven fifteen' – Ballard looked at his watch – 'I don't think there's another. Erskine-Brown, what am I going to do?'

'It's entirely up to you. Waltham Cross, eh? I'm afraid it's not on my route . . .' Erskine-Brown moved towards his own motor. 'Good-night, Ballard.'

Fate, for once, was on my side. Ballard consulted his wallet and found he had forgotten to go to the Bank and had indeed left his cheque book at home. He called out to Claude for a loan to pay a minicab, but my trusty ally had switched on his engine and was roaring out of the car park. Ballard put his car keys in his pocket and walked sadly off in the general direction of Chambers.

And there I found him the next morning. In fact I took him up a cup of tea as he awoke shivering slightly under an overcoat on a sofa in a corner of his room.

'Morning, Bollard,' I greeted him. 'Been sleeping rough?' I sat down on a chair which also contained his trousers. 'Kipping on the couch reserved for the clientele? What do you think this place is, the Sally Ann? I mean, what would the chaps think if they knew you were using our Chambers as a common boarding-house?' Ballard sat up, took the teacup and raised it to his lips. Then he said, 'You're not going to tell them?'

'It's my clear and definite professional duty to do so.' I can be remorseless on occasions. 'This is not living accommodation; you're in breach of the terms of our lease. What happened, old darling? Mrs Bollard had enough of you?

'There is no Mrs Ballard.'

'No. I don't suppose there is.'

Silence reigned while Ballard took another sip of tea. 'Rumpole,' he said, 'I've been thinking.'

'Don't overdo it.'

'I've been thinking' – he sounded judicial – 'it might be better if we approached the question of smoking in Chambers on a purely voluntary basis.'

'Well, now you're talking.'

'I mean, you were able to point out to me the provisions of the Magna Carta!'

'And the European Convention on Human Rights.'

'What's that got to say about it?' He frowned.

'No citizen shall be persecuted on the grounds of race, creed or colour or because he lights up occasionally.'

'Oh well. You may be right. So, having given the matter my mature consideration . . .'

'And I'm sure no consideration could be more mature than yours . . .'

'We needn't put smoking on the Agenda for our next meeting. In view of that, it may not be necessary for you to mention the question of any person . . .'

'Dossing down in Chambers?'

'Exactly! I'm sure we understand each other.'

I got up and moved to the door. 'Of course. That's what I admire about you, Bollard. You're absolutely firm on your principles. I hear the Bishop of Sidcup was a most tremendous hit.'

So I left him, still sipping thoughtfully. All that day I pondered on the simple observation by She Who Must Be Obeyed, which had put me on to the truth of *R*. v. *Lutterworth*. In the evening, believing that Dianne, our tireless typist, had really no further use for the geranium I had brought her from the Woodland Folk Garden Centre, I took it home to Froxbury Court, where I found Hilda comfortably ensconced and listening to *The Archers*.

'We won the case, you know,' I told her, after a pause, during which She looked not at all overjoyed by my return.

'So you should have.'

'I said *we* won it. You gave me the idea. I mean, you found the bull point. The way the girl looked at him.'

'I'm not Daddy's daughter for nothing! Daddy had forty-five years at the Bar.'

'Dear old C. H. Wystan. Knew nothing about bloodstains, but let that pass.'

'Daddy knew a good deal about human nature.'

'Yes. Well. All the same, I've got to give you the credit for our victory.'

'What are you doing here, Rumpole?' She looked at me doubtfully.

'Doing here? I came to give you a geranium. Hope you like it.' It was then I presented the plant. I can't say it was received with undiminished rapture.

'It looks as though it's seen better days.'

'Well. It happens to all of us. Anyway. I live here, don't I?'

'Do you? I haven't noticed you living here lately.'

'I expect you've been busy. Sweeping under beds. Listening

to everyday stories of country folk. That's what I've been doing too, come to think of it.'

'Well, you can't just come and go as you please.'

'Do you think I'm running a hotel?' I suggested a thought for her speech.

'How did you know I was going to say that?'

'Most people do. Let me pour you a G and T. Celebrate your great victory in Court. Not every day you win a case, Hilda.' I found the bottles and mixed a drink for her, taking the liberty of opening a bottle of Pommeroy's Ordinary for myself.

'Daddy once won a case,' Hilda said thoughtfully, as she raised her glass.

'Extraordinary!'

'What did you say?'

'Well, that was nothing out of the ordinary.'

'When C. H. Wystan, when Daddy was a young man at the Bar, he did a dock brief. He defended a pickpocket for nothing. Fellow who was accused of stealing a watch . . .'

'Oh, really?' Hilda was embarking on an anecdote, one of her few.

'Anyway, Daddy got the fellow off! His first real success and he was pleased as Punch. And as he was leaving the old London Sessions, this pickpocket came up to him and said, 'I'm so grateful to you, Mr Wystan. You've saved me from prison and I've got no money to pay you. But I can give you this.' So what do you think the pickpocket did?'

'I've no idea!' Well, I can occasionally lie in a good cause.

'Offered Daddy the watch!' She laughed and then stopped laughing, and looked at me with deep suspicion. 'You've heard it before?'

'No, Hilda. I promise you, never!'

'Do take that poor plant out to the kitchen and offer it some water. It looks exhausted.'

Of course, as ever, I obeyed her command.

Rumpole and the Official Secret

Lawyers and priests deal largely in secrets, being privy to matters which are not meant for the public ear. I don't know how it is in the religious life, or whether, when two or three prelates are gathered together, they regale each other with snatches from the Confessional, but barristers are mostly indiscreet. Go into Pommeroy's Wine Bar any evening when the Château Fleet Street is flowing and you may quickly discover who's getting a divorce or being libelled, which judge has got which lady pupil in the club or which Member of Parliament relaxes in female apparel. I don't join much in such conversations; my own clients' activities are, in the main, simple and uncomplicated trans-actions, and 'Who turned over Safeways?' or 'Which bloke sup-plies logbooks for stolen Cortinas?' are rarely questions which get much airing in the Mr Chatterbox column in the *Sunday Fortress*.

Of course, often the most closely guarded secrets turn out to be matters of such stunning triviality that you wonder why anyone ever bothered to keep quiet about them. Such, it seemed, was the closely guarded matter of the Ministry of Defence Elevenses which formed the basis for the strange prosecution of Miss Rosemary Tuttle. This was a case which, although it began with a laugh, and laughter was, as always, a weapon for the defence, certainly ended in what I will always think of as a tragedy.

But let me begin at the beginning, which was roughly Sunday lunchtime at 25b Froxbury Court, our alleged 'mansion' flat off the Gloucester Road. I was relaxing with the *Sunday Fortress* propped up against the Pommeroy's plonk bottle, and Hilda was removing what was left of the roast beef and two veg, when the following item met my eye under an alluring headline:

BISCUIT WAR IN THE MINISTRY OF DEFENCE

Government extravagance has been highlighted by the astonishing sums spent subsidizing tea and biscuits consumed by civil servants at the Ministry of Defence. The cost of elevenses plus the money spent on entertaining a long list of foreign visitors would, it is calculated, have paid for the Crimean War three times over.

Such was the item of what passes for news nowadays, leading the Mr Chatterbox column. Although I usually have a keen eye for crime, I can't say that I realized that this apparently harmless story was in itself, a breach of the Official Secrets Act.

And then Hilda was calling me from the kitchen to ask if I wanted 'afters'. 'Of course I want "afters",' I called back. 'Didn't I hear a rumour of baked jam-roll?'

'We need a hatch, Rumpole,' the voice from without called, and then She entered with the tray of pudding. 'If we had a hatch I shouldn't have to walk all the way round by the hall to get your "afters".'

Hilda had touched and reopened an old and sometimes bitter controversy. Personally, I am against hatches. We had one when I was a boy in the vicarage, a horrible thing that came trundling up from the bowels of the earth and smelled of stale cabbage. Besides which, hatches aren't things that are given away. The construction and the necessary excavation of the wall might run away with an alarming sum in legal aid fees. Hilda's argument, delivered with increasing volume as she went out again for the custard, was that the hatch wouldn't entail anything trundling up from anywhere, as it would go straight into the kitchen.

'If we hadn't spent all that money on biscuits at the Ministry of Defence, we might have had three Crimean Wars,' I called out to her as I thought she might have cared to know. 'Who do you imagine finds out these things?'

'I can't hear you, Rumpole,' Hilda called back. 'And that's because we haven't got a hatch.'

*

I should now go back to the start of the story of Miss Rosemary Tuttle and the great elevenses' leak at the Ministry of Defence. Miss Tuttle herself was a spinster lady in her fifties of vaguely central European extraction, whose parents had settled in Swiss Cottage shortly before the war. She lived alone, took her lunch in all weathers on a bench in St James's Park, being especially fond of fresh air and bright peasant-style knitted clothes, so that it was never difficult to spot Miss Tuttle in a crowd.

One night, a certain Thorogood, Private Secretary to the Minister of State, was working late and he heard the sound of a copying-machine from down the corridor. He went to investigate, but by the time he got there the room was empty, although he found one bright green, embroidered glove, later identified as the property of Miss Tuttle, by the still warm machine.

'Mr Chatterbox' masks the identity of a youngish, untidy, slightly dissolute old Etonian named Tim Warboys. At his office in the *Sunday Fortress*, Warboys received an anonymous typewritten message telling him that at 2 p.m. the next day he would, if he were to be in view of a certain bench in St James's Park, see a fifty-year-old lady in bright clothing arise from her seat. She would leave behind her a copy of the *Daily Telegraph* into which would be folded certain documents. Having done as he was instructed, Warboys discovered the newspaper in the appointed place and so came into the possession of figures concerning certain entertaining expenses in the Ministry of Defence, including the amount spent on coffee and biscuits. The biscuits alone, it seems, would have gone some way to financing the Navy. He was able to include this story in his next Sunday's column.

In due course Miss Tuttle was accused of the crime and a decision had to be taken as to her prosecution. Her immediate superior was the Assistant Under-Secretary, Oliver Bowling, an old Wykehamist, who, from time to time, went to the Opera with the Erskine-Browns. Bowling, when I came to meet him, appeared to be a thoroughly sensible sort of chap who was fond of Miss Tuttle and regarded her as a harmless eccentric. He took the reasonable view that to prosecute her for what was undoubtedly – so asinine can the law be on State Occasions – a breach of Section 2 of the Official Secrets Act would merely serve to bring the Civil Service in general, and the Ministry of Defence in particular, into ridicule and contempt. This view was not shared by Basil Thorogood who thought that whether the Secrets concerned biscuits or bombs, the safety of our Kingdom depended on the rigid application of the law and the consequent hounding of Miss Tuttle. Higher authority in the shape of Sir Frank Fawcett, K.C.B., the Permanent Under-Secretary, sent the papers to the Attorney-General who, somewhat to everyone's surprise, decided to prosecute.

When this decision was given to Oliver Bowling, he was apparently outraged at the crassness of our bureaucracy. Having prophesied that any prosecution would make the Ministry look absurd, he was secretly anxious to be proved right. He asked his old school-friend, Erskine-Brown, if he happened to know a barrister whose particular skill was getting cases laughed out of Court, and Claude, who felt he owed me a debt of gratitude for having returned to my matrimonial home, recommended the very one. The consequence was that I found myself briefed by the upmarket City firm of Farmilow, Pounsford & James for the defence of Miss Rosemary Tuttle on the sinister and mole-like activity of betraying our biscuits to the enemy.

The brief in this *cause célèbre* arrived in a peculiarly impressive manner. One day I entered our clerk's room to see Henry, Dianne and Uncle Tom staring respectfully at a heavy green safe.

'A present,' Uncle Tom explained, 'from Her Majesty the Queen.'

'No, Uncle Tom. A loan from the Ministry of Defence,' Henry corrected him with some pride.

'What's it got in it?' I asked. 'The Crown Jewels?'

'It's your brief, Mr Rumpole, in the Secrets trial. Government-issue safes are supplied to defence counsel when the matter is highly confidential. So that the papers don't fall into the wrong hands.' Henry's voice sank in awe.

'All right. How do we open it?'

'There's a number, for the combination. But' – Henry looked round nervously as the grey figure of Hoskins, the barrister, came into the room – 'it doesn't do, Mr Rumpole, to mention these things in public.'

'Well, just whisper it into the lock, Henry. There's a brief in there, a money brief with any sort of luck.'

'Four . . . five . . . three, eight, one,' Henry muttered, as he turned the dial on the safe. Then he pulled the handle, but it didn't open. Dianne almost shouted, 'Four, five, *two*, eight, *two* wasn't it, Henry?' Henry said, 'Dianne, *please*,' and tried again, but the safe still refused to divulge its contents.

'Open Sesame!' I thumped the green top with my fist. The door swung open and I collected a slender brief and went upstairs to meet the clientele.

'The number of gingernuts consumed in the Ministry of Defence! The amount spent on cups of tea in the Department of Arms Procurement! The free holidays charged up as entertaining foreign visitors!' I stood smoking a small cigar in Chambers in the company of Mr Jasper James, the instructing solicitor, a well-nourished fifty-year-old in an expensive city suiting; Miss Rosemary Tuttle, dressed apparently for the Hungarian gypsy encampment scene in *Balalaika*; and my faithful amanuensis, Liz Probert, who was trying hard to find the dread hand of the C.I.A. somewhere behind the biscuits.

'Miss Tuttle *is* bound by Section 2 of the Official Secrets Act. And it's alleged that she copied confidential documents and gave them to the Press. If that's a true bill, then . . .' Mr James, the solicitor, made a regretful clucking sound, apparently indicating that he wouldn't put 5p on our chances.

'Look, James, my dear old sweetheart' – I tried to cheer up the eminent solicitor – 'it's a well-known fact that Section 2 of the Official Secrets Act is the raving of governmental paranoia.'

'But if she's broken the law . . .'

'If Miss Tuttle's broken the law, the Jury are entitled to acquit her! It's their ancient and inalienable privilege, I shall tell them.

It's the light that shows the lamp of freedom burns.' I gave them a foretaste of my speech to the Jury: 'If you think it a sign of bureaucracy run mad, Members of the Jury, that this unfortunate lady, whom I represent, should be hounded through the Courts just because our masters in Whitehall can't restrain their revolting greed for Bath Olivers and Dundee shortbread, then you are fully entitled to return a resounding verdict of not guilty. She did what she did so that the tax-payer, that is you and I, Members of the Jury, should not be stung with an escalating bill for Maryland cookies and chocolate-covered digestives, and, God save us all, macaroons. She has been the guardian of our democracy and saved the waistlines of Whitehall!'

'Look, I'm awfully sorry to butt in . . .' Miss Tuttle butted in, interrupting my flow. 'You can say all that in Court, if you like.'

'I *do* like, Miss Tuttle. I like very much indeed. Strong stuff, perhaps, but I feel entirely justified.'

'But I didn't do it, don't you see? I didn't do anything!'

'Nothing?' I was, I confess, a little dashed to hear it.

'No. I never copied those figures, or sent them to the papers. I'm jolly well innocent, Mr Rumpole.'

'Innocent . . .' It was a disappointment, but then I saw a glimmer of hope. 'But your glove was found that night by the copying-machine!'

'I can't understand how it got there at all. It must have walked!' She smiled round at us, like a child who has just thought of a joke.

'Miss Tuttle. You copied those documents from the Personnel and Logistics Section of the Ministry of Defence and you gave them to Mr Tim Warboys of the *Sunday Fortress*, so he could make his little joke about the Crimean War in his Chatterbox column.' I was doing my best to convince her; if she were not guilty, there could be no hilarious speech.

'Would I do such a thing, Mr Rumpole?'

'It seems completely creditable to me. Why ever not?'

'I was in a position of trust.' Now she looked like a serious child, one who always keeps the school rules.

'Consider this. If you admit this noble act, I can turn you into a heroine, a Joan of Arc, Miss Tuttle, in shining armour doing battle against the forces of bureaucracy.' I made a last appeal to her.

'And if I deny it?'

'Then you're just an ordinary criminal, trying to lie your way out of trouble. Do think, Miss Tuttle. Do please think carefully.'

We sat in a minute's silence while Miss Tuttle thought it over. Then she said quietly, 'I've got to tell the truth.'

'Yes,' I agreed sadly. 'Oh, yes, Miss Tuttle. I suppose you have.' I looked at Jasper James in a resigned manner. 'We'd better check the evidence, Mr James. I suggest we do our own typewriter test . . .'

Whilst I was thus concerned with affairs of State, Claude Erskine-Brown was considering entering into secret negotiations of an entirely different nature. He plumped himself down next to Liz Probert, who was enjoying a solitary sandwich in the Taste-Ee-Bite café in Fleet Street, and told her that it was no picnic being married to a busy silk. Phillida was always away doing important cases in Manchester or Newport, or such far-flung outposts of the Empire, and he was left a great deal on his own. He then startled Mizz Probert by saying, as she told me much later, 'To be quite honest with you, Sue, it's a pretty ghastly situation. My wife has absolutely no time for it.' Mizz Probert could think of no suitable reply to this, except to say that her name was Liz.'

'Of course, I think I knew that. On the rare moments Phillida's at home, she's far too tired. I feel I'm missing a vital part of my life. Can you understand that at all?'

When Liz Probert said that she supposed she could, in a way, Claude carried on in a manner she found embarrassing, she told me at the time. 'I mean,' he said. 'it's not the sort of thing a fellow likes to do on his own.'

'No, I suppose not.'

'It'll be eighteen months now. I'm having the most terrible withdrawal symptoms.'

At which Liz tried to gobble her sandwich, but Claude was

relentless. 'All she could manage,' he told her, 'was a little bit of Offenbach at Christmas. You must know how it feels.'

'Well, not exactly.'

'To be honest with you,' Claude apparently told her then, 'I can't remember when my wife and I last sat down together to a decent Wagner opera.'

If this was an enigmatic conversation for Mizz Liz Probert, it was as nothing compared to the extraordinary encounter I had with Claude as I left Chambers after my work was done a few days later. Bear in mind the situation. I had no idea of the confidences my learned friend had bestowed on Mizz Probert, and he came popping out of his door and waylaid me in an urgent manner.

'Rumpole! A word in confidence!'

'Not another secret?' Secrets, it seemed, were in season around Equity Court.

'I've invited you to the Opera next month.' Erskine-Brown might have been passing on the recipe for Star Wars.

'Not Wagner?'

'Well, it does happen to be *Meistersinger*.'

'An entertainment about the length of a long firm fraud, tried through an interpreter. Who was it who said Wagner's music isn't nearly as bad as it sounds?'

'Don't worry, Rumpole. You won't actually have to *come* to the Opera.'

'You mean you're *not* going to ask me?' I wasn't entirely disappointed.

'Oh, I did ask you.'

'And I refused?'

'Oh no. You accepted. You'd like to get to know a good deal more about music drama.'

'White man speak in riddles.' The fellow was confusing me.

'It's just that if my wife asks you where I was on the twenty-eighth of next month we went to the Opera together,' Erskine-Brown explained as though to a slow-witted child.

'But I won't have been there!'

'Ssh!' – Erskine-Brown looked round nervously – 'that's the whole point!'

'Will *you* have been there?' I was doing my best to follow his drift.

'That's . . . something of a secret. I can count on you, can't I, Rumpole?' He began to move briskly away and out of Chambers, but I called out and came pounding after him. 'Why on earth should I assist you in this sordid little conspiracy?'

'Because I've done you an enormous favour, Rumpole. I recommended you to Batty Bowling.'

'Your old school-friend,' I remembered.

'Exactly. I was instrumental in getting you the brief in the Official Secrets case.'

'Civil of you. Claude' – I was considerably mollified – 'really remarkably civil. I suppose, if you can't get a hold of anyone else, I might as well not go to the Opera with you.'

DO YOU WANT TO HEAR ABOUT TEA AND SCANDAL, THEIR ANCIENT CUSTOM, IN THE MINISTRY OF DE-FENCE? IT'S ALL HIGHLY SECRET AND MIGHT MAKE A GOOD STORY FOR YOUR COLUMN. COME INTO ST JAMES'S PARK THURSDAY LUNCHTIME, FROM THE MALL. I'LL BE ON THE FIRST BENCH TO THE RIGHT AFTER YOU'VE CROSSED THE BRIDGE. DON'T SPEAK TO ME. I'M FIFTY YEARS OLD, BROWNISH HAIR GOING GREY, AND I WEAR SPECTACLES AND RATHER BRIGHTLY COLOURED CLOTHES. I'LL GET UP AT 2 P.M. WHAT YOU WANT WILL BE LEFT ON THE SEAT FOLDED INSIDE A COPY OF THE DAILY TELEGRAPH.

I was sitting by the gas-fire in the living-room of 25b Froxbury Court, with the brief *R*. v. *Tuttle* open on my knees. What I was reading was a photostat of the note, typed in capitals, that my client was alleged to have sent to Mr Chatterbox. One phrase stuck in my mind, 'tea and scandal'. It seemed too literary for Miss Tuttle, and had a sort of period flavour. No doubt it was a point of no importance and I dismissed it from my mind as the telephone rang and Hilda leapt to her feet and went out into the hall to answer it. This was somewhat odd, as there is a perfectly good extension in the living-room.

'Why not take it in here,' I called after her.

'Isn't a person entitled to a little privacy,' she called back, and kicked the door shut. I was left alone to wonder if even She Who Must Be Obeyed had secrets and what on earth those secrets could be. Was our mansion flat sheltering a mole, and could Hilda be selling off the secrets of my defence briefs to the Prosecution? My curiosity got the better of me and I gingerly lifted the sitting-room phone, but I got only an angry buzz and Hilda's voice behind me calling, 'Rumpole!' as she returned to the room. 'What's the matter with our phone?'

'It looks perfectly all right to me.' I surveyed the instrument I had hastily returned to its rest.

'It makes little hiccuping sounds. Have you paid the bill, Rumpole?'

'Perhaps not . . . Pressure of work lately.'

'If you haven't paid the bill it ought to be cut right off. It ought not to hiccup.' She looked at me severely as though any malaise of our telephone was undoubtedly my fault.

'To hear is to obey, O Mistress of the Blue Horizons,' I said, but not out loud.

The next day my journey to work was unusually eventful. I got off the tube, as usual, at Temple station and stopped to buy a *Times*. (They had been sold out at Gloucester Road.) A man in a cap and mackintosh, whom I had noticed on the train, seemed to loiter by the newsagent, and when I had bought my newspaper and set off towards Middle Temple Gardens, Fountain Court, and so to Equity Court, he seemed to be in casual pursuit. When I stopped to do up a shoelace, he stopped also. When I paused to admire the roses, he admired them also. I was wondering what I had done to earn the attention of the man with the cap, when a voice called out 'Rumpole', and Mizz Liz Probert engaged me in conversation. As we ambled on together, my unknown follower put on a sudden spurt, and walked past us.

'I wanted to tell you something.' Liz Probert was clearly in a confiding mood.

'Not a secret?' How many more could I take?

'It's about Claude Erskine-Brown. He's asked me to the Opera.'

'To *Meistersinger*?' I hazarded a guess.

'I think it's at Covent Garden actually.' Mizz Probert was clearly not a Wagnerite. 'What do you think . . .?'

'Well, at your age it's probably all right. For me, well, life's getting a bit short for Wagner.'

'It might be terribly embarrassing.'

'Why? I don't remember that they did much stripping-off at Nuremberg.'

'You don't think he'd use it as an excuse to project some sort of masculine aggression? Might he say I've got extremely nice eyes, or something horrible?'

'Oh, I don't think you need worry about that.' It was kindly meant, but I realize it wasn't exactly well put.

'Don't you?' She smiled.

'I didn't mean . . . they're *not* nice.'

'Rumpole' – she was no longer smiling – 'don't you start presenting as a male stereotype!'

'No, of course not. God forbid! Purely functional eyes, yours. Scarcely worth a mention.'

We had reached the door of Chambers and Mizz Probert changed the subject. 'How's your Secrets case?'

'A farce!' I told her. 'Anyone who calls it a Secrets case has had their brains addled by too many spy stories.'

I carried my battered old brief-case into the clerk's room to collect my letters which were mainly buff envelopes and sent to me by Her Majesty. As I filed a couple of them in the waste-paper basket, I noticed some sort of workman, a black man as I remember it, standing on a step-ladder and doing something to the electric light. I also saw Uncle Tom, our oldest inhabitant, who had just arrived with *his* brief-case, which, being dark brown and equally battered, seemed to be the twin of mine. As Uncle Tom had not, to my certain knowledge, received a brief of any sort for the last twenty years, I was prompted to ask what he carried in his brief-case, a question which had long been troubling me. 'Care to have a look?' Uncle Tom was ever obliging.

He opened his luggage to reveal a carton of milk, the green muffler his sister always insisted he took with him to Chambers, two golf balls, a packet of cheese and tomato sandwiches, the *Times* and a tin of throat pastilles.

'What are the zubes for?'

'Really, Rumpole! Doesn't *your* voice get tired when you speak in Court?'

'Yes. But you don't speak in Court.'

'One never knows, does one, when one might not get called on?'

As we left the clerk's room Uncle Tom said, 'That chap up the ladder was like you.'

'Well, not very like me.'

'He seemed extraordinarily interested in my brief-case.'

Events continued their unusual course when I got up to my room. I was hanging up the hat and mac when our Head of Chambers, Soapy Sam Ballard, slid in at the door and almost whispered, 'Thought I'd call in on you up here. Walls have ears you know, especially in the clerk's room. I'm prosecuting you in the Secrets case.'

'Oh, you mean the Biscuits case?'

'No, the Secrets.'

'The secret biscuits.' Entering into the spirit of the thing, I stabbed at the curtains with my umbrella and a cry of 'Dead for a ducat, dead!'

'What *are* you doing, Rumpole?'

'I thought there might be a couple of Russians behind the arras.'

'It's a particularly serious case.' Ballard looked pained; well he usually does. 'What's at stake isn't merely biscuits.'

'I know that. It's lavatory paper too.'

'Rumpole!'

'And cups of tea, naturally, and free holidays. And entertaining named persons.'

'It's a question of loyalty to the Crown. I'm sorry to have to tell you this but the Attorney-General himself takes a serious view.'

'Is the old darling keen on biscuits?' I suppose I shouldn't have said that, but as I did so Ballard became unexpectedly friendly. 'Look here, Rumpole, Horace . . .' he said. 'I don't know whether you know, I've just been elected to the Sheridan Club.'

'Great news, Bollard. Was it on telly?'

'I just wondered whether you'd care to join me there for a spot of luncheon.'

Usually I fear prosecuting counsel when they come offering lunch, but Ballard was extremely insistent and even paid for the taxi to the Sheridan, a rambling, grey building in the hinterland behind Trafalgar Square in need of a spring-clean, decorated with portraits of old actors and judges (the Judges looked more theatrical and the actors considerably more judicial), where that small, stage army of persons most closely engaged in running the nation's affairs meet to get mildly sloshed at lunchtime. In the small and crowded bar Sir Frank Fawcett from the M.O.D. was having a gin and tonic with Oliver Bowling, the Assistant Under-Secretary; an ex-Cabinet Minister was trying to persuade a publisher to buy his unreadable memoirs; Mr Chatterbox of the *Sunday Fortress* was giggling with a little group of journalists in the corner; and Ballard became almost unbearably excited when a sleepy-eyed, longish-haired man in a double-breasted suit and striped shirt – a middle-aged debs' delight – came wafting over to us. 'Mr Attorney!' Ballard greeted him loudly. 'This is Horace Rumpole. He's defending Tuttle.'

'Pink gin, thanks Sam. Lots of ice.' And when Ballard had gone about his business, Sir Lambert Syme, Her Majesty's Attorney-General, said, 'I imagine Tuttle's a plea of guilty.'

'Absolutely no harm in imagining.'

'It's only the tip of the iceberg, you know.'

'Of course. There's something far more serious at stake. Swiss Roll.'

'Molesworth!' The Attorney shook his head. He wasn't smiling.

'My name's Rumpole.'

'No. *Molesworth*.'

'No, really.'

'The American Air Force Base,' he explained carefully, 'where alleged protesters camp out with their thermoses, or is it "thermi"? I must say, if they're all genuine C.N.D. protesters, my name's Gorbachev. No point in going into Molesworth. I imagine Sam would take a plea on the biscuits. If she confesses to that, Lord Chief'll probably keep the old bat out of chokey.'

'The Lord Chief!' I was amazed at the compliment paid to me and Miss Tuttle. 'He's coming down to try it?'

'Oh, yes. Question of loyalty in the Civil Service. The Government's pretty concerned about it. It'll be quite a party.' And as Ballard returned to us with the drinks, the Attorney asked, 'Wouldn't you, Sam? Take a plea on the biscuits?'

'I'd be guided, of course, by the Law Officers of the Crown.' Ballard meant that he'd do as he was told.

Before we left him and went down to lunch, I had one other question to ask the Attorney-General: 'It's about my telephone at home,' I said. 'It's started to hiccup.'

'Perhaps it's had rather too much claret.' He looked down at the glass in my hand.

'What's more, I got a red notice at least a month ago and they haven't cut it off yet.'

'Well, you're in luck's way, aren't you, Rumpole?' The Attorney-General smiled and moved away from us. Ballard then bought me a perfectly good luncheon during which he continued to tell me how extremely grateful the Government of the day would be if Miss Tuttle put her hands up, and thus saved herself and all of us from further embarrassing revelations. I ploughed through the boiled beef, carrots and a suet dumpling, topped up with treacle tart, and offered the Government of the day no sort of comfort at all.

Miss Rosemary Tuttle used to keep her own portable Olivetti Lettera 22 typewriter in her office at the Ministry of Defence, and used it to do her own letters and reports when the typing pool was busy. This machine, a prosecution exhibit, was now incarcerated in New Scotland Yard, to which Jasper James and I took our client so that we might conduct our own typewriting test. While she sat typing placidly in her peasant attire, Detective Inspector Fallowes, the Officer-in-Charge of the case, started up a new mystery, drawing me a little apart from the clatter of the Olivetti.

'By the way, Mr Rumpole,' he muttered confidentially. 'A word of warning, sir. A gentleman of your stamp has to be careful of his position when he's on a sensitive case like this.'

'Has he?' I was perplexed.

'Oh, yes, sir. Does the name of O'Rourke mean anything to you? Seamus O'Rourke? Suspected I.R.A. sympathizer.'

'Absolutely nothing,' I said truthfully, whilst Miss Tuttle was resolutely typing I'LL BE ON THE FIRST BENCH TO THE RIGHT AFTER YOU'VE CROSSED THE BRIDGE.

'Perhaps it means something to your wife then.' Detective Inspector Fallowes smiled in a friendly fashion. 'We'd just like you to be extremely careful. There now' – he picked up Miss Tuttle's finished sheet and gave it to me – 'look at it all ways up, Mr Rumpole; no doubt it comes from the same machine as the note to the *Fortress*. So glad to have been able to help you.'

'Tea and scandal.' The words bothered me again, as I read them in the note Miss Tuttle had just typed. Back in Froxbury Court I looked up tea in the Index of my old *Oxford Dictionary of Quotations*: 'is there honey still for t.?' no, 'sometimes counsel take – and sometimes t.,' not that; and then I saw it: 't. and scandal'. Rather an obscure phrase in fact from Congreve's dedication to his play *The Double Dealer*: 'Retired to their tea and scandal, according to their ancient custom'. Well, there it was, but I couldn't see, for the moment, how it helped Miss Tuttle. So I called for my wife's assistance on another mystery. 'Hilda. It just crossed my mind. Have you by any chance an Irish friend called Seamus O'Rourke?'

'What sort of friend?'

'Any sort of friend.'

'Why do you ask that, Rumpole?' We were seated in the kitchen of our mansion flat, and She was dishing out stew.

'God knows.'

'What?'

'God knows why I ask. It's some sort of Official Secret.'

'What's that meant to mean?'

'That no one knows what the hell it's about except the Government and probably it's not of the slightest importance anyway.' Hilda sat down to her steaming plateful and looked at me, doubtfully.

'They haven't heard about the hatch, have they?' She wondered.

'What?'

'The Government haven't heard about my idea for a new kitchen hatch?'

'Oh, I expect so, Hilda. I expect your idea for a kitchen hatch ranks high in the list of classified information. Along with biscuits and the next American attack on somewhere or another!'

'I wish you'd stop talking nonsense, Rumpole.' Hilda then attacked her dinner and I could get no more out of her.

When I bought the next morning's *Times* and sat reading it on my journey to Temple station, I discovered that Whitehall was buzzing with rumours of a serious new leak from the Ministry of Defence. An article in the American magazine *Newsweek* had suggested that information concerning the sensitive N.A.T.O. 'Operation Blueberry' was already in the hands of the Russians. The matter was expected to be raised in Parliament during Prime Minister's Question Time ... So one mystery was solved at least; I thought I knew why the Lord Chief Justice of England was descending on the Old Bailey in person to try Miss Rosemary Tuttle.

Perhaps I had absorbed some of the general air of mystery surrounding the case, but I decided to carry my brief in *R. v. Tuttle* enclosed in my old brief-case, which I left for a while in the clerk's room whilst I went to refresh my memory of Section 2 of the Official Secrets Act. So I arrived at the door of the Court, with Liz Probert, who was to take a note for me, fully robed and carrying my brief-case, and there I met for the first time, Oliver Bowling, the pleasing and cultivated head of Miss

Tuttle's department, who had the good sense of having me briefed in the case. Although he had apparently borne the nickname Batty Bowling when at school with Claude, I could see no basis for any suggestion of insanity.

'This is a most ridiculous business,' Bowling told me. 'It's not going to do anyone the slightest good.' He was a quietly spoken man in a tweed suit which must have cost a good deal in its day, and he had wrinkles of amusement at the corners of his eyes; I thought Miss Tuttle was lucky to have him on her side. 'If there's anything I can do to help?' he said. 'Character witness. That sort of thing . . .?'

'There *is* something you can tell me. Miss Tuttle was eating her sandwiches in St James's Park. Is that where she always took her lunch?'

'Oh, I believe so. She was very regular in her habits.'

'By regular, you mean she always left the park at the same time?'

'Back in the office by ten past two. You could set your watch by her. Pretty rare nowadays . . .'

'Outdoor sandwich-eaters?'

'I really mean someone you can depend on. Utterly.' And then he excused himself saying he had to get back to the Ministry. Nearer the door of the Court I had a far less pleasant encounter. A pale and deeply disturbed Sam Ballard, Q.C., waylaid me.

'A word in your ear.' He took my arm and steered me apart.

'Bollard!' I sighed. 'We're not going into secret session again?' He was looking across at Liz, who was chattering to Jasper James, our solicitor, and he almost hissed, 'That girl Probert, she can't possibly come into Court!'

'She's taking a note for me.'

'Impossible!'

'She's a member of the Bar, Bollard. You can't keep her out.'

'We were grossly deceived.' Ballard's voice sank to a note of low tragedy. 'She's not a clergyman's daughter!'

'Oh? Is the Court only open to clergymen's daughters today? You and I'd better clear off home.'

'Detective Inspector Fallowes has just told me who she is.'

'Is it any of the Detective Inspector's business?'

'She's the daughter of Red Ron Probert!' The news came from him in an appalled whisper. 'Socialist Chairman of South-East London Council. Well, you do see? We can't have a girl like that in Court on a sensitive case.'

'You mean a case about sensitive biscuits?'

'It may not just be biscuits any more.' He sounded most grave. 'We may have to apply to add new charges!'

'Why don't you? And make this prosecution look even more fatuous.'

'Look, Rumpole. I would advise you to take this matter seriously. In the national interest!'

Then I used a phrase which I had planned for some time, and this seemed an ideal moment to trot it out: 'And I'd advise you, Bollard, if you can find a taxidermist willing to take on the work, to get stuffed.' I then called loudly to Mizz Liz Probert to follow me, and swept into Court.

We were only just in time. Ballard and his team followed us in, and then, at exactly twenty-nine minutes past ten, Lord Wantage took his seat on the Bench. I knew the Lord Chief Justice was a healthy-looking fellow who spent most of his spare time on the golf course, and who dispatched his business with a great reliance on short judgements and long sentences. His bluff and cheerful manner concealed an extremely conventional and sometimes brutal lawyer. He was also not noted for his criticisms of the Government's legislation, and I suspected that I would have to get the Jury, and not his Lordship, to laugh the case out of Court.

So, as Ballard rose to apply for certain parts of the evidence to be heard behind closed doors, I settled in my seat and opened the battered brief-case I had brought in with me, and as I did I gave what must have been an audible gasp of horror. My brief was notably absent, and all I had was a green muffler, a carton of milk, a *Times*, a packet of cheese and tomato sandwiches, two golf balls and some throat pastilles. Uncle Tom's brief-case had, at long last, got into Court.

*

Those who know me best around the Bailey will know that, when in full flood, I rarely consult my brief, and I did have most of the simple facts in *R. v. Tuttle* at my fingers' ends. However, it is somewhat unnerving to be in a Court crowded with reporters, appearing before the Lord Chief Justice of England, with nothing much to consult except a green muffler and a cheese sandwich. I sent Liz Probert off to phone Henry and get my effects sorted out, and then sat through an uneasy half-hour. Before the Jury was sworn in, the Lord Chief, who clearly knew more about the case than he let on, asked Ballard if he were applying to add more charges. Ballard answered that he wasn't going to do so for the moment, and although I reared up to protest, the Chief allowed the Prosecution to keep this threat of unknown and mysteriously serious allegations dangling.

The Jury assembled and Ballard opened his case. His first witness was Tim Warboys of the *Sunday Fortress*, and by the time I rose to cross-examine this star of journalism, Henry had come down from Chambers in a taxi, and I had my brief and Uncle Tom had his sandwiches.

'Mr Warboys . . . or should I call you Mr Chatterbox?' I began and Ballard rose to protest, 'There's no need for my learned friend to be offensive to the witness.'

'Oh, keep still, Bollard!' I growled at him. 'It's his name in the paper.'

'It would probably be better if you simply used the witness's name, Mr Rumpole.' The Chief started his interruptions politely and Ballard sat down, smiling with gratification.

'Oh, much obliged, my Lord. I'll try to remember.' I was also starting politely. 'Mr Warboys. You make your living by divulging secrets, don't you?'

'I don't know what you mean.' The investigative journalist clearly didn't like being investigated; he sounded narked.

'Who's sleeping with whom is one of your subjects. You keep your eye perpetually to the keyhole?'

'I write a gossip column, yes,' Mr Chatterbox admitted.

'And you know that some gossip is strictly protected by our Lords and Masters?'

'Some information is classified, yes.'

'Classified gossip. Exactly! And you are familiar with Section 2 of the Official Secrets Act?'

'I know something about it.' A very cautious chap, I thought, the dashing old Etonian, Warboys.

'You know that it's an offence to receive secret information?'

'I believe it is.'

'For which you can get two years in the nick.'

'Two years' imprisonment, Mr Rumpole,' the Chief Justice corrected me, still with smiling courtesy.

'Oh, I beg its pardon, my Lord. Imprisonment.'

'For a story about biscuits?' Warboys sounded incredulous.

'Oh, they're very protective of their biscuits in the Ministry of Defence.' I scored my first hit with that; there was some laughter from the Jury. The Chief turned to them and showed intense disapproval.

'Members of the Jury,' he said. 'You may hear a good deal from the Defence about biscuits in this case, and I suggest that, after Mr Rumpole has got his laugh, we take this matter seriously. This is a case about whether or not a servant of the Crown was loyal to the interests of the Government. Very well . . .'

'Your Lordship doesn't wish me to call a biscuit a biscuit?' I asked politely. 'Should we settle for *une petite pièce de pâtisserie*?' I got a suppressed titter for that from the twelve good citizens, and a cold 'What's your next question, Mr Rumpole?' from the Bench.

'Ah. Yes. I was so fascinated by your Lordship's address to the Jury that I have forgotten my next question. No! Now I remember it! Do you expect to be prosecuted for receiving secret information, Mr Warboys?'

'No. Not really.' Mr Chatterbox was hesitant.

'The police have set your mind at rest?'

'I've been told I have nothing to worry about.' He smiled modestly.

'In return for shopping Miss Tuttle?' At which the Lord Chief uttered a warning 'Mister Rumpole!' 'Oh, I do beg your Lordship's pardon. In return for giving evidence against the

middle-aged spinster lady whom I represent, you're saving your
own skin, Mr Warboys?' I suggested.

'I have agreed to cooperate with the police, yes.'

'Thus upholding the finest traditions of British journalism.'

'Mr Rumpole!' The Lord Chief's patience was in short supply.
'Have you any relevant questions to ask this witness?'

'Of course. About your alleged meeting with Miss Tuttle in St
James's Park. On that occasion you didn't speak to her at all. In
fact, by the time you reached her bench, she had gone?'

'That's what happened . . .'

'From the moment you saw her get up and go until you reached
the bench and collected the envelope . . .' – I picked up the
envelope containing the copied documents – '. . . was the newspaper folded round it always in your view?'

'I can't be sure,' he had to admit.

'There may have been other people passing in front of the
bench!'

'There may have been.'

I gave the Jury one of my most meaningful looks. 'So you
never really met Miss Tuttle at all?'

'Not if you put it like that. No.'

'And you have no doubt that it was Miss Tuttle, the defendant,
you saw.'

'No doubt at all. She . . .' He looked at the figure in the dock.

'What were you going to say?'

'I was going to say that she wears rather distinctive clothing.'

'So she could be easily identified?'

'Yes.'

'Rather a foolish thing to do, I suppose, if she was in the
business of leaking secrets?'

Ballard rose to protest, and the Judge smiled wearily at him, as
though they were both reasonable adults watching the antics of
an extremely tiresome child. 'I know, Mr Ballard,' he spoke
soothingly, 'but perhaps we should both possess our souls in
patience. No doubt the truth will finally emerge in this case,
despite Mr Rumpole's suppositions.'

'The truth! Yes. I'm so much obliged to your Lordship.' I

acted deep and humble gratitude. 'Let's see if we can discover the truth. Remember, Mr Warboys, you're on your oath; you had never seen Miss Rosemary Tuttle before?'

'No. I had had her letter, of course.'

'You say *her* letter. It wasn't signed by her?'

'No.'

'It didn't even have her name on it.'

'No.'

'So when you say it was her letter, it is a pure guess.'

'The letter said she would be sitting on the park bench, and would leave at two o'clock. And there she was!'

'But to say that the note was written by her is a pure guess!'

'I suppose Mr Ballard will say to the Jury that it's a reasonable deduction, Mr Rumpole.' The Lord Chief sounded the embodiment of common sense.

'My Lord! I really can't be held responsible for what my learned friend Mr Ballard may say to the Jury. Thank you, Mr Ch— Mr Warboys.'

I sat down then, fairly well satisfied, although I still had no clear idea which way the case was going. I wondered idly what you have to do to become Lord Chief Justice of England, and wear a golden lavatory chain on State occasions. Play remarkable golf? Shoot with the Lord Chancellor? Manners can't have anything to do with it. That means there might be a chance for Rumpole! Lord Rumpole of the Gloucester Road, Baron Rumpole of the Temple Station . . . I came down to earth to hear Warboys tell Lord Wantage, in answer to a flagrantly leading question, that he had no doubt at all that it was Miss Tuttle he had seen in St James's Park.

Before we had started to quarrel I had persuaded the Lord Chief to give Miss Tuttle bail during the lunch hour, and when I came out of Court there she was waiting patiently for instructions. I tried to cheer her up, told her that the case was going as well as possible and that, in any event, she had a good friend in old Batty Bowling.

'Oh, he is the most super boss,' she agreed, in her quaint English schoolgirl's lingo. 'Always listens to your problems, but never spares himself. Burns the midnight oil. Well, so do I. Often when I'm working late at the Ministry, he's still there. Sometimes I hear him singing to himself. He seems very happy.'

'Well . . .' I began to move off to the robing room. 'Care for a Guinness and a steak pie at the pub?'

'Oh, no. I brought sandwiches and there's a dear little churchyard across the road.'

'I'm sure there is. Oh. There was one thing I did mean to ask you. About Congreve.'

'Congreve?' Miss Tuttle looked blank. 'Is he at the Ministry?' There was clearly a gap in her English schoolgirl education.

'William Congreve, Miss Tuttle, an English dramatist of genius, born in Good King Charles's golden days, carried on rather shockingly with the Duchess of Marlborough. The name doesn't ring any kind of bell?'

'Sorry. I was an economist, actually.' I absorbed the information, and then asked, 'One other little matter. The bomb.'

'The what?'

'More politely known as the nuclear deterrent. Have you got any affection for it?'

'Oh golly yes!, Mr Rumpole.' She smiled enthusiastically. 'Like all the chaps at the Ministry. We're a hundred per cent behind the bomb.'

'Thank you, Miss Tuttle. That was all I wanted to know.' I moved away from her then, leaving her standing alone in the middle of the hall. I would do almost anything for a client, except share her sandwiches in the churchyard.

There was one part of *R. v. Tuttle* which I was looking forward to keenly. I may be a child when it comes to partnership agreements, a dolt about Real Property, and I may even have some difficulty construing the more opaque provisions of the Obscene Publications Act. But I do know about bloodstains, gunfire wounds and typewriters. The analysis of typewriting is a fascinating subject and one I have discussed with great enjoyment across many a crowded Court with Peter Royce-Williams, the uncrowned King of the questioned documents. Royce-Williams is no longer young; did he not, when we were both Juveniles, give evidence about the questioned suicide note in the Penge Bungalow Murders? But he is unrivalled in his field. He is a short, stout man with the pale face and strong, tinted spectacles of a man who spends his life with microscopes and darkrooms, pursuing forgeries.

That afternoon, Royce-Williams stood in the witness-box with his enlarged pictures of the two documents: the note sent to Mr Chatterbox and that typed by Miss Tuttle in New Scotland Yard. His conclusion was that both documents were typed on the sort of paper used in government departments on the Olivetti Lettera 22 portable, which, according to the evidence, belonged to my client, the defendant Tuttle.

When I got up to cross-examine, I knew that there would be no point whatever in a head-on clash with the witness. Peter Royce-Williams must be led gently and with the greatest respect to the point where we might, with any luck, agree. And having thought the matter over carefully, with the aid of a pint of Guinness during the luncheon adjournment, I now felt clear about what that point might be.

'Mr Royce-Williams,' I began. 'As an acknowledged expert, would you agree that a typewriter doesn't work itself, a human being is involved in the operation . . .?'

'Yes, of course, Mr Rumpole.' It was delightful to chat to old friends.

'And human operators have varying degrees of skill?'

'I should have thought that was obvious.'

'Bear with me if I have a very simple mind, Mr Royce-Williams.' The old boy smiled at that, although the Judge didn't. 'A highly experienced typist will, on the whole, type smoothly, hitting all the keys with equal force. A person not so used to the machine may hit harder, perhaps after a hesitation, or more faintly because their fingers are less skilled?'

'That's certainly possible.'

'Have you considered that, in relation to these documents?'

'No. I must confess I haven't.' Like all good experts he was completely candid about the limits of his research.

'Just look at the word "scandal" in the note to Mr Warboys, and in that typed by Miss Tuttle in Scotland Yard. In the one sent to the newspaper, aren't the 's' and 'c' heavier and the other letters lighter?'

Royce-Williams held the documents very close and raised his dark glasses, the better to peer at them with his naked and watery eyes.

'That would seem to be so,' he agreed at last.

'And in that typed in the Detective Inspector's office they all have the same clarity?'

'Yes. I think they have.'

'Might that not lead you to the conclusion that they were typed by different people using the *same machine and paper*?'

There was a pause that seemed to me to go on for ever, as Royce-Williams carefully put down his papers and polished his glasses. But he was too good at his job to exclude the possibility I had mentioned. 'I suppose it might,' he said.

'You suppose it might,' I repeated with suitable emphasis for the benefit to the Jury.

'Mr Rumpole. Where is this evidence leading us?' The Lord Chief clearly seemed to feel that the case was wandering out of his control.

'Your Lordship asks me that?' I would, if I'd been as honest as Royce-Williams, have gone on: 'Believe me, old darling, I wish I knew.' What I actually said was: 'To the truth, my Lord. Or isn't that what we want to discover?'

Furiously making a note, Lord Wantage then broke the point of his pencil. He whispered to the wigged Court Clerk below him, and when the man stood up to get him another, I thought I could hear him whisper, 'Is Rumpole always as outrageous as this?'

'I'm afraid so, my Lord,' I know the Clerk whispered back. 'Absolutely always.'

'Thank you, Mr Rumpole. I enjoyed that.' Oliver Bowling was waiting for me when I got out of Court that evening, having apparently taken an afternoon off from the defence of the Nation to sample some of the free entertainment the Old Bailey alone provides. Grateful for his support, I took him for a cup of tea in the unglamorous surroundings of the Old Bailey canteen, where the cheese rolls were just being stored away for the night.

'You had another leak from your Ministry? Anything important?' He smiled at me over his cup of strong Indian tea, made not, I imagined, how he really liked it.

'Sometimes I wonder what *is* important.' Bowling smiled at me. 'Wouldn't the world be a healthier, more peaceful place if we told everyone exactly what we'd got and stopped trying to frighten each other with a lot of spurious secrets? Mustn't say that in the Department, of course.'

'No. Of course not.' I crunched a chocolate biscuit; it's hungry work cross-examining experts in questioned documents. 'I've got to have a go at your big cheese tomorrow. The Permanent Under-Secretary. What sort of chap is he?'

'Comes from "a branch of one of your ante-diluvian families, fellows that the flood couldn't wash away". That sort of thing. He'll be immensely fair,' Bowling reassured me. 'Give me a ring if there's anything I can do.'

'I might call you at home, when Court's over.'

'Oh, right. Here's the number.' He took a card from his wallet and gave it to me. 'I'll be leaving the Ministry fairly early. Chap at the Foreign Office's got the use of the Royal Box at Covent Garden. You can dine there, you know. Rather fun.'

'Is it really?' I was prepared to take his word for it. When we parted I looked at the visiting card he had given me, then I turned it over and wrote, on the back, a sentence from our conversation. At home I paid another visit to *The Oxford Dictionary of Quotations*.

Sir Frank Fawcett, the Permanent Under-Secretary, walked solemnly into the witness-box the following afternoon in a Court from which the public had been excluded at Ballard's request. Could all this pomp and circumstance possibly be about so many thousand mid-morning snacks, or was it entirely occasioned by the activities of Miss Rosemary Tuttle, who sat, a small and somewhat garish figure, in the dock? I asked Sir Frank about her when I climbed to my feet and started to cross-examine.

'You know something about my client, Miss Tuttle?'

'Yes. I have the reports on her.'

'You have no reason to suppose that she would constitute any sort of danger to the State, have you?'

'May I refresh my memory, my Lord?' His Lordship gave permission and a file was handed up to the witness.

'Rosemary Alice Tuttle,' he read out. 'Born of Austrian parents, Franz and Maria Toller, who emigrated to this country when she was two years old and changed their name. Educated at Hampstead High School for Girls and the London School of Economics.'

'No mystery about that – except that they chose the name Tuttle.'

The Jury smiled at that and the Lord Chief was displeased. 'She was, of course, thoroughly vetted when she took up her post with us,' Sir Frank told him.

'Nothing else known against her?'

'Do you really want all this evidence in?' I had a whispered warning from Liz Probert, sitting beside me, who was rapidly turning into quite a conventional form of barrister. 'Keep your head, Mizz Probert, when all about you are losing theirs and blaming it on you.' I whispered back, and challenged the witness to tell us the worst.

'Unconfirmed reports that she was seen at Molesworth American Air Force Base in January 1986 . . .' Sir Frank sifted through the file.

'Taking part in an entirely peaceful demonstration?' I asked him.

'She was questioned about the matter and denied it. She suggested it might have been someone else similarly dressed.'

'Did that seem to you rather improbable?' The Lord Chief smiled understandingly at the witness.

'It did, my Lord, yes. After that she was not recommended for further promotion and kept under special surveillance.'

'Surveillance which in this case seems to have been somewhat ineffective?' His Lordship was telling Sir Frank that men of their stamp always had problems with incompetent underlings.

'I'm afraid so, my Lord.'

'She got at the biscuits . . .' I understood the full horror of the position and the Chief uttered a warning 'Mr Rumpole!'

'All right. Let's try to take this little scandal seriously. Have you been able to check whether the information leaked to the Press about money spent on refreshments and entertaining, and so on, is accurate?'

'It's not entirely accurate.' Sir Frank had blinked at an unexpected question and taken a while to answer. Now he seemed embarrassed.

'The report is exaggerated?'

'I'm afraid my inquiries have led me to believe that we spend a good deal more than has been suggested, my Lord.'

'So the secrets she's supposed to have leaked aren't accurate Official Secrets at all?' I went on, before My Lord could interrupt.

'Not . . . entirely accurate. No.'

'Sir Frank Fawcett' – I paused and looked seriously at the witness – 'there's something a good deal more significant than biscuits at the bottom of this case, isn't there?'

'I'm not sure what you mean exactly.'

'Neither am I, Mr Rumpole.' The Lord Chief wasn't going to be left out.

'We're not all assembled here – you, the Permanent Under-Secretary and my learned friend and the Lord Chief Justice of England – to sit in secret session in a Court which has now been closed to the public . . .'

'Mr Rumpole. It was I who decided that Sir Frank's evidence should be taken in camera,' the Judge reminded me, but I soldiered on: 'Denying the principle that justice should be seen to be done, just to discuss a few little white lies about the number of bikkies you took with your elevenses! Far more sensitive information than that has recently been leaked from the Ministry of Defence, hasn't it?'

'Mr Rumpole. Do you really think that question is in the

interests of your client?' The Judge wanted the Jury to know that, in his view, I was about to land Miss Tuttle in the soup.

'That's why I asked it. Now will you answer it, Sir Frank?'

'My Lord ...' The witness turned to the Lord Chief for guidance but he merely sighed heavily and said, 'You'd better answer Mr Rumpole's question. We *are* in camera.'

'The answer' – again it came after a long pause – 'is yes.'

'You don't know the source of that leak?'

'No ...'

'And no application has been made to add further charges against my client, Miss Tuttle?'

'Not as yet, my Lord,' Ballard interjected in a vaguely threatening manner, which was echoed by the Judge. 'No, Mr Rumpole, not as yet.'

'And when those charges are brought against whoever it is, these little leaks about Civil Service extravagance will seem even more paltry and insignificant.'

'Isn't that going to be a matter for the Jury?' The Lord Chief had had enough of Rumpole and wanted his tea.

'Oh, I entirely agree, my Lord.' I was at my most servile. 'It will be a matter for the Jury. If this petty prosecution lasts until the end.'

The Court rose then, not in the best of tempers, and the Usher intoned his usual rigmarole that marks the ending of another day: 'All persons who have anything further to do before my Lords, the Queen's Justices at the Central Criminal Court may depart hence and give their attendance here again tomorrow at ten thirty o'clock in the forenoon. God Save the Queen.' 'And protect her' – I joined silently in the prayer – 'from her civil servants.'

Back in Chambers, I sat at my desk with the curiously elated feeling of having solved the mystery and learned something, at least, of the secrets of *R.* v. *Tuttle*. I lifted the telephone and asked Dianne to ring Oliver Bowling's number for me.

In the long interval which took place before she called me back, Claude Erskine-Brown came into my room with the haunted and hangdog look of a man who has spent the past few nights being pursued by the Valkyries. 'I have to tell you, Rumpole,' he announced. 'We didn't go to the Opera together.'

'Pity. I was looking forward to it.'

'I mean, if you see my wife, if Phillida should happen to bump into you around Chambers, don't bother to tell her how much you enjoyed *Meistersinger*.'

'Snoozed off in it, did I?'

'She knows I didn't take you.'

'Been rumbled, Erskine-Brown?' I couldn't help looking at the man with pity.

'As I suppose you might say "grassed".' He gave a small and quite mirthless laugh. 'Well, I may as well tell you the horrible truth. Liz Probert rang up Phillida and said that I'd invited *her* to Covent Garden.'

'But hadn't you?'

'Of course I had.'

'And Mrs Phillida Erskine-Brown, the Portia of our Chambers, hasn't shown much of the quality of mercy?'

'She doesn't speak, Rumpole.' The fellow was clearly in distress. 'Breakfast passes by in utter silence. And I did nothing, you understand! Absolutely nothing.'

'Not even compliment Mizz Probert on her eyes?'

'How do you know?' He looked at me as though I had the gift of second sight.

'That was your mistake, Claude. Girls don't care for that sort of thing nowadays.'

'To go and blurt out the truth like that, to a chap's wife! It was totally uncalled for!'

'Perhaps Mizz Liz Probert doesn't believe in Official Secrets. Talking of which . . .'

'What?'

'Your friend Bowling,' I wondered. 'Why did you call him Batty?'

'No reason, really. He never minded what he said, questioned everything in class, that sort of thing. And he was a bit of a show-off.'

'Show-off? What about?

'Oh, his literary knowledge. Something like you, Rumpole.'

He looked up at me and finally asked in a tragic way, 'Do you think Philly will ever speak to me again?'

'Oh yes. I imagine so. If only to say goodbye.' And then the phone rang on my desk, and I was able to tell Batty Bowling that I wanted an urgent word with him about Miss Tuttle. He said he was about to leave home, but he would come out of *Tosca* quarter of an hour before the end of the first Act, and we could have a quiet word in the room behind the Royal Box. I told him that I would go anywhere for a client, and he rang off with every expression of goodwill.

So, after a few thoughtful glassfuls at Pommeroy's Wine Bar, I strolled through the gift shops and boutiques and bistros of Covent Garden (lamenting the days of ever-open pubs and old cabbage stalks) to the small Floral Street entrance to the Royal Box. At the mention of Bowling's name an ornately uniformed attendant pointed me up a back staircase, which led to a small dining-room. There, under a chandelier, the remnants of an excellent light dinner still littered the table, and whiffs of excited music came from a curtained doorway. At exactly the appointed time, Oliver Bowling emerged from the doorway wearing a black velvet dinner-jacket that might have seen some service. 'I can give you ten minutes.' He looked at his watch and I thought there was a certain irritation beneath the habitual charm. '*Tosca* doesn't really get going until the second Act, does it?'

'Until she kills him?'

'Well, exactly,' he smiled. 'How can I help you?'

'I wanted to defend Miss Tuttle on the basis that what she did was entirely public-spirited and honourable . . .' I began at the beginning.

'I'm inclined to agree.'

'But she's always maintained she did nothing' – I was looking at her Head of Department – 'and I believe her.'

'But my dear chap.' Bowling smiled tolerantly. 'The evidence!'

'What evidence exactly?' I asked him. 'Someone left her glove beside a copying-machine. Someone used her typewriter, someone who wasn't a trained typist. She went to the park as she always did, to feed the ducks. Perhaps she had no idea that Mr Chatterbox from the *Sunday Fortress* was there watching her. She got up as the clock struck two. Someone else could have passed the bench and dropped an envelope wrapped in the *Daily Telegraph*.'

'Why should anyone . . .?'

'Want to frame Miss Tuttle on a silly charge about biscuits?'

'Yes. Why?'

'Someone wanted to make her look ridiculous and dishonest, and totally unreliable,' I told him. 'Someone wanted her to appear in public as a gossiping little busybody who couldn't even get her facts right. So that, if she ever gave evidence about anything really important, no one would take a blind bit of notice!'

'Really important?' He was still smiling. Somehow I longed to dislodge his smile. 'The big leak . . . The great hole in the system. Whatever it was. Weapons. Submarine bases. Engines of death. Perhaps, after all, it was no more important than biscuits. Would the world be any more dangerous if we did without secrets all together? You don't think so, do you, Mr Bowling?'

'Did I say that to you?'

'Oh yes. I'm prepared to believe your intentions were honourable. The end of the arms race perhaps. The beginning of peace . . .'

A burst of music penetrated the curtain. Bowling looked at his watch; the smile had gone now. 'I really ought to get back to the Opera.'

'I don't know exactly when it was, but I'm sure it was some time when you ought to have been away on leave and out of the office. It was late at night and she heard you singing, whistling or whatever. So she came in and saw you with . . . perhaps she never realized what she saw you doing. But you couldn't be sure of her, could you? Bank robbers shoot witnesses. It's a great deal more subtle to make fools of them. Perhaps that's the sort of thing they teach you at Winchester.' I poured the remains of a bottle of wine into an empty glass. 'You want to go back to the Opera? Try and remember not to sing the tunes around the office. Opera appears to be the downfall of Englishmen who want to keep secrets.' I held up the glass to the chandelier. 'Perfectly decent bit of claret. It seems a pity to waste it.' I didn't.

'What are you going to do?' Bowling asked after a long silence.

'I suppose, recall Sir Frank and put the whole business to him. Remember Sir Frank whose family survived the flood. That was your quotation from Congreve. *Love for Love.*'

'Congreve . . .?'

'Who was also quoted in your note to Mr Chatterbox. That was what Erskine-Brown told me about you. You couldn't resist showing off your literary knowledge, even when engaged on forgery. Poor old Miss Tuttle; she's extremely conventional at heart and does her best to be an English spinster lady. She'd never dream of demonstrating at Molesworth; you should never have started that rumour. And I'm afraid she's never even heard of Congreve . . .'

Bowling said nothing. He turned back to the curtain. He seemed about to go and then said, almost pleading with me. 'Rumpole . . .'

'I'm sorry, I can't help you. It's a question of loyalty to my client. She has my allegiance; I can't worry about yours.' Far away from us, on the stage, the *Te Deum* was swelling from the Cathedral on the stage. The curtain was about to fall. 'You'd better get back to *Tosca*,' I told him. 'Isn't this where the melodrama begins?'

There was a small item in the next morning's *Times*. A man, later identified as Mr Oliver Bowling, O.B.E., Assistant Under-Secretary at the Ministry of Defence, had apparently slipped while waiting on the platform at Covent Garden underground station and fallen under a passing train. Mr Bowling had been quite alone at the time and foul play was not suspected. He was dead on his admission to hospital.

When I arrived, robed, that morning outside the Court, Sam Ballard came up to me. 'Rumpole' – he looked almost apologetic – 'there's been a development.'

'I know. A small accident at Covent Garden underground station. It was unnecessary,' I told him. 'Like everything else about this case.'

'I've been in touch with the Attorney-General.'

'Really? What did he feel like?'

'We're offering no further evidence. In view of the fact that the information leaked to the Press was apparently inaccurate.'

'Oh, that gives you the out, does it? Lucky for you, Ballard. And my client's discharged without a stain on her character?'

Ballard was silent and then forced himself to say, 'Yes.'

'Bowling finally told the truth, did he?'

'I'm not prepared to divulge that.'

'Old Batty Bowling. Bit of a literary show-off. But not a bad fellow, all the same. What did he do? Telephone Sir Frank from the Opera?'

'I told you. I'm not prepared to divulge . . .'

'Secrets! My God, Bollard. I wonder what we'd do without them. But they lead to death, don't they? Stupid, unnecessary secrets lead to death?'

So Miss Tuttle and the rest of us were released by the Judge and I went home to Froxbury Court. Hilda was not there, no doubt out on some shopping spree, and I felt un-usually tired. I pulled out my old India-paper edition of *The Oxford Book of English Verse*, and started to read by way of consolation: 'The clouds that gather round the setting sun/Do take a sober colouring from an eye/That hath kept watch o'er man's mortality;' – My thoughts were interrupted by the sound of hammering – 'Another race hath been, and other palms are won./Thanks to the human heart by which we live,/ Thanks to its tenderness, its joys, and fears, . . .' By now the hammering was building to a crescendo. I put down the book, and went to the window, opened it and looked out into the street where I thought the din must be coming from. But as I did so, there was a final crash from behind me, and I turned to see, to my horror, the end of a chisel appear through my living-room wall. Was the Secret Service getting its revenge? In a matter of moments I had doubled into the hall and flung open the kitchen door. There I was greeted with the spectacle of a small gnome-like person of undoubtedly Irish extraction, who, armed with a bag of tools, was tunnelling through my wall.

'A fair cop!'

'Mr Rumpole?' The man apparently recognized me.

'There's one thing to be said for a practice at the criminal Bar.' I told him. 'You don't expect to be burgled . . .'

'Burgled, Mr Rumpole?' He seemed shocked at the suggestion.

'You know the meaning of the word. Breaking and entering! Except you seem to have entered my kitchen and you're breaking out. Do you mind me telling you, that's an inside wall you're attacking. I suggest you give up your life of crime, old darling, you've clearly got very little talent for it.'

'Crime! I don't know what you're talking about, Mr Rumpole.'

'House-breaking instruments!' I was looking at his bag of tools. But at this moment we heard the front door open and the voice of Hilda calling 'Rumpole!'

'I might have sent you on your way with a promise of future good behaviour,' I told the intruder, 'but one is coming in whom the quality of mercy is considerably strained.'

'I thought you were in Court all day.' She came into the kitchen and viewed me with every sign of disfavour.

'Hilda! There is a man here.'

'Of course there's a man in here. He's come to do that hatch. How are you getting on, Mr O'Rourke?'

'O'Rourke? Not Seamus O'Rourke by any chance?' The name rang a pretty enormous bell. Then the man pulled out a smudged card and offered it to me. SEAMUS O'ROURKE, I read, ALL REPAIRS AND CONVERSIONS CHEERFULLY UNDERTAKEN. 'They've been listening to you on the telephone, Hilda.'

'Speaking of telephones, Rumpole . . .'

'Listening to you! On the subject of a kitchen hatch.' At which point, She moved to the wall, took down the telephone and held it out to me.

'The instrument has died on us at last! Listen to that! Silent as the tomb! I told you to pay the bill.'

'The bill? It must have slipped my mind. Pressure of business . . .'

'And now they've cut it off.'

I listened for a moment to the silent telephone, and then restored it to its place on the wall. 'They've cut it off at last,' I agreed with Hilda. 'No one's listening to us any more. No one wants to look in my brief-case. No one's following me from the tube station. The Secrets case is over. Old Batty Bowling is dead, and normal service will be resumed shortly.'

Rumpole and the Judge's Elbow

Up to now in these accounts of my most famous or infamous cases I have acted as a faithful historian, doing my best to tell the truth, the whole truth, about the events that occurred, and not glossing over the defeats and humiliations which are part of the daily life of an Old Bailey hack, nor being ridiculously modest about my undoubted triumphs. When it comes to the matter of the Judge's elbow, however, different considerations arise. Many of the vital incidents in the history of the tennis injury to Mr Justice Featherstone, its strange consequences and near destruction of his peace of mind, necessarily happened when I was absent from the scene, nor did the Judge ever take me into his confidence over the matter. Indeed as most of his almost frenetic efforts during the trial of Dr Maurice Horridge were devoted to concealing the truth from the world in general, and old Horace Rumpole in particular, it is a truth which may never be fully known. I have been, however, able to piece together from the scraps of information at my disposal (a word or two from a retired usher, some conversations Marigold Featherstone had with She Who Must Be Obeyed) a pretty clear picture of what went on in the private and, indeed, sheltered life of one of the Judges of the Queen's Bench. I feel that I now know what led to Guthrie Featherstone's curious behaviour during the Horridge trial, but in reconstructing some of the scenes that led up to this, I have had, as I say for the first time in these accounts, to use the art of the fiction writer and imagine, to a large extent, what Sir Guthrie or Lady Marigold Featherstone, or the other characters involved, may have said at the time. Such scenes are based, however, on a long experience of how Guthrie Featherstone was accustomed to behave in the face of life's little difficulties, that is to say, with anxiety bordering on panic.

I think it is also important that this story should be told to warn others of the dangers involved in sitting in Judgement on the rest of erring humanity. However, to save embarrassment to anyone concerned, I have left strict instructions that this account should not be published until after the death of the main parties, unless Mr Truscott of the Caring Bank should become particularly insistent over the question of my overdraft.

Guthrie Featherstone, then plain Mr Guthrie Featherstone, Q.C., M.P., became the Head of our Chambers in Equity Court on the retirement of Hilda's Daddy, old C. H. Wystan, a man who could never bring himself to a proper study of bloodstains. I had expected, as the senior member in practice, to take over Chambers from Daddy, but Guthrie Featherstone, a new arrival, popped in betwixt the election and my hopes.

I have forgotten precisely what brand of M.P. old Guthrie was; he was either right-wing Labour or left-wing Conservative until, in the end, he gave up politics and joined the S.D.P. He was dedicated to the middle of the road, and very keen on our Chambers 'image', which, on one occasion, he thought was being let down badly by my old hat. Finally, the Lord Chancellor, who was probably thinking of something else at the time, made Guthrie a scarlet judge, and the old darling went into a dreadful state of panic, fearing that there had been a premature announcement of this Great Event in the History of our Times.*

From that time, Sir Guthrie Featherstone was entitled to scarlet and ermine and other variously coloured dressing-gowns, to be worn at different seasons of the year, and sat regularly in the seat of Judgement, dividing the sheep from the goats with a good deal of indecision and anxiety. When his day's work was done, he returned to the block of flats in Kensington, where he lived with his wife, Marigold. The flats came equipped with a tennis court, and there the Judge and his good lady were accustomed to playing mixed doubles with their neighbours, the

* See 'Rumpole and the Genuine Article' in *Rumpole and the Golden Thread*, Penguin Books, 1983.

Addisons, during the long summer evenings. Mr Addison, I imagine, was excessively respectful of the sporting Guthrie and frequently called out 'Nice one, Judge,' or 'Oh, I say, Judge, what frightfully bad luck,' during the progress of the game.

What I see, doing my best to reconstruct the occasion which gave rise to the following chapter of accidents, is Guthrie and Marigold diving for the same ball with cries of 'Leave it, Marigold!' and 'Mine, Guthrie!'. These two rapidly moving bodies were set on a collision course and, when it happened, the Judge fell heavily to the asphalt, his wife stood over his recumbent figure, and the anxious Addisons came round the net with cries of 'Nothing broken I hope and trust?'. From then on, perhaps, it went something like this:

'Nothing broken is there, Guthrie?' from Marigold.

'My elbow.' The Judge sat up nursing the afflicted part.

'Such terrible luck when it was going to be such a super shot!' said the ever-sycophantic Addison.

'Twiddle your fingers, Guthrie, and let's see if anything is broken.' When the Judge obeyed, Marigold was able to tell him: 'There you are, nothing broken at all!'

'There's an extraordinary shooting pain. Ouch!' Guthrie was clearly suffering.

'Oh, you poor man, you are in the wars, aren't you?' Mr Addison was sympathetic. 'It'll wear off.' Lady Featherstone was not.

'It shows absolutely no sign of wearing off.'

'Rub it then, Guthrie! And for heaven's sake don't be such a baby!'

The next day I was at my business at the Old Bailey, making my usual final appeal on the subject of the burden of proof, that great presumption of innocence, which has been rightly called the golden thread which runs through British justice, when Mr Justice Featherstone, presiding over the trial, interrupted my flow to say, 'Just a moment, Mr Rumpole. I am in considerable pain.' He was, in fact, still rubbing his elbow. 'I have suffered a serious accident.'

'Did your Lordship say "pain"?' I couldn't, for the moment,

see how his Lordship's accident was relevant to the question of
the burden of proof.

'It's not something one likes to comment about,' the Judge
commented nobly, 'in the general course of events. I have, of
course, had some experience of pain, even at a comparatively
young age.'

'Did you say comparatively *young*, my Lord?' I thought he
was knocking on a bit, for a youngster.

'And if I was the only person concerned I should naturally
soldier on regardless . . .'

'Terribly brave, my Lord!' Leaving him to soldier on, I turned
back to the Jury. 'Members of the Jury. The question you must
ask about each one of these charges is "Are you certain sure?"'

'But I mustn't only think of myself,' the Judge interrupted me
again. 'The point is, am I in too much pain to give your speech
the attention it deserves, Mr Rumpole?'

'I don't know. Are you?' That was all the help I could give him.

'Exercising the best judgement I have, I have come to the
conclusion that I am not. I will adjourn now.'

'At three o'clock?' I must confess I was surprised. 'Pain,' his
Lordship told me solemnly, 'is no respecter of time. Till tomorrow morning, members of the Jury.'

'Would your Lordship wish us to send for Matron?' I was
solicitous.

'I think not, Mr Rumpole. I'm afraid in this particular instance
matters have gone rather beyond Matron.' Norman, the tall,
bald usher, called on us all to be upstanding. Guthrie rose, and
nursing his elbow, and faintly murmuring 'Ouch,' left us.

Norman the Usher was well known to me as a man of the
world, well used to judicial foibles and surprisingly accurate in
forecasting the results of cases. He was a man who took pleasure
in supplying the needs of others, often coming up to me during
lulls in cases to say he knew where to lay his hands on some
rubber-backed carpeting or a load of bathroom tiles. Although I
felt no need of any of Norman's contacts, he was able, on this
occasion, to put Mr Justice Featherstone in touch with a cure.
Long after his retirement Norman returned to the Bailey to look

up a few old friends and over a couple of pints of Guinness in the pub opposite he eventually told me of his part in the affair of the Judge's elbow. 'Muscular is it, your Lordship's affliction?' Norman asked when he had led Guthrie out of Court into the Judge's room, a leather and panelled sanctum furnished with law reports and silver-framed photographs of the children.

'Muscular, Norman,' the Judge admitted. 'One does not complain.'

'Only one thing for muscular pain, my Lord.'

'Aspirins?' The Judge winced as he started to unbutton his Court coat.

'Throw away the aspirins. It's a deep massage. That's what your Lordship needs. Here. Let me slip that off for you.' He removed Guthrie's coat delicately. 'Of course, your Lordship needs a massoose with strong fingers. One who can manipulate the fibres in depth.' At which point the Usher grasped the Judge's elbow with strong fingers, causing another stab of pain, heroically borne. 'I can feel that the fibres are in need of deep, deep manipulation. If your Lordship would allow me. I know just the massoose as'd get to your fibres and release the tension!'

'You know someone, Norman?' The Judge sounded hopeful.

'The wife's sister's daughter, Elsie. Thoroughly respectable, and fingers on her like the grab of a crane . . .'

'A talented girl?'

'Precisely what the doctor ordered. Our Elsie has brought relief to thousands of sufferers.'

'Where . . . does she carry on her practice?' The Judge started tentative inquiries, rather as some fellow in classical times might have said 'Who's got the key to Pandora's Box?'

'In a very hygienic health centre, my Lord. Only a stone's throw down the Tottenham Court Road, your Lordship.'

'Tottenham Court Road?' Guthrie was, at first, fearful. 'Not oriental in any way, this place, is it?'

'Bless you, no, my Lord. They're thoroughly reliable girls. Mostly drawn from the Croydon area. All medically trained, of course.' Norman had hung up the Court coat and was restoring the Judge to mufti.

'Medically trained? That's reassuring.'

'They have made a thorough study, my Lord, of the human anatomy. In all its aspects. Seeing as you've got no relief through the usual channels . . .'

'My doctor's absolutely useless!' The Chelsea G.P. had merely referred the Judge to time, the great healer. Guthrie lifted a brush and comb to his hair, and was again reminded of his plight. 'You're right, Norman. Why not try a little alternative medicine?'

'You wait, my Lord,' Norman told him. 'Just let our Elsie get her fingers on you.'

The address which Norman gave the Judge was situated in a small street running eastward from Tottenham Court Road. After a few days' more pain, Guthrie took a taxi there, got out and paid off the driver, wincing as he felt for his money. 'Had a bit of trouble with my elbow,' he said, as though to explain his visit to the Good Life Health Centre, Sauna and Massage. At which point, the cabby drove away, no doubt thinking it was none of his business, and Guthrie entered the establishment in some trepidation. He was reassured to some extent by the cleanliness of the interior. There was a good deal of light and panelling, photographs of fit-looking young blond persons of both sexes, and a kindly receptionist behind a desk, filing her nails.

'I rang for an appointment,' Guthrie told her. 'The name's Featherstone.' 'Elsie,' the receptionist called out, 'your gentleman's here. You can go right in, dear' – she nodded towards a bead curtain – 'and take off your things.' Later, after a brief spell in an airless and apparently red-hot wooden cupboard, the Judge was stretched out on a table, clad in nothing but a towel, whilst Elsie, a muscular, but personable, young lady, who might have captained a hockey team, manipulated his elbow, and asked him if he was going anywhere nice for his holiday.

'Hope so. I'm tired out with sitting,' Guthrie told her.

'Are you really?' Elsie, no doubt, had heard all sorts of complaints in her time.

'In fact I've been sitting almost continuously this year.'

'Fancy!'

'It gets tiring.'

'I'm sure it does.'

'Not how I did my elbow in, though. Tennis. When I'm not sitting, my wife and I play a bit of tennis.'

'Well, it makes a change, dear. Doesn't it?'

When Elsie had finished her manipulations, Guthrie got dressed and came back into the reception area. Being a little short of cash, and seeing the American Express sign on the counter, he decided to pay with his credit card. 'It feels better already,' he told her, as he signed without an 'ouch'. The receptionist banged the paperwork into her machine. 'There you are then.' She tore off his part of the slip and handed it and the credit card back to Guthrie, who thanked her again, and put the card and the slip carefully into his wallet. After he had left, Elsie came out from behind her curtain. 'He says he's tired out, done a lot of sitting,' she told the receptionist, who smiled and said, 'Poor bloke.'

I was not, of course, among those present when Mr Justice Featherstone had his treatment, and I have had to invent, or attempt to reconstruct, the above dialogue. I may have got it wrong, but of one thing I am certain, the Judge's massage was given in strict accordance with the Queensberry rules, and there was nothing below the belt.

Whilst Guthrie had undergone this satisfactory cure and almost forgotten his old tennis injury, much had changed in our old Chambers at 3 Equity Court. I had been away for a week or two, doing a long firm fraud in Cardiff, a case which had absolutely no bloodstains and a great deal of adding up. I returned from exile to find our tattered old clerk's room, with its dusty files, abandoned briefs, out-of-date textbooks and faded photograph of C. H. Wystan over the fireplace, had been greatly smartened up. Someone had had it painted white, given Henry a new desk and Dianne a new typewriter, hung the sort of coloured prints on the walls which they buy by the yard for 'modernized' hotels and introduced a large number of potted plants, at which

Dianne was, even as I arrived one morning in my old hat and mac, squirting with a green plastic spray.

'"Through the jungle very softly flits a shadow and a sigh –"': the shadow was Dianne, and the sigh came from Henry when I asked if this was indeed our old clerk's room or the tropical house at Kew.

'It's Mr Hearthstoke.' Henry pronounced the name as though it were some recently discovered malignant disease.

'Some old gardener?' I asked, clutching three weeks' accumulation of bills.

'The new young gentleman in Chambers. He reckons an office space needs a more contemporary look.'

'And I've been ticked off for putting.' Uncle Tom was in the corner as usual, trickling a golf ball across the carpet.

'Uncle Tom has been ticked off.' Dianne confirmed the seriousness of the situation.

'I've been asked to do it upstairs, but it isn't the same.' Uncle Tom sounded reasonable. 'Down here, you can see the world passing by.'

'Carry on putting, Uncle Tom,' I told him. 'Imagine you're on the fourth green at Kuala Lumpur.'

I forced my way through the undergrowth and went out into the passage; there I found that our clerk had followed me, and was whispering urgently, 'Could I have a word in confidence?'

'In the passage?'

'It's not only my clerk's room Mr Hearthstoke reckons should have a more contemporary look.' Henry started to outline his grievances. 'He says we could do with a smarter typist. Well, as you know, Mr Rumpole, Dianne has always been extremely popular with the legal executives.'

'A fine-looking girl, Dianne. A fine, sturdy girl. I always thought so.' I had the feeling that Henry felt a certain *tendresse* for our tireless typist, although I didn't think it right to inquire into such matters too deeply.

'Worse than that, Mr Rumpole, he wants to privatize the clerking.'

'To *what*?'

'Mr Hearthstoke's not over-enamoured, sir, with my ten per cent.'

For the benefit of such of my readers as may never have shared in the splendours and miseries of life at the Bar, I should explain that the senior clerk in a set of Chambers is usually paid ten per cent of the earnings of his stable of legal hacks. This system is frequently criticized by those who wish to modernize our profession, but I do not share their views. 'Good God!' I said, 'if barristers' clerks didn't get their ten per cent we'd have no one left to envy.'

'And he's got his criticism of you too, Mr Rumpole. That's why I thought, sir, we might be in the same boat on this one. Even if we'd had our differences in the past.'

'Of me?' I was surprised, and a little pained to hear it. 'What has this "Johnny Come Lately" got to criticize about me?'

'He's not enamoured of your old Burberry.'

Unreasonable I thought. My mac may not have been hand-tailored in Savile Row, but it has kept out the rain on journeys to some pretty unsympathetic Courts over the years. And then I looked at our clerk and saw a man apparently in the terminal stage of melancholia.

'Henry!' I asked him. 'Why this hang-dog look? What on earth's the need for this stricken whisper? If, whatever his name is, has only been here a few weeks . . .'

'Voted in when you were in Cardiff, Mr Rumpole . . .'

'Why does our learned Head of Chambers take a blind bit of notice?'

'Quite frankly, it seems to Dianne and me, Mr Ballard thinks, with great respect, that the sun shines out of Mr Hearthstoke's –' Perhaps it was just as well that he was prevented from finishing this sentence by our learned Head of Chambers, Soapy Sam Ballard, who popped out of his door and instructed Henry to rally the chaps for a Chambers meeting. He didn't seem exactly overjoyed to see me back.

Charles Hearthstoke turned out to be a young man in his early thirties, dark, slender and surprisingly goodlooking; he reminded me at once of Steerforth in the illustrations to *David Copperfield*.

Despite his appearance of a romantic hero, he was one of those persons who took the view, one fashionable with our masters in government, that we were all set in this world to make money. He might have made an excellent accountant or merchant banker; he wasn't, in my view, cut out for work at the Criminal Bar. He had been at some Chambers where he hadn't hit it off with the Clerk (a fact which didn't surprise me in the least) and now he sat at the right hand of Ballard and was clearly the apple of the eye of our pure-minded Head of Chambers.

'I've asked Hearthstoke to carry out an efficiency study into the working of Number 3 Equity Court, and I must say he's done a superb job!' My heart sank as Ballard told us this. 'Quite superb. Charles, would you speak to this paper?'

'He may speak to it,' I grumbled, 'but would it answer back?'

'What's that, Rumpole?'

'Oh, nothing, Ballard. Nothing at all . . .'

But Uncle Tom insisted on telling them. 'That was rather a good one! You heard what Rumpole said, Hoskins? Would it answer back?'

'Leave it, Uncle Tom,' I restrained him. Hearthstoke was now holding up some sort of document.

'In the first section of the report I deal with obvious reforms to the system. It's quite clear that our fees need to be computerized and I've made inquiries about the necessary software.'

'Oh, I'm all in favour of that.'

'Yes, Rumpole?' Ballard allowed my interruption with a sigh.

'Soft wear! Far too many stiff collars in the legal profession. Makes your neck feel it's undergoing a blunt execution.'

'Has Rumpole done another joke . . .?' Uncle Tom didn't seem to be sure about it.

'Do please carry on, Charles.' Ballard apologized to Hearthstoke for the crasser element in Chambers.

'I'm also doing a feasibility study in putting our clerking out to private tender,' Hearthstoke told the meeting. 'I'm sure we can find a young up-thrusting group of chartered accountants who'd take on the job at considerably less than Henry's ten per cent.'

'Brilliant!' I told him.

'So glad you agree, Rumpole.'

'Wonderful thing, privatization. Why not privatize the Judges while you're about it? I mean, they're grossly inefficient. Only give out about a hundred years' imprisonment a month, on the average. Why not sell them off to the Americans and step up production?'

'That, if I may say so,' – Hearthstoke gave a small, wintry smile – 'is the dying voice of what may well become a dying profession.'

'We've got to move with the times, Rumpole, as Charles has pointed out.' Ballard was clearly exercising a great self-control in dealing with the critics.

'As a matter of fact I'm entirely in favour of the privatization of Henry.' This was the colourless barrister, Hoskins. 'Speaking as a chap with daughters, I can ill afford ten per cent.'

'Those of us who have a bit of practice at the Bar, those of us who can't spend all our days doing feasibility studies on the price of paper-clips, know how important it is to keep our clerk's room happy.' That, at any rate, was my considered opinion. 'Besides, I don't want to go in there in the morning and find the place full of up-thrusting young chartered accountants. It'd put me off my breakfast.'

'Is that all you have to say on the subject?' Ballard looked as though he couldn't take much more.

'Absolutely. I'm going to work. Come along, Mizz Probert' – I rose to my feet – 'I believe you've got a noting brief.'

'There's a dingy-looking character in a dirty mac hanging about the waiting-room for you, Rumpole,' Erskine-Brown was at pains to tell me. 'And talking of dirty macs' – Hearthstoke looked at me in a meaningful fashion – 'There is one other point I have to raise,' he said, but I left him to raise it on his own. I was busy.

The client who was waiting for me was separated from his mac; all the same he cut a somewhat depressing figure. He wore thick, pebble glasses, a drooping bow-tie, and a cardigan which had claimed its fair share of soup. A baggy grey suit completed the get-up of a man who seemed to have benefited not at all from the programme of physical fitness which he sold to the public; neither did he seem to enjoy the prosperity which the Prosecution had suggested. He had a curiously high voice and the pained expression of a man who at least pretended not to understand why he was due to be tried at the Old Bailey.

'Dr Maurice Horridge. Where does the "Doctor" come from, by the way?' I asked him.

'New Bognor. A small seat of learning, Mr Rumpole. In the shadow of the Canadian Rockies . . .'

'You know Canada well?'

'I was never out of England, Mr Rumpole. Alas.'

'So this degree of yours. You wrote up for it?'

'I obtained my diploma by correspondence,' he corrected me. 'None the less valuable for that.'

'And it is a doctorate in . . .?'

'Theology, Mr Rumpole. I trust you find that helpful.' I got up and stood at the window, looking out at some nice, clean rain. 'Oh, very helpful, I'm sure. If you want to be well up in the Book of Job or if you want to carry on an intelligent chat on the subject of Ezekiel. I just don't see how it helps with the massage business.'

'The line of the body, Mr Rumpole, is the line of God.' My client spoke reverently. 'We are all of us created in His image.'

'Yes. I've often thought He must be quite a strange-looking chap.'

'Pardon me, Mr Rumpole?' Dr Horridge looked pained.

'Forget I spoke. But massage . . .'

'Spiritual, Mr Rumpole! Entirely spiritual. I could stretch you flat on the floor, with your head supported by a telephone directory, and lay your limbs out spiritually. All your aches and pains would be relieved at once. I don't know if you'd care to stretch out?'

'The girls in these massage parlours you run . . .' I got to the nub of the case.

'Trained! Mr Rumpole. All fully trained.'

'Medically?'

'In my principles, of course. The principles of the spiritual alignment of the bones.'

'What's alleged is that they so far forgot their spiritual mission as to indulge in a little hanky-panky with the customers.' I explained the nature of the charges to the good doctor; roughly it was alleged that he was living on immoral earnings and keeping a large number of disorderly houses. 'I cannot believe it, Mr Rumpole! I simply cannot believe it of my girls.' He spoke like a priest who has heard of group sex among the vestal virgins.

'So that your defence,' I asked him as patiently as possible, 'is that entirely without your knowledge your girls turned from sacred to profane massage?'

Dr Horridge nodded his head energetically. He seemed to think that I had put his case extremely well.

Now I must try to tell you how the troubles of Dr Maurice Horridge became connected with the painful matter of the Judge's elbow. Meeting his wife at the tennis court one night – he had so far improved in his health, thanks to Elsie, that he felt fit enough to resume mixed doubles with the Addisons – Guthrie found Marigold reading the *Standard*. 'Massage parlours,' she almost spat out the words with disgust.

'Well. Yes. In fact . . .' Guthrie hadn't yet confided the full facts of his visit to the Good Life Health Centre to his wife, who read aloud to him from the paper.

'"Doctor of Theology charged with running massage parlours as disorderly houses". How revolting! What was it you wanted to tell me, Guthrie?'

'Well, nothing really. Just that my elbow seems much better. I can really swing a racket now.'

'Well, just don't dislocate anything else.' She gave him more of the news. '"Thirty-five massage parlours alleged to offer immoral services in the Greater London area." Pathetic! Grown men having to go to places like that!'

'I'm quite sure some of them just needed a massage,' Guthrie tried to persuade her.

'If you'd believe that, Guthrie, you'd believe anything!' She read on regardless. '"Arab oil millionaires, merchant bankers and well-known names from television are said to be among those who used the cheap sex provided at Dr Horridge's establishments and paid by *credit card*"!' Guthrie stifled an agonized exclamation of terror. 'What's on earth's the matter? That elbow playing you up again?'

The next thing Guthrie did was to visit the tennis club Gents, and flush away the American Express slip which he had retained for the monthly check-up. He didn't want Marigold, searching for a bit of cash, to find the dreaded words 'Massage and Sauna' stamped on a bit of blue paper. The next day, in the privacy of the Judge's room, he made a telephone call, which I imagine went something like this.

'American Express? The name is Featherstone. Mr Justice Featherstone. No, not Justice-Featherstone with a hyphen. My name is Featherstone and I'm a justice. I'm a judge, that is. Yes. Well, actually I got into a bit of a muddle and paid someone with a credit card when I should have paid cash and if I could go and pay them now, could I get my credit-card slip back and you wouldn't need to have any record of it at all if it's a purely private matter, just a question of my own personal accounting? . . . Do I make myself clear? What's that? Oh. I don't . . .'

It is never easy to recall the past and rectify our mistakes. In this case, Guthrie was to find it impossible. Norman, the Usher, who started all the trouble, had suddenly retired and gone to live in the North of England, and when Guthrie revisited the address near Tottenham Court Road, in the hope that his credit-card transaction could be expunged from the records, he found that the Health Centre had sold up and the premises taken over by Luxifruits Ltd. He was offered some nice juicy satsumas by the greengrocer now in charge, but all traces of Elsie and the receptionist had vanished away.

Guthrie's cup of anxiety ran over when he bumped into Claude Erskine-Brown walking up from the Temple tube station. 'Always so good to see some of the chaps from my old Chambers,' the Judge was gracious enough to observe after Claude had removed his hat and then restored it to its position. 'See your wife was in the Court of Appeal again the other day. And Rumpole! What's old Horace doing?'

'Something sordid as usual,' Claude told him.

'Distasteful?'

'Downright disgusting. Rumpole's cases do tend to lower the tone of 3 Equity Court. This time it's massage parlours! Rumpole's acting for the King of the massage parlours. Of course, he thinks it's a huge joke.'

'But it's not, Erskine-Brown, is it?' The Judge was serious. 'In fact, it's not a joke at all!'

'I can't pretend my marriage is all champagne and opera. We've had our difficulties, Philly and I, from time to time, as I'd be the first to admit. But thank heavens I've never had to resort to massage parlours! I simply can't understand it.'

'No. It's a mystery to me, of course.'

'Anyway. That sort of thing simply lets down the tone of Chambers.'

'Yes. Of course, Claude. Of course it does. The honour of Equity Court is still extremely important to me, as you well know. Perhaps I should invite Horace Rumpole to lunch at the Sheridan. Have a word with him on the subject?'

'What subject?' Claude was apparently a little mystified.

'Massage ... No,' the Judge corrected himself, 'I mean Chambers, of course.'

'Oysters for Mr Rumpole ... and I'll take soup of the day. And Mr Rumpole will be having the grouse and I – I'll settle for the Sheridan Club Hamburger. I thought a Chablis Premier Cru to start with and then, would the Château Talbot '77 appeal to you at all, Horace?' The autumn sunlight filtered through the tall windows that badly needed cleaning and glimmered on the silver and portraits of old judges. Around us, actors hobnobbed with politicians and publishers. I sat in the Sheridan Club, amazed at the Judge's hospitality. As the waitress left us with my substantial order, I asked him if he'd won the pools.

'No. It's just that one gets so few opportunities to entertain the chaps from one's old Chambers. And now Claude Erskine-

Brown tells me you're doing this case about what was it . . . beauty parlours?'

'Massage parlours. Or, as I prefer to call them, Health Centres.'

'Oh, yes, of course. Massage parlours.' The Judge seemed to choke on the words and then recovered. 'Well, I suppose some of these places are quite respectable and above-board, aren't they? I mean, people might just drop in because they'd got . . .'

'A touch of housemaid's knee?' I was incredulous.

'That sort of thing, yes.'

'Someone who was as innocent and unsuspecting as that, they shouldn't be let off the lead.'

'Why do you say that?'

The waitress came with the white wine. Guthrie tasted it and she then poured. I tasted a cold and stony Chablis, no doubt at a price that seldom passes my lips. 'Well, to your average British jury, the words massage parlour mean only one thing,' I told Guthrie, without cheering him up.

'What?'

'Hanky-panky!'

'Oh. You think that, do you?'

'Everyone does.'

'Hanky-panky?' The words stuck in the Judge's throat.

'In practically every case.'

'Rumpole! Horace . . . Look, do let me top you up.' He poured more Chablis. 'You're defending in this case, I take it?'

'What else should I be doing?'

'And as such, as defending counsel, I mean, you'll get to see the prosecution evidence . . .'

'Oh, I've seen most of that already,' I assured him cheerfully.

'Have you?' He looked as though I'd already passed sentence on him. 'How extraordinarily interesting.'

'It's funny, really.'

'Funny?'

'Yes. Extremely funny. You know, all sorts of Very Important People visited my client's establishments. Nobs. Bigwigs.'

'Big *wigs*, Horace?' Guthrie seemed to take the expression personally.

'Most respectable citizens. And you know what? They actually paid with their credit cards! Can you imagine anything so totally dotty . . .'

'Dotty? No! Nothing.' The Judge laughed mirthlessly. 'So their names are all . . . in the evidence? Plain for all the world to see?' He broke off as the soup and the oysters were brought by the waitress, and then said thoughtfully, 'I don't suppose that *all* the evidence will necessarily be put before the Jury.'

'Oh no. Only a few little nuggets. The cream of the collection. It should provide an afternoon of harmless fun.'

'Not fun for the . . . big . . . big wigs involved . . .' He looked appalled.

'Well, if they were so idiotic as to use their *credit cards*!' There was a long pause during which my host seemed sunk in the deepest gloom. He then rallied a little, smiled in a somewhat ghastly manner, and addressed me with all his judicial charm and deep concern. 'Horace,' he said, 'don't you find this criminal work rather exhausting?'

'It's a killer!' I admitted. 'Only sometimes a bit of evidence turns up and makes it all worthwhile.'

'Have you ever considered relaxing a little?' He ignored any further reference to big wigs in massage parlours. 'Perhaps on the Circuit Bench?'

'You're joking!' He had amazed me. 'Anyway, I'm far too old.'

'I don't know. I could have a word with the powers that be. They might ask you to sit as a deputy, Rumpole. On a more or less permanent basis. A hundred and fifty quid a day and absolutely no worries.'

'Deputy Circus Judge?' I was still in a state of shock. 'Why should they offer me that?'

'As a little tribute, perhaps, to the tactful way you've always conducted your defences.'

'Tactful? No one's ever called me that before.' I squeezed lemon on an oyster and sent it sliding down.

'I've always found you extremely tactful in Court, Horace. And discreet. Oysters all right, are they?'

'Oh, yes, Judge.' I looked at him with some suspicion. 'Absolutely nothing wrong with the oysters.'

Walking back from the Sheridan Club to Chambers, I thought about Guthrie's strange suggestion and felt even more surprised. Deputy Circuit Judge! Why on earth should I want that? These thoughts flitted through my head. Judging people is not my trade. I defend them. All the same . . . One hundred and fifty smackers a day, the old darling did say a hundred and fifty, and you didn't even have to stand up for it. It could all be earned sitting down. With hacks constantly flattering you and saying 'If your Honour pleases', 'If your Honour would be so kind as to look at the fingerprint evidence.' No one has ever spoken to me like that. But what was the Judge up to exactly? Offering me grouse and oysters and Deputy Circus Judge. What, precisely, was Guthrie's game?

I could find no answer to these questions as I walked along the Strand. Then a voice hailed me and I turned to see a tall, bald man familiar to me from the Bailey. It was Norman, the ex-Usher, who had apparently called down to the old shop to collect his cards. He asked if Mr Justice Featherstone's elbow had improved.

'It seems to be remarkably recovered,' I told him.

'In terrible pain, he was,' Norman clucked sympathetically. 'Don't you remember? I was able to put him on to a place where they could give him a bit of relief. Get down to the deep fibres, you know. Have the Judge's bones stretched out properly . . .'

'You recommended a place?' I was suddenly interested.

'The wife's niece worked there. Nice type of establishment, it was really. Very hygienically run.' He looked down the road. 'Here comes a number 11. I'll be seeing you, Mr Rumpole. I don't know if you've got any use for a nice length of garden hose.'

'What place? What place did you recommend exactly?' I tried to ask him, but he skipped lightly on to his number 11 and left me.

The Prosecutor in *R.* v. *Dr Maurice Horridge* was a perfectly decent fellow called Brinsley Lampitt. I called on him at his

Chambers and he let me have a large cardboard box of documents, bank statements, accounts and credit-card slips all connected with the questioned massage parlours. My meetings with Guthrie Featherstone and Norman the Usher had given me the idea of a defence which seemed so improbable that at least it had to be tried. I carried the box of exhibits back to Chambers, and set Mizz Liz Probert to sift through them, with particular reference to the credit-card transactions. Then I went down to see Henry.

I found Charles Hearthstoke in the clerk's room asking for P.A.Y.E. forms and petty-cash vouchers for coffee consumed over the last two years. Henry was looking furious and Dianne somewhat flustered. I discovered much later that they had been surprised in a flagrant kiss behind a potted plant when Hearthstoke entered. On my arrival, he turned his unwelcome attentions on me. 'Sorry you had to slip away from the Chambers meeting, Rumpole.' 'What did I miss, Hearthrug?' I asked him. 'Have you replaced me with a reliable computer?'

'Not yet. But we did pass a resolution on the general standards of appearance in Chambers. Old macs are not acceptable now, over a black jacket and striped trousers.' The Pill then left us, and I looked after him with some irritation and contempt. 'I quite agree with you, Mr Rumpole,' Henry said, and I told him we stood together on the matter. 'Together,' I told him, 'we shall contrive to scupper Hearthrug.'

'It'll need a bit of working out,' Henry said, 'Mr Ballard being so pro . . .'

'Bollard? Leave Bollard to me! Providing, Henry, I can leave something to you.'

'I'll do my best, sir. What exactly?'

'Miss Osgood. The lady who arranges the lists down the Bailey. You know, your co-star from the Bromley amateur dramatics.'

'We're playing opposite each other, Mr Rumpole. In *Brief Encounter*.'

'Encounter her, Henry! Drop a word in her shell-like ear about the massage parlour case. What we need, above all things, is a sympathetic judge . . . "There is a tide in the affairs of barristers," Henry, "Which, taken at the flood, leads on to fortune; Omitted, all the voyage of their life is bound in shallows and in miseries . . ."' On such a full tide were we now afloat, and I took charge of the helm and suggested the name of the Judge whom I thought Miss Osgood would do well to assign to *R.* v. *Horridge.*

So it came about that when Guthrie Featherstone arrived for his next stint of work down the Bailey, and Harold, the new usher, brought him coffee in his room, he found the Judge staring, transfixed with horror, at the papers in the case he was about to try and muttering the words 'massage parlours' in a voice of deep distress. Not even the offer of a few nice biscuits could cheer him up. And when he entered Court and saw Dr Horridge in the dock, Rumpole smiling up at him benignly and the table of proposed exhibits loaded with credit-card slips, the Judge looked like a man being led to the place of execution.

'Mr Lampitt, Mr Rumpole.' His Lordship addressed us both in deeply serious tones before the Jury was summoned into Court. 'I feel I have a duty to raise a matter of personal nature.' I said I hoped he wasn't in pain.

'No. Not that, Mr Rumpole . . . Not that . . . The fact is, Mr Lampitt . . . Mr Rumpole . . . Gentlemen. I feel very strongly that I should *not* try this case. I should retire and leave the matter to some other judge.'

'Of course, we should be most reluctant to lose your Lordship,' I flattered Guthrie, and Brinsley Lampitt chimed in with 'Most reluctant.'

'Well, there it is. I'll rise now and . . .' Guthrie started to make his escape.

'May we ask . . . why?' I stopped him.

'May you ask what?'

'*Why*, my Lord. I mean, it's nothing about my client, I hope.'

'Oh no, Mr Rumpole. Nothing at all to do with him.' The Judge was back, despondently, in his seat.

'I can't imagine that your Lordship *knows* my client.'

'Know him? Certainly not!' The Judge was positive. 'Not that I'm suggesting I'd have anything against knowing your client. If I did, I mean. Which I most certainly don't!'

'Then, with the greatest respect, my Lord, where's the difficulty?'

'Where's the *what*, Mr Rumpole?' The Judge was clearly in some agony of mind.

'The difficulty, my Lord.'

'You wish to know where the difficulty is?'

'If your Lordship pleases!'

'And you, Mr Lampitt. You wish to know where the difficulty is?'

'If your Lordship pleases,' said the old darling for the Crown.

'It's a private matter. As you know, Mr Rumpole,' was the best the Judge could manage after a long pause.

'As ' *know*, my Lord? Then it can't be exactly private.'

'Perhaps I should make this clear in open Court. I happened to have lunch at my Club with counsel for the Defence.'

'The oysters were excellent! I'm grateful to your Lordship.'

There was a flutter of laughter and Harold called for silence as the Judge went on: 'And I happened to discuss this case, in purely general terms, with counsel for the Defence.' In the ensuing silence Lampitt was whispering to the police. I asked, 'Is that all, my Lord?'

'Yes. Isn't it enough?' The Judge sounded deeply depressed. Lampitt didn't cheer him up by telling him that he'd spoken to the Officer-in-Charge of the case, who had no objection whatever to the Judge trying Dr Horridge. He was sure that no lunchtime conversation with Mr Rumpole could possibly prejudice his Lordship in any way. 'In fact,' Brinsley Lampitt ended, to the despair of the Judge, 'the Prosecution wish your Lordship to retain this case.'

'And so do the Defence.' I drove in another nail.

'In fact I urge your Lordship to do so,' Lampitt urged.

'So do I, my Lord,' from Rumpole. 'It would be a great waste of public money if we had to fix a new date before a different judge. And in view of the Lord Chancellor's recent warnings about the high cost of legal aid cases . . .'

The Judge clearly felt caught then. He looked with horror at the exhibits and thought with terror of the Lord Chancellor. 'Mr Lampitt, Mr Rumpole,' he asked us without any real hope, 'are you *insisting* I try this case?'

'With great respect, yes,' from Lampitt.

'That's what it comes to, my Lord,' from me.

So the twelve honest citizens were summoned in and one of the strangest trials I have ever known began, because I could not tell who was more fearful of the outcome, the prisoner at the Bar, or the learned judge.

Picture Guthrie after the first day in Court, returning to play a little autumn tennis with his wife. Unfortunately the game was rained off, and he sat with Marigold in the bar of the tennis club and told her, when she asked if he'd had a good day, that he was sorry to say he had not. Then he looked out of the window at the grey sky and asked her if she didn't sometimes long to get away from it all. 'Fellow I was at school with runs a little bar in Ibiza. Wouldn't you like to run a little bar in Ibiza, Marigold?'

'I think I should hate it.'

'But you don't want to hang about around Kensington, in the rain, married to a judge who's away all day, sitting.'

'I like you being a judge, Guthrie,' Marigold explained patiently. 'I like you being away all day, sitting. And what's wrong with Kensington? It's handy for Harrods.'

'Marigold,' he started again after a thoughtful silence.

'Yes, Guthrie.'

'I was just thinking about that Cabinet Minister. You know. The fellow who had to resign. Over some scandal.'

'Did he run a little bar in Ibiza?'

'No. But what I remember about him is his wife stood by him. Through thick and thin. Would you stand by me, Marigold? Through thick and thin?'

'What's the scandal, Guthrie?' She was curious to know, but he answered, 'Nothing. Oh, no. Just a theoretical question. I just wondered if you'd stand by me. That's all.'

'Don't count on it, Guthrie,' she told him. 'Don't ever count on it.'

Meanwhile, back at 3 Equity Court, Liz Probert was working late, sorting through the prosecution exhibits of which we had not yet made a full list. Hearthstoke saw the light on in my room and, suspecting me of wasting electricity, called in to inspect. He apparently offered to help Liz with her task and, sitting beside her, started to sort out the credit-card slips. She remembered asking him why he was helping her, and hoping it had nothing to do with her eyes. She told him that Claude Erskine-Brown had taken her to the Opera and complimented her on her eyes, a moment she had found particularly embarrassing.

'Erskine-Brown's old-fashioned, like everything else in these Chambers,' he told her.

'Just because I'm a woman! I mean, I bet no one mentions *your* eyes. And Hoskins told me I could only do petty larceny and divorce; quite honestly he thinks that's all women are fit for.'

'Out of the ark, Hoskins. Liz, I know we'd disagree about a lot of things.'

'Do you?' She looked at him; I suppose it was not an entirely hostile gaze.

'I'm standing as a Conservative for Battersea Council,' he told her. 'And your father's Red Ron of South-East London! But we're both young. We both want things changed. When we've finished this, why don't you buy yourself a Chinese at the Golden Gate in Chancery Lane?'

'Why on earth?'

'I could buy one too. And we might even eat them at the same table. Oh, and I do promise you not to mention your eyes.'

'You can if you want to.'

'Mention your eyes?'

'No, you fool! Eat your Chinese at my table.' She was laughing as I came in after a little refreshment at Pommeroy's Wine Bar. I took in the scene with some surprise. 'Hearthrug! What's this, another deputation about my tailoring?'

'I was helping out your Pupil, Rumpole.' He was staring, with some distaste, at my old mac.

'Very considerate of you. I can take over now, after a pit-stop at Pommeroy's for refuelling. Why don't you two young things go home?' Liz Probert went, after Hearthstoke told her to wait for him downstairs. And then he revealed some of the results of his snooping round our Chambers. 'I was just going to ask you about Henry.'

'*What* about Henry?' I lit a small cigar.

'I was looking at his P.A.Y.E. returns. He *is* married, isn't he?'

'To a lady tax inspector in Bromley. That's my belief.'

'So what exactly is his relationship with Dianne, the typist?'

'Friendly, I imagine.'

'Just friendly?'

'That is a question I have never cared to ask.'

'There are lots of questions like that, aren't there, Rumpole?' With that, the appalling Hearthrug left me. I pulled the box of documents towards me and started working on them angrily. In the morning I would have to deal with further snoopers: police officers in plain clothes, or rather, in no clothes at all, as they lay on various massage tables and pretended to be in need of affection.

'Detective Constable Marten,' I asked the solid-looking copper with the moustache, 'that is not a note you made at the time?'

'No, sir.'

'Of course not! At the time this incident occurred, you were deprived of your clothing and no doubt of your notebook also?'

'I made the note on my return to the station.'

'After these exciting events had taken place?'

'After the incident complained of, yes.'

'And your recollection was still clear?'

'Quite clear, Mr Rumpole.'

'It started off with the lady therapist.'

'The masseuse, yes.'

'Passing an entirely innocent remark.'

'She asked me if I was going anywhere nice on holiday.'

'She asked you *that*?' The evidence seemed to have awakened disturbing memories in the Judge.

'Yes, my Lord.'

'Up to that time it appeared to be a perfectly routine, straight-forward massage?' I put it to the officer.

'I informed the young lady that I had a certain pain in the knee from playing football.'

'Was that the truth?' I asked severely.

'No, my Lord,' D.C. Marten told the Judge reluctantly.

'So you were lying, Officer?'

'Yes. If you put it that way.'

'What other way is there of putting it? You are an officer who is prepared to lie?'

'In the course of duty, yes.'

'And submit to sexual advances in massage parlours. In the course of duty.' I was rewarded by a ripple of laughter from the Jury, and a shocked sign from the Judge. 'Mr Rumpole,' he said politely, 'can I help?'

'Of course, my Lord.' I was suitably grateful.

'When the massage started, you told the young lady you had a pain in your knee?' The Judge recapped, rubbing in the point.

'Yes, my Lord.'

'From playing tennis?'

'Football, my Lord.'

'Yes. Of course. Football. I'm much obliged.' His Lordship made a careful note. 'So far as the lady masseuse was concerned, that might have been the truth?'

'She might have believed it, my Lord,' the Detective Constable admitted grudgingly.

'And so far as you know, quite a number of perfectly decent, respectable, happily married men may visit these ... health centres simply because they have received injuries in various sporting activities. Football ... tennis and the like!' The Judge was moved to express his indignation.

'Some may, I suppose, my Lord.' D.C. Marten was still grudging.

'Many may!'

'Yes.'

'Very well.' The Judge turned from the officer with distaste 'Yes, Mr Rumpole. Thank you.'

'Oh, thank *you*, my Lord. If your Lordship pleases.' I stopped smiling then and turned to the witness. 'So at first sight this appeared to be an entirely genuine health centre?'

'At first sight. Yes.'

'An entirely genuine health centre.' The Judge was actually writing it down, paying a quite unusual compliment to the Defence. 'Those were your words, Mr Rumpole?'

'My exact words, your Lordship. No doubt your Lordship is writing them down for the benefit of the Jury.'

'I am, Mr Rumpole. I am indeed.'

I saw Lampitt looking bewildered. Judges who brief themselves for the accused are somewhat rare birds down the Bailey.

'And the whole thing was as pure as the driven snow. In fact it was the normal treatment of a football injury until you made a somewhat distasteful suggestion?'

'Distasteful?' D.C. Marten appeared to resent the adjective.

'Just remind the Jury of what you said, Officer. As you lay on that massage table, clad only in a towel.'

'I said, "Well, my dear"' – the officer read carefully from his notebook – '"How about a bit of the other?"'

'The *what*, Officer?' The Judge was puzzled.

'The other, my Lord.'

'The other what?'

'Just. The other . . .'

'I must confess I don't understand.' His Lordship turned to me for assistance.

'You were using an expression taken from the vernacular,' I suggested to the Detective Constable.

'Meaning what, Mr Rumpole?' The Judge was still confused.

'Hanky-panky, my Lord.'

'I'm much obliged. I hope that's clear to the Jury?' Guthrie turned to the twelve honest citizens, who nodded wisely.

'You suggested some form of sexual intimacy might be possible?' The Judge was now master of the facts.

'I did, my Lord. Putting it in terms I felt the young lady would understand.'

'And if you hadn't made this appalling suggestion, the massage might have continued quite inoffensively?'

'It might have done.'

'To the considerable benefit of your knee!'

'There was nothing wrong with my knee, my Lord.'

'No. No, of course not! You were lying about that!' And then, high on his success, Guthrie asked the question that would have been better to leave unsaid. 'When you asked the young lady about "the other", what did she reply?'

'Her answer was, my Lord, "That'll be twenty pounds".'

'Very well, Officer,' Guthrie said hastily. 'No one wants to keep this officer, do they? The witness may be released.'

And as D.C. Marten left the box, Brinsley Lampitt whispered to me, 'Have you any idea why the Judge is batting so strenuously for the Defence?'

'Oh, yes,' I whispered back, 'it must be my irresistible charm.'

Two wives, Marigold Featherstone and Hilda 'She Who Must Be Obeyed' Rumpole, bumped into each other in Harrods, and had tea together, swapping news of their married lives. Hilda said she had been after a hat to wear when Rumpole was sitting. 'I thought I might be up beside him on the Bench occasionally.'

'Rumpole sitting?' For some reason Marigold appeared surprised.

'Yes. It was your Guthrie that mentioned it to him actually, when they took a spot of lunch together at the Sheridan Club. Rumpole said that it rather depended on his behaving himself in this case that's going on. But if he's a bit careful . . . well, Deputy County Court Judge! For all the world to see. It'll be one in the eye for Claude Erskine-Brown. That's what he's always wanted.'

'Guthrie seems to want to give up sitting.' Marigold told Hilda of their mysterious conversation. 'He speaks of going to Ibiza and opening a bar.'

'Ibiza!'

'Terrible place. Full of package tours and Spaniards.'

'Oh dear. I don't think Rumpole and I would like that at all.'

'Tell me, Mrs Rumpole. May I call you Helen?'

'Hilda, Marigold. And you and Guthrie always have.'

'Guthrie's been most peculiar lately. I wonder if I should take him to the doctor.'

'Oh dear. Nothing terribly serious, I hope.'

'He keeps asking me if I'd stand by him. Through thick and thin. Would you do that for Rumpole?'

'Well. Rumpole and I've been together nearly forty years . . .' she began judicially.

'Yes.'

'And I'd stand by him, of course.'

'Would you?'

'But thick and thin. No, I'm not sure about that.'

'Neither am I, Hilda. I'm not sure at all.'

'Have another scone, dear' – my wife passed the comforting plate – 'and let's hope it never comes to that.'

The next morning, Marigold's husband asked Rumpole (for the Defence) and Brinsley Lampitt (for the Prosecution) to see him in his room. 'I thought I'd just ask you fellows in to find out how much longer this case is going to last. Time's money you know. I don't think we should delay matters by going into a lot of unnecessary documents. Will you be producing documents, Lampitt?'

'Just Dr Horridge's bank accounts. Nothing else.' The words clearly brought great comfort to his Lordship. 'I don't think anything else is necessary.'

'Oh no. Absolutely right! I do so agree. I seem to remember hearing something about customers using credit cards. You won't be putting in any of the credit-card slips? Nothing of that nature?'

'No, Judge. I don't think we need bother with that evidence.'

'No. Of course not. That'd just be wasting the Jury's time. I'm sure you agree, don't you, Rumpole?'

'Well, yes.' I was more doubtful. 'That is. Not quite.'

'Not quite?'

'About the credit-card evidence.'

'Yes?' The Judge's spirits seemed to have sunk to a new low.

'I think I'd like to keep my options open.'

'Keep them . . . open?'

'You see, my argument is that no one who wasn't completely insane would pay by credit card in a disorderly house.'

'That's your argument?'

'So the fact that credit cards were used *may* indicate my client's innocence. It's a matter I'll have to consider, Judge. Very carefully.'

'Yes. Oh, yes. I suppose you will.' His Lordship seemed to have resigned himself to certain disaster.

'Was that all you wanted to see us about?' I asked cheerfully.

'How much longer?' was all the Judge could bring himself to say.

'Oh, don't worry, Judge. It'll soon be over!'

After we left, I imagined that Mr Justice Featherstone got out his Spanish Phrase Book and practised saying, '*Este vaso no esta limpio*. This glass is not clean.'

It must have been after the prosecution case was closed, and immediately before I had to put my client in the witness-box, that Guthrie Featherstone's view of life underwent a dramatic change. He had brought in the envelope containing his American Express accounts, a document that he had not dared to open. But, in the privacy of his room and after a certain amount of sherry and claret at the Judge's luncheon, he steeled himself to open it. Summing up a further reserve of courage, he looked and found the entry, his payment to the Good Life Health Centre. 'Good Life'? A wild hope rose in an unhappy judge, and he snatched up the papers in the case he was trying. There was no doubt about it. Maurice Horridge was charged with running a number of disorderly houses known as the Good Line Health Centre. It was clearly a different concern entirely. Guthrie felt like a man given six months to live, who discovers there's been a bit of a mix-up down the lab and all he's had is a cold in the head. He had never been to one of Dr Horridge's establishments, and there was no record of any judicial payment among the prosecution exhibits. 'I have no doubt,' he shouted, 'I'm in the clear,' and down the Bailey they still speak of the little dance of triumph Guthrie was executing when Harold, the new Usher, came to take him into Court.

Installed, happy now, on his Bench, Guthrie was treated to the Rumpole examination-in-chief of my distinctly shifty-looking client 'Dr Horridge'. I was saying, "If any of these young ladies misconducted themselves in your Health Centres . . .'

'They wouldn't,' the witness protested, 'I'm sure they wouldn't. They were spiritually trained, Mr Rumpole.'

'All the same, if by any chance they did, was it with your knowledge and approval?'

'Certainly not, my Lord. Quite certainly not!' Horridge turned to Guthrie, from whom I expected a look of sympathy. Instead, the Judge uttered a sharpish, 'Come now, Dr Horridge!'

'Yes, my Lord?' The theological doctor blinked.

'Come, come! We have had the evidence from that young officer, Detective Constable Marten, that he suggested to one of your masseuses . . . something of "the other"!'

'Something or other, my Lord?'

'No, Dr Horridge.' The Judge sounded increasingly severe. 'Something *of* the other. I'm sure you know perfectly well what that means. To which the masseuse replied, "That will be twenty pounds". A pretty scandalous state of affairs, I'm sure you'll agree?'

'Yes, my Lord.' What else could the wretched massage pedlar say?

'Are you honestly telling this jury that you had no idea whatever that was going on, in your so-called Health Centre?'

'No idea at all, my Lord.'

'And you didn't make it your business to find out?' Guthrie was now well and truly briefed for the Prosecution.

'Not specifically, my Lord.' It wasn't a satisfactory answer and the Judge met it with rising outrage. 'Not specifically! Didn't you realize that decent, law-abiding citizens, husbands and *rate-payers* might be trapped into the most ghastly trouble just by injuring an elbow – I mean, a knee?'

'I suppose so, my Lord,' came the abject reply.

'You suppose so! Well. The Jury will have heard your answer. What *are* you doing, Mr Rumpole?' His Lordship had some reason to look at me. I had wet my forefinger and now held it up in the air.

'Just testing the wind, my Lord.'

'The wind?' The Judge was puzzled.

'Yes. It seems to have completely changed direction.'

When the case was concluded, I returned to Chambers exhausted. Thinking I might try my client's recipe, I lay flat on the floor with my eyes closed. I heard the door open, and the voice of the Hearthrug from far away asking, 'Rumpole! What's the matter? Are you dead or something?'

'Not dead. Just laid out spiritually.' I opened my eyes. 'Losing a case is always a tiring experience.'

'I'm trying to see Ballard,' Hearthstoke alleged.

'Well, look somewhere else.'

'He always seems to be busy. I wanted to tell him about Henry.'

I rose slowly, and with some difficulty, to a sitting position, and thence to my feet. 'What about Henry?'

'Kissing Dianne in the clerk's room.' The appalling Hearthrug did his best to look suitably censorious. 'It's just not on.'

'Oh, I agree.' I was upright by now, but panting slightly.

'Do you?' He seemed surprised. 'I thought you'd say it was all just part of the freedom of the subject, or whatever it is you're so keen on.'

'Oh, good heavens, no! I really think he should stop rehearsing in his place of work.'

'Rehearsing?' He seemed surprised.

'Didn't you know? Henry's a pillar of the Bromley amateur dramatics. He's playing opposite Dianne in some light comedy or other. Of course, they both work so hard they get hardly any time to rehearse. I'll speak to them about it. By the way, how's the housemaid's knee?'

'The what?' Clearly, my words had no meaning for the man.

'The dicky ankle, dislocated elbow, bad back, tension in the neck. In a lot of pain, are you?'

'Rumpole! What *are* you talking about? I am perfectly fit, thank you!'

'No aches and pains of any sort?' It was my turn to sound surprised.

'None whatever.'

'How very odd! And you've been having such a lot of massage lately.'

'What on *earth* do you mean?' Hearthrug, I was delighted to note, was starting to bluster.

'Unfortunate case. The poor old theologian got two years, once the Judge felt he had a free hand in the matter. But we were looking through the evidence. Of course, you knew that. That was why you came in to give Mizz Probert a helping hand. I was after another name, as it so happens. But I kept finding yours, Charles Hearthstoke. In for a weekly massage at the Battersea Health Depot and Hanky-Panky Centre.'

'It was entirely innocent!' he protested.

'Oh, good. You'll be able to explain that to our learned Head of Chambers. *When* you can find him.'

But Hearthrug looked as though he was no longer eager to find Soapy Sam Ballard, or level his dreadful accusations against Henry and Dianne.

From time to time, and rather too often for my taste, we have Chambers parties, and shortly after the events described previously, Claude Erskine-Brown announced that he was to finance one such shindig; he had some particular, but unknown, cause for celebration. So we were all assembled in Ballard's room, where Pommeroy's most reasonably priced *Méthode Champenoise* was dished out by Henry and Dianne to the members of Chambers with their good ladies and a few important solicitors and such other distinguished guests as Mr Justice Featherstone, now fully restored to health both of mind and elbow. 'Hear you potted Rumpole's old brothel-keeper,' Uncle Tom greeted Sir Guthrie, making a gesture as though playing snooker, 'straight into the pocket!'

'It was a worrying case,' Guthrie admitted.

'It must have been for you, Judge. Extremely worrying.' I saw his point.

'There used to be a rumour about the Temple' – Uncle Tom was wandering down Memory Lane – 'that old Helford-Davis's clerk was running a disorderly house over a sweet-shop in High Holborn. Trouble was, no one could ever find it!' At which point, Hilda, in a new hat, came eagerly up to Guthrie and said, 'Oh, Judge. How we're going to envy you all that sunshine!' And she went on in spite of my warning growl. 'Of course, we'd love to retire to a warmer climate. But Rumpole's got all these new responsibilities. He feels he won't be able to let the Lord Chancellor down.'

'The Lord Chancellor?' Guthrie didn't seem quite to follow her drift.

'He's expecting great things, apparently, of Rumpole. Well' – she raised her glass – 'happy retirement.'

'Mrs Rumpole. I'm not retiring.'

'But Marigold distinctly told me that it was to be Ibiza.'

'Well. I had toyed with the idea of loafing about all day in an old pair of shorts and an old straw-hat. Soaking up the sun. Drinking Sangria. But no. I feel it's my duty to go on sitting.'

'Ibiza is no longer necessary,' I explained to Hilda, but she had to say, 'Your duty! Yes, of course. Rumpole is going to be doing his duty too.' At which point, our Head of Chambers banged a glass on his desk for silence. 'I think we are going to hear about Rumpole's future now,' Hilda said, and Ballard addressed the assembled company. 'Welcome! Welcome everyone. Welcome Judge. It's delightful to have you with us. Well, in the life of every Chambers, as in every family, changes take place. Some happy, others not so happy. To get over the sadness first. Young Charles Hearthstoke has not been with us long, only three months in fact.' 'Three months too long, if you want my opinion,' I murmured to Uncle Tom, and Bollard swept on with his ill-deserved tribute. 'But I'm sure we all came to respect his energy and drive. Charles has told me that he found the criminal side of our work here somewhat distasteful, so he is joining a commercial set in the Middle Temple.' At this news, Henry applauded with enthusiasm. 'I'm sure we're all sorry that Charles had to leave us before he could put some of his most interesting ideas for the reform of Chambers into practice . . .'

At this point, I looked at Mizz Probert. I have no idea what transpired when she and Hearthrug had their Chinese meal together, but I saw Liz's eyes wet with what I took for tears. Could she have been sorry to see the blighter go? I handed her the silk handkerchief from my top pocket, but she shook her head violently and preferred to sniff.

'Now I come to happier news,' Ballard told us. 'From time to time, the Lord Chancellor confers on tried and trusty members of the Bar . . .'

'Like Rumpole!' This was from Hilda, *sotto voce*.

'The honour of choosing them to sit as Deputy Circuit Judge.'

'We know he does!' Hilda again, somewhat louder.

'So we may find ourselves appearing before one of our colleagues and be able to discover his wisdom and impartiality on the Bench.'

'You may have Ballard before you, Rumpole,' Hilda called out in triumph, to my deep embarrassment.

'This little party, financed I may say,' Ballard smiled roguishly, 'by Claude Erskine-Brown . . .'

'So kind of Claude to do this for Rumpole,' was my wife's contribution.

'. . . Is to announce that he will be sitting, from time to time, at Snaresbrook and Inner London, where we wish him every happiness.'

Ballard raised his glass to Erskine-Brown, as did the rest of us, except for Hilda, who adopted a sort of stricken whisper to ask, '*Claude Erskine-Brown* will be sitting? Rumpole, what happened?' 'My sitting,' I tried to explain to her, 'like Guthrie Featherstone's Ibiza, is no longer necessary.' And then I moved over to congratulate the new Deputy Circus Judge.

'Well done, Claude.' And I told him, 'I've only got one word of advice for you.'

'What's that, Rumpole? Let everyone off?'

'Oh, no! Much more important than that. Always pay in cash.'

Rumpole and the Bright Seraphim

I know little of army life. It's true that I was able to serve my country during the last war (sometimes it seems only yesterday, the years rush by with such extraordinary speed) in the R.A.F. at Dungeness (ground staff, they never sent me up in the air). It was there that I met Bobby O'Keefe in the Women's Auxiliary Air Force, and was a little dashed in spirits when she was finally hitched to a pilot officer, 'Three-Fingers Dogherty' – events which I have described elsewhere.* Those years, in turn exciting, boring, alarming and uncomfortable, gave me no insight whatever into life in a 'good' cavalry regiment. I knew nothing of the traditions of the officers' Mess, and I had never even appeared at a court martial until the extraordinary discovery of the body of Sergeant Jumbo Wilson in the 37th and 39th Lancers, clad in women's attire outside the Rosenkavalier bar and discotheque in Badweisheim, West Germany, and the subsequent prosecution of Trooper Boyne for murder. It is a case which had its points of interest, notably in my cross-examination of an inexpert expert witness as to the time of death and the strange solution at which I arrived by an unaided process of deduction.

When we had any minor cause for celebration, or when the East wind was not blowing and conversation flowed freely between us, it was the practice of myself and She Who Must Be Obeyed to call in at the Old Gloucester pub (Good Food Reasonably Priced, Waitress Service and Bar Snacks), which is but the toss of a glass from our so-called 'mansion' flat at Froxbury Court. It was there we made the acquaintance of a major, recently

* See 'Rumpole and the Alternative Society' in *Rumpole of the Bailey*, Penguin Books, 1978.

retired and in his forties, named Johnnie Pageant, who had taken a flat in the Gloucester Road area, and who spent his days writing to various golf clubs, of which he would have liked to become secretary. I found him a most amiable fellow, an excellent listener to my fund of anecdotes concerning life at the Bailey, and never slow to stand his round consisting, invariably, of a large claret for me and jumbo-sized gin and tonics for himself and She.

One evening in the Old Gloucester I was holding forth as usual about the murderers and other friends I had made down the Bailey, explaining that those accused of homicide were usually less tiresome and ruthless customers than parties in divorce cases, and, having often killed the one person they found intolerable, they were mostly grateful for anything you could do for them. 'You've done a lot of murders?' the ex-Major wondered.

'More, perhaps, than you've had hot dinners.'

'Try not to show off, Rumpole,' She Who Must Be Obeyed warned.

'My nephew Sandy Ransom's got a bit of a murder in his regiment in Germany. Young trooper out there in a spot of bother.'

'Murder, in the Regiment, do you say?'

'Mention the word "murder" and you can see Rumpole pricking up his ears.' My wife, Hilda, of course, knew me of old. 'Murder's mother's milk to Rumpole.'

'Who's this young lad supposed to have murdered?' I wanted further and better particulars.

'His Troop Sergeant, apparently.'

'Murdered his sergeant; isn't that justifiable homicide?' I asked, being ignorant of army law.

'You should know. You've done a court martial or two, I suppose. Perhaps even more than I've had hot dinners,' Johnnie Pageant laughed.

'Court martials? Of course!' Then I thought it better to qualify the claim. 'Perhaps not more than you've had gin and tonics . . .'

'Point taken, Horace! Hilda, the other half?'

'Well. Just perhaps the tiniest, weeniest, Johnnie.' So, ex-Major Johnnie wandered off to the bar, and Hilda turned on me. 'What *are* you talking about, Rumpole? You've never done a court martial in your life.'

'Mum's the word, Hilda,' I warned her. 'I thought I could sniff, for a moment, the odour of a distant brief.'

And I was right. A week or so later, when I went into our clerk's room, Henry handed me the brief in a court martial in Germany, the charge being one of murder. I asked if there were any sort of rank attached: Lieutenant-Colonel or Major-General Rumpole? Henry said no, but there was a cheque under the tape and a first-class air ticket to Badweisheim. 'First class?' Well, it seemed only right and proper; an officer and a gent couldn't huddle with other ranks in steerage.

'The solicitors said it was a heavy sort of case and at first I thought they wanted a silk, Mr Ballard, perhaps, to lead you,' Henry said, as I thought tactlessly.

'Bollard to lead? He'd be following far behind.'

'But then they said no. What they wanted was just an ordinary barrister.'

'An *ordinary* barrister.' I was, I confess, somewhat irked. 'Then they've come to the wrong fellow!'

'Shall I return the brief then, Mr Rumpole?'

'No, Henry. We do not return briefs. When we are called to the colours, we do not hesitate. And if the Army needs me. Company ... Atten—shun! *Present Arms!*' So I marched out of the clerk's room with my umbrella over my shoulder, chanting, 'Boots, boots, boots, boots movin' up and down again. There's no discharge in the war!' much to the consternation of Bollard and that grey barrister, Hoskins, who had just come in and no doubt thought that 'Old Rumpole' had taken leave of his senses.

The 37th and 39th Lancers, the Duke of Clarence's Own, familiarly known as the Bright Seraphim because of the sky-blue plumes they still wore, in a somewhat diminished version, in their headgear, had been a crack cavalry regiment with a list of battle honours stretching back to the Restoration. Even now, when they were encased in rattling sardine tins and not mounted on horses, the Regiment was hugely proud of its reputation. Its officers ran to hunters, country estates and private incomes, its Mess silver and portraits were some of the most valuable, and its soldiers the best looked-after in the British forces stationed in Germany. Should one of the Bright Seraphim stray from the paths of righteousness, I learnt early in my preparation for the court martial, the whole regiment would close ranks to protect the boy in trouble and the high reputation of the Duke of Clarence's Own.

The scandalous circumstances surrounding the death of Sergeant James 'Jumbo' Wilson were therefore particularly unwelcome. Military police touring the streets of Badweisheim, the German town close to the Bright Seraphim's barracks, searched, as a result of a telephone call received at 3.45 a.m., an alleyway which ran by the side of the Rosenkavalier disco-bar. It was at 4 a.m. that they then found Sergeant Wilson's body. His short haircut, florid face and moustache indicated his military occupation; the scarlet, low-cut frock he wore did not. He had received a stab wound in the stomach which had penetrated the aorta, but the time of his death was a matter which would become the subject of some controversy. One other matter – the Sergeant was an extremely unpopular N.C.O. and few of those who came under his immediate command seemed to have much reason to love him.

One wing of the barracks at Badweisheim consisted of married quarters for the non-commissioned officers and men; on the whole the officers lived in various houses in the town. Sergeant Wilson and his wife – they were a childless couple – occupied a flat up a short, iron staircase at one end of the wing. Next door, but on a lower level, lived Danny Boyne, a good-looking Glasgow Irish trooper in his early twenties, with his wife and baby son.

Trooper Boyne had, unusually for anyone in the Regiment, married a German girl, and he was noted for his quick temper and his deep hatred of Sergeant Wilson, who, so many witnesses had noticed, lost no opportunity of picking on Danny and putting him on charges for a number of offences, many trivial but some more serious. Witnesses had also been found who had heard Danny threaten to cut the Sergeant up. He was, undoubtedly, present at the disco on the night the Sergeant died; and when the shirt he wore on that occasion was examined, a bloodstain of Sergeant Wilson's group was found on the cuff. For these cogent reasons, he was put under arrest and now had to face a general court martial with Horace Rumpole called to the colours to undertake his defence.

When I came out into the glass and concrete concourse of Badweisheim airport, a crisp, cheerful and thoroughly English voice called out to me, 'Horace Rumpole? Consider yourself under arrest, sir. The charge is smuggling an old wig through customs.'

The jokester concerned turned out to be a youngish, fair-haired captain, with a sky-blue cockade of the Seraphim in his beret and a lurcher at his heels. 'Very funny!' I hadn't smiled.

'Oh, do you think so? I can do much better than that. Sandy Ransom. I think you know my old uncle Johnnie?'

'Captain Ransom.' I didn't know if I should attempt a salute.

'I'm the Defending Officer.'

'Oh, really? I thought I was doing the defending.'

'Of course, you are. You're O/C Defence. I'm just your fag. Anything you want I'll run and get it. I'm the prisoner's friend. We are all the friends of any trooper in trouble. It's a question of regimental honour.'

'I see,' I said, although I didn't entirely, at the time.

'You'll need a porter, won't you?' He whistled to a man and said in what was, as far as I could tell, an impeccable German accent, '*Träger! Bitte nehmen sie das Gepäck.*' He also whistled to his obedient lurcher and led me to the jeep in which he was to drive me to the barracks. 'I told my Uncle Johnnie we were looking for an ordinary sort of barrister,' he told me when we were *en route*.

'Ordinary!' Again it seemed a most inadequate description of Rumpole's talents.

'The court-martial officers will be from other regiments,'

Sandy Ransom explained. 'Pay Corps. That sort of rubbish. Very downmarket. They're all highly suspicious of the Cavalry. Think we're all far too well-off, which is luckily quite true. Parade a flashy Q.C. and they'd convict Danny Boy before he got his hat off. Just to teach the Cavalry a lesson. Anyway, old Uncle Johnnie said you'd done loads of court martials.'

'Oh, yes, loads.' Well, we were far from home and no one, I hoped, would know any different.

At last we drew in at a gate house manned by a sergeant who saluted Sandy and got a brief acknowledgement, and then we were in a huge square surrounded by brick buildings erected, I learned, for the *Wehrmacht*. In the square there was a large collection of military vehicles – cars, jeeps, lorries and even tanks – and we passed various groups of the Duke of Clarence's Own, all of whom saluted us smartly. Some lines from the *Ancient Mariner* floated into my mind:

> This seraph-band, each waved his hand:
> It was a heavenly sight!
> They stood as signals to the land,
> Each one a lovely light.

> This seraph-band, each waved his hand,
> No voice did they impart –
> No voice; but oh! the silence sank
> Like music on my heart.

And I felt my own hand rising, irresistibly, to the brim of my hat.

'Steady on, sir,' Sandy told me. 'There's no need for you to return their salutes.'

That evening the candlelight gleamed on the silver and the paintings of long-gone generals and colonels wearing wigs and scarlet coats, three-cornered hats, swords and sashes, posed against gunmetal skies or on rearing horses. The few officers dining with us in the Mess that night wore elderly tweed suits as though they were guests in some rather grand country house, with the exception of a young lieutenant in uniform. Sandy

Ransom introduced me to a shortish, quietly spoken, amused and intelligent-looking man – considerably younger than me – as the Colonel of the Regiment, Lieutenant-Colonel Hugh Undershaft, a high-flier at Military College from whom even greater things were apparently expected. The Colonel performed the other introductions.

'Sandy you know, of course. And this is Major Graham Sykes.' A greying, rather sad-looking man who, I had been told, wouldn't rise higher in the service, nodded a greeting. 'And Lieutenants Tony Ross and Alan Hammick. Alan's Duty Officer, which is why he's all togged up. Is that all of us?'

'All we could rustle up, sir,' Sandy told him. The lurcher was also among those present, and was lapping up a bowl of water before going to sleep under the table.

'Can't lure many people into the Mess nowadays,' the Colonel admitted. 'They prefer to be at home with their wives or girl-friends. We felt we'd better turn out.'

'Very decent of you, Colonel.'

'I told Borrow to bring up some of the regimental Bollinger in honour of your visit. That suit you?' The elderly white-coated Mess Attendant handed round the champagne, which suited me admirably. I raised my glass and said, 'Well, here's to crime!'

'I think we'd prefer to drink to the Regiment . . .' the Colonel said quietly and the other officers muttered 'the Regiment', as they raised their glasses. 'The boy had to go to a court martial, of course. But we rely on you to get him off, Rumpole. It's a question of the honour of the Regiment.' It was not the first time I had been told this, and I looked at a gilded coat of arms and list of battle honours hanging on the wall: Malplaquet, Blenheim, Waterloo, Balaclava, Mons, El Alamein, I read and the Regiment's motto 'For the sake of honour'.

'Well, we can't have it said that we had a murderer in our ranks, can we?' the Colonel asked.

'Certainly not!' I found the courage to say. 'Not after you've killed so many people.' There was an uncomfortable silence, and then Sandy laughed. 'I say, you know. That was rather funny!'

'Was it really?' I asked him to reassure me.

.

'Oh yes. Distinctly humorous. Bit of a joker aren't you, sir, in your quiet way?' The Colonel looked at me and emptied his glass. 'Shall we start dinner,' he said. 'We heard you were a claret man, Rumpole.'

There was absolutely nothing wrong with the 1971 Margaux, and when the Cockburn 1960 was circulating, I was able to tell the assembled officers that I had done the State some service under battle conditions in the R.A.F., Dungeness. 'Ground staff merely,' I admitted, 'but that's not to say that we didn't have some pretty hairy nights.'

'Don't tell me' – Sandy was laughing – 'a bomb fell on the N.A.A.F.I.?'

'Well, as a matter of fact it did.' I was a little put out. 'Not a very laughable experience.'

'Of course not,' the Colonel rebuked Sandy mildly. 'The port seems to have stuck to the table . . .'

'I don't know exactly how many of you gentlemen served through the Second World War?' I was still a little stung by Sandy's joke.

'Too young for it, I'm afraid,' even Major Sykes admitted.

'I wasn't even a glint in my father's eye,' this from young Captain Sandy Ransom.

'*My* father was in Burma,' Lieutenant Ross boasted. 'He's inclined to be a terrible bore about it.'

'I suppose I was about one when it ended. Hardly in a position to join the Regiment,' the Colonel told me. 'And somehow we never even got invited to the Falklands . . .'

'Soldiers of the Queen,' I discovered. 'Born too late for a war.'

'Do you honestly think it's too late?' The Colonel looked at me; he was smiling gently.

'Too late for your sort of war, anyway,' I told him. 'Too late for Blenheim and Balaclava and the Thin Red Line, and hats off to you fuzzy-wuzzies 'cos you broke a British square. Even too late for Passchendaele and Tobruk . . . Next time some boffin will press a button, and good-night all. "Farewell the plumed troop and the big wars/That make ambition virtue!"' I was getting into my stride:

> 'O, farewell!
> Farewell the neighing steed and the shrill trump,
> The spirit-stirring drum, the ear-piercing fife,
> The royal banner, and all quality,
> Pride, pomp, and circumstance of glorious war! . . .
> Farewell! The Colonel's occupation's gone.'

I looked round at their slightly puzzled faces and said, 'Nowadays, let's face it, you're only playing at soldiers, aren't you?'

'Perhaps you're right,' the Colonel admitted. 'But while we're here, we may as well play the game as well as possible; it would be exceedingly boring if we didn't. And we have to do our best for the Regiment.'

'Oh, yes. Yes, of course.' I raised my glass. 'The Regiment!'

'It's not customary to drink to the Regiment after dinner,' Major Sykes corrected me quietly. 'Except on formal evenings in the Mess.'

So I drank, but not to the Regiment, and the Colonel got up and went to a small grand piano in the corner of the Mess. He sat on the piano stool, gently massaging his fingers and, as this was more as I expected an evening among soldiers would be, I started to sing 'Roll out the Barrel' just as we had sung it during the late war:

> 'Roll out the barrel,
> We'll have a barrel of fun
> Drink to the barrel
> We've got the blues on the run . . .'

And then I fell silent, feeling exceedingly foolish as Colonel Undershaft began to play what even I could recognize as Beethoven's Moonlight Sonata. Over a soft passage he spoke to no one in particular: 'Perhaps we are all practising idiotically for a war which would begin by obliterating us all. But we're still responsible, aren't we? Responsible for our soldiers. Boys like Danny Boy. We pick them out of a back-street in Glasgow and give them clean boots and a haircut. We feed them and water them and teach them to kill people in all sorts of ingenious ways, and then we can't even offer them a proper soldier's war to do it in. Can we expect them to turn into nice, quiet members of the Salvation Army? We're responsible for Danny Boy' – he stopped playing and looked at me – 'which is why we've got to take all possible steps to see that he's acquitted.'

'I'm sorry,' I said in the ensuing silence.

'Why?' the Colonel asked.

'Sorry about that "Roll out the Barrel" business. It seems that I got things rather wrong.'

Later Sandy took me across the square to a comfortable guest-room with a bathroom attached. On the way I asked him to show me the married quarters. I saw the late sergeant's flat up a short, iron staircase at the foot of which two or three large dustbins stood against a wall; and, on ground level, I saw Trooper Danny's small accommodation. There were lights on up and below the outside staircase. Two wives, parted from their husbands, were, it seemed, unable to sleep. When we got to my room, Sandy said we would see Danny in the morning and asked if I had all the 'paperwork' I needed.

'Oh yes. An interesting little brief, especially the post-mortem photographs. Quite a lot to be learned from them.'

'What about?' Captain Sandy Ransom didn't sound particularly interested.

'About the time of death. It's the hypostasis, you see, the post-mortem staining of the body that shows the time when the blood settles down to the lowest level.'

'Time of death? I shouldn't have thought it was the time that mattered. It's *who* dunnit.'

'Or it's *when* dunnit?' I suggested. 'Perhaps that's what makes this case interesting.'

The next morning I found myself alone at breakfast-time in the Mess with Major Sykes, who was now in uniform and methodically consuming eggs, bacon and sausages. 'Sandy told us you were brilliant at murders,' he said, an accusation to which I had to plead guilty.

'Of course Sandy's a great one for jokes, usually of the practical variety.'

'I can imagine that.'

'Oh yes.' The Major gave me an instance: 'We had some sort of man from the Ministry out here – Under-Secretary at Defence, something like that. And Sandy turned up in the Mess pretending to be a visiting German officer. He'd got hold of the uniform somewhere. God knows where. Of course Sandy speaks German. About the only one of us who does. Anyway, he started doing Nazi salutes and singing the "Horst Wessel". Nearly scared the fellow from the Ministry out of his few remaining wits.'

'Does your colonel allow that sort of thing?' I wondered.

'Oh, Hugh was away that night, somewhere at Brigade H.Q. But no one can really be angry with Sandy. He's a sort of licensed jester. Puts on the panto, you know. *Aladdin* last year. I was the Dame.' He turned and nodded to one of the many framed regimental photographs on the wall behind him. It showed Major Sykes with other members of the pantomime cast.

'You have hidden talents, Major,' I had to admit my surprise.

'Oh, it's Sandy brought it out in me. He's such a wonderful "producer" – is that the word for it? He can get the best out of everyone. Tell me. How do you find the U.K.?'

'Go out of that door, turn West and keep straight on.' I shouldn't have done it and the Major didn't smile.

'You're a joker, aren't you?' he said. 'Like Sandy. I only asked because I'm retiring next year. Got to. Back to live with my sister in Surrey. I never married – not to anyone except the Regiment.'

'Now you've got to divorce?'

'It'll be a bit of a wrench, although I wasn't born into it. I'm not like Sandy; his father was a colonel, of course, and his grandfather a lieutenant-general. Sandy was born into the Cavalry.'

'With a silver bit in his mouth?'

'Oh, he's got plenty of money. But generous with it. He's paying for you, you know . . .'

'For *me*? No. I didn't know that.' It came as a surprise, and I didn't know whether I wanted to feel so much indebted to the young Defending Officer.

'When anyone's in trouble, like this young Trooper Boyne' –

the Major explained the situation – 'Sandy'll always come to their rescue. He'd do anything for the Regiment.'

'Even making you a Dame?' At which point Major Sykes folded his arms and did a surprising Dame's North country accent.

'Where's that naughty boy Aladdin now?' he crowed, and then added, in his own voice, 'Yes. He'd even do that.'

After breakfast Sandy Ransom, an officer so popular, I later discovered, that it seemed inevitable that Trooper Danny Boyne should choose him for his defence, and I sat in a small office set aside in the guard room and interviewed our client. He seemed shy, indeed nervous, of me, and directed many of his answers to Captain Sandy Ransom, who perched on a small upright chair beneath which slept his favourite lurcher.

'You said Sergeant Jumbo Wilson picked on you,' I started at the beginning. 'Why do you think that was?'

'I don't know.'

'No idea?'

'I don't know, I told you.' And then he turned to Sandy as if to explain, 'I told him.'

'Mr Rumpole's here to help you. Trust him.' It was, I supposed, an order from a superior officer, but it didn't seem to have a great deal of effect. I picked up Danny's statement and went on to one of the most damaging parts of the evidence.

'Did you ever say you'd carve him up?'

'That was a long time ago.'

'About three weeks, apparently, before he died.'

'Jumbo Wilson came into the disco, throwing his weight about like he always did' – the Trooper started to talk more easily – 'shouting, so people'd notice him. I may have said that to some boys by the bar.'

'Some boys who're coming to give evidence!' I reminded him.

'Witnesses from another regiment,' Sandy said as though that disposed of the matter. 'Of course,' I remembered, 'seraphs wouldn't give evidence against each other – but you admit you said it?' I asked Danny.

'Like you'd say about anyone that picked on you: "I'll carve him up." It's like a common saying.'

'Danny comes from Glasgow.' Sandy supplied what must have seemed to him an obvious explanation. 'Is that going to be our defence?' Not if I had anything to do with it, I thought. I came on to the fatal occasion. 'On that evening, Saturday November 22nd . . .'

'We were practising for the panto Captain Ransom puts on at Christmas.' Danny now seemed more confident.

'I can confirm that.' Sandy confirmed it.

'Until when?'

'It was about nine o'clock.'

'Or 21.00 exactly.' I wasn't sure whether I was getting the answers from the client or the Defending Officer.

'I went back to the married quarters block. I changed and went out again. I was meeting my mates in the square. Just in front of my quarters.'

'Where?'

'Just on the square. In front of the quarters.'

'And there you met . . .?'

'Finchie and Goldie.'

'Troopers Finch and Goldsmith,' Sandy gave me the names and added, for good measure, 'I can confirm that too. I happened to see them. I stayed on a little while after the rehearsal and then I saw the three men when I came out.'

'Where did you three go to?'

'The disco.'

'The Rosenkavalier?'

'Got there about 21.30, didn't you?' Sandy asked, and Danny Boy said, 'About that. Yes, sir.'

'Did you see Sergeant Wilson?' I asked.

'He was there, yes. In a corner.'

'Your statement says the place was dark and very crowded. Are you sure you recognized the Sergeant?'

'I could tell that bastard anywhere.' At least he was sure about that, but I thought he could do with a little training as a witness. 'When you give your evidence, Trooper Boyne,' I told him, 'please try not to call the dear departed a bastard. It won't exactly endear you to the tribunal. How was the Sergeant dressed?'

'Casual – a sports jacket, I think. A shirt without a tie.'

'Not in a frock?'

'Not when I saw him.' He seemed a little puzzled, but when I asked, 'And then you saw this other man?', he answered with quiet conviction, 'I saw this German.'

'How did you know he was German?'

'He was speaking Kraut to the girl by the door. Then he spotted Wilson and went over to his table.'

'A man in a black leather jacket. With spiky hair . . .' I read from the statement our client had made to the Investigating Officer.

'This punk.' Danny spoke with a good deal of dislike. Basically, I thought, he was a very conventional young man.

'Did the Sergeant speak to him at all?'

'Just "Helmut". We heard him call out, "Helmut."'

'What else?'

'We didn't hear what they said. They sat together in the corner; they were still there when we left.'

'Which was at, approximately?'

'01.00 hours, wasn't it, Danny?' Again Captain Sandy Ransom supplied the time and our client nodded his head.

'And you never saw Sergeant Jumbo Wilson alive again?'

'Never!'

'And you got back into the barracks over the back wall?'

'We don't bother about booking in and out at the guard room.'

'Especially as you were confined to barracks.' Sandy smiled indulgently as a schoolmaster might at the prank of a favourite pupil.

'That was after a wee fight I had. A couple of weeks ago. Down at the disco . . .' Danny started to explain, but again the Defending Officer took up the story. 'That was the fight when he got the blood on his cuff. It's in the evidence.'

'Tell me' – I spoke to our client who wouldn't have a favourite captain to help him give evidence in Court – 'just tell me in your own words.'

'It was a German boy what was taking the mickey out of my

wife. Out of Hanni. I took him outside and gave him a couple of taps. He must have bled a bit.'

'A German boy with a Class AB Blood Group just like the Sergeant's?' I asked, feeling my side was getting over-confident. 'A blood group only enjoyed by 3 to 4 per cent of the population?' I stood up, put away my pen and started to tie up my brief. 'So it comes to this. You saw the Sergeant alive at one in the morning. And he was found at 4 a.m. after the Military Police got an anonymous phone call.'

'From a German,' Sandy reminded me.

'In German, anyway. So. Giving the Sergeant time to leave the bar, slip into his frock – wherever he did that – quarrel with whoever he quarrelled with . . .' 'His friend, Helmut. Isn't that the most likely explanation?' Sandy interrupted, but I went on. 'When he was found he couldn't have been dead much more than two and a half hours.'

'The fellows prosecuting accept that.' Sandy was reassuring me.

'But do I accept it?' I asked, and Danny, who had been looking at me doubtfully, spoke, for the first time I thought, his mind. 'Don't you believe me, Mr Rumpole?'

'I'm not here to believe anything, I'm here to defend you,' I told my client. 'But some time or another it might be a bit of a help, old darling, if you started to tell me the truth.'

After we had left our client, I asked Sandy to drive me to the scene of the crime. The Rosenkavalier disco-bar looked small and somewhat dingy by daylight with its neon sign – an outline of a silver rose – switched off. The place was locked up and we inspected the side alley which was, in fact, a narrow lane which joined the streets in front of and behind the disco, so a body might have been driven up from behind the building and delivered at the side entrance. On the other side of the lane was the high wall and regular windows of a tallish block of flats. Sandy's lurcher was sniffing at the side entrance, perhaps scenting old blood. I asked the Captain, 'None of the neighbours saw or heard anything?'

'They wouldn't, would they?'

'Why do you say that?'

'They're all Germans.'

'The telephone call was made in German.'

'By his boyfriend perhaps.' The Defending Officer clearly had his own explanation of the crime.

'Boyfriend?'

'Helmut. He might not have been sure if he'd killed Jumbo Wilson. Perhaps he had a fit of remorse.'

'Why do you think "Jumbo" had a boyfriend? He was married.'

'What's that got to do with it?' Sandy smiled and then said seriously, 'You were right, of course, Danny wasn't telling you the whole truth. You know why Jumbo picked on him?'

'Tell me.'

'Because the Sar'nt made a heavy pass and Danny Boy told him to satisfy his lust on the regimental goat, or words to that effect.'

I tried to think of the sequence of events. The Sergeant had left the disco and gone somewhere, perhaps into the block of flats, changed into a bizarre costume, been knifed and dumped in the lane. 'So Helmut stabbed Jumbo in a lovers' quarrel after a bit of convivial dressing up?' I considered the Captain's theory.

'Isn't that the obvious solution?' Sandy obviously regarded the problem as solved.

'I suppose it'd get you out of trouble,' I said, and when he laughed and asked, 'Me?', I explained, 'I mean, the Regiment, of course.'

I was tired that night and I left the Mess early. I got a torch from Borrow, the Mess Attendant, to light my way across the darkened square. As I left, Sandy had sat down to the piano, and I heard him singing: 'Kiss me goodnight, Sergeant Wilson, Tuck me in my little wooden bed . . .'

I came to the corner of the married quarters wing. I could hear the thin wail of the Boynes' baby, awake and crying, and I saw a curtain pulled back for a moment and a grey-haired, handsome woman, whom I took to be Mrs Wilson, looked out

frowning with anger towards the source of the sound. Then she
twitched the curtain across the window again, and I sank to my
knees behind the dustbins at the foot of the iron staircase, and
made a close examination, with the help of Borrow's torch, of
the ground and the bottom stair.

I was in that position when Lieutenant Tony Ross, the Duty
Officer in uniform that night, discovered me and looked down,
as I thought, rather strangely. 'Hail to thee, bright seraph,' I
greeted him. 'Thought I'd dropped a few marks down here.
Must've had a hole in my pocket.'

'Can I help at all, sir?' The young officer asked.

'Not at all. No.' I struggled to my feet. 'Sleep well, Lieutenant.
It's only money, isn't it?'

The court martial, which I don't think anyone suspected was
my first, took place in an ornate nineteenth-century German
civic building, and in a room with a great deal of carved stone-
work and a painted ceiling. Everyone was clearly identified, like
the members of a television chat-show panel, by a little board
with their title painted on it set on the table in front of them.
The tribunal appointed to try Danny Boyne consisted of a president (a Brigadier Humphries of the Transport Corps, Sandy
told me), a lieutenant-colonel, a major and two captains, one of
whom was a uniformed, lady W.R.A.C. officer. And seated
beside the President, I was surprised to see my old friend and
one-time Chamber mate, George Frobisher, who had deserted the
dusty arena down the Bailey (well, George was never much of a
cross-examiner) for the security of the Circuit Bench, and then,
apparently in search of adventure, become a judge advocate,
stationed in Germany advising court martials on the legal aspects
of soldiers' trials. George sat beside the President now, wearing
his wig and gown, and explained every point in the proceedings
with tireless courtesy to the accused trooper, in a way which
seemed to show the Military as more civilized than some of the
learned judges down the Bailey, notably his Honour Roger
Bullingham known to me as the Mad Bull.

So, 04916323, Trooper Boyne of the 37th and 39th, the Duke

of Clarence's Own Lancers, was charged with 'a civilian offence contrary to Section 70 of the Army Act 1955, that is to say, murder, in that on the 22nd and 23rd days of November last he murdered 75334188, Sergeant J. Wilson of the Duke of Clarence's Own'. A plea of not guilty was entered and after George had painstakingly explained the roles of everyone in Court, and advised Danny to relax and sit comfortably and make any comment that occurred to him to Mr Rumpole, his barrister, Lieutenant-Colonel Watford, was invited to rise from the prosecution table and outline the case against the Trooper.

Sandy Ransom (at last parted from his lurcher, who was being cared for in the Special Investigations Branch Office) and I sat at the defence table next to our client, who had an N.C.O. beside, and one behind him, holding his hat and belt, which he wouldn't wear, so Sandy explained, until he gave evidence. There was no dock, which again seemed a better arrangement than at the Bailey, where an accused person is penned into a sort of eminence which hints at their guilt. Taking George's advice, I sat comfortably and let the Prosecuting Officer begin.

And here was another plus. Lieutenant-Colonel Michael Watford, O.B.E., the Army Legal Services, was tall, youngish (almost everyone seems youngish to me), bespectacled and sensible. He had trained as a solicitor, and had, as it so happened, been well known to me as young Mike Watford, articled clerk with Butchers & Stringfellow, a firm who had often briefed me at the Bailey and who sent young Mike out to help with taking notes and witness statements, a task he performed a great deal better than the senior partners. So, from the whirligig of time, Mike Watford was known to me as a good egg; in fact, I would go so far as to say that he was a double yoker.

As Lieutenant-Colonel Mike outlined his case, my eyes strayed to our judges or, would they more correctly be called, the Jury of Army Officers, because they would decide all the facts and leave the law to George. I had never had to face a jury in uniform before. I tried flashing a charming smile at the W.R.A.C. officer but it had no effect on her whatever. She was listening to Mike's opening with a frown of fierce concentration.

Mike's first witness was a young lady with a good deal of rather dried-up blonde hair, tricked out in tight, artificial leopard-skin trousers and a low-cut black silk vest. Chains and bracelets clinked as she moved, and she looked as though she had better things to do than take part in the army exercises of a foreign power. Her English was, however, so much better than my non-existent German that it was fully equal to all the demands made on it that day.

Mike Watford got her to admit that her name was Greta Schmerz, and she worked at hanging up the coats in the Rosenkavalier; when business was brisk, apparently, she also helped out at the bar. She identified the photograph of Sergeant Wilson as someone she had seen on occasions at the disco-bar. Mike then went so far as to tell her that we knew that, on the night in question the Sergeant was stabbed outside the disco-bar.

'We know nothing of the sort,' I rose to protest, and drove on through a mild 'Don't we, Mr Rumpole?' from George. 'We know he was found dead outside the disco. We haven't the foggiest idea where he was stabbed.'

'Very well' – Mike Watford conceded the point – 'he was found dead. Had you seen him in the disco that night?'

'I can't remember,' Greta told us after a pause.

'And *that* young man, Trooper Boyne, sitting there, was *he* in the disco that night?' the Prosecutor asked.

'He was there, I remember him.' Miss Schmerz was sure. Having achieved this, Watford sat down and Rumpole arose.

'Fraulein Schmerz. So far as Sergeant Wilson, the man in the photograph, was concerned, he may have been there that night, or he may not. You simply don't know?'

'He was there. Danny and the other two saw him.' I got a loudly whispered reminder from the Defending Officer.

'Please, Captain. I do know your case!' I quietened Sandy and addressed the witness. 'Do you remember someone coming to the disco with spiky hair and black leather jacket?'

'I do remember.'

'Helmut!' Sandy whispered again triumphantly, and I muttered, 'I know it's much more exciting than manoeuvres, but do try and stay relatively calm.' I asked Miss Schmerz, 'What time did you see him?'

'How should I know that?'

'How indeed? Was it late?'

'I think . . . perhaps midnight . . .'

'Well, that's very helpful. Did he speak to you?'

'The punk man? He spoke to me.'

'In German?'

'Yes. He asked if I had seen the English sergeant.'

'Did he say the name Wilson?'

'He said that.'

'Tell me, Fraulein Schmerz.' I was curious to know. 'All the soldiers came to the disco in civilian clothes, didn't they? Jeans and anoraks and plimsolls – that sort of costume?'

'They weren't in soldier's dress,' she agreed.

'So you couldn't tell if that man in the photograph was a sergeant or not?'

'No.'

'Did you know his name was Wilson?'

'I didn't know his name.'

'So there seems very little point in the punk asking you the question? Yes, thank you, Fraulein Schmerz.'

I sat down, and Sandy looked at me with obvious displeasure. I was, it must have seemed to him, a very ordinary barrister indeed. 'What are you trying to do?' he asked me, and all I could whisper back was, 'Strangely enough, my dear old Defending Officer, I think I'm trying to find out the truth.'

The Court was still and respectful when the Sergeant's widow was called to give her evidence. George asked her if she'd care to sit, and when she preferred to stand, tall, grey-haired and dignified, by the witness chair, he assured her that she wouldn't be kept there long. In fact, Mike Watford only asked her a few questions. She identified the photograph of her dead husband, whom she had last seen alive when he left their flat in the married quarters not very long after nine o'clock on the night of 22 November. When I rose to cross-examine I told the witness that we all sympathized with her in the tragic situation in which she found herself, and went on to ask if Trooper Boyne and his German wife, Hanni, didn't live very near her little flat?

'Almost next door.' The voice was disapproving and the face stony.

'Did you see anything of them?'

'She was always at the dustbins. Putting things in them. Things the baby dirtied, most like.'

'Most likely.' I turned to another topic. 'You were at home all the evening and the night when your husband died?'

'Yes, I was. I never went out.'

'And Trooper Boyne was never in your flat at any time?'

'No.' The answer was decided.

'Did you ever ask either Mr or Mrs Boyne to your home?'

'Of course not.' The suggestion clearly struck her as ridiculous.

'Did you not invite them because your husband was a sergeant and my client was a humble trooper?'

'Not *just* because of that. She was one of them, wasn't she?'

'One of what?'

'One of them Germans.'

'You don't like Germans, Mrs Wilson?' The question seemed unnecessary; I asked it all the same.

'*They* did it.'

'They did what?'

'That's why he was out there in the street, out there dressed like that! They took him . . . He . . . He was gone . . . Gone . . .'

'Don't distress yourself, Madam.' George was using his best bedside manner. 'Which Germans do you mean killed your husband?'

'I don't know. How could I know?' She was talking very quietly and calmly, like someone, I thought, on the verge of tears.

'You say some Germans killed him?'

'With respect' – I had to correct him – 'she didn't say that. She said Germans "took" him. Perhaps the shorthand writer . . .'

The lady with the shorthand book stood and found the phrase

with unusual rapidity. 'She said "they took him . . . He was gone . . ."'

'I assume by "took" she meant kill.' George seemed to have little patience with my interruption.

'In my submission it would be extremely dangerous to assume anything of the sort,' I had to tell him. 'She said "took". The person who killed him may be someone entirely different.'

'What exactly are you suggesting, Mr Rumpole?' George frowned at me. It wasn't a fair question to an old Chambers mate who was, as yet, not entirely clear what he was suggesting. 'I hope that may become quite clear in my cross-examination of other witnesses,' I said to keep him quiet. 'I really don't want to prolong this witness's ordeal by keeping her in the witness-box a moment longer.' So I sat down and Sandy gave me another of his cross whispers, 'Why don't you ask her the vital question?'

'Which is?'

'Wasn't Jumbo Wilson a pooftah?'

'For a soldier, old darling,' I whispered back, 'you really know so little about murder. You don't endear yourself to the Court by asking the weeping widow if her husband wasn't a pooftah. It sort of adds insult to injury. No, I didn't ask the vital question. But I got the vital answer.'

'What was that?' Captain Sandy looked doubtful.

'They "took" him. That's what she said. Now wasn't that rather a curious way of putting it?' And as we sat in silence waiting for the next witness, some lines of old Robert Browning wandered idly into my mind: 'Some with lives that came to nothing, some with deeds as well undone,/ Death stepped tacitly and *took* them where they never see the sun . . .' So did Mrs Wilson mean that death had taken Jumbo, or did she mean something else entirely?

Now the door opened and an important-looking gentleman in the uniform of the Royal Army Medical Corps came to the witness table and was sworn by a member of the Court. I knew he would be the subject of my most important cross-examination, and I gazed at him with the close attention a matador gives to a bull as it enters the ring and does its preliminary business with the picadors. Lieutenant-Colonel Basil Borders, Doctor of Medicine and Fellow of The Royal College of Pathologists, was a tall, pale man with a thickening waist, ginger hair going thin, and rimless spectacles. He appeared, from the way he took the oath and answered Mike Watford's early questions, to have a considerable opinion of his own importance, and when he was asked to give his post-mortem findings he answered clearly enough.

'The deceased was a well-nourished man, forty-five years old, with no signs of disease,' Lieutenant-Colonel Borders told us. 'There were indications of a fairly recent high consumption of alcohol and a heavy meal. Death had been caused by a stab wound, with a flat, sharp object such as a knife which entered the abdomen and penetrated the abdominal aorta.'

I will not weary the reader with an account of the Army Pathologist's evidence-in-chief. It followed the lines of his statement and was thorough, painstaking and predictable. I opened my cross-examination with a dramatic performance which Captain Sandy had suggested and now staged with relish. He stood up with his back to me as I put an arm about his neck and appeared to stab him from behind with my pencil.

'One arm across the windpipe to stop the victim crying out and an upward stab from the back, penetrating the heart. Isn't that the accepted military manner of using a knife, Doctor?' I asked as I acted the commando role.

'That is the method taught in commando training.' Borders was clearly distressed by our courtroom histrionics.

'But the Sergeant had a knife jabbed into the stomach?'

'Yes, indeed.'

'So inexpertly that it might not even have been fatal?'

'It might not have been.'

'If it hadn't happened to penetrate the aorta?'

'Indeed.'

'It looks far more like a civilian than a military job, doesn't it, Doctor?'

'Perhaps,' was as far as the witness would go, but Sandy whispered, 'Oh, I like it,' as he resumed his seat, his great moment over. I just hoped he would enjoy the rest of my cross-examination as much.

'And the knife – there's nothing to indicate that it was a bayonet?' I asked the Pathologist.

'As I have said, I believe the blade was flat.'

'Not a bayonet or any sort of army knife?'

'There is no particular indication of that,' Borders agreed.

'It could've been the sort of sharp, pointed carving-knife available in any kitchen?'

'Yes, indeed.' He was finding the cross-examination easier than he had expected and was relaxed and smiling round the court. No one, I noticed, smiled back.

'Available to any civilian?'

'Available to Helmut!' the irrepressible Captain Sandy whispered as the witness answered, 'Yes.'

'So far so good but I knew I was coming to an area of likely disagreement. I decided to lull the witness into a feeling of false security, hoping he would be taken by surprise when the attack was launched. I leant forward, spoke in a silken voice and poured out a double dose of flattery: 'Lieutenant-Colonel Borders, you are a very distinguished and experienced patholigist and no doubt you carried out a most thorough post-mortem examination.'

'Thank you.' The witness preened himself visibly. 'Indeed I did.'

'And we are all *most* grateful for the enormous trouble you have clearly taken in this matter.' George joined in the smiles now and the witness was even more grateful. 'Thank you very much.'

'Rarely have I heard such absolutely expert evidence!' Well, *I* wasn't on oath.

'You're very kind.'

'Just one small detail. What were your conclusions about the frock?'

'The frock?' He looked puzzled and I knew I was on to something.

'There is a cut in the scarlet frock the Sergeant was wearing and a good deal of staining. Of course you fitted the hole in the dress to the hole in the body?' I assumed politely.

'I don't think I did.' The Lieutenant-Colonel looked at the Court as though it were a point of no importance, and I looked at him with rising and incredulous outrage. Finally, I managed a gasp of amazement on the word '*Indeed?*'

'The dress was a matter for the Scientific Officer. I don't believe I examined it at all.'

'Lieutenant-Colonel Borders!' I called the man to order. 'Are you representing yourself as an expert witness?'

'I am.' There was a flush now, rising to the roots of the ginger hair.

'A person capable of carrying out a post-mortem examination in a reasonably intelligent way?'

'Of course!'

'And you can't even tell this Court' – I spoke with rising fury – 'if the Sergeant was wearing the frock when he was stabbed, or if it was cut and put on him *after his death?*'

'No, I can't tell you that, I'm afraid.' Again he did his best to make it sound as irrelevant as the weather in Manchester.

'You're afraid?' I gave my best performance of contemptuous anger. 'Then I'm afraid you're unlikely to have sufficient expertise to be of much assistance to the Court on another vital matter.'

'Mr Rumpole . . .' George was trying to call a halt to this mayhem, but I had done with the cape and was moving in with the sword and not to be interrupted. 'I refer to the time of death. Have you any useful contribution to make on that matter?'

'Mr Rumpole.' George could contain himself no longer. 'I know that you are in the habit of conducting murder cases at the Old Bailey with all the lack of inhibition of, shall we say, a commando raid.'

'Oh, sir.' I smiled at the old darling. 'You're too kind.'

'I think I should make it clear that the Army expects far more peaceful proceedings.' George spoke as severely as he knew how. 'The Military Court is accustomed to seeing all witnesses treated with quiet courtesy. I hope you'll find yourself able to fall into our way of doing things.'

'I'm extremely grateful, sir.' I thought it best to apologize.

'The Court will excuse me if I showed myself, for a moment, to be as clumsy and inexpert in my profession as this officer clearly is in his . . .'

'Mr Rumpole!' George was about to launch another missile in my direction, but I turned to the witness. 'Lieutenant-Colonel. Tell me, is that higher than a colonel?'

'No, lower.' Borders was not pleased.

'Oh, I'm sorry. I'm sure you'll soon earn promotion. You came from England to do this post-mortem?'

'Yes. I was flown out from the U.K.'

'And were you told the brief facts of the case?'

'I was told that the suspect had been in a disco where the Sergeant had been seen by witnesses around 01.00 hours.'

'And a telephone call about the stabbing had been received by the Police at 03.45 hours. So when the Army Doctor arrived at 04.15 hours the Sergeant could only have been dead, say, about three hours?'

'That is so.'

'And yet there was a definite progress of rigor mortis?'

'Yes. That was found.' Borders was wary of another attack, and this was the vital part of my case. I pressed on quickly: 'Which you would not normally expect in the first three hours after death?'

'Rigor has been known to occur within thirty minutes,' he told *me*, who had won the Penge Bungalow case on rigor, among other factors.

'In *very* exceptional cases,' I told him.

'Well, yes . . .'

'And the temperature of the body had dropped by some six degrees.'

'Yes.'

'I have here Professor Ackerman's work *The Times of Death* in which he deals with falling temperatures.' In fact this volume, together with my old *Oxford Book of English Verse*, had been my constant bedtime reading in Germany. 'Let me put this to you. Normally wouldn't that indicate death at least six hours before?'

'It was a cold night in November, if you remember.'

'That is your answer?' I hope I sounded as though I couldn't believe it.

'Yes.' Borders looked at the faces of the Court members for comfort and received none. '*Hypostasis*,' I gave him the word as though I thought he might not have heard it before. 'The staining caused by blood settling down to the lower parts of the body after death. Were there not large areas of staining when the body was found? Just look at the photographs.' Borders opened the volume of post-mortem photographs on the witness table in front of him and I thought that he did so somewhat reluctantly. 'Isn't that degree of staining consistent with death, let's say, some six hours earlier?'

'It might be consistent with that, yes,' he admitted reluctantly. 'Hypostasis is subject to many variations.'

'In fact everything in those photographs is consistent with death having occurred around nine o'clock on the previous evening!'

'Mr Rumpole ...' George was now looking genuinely puzzled.

'Yes, sir?'

'Aren't you forgetting your own client's statement? And the statements of Troopers Finch and ...'

'Goldsmith, sir,' I helped him.

'Goldsmith. Exactly so. They saw the Sergeant in the disco at 1 a.m. He could hardly have died at nine the previous evening.'

'Oh, I don't know. Isn't there some sort of biblical parallel?' This was all the help I'd give old George. I said to the witness, 'One other little matter on the photographs. Are there not a number of pale patches on the stains?'

'Yes, there are.' He was looking at the pictures as though he hated them.

'Representing places where the body rested. Doesn't that indicate one thing clearly to you?'

'What do you mean exactly?'

'What do I mean? Exactly? I mean that the body had been moved after death. That's what I mean.'

There was a long pause, and then another reluctant admission from the witness who said, 'I think that may very well be so.'

It was over. A bit of a triumph, as I hope you will agree. I awarded myself two ears and a tail as I said, 'Thank you very much, Lieutenant Borders,' extremely politely and sat down.

Modestly satisfied as I had been with my cross-examination of the Army Pathologist, it had in no way delighted Captain Sandy Ransom, who sank lower in his seat during the course of it. As we came out of Court at the end of the day he was grumbling, 'Died by nine o'clock. He couldn't have! By nine o'clock he hadn't even met Helmut.'

'Helmut, of course.' I did my best to sound apologetic. 'Why do I always seem to forget about Helmut?'

'We thought we were getting an ordinary barrister. Do ordinary barristers try so damned hard to get their clients convicted?' Sandy was very angry. '*Someone*'s got to do something for that boy!' And he moved off to liberate his lurcher.

Then I heard the soft voice of a young woman who had clearly learnt to speak English with a Glasgow Irish accent.

'Mr Rumpole! About the blood on Danny's cuff . . .' I turned to her and it was impossible, in spite of Mrs Wilson's evidence, to think of her as English or German – she was just an extremely beautiful girl in very great distress. 'Yes, I am Hanni Boyne. It was the old shirt,' she told me. 'He wore it when he had the fight. I hadn't washed it, you see. Then he wore it again that night. He didn't remember. I will say all that to them.'

I bet you will, I thought. What lies love makes people tell, for I couldn't imagine Hanni failing to wash Danny Boy's shirts. 'I really shouldn't be talking to you about your evidence,' I told her. Out of the corner of my eye I could see Lieutenant-Colonel Mike Watford coming out of Court.

'You will do your best for Danny, sir. We have been so happy, so awfully happy. The three of us.' I knew she was telling the truth then, but all I could do was mutter something about the case going reasonably well – nothing of any real use to her when she was sick for certainties – and take Mike Watford's arm and steer him to a quiet end of a marble-paved corridor and under the ponderous stone arches.

'Soft you, a word or two before you go, Mike,' I started, doing my best to cash in on the past. 'We used to get on moderately well, didn't we, when you were an articled clerk with Butchers & Stringfellow.'

'I always enjoyed our cases,' Mike admitted.

'Went after the evidence, didn't we, and got at the truth on more than one occasion?'

'You always had a nose for the evidence, Mr Rumpole.'

'So did you, as a young lad, Mike.'

'All this flattery means you're after something.' Lieutenant-Colonel Watford was not born yesterday.

'Oh, young Mike, as astute as ever. Be honest, you're not happy about the evidence on the time of death are you?'

There was a silence then. Mike Watford stopped walking and looked at me. I knew it would not be his style to tell me anything less than the truth. 'To be honest, not particularly.' And then he asked me. 'When do you think it was?'

'The time? Around 21.00 hours, as you would say,' I told him. 'The place, the bottom of the iron staircase outside the Sergeant's married quarters. Looked for any blood traces round there, have you?'

'No. As a matter of fact.' He looked thoughtful. 'No.'

'Oh, young Mike Watford! What do you want to do? Win your case or discover the truth?'

'I think the Army would want us to discover the truth.' He had no doubt about it.

'Then, old darling, may I make a suggestion?' And I walked on with him, giving him a list of things to do as I had when we had worked together so happily down the Old Bailey.

When I got back to the barracks I sought an appointment with the Colonel. After I had seen him, I went back to my quarters and soaked for a long time in the excellently hot water provided by the British Army. I wondered how many times I had washed away the exhaustion of a day in Court, and the invisible grime which comes from a long association with criminal behaviour, in an early evening bath-tub. Then I put on a clean shirt and walked across the darkened barracks square to the Mess.

My journey was interrupted by the roar and rattle of a jeep which drew up beside me. Captain Sandy Ransom and his lurcher jumped out, and I saw, with some sinking of the heart, that he was holding a rather muddy black leather jacket. 'Triumph!' he shouted at me. 'I've found it. I've found the evidence.'

It seemed that he had gone for a walk by the old Badweisheim canal after what he regarded as an extremely unsatisfactory day in Court. The lurcher had started to sniff around in a pile of loose earth, and there, by chance, someone had tried to bury the clear indication of their guilt. 'It's Helmut's jacket.' Sandy had no doubt about it.

'Of course it is,' I agreed, and went on to a more important matter. 'I've spoken to your colonel and he's dining in the Mess tonight. I hope you can join us.'

'Aren't you going to ring Watford?' For a moment Sandy looked like a schoolboy deprived of a treat. 'Aren't you going to tell the Prosecution about the new evidence?'

'I really think that can wait until after dinner.'

We were once again a small gathering in the Mess: Colonel Undershaft, Major Sykes, Captain Ransom, Lieutenant Hammick and Ross, who was that night's Duty Officer. When the port was on the table I sat back and addressed them, having refused to answer any questions during the service of the usual excellent dinner. I felt that I was speaking to them as though I were in Court, and they formed the tribunal who would finally have to decide the strange case of the murder of Sergeant Jumbo Wilson. First I filled my glass and sent the decanter on round the table.

'I know you don't usually toast the Regiment after dinner,' I started, 'except on formal evenings in the Mess. But it's such a power over you all, isn't it, the Regiment? Blenheim, Malplaquet, Waterloo, Balaclava, El Alamein,' I intoned, looked round at them and raised my glass:

'This seraph-band . . .
It was a heavenly sight!
They stood as signals to the land,
Each one a lovely light.

And the Regiment always rallies round a seraph in trouble. You
told me that, didn't you, Sandy?'

'Of course we do.' Sandy was opposite me, nodding through
the candlesticks. 'That's why we got you out here. Not that
you've done much for the boy so far.'

'So when Sergeant Wilson was stabbed to death,' I went on
with my final speech, 'you couldn't have it said that it was done
by a seraph, could you? Not by one of the heavenly band. Far
better that the crime should have been committed by an unknown
German called Helmut with a black leather jacket and a punk
hairdo. Who better to take the blame, after all, than one of the
old enemy? An enemy from the war you're all too young to
remember.'

'Are you suggesting that the officers of this regiment . . .?'
The Colonel had never looked more deeply disturbed.

'Not the officers, Colonel,' I hastened to answer him. 'One
officer, the joker in the pack. Of course, pinning the crime on
the mysterious Helmut took a lot of organization and a good
many risks. But perhaps that was part of the attraction. It took
the place of war.'

The Mess was very quiet; Borrow had left us. Old generals
and defunct colonels on their rearing chargers looked down on
us. Behind the flickering candles, Sandy was smiling. Hugh
Undershaft asked me exactly what I knew.

'I'm not sure what I *know*, Colonel. Not for certain. But I'll
tell you what I think. I think Danny Boy and his mates met by
the dustbins at the foot of the Sergeant's staircase and found him
there. Dead. I think they told an officer. An officer who was
there. With a jeep – his usual method of transport. Danny helped
this officer move the body, hence the blood on his cuff. It was
the Sergeant's blood not the blood of another mysterious German.
Then the lads, the young seraphs, went into *Der Rosenkavalier*

so they could lie and say they'd seen the Sergeant there after midnight. Meanwhile, the Captain of the Seraphs was unloading a body in a dark alley . . .'

'Dressed in a frock?' the Colonel asked.

'That was your joker's contribution. Did he have a dress among the props for the pantomime, one large enough for the Dame? I think he dressed up a dead body.'

'Why on earth should anyone do that?' Sandy sounded incredulous.

'Why? To make some sort of homosexual crime of passion more credible, or as a sign of disapproval? The Sergeant brought no credit on the Regiment by having himself murdered, did he?'

There was a long silence then; the officers were looking at me, and I felt an intruder, never particularly welcome, in their private world. Then Sandy said, 'Aren't you forgetting Helmut?'

'Oh, I never believed in Helmut, the mysterious German who came so conveniently and asked for the Sergeant by name. All the girl remembered was the spiky hair. What do you use in the pantomime, Sandy? Hair lacquer? Hair gel? Was that your own black leather jacket you found so conveniently?' The port had returned to me and I refilled my glass. I felt tired after a long case, and I wanted to leave them, to go home and forget their problem. 'I suppose, in a way, you were a first-rate Defending Officer. You wanted to get Danny Boy out of trouble and you thought he was guilty. I always believed he was innocent; he was a boy from Glasgow with the good sense to marry a German girl because they loved each other.'

There was another long, thoughtful silence, and then the Colonel spoke to me, 'So, may we ask, who, in your opinion, killed Sar'nt Wilson?'

'Oh, don't worry,' I could reassure him, 'the joker never went so far as that. He could move his body, dress him in a frock, but not murder him.'

'Then *who* . . .'

'I always thought that it must've been bad enough to have been fancied by Sergeant Wilson. It must have been hell on earth to be married to him.' As I said it, in the warm Mess, I shivered slightly. I was doing a job which wasn't mine, making accusations and bringing home guilt.

While I was talking to the officers of the Duke of Clarence's Own Lancers, a Captain Betteridge of the Special Investigations Branch called at the flat up the iron staircase in the married quarters. He found it spotlessly clean and shining. He saw the polished furniture and the framed photographs of Sergeant and Mrs Wilson on their wedding day, and of Mrs Wilson's father, a sergeant-major who had been killed at Arnhem. He opened a drawer in the sideboard and saw the gleaming, black-handled carving-knife, and he told Mrs Wilson that he wanted to question her further about the events around nine o'clock on the evening her husband died. It was not long before she told him everything, as she had been secretly longing to do since the day she killed Sergeant Wilson.

> Farewell the plumed troop and the big wars,
> That make ambition virtue! O, farewell!
> Farewell the neighing steed and the shrill trump,
> The spirit-stirring drum, the ear-piercing fife,
> The royal banner, and all the quality,
>   Pride, pomp and circumstance of glorious war!

Farewell, anyway, to the barracks of the 37th and 39th Lancers at Badweisheim. Lieutenant Tony Ross drove me to the airport and Captain Ransom, for some reason, didn't turn out to say goodbye. Danny Boy thanked me a little brusquely, as though I had, after all, let down the Regiment. Only his wife, Hanni, was genuinely and, I expect, everlastingly, grateful. I went back to Civvy Street and, in due course, I was ensconced with Hilda in the bar of the Old Gloucester.

'Where's ex-Major Johnnie?' I asked her.

'He got a job as secretary of a golf club in Devon. We had a farewell lunch. He bought me champagne.'

'Decent of him.'

'We had a really good chat. When you're with us, he told me, you do all the chatting.'

'Oh, do I?'

'He got me wondering.'

'Oh, really. What about?'

'I suppose what my life would have been like if I hadn't got you to marry me, Rumpole.'

'Did you do that?'

'Of course. You don't decide things like that on your own.'

She was right. I can make all sorts of decisions for my clients, but practically none for Rumpole.

'I might have kept up my singing,' Hilda told me, 'if I hadn't married you, Rumpole. I can't help thinking about that.'

'No future in that, Hilda. No future at all in thinking about the past, or what we might have done. Let me give you a toast.' I raised my glass of indifferent claret. 'To the Regiment! Coupled,' I murmured under my breath, 'with the name of She Who Must Be Obeyed.'

Rumpole and the Winter Break

'What you need, Rumpole, is a break.'

My wife Hilda, known to me only as She Who Must Be Obeyed, was, of course, perfectly correct. I did need a break, a bit of luck, like not all my cases being listed before Judge Roger Bullingham, the Mad Bull of the Old Bailey, and not being led by an ineffective Q.C. named Moreton Colefax, not being prosecuted by Soapy Sam Ballard, the Savonarola of our Chambers, and not having as a client in my current little murder a short-sighted Kilburn greengrocer who admitted placing his hands about his wife's throat to reason with her. When this happened she dropped dead and he concealed her body, for some time, in a large freezer in the stock-room, that is, until he lost his nerve and called in the Old Bill.

'Of course, I need a break, Hilda. Anyone would think the Bull's the only judge left down the Bailey.'

'Not that sort of break. I mean a winter break. Now, for £236 each, we could have seven nights on Spain's Sunshine Coast, with sea-view, poolside barbecue, sports facilities and excursions, including cocktails aboard the hotel's old-time Pirate Galleon! Dodo's been to Marbella, Rumpole, and we never have a winter holiday.'

'Oh, yes,' I said. 'I can see your old school-friend, Dodo Mackintosh, with a cutlass between her teeth shinning up the ratlines to board the Pirate Galleon for a complimentary cocktail.'

'I'll book up,' Hilda said.

'Not yet,' I told her, and thought to avoid further argument with a perfectly safe bet. 'We'll go,' I promised, 'if I win *R. v. Gimlett*. We'll go as a celebration.' Hilda appeared, for the moment, to be satisfied and I knew that never, in the whole Rumpole career, had there been such a certain loser as the case of the gentle greengrocer from Kilburn.

'It's true, is it not?' I asked Professor Ackerman, pathologist *par excellence* and uncrowned King of the Morgues, across a crowded Courtroom a few days later, 'that a very slight pressure on the vagal nerve at the throat may stop the heart and death may follow speedily?'

'That would be so,' the Professor agreed. He and I had discussed many a deceased person together and so, over the years, although always opponents, we had achieved a great deal of rapport. 'But of course, my Lord, as Mr Rumpole knows, the pressure would have to be just on the right spot.'

'Of course Mr Rumpole knows that!' The Bull lowered his head in my direction and pawed the ground a little. 'Are you suggesting that your client sought out the right spot and pressed on it?'

'Certainly not, my Lord. He pressed on it by the sort of accident your Lordship or any of us might have – pressing on a gold collar-stud, say, putting on a winged collar before the start of a day in Court.'

'That sort of pressure?' I could see the Bull pale beneath his high blood pressure, and a nervous but stubby finger went to the space between the purplish folds of his neck and his off-white starched stand-up size nineteen. 'Do you mean by a collar-stud?' he asked the Professor.

'I think Mr Rumpole is exaggerating a little.' Ackerman gave me the tolerant smile he might reserve for a favourite pupil who had gone, for once, a little too far. 'But the pressure could be comparatively slight.'

'Mr Rumpole is exaggerating!' His Honour Judge Bullingham, senior Old Bailey judge, and as such, entitled to try murders, seemed to be remembering my previous convictions. 'That doesn't surprise me in the least.' And he gave the Jury one of his well-known meaningful smiles; no doubt it frightened the wits out of them.

'The sort of pressure which might arise if a man put his hand round his wife's neck for the purpose of restraining her?' I asked the witness.

'Restraining her, Mr Rumpole?' the Bull growled.

'Oh yes, my Lord. Restraining her from attacking him in one of her frequent outbursts of fury. Restraining her from following him into the shop and abusing him in front of the clientele as he weighed out a couple of pounds of Golden Delicious.'

I got a small titter from the Jury, a cry of 'Silence!' from the Usher, a glare from the Bull, and an absolutely charming answer from the fair-minded forensic expert.

'If he restrained her with some force, the vagal nerve might be inhibited, particularly if she were pressing against his hand. I suppose that is possible. Yes.'

'Thank you, Professor!' And I sat down silently wishing the pale Ackerman a long life and happy dissecting.

But why was I, Horace Rumpole, a junior barrister in status if not in years (I go back to the dawn of time when Lord Denning was a stripling judge in the Divorce Division), why was I, who had a none-too-learned leader in the shape of Moreton Colefax, Q.C., cross-examining the Pathologist called by the Crown?

The short answer was that Colefax, after a long delay, had been called to higher things, that is, the Bench, and, as our timid client appeared to feel safe in the Rumpole hands, I was left in the firing-line, a target for the Bull's blunderbuss and the sniping of my opponent and fellow member of Chambers, Sam Ballard, Q.C.

'You say your married life was unhappy, Mr Gimlett?' Ballard started his cross-examination when the prisoner at the Bar had given evidence.

'She had a terrible temper when roused.' Gimlett looked at the Jury in a woebegone sort of way. 'Her chief delight seemed to be to show me up in front of my customers. Talk about screaming; they say you could hear it all the way down to Sainsbury's.'

'You have some experience of married life though, haven't you? You have been married before?'

'My Lord. What on earth can be the relevance . . .?' I reared
to my hind legs to protest and the Bull bared his teeth in some
sort of grin. 'I don't know, Mr Rumpole. Unless Mr Ballard is
trying to suggest that your client is something of a Casanova.'

Ballard passed swiftly on to other matters and abandoned that
line of cross-examination, but I sat in a sort of glow because the
Bull had delivered himself into my hands. Nothing in the world
could have looked less like Casanova than the meek and middle-
aged Harold Gimlett, with his pinkish bald head and National
Health specs, who looked out of place without a brown overall, a
slightly runny nose and cold hands among the Jersey potatoes. I
would make him, before I finished with the Jury, the very image
and archetype of the hen-pecked husband.

'Members of the Jury,' I told them in my final speech. 'My
client has been presented to you as a Casanova, a Valentino, even
(I had got the name from Mizz Liz Probert, the youngest member
of our Chambers), a Jagger. Look at him! Can you imagine
teenagers swooning over him at the airport? (Laughter, at which
the Bull growled menacingly.) Is he a Lothario or a Bluebeard?
Does he fill you with terror, Members of the Jury, or is he
simply a put-on, timid and long-suffering human being who
only wanted peace in his home and prosperity for his little
grocery business? Of course, after this terrible accident, when he
managed to make contact with his wife's neck in a way that he
never dreamt could be so dangerous, he lost his head. For a
futile moment he tried to conceal the body in that freezing cabinet
you have all seen in the photograph, but soon he was his honest,
straightforward self again and walked, of his own free will, into
Kilburn Police Station, anxious only to face you fairminded,
sensible ladies and gentlemen of the Jury, and receive justice at
your hands . . .'

'You look tired, Mr Rumpole. You need a holiday.'

We sat together, Harold Gimlett and my learned self in the
cells under the Old Bailey, waiting for the Jury to come back
with a verdict. Such times are always embarrassing. You don't
quite know what to say to a client. You could say, 'Win a few,

lose a few,' or, 'See you again, in about fifteen years,' but such remarks would be scarcely welcome. On this occasion it was the greengrocer who kept up the small talk.

'I've always enjoyed a holiday, speaking personally,' he said. 'Things happen sometimes, on a holiday.'

'What sort of things?'

'Well, for instance. It was on holiday that I met the ladies who became my wives.'

I left him then and paced up and down outside the Court, smoking a small cigar and nervously dropping ash down the front of the waistcoat. I don't know why, after so many years of waiting for juries to return, it never gets any better. The sad face of Sam Ballard, my devout prosecutor, hoved into view.

'Ballard,' I said, 'why did you embark on that line about the previous wife? I mean, she died quite naturally, didn't she?'

'Natural causes, yes,' he agreed in a sepulchral tone. 'With quite a hefty life insurance made out in your client's favour. As was the case with the last Mrs Gimlett.'

'The trouble with you members of the Lawyers As Christians Society,' I told him, 'is that you have the most morbidly suspicious minds.' What he said had unsettled me a little, I confess. I felt a momentary sense of insecurity, but within ten minutes the Jury, to the Bull's evident chagrin, returned to find Harold Gimlett 'not guilty'. It was only then, and with a sickening heart, that I remembered the promise I had made to She Who Must Be Obeyed.

Three weeks later we had checked in at Gatwick airport, *en route* to the Costa del Sol.

'What you will find in the Hotel Escamillo, Mr and Mrs Rumpole, is never a dull moment. We lay on the usual wet-suit water-skiing on clear days – all that sort of activity. Hardly your line, Mr Rumpole, is it? Well, you'll be well pleased with the miniature golf, the Bingo and the bowling-green. We offer a full day, taking in Gibraltar and a packed lunch. The caves, now that makes a very nice excursion. And the hotel offers the Carmen Coffee Shop, the Mercedes Gourmet French Restaurant, the

Michaela for snacks and grills, and the usual solarium and gym equipment if you want to keep in trim, Mr Rumpole.'

'Thank you. I have no desire whatever to keep in trim.'

'And for Mrs Rumpole, the Beauty Parlour – not that you need that, Mrs Rumpole. I must say we all, in hospitality, take particular care of our more mature ladies. Tonight, just as a for instance, there's a Senior Citizens' Happy Hour in the Don José American Bar. Any problems at all, and you come straight to me. My name's Derek and I'm happy to host your stay.'

I could tell his name was Derek because he had it written in gold letters on a plastic label attached to his green blazer. He had soft brown eyes and a sort of Spanish-style gaucho moustache, although his accent was pure Ealing Broadway.

'Now, have you any questions at all, Mrs Rumpole, Mr Rumpole?'

'Yes,' I said. 'Where can I get *The Times*?'

'The Frasquita Drugstore on the mezzanine floor,' Derek told me, 'is continually at your service.'

But when I got there, they had nothing left but the *Mirror* and the *Sun*. I found the crosswords in those periodicals extremely puzzling.

'I don't know about you, Rumpole,' said She Who Must Be Obeyed, 'but I intend to take full advantage of all the facilities provided.'

'Pity I've got a touch of leg coming on.' I limped elaborately a few steps behind Hilda on the way to the lift. 'But of course, I want you to enjoy the full day in Gibraltar.'

So our days fell into a sort of pattern. The sun rose palely behind the tower blocks of the hotels, which in their turn cast a dark shadow upon the strip of beach. Each morning we took the Continental in the bedroom, as the Escamillo version of the full British breakfast arrived very cold and greasy, as though it had been flown out, tourist class, from England. I usually woke tired; the bedroom walls seemed made of thinnish hardboard, and the young family in the next room apparently enjoyed round games and pop music far into the night. Hilda was always in a hurry to get ready, to find her purse, her straw peasant-style shopping-basket, her hardly needed sun-hat and shaded specs, because the day's tour, or expedition, was always assembling round dawn in the foyer, to be taken by Derek on a bus journey to some distant point of interest.

I would skulk in bed until she had set out, and then get up slowly and wait for the hot water which apparently also arrived from a long way off. Once togged up in a pair of old flannels and a tweed jacket, I would leave the delights of the Escamillo Hotel. I would walk, my leg having rapidly recovered, into a sort of village where there were still dark and narrow streets, a dripping fountain and a square. On the square was a dark shop – a jumble of tinned food, sun-hats, paperback books, lilos and shrimping-nets – kept by an old woman in a black dress, with a gold tooth and a stubby moustache, who managed to save me copies of *The Times*. I would then go and sit in the comforting, incense-filled gloom of the church and do the crossword. Once it was finished, I transferred my patronage to a small, tiled bar which smelled of carbolic soap and wet dogs, where I ate shrimps, drank a red wine which bore about the same relationship to Pommeroy's plonk as Château Thames Embankment does to Latour 1961, and read my way backwards from the obituaries to the front-page news.

I was always back at the hotel in time to meet Hilda, who arrived home footsore and very weary with her basket full of fans, mantillas, bullfighting posters, sword-shaped paper-knives and other trophies of the chase. We had dinner together and after a terrible encounter with an antique hen lurking under a sweetish sauce, which called itself 'Caneton à l'Orange', in the Mercedes Gourmet Restaurant, we patronized the Michaela for snacks and grills. Every evening Hilda would recount the adventures of the day, repeat several of Derek's jokes, and tell me of the friendliness shown to her by everyone, but particularly by a Mr Waterlow, a visitor from England.

'Mr Waterlow's quite obviously a seasoned traveller. He came into the shop with me and managed to beat them down quite marvellously over the mantilla I bought as a present for Dodo Mackintosh.'

'I always thought old Dodo would look a lot better, heavily veiled.'

'What did you say?'

'You were going to tell me where you sailed . . .'

'Sailed? We didn't sail anywhere, Rumpole. We went on a bus. Mr Waterlow sat at my table at lunch in the Parador. Such a charming man and so distinguished-looking. He wears one of those white linen shirts with short sleeves. What do you call them? Bush-whacking shirts?' I said I didn't call them anything.

'I think it's "bush-whacking". Anyway, you ought to get a shirt like that, Rumpole.'

'Did you happen to tell this Waterlow person that you were here with your husband?'

'Oh, Rumpole! We didn't talk about my life; I don't suppose he even knows my name. He told me a little about himself though; he says he's all alone in the world now. He does seem rather sad about it.'

So life continued and each evening Hilda regaled me with her travels round the Iberian peninsula and told me of the charm and general helpfulness of the man Waterlow. Strangely we never saw this paragon about the hotel. He knew, Hilda told me, a lot of little restaurants along the coast. 'Places where the continentals go, Rumpole. But then, of course, Mr Waterlow speaks absolutely perfect Spanish.'

On the last but one night of our stay dinner was laid out in the nippy darkness beside the pool. The ladies pulled on cardigans over thin dresses, the men brought out sweaters, and a group of shifty-looking customers in big hats and frilly shirts sang 'Deep in the Heart of Texas' and such-like old Spanish folk-songs. Derek was tablehopping, telling his jokes and flirting in a nauseating manner with the female senior citizens, when Hilda looked up from a battle with a slice of singed bull which had no doubt weathered a good many corridas, and almost shrieked, 'Why, Rumpole. There he is!'

'There who is?'

'Why, Mr Waterlow, of course.'

I saw him then, sitting among the group who were so often poolside with their ladies. He saw Hilda and my back only. He raised his Sangría when she looked at him, but when he saw me he seemed to freeze, his glass an inch from his lower lip.

'Hilda,' I said, with all the determination I could muster, 'you must never speak to that man again!'

I looked back and he had gone, out of the poolside lights perhaps, and was still lingering in the shadows.

'But why, Rumpole? Why ever do you say that?'

I couldn't tell her about the man with whom she had struck up a friendship. Even if he had changed his name, substituted contact lenses for National Health specs and a safari suit and a gold medallion for a greengrocer's overall, I knew exactly who he was. I may have cherished uncharitable thoughts about She Who Must Be Obeyed at times, when a cold wind was blowing around Casa Rumpole, but I never wanted to see her end up in a freezer cabinet.

'Why mustn't I speak to him again?'

'Because I say so.'

'Rumpole, you silly old thing.' Hilda's face was wreathed in smiles. She looked some years younger, and intensely flattered. 'I do believe you're jealous.'

'Jealous?'

'Of Mr Waterlow. It's so silly, Rumpole. But it's nice to know that you really care as much as that. I do think that's awfully nice to know.' She's eyes were smiling. She put out her hand and took mine in a fairly moist embrace.

'You know, there's no one else really, don't you? Mr Waterlow was very charming, but what I really liked about him was he made you jealous! Would you like to dance with me, Rumpole?'

'No, Hilda.' I disengaged my hand as gently as possible. 'I don't really think I would.'

The next day was our last and Hilda forswore all trips. She came with me when I bought *The Times* and sat beside me in the church making some unhelpful suggestions for One Across. I didn't take her to the tiled bar, but we chose a restaurant by the sea where we ate calamares, food that tasted much like India rubber teething-rings. Hilda was smiling and cheerful all day. Harold Gimlett, the Kilburn greengrocer, seemed to have greatly improved my married life by giving Rumpole an undeserved reputation as a jealous husband.

Rumpole's Last Case

Picture, if you will, a typical domestic evening, *à côté de chez* Rumpole, in the 'mansion' flat off the Gloucester Road. I am relaxed in a cardigan and slippers, a glass of Jack Pommeroy's Very Ordinary perched on the arm of my chair, a small cigar between my fingers, reading a brief which, not unusually, was entitled, *R. v. Timson*. She Who Must Be Obeyed was staring moodily at the small hearthrug, somewhat worn over the ages I must admit, that lay in front of our roaring gas-fire.

'The Timsons carrying a shooter!' I was shocked at what I had just read. 'Whatever's the world coming to?'

'We need a new one urgently,' Hilda was saying, 'and we need it *now*.' She was still gazing at our hearthrug, scarred by the butt ends of the small cigars I was aiming at the bowl of water that stood in front of the fire.

'It's like music in lifts and wine in boxes.' I was lamenting the decline of standards generally. 'We'll be having Star Wars machines in Pommeroy's Wine Bar next. Decent, respectable criminals like the Timsons never went tooled up.'

'Rumpole, you've done it again!' Hilda recovered the end of my cigar from the rug and ground it ostentatiously out in an ashtray as I told her a bit of ash never did a carpet any harm, in fact it improved the texture.

'There's a perfectly decent little hearthrug going in Debenhams for £100,' Hilda happened to mention.

'Going to someone who isn't balancing precariously on the rim of their overdraft.'

'Rumpole, what on earth's the use of all these bank robberies and the rising crime-rate they're always talking about if we can't even get a decent little hearthrug out of it?' Hilda was clearly starting one of her campaigns, and I got up to recharge my glass from the bottle on the sideboard. 'Remember what they're paying for legal aid cases nowadays,' I told her firmly. 'It hardly covers the fare to Temple station. And there's Henry's ten per cent and the cost of a new brief-case . . .'

'You're never buying a new brief-case!' She was astonished.

'No. No, of course not. I can't afford it.' I took a quick sustaining gulp and carried the glass back to my armchair. '. . . And there's a small claret at Pommeroy's to recover from the terrors of the day.'

'That's your trouble, isn't it, Rumpole.' She looked at me severely. 'If it weren't for the "small claret" at Pommeroy's we'd have no trouble buying a nice new hearthrug, and if it weren't for those awful cheroots of yours we shouldn't need one anyway. I warn you I shall call in at Debenhams tomorrow; it's up to you to deal with the bank.'

'How do you suggest I deal with the bank?' I asked her. 'Tunnel in through the drains and rob the safe? Not carrying a shooter, though. A Timson carrying a shooter! It's the end of civilization as we know it.'

Counsel is briefed for Mr Dennis Timson. He will 'know the Timson family of old'. It appears that Dennis and his cousin Cyril entered the premises of the 'Penny-Wise Bank' in Tooting by masquerading as workers from British Telecom inspecting underground cables that were laid in Abraham Avenue. Whilst working underground the two defendants contrived to burrow into the 'strong-room' of the 'Penny-Wise' and open the safe, abstracting therefrom a certain quantity of cash and valuables. As they were doing so, they were surprised by a Mr Huggins, a middle-aged bankguard. It is clear from the evidence that Huggins was shot and wounded by a revolver, which was then left at the scene of the crime. The alarm had been given and the two Timson cousins were arrested by police officers who arrived at the scene of the crime.

Mr Dennis Timson admits the break-in and the theft. He says, however, that he had no idea that his cousin Cyril was carrying a 'shooter', and is profoundly shocked at such behaviour in a member of the family. He is most anxious to avoid the 'fourteen',

which he believes would be the sentence if the Jury took the view
he was party to the wounding of Mr Huggins. Cyril Timson,
who, instructing solicitors understand, is represented by Mrs
Phillida Erskine-Brown, Q.C., as 'silk' with Mr Claude Erskine-
Brown as her 'learned Junior', will, it seems likely, say that it is all
'down to' our client, Dennis. He has told the police (D.I. Broome)
that he had no idea Dennis came to the scene 'tooled up', and that
he was horrified when Dennis shot the bankguard. It seems clear
to those instructing that Cyril is also anxious to avoid the 'fourteen' at all costs.

Counsel will see that he is faced with a 'cut-throat' defence with
the defendants Timson blaming each other. Counsel will know
from his long experience that in such circumstances the Prosecution is usually successful, and both 'throat-cutters' tend to 'go
down'. Counsel may think it well to have a word or two with Mr
Cyril Timson's 'silk', Mrs Phillida Erskine-Brown, who happens
to be in Counsel's Chambers, to see if Cyril will 'see sense'
and stop 'putting it all down' to Mr Dennis Timson.

Counsel is instructed to appear for Mr Dennis Timson at the
Old Bailey, and secure his acquittal on the charges relating to the
firearm. Those instructing respectfully wish Learned Counsel 'the
best of British luck'.

Dear old Bernard, the Timsons' regular solicitor, was a great
one for the inverted comma. He had put the matter clearly enough
in his instructions with my brief in R. v. Timson, and the case as he
described it had several points of interest as well as a major worry.
Both Cyril and Dennis were well into middle-age and, at least so
far as Cyril was concerned, somewhat overweight. The whole
enterprise, setting up a tent over a manhole in the road and
carrying out a great deal of preliminary work in the guise of men
from British Telecom, seemed ambitious for men whom I should
never have thought of as bank robbers. It was rather as though the
ends of a pantomime horse had decided to get together and play
Hamlet. Den and Cyril Timson, I thought, should have stuck to
thieving frozen fish from the Cash & Carry. The Penny-Wise
affair seemed distinctly out of their league.

The fly in the ointment of our case had been accurately spotted
by the astute and experienced Bernard. In a cut-throat defence,
two prisoners at the Bar blame each other. The Prosecutor in-

variably weighs in with titbits of information designed to help
the mutual mayhem of the two defendants and the Jury pot them
both. The prospects were not made brighter by the fact that his
Honour Judge Bullingham was selected to preside over this
carnage. On top of all this anxiety, I was expecting my overdraft,
already bursting at the seams constructed for it by Mr Truscott
of the Caring Bank, to be swollen by Hilda's extravagant purchase of a new strip of floor-covering.

And then an event occurred which set me on the road to
fortune and so enabled me to call this particular account
'Rumpole's Last Case'.

My luck began when I called in at the clerk's room on the first
morning of *R*. v. *Timson* and found, as usual, Uncle Tom getting
a chip shot into the waste-paper basket, Dianne brewing up
coffee, and Henry greeting me with congratulations such as I
had never received from him after my most dramatic wins in
Court (barristers, according to Henry, don't win or lose cases,
they just 'do' them and he collects his ten per cent). 'Well done,
indeed, Mr Rumpole,' he said. 'You remember investing in the
barristers clerks' sweepstake on the Derby?' In fact I remembered his twisting my arm to part with two quid, much
better spent over the bar at Pommeroy's. 'You drew that Dire
Jeans,' Henry told me.

'I drew what?'

'Diogenes, Rumpole.' Uncle Tom translated from the original
Greek. 'Do you know nothing about the turf? It came in at a
canter. I said to myself, "That's old Rumpole for you. He has all
the luck!"'

'Oh. Got a winner, did I?' I tried to remain cool when Henry
handed me a bundle and told me that it was a hundred of the
best and asked if I wanted to count them. I told him I trusted
him implicitly and counted off twenty crisp fivers. It was an
excellent start to the day.

'You know what they say!' Uncle Tom looked on with interest
and envy. 'Lucky on the gee-gees, unlucky in love. You've never
been tremendously lucky in love, have you, Rumpole?'

'Oh, I don't know, Uncle Tom. I've had my moments. One

hundred smackers!' I put the loot away in my hip-pocket. 'It's not every day that a barrister gets folding money out of his clerk.' Uncle Tom looked at me a little sceptically. Perhaps he wondered what sort of moments I had had; after all he had enjoyed the privilege of meeting Mrs Hilda Rumpole at our Chambers parties.

> As I sat in the café I said to myself,
> They may talk as they please about what they call 'pelf',
> They may sneer as they like about eating and drinking,
> But I cannot help it, I cannot help thinking . . .
> How pleasant it is to have money, heigh ho!
> How pleasant it is to have money . . .
> So pleasant it is to have money . . .

The lines went through my head as I took my usual walk down Fleet Street to Ludgate Circus and then up to the Old Bailey. As I walked I could feel the comforting and unusual bulge of notes in my hip-pocket. As I marched up the back lanes to the Palais de Justice, I passed a newspaper kiosk which, I had previously noticed, seemed to mainly cater to the racing fraternity. There were a number of papers and posters showing jockeys whose memoirs were printed and horses whose exploits were described, and I noticed that morning the advertisement for a publication entitled *The Punter's Guide to the Turf* which carried a story headed FOUR-HORSE WINNER FATHER OF THREE TELLS HOW HE HIT QUARTER OF A MILLION JACKPOT.

Naturally, as a successful racing man (a status I had achieved in the last ten minutes), I took a greater interest in the familiar kiosk. I had, clearly, something of a talent for the turf. The Derby one day, perhaps the Grand National the next – was it the Grand National or the Oaks? With a few winners, I thought, a fellow could live pretty high on the hog – I took a final turning and the Old Bailey hoved into view – a fellow might even be able to consider giving up the delights of slogging down the Bailey for the dubious pleasure of doing a cut-throat defence before his unpredictable Honour Judge Roger Bullingham.

And then, walking on towards the old verdict factory, I heard the familiar voices of Phillida Erskine-Brown, Q.C., and her spouse; fragments of conversation floated back to me on the wind.

'Rumpole's got Probert taking a note for him,' our Portia said. 'Do try not to dream about taking her to the Opera again.'

'I only took her once. And then she didn't enjoy it.' This was Claude's somewhat half-hearted defence.

'I bet she didn't. You would have been better off inviting her to a Folk Festival at the Croydon Community Centre. *Much* more her style.'

'Philly! Look, aren't you ever going to forget it?'

'Frankly, Claude, I don't think I ever am.'

They crossed the road in front of me and their voices were lost, but I had heard enough to know that all was not sweetness and light in the Erskine-Brown household. I hoped that our Portia's natural irritation with her errant husband would not lead her to sharpen her scalpel for the cut-throat defence.

Half an hour later I knew the answer to that question. I was robed up with Liz Probert and Mr Bernard in tow on my way to a pre-trial conference with my client Dennis Timson, when we met Phillida Erskine-Brown and her husband on a similar mission to Den's cousin, Cyril.

'Ill met by moonlight, proud Titania.' I thought this was a suitable greeting to the lady silk in the lift.

'Rumpole! What's all this about proud Titania?'

'You're not going to listen to me?'

'I'll certainly listen, Rumpole. What've you got to say?'

'You know it's always fatal when two accused persons start blaming each other! A cut-throat defence with the Prosecutor chortling in his joy and handing out the razors. That's got to be avoided at all costs.'

'Why don't you admit it then?'

'Admit *what*?'

'Admit you had the shooter? Accept the facts.'

'Plead guilty?' I must admit I was hurt by the suggestion. 'And break the habit of a lifetime?' We were out of the lift now and waiting, at the gateway of the cells in the basement, for a fat and panting screw, who had just put down a jumbo-sized

sandwich, to unlock the oubliettes. 'Who's prosecuting?' I asked
Phillida.

'Young fellow who was in our Chambers for about five
minutes,' she told me. 'Charles Hearthstoke.'

'My life seems to be dominated by hearthrugs,' I told her.

'He's rather sweet.'

'If you can possibly think Hearthrug's sweet' – I must say I
was astonished – 'no wonder you suspect Dennis Timson of
carrying a shooter.'

'Dennis Timson was tooled up.' She was positive of the fact.

'Cyril was!' I knew my Dennis.

'Moreover, he shot the bankguard extremely inefficiently – in
the foot.'

'Come on, proud Titania. Plead guilty . . .' I tried a winsome
smile to a minus effect.

'Not for thy fairy kingdom, Rumpole!'

'What *do* you mean?'

'Isn't that what Titania tells him. At the end of the scene? I
suppose it means "no deal".' We parted then, to interview our
separate clients, and I was left wondering if, when she was a
white-wig, I had not taught young Phillida Trant, as she then
was, far too much.

We, that is to say, Liz, Mr Bernard and I, found Dennis in
one of the small interview rooms, smoking a little snout and
reading *The Punter's Guide to the Turf*. I thought I should do
best by an appeal to our old friendship and business association.
'You and I, Dennis,' I reminded him, 'have known each other
for a large number of years and I've never heard of you carrying
a shooter before.'

'You're a sporting man, Mr Rumpole,' the client said unexpectedly. I had to admit that I had enjoyed some recent success
on the turf.

'Bloke in here cleared quarter of a million on the horses.' And
Dennis was good enough to show me his *Punter's Guide*. 'Well,'
I told him, 'I've had handsome wins in my time, but nothing to
equal . . .'

'He's seen boarding an aeroplane for the Seychelles.' Dennis
showed me the picture in his *Punter's*.

'The Seychelles, eh?' I was thoughtful. 'Far from Judge Bullingham and the Old Bailey.'

'I could make more than that on a four-horse accumulator. If I had a ton,' our client claimed.

'A ton of what?'

'A hundred pound stake.'

'A hundred pounds?' That very sum was swelling in my back pocket.

'I reckon I could top three hundred grand in the next few days.'

I pulled myself together and reluctantly came back to the matter in hand. 'You know what's going to happen when you and Cyril blame each other for carrying the shooter? The Mad Bull's going to tell the Jury you agreed to go on an armed robbery together. He'll say that it doesn't really matter who was in charge of the equipment. You're *both* guilty! Did you say . . . three hundred thousand pounds?'

'From a four-horse accumulator.' Dennis made the point again.

'Four-horse what?'

'Accumulator.' He consulted his paper again. 'I could get 9 to 1 about Pretty Balloon at Goodwood this afternoon.'

'Do you want me to take this down?' Mizz Probert was puzzled at the course the conference was taking. I told her to relax but I pulled out a pencil and made a few notes on the back of my brief. I am ashamed to have to tell you they were not about the case.

'So there'd be a grand to go on Mother's Ruin at Redcar. 5 to 1, I reckon. That'd give us six thou.' Dennis went on as though it were peanuts. 'And that'd be on Ever So Grateful . . . which should get you fours at Yarmouth. So that's thirty grand!'

'Ever So Grateful, sounds a polite little animal.' I was taking a careful note.

'Now we need 10 to 1 for a bit of a gamble.' Dennis was studying the forecasts.

'What's it been up to now?'

'A doddle,' he told me calmly.

'Easy as tunnelling into a bank vault?' I couldn't help it.

'Do me a favour, Mr Rumpole, don't bring that up again.' His pained expression didn't last long. 'Kissogram at Newbury on

Wednesday,' he read out in triumph. 'Ante-post price should bring you, let's say three hundred and thirty grand! Give or take a fiver.'

'In round figures?'

'Oh, yes. In round figures.'

I put away my pen and looked at Dennis. 'Just tell me one thing.'

'About the shooter?' His cheerfulness was gone.

'We'll come back to the shooter in a minute; I was thinking that you've been in custody since that eventful night.'

'Six months, Mr Rumpole,' Bernard told me and Liz Probert added, 'We should get that off the sentence.'

'I suppose, being in Brixton and now here, it's difficult to place a small bet or two? Not to mention a four-horse accumulator?'

'Bless your heart, Mr Rumpole. There's always screws that'll do it for you, even down the Old Bailey cells.'

'Screws that'll put on bets?' I was surprised to hear it.

'You know Gerald, the fat one at the gate, the one that's always got his face in a bacon sarny?'

'Gerald.' I was grateful for the information. And then I stood up; we seemed to have covered all the vital points. 'Well, I think that's about all on the legal aspect of the case. Just remember one thing, Dennis. The Timsons don't carry weapons and they don't grass on each other.'

'That's true, Mr Rumpole. That has always been our point of honour.'

'So don't you go jumping into that witness-box and blame it all on your cousin Cyril. Let the Prosecution try and prove which of you had the gun; don't you two start cutting each other's throats.'

'Cyril goes in the first, don't he?' Dennis had a certain amount of legal knowledge gained in the hard school of experience.

'If he goes in at all, yes. You're second on the indictment.'

'I'll have to see what he says, won't I?'

'But you wouldn't grass on him?'

'Not unless I have to.' Dennis didn't sound so sure.

'"What is honour? A word. What is that word, honour? Air!"'
Happily the allusion was lost on my client, so I went off to try a
few passes at the Mad Bull after a word in confidence with the
stout warder at the gate.

'Gerald.' I accosted him after I had told Liz and Mr Bernard
to go on up and keep my place warm in Court. 'Yes, Mr Rumpole.
Got a busy day in Court ahead, have you?' The man's voice
came muffled by a large wadge of sandwich.

'I am a little hard-pressed; in fact I'm too busy to get to my
usual bookmakers.' 'Want me to put something on for you?'
Gerald seemed to follow my drift at once.

'A hundred pounds. Four-horse accumulator. Start this
afternoon at Goodwood' – I consulted the notes on my brief –
'with Pretty Balloon. I reckon you can get 9 to 1 about it.'

'Will do, Mr Rumpole. I'll be slipping out soon, for a bit of
dinner.'

'And I'm sure you'll need it . . .' I looked at the man with
something akin to awe and gave him the name of my four hopeful
horses. Then I put my hand in my back pocket, lugged out the
hundred pounds and handed it all to Gerald. As some old
gambler put it:

> He either fears his fate too much,
> Or his deserts are small,
> That puts it not unto the touch,
> To win or lose it all.

It was after I had placed the great wager with Gerald that I
went upstairs. Outside Judge Bullingham's Court, I found three
large figures awaiting me. I recognized Fred Timson, a grey-
haired man, his face bronzed by the suns of Marbella, wearing a
discreet sports jacket, cavalry-twill trousers and an M.C.C. tie.
He was the acknowledged head of the family, always called on
for advice in times of trouble, and with him I had also a long-
standing business relationship. Fred was flanked by two substantial ladies who had clearly both been for a recent tint and set at
the hairdressers; they were brightly dressed as though for a
wedding or some celebration other than their husbands' day in

Court. They, as I was reminded, were Den's Doris and Cyril's Maureen. Fred hastily told me of the family troubles. 'We're being made a laughing stock, Mr Rumpole. There's Molloys making a joke of this all over South London.' Of course, I knew the numerous clan Molloy, rival and perhaps more deft and successful villains, who were to the Timsons what the Montagues were to the Capulets, York to Lancaster or the Guelfs to the Ghibellines of old.

'I've been called out to in the street by Molloy women,' Den's Doris complained. 'Maureen's been called out to in Tesco's on several occasions.'

'They're laughing at our husbands' – this, from Cyril's Maureen – 'grassing on each other.'

'Is *that* what they're laughing at?' I wondered.

'Oh, the Molloys is doing very nicely, that's what we hear. They pulled off something spectacular.' Fred had the latest information.

'They got away with something terrific, they reckon,' Maureen and Doris added. 'And they calls out that all the Timsons can do is get nicked and then grass on each other.'

'These Molloys aren't ever going to let us hear the last of it.' Fred was gloomy. 'Young Peanuts Molloy, he called out that all the Timsons is good for is to use as ferrets.'

'Ferrets?' I looked at him with some interest. 'Why on earth did he say *that*, I wonder?'

'You know the way they talk.' Fred was full of contempt for Molloy boasting. 'We wants you to go in there, Mr Rumpole. And save our reputation.'

'I'll do my best,' I had to promise. After all, the Timson family had done more for the legal profession than a hundred Lord Chancellors.

A standard opening gambit, when faced with the difficulties of a cut-throat defence, is to apply to the Court, before the Jury is let in and sworn, for separate trials for the defendants. If they are tried on different occasions they cannot then give evidence which will be harmful to each other. Such applications are usually doomed, as the Judge is as keen as the Prosecution to see a couple of customers convicting each other without the need for outside assistance.

'A separate trial,' the Bull growled when I stood on my feet to make the application, 'for Dennis Timson? Any *reason* for that, Mr Rumpole, apart from your natural desire to spin out these proceedings as long as possible? I assume your client's on legal aid?'

I am sorry to say that not only the handsome young Hearthstoke but Phillida laughed at Bullingham's 'joke', and I thought that if I were to win the four-horse accumulator, I could tell his Lordship to shut up and not be so mercenary.

'The reason, my Lord,' I told him, 'is my natural desire to see that justice is done to my client.'

'Provided it's paid for by the unfortunate rate-payers of the City of London.' The Bull glared at me balefully. 'Go on, Mr Rumpole.'

'I understand that my co-defendant, Mr Cyril Timson, may give evidence accusing my client of having the gun.'

'And you, no doubt, intend to return the compliment?'

'I'm not prepared to say at this stage what my defence will be,' I said with what remained of my dignity.

'But it may be a cut-throat?' the Bull suggested artlessly.

'That is possible, my Lord.'

'These two . . .' – he looked at the dock with undisguised contempt – '*gentry!* Are going to do their best to cut each other's throats?'

Gazing at his Lordship, I knew how the Emperor Nero looked when he settled down in the circus to watch a gladiator locked in hopeless combat with a sabre-toothed tiger. I glanced away and happened to catch sight of a pale, weaselly-faced young man with lank hair and a leather jacket leaning over the rail of the Public Gallery, listening to the proceedings with interest and amusement. I immediately recognized the face, well known in criminal circles, of Peanuts Molloy, who also appeared to enjoy the circus. I averted my eyes and once more addressed the learned judge, 'Of course,' I told him, 'the statements the defendants made to the police wouldn't be evidence against each other.'

'But once they go into the witness-box in the same trial and repeat them on oath, then they become evidence on which the Jury could convict!' Bullingham added with relish.

'Your Lordship has my point.'

'Of course I do. You don't want your client sent down for armed robbery and grievous bodily harm, do you, Mr Rumpole?'

'I don't want my client sent down on evidence which may well be quite unreliable!' At that I sat down in as challenging a manner as possible and his Honour Judge Bullingham directed a sickly smile at Phillida. 'Mrs Erskine-Brown. Do you support Mr Rumpole's application?' he asked her in a voice like Guinness and treacle.

'My Lord. I do not!' Phillida rose to put her small stiletto heel into Rumpole. 'I'm sure that under your Lordship's wise guidance justice will be done to both the defendants. Your Lordship will no doubt direct the Jury with your Lordship's usual clarity.' When it came to buttering up the Bull our Portia could lay it on with a trowel. 'You may well warn them of the danger of convicting Mr Dennis Timson on the evidence of an accomplice. But, of course, they *can* do so if they think it right.'

'Oh yes, Mrs Erskine-Brown.' The Bull was purring like a kitten. 'I shall certainly tell them that. The Court is grateful for your most valuable contribution.'

So the two Timsons were ordered to be tried together and I thought that if only certain horses managed their races better than I was managing my case I might, in the not too distant future, be boarding an aeroplane for the Seychelles. In fact, that first day in Court was not an unmitigated disaster. As Hearthrug was drawing to the end of a distinctly unsporting address to the Jury, in the course of which he told them that the bankguard, Huggins, 'a family man, a man of impeccable character, who has sat upon his local Church Council, was wounded by these two desperate robbers, albeit in the foot', my client scribbled a note which was delivered to me by a helpful usher. I opened it and read the glad tidings: THE SCREWS TOLD ME, MR RUMPOLE. PRETTY BALLOON WON BY A SHORT HEAD AT GOODWOOD. One up, I thought as I crumpled the note and looked up at

Bullingham like a man who might not be in his clutches for ever – one up and three to go.

I have it on the good authority of Harry Shrimpton, the Court Clerk, that after he rose, Bullingham said to him, 'A really most attractive advocate, Mrs Erskine-Brown. Do you think it would be entirely inappropriate if I sent her down a box of chocolates?'

'Yes, Judge,' Shrimpton felt it his duty to tell him.

'You mean, "Yes", I can?'

'No. I mean "Yes", it would be entirely inappropriate.'

'Hm. She hasn't a sweet tooth?' The Bull was puzzled.

'The Lord Chancellor wouldn't like it.' The Court Clerk was expert on such matters, but the Judge merely growled, 'I wasn't going to send chocolates to the Lord Chancellor.'

Whilst the learned female Q.C. was being threatened by unsolicited chocolates from the Judge, she was sitting, at his express invitation, with Charlie Hearthstoke, in a quiet corner of Pommeroy's Wine Bar in the company of two glasses and a gold-paper-necked bottle in an ice bucket. The ruthless counsel for the Prosecution, she was able to tell me much later, had invited her there so that he could tell her that my client, Dennis, possessed a firearm without a licence, although it was unfortunately a shotgun and not a revolver, and that he had done malicious damage with an air rifle when he was fourteen. It was also thought that he had rung the hospital to inquire about Huggins's health; an event which, as interpreted by Hearthrug, showed not natural sympathy, but a desire to discover if he were likely to be charged with murder. All these facts were put at Phillida's disposal, so that she might be the better able to cut my client's throat. Then Charlie Hearthstoke told Phillida what a superb 'Courtroom technician' she was. 'The way you handled Bullingham was superb. He's dotty about you, naturally. Well, I can't blame him. I suppose everyone is.'

There was more of such flattery, apparently, and Hearthstoke made it clear that he wished he'd got to know Phillida better when he was in our Chambers, but of course she was always doing such important cases, and was 'very much married, naturally'.

'Not all *that* married,' Phillida now agrees she replied, and who knows what course the conversation might not have taken had I not hoved to with Liz Probert, seen the bottle in the bucket, and asked Jack Pommeroy's girl, Barbara, to bring us another couple of glasses. 'Champagne all round, eh, Hearthrug?' I said, as we settled in our places. 'And I know exactly what you're celebrating.'

'I can't imagine what that could be.' Phillida tried to sound innocent.

'Come off it,' I told her. 'You're celebrating the unholy alliance between Cyril Timson and the Prosecution, with a full exchange of information designed to send poor old Dennis away for at least fourteen years.'

'That's not fair!'

'Of course it's not fair, Portia. But it's true. And as the quality of mercy doesn't seem to be dropping like the gentle rain from heaven around here, we'll have to make do with Pommeroy's bubbly.' I pulled the bottle out of the bucket and looked at it with dismay. '*Méthode Champenoise*. Oh, Hearthrug. You disappoint me.'

'Actually, Charles, it's quite delicious.' I saw Phillida smile at the odious Prosecutor.

'Grape juice and gas,' I warned her. 'Wait for the headache. You know Mizz Probert, of course?' Of course she knew Liz only too well, but I wasn't in a mood to make life easy for Cyril Timson's silk.

'Of course,' Phillida spoke from the deep-freeze.

'There's one thing I've always wanted to ask you, Phillida.' Liz being extremely nervous, started to chatter. 'Now you're a Q.C. and all that. But when you started at the Bar, wasn't it terribly difficult being a woman?'

'Oh, no. Being a woman comes quite naturally, to some of us.' She smiled at Hearthstoke who laughed encouragingly. 'Not that I had much choice in the matter.'

'But didn't you come up against a load of fixed male attitudes?'

Liz stumbled on, doing herself no good at all. 'That's what made it all such tremendous fun,' Phillida told her. 'If you really want to know, I didn't get a particularly brilliant law degree but I never had the slightest trouble getting on with men.'

'Clearly not.' Hearthrug was prepared to corroborate her story. 'Oh, yes' – Phillida smiled at Liz in a particularly lethal way – 'and there's one question I wanted to ask *you*.'

'About the exploitation of women at the Bar?' A simple-minded girl, Mizz Probert.

'No. Just ... seen any good operas lately?' A deep old-fashioned blush spread across the face of that liberated lady Liz Probert, and I tried to help her by saying, 'You could have learned a great lesson from Portia today, Mizz Probert. How to succeed at the Bar by reducing Judge Bullingham to a trembling blob of sexual excitement. I've never been able to manage it myself.' Gazing idly about me, I saw Claude enter Pommeroy's, and I happened to tell his wife that he looked as though he'd lost her, a remark not lost on the egregious Hearthrug.

'Rumpole, lay off!' Phillida's aside was unusually angry. 'Are you going to lay off Dennis?' I was prepared to strike a bargain with her, but as she made no response, I invited Erskine-Brown to draw up a chair and sit next to Mizz Probert. He declined to do this, but squeezed himself, in a way welcomed by neither of the parties, between his wife and Hearthstoke. When we were all more or less uncomfortably settled, I asked Claude if I could borrow the copy of the *Standard*, which he was holding much as a drowning man clings to a raft.

'I went back to Chambers, Philly,' the unhappy man was saying. 'They said you hadn't been in.'

'No. I came straight here. I was discussing the case with prosecuting counsel.'

'Oh, yes.' Erskine-Brown was clearly cowed. 'Oh, yes. Of course.'

I wasn't listening to them. I was gazing like a man entranced at a stop-press item on the back of the *Standard*. The golden words read LATE RESULT FROM REDCAR. NUMBER ONE, MOTHER'S RUIN. Two down and two to go! Things were going so well that I suggested to Hearthrug he might order a bottle of the real stuff.

'Why? What are *you* celebrating?' Phillida asked.

'I don't know about you fellows,' I told them. 'But I've made a few investments which seem to have turned out rather well. In fact, my future is almost entirely secure. Perhaps I won't have to do this job any more.' I looked round the table, smiling. 'Suppose this should turn out to be Rumpole's positively last case!' At which point my learned friends, and one of my learned enemies, looked at me with a wild surmise, silent at a table in Pommeroy's Wine Bar, faced with what might well count as the most significant moment in recent legal history.

Events were moving quickly. Diogenes had won the Derby the previous Wednesday, and on Monday morning Henry had paid out my little bit of capital when I called into Chambers on my way to participate in *R. v. Timson*. By Monday night, two of my favoured horses had brought home the bacon: Pretty Balloon at Goodwood, and Mother's Ruin most recently at Redcar. The speed of my success had somewhat stunned me, but I began to feel, as anyone must half-way through a successful four-horse accumulator, that I had the Midas touch. I had listened to Dennis's advice perhaps, but I could certainly pick them. As I settled in my armchair at the gas-fireside in the Gloucester Road area that Monday evening I had no real doubt that Hilda and I were bound for some easy retirement by a sunkissed lagoon. We should soon, I thought, be boarding an aeroplane for the Seychelles. 'I've got it, Rumpole.' She broke into my reverie.

'What've you got, Hilda?'

'What I've been wanting for a long time, that little hearthrug. It looks smart, doesn't it?'

'If that's what you always wanted, I think you might be rather more ambitious!' The new arrival at our 'mansion' flat seemed hardly appropriate to our new-found wealth.

'Just don't you dare throw your cigar ends at it!'

'Don't you worry,' I told her. 'I shall be chucking my cigar ends, my Havana cigar ends, my Romeo y Julieta cigar ends, at the sparkling ocean, as I wander barefoot along the beach in a pair of old white ducks and knock the sweet oysters off the rocks.'

'You're hardly going to do that in the Gloucester Road.' Hilda seemed not to be following my drift.

'Forget the Gloucester Road! We'll move somewhere far away from Gloucester Road and the Old Bailey.' I rose to get a glass of Château Fleet Street from the bottle on the sideboard. 'It's not *real* Persian, of course, but I think it's a traditional pattern,' Hilda told me.

'"Courage!" he said,' – I gave her a taste of 'The Lotos-Eaters':

> 'and pointed toward the land,
> "This mounting wave will roll us shoreward soon."
> And in the afternoon they came unto a land
> In which it seemed always afternoon.
> All round the coast the languid air did swoon,
> Breathing like one that hath a weary dream.'

'I have absolutely no idea what you mean,' Hilda sighed and turned her attention to the *Daily Telegraph*.

'It's not the *meaning*, Hilda, it's the sounds we shall hear: the chatter of monkeys, the screech of parrots in the jungle, the hum of dragonflies, the rattle of grasshoppers rubbing their little legs together, the boom of breakers on the coral reef. And we shall sit out on the hotel verandah, drinking Planter's Punch and never having to wear a bloody winged collar again.'

'I don't wear a winged collar now.' Hilda tends to think first of herself. Then she said, as I thought, a little sharply, 'I wonder if the bank manager will have anything to say about the hearthrug.'

'Hardly, Hilda!' I reassured her. 'I rather suspect that when I next run into Mr Truscott of the Caring Bank, he'll be inviting me for a light lunch at the Savoy Grill. I just hope I can make time for him.'

'The bank manager inviting *you* to lunch? That'll be the day!' She suddenly looked at me. 'You have *got* the hundred pounds for our hearthrug, haven't you, Rumpole?'

'"Fear not, Hilda . . . I do expect return/Of thrice three times the value of this bond."'

'That's all very well. But have you got the hundred pounds?'

Tuesday dawned with only the case and Yarmouth races to worry about, but soon a new drama was unfolding itself before my eyes. I got to Chambers a little too late for my breakfast at the Taste-Ee-Bite in Fleet Street, so, once trapped again in the robes and the winged collar, I went down to the Old Bailey canteen, took my solitary coffee and bun to a corner table and sank behind *The Times*. I was soon aware of voices at the next table. It was Phillida again, but this time her companion was Charlie Hearthrug, and they both seemed blissfully unaware of old Rumpole at the table behind them.

'You might come back into the fold?' I heard Phillida say, and Hearthstoke answered, 'Well, without Rumpole there, I don't see why I shouldn't find my way back into your Chambers at Equity Court.'

'That'd be something to look forward to. I used to think nothing would ever change. Marriage and building up the practice and having the kids and taking silk and perhaps becoming one of the statutory women on the Circuit Bench – Circus Bench, Rumpole calls it . . .' Phillida was clearly choosing this unlikely time and place to pour out her heart to Hearthstoke, who encouraged her by asking in soft and meaningful tones, like a poorish actor, 'Doesn't that seem enough for you now?'

'Not really. You know' – more confidences were clearly to come from Mrs Erskine-Brown – 'sometimes I envy my clients getting into trouble and leaving home and doing extraordinary things, dreadful things sometimes. But their lives aren't dull. Nothing happens to us! Nothing adventurous, really.'

'Perhaps it will if this is really Rumpole's last case and we're in Chambers together. Almost anything can happen then.'

'Almost anything?' I saw Phillida's elegant hand, with its rosy nails and sparkling cuff, descend gently on to Hearthrug's. It was time to clear the throat, stand up and approach the couple.

'How are you enjoying our duel to the death, Portia?'

'Fighting you, Rumpole' – she withdrew her hand as casually as possible – 'is always a pleasure.'

'Of course, you've got one great advantage,' I told her.

'Have I?'

'Oh yes. You've got an excellent Junior. Good old Claude. He's always behind you. Working hard. I think you should remember that.' And with a brief nod to both of them, I swept on towards the corrida for another day's battle with the Bull.

When I rose to cross-examine Inspector Broome, the Officer-in-Charge of the case, a glance up at the Public Gallery told me that Peanuts Molloy was still *in situ* and apparently enjoying the proceedings. My gaze lingered on him for but a moment and then I turned my attention to the Inspector as I had done over so many cases and confronted a middle-aged, somewhat sardonic man who was capable of rare moments of humour and even rarer moments of humanity. He looked back at me, as always, with a sort of weary patience. Defence barristers in general, and Horace Rumpole in particular, were not among the Inspector's favourite characters.

'Inspector Broome,' I began my cross-examination. 'I understand that no fingerprints were found on the gun.' At which point the Bull couldn't resist weighing in with 'I imagine, Mr Rumpole, that these gentry would be too . . .' – for a wild moment I hoped he was going to say 'experienced' and then I'd have him on toast in the Court of Appeal, but his dread of that unjust tribunal made him say 'too *intelligent* to leave fingerprints?'

Something, perhaps it was the success I was enjoying with the horses, emboldened me to protest at the Judge's constant interruptions at the expense of my client. 'My Lord,' I ventured to point out, 'the prosecution in this case is in the hands of my learned friend, Mr Hearthrug.'

'Hearthstoke.' The young gentleman in question rose to correct me. 'Beg his pardon. Hearthstone. I'm sure he needs no assistance from your Lordship.'

There was the usual pause while the Bull lowered his head, snorted, pawed the ground and so on. Then he charged in with

'Mr Rumpole. That was an outrageous remark! It is one I may have to consider reporting as professional misconduct!'

Of course, by the time he did that, I might be safely on my way to the Seychelles, but I still had to get through Yarmouth that day and Newbury the next. I thought it best to return the retort courteous. 'I'm sorry if anything I might have said could possibly be construed as critical of your Lordship . . .'

'Very well! Let's get on with it.' Bullingham suspended his attack for the moment and I returned to the witness. 'Were the other areas of the strong-room examined for finger-prints, in particular the safe?'

'Yes, they were,' the Inspector told me.

'And again no fingerprints of either Mr Cyril or Mr Dennis Timson were found?' Bullingham roused himself to interrupt again, so I went on quickly, 'My Lord is about to say, of course, that they'd still be wearing their gloves when they opened the safe and that is a perfectly fair point. I needn't trouble your Lordship to make that interjection.'

'Isn't Rumpole going rather over the top?' I heard Phillida whispering to her husband, and she got the sensible reply, 'He's behaving like a chap who's got a secure future from investments.'

'No fingerprints identifiable as the defendant's were found, my Lord. That is true,' Broome told the Court.

'But no doubt a number of fingerprints *were* found on the door of the safe?' I asked.

'Of course.'

'And they were photographed?'

'Yes.'

'No doubt many of them came from bank employees?'

'No doubt about that, my Lord.'

'But did you take the trouble to check any of those fingerprints with criminal records?'

'Why should we have done that?' The Inspector looked somewhat pained at the suggestion.

'To see if they corresponded to the fingerprints of any known criminal, other than the two Mr Timsons.'

'No. We didn't.'

'Why not?'

'The two Mr Timsons were the only men we found at the scene of the crime and we had established that they were wearing gloves.'

'Because they had gloves on them when you caught them,' Bullingham explained to me as though I were a child, for the benefit of the Jury.

'We are so much obliged to the learned judge for his most helpful interjection, aren't we, Inspector? Otherwise you might have had to think of the answer for yourself.'

Of course that brought the usual warning rumble from the Bench, but I pressed on, more or less regardless, with, 'Let me ask you something else, Inspector. When the defendants were apprehended, they were carrying about three thousand pounds worth of cash and other valuables from various deposit boxes?'

'That is so.'

'Was that the total amount missing from the safe?'

'No. No, as a matter of fact, it wasn't.' For the first time Broome sounded puzzled. 'That particular safe had been almost entirely emptied when we came to inspect it.'

'Were its entire contents valued at something over sixty thousand pounds?'

'Well over that, my Lord.'

'Well over that . . .' The Judge made a grateful note.

'You have no idea when the sixty-thousand-pound worth was taken?' I heard Bullingham start with a menacing 'Perhaps . . .' and went on, 'My Lord is about to say perhaps they took it first and carried it out by the tunnel. That would be a sound point for my Lord to make.'

'Thank *you*, Mr Rumpole.' The Judge tried the retort ironical.

'Not at all, my Lord. I'm only too glad to be of assistance.' I smiled at him charmingly. 'But let me ask you this, Inspector. Your men came to the bank because an alarm went off in the strong-room?'

'That is so. The signal was received at Tooting Central at . . .'

'About 3 a.m. We know that. But it's clear, isn't it, that when your men invaded the bank they knew nothing about the tunnel?'

'That is quite right.'

'So they were admitted by the second guard on duty and went down to the vaults.'

'Yes.'

'No police officer ever entered by the tunnel?'

'Not so far as I am aware.'

'We all heard that evidence, Mr Rumpole. Or perhaps you weren't listening?' Nothing subtle, you see, about Judge Bullingham's little sallies.

'On the contrary, my Lord. I was listening most intently.' I turned back to the Inspector. 'And when your officers entered the vaults they found there two men running down a passage towards them?'

'That's what they reported.'

'Running *away* from the entrance to the tunnel.'

'Yes, indeed.'

'That is all I have to ask' – I gave Bullingham another of my smiles – 'unless your Lordship wishes to correct any of those answers . . .'

'Hadn't you better sit down, Mr Rumpole?'

'Sit down? Yes, of course. I'd be glad to. Your Lordship is most kind and considerate as always . . .' As I sat I thought that dear old Ever So Grateful had better get a spurt on or I would find myself up on a charge of professional misconduct. These thoughts were interrupted by Charlie Hearthstoke's re-examination of the witness.

'Mr Rumpole has asked you if you consulted criminal records on any of the fingerprints you *did* find on the safe.'

'Yes. I remember him asking me that,' Broome answered.

'Mr Rumpole no doubt felt that he had to ask a large number of questions in order to justify his fee from the legal aid.' Bullingham did one of his usual jokes to the Jury; it was a moderate success only with the twelve honest citizens.

'I suppose you *could* compare the photographs of fingerprints you have with criminal records, couldn't you?' Hearthstoke suggested, greatly to my relief.

'I could, my Lord. If the Court wishes it.' Inspector Broome turned politely to the Bench for guidance and the Judge did his best to sound judicial. 'Mr Hearthstoke has made a very fair suggestion, Inspector, as one would expect of a totally impartial prosecutor.' He said graciously, 'Perhaps you would be so kind as to make the inquiry. We don't want to give Mr Rumpole any *legitimate* cause for complaint.'

When we left Court at lunchtime, I followed the Inspector down the corridor in pursuit of the line of defence I had decided to adopt for Dennis Timson. When I caught up with him, I ventured to tell Inspector 'New' Broome what a thoroughly dependable and straightforward officer I had always found him. Quite rightly he suspected that I wanted something out of him and he asked me precisely what I had in my mind.

'A small favour,' I suggested.

'Why should I do you a favour, Mr Rumpole? You have been a bit of a thorn in my flesh over the years, if I have to be honest.'

'Oh yes, you have to be honest. But if I promised never to be a thorn in your flesh ever again?'

'Not making me and my officers look Charlies in front of the Jury?' Broome asked suspiciously.

'Never again.'

'Not letting the Timsons get away with murder?'

'Never murder, Inspector! Perhaps, occasionally, stolen fish.'

'Not getting my young D.C.s tied up in their own notebooks?' He pressed for specific assurances.

'If I swore on my old wig never to do anything of the sort again. In fact, Inspector Broome, if I were to promise you that this would be positively my last case!'

'Your last case, Mr Rumpole?' The Inspector was clearly reluctant to believe his ears.

'My positively last case!'

'You'd be leaving the Bailey after this for good?' Hope sprang in the officer's breast.

'I was thinking in terms of a warmer climate. So if I were to leave and never trouble you again . . .'

'Then I suppose I might be more inclined to help out,'

Inspector Broome conceded. 'But if it's that fingerprint business!'

'Oh, you won't get anything out of that. I just wanted to get somebody worried. No respectable thief's ever going to leave their prints on a Peter. No, what I was going to suggest, old darling, is something entirely different.'

'Nothing illegal, of course?'

'Illegal! Ask Detective Inspector Broome to do anything illegal?' I hope I sounded suitably appalled at the idea. 'Certainly not. This is only guaranteed to serve the interests of justice.'

After lunch, and after I had made my most respectful suggestions to the Inspector, Hearthstoke closed the prosecution case and Phillida called Cyril Timson to the witness-box. He agreed with most of the prosecution case and accepted the evidence, which we had heard, of Mr Huggins of having been shot at by some person and wounded in the foot. Phillida held the revolver in her hand and asked in her most solemn tones, 'Cyril Timson. Did you take this weapon with you when you tunnelled into the Penny-Wise Bank?' When he had, not unexpectedly, answered, 'No. I never,' I whispered a request to her to sit down and resist the temptation of cutting Dennis's throat. She was not in a temptation resisting mood.

'Did you ever,' she asked Cyril, 'have any idea that your cousin, the co-defendant, Dennis Timson, was armed with a pistol?'

'My Lord,' I objected, 'there is absolutely no evidence that Dennis was armed with anything!'

'The pistol was there at the scene of the crime, Mr Rumpole. *Someone* must have brought it,' Bullingham reasoned.

'Someone perhaps. But the question assumes . . .'

'Please continue, Mrs Erskine-Brown.' The Judge, ignoring me, almost simpered at Phillida, 'You may ask your question.'

'But you don't have to, Portia,' I whispered to her as I sat down. 'Remember the quality of mercy!'

'Did you have any idea that Dennis was armed?' She forgot it.

'No idea at all.' Cyril looked pained.

'And what would you have said if you had known?'

'My Lord' – I had another go – 'how can this be evidence? It's pure speculation!'

'Please, Mrs Erskine-Brown.' Again, I was ignored. 'Do ask the question.'

'What would you have said?'

'Leave that thing at home, Den.' Cyril sounded extraordinarily righteous. 'That's not the way we carry on our business.'

'Can you tell us if Dennis ever owned a firearm?'

'I don't object, my Lord. All objections are obviously perfectly useless.' I rose to tell the Court and got a look from the Judge which meant 'And that's another one for the report'. But now Cyril was saying, 'Dennis was always pretty keen on shooters. When he was a kid he had an airgun.'

'And probably a catapult as well,' I whispered as I subsided.

'Did you say something, Mr Rumpole?' the Judge was kind enough to ask.

'Nothing whatever, my Lord.'

'In his later years he bought a shotgun.' Cyril added to the indictment of his cousin.

'Did you know what he used that for?' Phillida asked.

'He said clay pigeons, my Lord.'

'He said clay pigeons. Did you believe him?' the judge asked and, looking up at the public gallery, I again saw Peanuts Molloy smiling.

'I had no means of checking the veracity of cousin Den's statement.'

'Thank you, Mr Timson, just wait there.' Phillida sat down, happily conscious of having done her worst, and I rose to cross-examine the witness. Bullingham sat back to enjoy further blood-shed.

'Mr Timson. When you were removing some of the property from the safe, you suddenly ran out of the strong-room into the corridor. Why was that?'

'We thought we heard a noise behind us.' Cyril frowned, as though he still found the situation puzzling.

'Coming from where?'

'He said "behind us", Mr Rumpole,' Bullingham reminded me.

'Thank you, your Lordship, so much! And it was that sound that made you retreat?'

'We thought we was being copped, like.'

'Why didn't you retreat back into the tunnel you came from? Was it by any chance because the sound was coming from that direction?'

'Yes. It might have been,' Cyril admitted.

'When you ran out into that corridor you were holding some boxes containing money and valuables.'

'Yes, I was.'

'And so was your cousin Dennis?'

'Yes.'

'You saw that?'

'Yes.'

'You never saw him with a gun in his hand?'

'No. I never saw it, like. But I knew *I* didn't have it.'

'Mr Cyril Timson, may I say at once that I accept the truth of that statement . . .' The Court went strangely silent; Bullingham looked disappointed, as though I had announced that throat-cutting was off and the afternoon would be devoted to halma. Phillida whispered to me, 'Rumpole, have you gone soft in your old age?'

'Not soft, Portia, I just thought it might be nice to win my last case,' I whispered back. Then I spoke to the witness, 'I agree that you didn't have the gun, and Dennis certainly didn't.'

'So where did it come from, Mr Rumpole?' The Judge gave me the retort sarcastic. 'Did it drop from the sky?'

'Yes, my Lord. In a manner of speaking, it did. Thank you, Mr Cyril Timson.'

I shot out of the Old Bailey, when Judge Bullingham rose at the end of that day, like a bat leaving hell. That was not my usual manner of departure, but careful inquiry at the sporting kiosk in the alley off Ludgate Circus had led me to believe that *The Punter's Guide*, out late on Tuesday afternoon, carried a full print-out of that very afternoon's results. If you can make one heap of all your winnings and risk it on one turn of pitch and toss, you will have some idea what I felt like as I hastened towards the news-stand and to what had rapidly become my favourite reading.

Meanwhile as Peanuts Molloy came out of the entrance of the Public Gallery, D.S. Garsington, an officer in plain clothes, peeled himself off a wall and followed at a discreet distance. When Peanuts mounted a bus going South of the river, the Detective Sergeant was also in attendance. This close watch on Peanuts' movements was something that the Detective Inspector had authorized on the understanding that I would be leaving the Bar after the present case and so would trouble the authorities no more.

While Peanuts was off on his bus journey with D.S. Garsington in attendance, I was watching the elderly, partially blind lady with the bobble hat try to undo the newly arrived parcel of *The Punter's Guide*, with swollen and arthritic fingers. At last I could bear it no longer. I seized the string and broke it for her. I fluttered *The Punter's* pages for the fly-away leaf of that afternoon's results, and there was the print-out from Yarmouth: 1.30 FIRST EVER SO GRATEFUL. 'Oh, my God,' I said devoutly as I paid the old lady. 'Thanks most awfully!'

At about opening time Peanuts Molloy was in a gym used to train young boxers over the Venerable Bede pub along the Old Kent Road. Peanuts was neither sparring nor skipping; he was reporting back to another deeply interested member of the Clan Molloy. What he said, as later recalled by D.S. Garsington, went something like this: 'Like I told you. No sweat. They're still just blaming it on each other. There's one old brief that thinks different, but the Judge don't take a blind bit of notice. Not of him.' At which point the Detective Sergeant intruded and asked, 'Are you Peter James Molloy?'

'What if I am?' said Peanuts.

'I must ask you to accompany me. My Inspector would like to ask you some questions.'

'Oh yes. What about?'

'I believe . . .' – D.S. Garsington was suitably vague – 'it's about a fingerprint.'

Wednesday morning passed as slowly as a discourse on the Christian attitude to Tort from Soapy Sam Ballard, or an afternoon in a rain-soaked holiday hotel with She Who Must Be Obeyed.

First of all, Judge Bullingham had some applications in another case to deal with and so we started late, and then Phillida had some other evidence of a particularly unimportant nature to call. At last it was lunchtime and I was ready for the final throw; this was the crunch, the crisis, the moment to win or lose it all. I couldn't get away to Newbury to cheer Kissogram on, but I had decided to do the next best thing. Discreet inquiries from the Ushers at the Bailey had revealed the fact that there was a betting shop recently opened by Blackfriars Station. I found it a curious establishment with painted-over windows and only a few visitors, who looked to be of no particular occupation, watching the television at lunchtime. They were joined by an ageing barrister in bands and a winged collar, who put a small cigar into his mouth but forgot to light it while watching the one-thirty.

I find it hard to recall my exact feelings while the race was going on and I supposed I have had worse times waiting for juries to come back with a verdict. Somewhere in the depths of my being I felt that I had come so far that nothing could stop me now, nor could it – Kissogram pulled it off by three lengths.

I hurried back to the Bailey repeating Dennis's magic figure: 'Let's say, three hundred and thirty grand! Give or take a fiver.' It was, of course, an extraordinary happening, and one which I intended to keep entirely to myself for the moment or God only knew how many learned friends would remember old Rumpole and touch him for a loan. Uppermost in my mind was the opening speech I was due to make of Dennis Timson's defence when the Bull, full of the City of London's roast beef and claret, returned to the seat of Judgement. It would be the last time I opened a defence in my positively last case. Why should I not do what a barrister who has his future at the Bar to think of can never do? Why should I not say exactly what I thought?

As I took the lift up to the robing room, the idea appealed to me more and more; it became even more attractive than the prospect of wandering along palm-fringed beaches beside the booming surf, although, of course, I meant to do that as well. Phrases, heartfelt sentiments, began to form in my mind. I was going to make the speech of a lifetime, Rumpole's last opening, and the Bull would have to listen. So, at exactly ten past two, I rose to my feet, glanced up at the Public Gallery, found that 'Peanuts' Molloy was no longer in his place, and began.

'Members of the Jury. You heard the prosecution case opened by my learned friend Mr Hearth—*stoke*. And I wish, now, to make a few remarks of a general nature before calling Mr Dennis Timson into the witness-box. I hope they will be helpful.'

'I hope so, too, Mr Rumpole. The Defence doesn't *have* to indulge in opening speeches.' The Judge was scarcely encouraging, but no power on earth was going to stop me now.

'Members of the Jury. You have no doubt heard of the presumption of innocence, the golden thread that runs through British justice. Everyone in this fair land of ours is presumed to be innocent until they're proved to be guilty, but against this presumption there is another mighty legal doctrine,' I told them. 'It is known as the Bullingham factor. Everyone who is put into that dock before this particular learned judge is naturally assumed to have done the deed, otherwise they wouldn't be there. Not only are those in the dock presumed to be guilty, defending barristers are assumed to be only interested in wasting time so they can share in the rich pickings of the legal aid system, an organization which allows criminal advocates to live almost as high on the hog as well-qualified shorthand typists. For this princely remuneration, Members of the Jury, we are asked to defend the liberty of the subject, carry on the fine traditions of Magna Carta, make sure that all our citizens are tried by their peers and no man nor woman suffers unjust imprisonment, and knock our heads, day in day out, against the rock solid wall of the Bullingham factor! For this we have to contend with a judge who invariably briefs himself for the Prosecution . . .'

During the flow of my oratory, I had been conscious of two main events in Court. One was the arrival of Detective Inspector Broome, who was in urgent and whispered consultation with Charlie Hearthstoke. The other was the swelling of the Bull like a purple gas balloon, which I had been pumping up to bursting point. Now he exploded with a deafening '*Mr Rumpole!*' But before he could deliver the full fury of his Judgement against me, Hearthstoke had risen and was saying, 'My Lord. I wonder if I may intervene? With the greatest respect . . .'

'Certainly, Mr Hearthstoke.' The Judge subsided with a gentle hiss of escaping air. 'Certainly you may. Perhaps you have a suggestion to offer on how I might best deal with this outrageous contempt?'

'I was only about to say, my Lord, that what I am going to tell your Lordship may make the rest of Mr Rumpole's opening speech unnecessary.'

'I have no doubt that *all* of his opening speech is unnecessary!' Judge Bullingham glared in my general direction.

'I am informed by Detective Inspector Broome, my Lord, that, after further inquiries, we should no longer proceed on the allegation that either Cyril or Dennis Timson used, or indeed carried, the automatic pistol which wounded Mr Huggins the bankguard.'

'*Neither* of them?' The Bull looked as though his constitution might not stand another shock.

'It seems that further charges will be brought, with regard to that offence, against another "firm", if I may use that expression,' Hearthstoke explained. 'In those circumstances, the only charge is one of theft.'

'To which Mr Cyril Timson has always been prepared to plead guilty,' Phillida stood up and admitted charmingly.

'Thank *you*, Mrs Erskine-Brown,' the Judge cooed, and then turned reluctantly to me. '*Mister* Rumpole?'

'Oh yes. Guilty to the theft, my Lord. With the *very greatest respect!*' I had said most of what I had always longed to say in Bullingham's Court, and my very last case was over.

*

'Ferrets! The Molloys said the Timsons were ferrets. They called it out after your wives in the street.' I was in the interview room again with Liz Probert and Mr Bernard, saying goodbye to our client Dennis Timson. 'I wonder why he used that particular expression. Ferrets are little animals you send down holes in the ground. Of course, the Molloys found out what you were up to and they simply followed you down the burrow. And after you'd got through the wall, what were they going to do? Use the gun to get the money off you and Cyril when you'd opened the safe? Anyway, it all ended in chaos and confusion, as most crimes do, I'm afraid, Dennis. You heard the Molloys and thought they were the Old Bill and ran towards the passage. The Molloys got their hands on the rest of the booty. Then Mr Huggins, the bankguard, appeared, some Molloy shot at him and dropped the gun and they scarpered back down the tunnel, leaving you and Cyril in hopeless ignorance, blaming each other.'

'But there weren't any fingerprints.' Liz Probert wondered about my cross-examination of Broome.

'Oh no. But the D.I. told Peanuts Molloy he'd found his and got him talking. In fact, Peanuts grassed on the rest of the Molloys.'

'Grassed on his family, did he?' Dennis was shocked. 'Bastard!'

'I'm afraid things aren't what they were in our world, Dennis. Standards are falling. When you've got this little stretch under your belt you'd do far better give it all up.'

'Never. I'd miss the excitement. You're all right, though, aren't you, Mr Rumpole?'

'What?' I was wondering whether I would miss the excitement, and decided that I could live without the thrills and spills of life with Judge Bullingham. 'I said *you're* all right,' Dennis repeated. 'On the old four-horse accumulator.'

'Oh yes, Dennis. I think I shall be all right. Thanks entirely to you. I shan't forget it. You were my last case.' I stood up and moved towards the door. 'Give me a ring when you get out, if you're ever passing through Lotus land.'

I had looked for Gerald as I arrived down the cells, but the gate had been opened by a thin turnkey without a sandwich. On my way out I asked for Gerald, anxious to collect my fortune, but was told 'It's Gerald's day off, Mr Rumpole. He'll be back tomorrow for sure.'

'Back tomorrow? You don't know the name of his bookmaker by any chance?'

'Oh no, Mr Rumpole. Gerald don't take us into his confidence, not as far as that's concerned.'

'Well, all right. I'll be back tomorrow too.'

'Dennis Timson well satisfied with his four years, was he?' the thin warder said as he sprang me from the cells.

'He seemed considerably relieved.'

'I don't know how you do it, Mr Rumpole. Honest, I don't.'

'Well,' I told him. 'I'm not going to do it any more.'

I gave the same news to Henry when I got back to our clerk's room and he looked unexpectedly despondent. 'I've done my positively last case, Henry,' I told him. 'I shan't ever be putting my head round the door again asking if you've got a spare committal before the Uxbridge Magistrates.'

'It's a tragedy, Mr Rumpole,' my former clerk said, and I must say I was touched. A little later he came up to see me in my room and explained the nature of his anxiety. 'If you leave, Mr Rumpole, we're going to have that Mr Hearthstoke back again. He's going to get your room, sir. Mr Ballard's already keen on the idea. It'll be a disaster for Chambers. And my ten per cent.' His voice sank to a note of doom. 'And Dianne's threatened to hand in her notice.'

'I delivered you from Hearthrug once before, Henry.' I reminded him of the affair of the Massage Parlours.

'You did, Mr Rumpole, and I shall always thank you for it. But he's due here at five o'clock, sir, for an appointment with Mr Ballard. I think they're going to fix up the final details.'

Well why should I have cared? By tomorrow, after a brief bit of business with Gerald and a word in the ear of my man of affairs at the Caring Bank, I would be well shot of the whole pack of them. And yet, just as a colonial administrator likes to leave his statue in a public park, or a university head might donate a stained-glass window to the Chapel, I felt I might give something to my old Chambers by which I would always be remembered. My gift to the dear old place would be the complete absence of Hearthrug. 'Five o'clock, eh?' I said. 'Courage, Henry! We'll see what we can do!'

Henry left me with every expression of confidence and gratitude, and at five o'clock precisely I happened to be down in our entrance hall when Hearthstoke arrived to squeeze Ballard and re-enter Equity Court.

'Well, Hearthrug,' I greeted him. 'Good win, that. An excellent win!'

'Who won?' He sounded doubtful.

'You did, of course. You were prosecuting. We pleaded guilty and you secured a conviction. Brilliant work! So you're going to have my old room in Chambers.'

'You *are* leaving, aren't you?' He seemed to need reassurance.

'Oh, yes, of course. Off to Lotos land! In fact, I only called in to pack up a few things.' I started up the stairs towards my room, calling to him over my shoulder, 'Your life's going to change too, I imagine. Have you had much experience as a father?'

'A father? No, none at all.'

'Pity. Ah, well, I expect you'll pick it up as you go along. That's the way you've picked up most things.'

I legged it up to the room then and had the satisfaction of knowing that he was in hot pursuit. Once in my sanctum, he closed the door and said, 'Now, Rumpole. Suppose you tell me exactly what you mean?'

'I mean it's clear to all concerned that you've fallen for Mrs Erskine-Brown hook, line and probably sinker. When you move into Chambers she'll be expecting to move into your bachelor pad in Battersea, bringing her children with her. Jolly brave of you to take her on, as well as little Tristan and Isolde.'

'Her children?' he repeated, dazed. The man was clearly in a state of shock.

'I suppose Claude will be round to take the kids off to the *Ring* occasionally. They'll probably come back whistling all the tunes.'

There was a long pause during which Hearthrug considered his position. Finally, he said, 'Perhaps, all things considered, these Chambers might not be *just* what I'm looking for . . .'

'Why don't you slip next door, old darling,' I suggested, 'and tell Bollard exactly that?'

I must now tell you something which is entirely to the credit of Mrs Phillida Erskine-Brown. She was determined, once the case was over, to save the neck of her old friend and one-time mentor, Horace Rumpole, despite the fact that she had only recently been merrily engaged in cutting his throat. She had no idea of my stunning success with the horses, so she took it upon herself to call on the Bull in his room, just as he was changing his jacket and about to set off for Wimbledon to terrorize his immediate family. When she was announced by Shrimpton, the Court Clerk, the learned Judge brushed his eyebrows, shot his cuffs and generally tried vainly to make himself look a little more appetizing.

When Phillida entered, and was left alone in the presence, an extraordinary scene transpired, the details of which our Portia only told me long after this narrative comes to an end. The, no doubt, ogling judge told her that her conduct of the defence had filled him with admiration, and said, 'I'm afraid I can't say the same for Rumpole. In fact, I shall have to report him for gross professional misconduct.' And the old hypocrite added, 'After such a long career too. It's a tragedy, of course.'

'A tragedy he was interrupted,' Phillida told him. She clearly had the Judge puzzled, so she pressed on. 'I read the second half of that speech, Judge. Rumpole was extremely flattering, but I think the things he said about you were no less than the truth.'

'Flattering?' The Bull couldn't believe his ears.

'"One of the fairest and most compassionate judges ever to have sat in the Old Bailey"; "Combines the wisdom of Solomon with the humanity of Florence Nightingale" – that's only a couple of quotations from the rest of his speech.'

'But . . . but that's not how he started off!'

'Oh, he was describing the sort of mistaken view the Jury

might have of an Old Bailey judge. Then he was about to put them right, but of course the case collapsed and he never gave the rest of that marvellous speech!'

'Florence Nightingale, eh? Can you tell me anything else' – the Bull was anxious to know – 'that Rumpole was *about* to say?'

'"With Judge Bullingham the quality of mercy is not strain'd, It droppeth as the gentle rain from heaven." Rather well put, I thought. Will you still be reporting Rumpole for professional misconduct?'

The Bull was silent then and appeared to reserve judgement. 'I shall have to reconsider the matter,' he said, 'in the light of what you've told me, Mrs Erskine-Brown.' And then he approached her more intimately: 'Phillida, may I ask you one question?'

'Certainly, Judge,' our Portia answered with considerable courage, and the smitten Bull asked, 'Do you prefer the hard or the creamy centres? When it comes to a box of chocolates?'

After this strange and in many ways heroic encounter, Phillida turned up, in due course, at Pommeroy's Wine Bar, and sat at the table in the corner where she had formerly been drinking with Hearthrug. She was there by appointment, but she didn't expect to meet me. I spotted her as soon as I came in, fresh from my encounter with the young man concerned, and determined to celebrate my amazing good fortune in an appropriate manner. I sat down beside her and, if she was disappointed that it was not someone else, she greeted me with moderate hospitality.

'Rumpole, have a choc?' I saw at once that she had a somewhat ornate box on the table in front of her. I was rash enough to take one with a mauve centre.

'Bullingham gave them to me,' she explained.

'The Mad Bull's in love! You're a *femme fatale*, Portia.'

'Don't ask me to explain yet, I'm not sure how it'll turn out,' she warned me. 'But I went to see him entirely in your interests.'

'And I've just been seeing someone entirely in yours. What are you doing here, anyway, alone and palely loitering?'

'I was just waiting for someone.' Phillida was non-committal.

'He's not coming.' I was certain.

'What?'

'Hearthrug's not coming. He's not coming into Chambers, either.' She looked at me, puzzled and not a little hurt. 'Why not?'

'Henry doesn't want him.'

'Rumpole! What've you done?' She suspected I had been up to something.

'Sorry, Portia. I told him you wanted to move into his bachelor pad in Battersea and bring Tristan and Isolde with you. I'm afraid he went deathly pale and decided to cancel his subscription.'

There was a longish silence and I didn't know whether to expect tears, abuse or a quick dash out into the street. I was surprised when at long last, she gave me a curious little half-smile and said, 'The rat!'

'I could have told you that before you started spooning with him all round the Old Bailey,' I assured her and added, 'Of course, I shouldn't have done that.'

'No, you shouldn't. You'd got no right to say any such thing.'

'It was Henry and Dianne I was thinking about.'

'Thank you very much!'

'They don't deserve Hearthrug. None of you deserve him.'

'I was only considering a small adventure . . .' she began to explain herself, a little sadly. But it was no time for regrets. 'Cheer up, Portia,' I told her. 'In all the circumstances, I think this is the moment for me to buy the Dom Perignon. *Méthode Champenoise* is a thing of the past.'

She agreed and I went over to the bar where Jack Pommeroy was dealing with the arrival of the usual evening crowd. 'A bottle of your best bubbles, Jack.' I placed a lavish order. 'Nothing less than the dear old Dom to meet this occasion.' And whilst he went about fulfilling it, I saw Erskine-Brown come in and look around the room. 'Ah, Claude,' I called to him. 'I'm in the chair. Care for a glass of vintage bubbly?'

'There you are!' he said, stating the obvious I thought. 'I took a telephone message for you in the clerk's room.'

'If it's about a murder tomorrow, I'm not interested.' My murdering days were over.

'No, this was rather a strange-sounding chap. I wouldn't have thought he was completely sober. Said his name was Gerald.'

'Gerald?' I was pleased to hear it. 'Yes, of course. Gerald . . .'

'Said he was calling from London airport.'

'From where?'

'He said would I give his thanks to Mr Rumpole for the excellent tips, and he was just boarding a plane for a warmer climate.'

'Gerald said that?' I have had some experience of human perfidy, but I must say I was shocked and, not to put too fine a point on it, stricken.

'Words to that effect. Oh, then he said he had to go. They were calling his flight.'

What do you do if your hopes, built up so bravely through the testing-time of a four-horse accumulator, are dashed to the ground? What do you do if the doors to a golden future are suddenly slammed in your face and you're told to go home quietly? I called for Jack Pommeroy and told him to forget the Dom Perignon and pour out three small glasses of the Château Thames Embankment. Then I looked at Phillida sitting alone, and from her to Erskine-Brown. 'Claude,' I told him, 'I have an idea. I think there's something you should do urgently.'

'What's that, Rumpole?'

'For God's sake, take your wife to the Opera!'

During the course of these memoirs I have stressed my article of faith: never plead guilty. Like all good rules this is, of course, subject to exceptions. For instance, readers will have noticed that having got Dennis Timson off the firearm charges, I had no alternative but to plead to the theft. So it was with my situation before She Who Must Be Obeyed. I knew that she would soon learn of my announced retirement from the Bar. If I wished to avoid prolonged questioning on this subject, no doubt stretching over several months, I had no alternative but to come clean and throw myself on the mercy of the Court. And so, that night, before the domestic gas-fire I gave Hilda a full account of the wager I had placed with Gerald, and of the fat screw's appalling treachery. 'But Rumpole,' she asked, and it was by no means a bad question, 'do you mean to say you've got no record of the transaction?'

'Nothing,' I had to admit. 'Not even a betting-slip. I trusted him. So bloody innocent! We look after our clients and we're complete fools about ourselves.'

'You mean' – and I could see that things weren't going to be easy – 'you lost my hundred pounds?'

'I'm afraid it's on its way to a warmer climate With about three hundred thousand friends.'

'The hundred pounds I spent on the new hearthrug!' She was appalled.

'*That* hundred pounds is still in the account of the Caring Bank, Hilda. Coloured red,' I tried to explain.

'You'll have to go and talk to Mr Truscott about it,' she made the order. 'I don't suppose he'll be inviting you to the Savoy Grill now, Rumpole?'

'No, Hilda. I don't suppose he will.' I got up then to recharge our glasses, and, after a thoughtful sip, Hilda spoke more reasonably.

'I'm not sure,' she told me, 'that I ever wanted to sit with you on a hotel verandah all day, drinking Planter's Punch.'

'Well. Perhaps not.'

'We might have run out of conversation.'

'Yes. I suppose we might.'

She had another sip or two and then, much to my relief, came out with 'So things could be worse.'

'They are,' I had to break it to her.

'What?'

'They are worse, Hilda.'

'What've you done now?' She sighed over the number of offences to be taken into consideration.

'Only promised Detective Inspector Broome that I'd done my last case. Oh, and told the Jury exactly what I thought of the Mad Bull. In open Court! I'll probably be reported to the Bar Council. For disciplinary action to be considered.'

'Rumpole!' Of course she was shocked. 'Daddy would be ashamed of you.'

'That's one comfort.'

'What did you say?'

'Your Daddy, Hilda, has already been called to account by the Great Benchers of the Sky. I hope he was able to explain his hopeless ignorance of bloodstains.'

There was a long silence and then She said, 'Rumpole.'

'Yes.'

'What are you going to be doing tomorrow?'

'Tomorrow?'

'I mean' – and Hilda made this clear to me – 'I hope you're not really going to retire or anything. I hope you're not going to be hanging round the flat all day. You will be taking your usual tube. Won't you? At eight forty-five?'

'To hear is to obey.' I lifted my glass of Pommeroy's Ordinary to the light, squinted at it, and noted its somewhat murky appearance. '"Courage!" he said, and pointed towards the Temple tube station.'

So it came about that at my usual hour next morning I opened the door of our clerk's room. Henry was telephoning, Dianne was brightening up her nails and Uncle Tom was practising chip shots into the waste-paper basket. Nothing had changed and nobody seemed particularly surprised to see me.

'Henry,' I said, when our clerk put down the telephone.

'Yes, Mr Rumpole?'

'Any chance of a small brief going today, perhaps a spot of indecency at the Uxbridge Magistrates Court?'

FOR THE BEST IN PAPERBACKS, LOOK FOR THE

In every corner of the world, on every subject under the sun, Penguin represents quality and variety – the very best in publishing today.

For complete information about books available from Penguin – including Puffins, Penguin Classics and Arkana – and how to order them, write to us at the appropriate address below. Please note that for copyright reasons the selection of books varies from country to country.

In the United Kingdom: Please write to *Dept E.P., Penguin Books Ltd, Harmondsworth, Middlesex, UB7 0DA.*

If you have any difficulty in obtaining a title, please send your order with the correct money, plus ten per cent for postage and packaging, to *PO Box No 11, West Drayton, Middlesex*

In the United States: Please write to *Dept BA, Penguin, 299 Murray Hill Parkway, East Rutherford, New Jersey 07073*

In Canada: Please write to *Penguin Books Canada Ltd, 2801 John Street, Markham, Ontario L3R 1B4*

In Australia: Please write to the *Marketing Department, Penguin Books Australia Ltd, P.O. Box 257, Ringwood, Victoria 3134*

In New Zealand: Please write to the *Marketing Department, Penguin Books (NZ) Ltd, Private Bag, Takapuna, Auckland 9*

In India: Please write to *Penguin Overseas Ltd, 706 Eros Apartments, 56 Nehru Place, New Delhi, 110019*

In the Netherlands: Please write to *Penguin Books Netherlands B.V., Postbus 195, NL–1380AD Weesp*

In West Germany: Please write to *Penguin Books Ltd, Friedrichstrasse 10–12, D–6000 Frankfurt/Main 1*

In Spain: Please write to *Longman Penguin España, Calle San Nicolas 15, E–28013 Madrid*

In Italy: Please write to *Penguin Italia s.r.l., Via Como 4, I-20096 Pioltello (Milano)*

In France: Please write to *Penguin Books Ltd, 39 Rue de Montmorency, F-75003 Paris*

In Japan: Please write to *Longman Penguin Japan Co Ltd, Yamaguchi Building, 2–12–9 Kanda Jimbocho, Chiyoda-Ku, Tokyo 101*